FLIGHTS OF FANCY

Jessica always does the sensible thing — until she meets James Strang . . . In Prague with friends, Jessica is grateful when a bag thief is foiled by James' intervention. Back home, although James lives in Birmingham and Jessica in Manchester, she finds herself agreeing to help James in his hour of need, and turning to him in hers. So when he suddenly vanishes from her life, Jessica is hurt and bewildered. Should she have just played it safe after all?

SHEILA HOLROYD

FLIGHTS OF FANCY

Complete and Unabridged

LINFORD
Leicester

First published in Great Britain in 2010

First Linford Edition
published 2011

Copyright © 2010 by Sheila Holroyd
All rights reserved

British Library CIP Data

Holroyd, Sheila.
 Flights of fancy. - - (Linford romance library)
 1. Vacations- -Czech Republic- -Prague- -
Fiction. 2. Long-distance relationships- -
England- -Fiction. 3. Love stories.
 4. Large type books.
 I. Title II. Series
 823.9′2–dc22

 ISBN 978–1–4448–0797–4

Published by
F. A. Thorpe (Publishing)
Anstey, Leicestershire

Set by Words & Graphics Ltd.
Anstey, Leicestershire
Printed and bound in Great Britain by
T. J. International Ltd., Padstow, Cornwall

1

Jessica peered at her guide book and then up at the clock. The crowd jostled around her, knocking her elbow, and a large man had stationed himself in front of her so she could barely see the famous monument. Then, as if at a signal, everybody fell quiet. It was noon. The ancient machinery creaked into action and little figures of the apostles were briefly visible as they passed two windows. Then the figures vanished, a cockerel appeared and flapped its wings and the clock struck the hour. There was a general satisfied sigh. The tourists had done their duty and observed one of Prague's most famous landmarks in action and now they could wander off to view other sights.

'Fifteenth century,' Jessica murmured, checking her guide book.

'Originally fifteenth century,' a voice said behind her. 'It's been repaired and altered many times since, though it's still the original clockwork.' A tall dark-haired man was gazing up at the clock, then he glanced down at her.

'I liked to think that it was genuinely mediaeval,' she replied reproachfully, but he shook his head.

'Isn't it more interesting to know how it's survived, how the people of Prague have restored it again and again, no matter how much effort it took?'

'Perhaps,' Jessica said coldly, turning to walk away.

The crowd was thinning but there were still plenty of people lingering in Prague's Old Square and she had to thread her way between them. Suddenly something thumped into her back and at the same time her handbag fell from her shoulder. Jessica felt herself falling towards the cobbles and gave a cry of panic, but before she hit the ground an arm caught her and steadied her. She was aware of a small

2

commotion around her. Thankfully she regained her balance and realised that she was being held by the man who had lectured her about the clock.

'Are you all right?' he asked anxiously.

She nodded, and he released her and held out her handbag, which he had grasped in his other hand. She saw that the shoulder strap was dangling in two pieces and she looked at her rescuer in bewilderment.

'A man cut the strap and then pushed you. He was going to grab your bag when you fell,' he informed her. 'It's a common trick in crowds. He ran away before anyone could stop him.'

Jessica gulped. Alone in a strange city, she suddenly felt very vulnerable.

'I think you need a coffee,' the man said firmly, and she found herself being led to one of the cafes that lined the ancient square. Gratefully she sank into a seat while her companion beckoned a waitress before picking up her bag and deftly knotting the ends of the handle together.

'I don't take sugar,' she said when their coffees appeared and he started to spoon some into both cups.

'You do this time,' he told her firmly, 'You've had a shock and the sugar will help you recover.' She was still too shaken to argue and obediently sipped the warm, sweet drink. 'My name is James Strang, by the way,' the dark-haired man said.

'Mine is Jessica Clarke. Thank you for rescuing me.'

He shrugged. 'Any city with a lot of tourists is bound to have plenty of pickpockets and petty thieves. It was just lucky that I saw what he was doing.' He paused. 'Are you in Prague by yourself?'

She shook her head slowly. 'No. I'm here with three friends just for a couple of nights.'

'But you are not looking round Prague together?'

'The others went to look at the shops in Wenceslas Square, but I wanted to explore the older part of the city.' She found herself warming to this stranger. 'This is the only time I have been abroad apart from a school trip to France years ago, and I want to see all I can. Are you here by yourself?'

'Yes, but I'm here on business. I work for a firm of architects and builders in Birmingham and I'm responsible for buying the special materials they require from time to time, so I'm here to buy some hand-made glass fittings for a luxury hotel.'

He picked up his coffee cup and Jessica briefly observed him while he drank. He was about thirty, with regular features below short, straight dark hair. He looked stern, serious, and she simply could not imagine anyone daring to call him Jimmy.

Her cup was empty. She wondered whether she should offer to pay for her coffee, but decided that he would probably be offended if she did so, and stood up to leave. 'Well, thank you again. I'll go and see a bit more of Prague and this time I shall be more

5

careful of my handbag.'

He put his cup down abruptly. 'Wait! I'll come with you. After all, we probably want to go to the same places. I've been to Prague before so I can tell you something about the city.'

Jessica looked at him doubtfully, her innate caution warning her that in spite of his kindness he was still a total stranger.

'Look, if you find you don't like me or I bore you, just tell me and I'll go away,' he assured her, and she couldn't help but smile. After all, he had saved her from a bag snatcher.

'Why not? I don't think my guide book is much use, anyway.' She glanced at her watch. 'I'm due back at my hotel in three hours' time.'

'Then we had better make a start.'

*　　*　　*

It was a packed three hours. They looked round the Old Square, wandered through the Jewish Quarter, and

6

then found their way to the famous Charles Bridge while James Strang told her all about the sights. He was knowledgeable and informative without overwhelming her with details. It was much pleasanter than wandering round by herself with only an inadequate guide book to help her. As she had told him, this was her first venture abroad as an adult and she delighted not only in the city's beauty but also in the contrast to her familiar surroundings back home.

At one point, as they gazed down an elegant street of houses incongruously dominated by a spire sprouting several smaller spires, she turned to him and threw her arms wide, struggling to find words to express how she felt. 'It's beautiful!' she managed. 'It's all just so beautiful!'

James smiled understandingly. 'I like Prague,' he commented as they gazed at the river. 'There's a marvellous vista down every street.'

But finally, when he suggested yet

another place to see, she had to admit that her feet were tired, and she needed to rest. They found a small bar and ordered red wine. 'Do you think you appreciate Prague more because you work for architects?' she enquired.

'Possibly, though I'm not much involved in the creative side. I'm practical and I help the designers turn their dreams into reality. What do you do?'

'Nothing special. The other girls and I all work in a hospital, in administration. I'm a secretary to one of the consultants.' She caught sight of the clock on the wall and gasped. 'Look at the time! I've got to get back to the hotel and get ready for this evening.'

'Where are you staying?' She told him and he nodded. 'I know the hotel. It's not far if we take a couple of short cuts I know of. I can get you there in ten minutes.'

He was true to his word and exactly ten minutes later he was ushering her through the plate-glass doors of her hotel. Once in the foyer, she turned to say goodbye. 'Thank you once again for rescuing my handbag, and thank you for showing me Prague. I really have enjoyed it.'

He smiled at her. 'Thank you for being such a pleasant companion. I hope I didn't bore you with too much information, and I hope you have a pleasant evening.'

He strode towards the doors, turned, waved briefly and was gone, leaving Jessica to make her way up to the room she was sharing with Tracey. Shannon and Susan, their two companions, were sharing another room, but she found all three of them in her bedroom, surrounded by shopping bags and relaxing with a bottle of wine.

'Welcome to the wanderer!' Shannon exclaimed, lifting her glass in greeting when Jessica came through the door. 'Did you enjoy all the old bits? We had a wonderful time!'

'I had fun too,' Jessica told her, and went through to the bathroom. In spite of the past few hours, she began to wonder yet again as she washed her hands whether she had after all made a mistake in coming to Prague with the other girls.

Although all four of them worked in the same office, Jessica knew that she was the outsider, regarded as far too careful and cautious for her age. The others didn't realise her desire for security and safety was due to the tragic car crash which had devastated her life when a drunken driver had rammed the side of the car driven by Jessica's father and killed him. Jessica had been seven, and in her nightmares could still remember the sound of the impact and her mother's screams.

The years that followed had been hard as her mother struggled to bring up her daughter on what she could earn as an unskilled worker. Then, when Jessica was fourteen, her mother had met and married John Clarke, and a new period of happy family life had followed. Jessica had started to dream of going to university, but just before her A-levels her step-father had had an accident and been unable to work for some time.

Once again, money had been scarce, so instead of applying for university Jessica started applying for jobs and was lucky enough to get one at the hospital. By the time her step-father had recovered and started work again Jessica had settled into the hospital, grateful for the security it offered. However, she had not completely given up her ambitions and hoped eventually to study at home with the Open University, though she wouldn't enrol until she had saved enough to pay for the whole course.

Shannon and Susan, the two youngest girls, were attractive and lively and saw work simply as a means of providing the money they needed to enjoy themselves. They talked of little but the boys they had met and the clothes they had bought.

Tracey had been engaged to Philip

for some time and plans for her wedding were beginning to figure prominently in her conversation. All three saw no point in Jessica's plans to go on studying when she didn't have to, and Shannon was frankly scornful about her ambitions.

'She's just pretending to be cleverer than us,' Jessica had once heard Shannon tell Susan. 'She'd soon give up all those crazy ideas if she could get a boyfriend.'

About a month earlier Jessica had come back from lunch to find the three friends studying some brochures. 'Are you planning your holidays?' she had enquired.

'We're planning a city break,' Tracey told her. 'We're going to Prague!'

Jessica's face lit up. 'Prague? Everybody says it's such a beautiful city.'

Tracey hesitated. 'Why don't you come with us?' she said politely.

Shannon snorted. 'Jessica go away to enjoy herself for a weekend? She'd rather stay at home and read a book!'

Jessica was stung. Why shouldn't she act on impulse and enjoy herself for once? She smiled at Tracey. 'Thank you. I'd love to come.'

Of course she had regretted it immediately, but she couldn't retract her words. Tracey explained what was involved. They would fly to Prague on Friday afternoon, have a quiet dinner somewhere, spend Saturday exploring or shopping, have a special meal on Saturday evening and fly back to England on Sunday afternoon. It all sounded very straightforward.

Jessica had been surprised by the enthusiasm her parents showed when she told them. 'Of course you must go! It's time you spent a bit of money on yourself,' her mother told her. 'You're only young once.'

'Have fun while you can,' her step-father added.

She knew that, although they had both been very grateful for her self-sacrifice when she had abandoned the prospect of university in order to

13

bring in a wage, they still felt somehow responsible for her blighted ambitions and wanted to see her do more things for her own pleasure.

She had forced a smile. 'Everybody says Prague is a marvellous place. I'll tell you all about it when I come back.'

Everything had gone to plan. The four girls arrived in Prague with time to wander through the streets before a quiet meal in the hotel, and even Shannon had been impressed. 'It all looks like the picture postcards,' she said, but next morning Jessica alone put sight-seeing before shopping.

Now it was time for the big celebration and Shannon and Susan went back to their own room to get ready, leaving Tracey and Jessica to shower and change.

'Did you really enjoy your day?' Tracey enquired.

'Very much, though I nearly had my bag . . . ' but before Jessica could say any more Tracey gave an angry exclamation.

'I've dropped an earring,' she complained, and by the time the missing object had been found, the topic of conversation had been forgotten.

Zipping up the simple black dress she had been wearing for special occasions for the past two years, Jessica admired the red chiffon concoction that Tracey was wearing, and told herself that next time she needed a special dress she would be more daring in her choice.

They had booked a table at a restaurant nearby and were warmly welcomed. Jessica looked around the agreeably old-fashioned restaurant, panelled with dark wood; candles supplied most of the subdued lighting. The waiter hovered unobtrusively while the girls debated whether to have venison steak or duck breast. They gave their orders and a bottle of wine was brought for them to enjoy while they waited. Jessica relaxed. It had been a pleasant day and now she was going to have a good meal. Coming to Prague had not been a mistake, after all.

'Wait a moment!' Shannon exclaimed, and dived into her handbag. 'Wait and see what I got for you, Tracey!'

Triumphantly she produced a white veil and head dress and insisted on Tracey putting it on.

'But I'm not getting married for months yet!' Tracey hissed, obviously embarrassed when people at nearby tables started to applaud, but she quickly recovered and stood up, waving to the other diners.

'After all, you are a bride-to-be,' Shannon pointed out. 'You say you don't want a proper big hen night, but it is traditional. Where would you like to go? How about Paris?'

Then the first course arrived to distract them.

To Jessica's relief, the evening was a success. They all wanted the rest of the trip to go just as well, and even Shannon restrained her sharp tongue. 'Just think, Tracey,' she said. 'Our next special meal together will probably be at your wedding reception. How long is it to go exactly?'

'Four months,' Tracey replied, and Jessica looked at her sharply. She had not sounded very happy.

'You haven't got any worries, have you? Practically everything is arranged, isn't it?' she queried.

'Of course it is,' Susan interrupted. 'We'd have certainly heard by now if there was any trouble!'

'There's no trouble. Everything is arranged and it's going to be a beautiful wedding,' Tracey said firmly. 'Jessica, see if you can catch the waiter's eye and order another bottle of wine.'

The wine and food were good, the service was excellent and the setting was very elegant. Finally, after they had been served coffee, the waiter appeared with a bottle of champagne, 'For the bride, with the compliments of the management.'

Jessica had decided not to tell the others about her encounter with James Strang. They would either laugh at the idea of her as the near-victim of a petty thief, or tell her how reckless she had been to go wandering round the city with a stranger.

As they strolled happily back to the hotel, Jessica even found herself wondering where she could go next for a city break!

She fell asleep rapidly, not surprising in view of her full day, but woke about three o'clock. She lay wondering what had disturbed her, then heard subdued sobs from Tracey's bed. She stretched out a hand, put on her bedside lamp, and struggled to sit up. 'Tracey? What's wrong?'

'Nothing!' came her muffled voice, but Jessica slipped out of bed and stood looking down at her friend. Tracey's face was clearly tear-stained.

'Whatever's the matter?' Jessica asked anxiously, gently sitting down on the side of Tracey's bed.

'Nothing!' Tracey insisted again.

'That's a silly thing to say when you're obviously lying there crying,' Jessica observed. She looked round at the tea-making tray the hotel provided. 'I'm going to make us a drink.'

By the time the tea was brewed Tracey was sitting up in bed, wiping her eyes and blowing her nose.

'Here,' Jessica said, handing her a cup. 'Drink this and tell me all about it. You shouldn't be crying. This is supposed to be the happiest time of your life. You're getting married in a few weeks.'

'That's just it,' snuffled Tracey. 'I'm not sure I want to get married!'

Jessica blinked. After listening so often to Tracey's wedding plans and her praise of her fiancé, Philip, this was the last thing she expected to hear.

'I'm sure it's just nerves,' she managed to say. 'Every bride has a moment when she wonders if she's doing the right thing.'

Tracey shook her head vigorously. 'I'm getting more and more sure that I'm not. When Philip asked me to marry him, I accepted him straight away. I liked him, but I think I really only said 'yes' because I was twenty-two, stuck in a dead-end job, and I couldn't think what else to do with my life. Getting married, having my own home, having children, it would be a fresh start, I thought, but now I just feel trapped.'

Jessica, at a loss what to say, hugged Tracey for a while. 'But you do at least love Philip,' she said at last. 'You'll enjoy being with him.'

Again Tracey shook her head. 'Every time I see him now I notice little things that annoy me — the way he laughs at his own jokes, the way he holds his knife and fork — then I get bad-tempered and he can't understand why.'

In spite of her concern, Jessica found herself yawning. 'It's just nerves,' she insisted. 'Now try to go to sleep and you'll feel better in the morning.'

Tracey seemed in no hurry to follow her advice. 'Jessica, you never talk about boyfriends. Have you had any?'

Jessica sighed. 'I'm twenty-two, and

in spite of what Shannon and Susan think, I have had a few boyfriends, though I haven't met anyone I've wanted to marry yet.'

'That's because you've got ambitions,' Tracey commented gloomily. 'You hope to teach. If you can't do that, what would you like to do?'

'Work my way round the world, write a book, go into social work . . . '

Tracey interrupted. 'You see? You can think of dozens of things you'd enjoy doing with your life. I'm not clever like you. That's why I'm going to marry Philip — because I can't think of anything else to do!'

Jessica looked at her seriously. 'If that's really how you feel, then it isn't fair to Philip and you must tell him that you aren't going to marry him. This talk of not being clever is nonsense. You're very competent and good at your job. You could use your skills in a hundred different ways.'

'But it's too late! Everything is arranged and there would be a terrible fuss if I backed out now!'

'It's not too late till you say, 'I do.' And a terrible fuss would be very exciting. You might even enjoy it.' Tracey looked doubtful as Jessica took her cup from her. 'Now lie down, I'll tuck you in, and we'll see how you feel in the morning,' Jessica instructed her, reflecting that she sounded just like her mother had when Jessica was suffering from some childish ailment.

2

Jessica woke to the sound of the shower in the bathroom. Soon Tracey emerged, wrapped in a bath-towel, and smiling brightly. 'Time to get up! It's our last day in Prague, so let's make the most of it.'

By the time Jessica had showered, Tracey was dressed and applying her lipstick. 'Where should we go this morning? The castle sounds nice . . . '

Jessica interrupted ruthlessly. 'Tracey, stop pretending that last night never happened. How do you feel now?'

Tracey's smile wavered and she put down her lipstick. 'You were right, Jessica. All that fuss was due to nerves and too much wine. I'm very fond of Philip and I know we'll be very happy together.'

Jessica wasn't sure that Tracey's tone was absolutely convincing, but she stayed diplomatically silent.

The four of them agreed over breakfast to go to Prague Castle.

'There's not just a castle,' Jessica said. 'There's at least one palace, a cathedral, a museum, a shopping street and lots more.'

'Perfect!' exclaimed Shannon. 'Culture and shopping! We'd better get going if we're to see all that.'

It was typical of Shannon and Susan that, even so, Tracey and Jessica found themselves waiting impatiently in the hotel reception area for the other two girls.

'I'll go and hurry them up,' Tracey said at last.

Left alone, Jessica was just wondering whether it was worth sitting down, when she heard a voice behind her.

'I hoped I'd find you still here.' It was James Strang, casually dressed like the day before. 'I was passing your hotel,' he told her, 'and it occurred to me that you might like to come sightseeing with me again.'

Jessica was immediately aware of

conflicting emotions. There was regret, because she really would have enjoyed seeing the city with him again, but she knew that there was no way she could possibly abandon the other girls when they seemed to be relying on her to tell them what they should see and do. She was also pleased because he had liked her enough to want her company again. That was flattering, and definitely a boost to her limited self-confidence.

'I'm sorry! I really would have liked to come with you again,' she said, 'but my friends and I had better stay together today to make sure we all get to the airport together.'

He shrugged. 'Oh, well. It was just an idea.'

But she was sure there was a shadow of disappointment on his face.

Just then she heard a small, polite cough, and turned to see Tracey, Shannon and Susan standing nearby, clearly curious about this stranger.

'We didn't know you had a friend in Prague,' Shannon said inquisitively.

'This is James Strang,' Jessica said quickly. 'We're not exactly friends. We only met yesterday.' She turned to James. 'These are the girls I told you about — Tracey, Shannon and Susan. We're just off to see the Castle.'

He smiled gravely at the trio. 'I'm sure you'll enjoy your visit.' Then he turned back to Jessica, as if an idea had just struck him. 'Perhaps we could ring each other in England? We might meet.' He fumbled in a pocket and produced a small card. 'My business address and telephone numbers.'

Aware of the other girls' scrutiny, she mumbled her thanks, took the card and slipped it into her handbag. Then she became aware that he was looking at her expectantly. 'And could I have your number?'

She blushed, felt in her bag, pulled out a pen and something to write on, scribbled her name and number and gave it to him. He looked as if he were about to say something more, but finally murmured a vague goodbye, turned on his heel, and left.

The other girls turned to Jessica for an explanation.

'We met in the Old Square,' she said airily. 'He's quite nice.' She held up her bag so that they could see the knotted strap. 'He saved me from a petty thief. I might phone him sometime.'

'That will be difficult,' Shannon said crisply. 'You can't call him because you wrote your name and number on the back of his card. I should think he'll take that as a definite hint that you aren't interested in seeing him again.'

Taken aback, Jessica managed a laugh. 'Oh, well, I'm not bothered. He was all right for a couple of hours, but Birmingham is a long way from Manchester so I don't expect I'd ever have seen him again, anyway. Now, are we ready for the castle?'

★ ★ ★

The wide range of buildings which included the actual Prague Castle was both overwhelming and fascinating, with enough variety to please everyone in their group — even shops where the girls could spend their remaining currency — and the morning passed rapidly. They found it was time to make their way back to the hotel to collect their luggage, then they climbed into the taxi Tracey had insisted on hiring, and soon they were back at Prague Airport waiting for their flight.

'Well, that was great!' sighed Shannon as they thirstily drank some coffee. 'I enjoyed the hotel, the shopping, the food — and even the sight-seeing! Let's hope your wedding goes as smoothly, Tracey.'

They touched down in Manchester on time. Shannon and Susan were picked up by boyfriends who already had an evening out planned for them, and Philip was waiting for Tracey. Jessica was secretly pleased to see how warmly Tracey greeted her fiancé. She herself picked up her case and looked round for directions to the buses, but a familiar voice stopped her.

'This way for your very own taxi, petal.' Her parents stood there smiling broadly and she embraced them with delight.

'I did say I'd make my own way back,' she said in mild reproach.

'But a car waiting for you is much better,' her step-father told her. 'Anyway, we couldn't wait to see you and hear about Prague.'

'It was wonderful!' Jessica said as she settled into the old but cherished family car. She told them about the various sites, about the comfortable hotel and the meals they had enjoyed. She did mention briefly that a bystander had stopped a thief from snatching her bag, but did not say any more about James Strang.

Her mother always wanted every scrap of information about any young man who met her unmarried only child, which could get exhausting. Anyway, a chance encounter with an attractive stranger was an episode Jessica preferred to keep to herself rather than sharing it with her parents.

The next day it was back to work as usual, though Jessica could not help feeling that she had been away for far longer than a weekend. At lunchtime she tried to explain this feeling to George, a hospital administrator with whom she sometimes chatted. 'There are so many things to see, and they cover so many centuries that time somehow seems to have been condensed there.'

George, scrupulously neat and tidy, frowned. 'I prefer to study a few things in depth,' he observed, carefully moving the salt, pepper and ketchup containers into a straight line.

'Well, yes. I'd like to go back to see some parts of the Palace again.'

'Duplicating the experience? Isn't that rather wasteful?'

Jessica pressed her lips together and then picked up the salt, shook a little on her food, and replaced it slightly out of alignment. George moved it back into place.

Jessica decided that, although George was intelligent and hard-working and would probably do well in his career, he could be very irritating.

There was a slight but definite change in the office atmosphere. Shannon and Susan now seemed to accept her into their circle of friends, but Jessica was still worried about Tracey. She seemed tense and brittle, easily upset, though she blamed everything on the run-up to the wedding.

'I never realised that people could have so many allergies,' she complained. 'I'm tired of ringing up the hotel to make sure they can provide food that doesn't contain meat, or cheese, or onions, or half a dozen other ingredients! And now the printer has messed up the wedding invitations!'

One day, when Tracey was out of the office, Shannon came over to Jessica's desk. 'Something's wrong with Tracey. I know she's got a lot on, but most brides don't get in such a state months before the wedding. She talks to you more than she does to us. Do you think she doesn't really want to get married?'

'I think it's just that she wants everything to be perfect,' Jessica answered, hoping that was true.

Shannon pursed her lips. 'I hope you are right. After all, I think she and Philip make a good couple.'

★   ★   ★

Ten days after her return from Prague, Jessica came home after a particularly wearing day. There had been an emergency and she had to reschedule the whole of the consultant's programme as well as dealing with those who didn't see why they should be inconvenienced by his problems. She wanted tea, then a long soak in a hot bath, then bed, but as soon as she put her key in the front door her step-father opened it, his finger on his lips.

'You've got a visitor!' he hissed.

Her heart sank. 'A visitor? Who?'

'I've never seen him before. He's in

the front room with your mother.'

Jessica slipped her coat off and reluctantly prepared to find out who the unexpected visitor was. She could hear her mother's voice, obviously a little nervous as she entertained the stranger.

'I'm sure Jessica won't be long now,' she was saying.

'In fact I'm here now, Mother,' Jessica told her, and looked curiously at the man who stood up as she came in. He was neatly dressed in a dark business suit and sober tie, and it was a second before she recognised him.

'James! James Strang!'

'So you have met?' her mother said.

'Of course. We met in Prague,' Jessica told her, and saw from her mother's expression that she would face a long interrogation at the first available opportunity.

She turned back to James. 'It's a surprise to see you, but a nice one. What are you doing in Manchester?'

'I'm looking for suppliers again. As I'm staying in Manchester overnight, I wondered whether you would care to have dinner with me.'

Jessica heaved a sigh. 'It has been a hard day . . . ' she began. James' face did not fall, rather it became completely expressionless, and Jessica reproached herself. After all, this was the man who had rescued her from a thief and then given her an enjoyable tour round Prague. She owed him something. ' . . . so I need a shower first,' she went on smoothly. 'Are you prepared to wait for half an hour?'

'No problem,' he responded, his face lighting up.

'Then I'll make a cup of tea,' Mrs Clarke told him, a lot happier now the stranger had been identified and approved by her daughter.

Jessica managed to shower, apply a little make-up and slip into a suitable dress for dinner in slightly less than half an hour, and then rescued James from her step-father, who had embarked on a long monologue about the best ways to fish for trout. A taxi was rapidly summoned and James directed it to a well-known restaurant near the city centre.

'It may be full,' Jessica said anxiously. 'I hear it is very popular.'

'I booked a table,' he told her. 'That doesn't mean I took it for granted you would come out with me,' he added hastily. 'If you'd refused, I would be sitting alone at a table for two.'

'Does that often happen when you are travelling?'

'More often than not, so I'm very grateful you agreed to come tonight.'

At the restaurant they were shown to a well-placed, roomy table. The chef specialised in classic British dishes and they agreed on soup as a first course, with pheasant to follow. James recommended which wines they should drink and Jessica accepted his choice. The soup was excellent, and Jessica began to relax and enjoy herself. Perhaps this really was what she needed to compensate for the awful day!

'Do I call you Jessica, or is there

some other version of the name which you prefer?' James enquired.

'You can call me Jessica,' she said firmly. 'I warn you that if you call me Jess I shall stand up, scream, and pour my soup over you.'

He laughed. 'And if you call me anything but James I'll do the same.'

She sipped a little more soup and then looked at him inquisitively. 'Are you here trying to find something for your firm?'

He nodded. 'I have quite a shopping list this time, but at the moment I'm on my way to Wales to try to buy enough slate to roof a large house.'

'I thought slate was out-of-date.'

He looked at her with horror. 'Out-of-date? It's a beautiful material on the right house. Why do you think slate tiles are stolen so often?'

Before she could not think of a reply there was a brief silence before they were suddenly interrupted.

'Jessica! It is you! We just dropped in for a drink at the bar.' It was Tracey, with Philip in tow. Tracey turned to James. 'Have we met before?'

'Briefly, in Prague,' Jessica said. 'James called at the hotel just as we were leaving for the Palace.'

'Oh! I remember! The mystery man.'

'Tracey, shall we leave them to have their meal in peace?' Philip interrupted, but Tracey was looking enviously at the table.

'I keep telling Philip I'd like to eat here, but it looks as if I'll have to settle for a pizza again tonight.'

'Then, please, why don't you join us?' James asked them politely.

'What a brilliant idea! Where can we get some chairs?' Tracey exclaimed before Philip could respond, and James lifted a hand to summon a waiter. Soon the table was set for four.

'We'll skip the first course, and then you won't have to wait for us,' Philip said firmly, giving Tracey a sharp look.

Jessica was beginning to suspect that Tracey had already had more than one drink and she certainly insisted on having a generous amount of wine as the meal progressed.

Philip looked annoyed, James was carefully polite, and Jessica felt a headache coming on as Tracey chattered relentlessly about her forthcoming wedding. Jessica already knew of the difficulties with the bridesmaids' dresses and she was sure that James was not interested. It was a relief when the meal was over and coffee was served.

The waiter brought the bill and presented it to James.

'We must pay our share,' Philip insisted, reaching for the piece of paper. Then he looked at it and swallowed hard, trying to cover his own embarrassment. James deftly twitched the bill away from him.

'I asked you to join us,' he said firmly. 'You are my guests.'

Philip's protests were half-hearted, and he thanked James profusely before tearing Tracey away.

'I should think they'll have the most awful row about this later on,' Jessica said thoughtfully.

'I hope so. This is the second time I've tried to take you out, only to have your friends ruin my plans,' James commented. 'And your parents treated me with great suspicion. What's wrong with me?'

'My parents still regard me as a little girl who has to be protected from strangers,' she told him, and then frowned. 'There's nothing wrong with you, but I don't know what's wrong with Tracey lately. At least she won't be able to go on talking about her wedding plans once she's married.'

'No,' James said glumly. 'She'll probably spend the next few years talking about what happened at her wedding — and she'll have photographs to bore you with endlessly.'

They smiled at each other warmly, but then Jessica tried to conceal a yawn and failed.

'It's time to take you home,' James said resignedly.

'I'm sorry, it's been a bit of a

disastrous evening,' she said sadly.

James smiled comfortingly. 'It wasn't all disastrous. I thoroughly enjoyed the beginning.'

'Perhaps we could meet some other time while you are in Manchester?' she said hesitantly, but he shook his head.

'Unfortunately I leave for Wales early tomorrow.' He felt in his pocket and held out a card. 'But here is my card — again. Call me if you're ever in Birmingham, and next time I'm in Manchester I'll contact you.' He stood up. 'Now, we need a taxi.'

They were silent during the drive until she tentatively mentioned money. She was worried about the bill, afraid that James had booked that particular restaurant because he wanted to impress her and that unexpectedly having to pay for four might be more than he could comfortably afford.

'I'm a modern girl, you know' she told him. 'I'm willing to pay half the bill. After all, why should you pay for my friends?'

'I'm paying,' he said with finality.

When they reached her home he asked the taxi to wait, an indication that he didn't want to be invited in. Perhaps he saw the lights on downstairs and realised that her parents were waiting up for her.

'Well, thank you and good night,' Jessica said, wondering whether that was enough, or if he expected some other form of farewell.

He settled the matter by leaning forward and taking her gently by the shoulders, then he bent and kissed her briefly on the cheek. 'Good night, Jessica.' Then he slipped into the taxi and was gone.

Jessica sighed, let herself in, and prepared for her parents' inquisition.

She stuck to the facts when it came to describing the evening, listing the dishes they had eaten, describing the restaurant's décor, and telling them how Tracey and Philip had joined them.

'I didn't tell you about meeting him in Prague because it was a minor incident and I didn't expect to see him again,' she protested when her mother reproached her for leaving them ignorant of James' existence.

'Why can't you have a boyfriend we know, someone local?' her mother complained. 'All you know about this man is that he's a travelling salesman, and you know what their reputation is like.'

'James doesn't sell things, he buys them,' Jessica pointed out.

'That's nearly the same,' her mother said triumphantly.

Finally she pleaded exhaustion and escaped to her bedroom, but it was difficult to sleep. Her mother was right, of course. She knew little about James and didn't even know if what he had told her was true. But she liked him and her instinct was to trust him. Anyway, what did it matter? It had been obvious that he'd only invited her out because he didn't want to spend another lonely evening by himself.

She thought about the few boyfriends

she'd had — they had all been known to her family, pleasant, hard-working and reliable, and they made it clear that they were dating her because they saw the same qualities in her. Her parents would have welcomed any one of them as a son-in-law. But whenever one of them had shown signs of getting really serious and had started hinting at marriage, Jessica found some excuse to end the relationship. The truth was that she had found them all rather boring.

One of the reasons she'd wanted to go to university was to meet new people from different backgrounds, to experience the excitement of new attitudes to life without having to take risks herself. In a way, she regretted missing out on that even more than she regretted the academic qualifications she could have achieved.

3

Tracey looked very heavy-eyed the next day and required several cups of coffee before she could start work properly, nodding very carefully when Jessica asked if she had enjoyed herself last night.

'It was a good meal.' But she did not look as if she was remembering the evening with pleasure. 'The trouble was,' she confided, 'that afterwards Philip kept saying we shouldn't have joined you, and that your friend only asked us to out of politeness. But I told him it would've been rude of us to refuse the invitation.'

'So you had an argument?' Jessica enquired, feeling rather guilty at the fact that her prediction had come true.

'We had yet another argument,' Tracey said moodily. 'It's all we seem to do nowadays.' But by lunchtime she had recovered enough to give the other girls a full account.

'So I hear that man you met in Prague took you to one of the best restaurants in town last night,' Shannon commented, perching herself on the edge of Jessica's desk.

'Yes,' Jessica said curtly, but Shannon stayed where she was.

'And then Tracey dragged Philip over to you and they ended up spending the rest of the evening with you. How did your boyfriend feel about that?'

'He's not my boyfriend,' Jessica said patiently. 'He just happened to be in Manchester. I very much doubt if I'll see him again.'

'But you might have done if Tracey hadn't butted in,' Shannon said shrewdly. 'I still think there's something wrong, something worrying her.'

'Well, she'll soon be on her honeymoon, and we'll just have to hope that solves the problem.'

'Two weeks of sun and Philip? Maybe it'll work at that,' and Shannon produced a surprisingly dirty laugh.

In spite of the fact that George gave the impression he cared only about his work, Jessica had noticed that he did manage to hear all the hospital gossip and she was not surprised when he referred to her evening out.

'I think this man should have phoned to ask you out. Actually appearing at your house without warning put you under unwarranted pressure to accept his invitation.'

'Perhaps he wanted me to have dinner with him so much that he didn't want to risk a refusal,' she said flippantly, but his face remained disapproving. 'Anyway, I had an excellent meal at a very good restaurant. I enjoy a treat like that sometimes.'

George's expression grew even blacker. 'Do you realise that a place like that charges at least three times the value of the food? I see no point in paying other people to cook food for you when you could cook it at home for a fraction of the cost and be sure about the hygiene.'

Jessica looked at him dispassionately.

'You've dropped something on your tie,' she told him, and took a guilty pleasure in his agitated search for the non-existent spot.

★ ★ ★

It looked as though Jessica was going to have an unusually busy social week, for the next day her mother welcomed her home with the news that they were having an early tea because Mrs Mallory had invited them round later that evening.

'What's the occasion?' Jessica asked as she shrugged off her coat. 'I thought we were only asked round there at Christmas.'

'It's not a special occasion, but she said it was a long time since she had seen us and it would be nice to have a friendly chat.'

Mrs Mallory lived a few doors away in an identical semi-detached house, though she always gave the impression that she felt slightly socially superior to her neighbours, and neither Jessica nor her step-father looked forward to the evening. Her mother would probably enjoy spotting Mrs Mallory's latest purchases and Mrs Mallory would enjoy telling her about them.

So Jessica found herself, a little after seven, obediently accompanying her mother and step-father along the road. It was only as her mother was about to knock on the door that she turned to Jessica and said brightly and innocently, 'Oh! I forgot to tell you — Brian will be here this evening, too.'

Jessica could not turn and run because her step-father was behind her, blocking the path, and anyway it was too late because Mrs Mallory was already opening the door. Jessica followed her mother into the hall, trying to keep her smile in place.

Brian Mallory was a year older than she was and they had gone to the same school. He had been an unpleasant, cocky little boy who had enjoyed teasing her and playing unkind tricks on their journeys to and from school when she was young, and when she became a teenager he had seen her as a possible target for his fumbling sexual experiments until she'd threatened to tell her step-father if he tried to touch her again. He had gone to university, managed a third-class degree, and she'd heard that for the past year he had been working for a large building firm. Jessica's mother, blissfully unaware of how her daughter felt about him, had long thought that he would make a good match for Jessica.

Now he embraced Jessica as if they had been dear friends for years and managed to plant a wet kiss on her cheek before she could dodge. He also sat close beside her on the couch until she shifted away from him. At least with their parents sitting with them there was nothing else he could try.

The conversation covered the weather, the state of the gardens, and the prospects of the local football teams. Then Mrs Mallory asked Jessica about her trip to Prague and listened politely, but as soon as Jessica finished her description, Mrs Mallory moved on to her favourite topic — Brian.

While her son sat complacently by, she told the Clarkes how well he was doing and how bright his future prospects were. When asked, Brian told them how many hundreds of speculative buildings his firm had planned, and how much better they were doing than their rivals. A thought struck Jessica. Maybe he could give her some information about James's firm. 'Do you know of a Birmingham firm of architects called Hinton?' she enquired politely. 'I met someone recently who was buying supplies for them.'

Brian frowned and shook his head. 'Hinton? Never heard of them. Probably one of these firms that build a few houses where they can. My firm takes over dozens of them every year.' This casual dismissal of James's firm did not mean much apart from showing that it was not well-known to minor employees of large firms but, still, it was not reassuring and her mother's expression showed this.

Later that evening Mrs Mallory insisted on showing her guests how her kitchen had been refitted. Jessica, lagging behind, found herself with Brian. Pushing the kitchen door shut with his foot, he slid an arm round her. 'Perhaps we could go out together some evening,' he murmured. 'We could enjoy ourselves without the oldies.'

'I'm busy,' she said curtly.

'I haven't suggested a date yet, so how do you know if you'll be busy?'

'Whatever date you say, I'll be busy,' she said coldly. 'And if you don't take your hand off my backside I'll put my high heel through your foot.'

Hastily he stood away from her and sulked the remainder of the evening.

Her mother reproached her on the way home. 'Brian's a nice boy,' she said. 'What did you do to upset him?'

Jessica was tempted to tell her exactly what she had said to Brian, but knew that this would spoil her mother's evening and probably lead to a feud with the Mallorys. 'I don't like him,' was all she said. 'He's not my type.'

'He's not my type either,' said her step-father in unexpected support. 'He's got far too high an opinion of himself.'

Faced with this united opposition, her mother dropped the subject.

★ ★ ★

In the morning Jessica took out the card James had given her. It had his name and two telephone numbers, the words 'Hinton Architects', and an address in Birmingham. Certainly not enough information to satisfy her mother. It was curiosity, nothing else, Jessica told herself, that made her call Hinton's. After all, she should thank James properly for taking her out.

The phone was answered promptly and with professional courtesy. 'Hintons, architects. How may I help you?' It was a confident, female voice.

'May I speak to Mr James Strang?'

Jessica replied, trying to sound as business-like as a possible customer.

There was a pause. 'Who?'

'Mr James Strang. He does work there, doesn't he?'

Another pause. 'I'll just see if Mr Strang is available.' There was a longer pause this time. 'I'm sorry. Mr Strang is out of the office at the moment. Can I take a message?'

'No, thank you. I needed to talk to Mr Strang himself.'

The voice grew more insistent. 'Perhaps I can help? If you would like to give me your name . . . '

'No, thank you,' Jessica repeated, and put the phone down. Well, she would probably never see James Strang again, or hear from him, but at least she had confirmed that he did work at Hintons. She looked at the little card with the name and telephone numbers, dropped it in the waste-paper basket and then, a minute later, picked it out and put it back in her bag, though she didn't know why.

A couple of days later, Jessica was surprised when George drew her aside and asked her if she would go to the cinema with him.

'I may not be able to afford fancy expensive restaurants,' he said, 'but this film has received very good reviews.'

She had actually wanted to see the film and had no good reason to refuse, so accepted the invitation without expecting to enjoy the evening too much, but was pleasantly surprised. George ushered her to good seats where they found themselves laughing in unison at the comedy and enjoying the musical interludes. She came out of the cinema in a good mood and agreed to a coffee in a nearby restaurant.

'Thank you for taking me to see that,' she said to George.

'It was a pleasure. I don't go out much, and having your company this evening made it much more enjoyable.'

It was stiff, it was stilted, but it was definitely a compliment and it was definitely sincere. Perhaps the smile

Jessica gave him in return helped George to relax and open up more than usual.

'I know the people at the hospital think that all I care about is my work, but I know from what I have heard that you have reasons for playing safe and wanting security, and so have I. My father was a gambler. Sometimes he won, and then he would shower us with presents, but more often he lost and I have some painful memories of creditors coming to our house and demanding money, reducing my mother to tears. As a result, I don't take risks and I don't waste money.'

Jessica found herself patting his hand. 'I understand how you must feel,' she said softly, and he smiled at her gratefully.

'Perhaps we can go out together again,' he said hopefully.

She refused his offer to see her home, assuring him that it would be a waste of his time as the bus would drop her almost at her door. She decided that she might go out with him again, but not too frequently, and only as a companion, as she certainly could not regard him as a possible boyfriend.

* ★ ★

One Tuesday Jessica found herself in the fortunate position of not having to work. The consultant had decided at the last minute to go to a conference and would not be back till the evening.

'You needn't come in, Jessica. You've worked enough extra hours to deserve a day off,' he told her the previous day. She thanked him, though wishing she had been given more notice so she could decide what to do. Looking through the papers that evening, she saw that Birmingham Museum was having a special exhibition of Anglo-Saxon gold artefacts, whose barbaric splendour she had always admired.

'I think I'll go and see it,' she told her mother. 'There are plenty of trains.'

'It takes a couple of hours. What will you do in that time?'

'Read a book. It's probably what I'd do if I stayed here anyhow.'

Jessica followed this plan, but even after she had admired the exhibition, looked round other galleries in the museum, and had a snack in the coffee shop, it was only mid-afternoon. What else could she do in Birmingham? It was time to admit that she knew very well what she intended to do and that it had been a major reason why she had decided to come to Birmingham.

'Do you know where this address is?' she asked an attendant, showing him James's card. He peered at it and then nodded.

'It's very near here. Go out, turn right, walk down the road and take the second turning on the left.'

She followed his directions and found herself in a cul-de-sac whose impressive nineteenth-century buildings had been converted into offices. The address she was looking for was in a building whose brickwork glowed from a recent cleaning. She hesitated, wondering if she was doing the right thing or risking a humiliating encounter, but then hoisted her shoulder bag higher and walked across the road into the building.

The small panelled lobby had two lifts and a list of the tenants. 'Hinton Architects' was on the top floor. When Jessica stepped out of the lift she was in an elegant reception area and was greeted immediately by an equally elegant receptionist.

'I'd like to speak to James Strang, if he is here,' she told the woman and after admitting that she didn't have an appointment she was invited to take a seat on a sleekly designed chair while the receptionist picked up her telephone and pressed various keys.

'A young lady would like to see Mr Strang,' she said. Then she turned to Jessica, lifting her eyebrows interrogatively.

'My name is Jessica Clarke.'

'Miss Jessica Clarke,' the receptionist repeated. 'Yes,' she said slowly, in response to some question, then, 'Yes,' again, followed by, 'Probably.' Then she put the phone down. 'Miss Chalmers will be with you directly,' she smiled, and seconds later an equally smart but rather older woman came through one of the doors leading off the area. Jessica rose.

'Miss Clarke?' said the newcomer, without a smile. 'Will you come this way, please?' and Jessica was ushered into an office where Miss Chalmers saw her seated before taking her own place behind the desk.

'I'm Mr Strang's secretary. He should be here soon, but perhaps I can help you,' she said coolly, and frowned when Jessica declined. 'If you're here on a business matter, I can ask Mr Hinton himself to see you.'

'It's a personal matter,' Jessica said firmly. 'I'll wait for Mr Strang.' After all, what else could she do now?

It was an uncomfortable wait but she couldn't see how she could leave with dignity now. Jessica had never imagined that James would have an impressive secretary and his own office. Her mental picture of his probable base had been of a neglected desk in the corner of a large general office which he would visit only at intervals when he was not out buying materials,

Five minutes passed, then ten. Miss Chalmers was fidgeting and casting glances at Jessica from time to time, and Jessica began to feel that she was a fool, wasting her time, and that she should save what dignity she could and leave and go home. But just as she decided that she definitely was going to stand up and leave, the door opened and James strode in.

'Hello, Agnes, anything new?' he said breezily, and then stopped short when he saw Jessica.

'Miss Clarke wishes to see you on a personal matter,' Miss Chalmers said freezingly, but James did not hear her. He took Jessica's hands in his and she smiled at him, warmed by his obvious pleasure at the sight of her.

'Jessica, how marvellous! I was

thinking of you earlier,' he said and slipped his arm round her shoulder to guide her through yet another door. 'Coffee for two, please, Agnes,' he said.

His office was big, with two adjoining walls of floor-to-ceiling windows that provided stunning views over the city. His desk was large and plain, but made of beautiful mahogany. There was a computer desk and two filing cabinets made of the same wood. By the windows were some comfortable chairs around a coffee table. Jessica gazed around almost in awe, and then turned challengingly to James.

'You're not just a buyer or a company rep, are you?'

He grinned. 'Is that what you thought? No, in fact I'm the junior partner. Edward Hinton is my uncle. My father used to work with him and married his sister.' He settled her into one of the chairs by the coffee table, sat down himself and leant forward. 'Now, what brings you here?'

This was difficult. A humble buyer

might be flattered if a young woman came looking for him, but the partner in a successful firm might feel that he was being pursued. She settled for most of the truth.

'I came to see the exhibition at the Museum, found I had time to spare, and decided to look you up.'

'I'm glad you did. What did you think of the exhibition? I was amazed by the sheer quantity of the gold.'

They chatted about the exhibition while they enjoyed the coffee Miss Chalmers had produced — proper china cups, Jessica noted; her mother would have been impressed.

'What train do you plan to catch?' James asked, noting her swift glance at her watch.

'There's one just before seven.'

'The office will be closing soon. There's a pleasant hotel near the station. If we leave now we'll have time for a quick drink together to celebrate this unexpected meeting.'

Just then his door opened to admit a

slender, white-haired man in shirtsleeves. 'James, did I ask you about the Neils enquiry?' he asked, and stopped short when he saw Jessica. 'I'm so sorry, I didn't realise you had a client with you.'

James stood. 'You're not interrupting, Uncle. Jessica is a friend, not a client, and I'm just about to take her for a drink.'

The newcomer pushed his spectacles back into place and smiled amiably at Jessica. 'I'm glad to hear it. James works too hard, my dear. He should spend more time with pretty girls like you.'

It was obvious flattery; Jessica laughed, and was rewarded by a shameless and attractive grin.

'Uncle, stop flirting with the girl,' James said with mock severity. 'Come on, Jessica, or he'll be offering to take you out himself.'

4

The hotel to which James took her was very pleasant indeed, with large and comfortable studded leather armchairs, in which they now sat with their drinks on the table in front of them.

'I was impressed by your office,' Jessica remarked as they waited for their drinks to arrive. 'Tell me about Hinton's. What does it specialise in?'

James's eyes lit up. Obviously this was a favourite subject. 'My uncle started the firm about thirty years ago with the aim of creating beautiful buildings, and my father joined him soon afterwards. They were both architects, and they had similar aims. It was difficult at first but gradually their work became known and has prospered. The firm specialises in one-off houses and the occasional office or small hotel, but never anything bigger. I joined the firm when I left university, and Uncle Edward made me a partner soon after my father died five years ago.'

'But you're not an architect?' she asked.

He shook his head a little sadly. 'I wanted to be. I would have been perfectly competent designing the usual, run-of-the-mill stuff, but I just hadn't got the spark that helps people design special, unique buildings. However, I have got an eye for detail and materials, so I specialise in that. It gives me an excuse to travel occasionally. I'm gradually taking on more responsibility, however, and eventually I'll take over from my uncle.' His face grew grim. 'The only real fly in the ointment is that one of the country's largest building firms would like to buy us up. They build big estates of identical houses all over the country, and I think they believe that if our firm were to become part of them it would improve their image.'

'And you don't want that?'

'No!' he said vehemently. 'How long

do you think it would be before their accountants started looking at our figures and having heart attacks at the amounts we spend on what they would consider inessentials? Soon they would be suggesting how we could cut our costs by lowering our standards a little, and that, I'm afraid, is the slippery slope.'

'Who will decide whether Hinton's is sold or not?'

'I have a third of the shares, Uncle Edward has half, and my mother has the rest. My uncle is undecided, but he'll be retiring before long, so it wouldn't affect him much as far as work goes, though it would mean he would retire with a lot more money. My mother has moved to St Mawes, in Cornwall, and spends her time paint-ing. She says she'll let me decide. So I've just got to wait for my uncle to make up his mind.'

He shook his head. 'Let's change the subject. Can I ask a personal question? You're here alone — you haven't got a boyfriend, or is he at work?'

'I haven't got a boyfriend at the moment.'

He smiled wryly. 'I'm not going out with anyone either. I was for some time, but then she ended it. She said being with me was fun, but I wasn't the person she wanted to spend her life with.' He frowned. 'She said she couldn't imagine discussing children's names with me or deciding which school they should go to!' He shrugged. 'I suppose she was right. I was rather annoyed that she dropped me, but I wasn't exactly heartbroken.'

They looked at each other, on the verge of a mutual understanding, and then a voice broke in. 'So, Miss Jessica Clarke, you seem to be enjoying Birmingham. Who's your friend?' Looking down at the two of them with a sneering smile was Brian Mallory.

'What are you doing here?' Jessica demanded.

'Enjoying an evening out with friends,' he responded, nodding to a large group.

He looked at James, who was frowning up at him. 'The folks at home will be interested to hear how you're spending your time, Jessica. Bye.'

He was gone, back to his friends, and the mood was ruined.

'Who was that?' James demanded.

'An idiot whom I have loathed since we were at school together,' she told him. 'Incidentally, he works for a large building firm.'

'Is he an accountant?'

'He's something in an office, but I'm not sure what.' James snorted and she looked at him reprovingly. 'Remember, so am I.' She looked at her watch. 'Well, thank you for the drink, but I'd better get to the station now.'

He waited with her until her train arrived and saw her safely on board. 'I'm glad you thought it worth coming to see me.'

He was holding her hands, she realised, and his grip was warm and firm. Their eyes met, and suddenly there seemed a lot to say, but it was too late because the train was about to leave.

'It's been a very pleasant few hours.'

'Perhaps we can meet again?'

That was unlikely, she thought as the train drew out of the station, and she assumed that he was just being polite. It was a pity, because she had enjoyed his company and would have liked to know him better, but geographical facts could not be altered. Manchester was still a long way from Birmingham.

★   ★   ★

'Was the exhibition worth the train journey?' her mother enquired when she got home.

'Well worth it,' she replied, a little cagey.

'Did you spend the whole day in the museum?' her mother pushed.

It was confession time. 'Well — not all of it. I met James Strang for a drink. You remember him. He called here and took me out for dinner.'

Her mother's lips tightened. 'I remember — the rep.'

'Not exactly a rep,' and she told her mother about Hinton's.

Her mother was quiet for a while after she had finished. 'So this Mr Strang — James — isn't just a rep or a buyer after all. He's actually a partner in the firm?' she said at last. 'And the firm's doing quite well?'

'Extremely well, according to what he told me. He's certainly got all the trimmings — a big office and a dragon for a secretary.' Jessica looked at her mother sharply. 'Forget it, Mother. I'm very unlikely to ever see him again, so stop thinking of him as a possible boyfriend for me.'

Her mother sighed. 'It's a pity. You haven't met many presentable, well-mannered and rich young men.'

'The world is full of them. I'll meet another,' Jessica giggled.

★   ★   ★

Life went on as usual. She went to work each day at the hospital, which was singularly lacking in eligible young men, went out with George a couple of times and then found herself trying to avoid him because she was afraid he was growing too serious, even showing signs of possessiveness at work, which amused the other girls but annoyed her considerably.

As her wedding drew nearer, Tracey stopped talking about anything else, until one Friday afternoon Shannon threatened to scream if she heard any more about bridesmaids and their dresses. Tracey was hurt and grew tearful, and Jessica was relieved when it was time to go home for the weekend. That evening, about eight o'clock, the telephone rang. Her mother answered and then put her hand over the receiver.

'It's for you, Jessica,' she hissed. 'It's that young architect.'

It was indeed James, and he sounded very agitated.

'Jessica! Are you doing anything this weekend?'

Was he coming to Manchester? Did

this mean another dinner date? Well, at least she would have time to get ready properly. 'I hadn't planned anything special. Why?'

'Can you meet me at Manchester Airport, Terminal One, at seven tomorrow morning? I'm going to Madrid and I need a secretary.'

She held the receiver away from her and looked at it in disbelief for a moment. 'What on earth are you talking about?'

She heard a deep sigh and then he started again. 'I've got to go to Madrid to meet an important client who wants us to build a house for him. I need a secretary to take notes while we discuss things. Miss Chalmers was coming with me but she's just phoned to say she can't come because her mother has taken ill, but unless I have someone to write down details of the discussion something may be forgotten. So I thought of you. You're a secretary, and you liked Prague so I know you'll like Madrid.'

His tone became wheedling. 'I'm offering you a free trip to Madrid, with spending money as well because I'll pay you. We'll see the client tomorrow afternoon and then we can spend the evening and Sunday morning looking round the city. We'll be back in Manchester by six on Sunday.'

Jessica was silent, wondering what to say, and his voice developed a note of desperation. 'Jessica! You can't let me down, I need you! And I know that you've never been to Madrid. Say you will come!'

She was a sensible girl who never took risks. How could she agree to his ridiculous last-minute pleas? But how could she refuse? After all, it would be work and she would be paid. 'Yes,' she said abruptly. 'I'll come.'

'Great! Remember — seven o'clock at Terminal One — and remember your passport!' and the line went dead.

Her parents were watching television when she stepped back into the lounge. 'Dad,' she said casually, 'can you give me a lift to the airport tomorrow morning?'

'I suppose so,' her step-father said absent-mindedly before both parents looked up at her, startled. 'Why?'

'Because I'm going to Madrid for the weekend.'

Then, of course, she had to explain. Her parents, especially her mother, were not happy, but she brushed their objections aside. 'It's a working weekend, plus time to look round Madrid — and I won't have to pay a penny for it.' She glared at them. 'I know that what you really want to do is ask if Mr Strang's intentions include getting me into bed. Well, I'm twenty-two and I can deal with him if he gets out of line. Now I'm going to pack.'

*   *   *

The next morning, driven to the airport by a step-father who complained all the way at having to get up so early on a Saturday, she found James waiting in the check-in area and saw the lines of anxiety on his face vanish as she appeared. So he had been afraid she might not come.

The flight was on time and she was delighted to find that they were travelling business class. She was aware of other passengers looking at them, seeing a good-looking young couple and assuming they were going away for a pleasant weekend. She looked sideways at James. If he had invited her to go to Madrid with him just so they could be together, would she have accepted? Well, he was an attractive man; she might have. James saw her smiling to herself and raised an eyebrow, but she laughed and shook her head. There was no way she was going to tell him what she had just been thinking.

When they landed at Madrid a chauffeur-driven car was waiting to take them to an imposing hotel opposite the Royal Palace where she had been assigned a room on the third floor.

James had booked a suite for himself. He apologised for the difference in their accommodation.

'A suite gives us a room suitable for meeting the client,' he explained.

A light lunch was served in the suite and James told her about the client, who she gathered was something to do with football and wanted a house built in Manchester which he could use as a base when he visited the city, which he apparently planned to do fairly frequently. They were there to find out exactly what the client wanted and then take the details back to England, where an architect would draw up the final plans for the house.

The client, Señor Perez, appeared at two o'clock. He was tall, thin and dark, with an air of total self-confidence. Unexpectedly he was accompanied by his wife, also tall, thin and dark, carefully made-up, and dressed in very elegant and clearly very expensive clothes.

Apparently the house would replace an old terraced building and would be on three floors, with a built-in garage and foyer on the ground floor, a reception room and small kitchen on the first floor, and two bedrooms with en suite bathrooms on the third floor. This basic plan had already been agreed, but the discussion of the details became very complicated. Jessica just managed to keep up with the various suggestions; the sudden realisation that the master bedroom had to have a linked dressing room, the long debate over whether the staircase should be wooden or an iron spiral, returning to something Señora Perez considered absolutely essential that had not been mentioned earlier . . . after nearly three hours Jessica was exhausted, although Señora Perez was obviously ready to continue for another hour at least.

'You'll receive the detailed plans very soon,' James assured the couple when all possible points had finally been debated. 'I'm sure you'll be delighted.' He shook hands, closed the door, and then collapsed on the couch. 'What a woman! When she casually mentioned that she had to have a fountain in the foyer I nearly gave up.'

'Can you do what she wants?'

'Most of it, and I can give her husband very good reasons why we can't do everything.' He sighed. 'We need him to give us the contract to build this house. With his connections, it would give us invaluable publicity and I might be able to convince my uncle that Hinton's should be kept out of the clutches of that building firm.' He sat up. 'Come on. Now we've got to make sense of everything.'

For two hours they laboured over Jessica's notes and James's scrawled designs until they had assembled an organised series of guidelines for the architect. Finally James snapped shut his laptop computer. 'That's it for one day! I need a drink!'

'We haven't eaten for a long time either,' Jessica reminded him.

'True. We'll see what the hotel has to offer.'

The hotel offered a very acceptable dinner, even though the dining-room was almost empty. 'Where is everybody?' she asked.

James looked round and laughed. 'Jessica, we're only able to eat now because the hotel is prepared to cater for the strange whims of foreigners. You won't find many restaurants open in Madrid at this hour because most Spaniards won't be eating until about ten o'clock.' He offered her another glass of wine. She refused, but he poured himself one. 'Now, the work is over and we can see Madrid. You'll find that wandering round a Spanish city in the evening is very enjoyable.'

Just at that moment his mobile phone rang. He took it out of his pocket and listened, and then looked at Jessica in mock despair. 'Perez!' he mouthed. Then followed five minutes when he listened, made an occasional comment, and finally ended with, 'We'll see you then.'

Putting his phone away, he broke the

bad news. 'Work is not yet over after all. Perez wants to see us tomorrow at ten o'clock. He has thought of a few more things.' He gritted his teeth. 'At least we have this evening. Let's get out of here and see Madrid.'

They sauntered through the evening crowds in the heart of the city, gazing up at the buildings as James gave her an analysis of their architecture. She only half-listened, preferring just to look at the scenes and the people. At one point he took her hand to guide her across a busy road. Afterwards her hand remained in his warm clasp. Her awareness of his nearness added to the pleasure of the evening.

Finally they sank down at a little table outside a café in a floodlit colonnaded square and James ordered coffee and brandy. They sat side by side viewing the constantly-moving spectacle till Jessica turned and found James looking at her.

'I like this,' she said with feeling. 'I love just being here and watching the people, hearing a different language.'

'I love being here with you,' he said quietly. She stared at him, wondering if she had heard correctly. He smiled at her. 'Do you remember when we met in Prague?'

'Yes. You were eager to correct my guide book.'

'Well, I had spent ten minutes wondering what excuse I could find to talk to you, get to know you. The moment I saw you I was attracted to you.' He smiled fleetingly. 'I think it was the nape of your neck. I wanted to stroke it.'

Jessica was scarlet, half-amused and half-indignant.

'And I let you take me off, show me round Prague . . . You didn't show any sign of wanting to . . . '

'Take you in my arms, feel your body against mine? I have some sense of self-preservation; I didn't want to frighten you off! Then the next day you went off with your friends, and when I did manage to take you out to dinner in

Manchester that couple insisted on joining us and ruined any romantic possibilities. But now I've finally got you to myself.'

Jessica realised that he was holding her hand, stroking it gently, and she closed her eyes, thrilling to his touch. She did like this man very much, and, clearly, he wanted her. But although she was attracted to him she was not sure that she was yet ready to accept him as a lover. Her innate caution warned her against being swept away by the glamour and the strangeness of her surroundings.

Abruptly he sat back, breaking the physical contact. 'But we're not going to spend the night together, Jessica, for two very good reasons. Firstly, I can see how it would appear to other people — the boss taking his secretary away for a dirty weekend and putting it on expenses. And secondly . . . ' he laughed self-consciously, 'I'm just too tired. I was up half the night preparing for this meeting with Perez, which was exhausting in itself.'

Jolted, she sat up straight, anxious to reclaim her dignity. 'There is a third reason. You haven't actually asked me if I would be willing and I might have said 'no'.'

He looked surprised, and then started to laugh ruefully. 'You're right, of course. I do apologise.' He gestured at the table. 'I'm afraid I'm so weary that the brandy is affecting me — loosening my tongue.' He took some money from his pocket and beckoned the waiter. 'Let's get back to the hotel for a good night's sleep.' He turned back to her challengingly. 'But as a matter of interest, what would you have said if I had asked you?'

She raised her eyebrows. 'You didn't ask me, so I don't have to decide.'

This time his laugh was one of genuine amusement. He saw her to the door of her room and she slipped the key card in the lock.

'Good night, sleep well,' he said, and bent forward to kiss her lightly on the lips. Then suddenly his arms were round her. 'I can do better than that,' he muttered, his voice thickening, but her palms were flat on his chest, pushing him away.

'Goodnight!' she said firmly, then slipped through her open door and closed it behind her. She leant against it, breathing deeply, and waited. After a few seconds she heard his footsteps going away towards the stairs. She sighed, telling herself that if she had welcomed him into her room, knowing that his self-control had been undermined by the brandy, they would both have regretted it the next day.

She went downstairs a little reluctantly the next morning, hoping that what had happened the previous evening would not make the day difficult, but James greeted her cheerfully at the breakfast buffet as if that last part of the evening had never happened, and she relaxed.

'Eat well. Señora Perez may have decided to have the garage silver-plated.

It could be a long morning.'

In fact, to their relief it was Señor Perez alone who appeared and who soon made it clear that his main aim was to indicate which of his wife's ideas he considered unnecessary.

'I will be coming to Manchester on business and my wife will rarely accompany me,' he explained. 'Therefore I think that in this case my wishes should take precedence.' The meeting lasted barely an hour and left James feeling much happier about the plans.

'We ought to get to the airport by just after two. Now, there's a small group of old houses near the Puerta del Sol . . . '

'I'm going to the Prado,' Jessica told him.

'The Prado? But everyone goes there!'

'With good reason. It has some of the greatest pictures in the world. We looked at buildings yesterday evening. Now it's my turn to choose. Anyway, you should like its building.'

He gave in but with bad grace. They

spent two hours in the gallery and Jessica was enthralled, barely aware of him following her around reluctantly.

'Wasn't that marvellous?' she breathed when they emerged.

'All those saints and angels one after the other? It was boring.'

She was unable to convince him that this point of view was artistic heresy and they wandered into the park behind the Prado for a snack, then just had time to hail a taxi to the hotel to collect their luggage, then on to the airport.

'You coped very well with the Perezes. I'm very glad you agreed to come because I would have been lost without you,' he complimented her as they sat in the airport waiting for their flight. 'I hope you've enjoyed yourself, in spite of my stupid behaviour yesterday evening.'

The apology was rather late, but at least he had made it.

'Let's forget that. A strange, exciting place does tend to loosen one's inhibitions,' she told him.

'But not yours.'

She smiled to herself. He did not know how close she had come to forgiving his masculine arrogance last night and flinging the door open to call him back before he reached the stairs.

5

Once again they had a trouble-free flight. James was planning to return to Birmingham by train but insisted on seeing Jessica to a taxi at Manchester Airport. He handed the driver enough to cover the fare and then stood by the vehicle as if wondering how to say goodbye. He smiled down at her. 'Thank you for everything, particularly for the way you stopped me making too big a fool of myself.'

Suddenly he opened his briefcase and gave Jessica a white foolscap envelope. 'I nearly forgot. Here are your wages for the weekend.'

She pushed the envelope away. 'You don't have to pay me. I've had a marvellous free city break.'

'You earned it twice over.' He tossed it on to her lap and stood back. 'Goodbye, Jessica. Look after yourself.'

His voice had a note of finality. Perhaps he felt that it would be embarrassing to see her again. She could not decide whether she was relieved or disappointed. Fingering the envelope, she was glad she had not called him back to her room the previous night. To have taken money from him afterwards would have left a bitter aftertaste.

Back home she was received with a certain stiffness which rapidly vanished as she chatted on about what she had seen in Madrid and how difficult the clients had been.

'Did you say he was called Juan Perez?' interrupted her step-father.

'Yes. Have you heard of him? He's something to do with football in Madrid,' she told him, recalling his addiction to the game.

'Something to do with football? He's the big boss there! And you say he's going to be coming to Manchester? There was a rumour about that.'

'His wife is always in the fashion pages in magazines,' Jessica's mother added eagerly, and implored Jessica to tell them every detail that she could remember about Señor and Señora Perez and their new house.

However, when she later found herself alone with her mother, Mrs Clarke lifted one eyebrow and said, 'Well?'

'Nothing happened,' her daughter replied, though honesty compelled her to add, 'It might have done if he hadn't been so conceited and taken it for granted that I was his for the asking. So I slapped him down.'

'Good!' said her mother.

At that point Jessica remembered the envelope James had given her. She ripped it open and stared at the cheque it contained. 'But this is too much!' she exclaimed.

Her mother peered at it. 'I don't think so. You gave up your weekend at very short notice and did some useful work for him. Keep it and treat yourself. Buy a new dress for Tracey's wedding.'

Jessica groaned. 'For two whole days I was able to forget about Tracey's wedding. Just remember, Mother, that if I do ever decide to get married I shall either elope or have the quietest wedding possible.'

'Let's wait and see,' was her mother's rejoinder.

★   ★   ★

Jessica was very careful to keep her visit to Madrid a secret from the people she worked with, being very well aware of the gossip and speculation that would sweep the department if her mini-adventure became known, and she hated to think how George would react if he learnt about it. However, she could not swear her mother to secrecy and, one Saturday afternoon when she was helping her mother arrange seating in the church hall for a meeting, Brian Mallory came looking for her. At first she assumed he had come with his mother, who was also helping, but he placed himself near Jessica so that she could not move the next pile of chairs without asking him to get out of the way.

'I'll go in a minute,' he told her, 'but I want to have a word with you first.'

'We have nothing to talk about.'

'Yes, we have. I want to talk to you about Hinton's.'

She stared at him, taken aback, and he smiled smugly. 'Your mother couldn't wait to tell mine that you were getting very friendly with one of the partners at Hinton's. Now, I'd checked on that firm after you asked me about it, and I found out that my firm wants to take it over — in fact, they are very keen to do so. So I was thinking that you could use your influence to persuade young Mr Strang to sell. My firm would be very grateful to you, and to me for getting you to help us.'

Jessica picked up a chair and forced herself past him. 'You're wasting your time. I won't be seeing James Strang again, and even if I were I would not try to influence his decision. Now, either help me carry these chairs or stop annoying me before I scream!' She left him gazing after her angrily.

★　★　★

It was two weeks before Tracey's wedding, and to the relief of the other girls in the office she'd fallen very quiet, though Jessica noticed that she seemed to spend a lot of time staring out of the window, her work forgotten. Tracey had arranged to take the week before the wedding off, and Shannon pointed out with some annoyance that she and Susan would definitely be overworked, as Jessica had already arranged to take that week as part of her annual holiday leave. She was planning a quiet break doing nothing very much except relax and read.

Jessica was tidying her desk in the last minutes before the office closed on Friday afternoon when she became aware of Tracey hovering nearby. 'Did you want something?' she enquired.

Tracey shook her head but didn't move away. 'I was just wondering,' she said at last, 'if you'd like to come for a coffee before we go home?'

Jessica sighed. Tracey had been almost silent all day. Now she obviously wanted to talk about something, but Jessica felt she just couldn't stand listening to the other girl's worries about her wedding. She wanted to go home. Tracey would have to find someone else to listen to her woes.

'I'm sorry, Tracey, I'd like to but I haven't got the time to spare,' she said firmly. Tracey's face fell, and for a moment Jessica almost relented. Couldn't she spare a few minutes? But she told herself that the few minutes would probably stretch to an hour or more and hardened her heart. 'I'll see you next week — at your wedding,' she added, gathering up her bag.

'Yes, of course,' Tracey said apathetically and Jessica left, reflecting that things must be bad if Tracey wasn't even sparked into life by the mention of the wedding.

* * *

Jessica enjoyed her peaceful weekend but on Monday afternoon, when she returned from a visit to the library, she found her mother in the kitchen with her arms round a woman who was in tears. Mrs Clarke looked up with relief when Jessica came in. 'Look, Mrs Ellis, here's Jessica. She'll be able to help you.'

'Help with what?' Jessica asked, concerned.

'With Tracey!' the woman wailed, deeply distressed. 'She's run away!'

Light dawned. 'You're the mother of Tracey from the office — Tracey Ellis? What's happened?'

Mrs Ellis prepared to repeat her story to Jessica while Mrs Clarke seized the opportunity to put the kettle on for a cup of tea.

'Tracey went off this morning. She

was supposed to see the hairdresser and show her the tiara she'll be wearing with her veil on Saturday, but then I got a call from the hairdresser saying Tracey hadn't come in and asking if she was going to be late. So I went up to Tracey's room, and there was an envelope on her bed addressed to me!' She paused dramatically and Mrs Clarke made soothing noises while she counted out the teabags. 'It said that she had decided she needed time to think about things so she was going to stay with her friend, Elaine Pitt, for a night or two.' Fresh tears welled up. 'How could she vanish now — just days before her wedding?' She gulped and went on. 'I rang Elaine up but there was no reply. I tried again later and still nothing. So I don't know where Tracey is, or what's the matter with her. I don't know what to do!'

'I'm sorry to hear that, but why did you think I could help?' Jessica asked, puzzled.

'Well, I rang your office before I

found the letter, just in case Tracey had called in to do something. That girl Shannon said Tracey was talking to you last thing on Friday, so she thought Tracey might have confided in you and she gave me your address.'

The guilty feeling returned. If only she had agreed to have that coffee with Tracey, perhaps this crisis could have been avoided. 'I'm afraid she didn't tell me anything. What does Philip say?'

Mrs Pitt's eyes widened. 'I can't tell Philip that Tracey has run away! It might be about something she doesn't want him to know. He might even call the wedding off! No, Tracey has to be found and brought back as quickly and quietly as possible.'

'So are you going after her?'

'How can I? I've got my husband to look after and people keep ringing up and asking me questions about the wedding.'

'Then who . . . ?' Jessica saw the two older women looking at her. 'But I can't go anywhere! I've made plans!'

Mrs Clarke looked at her daughter with deep disapproval. 'You haven't got anything important on and you are free for the rest of the week. It's clear that your friend needs help. Of course you'll go!'

Mrs Ellis was nodding vigorously. Faced with the two of them and still feeling guilty about the way she had brushed Tracey aside — and she had to admit, eager to know exactly what had sent Tracey off — Jessica attemped to offer a compromise.

'She's probably at her friend's. You may have just missed them when you rang. Suppose we leave it till the morning. You can keep trying to contact her and, if you don't succeed, perhaps I can try to do something.'

Mrs Clarke poured out the tea and handed round biscuits. 'So that's settled then, dear. If there's no answer by tomorrow morning, Jessica will go to Birmingham.'

'Birmingham?' Jessica demanded.

'That's where Elaine lives.'

Jessica looked aghast at her mother and got a steely glare in return. Mrs Clarke had set her mind that it was her daughter's duty to help, so there could be no argument.

Jessica hoped against hope that Mrs Ellis had somehow got everything wrong and that Tracey would return home that night with some simple explanation, but the following morning's call from a distraught Mrs Ellis only confirmed that she had not heard from Tracey and still could not contact Elaine Pitt. Resignedly, Jessica took down the Birmingham address and telephone number and prepared to go to the train station. Her mother insisted she take a few basic necessities in her shoulder bag in case she had to spend the night away.

'You never know,' she said in response to Jessica's objections. 'Tracey may take some persuading. We don't know what's caused this. If only she'd talked to someone here!'

Her guilt reawakened, Jessica set off.

It was a dull journey to Birmingham, and she treated herself to a taxi to Elaine's address, a couple of miles from the city centre. It turned out to be a large Victorian terraced house that had been converted into flats and a neatly-printed card informed her that Elaine Pitt lived on the first floor, so Jessica trudged upstairs and knocked on the door of the flat. There was no response and no sound from within. She knocked again. Still there was no reply. Angry that she might have come all this way for nothing, she hammered on the door. It still did not open, but the neighbouring door flew open.

'Will you please be quiet? I'm trying to get the baby to sleep!'

The young woman glared indignantly at Jessica, who immediately felt very foolish. 'I'm sorry, but I'm trying to contact Elaine Pitt. I believe that she lives here.'

'She does, but she's away.'

Jessica blinked. 'Do you know when she's due back?'

'I'm afraid not. There was some family problem, so she wasn't sure when she would be back.' There was the sound of a baby wailing and the neighbour started to close her door. 'I wish she'd told her friends she would be away. There was another girl here looking for her yesterday,' were her parting words.

Galvanised, Jessica knocked at her door and was greeted with a thunderous frown when it reopened. 'Do you know where the other girl went when she found Elaine wasn't here?' Jessica asked her urgently.

'No.' The door closed very firmly.

Jessica wandered downstairs and out into the street. She found a small café and sat brooding over a cup of coffee. If she just went back and said she didn't know where Tracey was, she knew that both her mother and Mrs Ellis would reproach her for not trying harder. But what could she do now? She sighed heavily. Tracey had obviously intended to take Elaine into her confidence and also had hoped to stay with her friend. Finding Elaine gone and reluctant to return to face her mother, she would have had to look for accommodation for the night.

Jessica ordered another cup of coffee and asked if she could look at the café's Yellow Pages, but when she looked at the vast number of hotels listed in Birmingham she felt overwhelmed. Tracey would probably have avoided five and four-star hotels as too expensive, but Jessica thought she was a fussy girl who would certainly not have settled for fewer than three stars. Unfortunately there were over a hundred three-star hotels in Birmingham. Jessica started to list those she knew were in the immediate area but then gave up. Even if she started trudging from hotel to hotel, what could she do? If Tracey wanted to avoid discovery she might have used another name and Jessica hadn't thought there was any need to bring a photograph of Tracey, even if she had been able to get one from Mrs Ellis, so she would have to rely on her own powers of description when enquiring about her. Anyway, would a hotel tell her if Tracey was one of their guests? Wouldn't they consider it their duty to safeguard her privacy, especially as Jessica could not claim any official reason for her search?

Jessica stood up, closed the Yellow Pages and handed it back to the waitress. Then she spent some time looking in her bag for an elusive scrap of card before leaving the restaurant. It was on a busy road and it was not long before a taxi responded to Jessica's signals.

'Where to?' the driver said tersely and Jessica showed him the little white oblong.

'I want to go to this firm, Hinton's.'

He looked at the address. 'No trouble. It's only a couple of miles.'

Winding expertly through the traffic, in a few minutes he deposited her near James's office. Jessica paid him, thanked him, and made for the building. She stepped into the lift and pressed a button.

The receptionist welcomed her with a warm, professional smile, and then recognition dawned. 'Oh! You came to see Mr Strang once before, didn't you? Do you want to see him again?'

'Yes, please.'

Miss Chalmers was summoned and took Jessica through to her office. Her attitude, however, was as unwelcoming as the first time.

'Mr Strang is with Mr Hinton, but will be back soon.'

There was a silence. 'I hope your mother is better,' Jessica said politely, and got a startled look.

'What? Oh, yes. Thank you, she is much better.'

This time there was a significant silence.

'Of course, you went to Madrid with Mr Strang, didn't you? I hope he wasn't too demanding.'

Both women considered the possible implications of this remark, before

Jessica said sweetly, 'Not at all. I enjoyed the experience,' and then wondered whether her own choice of words had been equally unfortunate.

She could imagine the gossip that had gone on in Hinton's when it had been discovered that James had gone to Spain with the girl who had walked into the office a few weeks earlier!

Fortunately at this point James came in. Jessica had been wondering whether he would resent her sudden appearance, but he seemed genuinely pleased to see her.

'This is a pleasant surprise. Come into my office. Miss Chalmers . . . '

'You want coffee,' his secretary said resignedly.

Seated at the coffee table, James looked at Jessica searchingly. 'If you don't mind my saying so, you don't look as if you have come here just for the pleasure of seeing me. What's the matter?'

She was beginning to feel that she had made a mistake in coming to him.

After all, he was a busy man and Tracey was nothing to him, but she was here now so she might as well go ahead.

'I need your help.'

To her great relief he simply nodded, and then waited till Miss Chalmers had put the coffee tray down in front of them and he had thanked her. Then he turned back to Jessica. 'How can I help you?'

'It's expecting a lot of you. Do you remember Tracey, the girl who interrupted our dinner date? She's supposed to be getting married on Saturday, but she's disappeared, apparently in Birmingham.'

'All right, that's obviously the bare outline,' James commented. 'Now give me the details.'

So she told him the whole story, from Tracey's restlessness to Mrs Ellis's appearance at her home to her discovery that Elaine Pitt was away on holiday. 'Once I found she wasn't at her friend's place I didn't know what to do. There are so many hotels in Birmingham. Then it occurred to me that you must know something about Birmingham hotels. It would help if you could narrow it down to about a dozen probables.'

He nodded, pressed a button by his chair, and immediately Miss Chalmers reappeared.

'Agnes, could you find me a large-scale map of Birmingham and a guide to its hotels?' James requested. Both articles appeared rapidly, though there was still an aura of disapproval about the secretary.

'I don't think she likes me,' murmured Jessica, and James laughed.

'Agnes used to be my father's secretary and has known me since I was a gangling young lad. She still thinks I need protection from the world, and especially from predatory young ladies.'

'Well, I'm not one!'

He smiled into her eyes. 'You are young and attractive. Of course you are a threat to the young master.' He turned back to the map without waiting for her reaction. 'Now, show me where this Miss Pitt lives.'

Between them they selected ten hotels within a reasonable range of Elaine Pitt's flat.

'That's enough to start with,' James commented. 'I'll just tell Agnes that I'll be out for the rest of the afternoon.'

'No!' Jessica exclaimed. 'That's asking too much of you. I'll take this list and try to persuade them to tell me if anybody like Tracey is staying there.'

'Nonsense! You don't know Birmingham. I can get you round in half the time you would take by yourself. Besides, I'm intrigued. I want to know what has happened to your Tracey.'

Miss Chalmers received his news with a carefully expressionless face. 'What shall I tell Mr Hinton if he asks for you?' she enquired.

'Tell him I'm trying to rescue a damsel in distress,' he said cheerfully, and swept Jessica out of the office.

6

James hailed a taxi and asked for the first hotel on the list. Once there, he asked if a Miss Tracey Ellis was currently a guest, and when he was told there was no one of that name he went on to describe her. 'It's important that we find this lady,' he murmured, and without actually saying so he somehow managed to imply that he possessed some significant official status and was deeply involved in important matters. However, there was still no success and they went on to the second hotel and repeated the process, then on to the third, still with no luck.

Coming out of that hotel, Jessica sank wearily into the taxi, and then as it inched out into the traffic she sat up in embarrassment as her stomach gurgled loudly. 'I'm sorry.'

James smiled. 'Are you hungry? What

did you have for lunch?'

'I didn't have lunch,' she confessed. 'What with going to the flat, then wondering what to do, and then going to your office, I forgot about eating.'

At the next hotel, instead of going to the receptionist's desk he conducted Jessica to its restaurant and ordered sandwiches, cakes and tea. Jessica's eyes lit up and she began to work her way steadily through the food. James nibbled at some himself and waited until she sat back with a satisfied sigh. 'Now, while we have a few minutes, tell me something. Why are you looking for Tracey? Why not her parents or other friends? Above all, why isn't her fiancé here?'

'Her mother claims she's busy with last-minute details of the wedding and Tracey has acquaintances rather than friends. I was on holiday and my mother decided I could come looking. Anyway, I feel guilty because I may have let Tracey down.' She explained how she had rejected Tracey's invitation to coffee. 'As for Philip, how is he going to feel now his fiancée has run away days before the wedding? He might start having doubts as well!'

James was frowning. 'I think he has a right to know,' he said firmly.

'Well, I think it would only cause trouble. Anyway, we'd better get a move on! We'll never get through the list at this rate!'

At the sixth hotel they had a glimmer of hope. The receptionist thought that James's description did remind him of a woman who had checked in the previous day. Unfortunately the guest in question walked through the foyer at that moment and proved to look nothing like Tracey.

Jessica's shoulders sagged. 'We're not going to find her,' she said flatly. Then she caught sight of the clock on the wall. 'Look at the time! If I'm to get back to Manchester tonight I'll have to leave now!'

She felt tears of weariness and frustration well up, but then James's arm was round her, comforting and reassuring. 'We can't give up now,' he told her. 'Forget about Manchester and stay here for the night. Then we can finish this list today and think about the next step if we don't find Tracey.'

'I suppose I could,' Jessica said slowly. 'Mother was half-expecting me to do that anyway.' She started to turn back to the hotel's reception desk. 'I'll see if they have a room here.'

'There's no need for that,' James informed her. 'Hinton's have a room permanently reserved at a small hotel not far from our offices. It comes in handy if a client needs somewhere to stay. I know nobody is using it at the present so you may as well stay there.'

Jessica thought of the expensive offices and wondered what standard of accommodation clients might expect.

'Does it cost much?' she asked tentatively, but James laughed.

'Not for you. We pay them a fee to keep it available for us, so you can be treated like a client and stay there for nothing.' He brushed aside her protests and produced a mobile phone and after a short conversation informed her that the hotel room would be waiting for her. 'Now, let's see if one of these last four hotels is currently sheltering your friend Tracey.'

None of them were, so a final taxi ride took them to the hotel where she was to stay for the night. It was small, discreetly hidden away in a side street, but Jessica saw the five stars by the entrance.

'I suggest I see you to your room, and we can discuss what to do tomorrow morning.'

Jessica nodded gratefully. She was almost exhausted, and when she saw her room, beautifully furnished as well as comfortable, all she really wanted to do was climb into the enormous bed, but she made a quick phone call to her mother, saying briefly that she had not yet found Tracey but would continue the search the following day and asking her to pass the message on to Mrs Ellis.

Then she excused herself and went into the bathroom to wash and apply a little fresh make-up while James waited in the room. She came out of the bathroom and saw that he was sipping a gin and tonic, while another was waiting for her. Suddenly she remembered Madrid and how James Strang had told her there that he found her desirable. Now she had come to him, putting herself in his debt. Had he brought her to this hotel thinking that a night with her would be a fair reward for his efforts to help her search? Had she been stupidly naïve?

But then she thought of the consideration and support he had shown that afternoon. A night in the shelter of his arms would certainly make her forget the trials of the day — and he was a very attractive man. As she hesitated, wondering what to say, James put down his glass and stood up.

'I thought you might like a drink. Please don't hesitate to call room service when you want something to eat. I'll see you in the morning.'

She gazed at him, confused. This was the last thing she expected. 'You are going now?'

He nodded. 'I decided there wasn't much we could discuss now after all, so I'm going back to the office to catch up with some of the work I should have done this afternoon.'

So he hadn't planned a seduction. Irrationally, Jessica felt angry with him for making her judge him so unfairly — as well as just slightly disappointed.

'Will it be all right if I get here about nine?' he asked.

'There's no need for you to take any more time off. I'll try to find Tracey by myself tomorrow,' she said stiffly.

'I'll see you in the morning,' he repeated firmly, and she was silent.

In spite of her exhaustion, she spent some time fidgeting restlessly, unable to sleep. Had she misjudged James? She told herself to forget him, to remember that she was here to find Tracey, but then she wondered helplessly how she was going to go about that. Tracey might have gone off to London or some other city for all she knew.

Finally she fell asleep, only to wake up abruptly in the middle of the night. She sat up. There *was* something she could do! She lay down, closed her eyes, and fell fast asleep.

★   ★   ★

The next morning she had showered and breakfasted and was waiting impatiently in the foyer when James appeared soon after nine o'clock. He started to greet her, but she brushed his formalities aside, telling him urgently, 'We need a taxi — quickly!'

'Have you heard from Tracey? Do you know where she is?'

She shook her head impatiently. 'No — but I've had an idea!'

Without further questions he turned, went through the door, and waved down a taxi. They climbed in and he listened as she gave Elaine Pitt's address before turning to him.

'It suddenly dawned on me. Elaine seems to be Tracey's only acquaintance in Birmingham, but nobody knows when she'll be back. If Tracey is still in Birmingham, then I think she'll go back to Elaine's flat each day in the hope that she's returned.'

'But how are we to know when she'll be there?'

Jessica looked at him impatiently. 'We don't, but I think she will go there first thing in the morning before she has to decide what to do for the rest of the day. Anyway, we can put a note on the door, telling her I'm looking for her and giving my mobile number — and the sooner the better!'

She was sitting on the edge of her seat, urging the taxi along, only vaguely aware of the way James was smiling at her.

No one was loitering outside the building but Jessica pushed the front door open impatiently and hurried up the stairs. Then she stopped abruptly.

Outside Elaine Pitt's door a huddled figure was sitting on the floor, her head resting on her knees.

'Oh, Tracey!' Jessica flung herself down beside the sad girl and gathered her in her arms. Her friend gulped convulsively and buried her head in Jessica's shoulder and Jessica could feel her shaking with sobs.

'I've been such a fool and now I just don't know what to do,' came Tracey's muffled voice.

'Don't worry. I'm here now,' Jessica said soothingly, stroking the dishevelled hair. She looked up as she became aware of James standing over her. 'Where can we take her?'

'Your hotel room is the obvious place and I told the taxi to wait. Come on, I'll help you with her.'

With James holding Tracey's travel bag in one hand, they helped her down the stairs and into the taxi. The hotel receptionist looked at them with curiosity but Jessica smiled blandly at her and ushered Tracey into the lift. Once in her room, Tracey collapsed into an armchair and Jessica turned to James, eager to be free to give Tracey her full attention.

'Thank you so much, James. I don't think there is anything else for you to do just now. I'll phone Mrs Ellis and let her know I've found her daughter and that she's safe with me.'

James didn't move. 'What about her fiancé? Are you going to call him?'

Jessica shook her head. 'Unless the wedding is actually called off, he doesn't need to know about this. Now, I really must see to Tracey. Can you phone me later?'

He turned on his heel and left and Jessica forgot about him in seconds. Maybe he had earned more than her brief thanks, but Tracey was her priority now. She swept the cover off the bed, wrapped it round Tracey and made her a hot drink, grateful for the tea-making tray. While Tracey drank, Jessica called Mrs Ellis to tell her she'd found Tracey but couldn't tell her anything else at the moment, but promised to call again later.

She sat by Tracey, waiting. Eventually the sobs stopped and were replaced by snuffles. Jessica handed over some tissues. Finally Tracey blew her nose loudly and looked up. 'Do you know what I did?'

'Instead of going to the hairdresser you ran away to see a friend, but the friend wasn't there.'

Tracey nodded dolefully. 'When I phoned and didn't get a reply, it never occurred to me that Elaine might be away. I just thought she'd gone shopping or something. All I wanted was someone I could talk to who wasn't involved in the wedding, and instead I've spent two nights in a horrible bed-and-breakfast and the days sitting in cheap cafes wondering what to do and where to go.'

'Tracey, I'm sorry I couldn't go out with you after work on Friday, but I'm here now, so what is it that you want to talk about so badly?'

120

There was a pause before Tracey started to speak. 'This wedding — it will all be over in a few hours next Saturday — but it has taken over my life. I've worried myself sick about flowers and food, but I suddenly realised the other day that I haven't thought properly since Prague about whether I actually want to get married, or about my life afterwards.'

Jessica put the kettle on again. She felt she needed a hot drink as well. 'But surely you must want to get married. After all, you did say yes when Philip asked you, and that must have been before you even started to think of the wedding.'

Tracey was fidgeting uneasily. 'I told you in Prague I wasn't sure I was marrying Philip for the right reasons. You see, as soon as he asked me I did think of the wedding. I had this vision of myself in a beautiful dress, with everyone looking at me and admiring me. It wasn't the only reason I accepted Philip, but it was one reason.' She accepted a fresh cup of tea. 'The other thing is, I'm not sure Philip asked me to marry him for the right reasons. We had been going out together for some time, people were beginning to take it for granted that we would get married, and I think Philip asked me because he thought he should, not because I was the only girl in the world for him.'

Jessica pushed her fingers through her hair. 'Lots of people get married without it being a grand melodramatic romance.'

'But suppose one of us falls in love properly with someone else? Suppose we split up because we bore each other silly?' Tracey's lips trembled. She was clearly on the point of tears again.

'Suppose the world comes to an end on Friday afternoon? Come on, Tracey. Nobody knows what the future holds for them. Now, think back instead. Did you like Philip when you were first going out together?'

For the first time, Tracey smiled. 'Oh, yes! He's so good-looking!'

'And when did you start to think you might have made a mistake?'

'Just before we went to Prague. We were arguing about the menu for the reception, and suddenly he seemed to be the most boring person on Earth.'

'He might've been thinking the same about you! It seems to me that the two of you should have eloped, or had a very quiet registry office wedding with only your parents there. It would've saved a lot of trouble and it's what I intend to do if I ever get married.'

Tracey's eyes widened in horror. 'No wedding dress?'

Jessica groaned. 'Tracey, go and have a long, hot bath while I order something to eat from room service.'

Tracey stood up obediently, and then looked round the room as a thought struck her. 'Jessica, what was that man James Strang doing with you this morning? And isn't this a very expensive hotel? How much are you paying for it?'

Jessica gritted her teeth. 'When you

disappeared, our mothers sent me after you, but when I got to Birmingham you had vanished off the face of the earth. James was the only person I knew in Birmingham so I asked him for help. And his firm is paying for the hotel room. Now go and have a bath!'

Tracey would plainly have liked to ask more questions, but Jessica's tone warned her not to and she made for the bathroom, emerging later in the hotel's towelling wrap and looking much more like the Tracey that Jessica was accustomed to.

The discussion continued. Most of the time Tracey was speculating on how she and Philip really felt about each other, but from time to time she started talking about her hope that her mother was coping adequately with the final preparations for the wedding that might not take place. There was a fresh burst of tears as she contemplated the awful tasks that would be involved if the wedding were to be cancelled and how the guests would feel and, more importantly, what they would say. Jessica listened and made soothing noises until her head was aching and she was repressing a desire to shake the other girl.

Tracey had still not decided what she wanted to do by four o'clock when there was a knock on the door. Jessica assumed that James had come in person to see how she was getting on but when she opened the door it was Philip Beech who was standing outside. Philip ignored her, in fact she doubted if he actually saw her. He looked past her at Tracey, who had scrambled to her feet and stood staring at him in disbelief.

'Tracey!' he said simply, and advanced towards her. Tracey made a sound that could only be described as a squeak and walked into his arms, and Philip enfolded her eagerly. Jessica looked at the scene and took a step towards the entwined couple but was stopped by a hand grasping her arm.

'Leave them to it!' James ordered and drew her out of the room, shutting the door behind them. Without a word he took her downstairs to a quiet corner of the lounge.

'Well, from the initial reaction it looks as if their problems are going to be solved,' he observed, but Jessica was looking at him with deep suspicion.

'How did Philip know Tracey was here?' she demanded of him.

He looked her in the eye. 'I looked up his name in the phone book, got his mother, and she gave me his mobile number so I called him and told him where Tracey was.'

Jessica's face flushed with anger. 'But I had already told you that we didn't want him to know what was happening!' she told him angrily.

'I thought you were wrong and that he was entitled to know. It was his future that was being decided as well as that silly little girl's.'

'And you didn't even think you should tell me first that you were planning to call him?'

He shrugged. 'Arguing about it

would just have wasted time.'

Jessica was furious. He was so arrogant! True, she had asked James for help, but after that it had been him who had decided how they should set about searching, had chosen the hotels and interrogated the receptionists. He had arranged for her to spend the night here. She had been the one who had had the idea that finally led them to Tracey, but then he had ignored what she had said about Philip. He was too high-handed, too accustomed to getting his own way. She remembered her suspicions about his motives.

'Tell me,' she narrowed her eyes. 'Why did you bring me to this hotel?'

He was startled, and then his lips set. 'All I wanted to do when I brought you here was make sure you had somewhere safe and comfortable to spend the night. I did not intend to drag you into bed.' She began to feel foolish, but then he went on. 'All right, I did think you would feel more grateful than if I had dumped you in a cheap hotel. But I was only trying to give you a good opinion of me.'

'Thank you,' she said coldly, pushing back her chair. 'Now I'm going to see what is happening upstairs.'

She had reached the lift before it occurred to her that Tracey and Philip might be celebrating their reunion and not welcome her intrusion. However, she had nowhere to retreat to, so she knocked on the bedroom door and was relieved when it was flung open by a beaming Tracey.

'Come in, Jessica! Everything's all right now. Do you know, even Philip was beginning to get fed up with all the fuss about the wedding and it was making him wonder whether he wanted to go through with it too! Anyway, we've decided that we love each other and that it's our life together that is important, not the wedding.'

Philip came forward and kissed Jessica on the cheek. 'Thank you for finding her and looking after her. We've phoned our parents and told them that we're coming back this evening. Can I give you a lift back to Manchester or do you want to stay here with Mr Strang?'

'I'll come with you,' Jessica said firmly. 'Just give me a minute to pack.'

James was standing in Reception when they went down and before he could avoid her Tracey had seized his hands and kissed him on the cheek.

'Thank you for all you have done for Philip and me, and for Jessica,' she said. 'Everything is going to be all right now.'

Philip shook James's hand, but was apparently at a loss for words. Finally Jessica and James were left facing each other.

'Thank you for your help,' she said. There seemed nothing else to say.

'Glad to be of assistance — and I wasn't going to demand any reward!' He came to the car with them and, as they drove away, Jessica could see him watching until they rounded a bend.

'What a nice man!' Tracey said. 'It was lucky you met him, Jessica.'

'He was very useful,' Jessica said in a

tone that clearly forbade any further discussion.

Tracey sat in the front passenger seat while Philip drove and Jessica had to endure a journey listening to tender murmurs between the two of them. Finally they stopped outside her home.

'See you at the wedding!' was Tracey's parting shot.

Mrs Clarke greeted her daughter eagerly, full of impatient questions, but Jessica pleaded exhaustion and just gave her mother the bare outlines of what had happened.

'So the marriage is going ahead?'

Jessica sighed. 'It's going ahead as planned and I'll be there. Now, what's for tea?'

Mrs Clarke would not be denied forever, and the next morning Jessica gave her mother an almost full account of her time in Birmingham, discreetly omitting some details of her exchanges with James.

'Well,' her mother said at the end, 'I just hope Tracey is grateful to you.'

'She just needed someone that she could talk to. If I'd been willing to listen earlier she would never have gone to Birmingham.'

'I think Mr Strang was right to tell Philip what was happening, though. If his fiancée was thinking of cancelling the wedding, then he should have been the first person to know. It was a bit cowardly and selfish of her not to tell him herself.'

Jessica made no comment and her mother changed the subject, but Jessica was feeling a little uncomfortable. She had been furious with James when she left Birmingham because he had not consulted her before he rang Philip. But his action had turned out well, leading to a happy reunion, and her mother was not the only person who would say that Philip had been entitled to know what was happening.

James had neglected his work to help her when he was under no obligation to do so, had arranged free accommodation for her in a very comfortable hotel after chasing round a series of Birming-ham hotels, and his reward had been to be virtually abandoned in the hotel car park with only the most meagre thanks for what he had done. He deserved better.

Jessica spent a lot of time that afternoon writing a letter to James thanking him profusely for all he had done. She apologised for her ungra-cious behaviour, blaming it on tiredness and anxiety, told him that apparently all was going well for Tracey and Philip, and concluded by saying that if they met again she hoped nothing would spoil the meeting.

She read it through carefully and then slowly tore the letter into little pieces. It was too late to repair matters. Instead she wrote a brief note, thanking him for his help and assuring him that the wedding was going ahead as planned. Then she put it in an envelope, sealed it, put a stamp on it and posted it. As she heard it plop down on to the other letters in the box she mentally said good-bye to James Strang.

7

The restful week that Jessica had planned continued to spiral out of her control. Tracey rang her several times the next day to tell her how things were progressing and to tell her again and again how happy she was at the prospect of marrying Philip. Even when she did have some quiet uninterrupted time, Jessica found she could not settle down to reading the books she had chosen.

Jessica was beginning to have second thoughts about the future she had planned for herself. She had decided she wanted to be a teacher eventually because it was a steady, worthwhile job that people respected and she couldn't really think of anything else she wanted to do. But now she was beginning to wonder if teaching was really the career for her. Jessica knew she did not have the endless patience that teaching required, and although she enjoyed learning she was not sure that she wanted to spend her life passing on what she had learned to others. She did enjoy her work as a secretary and knew she did it well. First-class secretaries were always in demand everywhere and if she decided to pursue that career she would not need to study for a degree and therefore would not have to save all her spare cash for the necessary fees.

But the idea of abandoning her long-cherished plans and taking risks daunted her. She could not forget the unhappy times when her father had died and then when her step-father was in hospital and the family's future had been so uncertain. Security was still something to cling to. Still, she did find herself reading the advertisements for secretarial posts in the papers, wondering whether some captain of industry would like her as his personal assistant, even wondering whether she could develop her organisational skills and move into management herself.

She mentioned her doubts about her future plans over the family's evening meal. Her mother listened, looked meaningfully at her husband, but did not comment directly. 'I think we need to have a discussion, Jessica. If you and John go into the living-room, I'll bring in the tea-tray.'

This was portentous! Tea in the living-room was for visitors and very special occasions. When they were settled and the tea had been duly poured, Mrs Clarke turned to Jessica. 'I'm glad you've been thinking about the future, Jessica, because John and I have been thinking about our future plans as well.'

Future plans? What was she talking about? She and John would continue to lead their quiet lives until her step-father retired in about five years, and then the only difference would be that he would go out fishing instead of to work. There would always be this house to come home to, with these two waiting for her. But now her mother was destroying this comfortable illusion.

'You know how uncertain business is recently. Well, John has been offered early retirement with a good lump sum. His sister runs a boarding-house in Windermere, overlooking the lake, and has suggested we move up there and help during the busy season. I could cook and John would be handyman. She would pay us and it would help eke out our pensions.'

Jessica frowned, but quickly told herself that early retirement for John would not mean major changes for her. 'You mean you would go and stay with her during the summer?

'No, dear,' her mother said patiently. 'I mean that we would sell this house and buy a cottage in Windermere.'

Jessica's eyes widened. 'But that means that I . . . '

'Will have to find somewhere else to live, I'm afraid. We were worried about that, but if you're thinking of another job and possibly moving away from the area then there won't be a problem. And you'll always be able spend your holidays with us in the Lakes.' She looked at her daughter's face. 'After all, my dear,' she said with a hint of steel, 'someday you'll get married and leave anyway. We can't just sit here waiting for you to move on.'

Jessica spent another sleepless night. She realised that she had become too complacent, accepting her life in her parents' home as her right. She did pay for her keep and help with some of the housework but she knew that renting a flat would be much more expensive, but she couldn't be selfish and begrudge her mother and step-father this opportunity for a new chance. She was facing fundamental changes to her life.

★　★　★

In spite of Susan and Shannon's pleas, Tracey had refused to have a big hen night and arranged instead to have dinner at a city-centre restaurant on the

Thursday evening with her three fellow workers.

'Prague was the big event,' Tracey had announced. 'I just want a pleasant, quiet meal and no hangovers.'

Tracey was waiting in the restaurant and hugged Jessica warmly. 'If it hadn't been for you, I wouldn't be here,' she whispered.

Shannon and Susan knew nothing about the events earlier in the week. Mrs Ellis's phone call had been put down to a brief failure in communications. The meal was pleasant but was dominated by the feeling that an era was coming to an end.

'Once you're married you'll have different interests from the rest of us,' Susan commented a little sadly. 'You'll be worrying about the mortgage and rushing home to cook the supper instead of going out having fun.'

'Going home to Philip will be fun,' Tracey retorted, 'but I know what you mean. I'm moving on to a new stage in my life.'

Jessica came to a sudden decision. 'So am I,' she announced. 'I've decided it's time I moved on and tried something new. I'm going to start applying for jobs in other parts of the country — possibly even abroad.'

This caused a stir, and Jessica saw a gleam in Shannon's eyes. 'Are you thinking of Birmingham?' she asked, and laughed when Jessica denied this. 'So your boss will be looking for a new secretary,' Shannon said. 'How about putting in a good word for me? It's a couple of grades higher than my present post.'

'Let me find somewhere else first!'

Susan sighed. 'So everybody else wants to move on. What can I do?'

'Do what makes you happy,' Shannon told her friend. 'If you like what you are doing, stay with it.'

'I suppose I shall,' Susan said as she looked round dolefully. 'I expect this definitely means this is the last time the four of us will meet like this. Well, at least we went to Prague together.'

The evening ended fairly early and Tracey and Jessica resisted pressure from the younger two to go on to a club afterwards.

'Well, see you in the church,' was Shannon's farewell.

Jessica and Tracey were briefly alone. 'Only one more day to wait,' Jessica commented.

'I think I'm going to spend tomorrow curled up in a chair watching television,' Tracey told her. 'Particularly the weather forecasts.'

* * *

At lunchtime on Friday George came to sit with Jessica. 'Can we go for a short walk when we've finished lunch?' he asked her. 'We need to talk.'

'Is something the matter?'

'I've been talking to Shannon,' was all he would say, but it was enough.

Pacing round the hospital grounds, he told her how sorry he was to hear that she was to lose her home. 'I know how devastated you must be to have your life disrupted like this by your parents, so that you feel you are being driven away from the life you know,' he said heavily.

'You make it sound worse than it is,' she responded, trying to sound cheerful. 'After all, if I got married I'd move on to a new life, and it wouldn't be a tragedy, you know.'

'Exactly,' he said meaningfully, and stopped pacing to face her. 'I know it's too soon for you to make any commitment, Jessica, because we're still little more than acquaintances, but just be sure that if you don't want to leave Manchester, there could be another home waiting for you here.'

Jessica almost panicked. His message could not have been clearer. George had decided that she would make him a suitable wife and he saw her parents' plans as a good opportunity to persuade her to consider him as a partner for life.

'Thank you, George,' she gulped.

'But I can't talk about that now — I've got to get back to the office,' she blustered and then she almost fled.

Shannon saw her flushed face and sidled over to her desk. 'I saw you out with George,' she murmured. 'Did he have anything interesting to say?'

'He practically proposed!' Jessica blurted out.

'And you're not interested? He's worth considering.'

Jessica shot her a disbelieving look. 'He's not my type, and I wouldn't have thought he was yours!'

Shannon shrugged. 'I've had enough of exciting but unreliable boyfriends. George would make a very good husband — very dependable — and he would always take good care of his family.'

'And what about love?' Jessica found herself saying.

'He's a lonely man, Jessica, and he doesn't always know how to relate to people. I believe that he would always be grateful to someone who showed that they thought he was worth caring for. He's not bad-looking, either. I think love might come.'

'Then you are welcome to him!'

'I'll remember that,' Shannon said as she strolled away. 'See you at the wedding tomorrow,' she said as an afterthought.

★ ★ ★

Fate was kind to Tracey, and the day of her wedding was clear and bright. Jessica had listened to her mother and bought herself a light dress printed with big, green, splashy flowers and a wide-brimmed white hat which, she told herself, would be useful on summer holidays.

The wedding was to be at eleven-thirty in an ancient church which Shannon believed had been chosen because it was so picturesque and would therefore look good in the photographs. Jessica got there in plenty of time and was greeted by Shannon and Susan. They admired each others' outfits, speculated on Tracey's wedding dress, and covertly inspected the other guests.

'Remember, if you catch the bride's bouquet, you'll be the next to get married,' Susan told them.

Shannon looked round. 'Well, I've just got rid of my boyfriend and Susan's has told her he doesn't believe in marriage, so it's up to you to catch it, Jessica.'

Jessica laughed cheerfully and shook her head. 'I'm going to end up as an elderly unmarried teacher,' she proclaimed. 'I'll be Aunt Jessica to all your children.'

'Can I book you as babysitter now?' Shannon asked, and then shook her head in turn. 'No, you'll get married, Jessica. Remember when we went to Prague? You were the only one who met someone.'

'Prague was all very well, but I still think Tracey should have had a big hen night,' grumbled Susan.

'It looks as if they want us to go in now,' Shannon murmured, indicating the ushers beckoning to the guests who were still lingering in the sunlit churchyard. Jessica had seen George hovering near their little group, and as they made their way in to the church he took Jessica's arm and seated himself next to her. The congregation waited while the organ played and gradually the church filled. The sound of the organ swelled as Philip and his best man took their places in front of the altar, the church door opened wide, and Tracey entered on her father's arm.

Everything else forgotten, Jessica stared at the bride, finally understanding why Tracey had thought it worthwhile to spend months planning her big day. Her full-skirted dress was of lace-covered silk, her veil held in place by a sparkling tiara and she grasped a bouquet of white lilies. She looked like a princess. Slowly she made her way up the aisle, the cyno-sure of all eyes.

The bridesmaids' mothers might

have looked at their four daughters as they followed the bride, but Tracey was the centre of attention as she reached the altar and smiled shyly up at Philip before the pair turned to face the vicar. Bride and groom spoke the same words as thousands of other couples do each year but, like every wedding, the measured sentences seemed fresh and full of meaning as Philip and Tracey made their vows to each other. Jessica realised a tear was creeping down her cheek and had to dab at it hastily with a handkerchief.

Just as Philip slipped the wedding ring on Tracey's finger, Jessica was conscious of a latecomer slipping quietly into the pew. As the blessing was pronounced, she glanced sideways, and her eyes widened. It was James, neatly dressed in a suit but without a wedding flower in his buttonhole. He gave her a brief smile before his attention turned to the couple at the altar. Afterwards Jessica could not have said how the service ended because her mind was full of the questions raised by his sudden appearance. Who had invited him? Had he come all the way from Birmingham just to see Philip and Tracey married?

The newly-married couple made their triumphant progress from the altar to the church door, and then their guests were free to pour out after them into the sunlight. Forgetting George, Jessica followed James and they confronted each other on a patch of grass.

'I didn't expect to see you here,' Jessica said, and then regretted making such a stupidly obvious remark.

'Philip phoned me and said that both he and Tracey would like me to come if I could. I hoped to get here earlier, but the train was held up.'

There was a pause. 'You were right to tell Philip about Tracey going to Birmingham,' Jessica said abruptly.

'And you were right as well. I should have discussed it with you first.'

With mutual apologies over, Jessica

relaxed a little. 'I'm sorry I was in such a foul mood that day,' she said with sincerity. 'I didn't want to go to Birmingham anyway, but then when we found Tracey in such a state I was very worried about her, and her mother had been so convinced earlier that we should not tell Philip.'

'Then let's forgive each other and start again.'

They smiled at each other, and then an usher bustled up and asked them to take their places for the photographs that were being taken in front of the church. Jessica moved obediently towards the church porch, but James looked at his wristwatch and frowned. 'I have to go. A taxi is picking me up in five minutes to take me to the airport.'

She was conscious of crushing disappointment. 'Where are you going this time?' she asked him.

'South America, just for a few days.' With sudden resolution he seized her hand. 'Jessica, when I come back we must meet and have a good talk, somewhere

where we won't be interrupted by your friends or my work, though that is surprisingly difficult. I may even have to carry you off to Paris or Barcelona to do it!'

Jessica found herself laughing. 'James, I think there are places nearer than Spain or France where we can talk!'

He grinned, then they saw a taxi draw up next to the ribbon-bedecked wedding car. 'I must go and you have to have your photograph taken.' He bent and kissed her lightly on the lips. 'I'll call you when I get back.'

She watched him hurry to the taxi, her hand to her lips, savouring the memory of his kiss, and then, turning away, saw George staring at her. She gave an apologetic smile but he walked away abruptly. In response to the usher's urgent pleas, Jessica took her place for the group photographs.

'I saw that, and I recognised him. What did the man from Birmingham want this time?' hissed Shannon.

'He just wanted to wish Tracey

and Philip well,' Jessica responded, and Shannon gave her a disbelieving look.

'Well, I think you've ruined your chances with George,' she said tartly.

For Jessica, the wedding reception was an anti-climax, though everybody else seemed to be enjoying themselves. She saw the way Shannon stayed close to George and wished her well.

'All that planning seems to have paid off,' Tracey said gratefully when the two girls found themselves briefly together.

'It's all gone smoothly. You can congratulate yourself.'

Tracey smiled. 'But you know, even if I'd tripped over my dress and gone sprawling when I walked up the aisle, or we'd all arrived at the hotel and found it closed because of a power failure, it wouldn't have spoilt my happiness today.'

Jessica stared at her. 'Was that what you were worrying about?'

Tracey put a hand on her friend's arm. 'But you and your friend James rescued me and sorted me out, and I'll always be grateful for that.' She looked round. 'We did invite him, and I thought I saw him when we came out of the church.'

Jessica explained James's brief appearance and why he had left.

'South America? That's a big place. Why is he going?'

'Probably to find some special wood. He'll only be gone a few days.'

The festivities proceeded. A distant cousin of Philip caught the bride's bouquet, and Jessica went home to wait for James's call.

★ ★ ★

It never came.

After a week Jessica was jumping up to answer the phone whenever it rang. After a fortnight she was hovering nearby, willing it to ring.

'What on earth is the matter with you?' her mother said impatiently after one disappointment. 'You nearly fell over the coffee table trying to get to the phone when it rang. You know Maggie always calls me on a Sunday. Who else did you expect it to be?'

Jessica tried to shrug casually. 'Oh, somebody said they might call me.'

'Who?'

Challenged like that, Jessica told her mother all about the encounter with James at the church. 'He did say he would call,' she finished.

Her mother pursed her lips. 'Well, he could scarcely say he never wanted to see you again, could he? Face it, Jessica, the only times he contacted you were when he found himself in Manchester with nothing to do and when he urgently needed a secretary. He found you useful, that's all.'

'Then why did he come to the wedding?' Jessica asked despondently.

'To see for himself if that pair actually did get married? And he had to come up to the airport anyway. Then he was polite to you, but got away as soon as he could.' She put an arm round

Jessica's drooping shoulders. 'Be practical, love. Forget him.'

This was sensible, sound advice, though hard to take, but as the days passed and no call came, there seemed to be no alternative.

8

One day Jessica had gone out to the city centre at lunch time to do some shopping and was walking through the streets of Manchester when a street name caught her attention. She remembered that this was the street where Señor Perez of Madrid had bought a house. She wondered if he had finally decided to hire Hinton's to renovate it, and curiosity made her wander down the street until she saw a building covered in scaffolding, the name 'Hinton' on a sign. So she and James had not wasted their time in Madrid and Hinton's had secured the contract.

She moved closer and gazed up at the building, wondering how many of the details she and James had worked so hard to incorporate were actually being included by the builders. She sighed, momentarily envying the architects who could see and touch the solid result of their work. She herself simply sent out and received piles of paperwork on behalf of her employer, though presumably her painstaking accuracy helped his patients.

Jessica took a step back and collided with someone. She looked round to apologise, only to find herself looking at Edward Hinton, James's uncle and partner. He was dressed in a sweater and jeans, with a hard hat hiding his white hair. 'I'm sorry,' she began, but he was already shaking his head.

'It was my fault entirely. I should have looked where I was going.' He looked at her more closely. 'Haven't I seen you before?'

This was embarrassing. If he told James he'd seen her, his nephew might think she had come there hoping to find him. She gave a non-committal murmur and began to turn away, but it was too late.

'I remember! I met you in James's office!'

Trapped, Jessica managed a smile.

'Oh, yes! How nice to see you. I just came down this street by chance and saw your name on the sign.'

Edward Hinton looked at the building proudly. 'It's going well. I'm surprised by how much we have managed to pack into a fairly small house.'

It was impossible to resist the temptation and Jessica asked, 'Is James working with you or are you supervising it by yourself?'

Edward Hinton's expression changed suddenly. He looked at her sadly. 'Oh, my dear! Haven't you heard about James?'

Suddenly Jessica felt very cold. 'Heard what? I saw James three or four weeks ago and he said he was going to South America. I haven't heard anything since.'

He blinked, almost as if he were on the point of tears. 'Oh, yes. He went to South America. But he vanished. We don't know what's happened.'

Jessica suddenly felt giddy. She shook

her head to clear it, and felt Edward Hinton's arm go round her.

'I've given you a shock, my dear. Let me take you into the house and get you a glass of water.'

The future ground-floor foyer provided rough seating on packing-cases, and Jessica sank down gratefully while Edward Hinton went in search of some water. 'How can he just have vanished?' she asked.

Edward Hinton shook his head sadly. 'He was looking at various possible sources of timber in the Amazon rain forest so we don't even know exactly where he was when the area was hit by torrential rains — you may have heard about them on the news about ten days ago. There were floods and landslides and a lot of roads were cut off. Since then we've heard nothing. We made enquiries through the local consul and the firms he was supposed to visit, but it's an enormous area and communications are still completely disorganised. We're hoping for a phone call or email to tell us he's safe.'

'But the more time passes, the more unlikely that is?' Jessica said bleakly. Suddenly Jessica recalled the events that changed her life — the violent car crash and the knock on the door that had brought news of her step-father's accident. Now James had disappeared in the stormy violence of South America. She was shivering and Edward Hinton hugged her as she struggled to pull herself together and managed a travesty of a smile. 'I'm sorry; I'm being a fool. It was just such a shock!'

He sighed. 'Each day I think we must hear within a few hours. Every time the phone rings I think it must be him. His mother is the same.' He looked round sadly. 'Without James there'll be no point in carrying on with the firm. I want to see this project completed because it was important to him, but if he doesn't come back I'll probably sell up and retire.' He shook himself. 'Now I am being pessimistic! Look, give me your number and I'll call you when we get news, I promise.'

He wrote her number down in a notebook then Jessica stood up and said, 'Thank you for the water. I feel better now so I'll go back to work.'

He frowned. 'You don't look much better. Wait a minute.' He went out, returning moments later. 'I've called a taxi. Don't argue. It's what you need.'

His decisiveness reminded her of James, and she found herself smiling and crying at the same time as he ushered her into the taxi. 'Remember, there's still hope, and I will call you with any news,' were his parting words.

Shannon saw the taxi drop her off at the hospital and tracked her down to the ladies' room where she was trying to repair her make-up and brace herself to face the office.

'Tell me what's the matter,' was Shannon's curt command, and Jessica, with no one else to turn to, did just that. Shannon crossed her arms and grimaced. 'You liked him, didn't you?'

'We hadn't met that often, but we did

seem to suit each other. Anyway, I hate the idea of his disappearing like this, so that nobody may ever know what has happened to him.'

'Of course you do and, as his uncle said, he may yet turn up safe and sound. But if he doesn't . . . ' She paused significantly, and then began again. 'Jessica, you're too good for your job. It isn't using half your abilities. You said you were planning to look for somewhere else, and if this man doesn't reappear, then I think you should make a fresh start as soon as possible. Leave this hospital, leave town. Take a chance, and don't waste yourself.'

'You know that I've been thinking about moving,' Jessica admitted, 'but I'm beginning to have second thoughts and wondered if it would be the right thing to do. My boss has come to rely on me.'

Shannon grinned wickedly. 'Don't worry. You are not the only competent secretary here. Remember, if you leave, I'll probably take over your job

— though that's not the reason I am advising you to go,' she added hastily.

'I thought work wasn't important to you?' Jessica queried.

'Perhaps I'm growing up at last. And with you gone, I'll have a better chance with George too. Now, let's get back before we both get sacked!'

★   ★   ★

That evening Jessica decided to bring her mother up to date with her intentions. 'Mother,' she began cautiously, 'what would you think if I said I'm thinking of getting a job in another city, possibly even another country?'

Her mother put her magazine down. 'I'd say that's a very good idea.' Jessica was taken aback, but her mother carried on. 'I know you're good at your job, but I think you've stayed there for the wrong reasons. We've had some hard times and for that reason you're inclined to avoid risk, but your father's death and John's accident were sheer

161

chance, and nothing we could have done would have prevented them. You're young and you should be enjoying life, not being careful all the time. Now John and I are thinking of moving it's a good time for you to try something completely new, and we'd be much happier about moving ourselves once you've got your future sorted out. Of course,' she added hastily. 'You don't have to sail round the world single-handed or walk to the North Pole, but I do think you should experiment and experience life more before you settle down.'

So both her mother and her work-mates thought she was a timid stick-in-the-mud! This was food for thought and Jessica brooded for a couple of days, then combed the 'Situations Vacant' columns and drew up a CV and letter of application which she sent to four advertisers. Two sent polite letters of regret, one reply said she would be hearing from them in the near future, and one invited her to an interview in

London in a week's time. She wrote telling them she would be there.

'London?' said Shannon with interest. 'That would be a change! The only trouble is living there is expensive.'

'It is an international firm,' Jessica explained. 'I could be sent to any of their branches abroad, and then accommodation would be provided.'

Shannon raised her eyebrows. 'Can I make a note of their address? Perhaps I'll be trying to get away from Manchester as well.'

All the time Jessica felt that she was just going through the motions of looking for a new job, because at any moment she expected the phone to ring and Edward Hinton's voice to tell her that James had been found safe and well, and somehow — she wasn't sure how — this would affect her plans for the future. But time was passing and Mr Hinton did not call.

Jessica's interview was at one o'clock, so she calculated that she would be able to get to London and back by train the same day and avoid the expense of a London hotel. She had her neat grey suit cleaned, decided to wear a long-sleeved blouse with a small floral pattern, and persuaded her step-father to polish her plain court shoes till they shone. Trying on the ensemble, she decided she looked satisfactory; then she took another look and told herself she looked dull and dowdy, and treated herself to a scarlet blouse and a big, fashionable handbag.

Jessica was determined that the evening before her London interview should be quiet and restful. Her mother and step-father had gone to bed and Jessica had settled down to watch TV before going to bed herself, when the phone rang. She picked up the receiver a little impatiently and then nearly dropped it when she heard the excited voice.

'Miss Clarke? It's me, Edward Hinton. He's been found! James is alive and well and coming back to England!'

She gripped the telephone tightly.

'What happened to him?'

'I haven't heard the whole story yet. We just got a call from him today, saying that he is well and coming home.'

'When is he due back?'

'Tomorrow. He is flying to Manchester Airport. Hold on, I can give you the flight number. It should arrive about two o'clock.'

★   ★   ★

The next morning her mother was pounding on her bedroom door. 'Jessica, get up! You're going to miss your train!'

Jessica, heavy-eyed, opened her door. 'I'm not going to London. I've been thinking it over and I've decided I don't want to move so far.'

And that was all Jessica would say, in spite of her mother's indignation at her unreasonable behaviour, though Jessica did say that as she had the day off work anyway she would be going out for the afternoon. She found it difficult to explain to herself why she was so reluctant to confide in her mother, but decided that her mother would have told her not to throw away the chance of the London job for no good reason, that she could go to the interview and see James another time. It would have been perfectly sound advice, after all, but Jessica just knew that she had to be at the airport that afternoon to greet him when he returned to England.

She phoned the London firm and informed them that she would not be there for the interview and could hear their unspoken disapproval of a candidate who cancelled at such short notice. It was nearly noon and she was in her bedroom, wondering whether it was too early to leave for the airport, when she heard a scream, followed by a crash. She rushed downstairs and found her step-father crouched over her mother, who lay unconscious on the kitchen floor.

'She stood on a chair to reach that

high shelf and slipped! I've told her again and again not to do it. Annie, my love, wake up!'

Jessica was already dialling 999 and the ambulance arrived within fifteen minutes to take Mrs Clarke to the hospital, where she was rapidly wheeled away for examination while Jessica and her step-father waited helplessly for news, but it was a good half-hour before an orderly came with information.

'It is good news,' he assured them first, before going into details. 'Mrs Clarke obviously struck her head and knocked herself unconscious, but she didn't fracture her skull. We'll keep her in overnight for observation.'

John and Jessica were allowed to see her, tucked up in bed, though still a little dazed.

'Well, it looks as if it isn't as bad as we feared,' John commented as they stood on the hospital steps. Jessica saw how white and shaken he looked and slipped her arm through his. 'Come on,

Dad. Let's go home and I'll make you a cup of tea,' she coaxed him.

'Good idea. What's the time?' he asked as they reached the taxi rank.

She glanced at her watch. 'Two o'clock.' James's plane should be landing about now.

Jessica settled her step-father comfortably, and in due course went to see what they could have for tea. As she sliced and buttered bread, she reflected on the changes the past twenty-four hours had made to her plans. She had thrown away her chances of the job in London for nothing, because it was unlikely that James would ever learn that she had intended to meet him at the airport. Now she had to go on looking for another job because the hospital knew she wanted to leave. Depending on where she found work, she would then have to find somewhere to live. She sighed, feeling very sorry for herself.

When she returned to work she was uncertain how the other girls would react, but when they heard her story they were sympathetic, but there was little attention to spare, for that day also marked Tracey's return from her honeymoon, complete with dozens of pictures of the wedding and the Caribbean resort where she and Philip had passed an apparently idyllic fortnight. The girls spent their break exclaiming over the pictures and searching for those that included themselves.

It was only at the end of the day that Shannon, shrugging on her coat, turned to Jessica and casually asked her what she planned to do next.

'I'll go back to looking for work somewhere a little nearer than London.'

'How about Birmingham?'

Jessica shook her head. 'There's nothing there for me.'

'Are you sure? Don't give up too easily.'

'Unfortunately I'm quite sure.' Jessica was not going to go anywhere near Birmingham or Hinton's. Any initiative would have to come from James, and he had made no attempt to contact her.

At least her mother had recovered well. She had been brought home the day after her accident, a little subdued, and made to promise that she would never stand on a chair again. For a couple of days she moved stiffly, complaining of her bruises, but then woke up one day, announced she was perfectly all right, and started to rule the house with her usual vigour.

9

Jessica came home from work one evening to find that her mother had announced she wanted to go to the cinema to see a particular film. As they got ready to go out, John asked, 'Are you coming, Jessica?'

'No, she isn't,' her mother said firmly before Jessica could reply. 'It's going to be just the two of us, John — a romantic evening. In fact, you can take me somewhere for a drink afterwards.' She eyed Jessica. 'You could do with a bit more lipstick, Jessica. There's no need to neglect yourself just because you are staying in.'

She repeated this advice just before they left, but after she had shut the door behind them Jessica sank into a chair with a contented sigh. She rarely had any time alone, so what would she do with this evening? Her mother had seemed worried about her appearance so she decided on a few hours of beautification. First of all she would wash her hair, and then give herself a face-mask, then a manicure. A little self-indulgence was good for you.

She stood up ready to put this plan into operation just as the door bell rang. She was annoyed at the disturbance, and even more annoyed when she found it was Brian Mallory on the doorstep.

'What do you want?' she demanded, deliberately being as unwelcoming and ungracious as possible.

He gave a rather sickly smile. 'Can't I come in?'

'No. I'm busy. Tell me why you're here.'

He hesitated. 'I just wondered whether you'd heard any more about Hinton's — you know, the firm my employers want to buy — whether you know if they've decided to sell or not? I kind of gave my boss the impression that I might have some influence in the matter and now he keeps asking me for information.'

Jessica gave him a long withering look. 'Then I'm afraid you are going to have to disappoint him. I heard some news recently that suggests they definitely will not be selling. Goodbye.'

She shut the door on his crestfallen face and went upstairs, where she took off her top and skirt, shampooed and conditioned her hair, then wrapped a towel round her head before putting on her old dressing-gown. Just as she had applied the first few dollops of face mask, the door bell rang again. Jessica hesitated. Was it Brian again — could she just ignore it? She heard the bell peal out once more. Whoever was at the door was impatient and would know the house was not empty because of the lights in various rooms. Grimly Jessica seized a towel, wiped her face, stamped down the stairs, and then half-opened the door, peering through the gap to see who the unwanted caller was. 'Well?' she challenged, and then stared in disbelief at the silhouetted figure before opening the door wide.

It was James Strang on the doorstep, his shoulders hunched against the fine rain and clutching two shopping bags. Jessica gaped at him and then almost shut the door in his face as she remembered what she looked like.

'Jessica, will you please let me in? I'm getting soaked here!' he demanded irritably.

She opened the door and stood back as he entered, shaking himself like a dog to get rid of the raindrops. Then she ran for the stairs.

'I'll be down in ten minutes,' she shouted over her shoulder, abandoning him on the doormat. In fact it was twenty minutes before she came down, wearing a soft, clinging dress, make-up on and with her damp hair combed back. James was in the kitchen. He had made himself at home and was opening various dishes in containers. He stood up and surveyed Jessica.

'That looks better. We'll eat and then

we'll talk. Here, take this.' He handed her a glass of wine. 'I've brought a Chinese takeaway. I was going to get Indian, but your mother said you preferred Chinese.'

She opened her mouth to say something, decided she was beyond words, and sipped her wine while she waited for an explanation.

'I'm sorry to have given you such a shock, but I did phone this morning,' he said. 'Your mother answered and we had quite a talk.' He smiled at the memory. 'Anyway, she assured me that she and your step-father will not be back before eleven o'clock at the earliest, so for once we should have a quiet, uninterrupted evening.'

'You mean my mother knew you were coming here tonight and didn't warn me?' Jessica thought of various things she'd like to do to her mother.

'She must have thought you would enjoy the surprise.' James laughed. 'She obviously didn't know what you planned to do with your evening.'

175

Jessica collected various bits of crockery and cutlery and took them into the dining-room, while James followed with two trays of Chinese dishes. They ate in almost perfect silence, broken only when James offered Jessica another glass of wine.

Finally James pushed his plate aside and leant forward. 'Now, can we begin to sort things out?'

'It's about time,' Jessica said bitterly. 'First I heard you were lost in the South American jungle, then that you had reappeared and were coming home, but since then there has been nothing but silence.'

'I haven't contacted you,' James began, 'because my uncle told me that he had made sure you knew I was coming to Manchester and had even told you the flight and time, but you weren't there when I landed.' He held up a hand as she began to speak. 'Let me finish. I knew that possibly you couldn't get away from work, but when you didn't call either I naturally assumed you didn't want anything more to do with me, so I thought it would be better not to phone.' He looked down at the table. 'But it was no use. I decided I had to find out once and for all whether we had a future or not, and I had to hear it directly from you, so I called and, as I said, I spoke to your mother. She thought we should meet, that there were matters we should clear up face to face.'

Jessica sipped her wine and put her glass down carefully before speaking. 'When your plane landed at Manchester I was at the hospital. My mother had had a fall and we were waiting to see if she was badly injured. I didn't call because I think I was trying to preserve my dignity by leaving it to you to decide whether we met again. So it seems we've both been waiting for the other one to make the first move.'

He looked thoughtful. 'If your mother hadn't had her accident, would you have met me?'

'Yes,' Jessica said. 'I even cancelled an

interview for a very good job so I could meet you when your plane landed, and then Mother fell off a chair.'

James released a heart-felt sigh. 'You don't know what it means to me to hear you say that! When I got off the plane I didn't know if you had any idea why I hadn't phoned you as I promised, if you knew what had happened to me, or when I was coming home, yet I still found myself looking for you, hoping by some miracle you'd be there.'

'I wasn't sure you'd want me there, but I desperately wanted to see for myself that you were safe and well.'

He smiled and stretched across to cover her hand with his. 'Pride has made us both stupid. Come on. Let's leave the dishes where they are.'

They sat on the couch, with his arm round her and her head resting on his shoulder. She felt his hand slowly stroking her arm and moved closer to him, rejoicing in his nearness. It was a time of calm and reassurance.

She stirred. 'Incidentally, what did

happen to you? All I knew was that you had disappeared.'

'Nothing terribly exciting. A man had driven me into the forest to inspect some trees. We planned to spend one or two nights in the forest, and then torrential rains came down, landslides blocked the road and we couldn't get back. We waited a couple of days, sheltering in the Land Rover.' He grimaced. 'We lived on tins of cold beans and hard biscuits that we'd taken as emergency supplies — not a pleasant diet. As the roads were impassable we had to abandon the vehicle and start walking back. Unfortunately the man I was with fell and broke his ankle. I managed to get him to a village, but it had been cut off from the outside world for a time, so we just had to wait until the road was cleared and we could get a lift back to the town. Even then it was difficult to get on a flight. Do you know, it took me five planes to get back to Manchester?'

'I'm glad you finally managed it. Your

uncle was worried sick about you. He was talking about selling Hinton's if you didn't reappear. Incidentally, that idiot who spoke to me in the Manchester hotel has been trying to find out what's happening to your firm.'

'We talked it over when I got back. My uncle will retire before the end of the year and I'll take over. We're not selling and that's definite. Now, what have you been doing while I was away?'

She laughed. 'I found out my parents are planning to move and sell my home, I started applying for other jobs, received a virtual proposal of marriage — and, incidentally, Tracey and Philip had a lovely honeymoon and are very happy.'

He blinked. 'Nothing too exciting, then. And what did you say to the virtual proposal of marriage?'

'I said a virtual 'no'.'

Jessica felt him relax. 'Very sensible. Now, let's forget dignity and admit that it's obvious we're growing very important to each other. I'm going to be spending a lot of time in Manchester in the next few months, overseeing the completion of the house for Señor and Señora Perez. It'll give us the chance to meet frequently and get to know each other. Little things can be surprisingly important.' She felt rather than heard his laugh. 'Would you send our children to private schools? What's your favourite boy's name?'

'And what about you?' she interpolated. 'Do you watch football and shout at the screen like my father?' She smiled up at him. 'James, are we getting too serious? Remember, we've only met a few times.'

'That's why we are going to meet whenever we have a chance — ' Then the door bell rang again. James scowled. 'Who's calling at this time?'

It was Brian Mallory. 'Look, Jessica,' he began, 'I know you don't have much time for me, but our mothers are friends, and for their sakes I think you might help me with more information about Hinton's.'

A figure loomed up behind Jessica and moved her gently but firmly aside. 'Hinton's is not being sold, and that's all you need to know. Now, go away and stop cluttering up the doorstep!'

Brian Mallory retreated rapidly and James shut the door. Jessica was shaking her head.

'What's the matter?' James asked.

'He'll tell his mother and she'll complain to my mother.'

'Let them sort it out,' he said comfortably and led her back to the couch. 'Now, do you remember that when I first saw you in Prague I wanted to touch you, to stroke the back of your neck?'

She nodded, her eyes smiling. 'I remember, and I know how you feel, because I want to touch your mouth, to feel its shape with my fingers . . . '

And then his arms were round her and he was kissing her. She felt his hands move over her and closed her eyes, aware of the sensuous pleasure of the feel and the smell of him.

Time passed, neither of them aware of it until Jessica suddenly struggled to free herself. 'It's nearly eleven o'clock! My parents will be back soon!'

When her parents did return — Mr Clarke making far more noise than usual when he put his key in the lock — they found Jessica and James in the kitchen washing up their supper dishes.

While Mr Clarke made tea for the four of them, his wife drew Jessica out of the kitchen. 'Well?' she demanded.

'Very well,' Jessica told her, 'though you might have given me a clue he was coming. Incidentally, you may have trouble with Mrs Mallory over Brian. We were both very rude to him.'

Tea was served and the four of them sat making polite conversation. Jessica was aware of her mother's deep desire to take her away for a thorough inquisition. Mr Clarke had been given a quick summary of what his wife knew of the situation and was still trying to work it out, while James was trying to make a good impression and therefore sounded very stilted.

'What are you doing in Manchester?' Mr Clarke asked James. 'Jessica did tell us you were doing some work for Juan Perez. What's he like?'

'He's a very agreeable man. I see him and his wife quite often.' James brightened up, seeing a chance of earning Mr Clarke's interest. 'In fact, I can introduce you to him, if you're interested in football. He has said he wants to meet some of the fans.'

Mr Clarke gave a beatific smile. 'I would indeed like to meet him.'

James turned to Mrs Clarke. 'He's coming over with his wife very soon. You could both meet them at his house. Señora Perez loves showing people round it and telling them what it will be like when it's finished.'

Jessica could see her mother deciding that an introduction to the elegant Señora Perez and the fact that Jessica's suitor was a partner in a prosperous architects' firm would trump anything Mrs Mallory could come up with, while

Mr Clarke was rejoicing in the prospect of actually meeting Juan Perez. It was clear that James was going to be very welcome indeed in the Clarkes' house.

Jessica stirred. 'It's getting rather late,' she pointed out, 'and Dad and I have to go to work in the morning.'

James stood up hastily. 'Me too. I'm sorry I have kept you up so late.'

'Not at all, lad. It's been a pleasure to meet you again,' Mr Clarke assured him as James turned to say goodbye at the front door.

'It has been a very enjoyable evening,' he assured them, and saw Jessica's lips twitch appreciatively at the memory of some particularly enjoyable moments. He grinned at her. 'I'll call tomorrow, Jessica, to arrange our next meeting — and when your parents can meet the Perezes.'

As the sound of his footsteps faded down the path, Mrs Clarke took her daughter's arm. 'I think we should have a talk,' she stated, but Jessica shook her head.

'Not now, Mother, please. I'm just too tired. I promise you I will tell you everything tomorrow.'

Mrs Clarke released her reluctantly. 'Very well. Just answer me one question. What do you think of wedding dresses now?'

Jessica's eyes were full of dreams. 'White silk, no lace, but a full train.'

Her mother gave a satisfied smile.

★ ★ ★

'I thought Jessica looked lovely,' Susan commented after the wedding. 'Her dress suited her, though it was a lot plainer than yours, Tracey.'

Tracey nodded, stroking the bump that betrayed her pregnancy.

'I know she thought my wedding was a bit over the top — in fact she took it as an awful warning. Still, this is very pleasant.'

They looked round at the guests. Mr Hinton was chatting to James's mother and Miss Chalmers was smiling at

186

something Mrs Clarke said.

'I think James and Jessica make a good couple,' George said soberly.

Shannon reached up and twitched his tie a few millimetres so that it was perfectly central, letting her hand rest on his chest for a moment.

'And to think they met by chance in Prague — that was very romantic.'

George smiled at her fondly. 'Sometimes you find love where you least expect it,' he murmured. 'Where are they going for their honeymoon?'

'Barcelona,' Shannon told him. 'Apparently there are a lot of buildings that James wants to look at as well as a lot of history and art for Jessica.'

'Well, it's not what I would want but they should enjoy it.'

Philip lifted his glass in a toast. 'Anyway, here's to the bride and groom and here's to all of us. Here's to a happy future.'

TRANSWORLD PUBLISHERS
61–63 Uxbridge Road, London W5 5SA
www.penguin.co.uk

Transworld is part of the Penguin Random House group of companies
whose addresses can be found at global.penguinrandomhouse.com

First published in Great Britain in 2019 by Bantam Press
an imprint of Transworld Publishers
Bantam edition published 2020

A CIP catalogue record for this book
is available from the British Library.

ISBN
9780857503527

Typeset in 11/13pt Sabon by Jouve (UK), Milton Keynes
Printed and bound in Great Britain by Clays Ltd, Elcograf S.p.A.

Penguin Random House is committed to a sustainable
future for our business, our readers and our planet. This book
is made from Forest Stewardship Council® certified paper.

1 3 5 7 9 10 8 6 4 2

SUNFALL

JIM AL-KHALILI

BANTAM BOOKS

By Mary Higgins Clark

Moonlight Becomes You
Let Me Call You Sweetheart
Remember Me
I'll Be Seeing You
All Around the Town
Loves Music, Loves to Dance
The Anastasia Syndrome and Other Stories
While My Pretty One Sleeps
Weep No More, My Lady
Stillwatch
A Cry in the Night
The Cradle Will Fall
A Stranger is Watching
Where Are the Children?

STILLWATCH

Mary Higgins Clark

POCKET
BOOKS

New York London Toronto Sydney Tokyo Singapore

First published in Great Britain by William Collins Sons and Co.
Ltd, 1984
First published by Pocket Books, 1996
An imprint of Simon & Schuster
A Viacom Company

Simon & Schuster Ltd
West Garden Place
Kendal Street
London W2 2AQ

Simon & Schuster of Australia Pty Ltd
Sydney

A CIP catalogue record for this book is available from the British
Library.

ISBN 0 671 85397 X

Printed and bound in Great Britain by Caledonian International
Book Manufacturing, Glasgow

To Pat Myrer, my agent
and
Michael V. Korda, my editor

For their inestimable expertise, support,
help and encouragement I joyfully offer
"the still small voice of gratitude."

1

Pat drove slowly, her eyes scanning the narrow Georgetown streets. The cloud-filled sky was dark; streetlights blended with the carriage lamps that flanked doorways; Christmas decorations gleamed against ice-crusted snow. The effect was one of Early American tranquillity. She turned onto N Street, drove one more block, still searching for house numbers, and crossed the intersection. That must be it, she thought—the corner house. Home Sweet Home.

She sat for a while at the curb, studying the house. It was the only one on the street that was unlighted, and its graceful lines were barely discernible. The long front windows were half-hidden by shrubbery that had been allowed to grow.

After the nine-hour drive from Concord her body ached every time she moved, but she found herself putting off the moment when she opened the front door and went inside. It's that damn phone call, she thought. I've let it get to me.

A few days before she'd left her job at the cable

station in Boston, the switchboard operator had buzzed her: "Some kind of weirdo insists on talking to you. Do you want me to stay on the line?"

"Yes." She had picked up the receiver, identified herself and listened as a soft but distinctly masculine voice murmured, "Patricia Traymore, you must not come to Washington. You must not produce a program glorifying Senator Jennings. And you must not live in *that* house."

She had heard the audible gasp of the operator. "Who is this?" she asked sharply.

The answer, delivered in the same syrupy murmur, made her hands unpleasantly moist. "I am an angel of mercy, of deliverance—and of vengeance."

Pat had tried to dismiss the event as one of the many crank calls received at television stations, but it was impossible not to be troubled. The announcement of her move to Potomac Cable Network to do a series called *Women in Government* had appeared in many television-news columns. She had read all of them to see if there was any mention of the address where she would live, but there had been none.

The Washington Tribune had carried the most detailed story: "Auburn-haired Patricia Traymore, with her husky voice and sympathetic brown eyes, will be an attractive addition to Potomac Cable Network. Her profiles of celebrities on Boston Cable have twice been nominated for Emmys. Pat has the magical gift of getting people to reveal themselves with remarkable candor. Her first subject will be Abigail Jennings, the very private senior Senator from Virginia. According to Luther Pelham, news director and anchorman of Potomac Cable, the program will include highlights of the

Senator's private and public life. Washington is breathlessly waiting to see if Pat Traymore can penetrate the beautiful Senator's icy reserve."

The thought of the call nagged at Pat. It was the cadence of the voice, the way he had said *"that* house."

Who was it who knew about the house?

The car was cold. Pat realized the engine had been off for minutes. A man with a briefcase hurried past, paused when he observed her sitting there, then went on his way. I'd better get moving before he calls the cops and reports a loiterer, she thought.

The iron gates in front of the driveway were open. She stopped the car at the stone path that led to the front door and fumbled through her purse for the house key.

She paused at the doorstep, trying to analyze her feelings. She'd anticipated a momentous reaction. Instead, she simply wanted to get inside, lug the suitcases from the car, fix coffee and a sandwich. She turned the key, pushed the door open, found the light switch.

The house seemed very clean. The smooth brick floor of the foyer had a soft patina; the chandelier was sparkling. A second glance showed fading paint and scuff marks near the baseboards. Most of the furniture would probably need to be discarded or refinished. The good pieces stored in the attic of the Concord house would be delivered tomorrow.

She walked slowly through the first floor. The formal dining room, large and pleasant, was on the left. When she was sixteen and on a school trip to Washington, she had walked past this house but hadn't realized

how spacious the rooms were. From the outside the house seemed narrow.

The table was scarred, the sideboard badly marked, as if hot serving dishes had been laid directly on the wood. But she knew the handsome, elaborately carved Jacobean set was family furniture and worth whatever it would cost to restore.

She glanced into the kitchen and library but deliberately kept walking. All the news stories had described the layout of the house in minute detail. The living room was the last room on the right. She felt her throat tighten as she approached it. Was she crazy to be doing this—returning here, trying to recapture a memory best forgotten?

The living-room door was closed. She put her hand on the knob and turned it hesitantly. The door swung open. She fumbled and found the wall switch. The room was large and beautiful, with a high ceiling, a delicate mantel above the white brick fireplace, a recessed window seat. It was empty except for a concert grand piano, a massive expanse of dark mahogany in the alcove to the right of the fireplace.

The fireplace.

She started to walk toward it.

Her arms and legs began to tremble. Perspiration started from her forehead and palms. She could not swallow. The room was moving around her. She rushed to the French doors at the far end of the left wall, fumbled with the lock, yanked both doors open and stumbled onto the snow-banked patio.

The frosty air seared her lungs as she gulped in short, nervous breaths. A violent shudder made her hug her arms around her body. She began to sway and

needed to lean against the house to keep from falling. Light-headedness made the dark outlines of the leafless trees seem to sway with her.

The snow was ankle-deep. She could feel the wetness seep through her boots, but she would not go back in until the dizziness receded. Minutes passed before she could trust herself to return to the room. Carefully she closed and double-locked the doors, hesitated and then deliberately turned around and with slow, reluctant steps walked to the fireplace. Tentatively she ran her hand down the rough whitewashed brick.

For a long time now, bits and pieces of memory had intruded on her like wreckage from a ship. In the past year she had persistently dreamed of being a small child again in this house. Invariably she would awaken in an agony of fear, trying to scream, unable to utter a sound. But coupled with the fear was a pervading sense of loss. The truth is in this house, she thought.

It was here that it had happened. The lurid headlines, gleaned from newspaper archives, flashed through her mind. "WISCONSIN CONGRESSMAN DEAN ADAMS MURDERS BEAUTIFUL SOCIALITE WIFE AND KILLS SELF. THREE-YEAR-OLD DAUGHTER FIGHTS FOR LIFE."

She had read the stories so many times, she knew them by heart. "A sorrowful Senator John F. Kennedy commented, 'I simply don't understand. Dean was one of my best friends. Nothing about him ever suggested pent-up violence.'"

What had driven the popular Congressman to murder and suicide? There had been rumors that he and

his wife were on the verge of divorce. Had Dean Adams snapped when his wife made an irrevocable decision to leave him? They must have wrestled for the gun. Both their fingerprints, smudged and overlapping, were found on it. Their three-year-old daughter had been found lying against the fireplace, her skull fractured, her right leg shattered.

Veronica and Charles Traymore had told her that she was adopted. Not until she was in high school and wanted to trace her ancestry had she been given the whole truth. Shocked, she learned that her mother was Veronica's sister. "You were in a coma for a year and not expected to live," Veronica told her. "When you finally did regain consciousness you were like an infant and had to be taught everything. Mother—your grandmother—actually sent an obituary notice to the newspapers. That's how determined she was that the scandal wouldn't follow you all your life. Charles and I were living in England then. We adopted you and our friends were told you were from an English family."

Pat recalled how furious Veronica had been when Pat insisted on taking over the Georgetown house. "Pat, it's wrong to go back there," she'd said. "We should have sold that place for you instead of renting it all these years. You're making a name for yourself in television—don't risk it by raking up the past! You'll be meeting people who knew you as a child. Somebody might put two and two together."

Veronica's thin lips tightened when Pat insisted. "We did everything humanly possible to give you a fresh start. Go ahead, if you insist, but don't say we didn't warn you."

In the end they had hugged each other, both shaken

and upset. "Come on," Pat pleaded. "My job is digging for the truth. If I hunt for the good and bad in other people's lives, how can I ever have any peace if I don't do it in my own?"

Now she went into the kitchen and picked up the telephone. Even as a child she had referred to Veronica and Charles by their first names, and in the past few years had virtually stopped calling them Mother and Dad. But she suspected that that annoyed and hurt them.

Veronica answered on the first ring. "Hi, Mother. I'm here safe and sound; the traffic was light all the way."

"Where is *here?*"

"At the house in Georgetown." Veronica had wanted her to stay at a hotel until the furniture arrived. Without giving her a chance to remonstrate, Pat rushed on. "It's really better this way. I'll have a chance to set up my equipment in the library and get my head together for my interview with Senator Jennings tomorrow."

"You're not nervous there?"

"Not at all." She could visualize Veronica's thin, worried face. "Forget about me and get ready for your cruise. Are you all packed?"

"Of course. Pat, I don't like your being alone for Christmas."

"I'll be too busy getting this program together even to think about it. Anyway, we had a wonderful early Christmas together. Look, I'd better unload the car. Love to both of you. Pretend you're on a second honeymoon and let Charles make mad love to you."

"*Pat!*" Disapproval and amusement mingled in her voice. But she managed one more piece of advice before hanging up. "Keep the double locks on!"

Buttoning her jacket, Pat ventured out into the chilly evening, and for the next ten minutes she tugged and hauled the luggage and cartons. The box of linens and blankets was heavy and ungainly; she had to rest every few steps on the way to the second floor. Whenever she tried to carry anything heavy her right leg felt as though it might give way. The carton with dishes and pans and groceries had to be hoisted up to the kitchen counter. I should have trusted the movers to arrive tomorrow on time, she thought—but she had learned to be skeptical of "firm" delivery dates. She had just finished hanging up her clothes and making coffee when the phone rang.

The sound seemed to explode in the quiet of the house. Pat jumped and winced as a few drops of coffee touched her hand. Quickly she put the cup on the counter and reached for the phone. "Pat Traymore."

"Hello, Pat."

She clutched the receiver, willing her voice to sound only friendly. "Hello, Sam."

Samuel Kingsley, Congressman from the 26th District of Pennsylvania, the man she loved with all her heart—the *other* reason she had decided to come to Washington.

Forty minutes later Pat was struggling with the clasp of her necklace when the peal of the door chimes announced Sam's arrival. She had changed to a hunter green wool dress with satin braiding. Sam had once told her that green brought out the red in her hair.

The doorbell rang again. Her fingers were trembling too much to fasten the catch. Grabbing her purse, she dropped the necklace into it. As she hurried down the stairs she tried to force herself to be calm. She reminded herself that during the eight months since Sam's wife, Janice, had died Sam hadn't called once.

On the last step she realized that she was again favoring her right leg. It was Sam's insistence that she consult a specialist about the limp that had finally forced her to tell him the truth about the injury.

She hesitated momentarily in the foyer, then slowly opened the door.

Sam nearly filled the doorway. The outside light caught the silver strands in his dark brown hair. Under

unruly brows, his hazel eyes looked wary and quizzical.
There were unfamiliar lines around them. But the
smile when he looked at her was the same, warm and
all-embracing.

They stood awkwardly, each waiting for the other to
make the first move, to set the tone for the reunion.
Sam was carrying a broom. Solemnly he handed it to
her. "The Amish people are in my district. One of
their customs is to carry a new broom and salt into a
new home." He reached into his pocket for a salt cellar. "Courtesy of the House dining room." Stepping
inside, he put his hands on her shoulders and leaned
down to kiss her cheek. "Welcome to our town, Pat.
It's good to have you here."

So this is the greeting, Pat thought. Old friends
getting together. Washington is too small a town to try
to duck someone from the past, so meet her head on
and establish the rules. Not on your life, she thought.
It's a whole new ball game, Sam, and this time I plan to
win.

She kissed him, deliberately, leaving her lips against
his just long enough to sense the intensity gathering in
him, then stepped back and smiled easily.

"How did you know I was here?" she asked. "Have
you got the place bugged?"

"Not quite. Abigail told me you were going to be in
her office tomorrow. I called Potomac Cable for your
phone number."

"I see." There was something intimate in the way
Sam sounded when he mentioned Senator Jennings.
Pat felt her heart give a queer twist and looked down,
not wanting Sam to see the expression on her face.
She made a business of fishing in her purse for her

necklace. "This thing has a clasp that Houdini couldn't figure out. Will you?" She handed it to him.

He slipped it around her neck and she felt the warmth of his fingers as he fastened it. For a moment his fingers lingered against her skin.

Then he said, "Okay, that should stay put. Do I get the Cook's Tour of the house?"

"There's nothing to see yet. The moving van delivers tomorrow. This place will have a whole new look in a few days. Besides, I'm starving."

"As I remember, you always were." Now Sam's eyes betrayed genuine amusement. "How a little thing like you can put away hot-fudge sundaes and buttered biscuits and still not put on an ounce . . ."

Very smooth, Sam, Pat thought as she reached into the closet for her coat. You've managed to ticket me as a little thing with a big appetite. "Where are we going?" she asked.

"I made a reservation at Maison Blanche. It's always good."

She handed him her jacket. "Do they have a children's menu?" she asked sweetly.

"*What?* Oh, I see. Sorry—I thought I was paying you a compliment."

Sam had parked in the driveway behind her car. They walked down the path, his hand lightly under her arm. "Pat, are you favoring your right leg again?" There was concern in his tone.

"Just a touch. I'm stiff from the drive."

"Stop me if I'm wrong. But isn't this the house you own?"

She had told him about her parents the one night they had spent together. Now she nodded dis-

tractedly. She had often relived that night in the Ebb
Tide Motel on Cape Cod. All she needed was the scent
of the ocean, or the sight of two people in a restaurant,
their fingers linked across the table, smiling the secret
smile of lovers. And that one night had ended their
relationship. In the morning, quiet and sad at breakfast, on their way to separate planes, they had talked it
out and agreed they had no right to each other. Sam's
wife, already confined to a wheelchair with multiple
sclerosis, didn't deserve the added pain of sensing that
her husband was involved with another woman. "And
she'd know," Sam had said.

Pat forced herself back to the present and tried to
change the subject. "Isn't this a great street? It reminds me of a painting on a Christmas card."

"Almost any street in Georgetown looks like a
Christmas card at this time of year," Sam rejoined.
"It's a lousy idea for you to try to dredge up the past,
Pat. Let go of it."

They were at the car. He opened the door and she
slipped in. She waited until he was in the driver's seat
and pulling away before she said, "I can't. There's
something that keeps nagging me, Sam. I'm not going
to have any peace until I know what it is."

Sam slowed for the stop sign at the end of the block.
"Pat, don't you know what you're trying to do? You
want to rewrite history, remember that night and decide it was all a terrible accident, that your father
didn't mean to hurt you or kill your mother. You're
just making it harder for yourself."

She glanced over and studied his profile. His features, a shade too strong, a hairbreadth too irregular
for classic good looks, were immensely endearing. She

had to conquer the impulse to slide over and feel the fine wool of his overcoat against her cheek.

"Sam, have you ever been seasick?" she asked.

"Once or twice. I'm usually a pretty good sailor."

"So am I. But I remember coming back on the *QE 2* with Veronica and Charles one summer. We hit a storm and for some reason I lost my sea legs. I don't ever remember being so miserable. I kept wishing I could be sick and have done with it. And you see, that's the way it's getting to be for me now. Things keep coming back to me."

He turned the car onto Pennsylvania Avenue. "What things?"

"Sounds . . . impressions . . . sometimes so vague; other times, especially when I'm just waking up, remarkably clear—and yet they fade before I can get hold of them. I actually tried hypnosis last year, but it didn't work. Then I read that some adults can remember accurately things that happened when they were as young as two. One study said the best way to recapture the memory is to reproduce the environment. Fortunately or unfortunately, that's something I can do."

"I still think it's a lousy idea."

Pat gazed out the car window. She had studied street maps to get a sense of the city and now tried to test herself on the accuracy of her impressions. But the car was moving too swiftly, and it was too dark to be sure of anything. They didn't speak.

The maître d' at Maison Blanche greeted Sam warmly and escorted them to a banquette.

"The usual?" Sam asked after they were seated.

Pat nodded, acutely aware of Sam's nearness. Was

this his favorite table? How many other women had he brought here?

"Two Chivas Regals on the rocks with a splash of soda and a twist of lemon, please," Sam requested. He waited until the maître d' was out of earshot, then said, "All right—tell me about the last few years. Don't leave anything out."

"That's a tall order. Give me a minute to think." She would eliminate those first few months after they had agreed not to see each other, when she'd gotten through the day in a fog of sheer, hopeless misery. She could and did talk about her job, about getting an Emmy nomination for her program on the newly elected woman mayor of Boston, about her growing obsession to do a program about Senator Jennings.

"Why Abigail?" Sam asked.

"Because I think it's high time a woman was nominated for President. In two years there'll be a national election and Abigail Jennings should lead the ticket. Just look at her record: ten years in the House; in her third term in the Senate; member of the Foreign Relations Committee; the Budget Committee; first woman to be Assistant Majority Leader. Isn't it a fact that Congress is still in session because the President is counting on her to get the budget through the way he wants it?"

"Yes, it's true—and what's more, she'll do it."

"What do *you* think of her?"

Sam shrugged. "She's good. She's damn good, as a matter of fact. But she's stepped on a lot of important toes, Pat. When Abigail gets upset, she doesn't care who she blasts, and where and how she does it."

"I assume that's also true of the majority of the men on the Hill."

"Probably."

"Exactly."

The waiter came with menus. They ordered, deciding to share a Caesar salad. And that was another memory. That last day together Pat had made a picnic lunch and asked Sam what salad she should bring. "Caesar," he'd said promptly, "and lots of anchovies, please." "How can you eat those things?" she'd demanded. "How can you not? It's an acquired taste, but once you have it, you'll never lose it." She'd tried them that day and decided they were good.

He remembered too. As they handed back the menus, he commented, "I'm glad you didn't give up on the anchovies." He smiled. "Getting back to Abigail, I'm amazed she agreed to go along with the documentary."

"Frankly, I'm still amazed myself. I wrote to her about three months ago. I'd done a lot of research on her and was absolutely fascinated by what I uncovered. Sam, how much do you know about her background?"

"She's from Virginia. She took her husband's seat in Congress when he died. She's a workaholic."

"Exactly. That's the way everyone sees her. The truth is that Abigail Jennings comes from Upstate New York, *not* Virginia. She won the Miss New York State beauty contest but refused to go to Atlantic City for the Miss America pageant because she had a scholarship to Radcliffe and didn't want to risk wasting a year. She was only thirty-one when she was widowed. She

was so in love with her husband that twenty-five years later she still hasn't remarried."

"She hasn't remarried, but she hasn't lived in a cloister either."

"I wouldn't know about that, but judging from the information I've gathered, the vast majority of her days and nights are strictly work."

"That's true."

"Anyhow, in my letter I wrote that I'd like to do a program that would give viewers the feeling of knowing her on a personal level. I outlined what I had in mind and got back about the frostiest rejection I've ever read. Then a couple of weeks ago Luther Pelham phoned. He was coming to Boston specifically to take me to lunch and wanted to talk about my coming to work for him. Over lunch he told me the Senator had showed him my letter; he'd already been mulling over the idea of a series called *Women in Government.* He knew and liked my work and felt I was right for the job. He also said that he wanted to make me a regular part of his seven-o'clock news program.

"You can imagine how I felt. Pelham is probably the most important commentator in the business; the network is as big as Turner's; the money's terrific. I'm to kick off the series with a documentary on Senator Jennings and he wants it as fast as possible. But I still don't know why the Senator changed her mind."

"I can tell you why. The Vice President may be on the verge of resigning. He's much sicker than people realize."

Pat laid down her fork and stared at him. "Sam, do you mean . . . ?"

"I mean the President has less than two years left in

his second term. How better to make every woman in the country happy than by appointing the first woman Vice President?"

"But that means . . . if Senator Jennings is Vice President, they almost couldn't deny her the nomination for President next time."

"Hold on, Pat. You're going too fast. All I've said is that *if* the Vice President resigns, there's a damn good chance he'll be replaced by either Abigail Jennings or Claire Lawrence. Claire is practically the Erma Bombeck of the Senate—very popular, very witty, a first-rate legislator. She'd do an excellent job. But Abigail's been there longer. The President and Claire are both from the Midwest, and politically that isn't good. He'd rather appoint Abigail, but he can't ignore the fact that Abigail really isn't well known nationally. And she's made some powerful enemies in Congress."

"Then you believe Luther Pelham wants the documentary to let people see Abigail in a warmer, more personal way?"

"From what you've just told me, that's my guess. I think he wants to generate popular support for her. They were pretty cozy for a long time, and I'm sure he'd like to have his dear friend in the Vice President's chair."

They ate silently as Pat mulled the implications of what Sam had told her. Of course it explained the sudden job offer, the need for haste.

"Hey, remember me?" Sam finally said. "You haven't asked me what *I've* been doing these past two years."

"I've been following your career," she told him. "I toasted you when you were reelected—not that I was

surprised. I wrote and tore up a dozen notes to you when Janice died. I'm supposed to have a way with words, but nothing sounded right. . . . It must have been very bad for you."

"It was. When it was obvious Janice didn't have much time, I cut my schedule to the bone and spent every possible minute with her. I think it helped."

"I'm sure it did." She had to ask: "Sam, why did you wait so long to call me? In fact, would you ever have called me if I hadn't come to Washington?"

The background sounds of the other diners' voices and the faint clinking of glasses, the tempting aromas of the food, the paneled walls and frosted-glass partitions of the attractive room faded as she waited for his answer.

"I did call you," he said, "a number of times, but I had the guts to break the connection before your phone rang. Pat, when I met you, you were about to become engaged. I spoiled that for you."

"With or without you it wouldn't have happened. Rob is a nice guy, but that's not enough."

"He's a bright young lawyer with an excellent future. You'd be married to him now if it weren't for me. Pat, I'm forty-eight years old. You're twenty-seven. I'm going to be a grandfather in three months. You know you would want to have children, and I simply don't have the energy to raise a new family."

"I see. Can I ask you something, Sam?"

"Of course."

"Do you love me, or have you talked yourself out of that too?"

"I love you enough to give you a chance to meet someone your own age again."

"And have you met someone *your* own age yet?"

"I'm not seeing anyone specifically."

"I see." She managed a smile. "Well, now that we have everything out in the open, why don't you buy me that nice gooey dessert I'm supposed to crave?"

He looked relieved. Had he expected her to badger him? she wondered. He seemed so tired. Where was all the enthusiasm he'd had a few years ago?

An hour later when he was dropping her at home, Pat remembered what she'd been meaning to discuss. "Sam, I had a crazy phone call at the office last week." She told him about it. "Do people in Congress get much hate mail or calls?"

He didn't seem especially concerned. "Not that many, and none of us takes them very seriously." He kissed her cheek and chuckled. "I was just thinking. Maybe I'd better talk to Claire Lawrence and see if she's been trying to scare off Abigail."

Pat watched him drive away, then closed and latched the door. The house reinforced her feeling of emptiness. The furniture will make a difference, she promised herself.

Something on the floor caught her eye: a plain white envelope. It must have been slipped under the door while she was out. Her name was printed in heavy black lettering that was sharply slanted from left to right. Probably someone from the realtor's office, she tried to tell herself. But the usual business name and address were missing from the upper left-hand corner, and the envelope was of the cheapest dime-store sort.

Slowly she ripped it open and pulled out the single sheet of paper. It read: "I TOLD YOU NOT TO COME."

3

The next morning the alarm went off at six. Pat
slipped willingly out of bed. The lumpy mattress had
not been conducive to sleep, and she had kept waking,
aware of the creaking, settling sounds in the house and
the thumping activity of the oil burner as it snapped
off and on. Try as she would, she could not dismiss the
note as the work of a harmless eccentric. Somebody
was observing her.

The movers had promised to arrive by eight. She
planned to move the files stored in the basement up to
the library.

The basement was dingy, with cement walls and
floor. Garden furniture was stacked neatly in the center. The storage room was to the right of the furnace
room. A heavy padlock on its door was grimy with the
accumulated soot of years.

When Charles had given her the key, he'd warned,
"I don't know exactly what you'll find, Pat. Your
grandmother instructed Dean's office to send all his

personal effects to the house. We never did get around to sorting them."

For a moment it seemed as though the key would not work. The basement was damp, with a vague smell of mildew. She wondered if the lock had rusted. She moved the key back and forth slowly and then felt it turn. She tugged at the door.

Inside the storeroom, a stronger smell of mildew assailed her. Two legal-size filing cabinets were so covered with dust and cobwebs she could barely determine their color. Several heavy cartons, haphazardly piled, stood next to them. With her thumb she rubbed at the grime until the labels appeared: CONGRESSMAN DEAN W. ADAMS, BOOKS. CONGRESSMAN DEAN W. ADAMS, PERSONAL EFFECTS. CONGRESSMAN DEAN W. ADAMS, MEMORABILIA. The inserts on the file drawers read the same: CONGRESSMAN DEAN W. ADAMS, PERSONAL.

"Congressman Dean W. Adams," Pat said aloud. She repeated the name carefully. Funny, she thought, I really don't think of him as a Congressman. I only place him here in this house. What kind of Representative was he?

Except for the formal picture the newspapers used at the time of the deaths, she'd never seen even a snapshot of him. Veronica had shown her albums filled with pictures of Renée as a child, as a young woman at her debut, at her first professional concert, with Pat in her arms. It hadn't been hard to guess why Veronica had kept no reminder of Dean Adams around.

The key to the files was on the ring Charles had given her. She was about to unlock the first one when she began to sneeze. She decided it was crazy to try to

examine anything in that cellar. Already her eyes were itching from the dust. I'll wait until it's all in the library, she thought. But first she would wash the outside of the cabinets and get the worst of the dust off the cartons.

It turned out to be a messy, exhausting job. There was no sink in the basement, and she trudged repeatedly upstairs to the kitchen, bringing down a pail of sudsy hot water and returning a few minutes later with both water and sponge blackened.

On the last trip she brought down a knife and carefully scraped the identifying labels from the cartons. Finally she removed the inserts from the fronts of the file drawers. Satisfied, she surveyed her work. The cabinets were olive green and still in decent condition. They would fit along the east wall of the library. The cartons could go there too. No one would have any reason to think they hadn't come from Boston. Veronica's influence again, she thought wryly. "Don't tell anyone, Pat. Think ahead, Pat. When you marry, do you want your children to know that the reason you limp was that your father tried to kill you?"

She had barely time to wash her hands and face before the movers arrived. The three men on the truck hauled in the furniture, unrolled carpets, unpacked china and crystal, brought up the contents of the storage room. By noon they had gone, manifestly pleased with their tip.

Alone again, Pat went directly to the living room. The transformation was dramatic. The fourteen-by-twenty-four-foot Oriental carpet with its brilliant designs of apricot, green, lemon and cranberry against a black background dominated the room. The green

velvet love seat stood against the short wall at a right angle to the long apricot satin sofa. The matching high-backed wing chairs flanked the fireplace; the Bombay chest was to the left of the patio doors.

The room was well nigh a restoration of its former self. She walked through it, touching the tops of the tables, adjusting the angle of a chair or lamp, running her hands over the fabric of the upholstered pieces. What was she feeling? She couldn't be sure. Not fear exactly—though she had to force herself to pass the fireplace. What then? Nostalgia? But for what? Was it possible that some of those blurred impressions were memories of happy times spent in this room? If so, what else could she do to retrieve them?

At five minutes to three she stepped out of a cab in front of the Russell Senate Office Building. The temperature had dropped sharply in the last several hours and she was glad to enter the heated foyer. The security guards passed her through the metal detector and directed her to the elevator. A few minutes later she was giving her name to Abigail Jennings' receptionist.

"Senator Jennings is running a little behind," the young woman explained. "She has several constituents who stopped in to see her. It won't be long."

"I don't mind waiting." Pat selected a straight-backed chair and looked around. Abigail Jennings clearly had one of the most desirable of the senatorial offices. It was a corner unit and had a feeling of airiness and space that she knew was in short supply in the overcrowded building. A low railing separated the waiting area from the receptionist's desk. A corridor to the right led to a row of private offices. The walls

were covered with framed news photos of the Senator.
The small table by the leather couch held pamphlets
explaining Senator Jennings' positions on pending
legislation.

She heard the familiar voice, softly modulated by
the faintest touch of a Southern accent, easing visitors
out of an inner office. "I'm delighted you were able to
stop by. I only wish we had more time. . . ."

The visitors were a well-dressed sixtyish couple, ef-
fusive in their thanks. "Well, at the fund-raiser you did
say to stop in anytime, and I said, 'Violet, we're in
Washington, let's just do it.' "

"You're sure you're not free for dinner?" the
woman visitor interjected anxiously.

"I only wish I were."

Pat watched as the Senator steered her guests to the
outer door, opened it and slowly closed it, forcing
them out. Well done, she thought. She felt her adrena-
line rise.

Abigail turned and paused, giving Pat an opportunity to study her closely. Pat had forgotten how tall the
Senator was—about five feet nine, with a graceful,
erect carriage. Her gray tweed suit followed the lines
of her body; broad shoulders accentuated a taut waistline; angular hips ended in slender legs. Her ash blond
hair was cut short around the thin face dominated by
extraordinary china-blue eyes. Her nose was shiny,
her lips pale and undefined. She seemed to use absolutely no makeup, as though trying deliberately to un-
derstate her remarkable beauty. Except for the fine
lines around her eyes and mouth, she looked the same
as she had six years earlier.

Pat watched as the Senator's glance came to rest on her.

"Hello," the Senator said, moving quickly toward her. With a reproachful glance at the receptionist she said, "Cindy, you should have told me that Miss Traymore was here." Her chiding expression turned rueful. "Well, no harm done. Come inside, please, Miss Traymore. May I call you Pat? Luther has recommended you so highly I feel I know you. And I've seen some of the specials you've done in Boston. Luther ran them for me. They're splendid. And as you mentioned in your letter, we did meet some years ago. It was when I spoke at Wellesley, wasn't it?"

"Yes, it was." Pat followed the Senator into the inner office and looked around. "How lovely!" she exclaimed.

A long walnut console desk held a delicately painted Japanese lamp, an obviously valuable figurine of an Egyptian cat, a gold pen in a holder. The crimson leather chair, wide and comfortable with arched arms and intricate nailheads, was probably seventeenth-century English. An Oriental carpet had predominant tones of crimson and blue. The flags of the United States and the Commonwealth of Virginia were on the wall behind the desk. Blue silk tieback draperies softened the bleakness of the cloudy winter day beyond the windows. One wall was covered with mahogany bookshelves. Pat chose a chair nearest the Senator's desk.

The Senator seemed pleased at Pat's reaction to the office. "Some of my colleagues feel that the shabbier and more cluttered their offices appear, the busier and more down-to-earth their constituents will think they

are. I simply can't work in confusion. Harmony is very important to me. I get a lot more accomplished in this atmosphere."

She paused. "There's a vote coming up on the floor within the hour, so I guess we'd better get down to business. Has Luther told you that I really *hate* the idea of this special?"

Pat felt on safe ground. Many people resisted programs about themselves. "Yes, he has," she said, "but I honestly believe you'll be pleased with the result."

"That's the only way I'd even consider this. I'll be perfectly honest: I prefer to work with Luther and you rather than have another network decide to produce an unauthorized story. But even so, I wish the good old days were here when a politician could simply say 'I stand on my record.' "

"They're gone. At least, they are for the people who count."

Abigail reached into her desk drawer and pulled out a cigarette case. "I never smoke in public anymore," she observed. "Just once—*once*, mind you—a paper printed a picture of me with a cigarette in my hand. I was in the House then, and I got dozens of irate letters from parents in my district saying I was setting a bad example." She reached across the desk. "Do you . . . ?"

Pat shook her head. "No, thanks. My father asked me not to smoke till I was eighteen, and by then I'd lost interest."

"And you kept your word? No puffing away behind the garage or whatever?"

"No."

The Senator smiled. "I find that reassuring. Sam

Kingsley and I share a great distrust of the media. You know him, don't you? When I told him about this program, he assured me you were different."

"That was kind of him," Pat said, trying to sound casual. "Senator, I suspect the shortest way to go about this is for you to tell me exactly why the idea of the program is so abhorrent to you. If I know in advance what you find objectionable we're bound to save a lot of time."

She watched as the Senator's face became thoughtful. "It's infuriating that no one is satisfied with my personal life. I've been a widow since I was thirty-one years old. Taking my husband's place in Congress after his death, then being elected myself and going on to the Senate—all of it has always made me feel I'm still partners with him. I love my job and I'm married to it. But of course I can't very well tearfully describe little Johnny's first day at school because I never had a child. Unlike Claire Lawrence, I can't be photographed with an army of grandchildren. And I warn you, Pat, I will not allow a picture of me in a bathing suit, high heels and a rhinestone crown to be used in this program."

"But you *were* Miss New York State. You can't ignore that."

"Can't I?" The incredible eyes flashed. "Do you know that shortly after Willard's death, some rag printed that picture of me being crowned Miss New York State with the caption *"And your real prize is to go to Congress for the South?"* The Governor almost changed his mind about appointing me to complete Willard's term. It took Jack Kennedy to persuade him that I'd been working side by side with my husband from the

day he was elected. If Jack hadn't been so powerful, I might not be here now. No, thank you, Pat Traymore. No beauty-queen pictures. Start your special when I was a senior at the University of Richmond, just married to Willard and helping him campaign for the first seat in Congress. That's when my life began."

You can't pretend the first twenty years of your life don't exist, Pat thought. And why? Aloud she suggested, "I came across one picture of you as a child in front of your family home in Apple Junction. That's the kind of early background I plan to use."

"Pat, I never said that was *my* family home. I said I had *lived* there. In point of fact, my mother was the housekeeper for the Saunders family and she and I had a small apartment in the back. Please don't forget I'm the senior Senator from Virginia. The Jennings family has been prominent in Tidewater Virginia since Jamestown. My mother-in-law always called me Willard's Yankee wife. I've gone to great effort to be considered a Jennings from Virginia and to forget Abigail Foster from Upstate New York. Let's leave it that way, shall we?"

There was a knock at the door. A serious-looking, oval-faced man in his early thirties entered, wearing a gray suit with a faint pin stripe that accentuated the leanness of his body. Thinning blond hair carefully combed across his pate failed to conceal his bald spot. Rimless glasses added to the middle-aged effect. "Senator," he said, "they're about to take the vote. The fifteen-minute bell just went off."

The Senator stood up abruptly. "Pat, I'm sorry. Incidentally, this is Philip Buckley, my administrative assistant. He and Toby have put together some mate-

rial for you—all sorts of stuff: press clippings, letters, photo albums, even some home movies. Why don't you look them over, and then let's talk again in the next few days?"

Pat could do nothing except agree. She would talk to Luther Pelham. Between them, they must convince the Senator that she could not sabotage the program. She realized Philip Buckley was studying her carefully. Did she detect a certain hostility in his manner?

"Toby will drive you home," the Senator continued hurriedly. "Where *is* he, Phil?"

"Right here, Senator. Keep your shirt on."

The cheerful voice came from a barrel-chested man who immediately gave Pat the impression of being an overage prize-fighter. His big face was beefy, with the flesh beginning to puff under small, deep-set eyes. Fading sandy hair was abundantly mixed with gray. He was wearing a dark blue suit and holding a cap in his hands.

His hands—she found herself staring at them. They were the largest she had ever seen. A ring with an onyx an inch square accentuated the thickness of his fingers.

Keep your shirt on. Had he really said that? Aghast, she looked at the Senator. But Abigail Jennings was laughing.

"Pat, this is Toby Gorgone. He can tell you what his job is as he drives you home. I've never been able to figure it out and he's been with me for twenty-five years. He's from Apple Junction too, and besides me, he's the best thing that ever came out of it. And now I'm off. Come on, Phil."

They were gone. This special is going to be sheer hell to make, Pat thought. She had three solid pages of

points she'd wanted to discuss with the Senator and had gotten to bring up exactly one. Toby had known Abigail Jennings since childhood. That she put up with his insolence was incredible. Maybe he'd answer some questions on the drive home.

She had just reached the reception area when the door was flung open and Senator Jennings rushed back in, followed by Philip. The relaxed manner was gone. "Toby, thank God I caught you," she snapped. "Where did you get the idea I'm not due at the Embassy until seven?"

"That's what you told me, Senator."

"That's what I *may* have told you, but you're supposed to double-check my appointments, aren't you?"

"Yes, Senator," Toby said genially.

"I'm due at *six*. Be downstairs at quarter to." The words were spat out.

"Senator, you'll be late for the vote," Toby said. "You'd better get a move on."

"I'd be late for everything if I didn't have eyes in the back of my head to double-check on you." This time the door slammed behind her.

Toby laughed. "We'd better get started, Miss Traymore."

Wordlessly, Pat nodded. She could not imagine one of the servants at home addressing either Veronica or Charles with such a familiarity or being so unconcerned about a reprimand. What circumstances had created such a bizarre relationship between Senator Jennings and her oxlike chauffeur?

She decided to find out.

4

Toby steered the sleek gray Cadillac Sedan de Ville through the rapidly gathering traffic. For the hundredth time he brooded on the fact that Washington in the late afternoon was a driver's nightmare. All the tourists in their rented cars who didn't realize that some of the streets became one-way on the dot of four created havoc for the people who worked here.

He glanced into the rearview mirror and liked what he saw. Patricia Traymore was all right. It had taken all three of them—himself, Phil and Pelham—to talk Abby into agreeing to this documentary. So Toby felt even more than usually responsible to see that it worked out.

Still, you couldn't blame Abby for being nervous. She was within an eyelash of everything she'd ever wanted. His eyes met Pat's in the mirror. What a smile that girl had! He'd heard Sam Kingsley tell Abigail that Pat Traymore had a way of making you tell things you never thought you'd share with another human being.

Pat had been considering what approach to take with Toby and had decided the straightforward one was the best. As the car stopped for a light on Constitution Avenue, she leaned forward. There was a chuckle in her voice as she said, "Toby, I have to confess I thought I wasn't hearing straight when you told the Senator to keep her shirt on."

He turned his head to look at her directly. "Oh, I shouldn't a said that first time you met me. I don't usually do that. It's just I knew Abby was uptight about this program business and on her way in for the vote, and a bunch of reporters were going to be all over her about why she wasn't going along with the rest of the party—so I figured if I got her to let down for a minute it'd do her good. But don't misunderstand. I respect the lady. And don't worry about her blowing up at me. She'll forget it in five minutes."

"You grew up together?" Pat prodded gently.

The light turned green. Smoothly the car moved forward; Toby maneuvered into the right lane ahead of a station wagon before answering. "Well, not exactly that. All the kids in Apple Junction go to the same school—'cept, of course, if they go to parochial school. But she was two years ahead of me, so we were never in the same classes. Then when I was fifteen I started doing yard work in the rich part of town. I guess Abby told you she lived in the Saunders house."

"Yes, she did."

"I worked for the people about four places away. One day I heard Abby screaming. The old guy who lived opposite the Saunderses' had taken in his head he needed a watchdog and bought a German shepherd. Talk about vicious! Anyway, the old guy left the

gate open and the dog got out just as Abby was coming down the street. Made straight for her."

"And you saved her?"

"I sure did. I started shouting and distracted him. Bad luck for me I'd dropped my rake, 'cause I got half chewed to rags before I got a grip on his neck. And then"—Toby's voice filled with pride—"and then, no more watchdog."

With one hand, Pat slipped her tape recorder out of her shoulder bag and turned it on. "I can see why the Senator must feel pretty strongly about you," she commented. "The Japanese believe that if you save someone's life you become somehow responsible for them. Do you suppose that happened to you? It sounds to me as though you feel responsible for the Senator."

"Well, I don't know. Maybe that did happen, or maybe she stuck her neck out for me when we were kids." The car stopped. "Sorry, Miss Traymore. We should a made that light, but the jerk ahead of me is reading street signs."

"It doesn't matter. I'm not in any hurry. The Senator stuck her neck out for you?"

"I said *maybe* she did. Look, forget it. The Senator doesn't like me to talk about Apple Junction."

"I'll bet she talks about how you helped her," Pat mused. "I can imagine how *I'd* feel if an attack dog was charging at me and someone threw himself in between."

"Oh, Abby was grateful, all right. My arm was bleeding, and she wrapped her sweater around it, then insisted on coming to the emergency room with me and

even wanted to sit in while they sewed it. After that we were friends for life."

Toby looked over his shoulder. *"Friends,"* he repeated emphatically, "not boyfriend-girlfriend. Abby's out of my league. I don't have to tell you that. There was no question of any of that stuff. But sometimes in the afternoon she'd come over and talk while I was working around the yard. She hated Apple Junction as much as I did. And when I was flunking English, she tutored me. I never did have any head for books. Show me a piece of machinery and I'll take it apart and put it together in two minutes, but don't ask me to diagram a sentence.

"Anyhow, Abby went off to college and I drifted down to New York and got married and it didn't take. And I took a job running numbers for some bookies and ended up in hot water. After that I started chauffeuring for some fruitcake on Long Island. By then Abby was married and her husband was the Congressman and I read that she'd been in an automobile accident because her chauffeur had been drinking. So I thought, What the hell. I wrote to her and two weeks later her husband hired me and that was going on twenty-five years ago. Say, Miss Traymore, what number are you? We're on N Street now."

"Three thousand," Pat said. "It's the corner house on the next block."

"That house?" Too late, Toby tried to cover the shock in his voice.

"Yes. Why?"

"I used to drive Abby and Willard Jennings to that house for parties. Used to be owned by a Congress-

man named Dean Adams. Did they tell you about him killing his wife and committing suicide?"

Pat hoped her voice was calm. "My father's lawyer arranged the rental. He mentioned there had been a tragedy here many years ago, but he didn't go into it."

Toby pulled up to the curb. "Just as well to forget it. He even tried to kill his kid—she died later on. Cute little thing. Her name was Kerry, I remember. What can you do?" He shook his head. "I'll just park by the hydrant for a minute. Cops won't bother as long as I don't hang around."

Pat reached for the handle of the door, but Toby was too quick for her. In an instant he was out the driver's side, around the car and holding the door open, putting a hand under her arm. "Be careful, Miss Traymore. Plenty icy here."

"Yes, I see that. Thank you." She was grateful for the early dusk, afraid that her expression might send some signal to Toby. He might not have a head for books but she sensed he was extremely perceptive. She had thought of this house only in the context of that one night. Of course there had been parties here. Abigail Jennings was fifty-six. Willard Jennings had been eight or nine years her senior. Pat's father would have been in his early sixties now. They had been contemporaries in those Washington days.

Toby was reaching into the trunk. She longed to ask him about Dean and Renée Adams, about "the cute little kid, Kerry." But not now, she cautioned herself.

Toby followed her into the house, two large cartons in his arms. Pat could see that they were heavy, but he carried them easily. She led him into the library and indicated the area next to the boxes from the store-

room. She blessed the instinct that had made her scrape off the labels with her father's name.

But Toby barely glanced at the boxes. "I'd better be off, Miss Traymore. This box"—he pointed—"has press clippings, photo albums, that sort of thing. The other one has letters from constituents—the personal kind, where you can see the sort of help Abby gives them. It had some home movies too, mostly of when her husband was alive. The usual stuff, I guess. I'll be glad to run the movies for you anytime and tell you who's in them and what was going on."

"Let me sort them out and I'll get back to you. Thanks, Toby. I'm sure you're going to be a big help in this project. Maybe between us, we'll put together something the Senator will be happy about."

"If she's not, we'll both know it." Toby's beefy face lit up in a genial smile. "Good night, Miss Traymore."

"Why not make it 'Pat'? After all, you do call the Senator 'Abby.' "

"I'm the only one who can call her that. She hates it. But who knows? Maybe I'll get a chance to save your life too."

"Don't hesitate for a minute if the opportunity comes your way." Pat reached out her hand and watched it disappear into his.

When he had left, she stood in the doorway, lost in thought. She would have to learn not to show any emotion when Dean Adams was mentioned. She had been lucky that Toby had brought up his name while she was still in the protective darkness of the car.

From the shadow of the house directly opposite, another observer watched Toby drive away. With an-

gry curiosity he studied Pat as she stood in the doorway. His hands were thrust into the pockets of his skimpy overcoat. White cotton pants, white socks and white rubber-soles blended into the snow that was banked against the house. His bony wrists tightened as he closed his fingers into fists, and tension rippled through the muscles in his arms. He was a tall, gaunt man with a stiff, tense stance and a habit of holding his head unnaturally back. His hair, a silvery gray that seemed incongruous over a peculiarly unlined face, was combed forward over his forehead.

She was here. He had seen her unloading her car last night. In spite of his warnings, she was going ahead with that program. That was the Senator's car, and those boxes probably had some kind of records in them. And she was going to stay in that house.

The memory of that long-ago morning sprang into his mind: the man lying on his back, wedged between the coffee table and sofa; the woman's eyes, staring, unfocused; the little girl's hair matted with dried blood . . .

He stood there silently, long after Pat had closed the door, as if he were unable to tear himself away.

Pat was in the kitchen broiling a chop when the phone began to ring. She didn't expect to hear from Sam but . . . With a quick smile she reached for the receiver. "Hello."

A whisper. "Patricia Traymore."

"Yes. Who is this?" But she knew that syrupy, whispering voice.

"Did you get my letter?"

She tried to make her voice calm and coaxing. "I don't know why you're upset. Tell me about it."

"Forget your program on the Senator, Miss Traymore. I don't want to punish you. Don't make me do it. But you must remember the Lord said, 'Whoever harms one of these my little ones, better a millstone be put around his neck and he be drowned in the depth of the sea.' "

The connection went dead.

5

It was only a crank call—some wacko who probably thought women belonged in the kitchen, not in public office. Pat recalled the character in New York who used to parade on Fifth Avenue with signs quoting Scripture about women's duty to obey their husbands. He had been harmless. So was this caller. She wouldn't believe it was anything more than that.

She brought a tray into the library and ate dinner while she sorted out Abigail's records. Her admiration for the Senator increased with every line she read. Abigail Jennings had meant it when she said she was married to her job. Her constituents *are* her family, Pat thought.

Pat had an appointment with Pelham at the network in the morning. At midnight she went to bed. The master bedroom suite of the house consisted of a large bedroom, a dressing room and bath. The Chippendale furniture with its delicate inlays of fruitwood had been easy to place. It was obvious that it had been purchased for this house. The highboy fitted between the

closets; the mirrored dresser belonged in the alcove, the bed with its elaborately carved headboard on the long wall facing the windows.

Veronica had sent a new spring and mattress, and the bed felt wonderfully comfortable. But the trips to the basement to clean the filing cabinets had taken their toll on her leg. The familiar nagging pain was more acute than usual, and even though she was very tired it was hard to fall asleep. Think about something pleasant, she told herself as she stirred restlessly and turned on her side. Then in the dark she smiled wryly. She'd think about Sam.

The offices and studio of the Potomac Cable Network were just off Farragut Square. As she went in, Pat remembered what the news director at the Boston station had told her: "There's no question you should take the job, Pat. Working for Luther Pelham is a once-in-a-lifetime break. When he left CBS for Potomac, it was the biggest upset in the industry."

At the lunch with Luther in Boston, she'd been astonished at the frank stares of everyone in the dining room. She had become used to being recognized in the Boston area and having people come to her table for autographs. But the way virtually every pair of eyes was absolutely riveted on Luther Pelham was something else. "Can you go anywhere without being the center of attention?" she'd asked him.

"Not too many places, I'm happy to say. But you'll find out for yourself. Six months from now, people will be following *you* when you walk down the street and half the young women in America will be imitating that throaty voice of yours."

Exaggerated, of course, but certainly flattering. After the second time she called him "Mr. Pelham," he'd said, "Pat, you're on the team. I have a first name. Use it."

Luther Pelham had certainly been charming, but on that occasion he had been offering her a job. Now he was her boss.

When she was announced, Luther came to the reception area to greet her. His manner was effusively cordial, the familiar well-modulated voice exuding hearty warmth: "Great to have you here, Pat. I want you to meet the gang." He took her around the newsroom and introduced her. Behind the pleasantries, she sensed the curiosity and speculation in the eyes of her new co-workers. She could guess what they were thinking. Would she be able to cut the mustard? But she liked her immediate impressions. Potomac was rapidly becoming one of the largest cable networks in the country, and the newsroom whirred with activity. A young woman was giving on-the-hour headlines live from her desk; a military expert was taping his bi-weekly segment; staff writers were editing copy from the wire services. She well knew that the apparently calm exterior of the personnel was a necessary ploy. Everyone in the business lived with constant underlying tension, always on guard, waiting for something to happen, fearful that somehow a big story might be fumbled.

Luther had already agreed that she could write and edit at home until they were ready for actual taping. He pointed out the cubicle that had been reserved for her, then led her into his private office, a large oak-paneled corner room.

"Make yourself comfortable, Pat," he directed. "There's a call I have to return."

While he was on the phone, Pat had a chance to study him closely. He was certainly an impressive and handsome man. His thick, carefully barbered stone gray hair contrasted with his youthful skin and probing dark eyes. She knew he had just had his sixtieth birthday. The party his wife had given at their Chevy Chase estate had been written up in all the columns. With his aquiline nose and long-fingered hands that tapped impatiently on the desk top, he reminded her of an eagle.

He hung up the phone. "Have I passed inspection?" His eyes were amused.

"With flying colors." Why was it, she wondered, that she always felt at ease in a professional situation and yet so often had a sense of alienation in personal relationships?

"Glad to hear it. If you weren't sizing me up, I'd be worried. Congratulations. You made a great impression on Abigail yesterday."

A quick pleasantry and then he was down to business. She liked that and wouldn't waste his time leading up to the problem. "I was very impressed with her. Who wouldn't be?" Then she added significantly— "for as long as I had the chance to be with her."

Pelham waved his hand as though to remove an unpleasant reality. "I know. I know. Abigail is hard to pin down. That's why I told them to put together some of her personal material for you. Don't expect much cooperation from the lady herself because you won't get it. I've scheduled the program for the twenty-seventh."

"The twenty-seventh? December twenty-seventh!" Pat heard her voice rising. "Next Wednesday! That would mean all the taping, editing and scoring will have to be done in a week!"

"Exactly," Luther confirmed. "And you're the one who can do it."

"But why the rush?"

He leaned back, crossed his legs and smiled with the relish of a bearer of momentous news. "Because this isn't going to be just another documentary. Pat Traymore, you have the chance to be a kingmaker."

She thought of what Sam had told her. *"The Vice President?"*

"The Vice President," he confirmed, "and I'm glad you have your ear to the ground. That triple bypass last year hasn't done the job for him. My spies at the hospital tell me he has extensive heart damage and if he wants to live he's going to have to change his lifestyle. That means he's virtually certain to resign—and now. To keep all factions of the party happy, the President will go through the motions of having the Secret Service check out three or four serious contenders for the job. But the inside bet is that Abigail has the best shot at it. When we air this program we want to motivate millions of Americans to send telegrams to the President in Abigail's behalf. That's what the program must do for her. And think about what it can do for *your* career."

Sam had talked about the *possibility* of the Vice President's resignation and Abigail's candidacy. Luther Pelham clearly believed both were imminent *probabilities*. To be at the right place at the right time, to be there when a story was breaking—it was the dream of

every newswoman. "If words leaks out about how sick the Vice President is . . ."

"It's more than leaking out," Luther told her. "I'm carrying it on my newscast tonight, including the rumors that the President is considering a woman replacement."

"Then the Jennings program could sweep the ratings next week! Senator Jennings isn't that well known to the average voter. Everyone's going to want to find out about her."

"Exactly. Now you can understand the need to put it together fast and make it something absolutely extraordinary."

"The Senator . . . If we make this program as bloodless as she seems to want, you won't get fourteen telegrams, never mind millions. Before I proposed this documentary I did some extensive surveying to find out what people think about her."

"And?"

"Older people compared her to Margaret Chase Smith. They called her impressive, gutsy, intelligent."

"What's wrong with that?"

"Not one of the older people felt they knew her as a human being. They think of her as being distant and formal."

"Go on."

"The younger people have a different approach. When I told them about the Senator being Miss New York State, they thought it was great. They want to know more about it. Remember, if Abigail Jennings is chosen to be Vice President, she'll be second in command of the whole country. A number of people who know she is from the Northeast resent the fact that she

never talks about it. I think she's making a mistake. And we'll compound it if we ignore the first twenty years of her life."

"She'll never let you mention Apple Junction," Luther said flatly. "So let's not waste time on that. She told me that when she resigned her Miss New York State title, they wanted to lynch her there."

"Luther, she's wrong. Do you seriously think anyone in Apple Junction gives a damn anymore that Abigail didn't go to Atlantic City to try to become Miss America? Right now I'll bet every adult there is bragging that he or she knew Abigail when. As for resigning the title, let's face it head on. Who wouldn't sympathize with an answer like Abigail saying it had been a lark entering the contest but she found she hated the idea of parading around in a bathing suit and having people judge her like a side of beef? Beauty contests are passé now. We'll make her look good for realizing it before anyone else did."

Luther drummed his fingers on the desk. Every instinct told him Pat was right, but Abigail had been definite on this point. Suppose they talked her into doing some material on her early life and it backfired? Luther was determined to be the power that put Abigail across as Vice President. Of course the party leaders would exact a promise from Abigail not to expect to run for the number one spot next time, but hell, those promises were made to be broken. He'd keep Abigail front and center until the day came when she was sitting in the Oval Office—and she'd owe it to him. . . .

He suddenly realized that Pat Traymore was watching him calmly. Most of the people he hired were

trying not to swallow their own spit in the first private session in this office. The fact that she seemed totally at ease both pleased and annoyed him. He had found himself doing a lot of thinking about her in the two weeks since he'd offered her the job. She was smart; she'd asked all the right questions about her contract; she was damn good-looking in an interesting, classy kind of way. She was a born interviewer; those eyes and that raspy voice gave her a kind of sympathetic, even naive quality that created a "tell all" atmosphere. And there was a smoldering sexiness about her that was especially intriguing.

"Tell me how you see the overall approach to her personal life," he ordered.

"First Apple Junction," Pat said promptly. "I want to go there myself and see what I can find. Maybe some shots of the town, of the house where she lived. The fact that her mother was a housekeeper and that she went to college on scholarship is a plus. It's the American dream, only for the first time we're applying it to a national leader who happens to be a woman."

She pulled her notebook from her purse. Flipping it open, she continued. "Certainly we'll emphasize the early years when she was married to Willard Jennings. I haven't run the films yet, but it looks as though we'll pick up quite a bit of both their public and private lives."

Luther nodded affirmatively. "Incidentally, you'll probably see a fair amount of Jack Kennedy in those pictures. He and Willard Jennings were close friends. That's when Jack was a Senator, of course. Willard and Abigail were a part of the pre-Camelot years. People don't realize that about her. Leave in as many clips as

you can find of them with any of the Kennedys. Did you know that when Willard died, Jack escorted Abigail to the memorial service?"

Pat jotted a few words on her pad. "Didn't Senator Jennings have any family?" she asked.

"I guess not. It never came up." Luther impatiently reached for the cigarette case on his desk. "I keep trying to give up these damn weeds." He lit one and for the moment looked somewhat relaxed. "I only wish I'd headed to Washington at that time," he said. "I thought New York was where the action was. I've done all right, but those were great Washington years. Crazy, though, how many of those young men died violently. The Kennedy brothers. Willard in a plane crash. Dean Adams a suicide . . . You've heard about him?"

"Dean Adams?" She made her voice a question.

"Murdered his wife," Luther explained. "Killed himself. Nearly killed his kid. She did die eventually. Probably better off, too. Brain-damaged, no doubt. He was a Congressman from Wisconsin. Nobody could figure the reason. Just went nuts, I guess. If you come across any pictures of him or his wife in a group shot, edit them out. No one needs to be reminded of that."

Pat hoped her face didn't betray distress. Her tone remained determinedly brisk as she said, "Senator Jennings was one of the moving forces in getting the Parental Kidnapping Prevention Act passed. There are some wonderful letters in her files. I thought I'd look up some of the families she's reunited and pick the best one for a segment on the program. That will counteract Senator Lawrence and her grandchildren."

Luther nodded. "Fine. Give me the letters. I'll get

someone around here to do the legwork. And by the way, in your outline you didn't have anything about the Eleanor Brown case. I absolutely want that in. You know she came from Apple Junction too—the school principal there asked Abigail to give her a job after she'd been caught shoplifting."

"My instinct is to let that alone," Pat said. "Think about it. The Senator gave a convicted girl a new start. That much is fine. Then Eleanor Brown was accused of stealing seventy-five thousand dollars in campaign funds. She swore she was innocent. Essentially it was the Senator's testimony that convicted her. Did you ever see that girl's pictures? She was twenty-three when she went to prison for the embezzlement but looked about sixteen. People have a natural inclination to feel sorry for the underdog—and the whole purpose of this program is to make everyone love Abigail Jennings. In the Eleanor Brown case, she comes through as the heavy."

"That case shows that some legislators don't cover up for the crooks on their staff. And if you want Abigail's image softened, play up the fact that thanks to her, that kid got off a lot lighter than anyone else I know who stole that much money. Don't waste your sympathy on Eleanor Brown. She faked a nervous breakdown in prison, was transferred to a psychiatric hospital, was paroled as an outpatient and took off. She was some cool cookie. What else?"

"I'd like to go to Apple Junction tonight. If there's anything worthwhile there, I'll call you and we'll arrange for a camera crew. After that, I want to follow

the Senator through a day in her office, plan some shots and then tape her there a day or two later."

Luther stood up—a signal that the meeting was over. "All right," he said. "Fly up to . . . What is the place . . . Apple Junction? What a hell of a name! See if you can get good copy. But play it low key. Don't let the natives get the idea they're going to be on camera. The minute they think you might have them on the program, they'll start using all the big words they know and planning what leisure suit to wear." He twisted his face into a worried frown, made his voice nasal. "Myrtle, get the lighter fluid. There's a gravy stain on my jacket."

"I'm sure I'll find some pretty decent people there." Pat forced a faint smile to take the implied rebuke out of her words.

Luther watched her leave, noting the burgundy-and-gray tweed suit, obviously a designer original; the burgundy leather boots with the small gold Gucci trademark; the matching shoulder bag; the Burberry over her arm.

Money. Patricia Traymore had family money. You could always tell. Resentfully, Luther thought of his own humble beginnings on a farm in Nebraska. They hadn't had indoor plumbing until he was ten. No one could sympathize more than he with Abigail about not wanting to resurrect the early years.

Had he done the right thing in allowing Pat Traymore to have her way in this? Abigail would be sore—but she'd probably be a lot sorer when she found out they hadn't told her about the trip.

Luther turned on his intercom. "Get me Senator

Jennings' office." Then he hesitated. "No, hold it; don't bother."

He put down the phone and shrugged. Why start trouble?

6

Pat felt the sidelong glances of the people in the newsroom as she left Pelham's office. Deliberately she set her face in a half-smile and made her step brisk. He'd been very cordial; he had risked Senator Jennings' anger by letting her go to Apple Junction. He had expressed his faith in her ability to put the program together on a breakneck schedule.

Then what's the matter? she wondered. I should feel great.

Outside, it was a cold, bright day. The streets were clear, and she decided to walk home. It was a couple of miles, but she wanted the exercise. Why not admit it? she thought. It's what Pelham just said about the Dean Adams mess; it's what Toby said yesterday. It's the feeling of everyone stepping back when Dean Adams' name is mentioned, of no one wanting to admit having known him. What had Luther said about her? Oh, yes —he thought the child had died, and it was better that way; she was probably brain-damaged.

I'm not brain-damaged, Pat thought as she tried to

avoid a spray of dirty slush. But I *am* damaged. My leg is the least of it. I hate my father for what he did. He killed my mother and he tried to kill me.

She had come here thinking she only wanted to understand what had caused him to crack up. Now she knew better. She had to face the anger she had been denying all these years.

It was a quarter to one when she got home. It seemed to her that the house was taking on a certain comfortable aura. The antique marble table and Serapi rug in the foyer made the faded paint seem insignificant. The kitchen counters were cheerful now with canisters; the oval wrought-iron table and matching soda-parlor chairs fitted exactly into the area beneath the windows and made it easy to ignore the worn spots on the aging tiles.

Quickly she fixed a sandwich and tea while phoning for a plane reservation. She was fully seven minutes on "hold" listening to a particularly poor selection of canned music before a clerk finally came on the line. She arranged for a four-forty flight to Albany and a rental car.

She decided to use the few hours before flight time to begin going through her father's effects.

Slowly she pulled aside the flaps of the first box and found herself staring down at the dust-covered picture of a tall, laughing man with a child on one shoulder. The child's eyes were wide with delight; her mouth half-open and smiling. Her palms were facing each other as though she might have just clapped them. Both man and child were in swimsuits by the water's edge. A wave was crashing behind them. It was late afternoon. Their shadows on the sand were elongated.

Daddy's little girl, Pat thought bitterly. She had seen children on their fathers' shoulders, hanging on to their necks or even twining their fingers in their hair. Fear of falling was a basic instinct. But the child in this picture, the child she had been, clearly had trusted the man holding her, trusted him not to let her fall. She laid the picture on the floor and continued emptying the box.

When she had finished, the carpet was covered with memorabilia from the private office of Congressman Dean Adams. A formal portrait of her mother at the piano. She was beautiful, Pat thought—I resemble him more. There was a collage of snapshots of Pat as a baby and toddler that must have hung on his office wall; his appointment diary, dark green leather with his initials in gold; his silver desk set, now so terribly tarnished; the framed diploma from the University of Wisconsin, a B.A. in English with high honors; his law-school degree from the University of Michigan, proclaiming him an LL.B; a citation from the Episcopal Bishops' Conference for generous and unstinting work for minorities; a Man of the Year plaque from the Madison, Wisconsin, Rotary Club. He must have been fond of seascapes. There were several excellent old prints of sailing vessels, billowing over turbulent waters.

She opened the appointment book. He had been a doodler; almost every page contained swirls and geometric figures. So that's where I got the habit, Pat thought.

Her eyes kept returning to the picture of herself and her father. She looked so blissfully happy. Her father

was looking up at her with so much love. His grip on her arm was so firm.

The telephone broke the spell. She scrambled to her feet, alarmed to realize that it was getting late, that she'd have to put all this away and pack a few things in a bag.

"Pat."

It was Sam.

"Hi." She bit her lip.

"Pat, I'm on the run as usual. I've got a committee meeting in five minutes. There's a dinner at the White House Friday night honoring the new Canadian Prime Minister. Would you like to go with me? I'll have to phone your name in to the White House."

"The White House! That would be wonderful. I'd love to go." She swallowed fiercely, trying to suppress the quiver in her voice.

Sam's tone changed. "Pat, is anything wrong? You sound upset. You're not crying, are you?"

At last she could control the tremor in her voice. "Oh, no. Not at all. I guess I'm just getting a cold."

7

At the Albany airport, Pat picked up her rental car, pored over a road map with the Hertz attendant and worked out the best route to Apple Junction, twenty-seven miles away.

"Better get going, Miss," the clerk warned. "We're supposed to have a foot of snow tonight."

"Can you suggest the best place to stay?"

"If you want to be right in town, the Apple Motel is it." He smirked. "But it's nothing fancy like you'd find in the *Big* Apple. Don't worry about phoning ahead for a reservation."

Pat picked up the car key and her bag. It didn't sound promising, but she thanked the clerk all the same.

The first flakes were falling as she pulled into the driveway of the dreary building with the flickering neon sign APPLE MOTEL. As the Hertz attendant had predicted, the VACANCY sign was on.

The clerk in the tiny, cluttered office was in his seventies. Wire-framed glasses drooped on his narrow

nose. Deep lines creased his cheeks. Clumps of gray-white hair sprouted from his skull. His eyes, rheumy and faded, brightened in surprise when Pat pushed open the door.

"Do you have a single for the next night or two?" she asked.

His smile revealed a worn, tobacco-stained dental plate. "Long as you want, Miss; you can have a single, a double, even the Presidential suite." A braying laugh followed.

Pat smiled politely and reached for the registration card. Deliberately she omitted filling the blank spot after PLACE OF BUSINESS. She wanted to have as much chance as possible to look around for herself before the reason for her presence here became known.

The clerk studied the card, his curiosity disappointed. "I'll put you in the first unit," he said. "That way you'll be near the office here in case the snow gets real heavy. We have a kind of dinette." He gestured toward three small tables against the rear wall. "Always have juice and coffee and toast to get you started in the morning." He looked at her shrewdly. "What brings you here, anyway?"

"Business," Pat said, then added quickly, "I haven't had dinner yet. I'll just drop my bag in my room and maybe you can tell me where I can find a restaurant."

He squinted at the clock. "You better hurry. The Lamplighter closes at nine and it's near eight now. Just go out the drive, turn left and go two blocks, then turn left again on Main. It's on the right. Can't miss it. Here's your key." He consulted the registration card. "Miss Traymore," he concluded, "I'm Travis Blodg-

ett. I own the place." Pride and apology blended in his voice. A slight wheeze suggested emphysema.

Except for a dimly lit movie marquee, the Lamplighter was the only establishment open in the two blocks embracing the business district of Apple Junction. A greasy, handprinted menu posted on the front door announced the day's special, sauerbraten and red cabbage for $3.95. Faded linoleum lay underfoot just inside. Most of the checkered cloths on the dozen or so tables were partially covered with unpressed napkins—probably, she guessed, to hide stains caused by earlier diners. An elderly couple were munching on dark-looking meat from overfilled plates. But she had to admit the smell was tantalizing, and she realized she was very hungry.

The sole waitress was a woman in her mid-fifties. Under a fairly clean apron, a thick orange sweater and shapeless slacks mercilessly revealed layers of bulging flesh. But her smile was quick and pleasant. "You alone?"

"Yes."

The waitress looked uncertainly around, then led Pat to a table near the window. "That way you can look out and enjoy the view."

Pat felt her lips twitch. The view! A rented car on a dingy street! Then she was ashamed of herself. That was exactly the reaction she would expect of Luther Pelham.

"Would you care for a drink? We have beer or wine. And I guess I'd better take your order. It's getting late."

Pat requested wine and asked for a menu.

"Oh, don't bother with a menu," the waitress urged. "Try the sauerbraten. It's really good."

Pat glanced across the room. Obviously that was what the old couple were eating. "If you'll give me about half much as . . ."

The waitress smiled, revealing large, even white teeth.

"Oh, sure." She lowered her voice. "I always fill those two up. They can only afford to eat out once a week, so I like to get a decent meal into them."

The wine was a New York State red jug wine, but it was pleasant. A few minutes later the waitress came out of the kitchen carrying a plate of steaming food and a basket of homemade biscuits.

The food was delicious. The meat had been marinated in wines and herbs; the gravy was rich and tangy; the cabbage pungent; the butter melted into the still-warm biscuits.

My God, if I ate like this every night, I'd be the size of a house, Pat thought. But she felt her spirits begin to lift.

When Pat had finished, the waitress took her plate and came over with the coffeepot. "I've been looking and looking at you," the woman said. "Don't I know you? Haven't I seen you on television?"

Pat nodded. So much for poking around on my own, she thought.

"Sure," the waitress continued. "You're Patricia Traymore. I saw you on TV when I visited my cousin in Boston. *I know why you're here!* You're doing a program on Abby Foster—I mean Senator Jennings."

"You knew her?" Pat asked quickly.

"Knew her! I should say I did. Why don't I just have

coffee with you?" It was a rhetorical question. Reaching over to the next table for an empty cup, she sank heavily into the chair opposite Pat. "My husband does the cooking; he can take care of closing up. It was pretty quiet tonight, but my feet hurt anyhow. All this standing . . ."

Pat made appropriate sympathetic sounds.

"Abigail Jennings, huh. Ab-by-gail Jennings," the waitress mused. "You gonna put folks from Apple Junction in the program?"

"I'm not sure," Pat said honestly. "Did you know the Senator well?"

"Not well, exactly. We were in the same class at school. But Abby was always so quiet; you could never figure what she was thinking. Girls usually tell each other everything and have best friends and run in cliques. Not Abby. I can't remember her having even one close friend."

"What did the other girls think about her?" Pat asked.

"Well, you know how it is. When someone is as pretty as Abby was, the other kids are kind of jealous. Then everybody got the feeling she thought she was too good for the rest of us, so that didn't make her any too popular either."

Pat considered her for a moment. "Did *you* feel that way about her, Mrs. . . . ?"

"Stubbins. Ethel Stubbins. In a way I guess I did, but I kind of understood. Abby just wanted to grow up and get out of here. The debating club was the only activity she joined in school. She didn't even dress like the rest of us. When everyone else was going around in sloppy joe sweaters and penny loafers, she wore a

starched blouse and heels to school. Her mother was the cook at the Saunders house. I think that bothered Abby a lot."

"I understood her mother was the housekeeper," Pat said.

"The *cook*," Ethel repeated emphatically. "She and Abby had a little apartment off the kitchen. My mother used to go to the Saunders place every week to clean, so I know."

It was a fine distinction: saying your mother had been the housekeeper rather than the cook. Pat shrugged mentally. What could be more harmless than Senator Jennings' upgrading her mother's job a notch? She debated. Sometimes taking notes or using a recorder had the immediate effect of causing an interviewee to freeze. She decided to take the chance.

"Do you mind if I record you?" she asked.

"Not at all. Should I talk louder?"

"No, you're fine." Pat pulled out her recorder and placed it on the table between them. "Just talk about Abigail as you remember her. You say it bothered her that her mother was a cook?" She had a mental image of how Sam would react to that question. He would consider it unnecessary prying.

Ethel leaned her heavy elbows on the table. "Did it ever! Mama used to tell me how nervy Abby was. If anyone was coming down the street, she used to walk up the path to the front steps just as though she owned the place and then when no one was looking, she'd scoot around to the back. Her mother used to holler at her, but it didn't do any good."

"Ethel. It's nine o'clock."

Pat looked up. A squat man with pale hazel eyes set

in a cheerful round face was standing at the table, untying a long white apron. His eyes lingered on the recorder.

Ethel explained what was happening and introduced Pat. "This is my husband, Ernie."

Clearly Ernie was intrigued by the prospect of contributing to the interview. "Tell how Mrs. Saunders caught Abby coming in the front door and told her to know her place," he suggested. "Remember, she made her walk back to the sidewalk and come up the driveway and go around to the back door."

"Oh, yeah," Ethel said. "That was lousy, wasn't it? Mama said she felt sorry for Abby until she saw the look on her face. Enough to freeze your blood, Mama said."

Pat tried to imagine a young Abigail forced to walk to the servants' entrance to show that she "knew her place." Again she had the feeling of intruding on the Senator's privacy. She wouldn't pursue that topic. Refusing Ernie's offer of more wine, she suggested, "Abby—I mean the Senator—must have been a very good student to get a scholarship to Radcliffe. Was she at the head of her class?"

"Oh, she was terrific in English and history and languages," Ethel said, "but a real birdbrain in math and science. She hardly got by in them."

"Sounds like me," Pat smiled. "Let's talk about the beauty contest."

Ethel laughed heartily. "There were four finalists for Miss Apple Junction. Yours truly was one of them. Believe it or not, I weighed one hundred eighteen pounds then, and I was darn cute."

Pat waited for the inevitable. Ernie did not disappoint her. "You're still darn cute, honey."

"Abby won hands down," Ethel continued. "Then she got into the contest for Miss New York State. You could have knocked everyone over with a feather when she won *that!* You know how it is. Sure, we knew she was beautiful, but we were all so used to seeing her. Was this town ever excited!"

Ethel chuckled. "I must say Abby kept this town supplied with gossip all that summer. The big social event around here was the country-club dance in August. All the rich kids from miles around went to it. None of *us,* of course. But that year Abby Foster was there. From what I hear, she looked like an angel in a white marquisette gown edged with layers of black Chantilly lace. And guess who took her? Jeremy Saunders! Just home after graduating from Yale. And he was practically engaged to Evelyn Clinton! He and Abby held hands all night and he kept kissing her when they danced.

"The next day the whole town was buzzing. Mama said Mrs. Saunders must have been spitting nails; her only son falling for the cook's daughter. And then"— Ethel shrugged—"it just ended. Abby resigned her Miss New York State crown and took off for college. Said she knew she'd never become Miss America, that she couldn't sing or dance or act for the talent part and there was no way she wanted to parade around in Atlantic City and come back a loser. A lot of people had chipped in for a wardrobe for her to wear to the Miss America contest. They felt pretty bad."

"Remember Toby threw a punch at a couple of guys

who said Abby let the folks around here down?" Ernie prompted Ethel.

"Toby Gorgone?" Pat asked quickly.

"The same," Ernie said. "He was always nuts about Abby. You know how kids talk in locker rooms. If any guy said anything fresh about Abby in front of Toby, he was sorry fast."

"He works for her now," Pat said.

"No kidding?" Ernie shook his head. "Say hello to him for me. Ask him if he's still losing money on the horses."

It was eleven o'clock before Pat got back to the Apple Motel, and by then Unit One was chilly. She quickly unpacked—there was no closet, only a hook on the door—undressed, showered, brushed her hair and, propping up the narrow pillows, got into bed with her notebook. As usual, her leg was throbbing—a faint ache that began in her hip and shot down her calf.

She glanced over the notes she had taken during the evening. According to Ethel, Mrs. Foster had left the Saunders home right after the country-club dance and gone to work as a cook in the county hospital. Nobody ever did know whether she'd quit or been fired. But the new job must have been hard on her. She was a big woman—"You think *I'm* heavy," Ethel had said, "you should've seen Francey Foster." Francey had died a long time ago and no one had seen Abigail after that. Indeed, few had seen her for years before that.

Ethel had waxed eloquent on the subject of Jeremy Saunders—"Abigail was lucky she didn't marry him. He never amounted to a hill of beans. Lucky for him he had the family money: otherwise he'd probably

have starved. They say his father tied up everything in trusts, even made Evelyn the executor of his will. Jeremy was a big disappointment to him. He always looked like a diplomat or an English lord and he's just a bag of wind."

Ethel had insinuated that Jeremy was a drinker, but suggested that Pat call him: "He'd probably love company. Evelyn spends most of her time with their married daughter in Westchester."

Pat turned out the light. Tomorrow morning she would try to visit the retired principal who'd asked Abigail to give Eleanor Brown a job, and she'd attempt to make an appointment with Jeremy Saunders.

It snowed during the night, some four or five inches, but the plows and sanders had already been through by the time Pat had coffee with the proprietor of the Apple Motel.

Driving around Apple Junction was a depressing experience. The town was a particularly shabby and unattractive one. Half the stores were closed and had fallen into disrepair. A single strand of Christmas lights dangled across Main Street. On the side streets, houses were jammed together, their paint peeling. Most of the cars parked in the street were old. There seemed to be no new building of any kind, residential or business. There were few people out; a sense of emptiness pervaded the atmosphere. Did most of the young people flee like Abigail as soon as they were grown? she wondered. Who could blame them?

She saw a sign reading THE APPLE JUNCTION WEEKLY and on impulse parked and went inside. There were two people working, a young woman who

seemed to be taking a want ad over the phone and a sixtyish man who was making an enormous clatter on a manual typewriter. The latter, it developed, was Edwin Shepherd, the editor-owner of the paper and perfectly happy to talk to Pat.

He could add very little to what she already knew about Abigail. However, he willingly went to the files to hunt up issues that might refer to the two contests, local and state, that Abigail had won.

In her research Pat had already found the picture of Abigail in her Miss New York State sash and crown. But the full-length shot of Abigail with the banner MISS APPLE JUNCTION was new and unsettling. Abigail was standing on a platform at the county fair, the three other finalists around her. The crown on her head was clearly papier-mâché. The other girls had pleased, fluttery smiles—Pat realized that the girl on the end was the youthful Ethel Stubbins—but Abigail's smile was cold, almost cynical. She seemed totally out of place.

"There's a shot of her and her maw inside," Shepherd volunteered, and turned the page.

Pat gasped. Could Abigail Jennings, delicate-featured and bone-slender, possibly be the offspring of this squat, obese woman? The caption read: PROUD MOTHER GREETS APPLE JUNCTION BEAUTY QUEEN.

"Why not take those issues?" Edwin Shepherd asked. "I've got more copies. Just remember to give us credit if you use anything on your program."

It would be awkward to refuse the offer, Pat realized. I can just see using *that* picture, she thought as she thanked the editor and quickly left.

A half-mile down Main Street, the town changed

dramatically. The roads became wider, the homes stately, the grounds large and well tended.

The Saunders house was pale yellow with black shutters. It was on a corner, and a long driveway curved to the porch steps. Graceful pillars reminded Pat of the architecture of Mount Vernon. Trees lined the driveway. A small sign directed deliveries to the service entrance in the rear.

She parked and went up the steps, noticing that on closer inspection the paint was beginning to chip and the aluminum storm windows were corroded. She pushed the button and from somewhere far inside could hear the faint sound of chimes. A thin woman with graying hair wearing a half-apron over a dark dress answered the door. "Mr. Saunders is expecting you. He's in the library."

Jeremy Saunders, wearing a maroon velvet jacket, was settled in a high-backed wing chair by the fire. His legs were crossed, and fine dark blue silk hose showed below the cuffs of his midnight-blue trousers. He had exceptionally even features and handsome wavy white hair. A thickened waistline and puffy eyes alone betrayed a predilection for drink.

He stood up and steadied himself against the arm of the chair. "Miss Traymore!" His voice was so pointedly well bred as to suggest classes in elocution. "You didn't tell me on the phone that you were *the* Patricia Traymore."

"Whatever that means," Pat said, smiling.

"Don't be modest. You're the young lady who's doing a program on Abigail." He waved her to the chair opposite his. "You *will* have a Bloody Mary?"

"Thank you." The pitcher was already half-empty.

The maid took her coat.

"Thank you, Anna. That will be all for now. Perhaps a little later Miss Traymore will join me in a light lunch." Jeremy Saunders' tone became even more fatuous when he spoke to the servant, who silently left the room. "You can close the door if you will, Anna!" he called. "Thank you, my dear."

Saunders waited until the latch clicked, then sighed. "Good help is impossible to find these days. Not as it was when Francey Foster was presiding over the kitchen and Abby was serving the table." He seemed to relish the thought.

Pat did not reply. There was a gossipy kind of cruelty about the man. She sat down, accepted the drink and waited. He raised one eyebrow. "Don't you have a tape recorder?"

"Yes, I do. But if you prefer I won't use it."

"Not at all. I prefer that every word I say be immortalized. Perhaps someday there'll be an Abby Foster— forgive me, à *Senator Abigail Jennings*—Library. People will be able to push a button and hear me tell of her rather chaotic coming of age."

Silently Pat reached into her shoulder bag and pulled out the recorder and her notebook. She was suddenly quite sure that what she was about to hear would be unusable.

"You've followed the Senator's career," she suggested.

"Breathlessly! I have the utmost admiration for Abby. From the time she was seventeen and began offering to help her mother with household duties, she had won my utmost respect. She's ingenious."

"Is it ingenious to help your mother?" Pat asked quietly.

"Of course not. If you *want* to *help* your mother. On the other hand, if you offer to serve only because the handsome young scion of the Saunders family is home from Yale, it does color the picture, doesn't it?"

"Meaning you?" Pat smiled reluctantly. Jeremy Saunders had a certain sardonic, self-deprecating quality that was not unattractive.

"You've guessed it. I see pictures of her from time to time, but you can never trust pictures, can you? Abby always photographed very well. How does she look in person?"

"She's absolutely beautiful," Pat said.

Saunders seemed disappointed. He'd love to hear that the Senator needs a face lift, Pat reflected. Somehow she could not believe that even as a very young girl Abigail would have been impressed by Jeremy.

"How about Toby Gorgone?" Saunders asked. "Is he still playing his chosen role as bodyguard and slave to Abby?"

"Toby works for the Senator," Pat replied. "He's obviously devoted to her, and she seems to count on him very much." *Bodyguard and slave,* she thought. It was a good way to describe Toby's relationship to Abigail Jennings.

"I suppose they're still pulling each other's chestnuts out of the fire."

"What do you mean by that?"

Jeremy raised his hand in a gesture of dismissal. "Nothing, really. He probably told you how he saved Abby from the jaws of the attack dog our eccentric neighbor kept."

"Yes, he did."

"And did he tell you that Abigail was his alibi the night he may have gone joyriding in a stolen car?"

"No, he didn't, but joyriding doesn't seem to be a very serious offense."

"It is when the police car chasing the 'borrowed' vehicle goes out of control and mows down a young mother and her two children. Someone who looked like him had been observed hanging around the car. But Abigail swore that she had been tutoring Toby in English, right here in this house. It was Abigail's word against an uncertain witness. No charge was brought and the joyrider was never caught. Many people found the possible involvement of Toby Gorgone quite credible. He's always been obsessed with machinery, and that was a new sports car. It makes sense he'd want to give it a spin."

"Then you're suggesting the Senator may have lied for him?"

"I'm suggesting nothing. However, people around here have long memories, and Abigail's fervent deposition—taken under oath, of course—is a matter of record. Actually, nothing much could have happened to Toby even if he had been in the car. He was still a juvenile, under sixteen. Abigail, however, was eighteen and if she had perjured herself would have been criminally culpable. Oh, well, Toby may very well have spent that evening diligently drilling on participles. Has his grammar improved?"

"It sounded all right to me."

"You couldn't have spoken to him very long. Now, fill me in on Abigail. The endless fascination she evokes in men. With whom is she involved now?"

"She's not involved with anyone," Pat said. "From what she tells me, her husband was the great love of her life."

"Perhaps." Jeremy Saunders finished the last of his drink. "And when you consider that she had absolutely no background—a father who drank himself to death when she was six, a mother content among the pots and pans . . ."

Pat decided to try another tack to get some sort of usable material. "Tell me about this house," she suggested. "After all, Abigail grew up here. Was it built by your family?"

Jeremy Saunders was clearly proud of both house and family. For the next hour, pausing only to refill his glass and then to mix a new pitcher of drinks, he traced the history of the Saunderses from "not quite the *Mayflower*—a Saunders was supposed to be on that historic voyage, but fell ill and did not arrive till two years later"—to the present. "And so," he concluded, "I sadly relate that I am the last to bear the Saunders name." He smiled. "You are a most appreciative listener, my dear. I hope I haven't been too long-winded in my recitation."

Pat returned the smile. "No, indeed. My mother's family were early settlers and I'm very proud of them."

"You must let me hear about *your* family," Jeremy said gallantly. "You will stay for lunch."

"I'd be delighted."

"I prefer having a tray right here. So much cozier than the dining room. Would that do?"

And so much nearer the bar, Pat thought. She hoped she could soon steer the subject back to Abigail.

Her opportunity came as she made a pretense of sipping the wine Jeremy insisted they have with the indifferently served chicken salad.

"It helps to wash it down, my dear," he told her. "I'm afraid when my wife is away, Anna doesn't put her best foot forward. Not like Abby's mother. Francey Foster took pride in everything she prepared. The breads, the cakes, the soufflés . . . Does Abby cook?"

"I don't know," Pat said. Her voice became confidential. "Mr. Saunders, I can't help feeling that you are angry at Senator Jennings. Am I wrong? I had the impression that at one time you two cared a great deal about each other."

"Angry at her? Angry?" His voice was thick, his words slurred. "Wouldn't *you* be angry at someone who set out to make a fool of you—and succeeded magnificently?"

It was happening now—the moment that came in so many of her interviews when people let down their guard and began to reveal themselves.

She studied Jeremy Saunders. This sleekly overfed, drunken man in his ridiculous formal getup was mulling a distasteful memory. There was pain as well as anger in the guileless eyes, the too soft mouth, the weak, puffy chin.

"Abigail," he said, his tone calmer, "United States Senator from Virginia." He bowed elaborately. "My dear Patricia Traymore, you have the distinction of addressing her former fiancé."

Pat tried unsuccessfully to hide her surprise. "You were *engaged* to Abigail?"

"That last summer she was here. Very briefly, of course. Just long enough for her overall scheme.

She'd won the state beauty contest but was smart enough to know she wouldn't go any further in Atlantic City. She'd tried to get a scholarship to Radcliffe, but her math and science marks weren't scholarship level. Of course, Abby had no intention of day-hopping to the local college. It was a terrible dilemma for her, and I still wonder if Toby didn't have a hand in planning the solution.

"I had just been graduated from Yale and was due to go into my father's business—a prospect which did not intrigue me; I was about to become engaged to the daughter of my father's best friend—a prospect which did not excite me. And here was Abigail right in my own home, telling me what I could become with her at my side, slipping into my bed in the dark of the night, while poor, tired Francey Foster snored away in their service apartment. The upshot was that I bought Abigail a beautiful gown, escorted her to the country-club dance and proposed to her.

"When we came home we woke our parents to announce the joyous news. Can you imagine the scene? My mother, who delighted in ordering Abigail to use the back door, watching all her plans for her only son dissolving. Twenty-four hours later, Abigail left town with a certified check from my father for ten thousand dollars and her bags filled with the wardrobe the town people had donated. She was already accepted by Radcliffe, you see. She only lacked the money to attend that splendid institution.

"I followed her there. She was quite explicit in letting me know that everything my father was saying about her was accurate. My father to his dying day never let me forget what a fool I'd made of myself. In

thirty-five years of married life, whenever Evelyn hears Abigail's name she becomes quite shrewish. As for my mother, the only satisfaction she could get was to order Francey Foster out of the house—and that was cutting off her nose to spite her face. We never had a decent cook after that."

When Pat tiptoed out of the room, Jeremy Saunders was asleep, his head bobbing on his chest.

It was nearly a quarter to two. The day was clouding up again, as though more snow might be in the offing. As she drove toward her appointment with Margaret Langley, the retired school principal, she wondered how accurate Jeremy Saunders' version of Abigail Foster Jennings' behavior as a young woman had been. Manipulator? Schemer? Liar?

Whatever, it didn't jibe with the reputation for absolute integrity that was the cornerstone of Senator Abigail Jennings' public career.

8

At a quarter of two, Margaret Langley took the unusual step of making a fresh pot of coffee, knowing full
well that the burning discomfort of gastritis might
plague her later.

As always when she was upset, she walked into her
study, seeking comfort in the velvety green leaves of
the plants hanging by the picture window. She'd been
in the midst of rereading the Shakespeare sonnets
with her after-breakfast coffee when Patricia Traymore
phoned asking permission to visit.

Margaret shook her head nervously. She was a
slightly stooped woman of seventy-three. Her gray
hair was fingerwaved around her head, with a small
bun at the nape of her neck. Her long, rather horsey
face was saved from homeliness by an expression of
good-humored wisdom. On her blouse she wore the
pin the school had given her when she retired—a gold
laurel wreath entwined around the number 45 to sig-
nify the years she'd served as teacher and principal.

At ten minutes past two she was beginning to hope

that Patricia Traymore had changed her mind about stopping in when she saw a small car coming slowly down the road. The driver paused at the mailbox, probably checking the house number. Reluctantly Margaret went to the front door.

Pat apologized for being late. "I took a wrong turn somewhere," she said, gladly accepting the offer of coffee.

Margaret felt her anxiety begin to subside. There was something very thoughtful about this young woman, the way she so carefully scraped her boots before stepping onto the polished floor. She was so pretty, with that auburn hair and those rich brown eyes. Somehow Margaret had expected her to be terribly aggressive. When she explained about Eleanor, maybe Patricia Traymore would listen. As she poured the coffee she said as much.

"You see," Margaret began, and to her own ears her voice sounded high-pitched and nervous, "the problem at the time the money disappeared in Washington was that everyone talked about Eleanor as though she were a hardened thief. Miss Traymore, did you ever hear the value of the object she supposedly stole when she was a high school senior?"

"No, I don't think so," Pat answered.

"*Six dollars.* Her life was ruined because of a six-dollar bottle of perfume! Miss Traymore, haven't you ever started to walk out of a store and realized you were holding something you meant to buy?"

"A few times," Pat agreed. "But surely no one is convicted of shoplifting for being absentminded about a six-dollar item."

"You are if there's been a wave of shoplifting in

town. The shopkeepers were up in arms, and the district attorney had vowed to make an example of the next person caught."

"And Eleanor was the next person?"

"Yes." Fine beads of perspiration accentuated the lines in Margaret's forehead. Alarmed, Pat noticed that her complexion was becoming a sickly gray.

"Miss Langley, don't you feel well? May I get you a glass of water?"

The older woman shook her head. "No, it will pass. Just give me a minute." They sat silently as the color began to return to Miss Langley's face. "That's better. I guess just talking about Eleanor upsets me. You see, Miss Traymore, the judge made an example of Eleanor; sent her to the juvenile home for thirty days. After that she was changed. Different. Some people can't take that kind of humiliation. You see, nobody believed her except me. I know young people. She wasn't daring. She was the kind who never chewed gum in class or talked when the teacher was out of the room or cheated on a test. She wasn't only good. She was *timid.*"

Margaret Langley was holding something back. Pat could sense it. She leaned forward, her voice gentle. "Miss Langley, there's a little more to the story than you're telling."

The woman's lip quivered. "Eleanor didn't have enough money to pay for the perfume. She explained that she was going to ask them to wrap it and put it aside. She was going to a birthday party that night. The judge didn't believe her."

Neither do I, Pat thought. She was saddened she couldn't accept the explanation that Margaret Langley

so passionately believed. She watched as the former principal put her hand on her throat as though to calm a rapid pulsebeat. "That sweet girl came here so many evenings," Margaret Langley continued sadly, "because she knew I was the one person who absolutely believed her. When she was graduated from our school, I wrote and asked Abigail if she could find a job for her in her office."

"Isn't it true that the Senator gave Eleanor that chance, trusted her, and then Eleanor stole campaign funds?" Pat asked.

Margaret's face became very tired. The tone of her voice flattened. "I was on a year's sabbatical when all that happened. I was traveling in Europe. By the time I got home, it was all over. Eleanor had been convicted and sent to prison and had a nervous breakdown. She was in the psychiatric ward of the prison hospital. I wrote to her regularly, but she never answered. Then, from what I understand, she was paroled for reasons of poor health, but only on condition she attend a clinic as an outpatient twice a week. One day she just disappeared. That was nine years ago."

"And you never heard from her again?"

"I . . . No . . . uh . . ." Margaret stood up. "I'm sorry—wouldn't you like a little more coffee? There's plenty in the pot. I'm going to have some. I shouldn't, but I will." With an attempt at a smile Margaret walked into the kitchen. Pat snapped off the recorder. She *has* heard from Eleanor, she thought, and can't bring herself to lie. When Miss Langley returned, Pat asked softly, "What do you know about Eleanor now?"

Margaret Langley set down the coffeepot on the table and walked over to the window. Would she hurt

Eleanor by trusting Pat Traymore? Would she in effect point out a trail that might lead to Eleanor?

A lone sparrow fluttered past the window and settled forlornly on the icy branch of an elm tree near the driveway. Margaret made up her mind. She would trust Patricia Traymore, show her the letters, tell her what she believed. She turned and met Pat's gaze and saw the concern in her eyes. "I want to show you something," she said abruptly.

When Margaret Langley returned to the room, she held in each hand a folded sheet of notepaper. "I've heard from Eleanor twice," she said. "This letter"— she extended her right hand—"was written the very day of the supposed theft. Read it, Miss Traymore; just read it."

The cream stationery was deeply creased as though it had been handled many times. Pat glanced at the date. The letter was eleven years old. Pat skimmed the contents quickly. Eleanor hoped that Miss Langley was enjoying her year in Europe; Eleanor had received a promotion and loved her job. She was taking painting classes at George Washington University and they were going very well. She had just returned from an afternoon in Baltimore. She'd had an assignment to sketch a water scene and decided on Chesapeake Bay. Miss Langley had underlined one paragraph. It read:

I almost didn't get there. I had to run an errand for Senator Jennings. She'd left her diamond ring in the campaign office and thought it had been locked in the safe for her. But it wasn't there, and I just made my bus.

This was proof? Pat thought. She looked up, and her eyes met Margaret Langley's hopeful gaze. "Don't you see?" Margaret said. "Eleanor wrote to me the very night of the supposed theft. Why would she make up that story?"

Pat could find no way to soften what she had to say. "She could have been setting up an alibi for herself."

"If you're trying to give yourself an alibi, you don't write to someone who may not get the letter for months," she said spiritedly. Then she sighed. "Well, I tried. I just hope you'll have the goodness not to rake up that misery again. Eleanor apparently is trying to make some sort of life for herself and deserves to be let alone."

Pat looked at the other letter Margaret was holding. "She wrote you after she disappeared?"

"Yes. Six years ago this came."

Pat took the letter. The typeface was worn, the paper cheap. The note read:

Dear Miss Langley. Please understand that it is better if I have no contact with anyone from the past. If I am found, I will have to go back to prison. I swear to you I never touched that money. I have been very ill but am trying to rebuild my life. Some days are good. I can almost believe it is possible to become well again. Other times I am so frightened, so afraid that someone will recognize me. I think of you often. I love and miss you.

Eleanor's signature was wavering, the letters uneven—a stark contrast to the firm and graceful penmanship of the earlier letter.

It took all Pat's persuasive powers to coax Margaret

Langley to let her take the letters. "We are planning to include the case in this program," she said, "but even if Eleanor is recognized and someone turns her in, perhaps we can have her parole reinstated. Then she wouldn't have to hide for the rest of her life."

"I would love to see her again," Margaret whispered. Now tears brightened her eyes. "She's the nearest thing I ever had to a child of my own. Wait—let me show you her picture."

On the bottom shelf of the bookcase were stacks of yearbooks. "I have one for every year I was in school," she explained. "But I keep Eleanor's on top." She riffled through the pages. "She graduated seventeen years ago. Isn't she sweet-looking?"

The girl in the photo had fine, mousy hair; soft, innocent eyes. The caption read:

Eleanor Brown—Hobby: painting. Ambition: secretary. Activities: choir. Sport: roller skating. Prediction: right-hand gal for executive, marry young, two kids. Favorite thing: Evening in Paris perfume.

"My God," Pat said, "how cruel."

"Exactly. That's why I wanted her to leave here."

Pat shook her head, and her glance caught the other yearbooks. "Wait a minute," she said, "by any chance do you have the book Senator Jennings is in?"

"Of course. Let's see—that would be over here somewhere."

The second book Margaret Langley checked was the right one. In this photo Abigail's hair was in a pageboy on her shoulders. Her lips were parted slightly as

though she had obediently followed the photographer's direction to smile. Her eyes, wide and thick-lashed, were calm and inscrutable. The caption read:

Abigail Foster ("Abby")—Hobby: attending state legislature. Ambition: politics. Activities: debating. Prediction: will become state assemblywoman from Apple Junction. Favorite thing: any book in the library.

"State assemblywoman," Pat exclaimed; "that's great!"

A half-hour later she left, the Senator's yearbook under her arm. As she got into the car, she decided that she'd send a camera crew to get some background footage of the town, including Main Street, the Saunders home, the high school and the highway with the bus to Albany. Under the footage she'd have Senator Jennings speak briefly about growing up there and her early interest in politics. They'd close that segment with the picture of the Senator as Miss New York State, then her yearbook picture and her explanation that going on to Radcliffe instead of Atlantic City was the most important decision of her life.

With the unfamiliar and disquieting feeling that somehow she was glossing over the full story, Pat drove around town for an hour and marked locations for the camera crew. Then she checked out of the Apple Motel, drove to Albany, turned in the rental car and with relief got on the plane back to Washington.

9

Washington is beautiful, Pat thought, from any view, at any hour. By night the spotlights on the Capitol and monuments seem to impart a sense of tranquil agelessness. She'd been gone from here only thirty hours, yet felt as though days had passed since she'd left. The plane landed with a slight bump and taxied smoothly across the field.

As she opened the door to her house, Pat heard the phone ringing and scrambled to answer it. It was Luther Pelham. He sounded edgy.

"Pat, I'm glad I've reached you. You never did let me know where you were staying in Apple Junction. When I finally tracked you down, you had checked out."

"I'm sorry. I should have phoned you this morning."

"Abigail is making a major speech before the final vote on the budget tomorrow. She suggested you spend the entire day at her office. She gets in at six-thirty."

"I'll be there."

"How did you do in the hometown?"

"Interesting. We can get some sympathetic footage that won't raise the Senator's hackles."

"I'd like to hear about it. I've just finished dinner at the Jockey Club and can be at your place in ten minutes." The phone clicked in her ear.

She had barely time to change into slacks and a sweater before he arrived. The library was cluttered with the Senator's material. Pat brought him back to the living room and offered him a drink. When she returned with it, he was studying the candelabrum on the mantel. "Beautiful example of Sheffield," he told her. "Everything in the room is beautiful."

In Boston, she had had a studio apartment similar to those of other young professionals. It had not occurred to her that the costly furnishings and accessories in this house might arouse comment.

She tried to sound casual. "My folks are planning to move into a condominium soon. We have an attic full of family stuff and Mother told me it's now or never if I want it."

Luther settled on the couch and reached for the glass she placed in front of him. "All I know is that at your age I was living at the Y." He patted the cushion beside him. "Sit here and tell me all about Our Town."

Oh, no, she thought. There'll be no passes tonight, Luther Pelham. Ignoring the suggestion, she sat on the chair across the table from the couch and proceeded to give Luther an accounting of what she had learned in Apple Junction. It was not edifying.

"Abigail may have been the prettiest girl in those parts," she concluded, "but she certainly wasn't the

most popular. I can understand now why she's nervous about stirring things up there. Jeremy Saunders will bad-mouth her till the day he dies. She's right to be afraid that calling attention to her being Miss New York State will get the old-timers again talking about how they contributed their two bucks to dress her up for Atlantic City and then she bugged out. Miss Apple Junction! Here, let me show you the picture."

Luther whistled when he saw it. "Hard to believe that blimp could be Abigail's mother." He thought better of the remark. "All right. She has a valid reason for wanting to forget Apple Junction and everyone in it. I thought you told me you could salvage some human-interest stuff."

"We'll cut it to the bone. Background shots of the town, the school, the house where she grew up; then interview the school principal, Margaret Langley, about how Abigail used to go to Albany to sit in on the legislature. Wind up with her school picture in the yearbook. It's not much, but it's something. The Senator's got to be made to understand she's not a UFO who landed on earth at age twenty-one. Anyhow, she agreed to cooperate in this documentary. We didn't give her creative control of it, I hope."

"Certainly not creative control, but some veto power. Don't forget, Pat. We're not just doing this *about* her; we're doing it *with* her, and her cooperation in letting us use her personal memorabilia is essential."

He stood up. "Since you insist on keeping that table between us . . ." He walked around it, and came over to her, put his hands on hers.

Quickly she jumped to her feet, but she was not fast

enough. He pulled her against him. "You're a beautiful girl, Pat." He lifted her chin. His lips pressed down on hers. His tongue was insistent.

She tried to pull away, but his grip was viselike. Finally she managed to dig her elbows into his chest. "Let go of me."

He smiled. "Pat, why don't you show me the rest of the house?"

There was no mistaking his meaning. "It's pretty late," she said, "but on the way out you can poke your head into the library and dining room. I do sort of wish you'd wait until I've had a chance to get pictures hung and whatever."

"Where's your bedroom?"

"Upstairs."

"I'd like to see it."

"As a matter of fact, even when it's fixed up, I'd like you to think of the second floor of this house the way you had to think about the second floor of the Barbizon for Women in your salad days in New York: off-limits for gentlemen callers."

"I'd rather you didn't joke, Pat."

"I'd rather we treat this conversation as a joke. Otherwise I can put it another way. I don't sleep on the job nor do I sleep off the job. Not tonight. Not tomorrow. Not next year."

"I see."

She preceded him down the hall. In the foyer she handed him his coat.

As he put it on, he gave her an acid smile. "Sometimes people who have your kind of insomnia problem find it impossible to handle their responsibilities," he said. "They often discover they're happier at some

backwoods station than in the big time. Does Apple Junction have a cable station? You might want to check it out, Pat."

Promptly at ten to six, Toby let himself in the back door of Abigail's house in McLean, Virginia. The large kitchen was filled with gourmet equipment. Abigail's idea of relaxing was to spend an evening cooking. Depending on her mood, she'd prepare six or seven different kinds of hors d'oeuvre or fish and meat casseroles. Other nights she'd make a half-dozen different sauces, or biscuits and cakes that would melt in your mouth. Then she'd pop everything into the freezer. But when she gave a party she never admitted that she'd prepared everything herself. She hated any association with the word "cook."

Abigail herself ate very little. Toby knew she was haunted by the memory of her mother, poor old Francey, that groaning tub of a woman whose trunklike legs settled into fat ankles and feet so wide it was hard to find shoes to fit them.

Toby had an apartment over the garage. Nearly every morning he'd come in and start the coffeepot and squeeze fresh juice. Later on, after he had Abby settled in her office, he'd have a big breakfast, and if she wasn't going to need him, he'd find a poker game.

Abigail came into the kitchen, still fastening a crescent-shaped gold pin on her lapel. She was wearing a purple suit that brought out the blueness of her eyes.

"You look great, Abby," he pronounced.

Her smile was quick and instantly gone. Whenever Abby had a big speech planned in the Senate she was like this—nervous as a cat before it, ready to be irri-

tated at anything that went wrong. "Let's not waste time on coffee," she snapped.

"You've got plenty of time," Toby assured her. "I'll have you there by six-thirty. Drink your coffee. You know how crabby you get without it."

Later he left both cups in the sink, knowing Abby would be irritated if he took time to rinse them out.

The car was at the front entrance. When Abby went to get her coat and briefcase, he hurried outside and turned on the heater.

By six-ten they were on the parkway. Even for a day when she was making a speech, Abby was unusually tense. She'd gone to bed early the night before. He wondered if she'd been able to sleep.

He heard Abby sigh and snap her briefcase closed. "If I don't know what I'm going to say by now I might as well forget it," she commented. "If this damn budget doesn't get voted on soon, we'll still be in session on Christmas Day. But I *won't* let them ax any more of the entitlement programs."

Toby watched in the rearview mirror as she poured some coffee from a thermos. From her attitude he knew she was ready to talk.

"Did you get a good rest last night, Senator?" Once in a while, even when they were alone, he threw in the "Senator." It reminded her that no matter what, he knew his place.

"No, I didn't. I started thinking about this program. I was stupid to let myself get talked into it. It's going to backfire. I feel it in my bones."

Toby frowned. He had a healthy respect for Abby's bones. He still hadn't told Abby that Pat Traymore lived in the Dean Adams house. She'd get real super-

stitious about that. This wasn't the time for her to lose
her cool. Still, at some point she'd have to know. It was
bound to come out. Toby was starting to get a lousy
feeling about the program himself.

Pat had set the alarm for five o'clock. In her first
television job, she'd discovered that being calm and
collected kept her energy directed to the project at
hand. She could still remember the burning chagrin of
rushing breathlessly to interview the Governor of
Connecticut and realizing she'd forgotten her carefully prepared questions.

After the Apple Motel, it had felt good to be in the
wide, comfortable bed. But she'd slept badly, thinking
about the scene with Luther Pelham. There were
plenty of men in the television-news business who
made the obligatory pass, and some of them were
vengeful when rejected.

She dressed quickly, choosing a long-sleeved black
wool dress with a suede vest. Once again it looked as
though it would be one of the raw, windy days that had
characterized this December.

Some of the storm windows were missing, and the
panes on the north side of the house rattled as the
wind shrieked against them.

She reached the landing of the staircase.

The shrieking sound intensified. But now it was a
child screaming. *I ran down the stairs. I was so frightened,
and I was crying. . . .*

A momentary dizziness made her grasp the banister.
It's starting to happen, she thought fiercely. It *is* coming back.

En route to the Senator's office she felt distracted,

out of sync. She could not rid herself of the over-whelming fear that was the result of the fleeting memory.

Why should she experience fear now?

How much had she seen of what happened that night?

Philip Buckley was waiting for her in the office when she arrived. In the gloom of the early morning, his attitude toward her seemed even more cautiously hostile than before. What is he afraid of? Pat wondered. You'd think I was a British spy in a Colonial camp. She told him that.

His small, cold smile was humorless. "If we thought you were a British spy, you wouldn't be anywhere near this Colonial camp," he commented. "The Senator will be here any minute. You might want to have a look at her schedule today. It will give you some idea of her workload."

He looked over her shoulder as she read the crammed pages. "Actually we'll have to put off at least three of these people. It's our thought that if you simply sit in the Senator's office and observe, you'll be able to decide what segments of her day you might want to include in the special. Obviously, if she has to discuss any confidential matters, you'll be excused. I've had a desk put in her private office for you. That way you won't be conspicuous."

"You think of everything," Pat told him. "Come on, how about a nice big smile? You'll have to have one for the camera when we start to shoot."

"I'm saving my smile for the time when I see the

final edited version of the program." But he did look a little more relaxed.

Abigail came in a few minutes later. "I'm so glad you're here," she said to Pat. "When we couldn't reach you, I was afraid you were out of town."

"I got your message last night."

"Oh. Luther wasn't sure if you'd be available."

So that was the reason for the small talk, Pat decided. The Senator wanted to know where'd she been. She wasn't going to tell her. "I'm going to be your shadow until the program's completed," she said. "You'll probably get sick of having me around."

Abigail didn't look placated. "I must be able to reach you quickly. Luther told me you had some questions to go over with me. With my schedule the way it is, I don't often know about free time until just before it's available. Now let's get to work."

Pat followed her into the private office and tried to make herself inconspicuous. In a few moments the Senator was in deep discussion with Philip. One report that he placed on her desk was late. Sharply, she demanded to know why. "I should have had that last week."

"The figures weren't compiled."

"Why?"

"There simply wasn't time."

"If there isn't time during the day, there's time in the evening," Abigail snapped. "If anyone on my staff has become a clock-watcher, I want to know about it."

At seven o'clock the appointments started. Pat's respect for Abigail grew with each new person who came into the office. Lobbyists for the oil industry, for environmentalists, for veterans' benefits. Strategy sessions

for presenting a new housing bill. A representative from the IRS to register specific objections to a proposed exemption for middle-income taxpayers. A delegation of senior citizens protesting the cutbacks in Social Security.

When the Senate convened, Pat accompanied Abigail and Philip to the chamber. Pat was not accredited to the press section behind the dais and took a seat in the visitors' gallery. She watched as the Senators entered from the cloakroom, greeting one another along the way, smiling, relaxed. They came in all sizes—tall, short; cadaver-slender, rotund; some with manes of hair, some carefully barbered, some bald. Four or five had the scholarly appearance of college professors.

There were two other women Senators, Claire Lawrence of Ohio and Phyllis Holzer of New Hampshire, who had been elected as an independent in a stunning upset.

Pat was especially interested in observing Claire Lawrence. The junior Senator from Ohio wore a three-piece navy knit suit that fitted comfortably over her size 14 figure. Her short salt-and-pepper hair was saved from severity by the natural wave that framed and softened her angular face. Pat noted the genuine pleasure with which this woman was greeted by her colleagues, the burst of laughter that followed her murmured greetings. Claire Lawrence was eminently quotable; her quick wit had a way of taking the rancor out of inflammatory issues without compromising the subject at hand.

In her notebook, Pat jotted *"humor"* and underlined the word. Abigail was rightly perceived to be serious,

intense. A few carefully placed light moments should be included in the program.

A long, insistent bell was calling the Senate to order. The senior Senator from Arkansas was presiding in place of the ailing Vice President. After a few short pieces of business had been completed, the Presiding Officer recognized the senior Senator from Virginia.

Abigail stood up and without a trace of nervousness carefully put on blue-rimmed reading glasses. Her hair was pulled back into a simple chignon that enhanced the elegant lines of her profile and neck.

"Two of the best-known sentences in the Bible," she said, "are 'The Lord giveth and the Lord taketh away. Blessed be the name of the Lord.' In recent years our government, in an exaggerated and ill-considered manner, has given and given. And then it has taken away and taken away. But there are few to bless its name.

"Any responsible citizen would, I trust, agree that an overhaul of the entitlement programs has been necessary. But now it is time to examine what we have done. I maintain that the surgery was too radical, the cuts too drastic. I maintain that this is the time for restoration of many necessary programs. Entitlement by definition means 'to have a claim to.' Surely no one in this august chamber will dispute that every human being in this country has a rightful claim to shelter and food. . . ."

Abigail was an excellent speaker. Her address had been carefully prepared, carefully documented, sprinkled with enough specific anecdotes to keep the attention of even these professionals.

She spoke for an hour and ten minutes. The ap-

plause was sustained and genuine. When the Senate recessed, Pat saw that the Majority Leader hurried over to congratulate her.

Pat waited with Philip until the Senator finally broke away from her colleagues and the visitors who crowded around her. Together they started back to the office.

"It was good, wasn't it?" Abigail asked, but there was no hint of question in her voice.

"Excellent, Senator," Philip said promptly.

"Pat?" Abigail looked at her.

"I felt sick that we couldn't record it," Pat said honestly. "I'd love to have had excerpts of that speech on the program."

They ate lunch in the Senator's office. Abigail ordered only a hard-boiled egg and black coffee. She was interrupted four times by urgent phone calls. One was from an old campaign volunteer. "Sure, Maggie," Abigail said. "No, you're not interrupting me. I'm always available to you—you know that. What can I do?"

Pat watched as Abigail's face became stern and a frown creased her forehead. "You mean the hospital told you to come get your mother when the woman can't even raise her head from the pillow? . . . I see. Have you any nursing homes in mind? . . . Six months' wait. And what are you supposed to do in those six months . . . Maggie, I'll call you back."

She slammed the phone down on the hook. "This is the kind of thing that drives me wild. Maggie is trying to raise three kids on her own. She works at a second job on Saturdays and now she's told to take home a senile, bedridden mother. Philip, track down Arnold

Pritchard. And I don't care if he's having a two-hour lunch somewhere. Find him now."

Fifteen minutes later the call Abigail was waiting for came through. "Arnold, good to talk to you. . . . I'm glad you're fine. . . . No, I'm not fine. In fact, I'm pretty upset. . . ."

Five minutes later Abigail concluded the conversation by saying, "Yes, I agree. The Willows sounds like a perfect place. It's near enough so that Maggie can visit without giving up her whole Sunday to make the trip. And I know I can count on you, Arnold, to make sure the old girl gets settled in. . . . Yes, send an ambulance to the hospital for her this afternoon. Maggie will be so relieved."

Abigail winked at Pat as she hung up the phone. "This is the aspect of the job that I love," she said. "I shouldn't take time to call Maggie myself, but I'm going to. . . ." She dialed quickly. "Maggie, hello. We're in good shape . . ."

Maggie, Pat decided, would be a guest on the program.

There was an environmental-committee hearing between two and four. At the hearing, Abigail got into a verbal duel with one of the witnesses and quoted from her report. The witness said, "Senator, your figures are dead wrong. I think you've got the old quotes, not the revised ones."

Claire Lawrence was also on the committee. "Maybe I can help," she suggested. "I'm pretty sure I have the latest numbers, and they do change the picture somewhat. . . ."

Pat observed the rigid thrust of Abigail's shoulders,

the way she clenched and unclenched her hands as Claire Lawrence read from her report.

The studious-looking young woman seated behind Abigail was apparently the aide who had compiled the inaccurate report. Several times Abigail turned to look at her during Senator Lawrence's comments. The girl was clearly in an agony of embarrassment. Her face was flushed; she was biting her lips to keep them from trembling.

Abigail cut in the instant Senator Lawrence stopped speaking. "Mr. Chairman, I would like to thank Senator Lawrence for her help, and I would also like to apologize to this committee for the fact that the figures given to me were inaccurate and wasted the valuable time of everyone here. I promise you it will never happen again." She turned again to her aide. Pat could read Abigail's lips: "You're fired." The girl slipped out of her chair and left the hearing room, tears running down her cheeks.

Inwardly Pat groaned. The hearing was being televised—anyone seeing the exchange would surely have felt sympathy for the young assistant.

When the hearing was over, Abigail hurried back to her office. It was obvious that everyone there knew what had happened. The secretaries and aides in the outer office did not lift their heads as she roared through. The hapless girl who had made the error was staring out the window, futilely dabbing at her eyes.

"In here, Philip," Abigail snapped. "You too, Pat. You might as well get a full picture of what goes on in this place."

She sat down at her desk. Except for the paleness of her features and the tight set of her lips, she appeared

totally composed. "What happened, Philip?" she asked, her tone level.

Even Philip had lost his usual calm. He gulped nervously as he started to explain. "Senator, the other girls just talked to me. Eileen's husband walked out on her a couple of weeks ago. From what they tell me, she's been in a terrible state. She's been with us three years, and as you know, she's one of our best aides. Would you consider giving her a leave of absence until she pulls herself together? She loves this job."

"Does she, indeed? Loves it so much she lets me make a fool of myself in a televised hearing? She's finished, Philip. I want her out of here in the next fifteen minutes. And consider yourself lucky you're not fired too. When that report was late, it was up to you to dig for the real reason for the problem. With all the brainy people hungry for jobs, *including mine,* do you think I intend to leave myself vulnerable because I'm surrounded by deadwood?"

"No, Senator," Philip mumbled.

"There are no second chances in this office. Have I warned my staff about that?"

"Yes, Senator."

"Then get out of here and do as you're told."

"Yes, Senator."

Wow! Pat thought. No wonder Philip was so on guard with her. She realized the Senator was looking over at her.

"Well, Pat," Abigail said quietly, "I suppose you think I'm an ogre?" She did not wait for an answer. "My people know if they have a personal problem and can't handle their job, their responsibility is to report it and arrange for a leave of absence. That policy is in

effect to prevent this sort of occurrence. When a staff member makes a mistake, it reflects on me. I have worked too hard, for too many years, to be compromised by anyone else's stupidity. And Pat, believe me, if they'll do it once, they'll do it again. And now, for God's sake, I'm due on the front steps to have my picture taken with a Brownie troop!"

10

At a quarter to five, a secretary timidly knocked on the door of Abigail's office. "A call for Miss Traymore," she whispered.

It was Sam. The reassuring heartiness of his voice boosted Pat's spirits immediately. She had been unsettled by the unpleasant episode, by the abject misery in the young woman's face.

"Hello, Sam." She felt Abigail's sharp glance.

"My spies told me you're on the Hill. How about dinner?"

"Dinner . . . I can't, Sam. I've got to work tonight."

"You also have to eat. What did you have for lunch? One of Abigail's hard-boiled eggs?"

She tried not to laugh. The Senator was clearly listening to her end of the conversation.

"As long as you don't mind eating fast and early," she compromised.

"Fine with me. How about if I pick you up outside the Russell building in half an hour?"

When Pat hung up, she looked over at Abigail.

"Have you reviewed all the material we gave you?— the films?" Abigail demanded.

"No."

"Some of them?"

"No," Pat admitted. Oh, boy, she thought. I'm glad I don't work for you, lady.

"I had thought you might come back to my place for dinner and we could discuss which ones you might be interested in using."

Again a pause. Pat waited.

"However, since you haven't seen the material, I think it would be wiser if I use tonight for some reading I must do." Abigail smiled. "Sam Kingsley is one of the most eligible bachelors in Washington. I didn't realize you knew him so well."

Pat tried to make her answer light. "I really don't." But she couldn't help thinking that Sam was finding it hard to stay away from her.

She glanced out the window, hoping to hide her expression. Outside it was almost dark. The Senator's windows overlooked the Capitol. As the daylight faded, the gleaming domed building framed by the blue silk draperies resembled a painting. "How lovely!" she exclaimed.

Abigail turned her head toward the window. "Yes, it is," she agreed. "That view at this time of day always reminds me of what I'm doing here. You can't imagine the satisfaction of knowing that because of what I did today an old woman will be cared for in a decent nursing home, and extra money may be made available for people who are trying to eke out an existence."

There was an almost sensual energy in Abigail Jennings when she spoke about her work, Pat thought. She means every word.

But it also occurred to her that the Senator had already dismissed from her memory the girl she had fired a few hours earlier.

Pat shivered as she hurried down the few steps from the Senate office building to the car. Sam leaned over to kiss her cheek. "How's the hotshot filmmaker?"

"Tired," she said. "Keeping up with Senator Jennings is not the recipe for a restful day."

Sam smiled. "I know what you mean. I've worked with Abigail on a fair amount of legislation. She never wears down."

Weaving through the traffic, he turned onto Pennsylvania Avenue. "I thought we'd go to Chez Grandmère in Georgetown," he said. "It's quiet, the food is excellent and it's near your place."

Chez Grandmère was nearly empty. "Washington doesn't dine at quarter to six." Sam smiled as the maître d' offered them their choice of tables.

Over a cocktail Pat told him about the day, including the scene in the hearing room. Sam whistled. "That was a rotten break for Abigail. You don't need someone on your payroll to make you look bad."

"Could something like that actually influence the President's decision?" Pat asked.

"Pat, *everything* can influence the President's decision. One mistake can ruin you. Well, figure it out for yourself. If it weren't for Chappaquiddick, Teddy Kennedy might be President today. Then, of course, you have Watergate and Abscam, and way back, vicuña

coats and home freezers. It never ends. Everything reflects on the man or woman who holds the office. It's a miracle Abigail survived that scandal about the missing campaign funds, and if she had tried to cover up for her aide, it would have been the end of her credibility. What was the girl's name?"

"Eleanor Brown." Pat thought of what Margaret Langley had said. *"Eleanor couldn't steal. She's too timid."*

"Eleanor always claimed she was innocent," she told Sam now.

He shrugged. "Pat, I was a county prosecutor for four years. You want to know something? Nine out of ten criminals swear they didn't do it. And at least eight out of nine of them are liars."

"But there is always that one who *is* innocent," Pat persisted.

"Very occasionally," Sam said. "What do you feel like eating?"

It seemed to her that she could watch him visibly unwind in the hour and a half they were together. I'm good for you, Sam, she thought. I can make you happy. You're equating having a child with the way it was when you were doing everything for Karen, because Janice was sick. It wouldn't be that way with me. . . .

Over coffee he asked, "How do you find living in the house? Any problems?"

She hesitated, then decided to tell him about the note she'd found slipped under the door and the second phone call. "But as you say, it's probably just some joker," she concluded.

Sam didn't return her attempt at a smile. "I said that one random call to the Boston station might not be

important. But you're saying that in the last three days you've had a second phone call, and a note pushed under the door. How do you think this nut got your address?"

"How did *you* get it?" Pat asked.

"I phoned Potomac Cable and said I was a friend. A secretary gave me your phone number and street address here and told me when you were arriving. Frankly, I was a little surprised they were that casual about giving out so much information."

"I approved it. I'll be using the house as an office for this program, and you'd be surprised how many people volunteer anecdotes or memorabilia when they read about a documentary being prepared. I didn't want to take the chance of losing calls. I certainly didn't think I had anything to worry about."

"Then that creep could have gotten it the same way. By any chance do you have the note with you?"

"It's in my bag." She fished it out, glad to be rid of it.

Sam studied it, frowning in concentration. "I doubt whether anybody could trace this, but let me show it to Jack Carlson. He's an FBI agent and something of a handwriting expert. And you be sure to hang up if you get another call."

He dropped her off at eight-thirty. "You've got to get timers for the lamps," he commented as they stood at the door. "Anybody could come up here and put a note under the door without being noticed."

She looked up at him. The relaxed expression was gone, and the newly acquired creases around his mouth had deepened again. You've always had to

worry about Janice, she thought. I don't want you worrying about me.

She tried to recapture the easy companionship of the evening. "Thanks for being the Welcome Wagon again," she said. "They're going to make you chairman of the Hospitality Committee on the Hill."

He smiled briefly and for that moment the tension disappeared from his eyes. "Mother taught me to be courtly to the prettiest girls in town." He closed his hands around hers. For a moment they stood silently; then he bent down and kissed her cheek.

"I'm glad you're not playing favorites," she murmured.

"What?"

"The other night you kissed me below my right eye —tonight the left."

"Good night, Pat. Lock the door."

Pat had barely reached the library when the telephone began to ring insistently. For a moment she was afraid to answer.

"Pat Traymore." To her own ears her voice sounded tense and husky.

"Miss Traymore," a woman's voice said, "I'm Lila Thatcher, your neighbor across the street. I know you just got home, but would it be possible for you to come over now? There's something quite important you should know."

Lila Thatcher, Pat thought. *Lila Thatcher.* Of course. She was the clairvoyant who had written several widely read books on ESP and other psychic phenomena. Only a few months ago she'd been celebrated for her assistance in finding a missing child.

"I'll be right there," Pat agreed reluctantly, "but I'm afraid I can't stay more than a minute."

As she threaded her way across the street, taking pains to avoid the worst of the melting slush and mud, she tried to ignore the sense of uneasiness.

She was sure she would not want to hear what Lila Thatcher was about to tell her.

11

A maid answered Pat's ring and escorted her to the living room. Pat didn't know what kind of person to expect—she'd visualized a turbaned Gypsy; but the woman who rose to greet her could be described simply as cozy. She was gently rounded and gray-haired, with intelligent, twinkling eyes and a warm smile.

"Patricia Traymore," she said, "I'm so glad to meet you. Welcome to Georgetown." Taking Pat's hand, she studied her carefully. "I know how busy you must be with the program you're preparing. I'm sure it's quite a project. How are you getting on with Luther Pelham?"

"Fine so far."

"I hope that continues." Lila Thatcher wore her glasses on a long silver chain around her neck. Absently she picked them up in her right hand and began to tap them against her left palm. "I have only a few minutes myself. I have a meeting in half an hour, and in the morning I have to catch an early flight to California. That's why I decided to phone. This is not the

sort of thing I usually do. However, in conscience I can't go away without warning you. Are you aware that twenty-three years ago a murder-suicide took place in the house you're now renting?"

"I've been told that." It was the answer nearest the truth.

"It doesn't upset you?"

"Mrs. Thatcher, many of the houses in Georgetown must be about two hundred years old. Surely people have died in every one of them."

"It's not the same." The older woman's voice became quicker, a thread of nervousness running through it. "My husband and I moved into this house a year or so before the tragedy. I remember the first time I told him that I was beginning to sense a darkness in the atmosphere around the Adams home. Over the next months it would come and go, but each time it returned it was more pronounced. Dean and Renée Adams were a most attractive couple. He was quite splendid-looking, one of those magnetic men who instantly attract attention. Renée was different—quiet, reserved, a very private young woman. My feeling was that being a politician's wife was all wrong for her and inevitably the marriage became affected. But she was very much in love with her husband and they were both devoted to their child."

Pat listened motionless.

"A few days before she died, Renée told me she was going to go back to New England with Kerry. We were standing in front of your house, and I can't describe to you the sense of trouble and danger I experienced. I tried to warn Renée. I told her that if her decision was irrevocable, she should not wait any longer. And then

it was too late. I never again felt even a suggestion of trouble concerning your house until this week. But now it's coming back. I don't know why but it's like last time. I sense the darkness involves you. Can you leave that house? *You shouldn't be there.*"

Pat chose her question carefully. "Do you have any reason, other than sensing this aura around the house, for warning me not to stay there?"

"Yes. Three days ago my maid observed a man loitering on the corner. Then she saw footprints in the snow along the side of this house. We thought there might be a prowler and notified the police. We saw footprints again yesterday morning after the fresh snowfall. Whoever is prowling about only goes as far as that tall rhododendron. Standing behind it anyone can watch your house without being observed from our windows or from the street."

Mrs. Thatcher was hugging herself now as if she were suddenly chilled. The flesh on her face had hardened into deep, grave lines. She stared intently at Pat and then, as Pat watched, her eyes widened; an expression of secret knowledge crept into them. When Pat left a few minutes later, the older woman was clearly upset and again urged Pat to leave the house.

Lila Thatcher knows who I am, Pat thought. I'm sure of it. She went directly to the library and poured a fairly generous brandy. "That's better," she murmured as warmth returned to her body. She tried not to think of the dark outside. But at least the police were on the lookout for a prowler. She tried to force herself to be calm. Lila had begged Renée to leave. If her mother had listened, had heeded the warning,

could the tragedy have been averted? Should she take Lila's advice now and go to a hotel or rent an apartment? "I can't," she said aloud. "I simply can't." She had so little time to prepare the documentary. It would be unthinkable to waste any of that time relocating. The fact that, as a psychic, Lila Thatcher *sensed* trouble did not mean she could *prevent* it. Pat thought, If Mother had gone to Boston, Daddy would probably have followed her. If someone is determined to find me, he'll manage it. I'd have to be just as careful in an apartment as here. And I *will* be careful.

Somehow the thought that Lila might have guessed her identity was comforting. She cared about my mother and father. She knew me well when I was little. After the program is finished I can talk to her, probe her memory. Maybe she can help me piece it all together.

But now it was absolutely essential to begin reviewing the Senator's personal files and select some for the program.

The spools of film were jumbled together in one of the cartons Toby had brought in. Fortunately, they were all labeled. She began to sort them. Some were of political activities, campaign events, speeches. Finally she found the personal ones she was most interested in seeing. She started with the film labeled WILLARD AND ABIGAIL—HILLCREST WEDDING RECEPTION.

She knew they had eloped before his graduation from Harvard Law School. Abby had just finished her junior year at Radcliffe. Willard had run for Congress a few months after their wedding. She'd helped him campaign, then completed college at the University of

Richmond. Apparently there had been a reception when he brought her to Virginia.

The film opened on the panorama of a festive garden party. Colorful umbrella-covered tables were arranged against the tree-shaded background. Servants moved among the clusters of guests—women in summer gowns and picture hats, men in dark jackets and white flannel trousers.

In the reception line on the terrace, a breathtaking young Abigail wearing a white silk tunic-style gown stood next to a scholarly-looking young man. An older woman, obviously Willard Jennings' mother, was to Abigail's right. Her aristocratic face was set in taut, angry lines. As the guests moved slowly past her, she introduced them to Abigail. Never once did she look directly at Abigail.

What was it the Senator had said? "My mother-in-law always considered me the Yankee who stole her son." Clearly, Abigail had not exaggerated.

Pat studied Willard Jennings. He was only slightly taller than Abigail, with sandy hair and a thin, gentle face. There was something rather endearingly shy about him, a diffidence in his manner as he shook hands or kissed cheeks.

Of the three, only Abigail seemed totally at ease. She smiled constantly, bent her head forward as if carefully committing names to memory, reached out her hand to show her rings.

If there were only a sound track, Pat thought.

The last person had been greeted. Pat watched as Abigail and Willard turned to each other. Willard's mother stared straight ahead. Now her face seemed less angry than thoughtful.

And then she smiled warmly. A tall auburn-haired man approached. He hugged Mrs. Jennings, released her, hugged her again, then turned to greet the newlyweds. Pat leaned forward. As the man's face came into full view, she stopped the projector.

The late arrival was her father, Dean Adams. He looks so young! she thought. He can't be more than thirty! She tried to swallow over the lump in her throat. Did she have a vague memory of him looking like this? His broad shoulders filled the screen. He was like a handsome young god, she thought, towering over Willard, exuding magnetic energy.

Feature by feature she studied the face, frozen on the screen, unwavering, open to minute examination. She wondered where her mother was, then realized that when this film was taken, her mother had still been a student at the Boston Conservatory, still planning a career in music.

Dean Adams was then a freshman Congressman from Wisconsin. He still had the healthy, open look of the Midwest in him, a larger-than-life outdoorsy aura.

She pushed the button and the figures sprang to life —Dean Adams joking with Willard Jennings, Abigail extending her hand to him. He ignored it and kissed her cheek. Whatever he said to Willard, they all began to laugh.

The camera followed them as they walked down the flagstone steps of the terrace and began to circulate among the guests. Dean Adams had his hand under the arm of the older Mrs. Jennings. She was talking to him animatedly. Clearly they were very fond of each other.

When the film ended, Pat reran it, marking off seg-

ments that might be used in the program. Willard and Abigail cutting the cake, toasting each other, dancing the first dance. She couldn't use any of the footage from the reception line—the displeasure on the face of the senior Mrs. Jennings was too obvious. And of course there was no question of using the film that involved Dean Adams.

What had Abigail felt that afternoon? she wondered. That beautiful whitewashed brick mansion, that gathering of Virginia gentry and she only a few years removed from the service apartment of the Saunders house in Apple Junction.

The Saunders house. Abigail's mother, Francey Foster. Where was she that day? Had she declined to be at her daughter's wedding reception, feeling she would seem out of place among these people? Or had Abigail made that decision for her?

One by one Pat began to view the other reels, steeling herself against the shock of watching her father regularly appear in those which had been taken on the estate.

Even without the dates, it would have been possible to arrange the films in a time sequence.

The first campaign: professional newsreels of Abigail and Willard hand in hand walking down the street, greeting passersby . . . Abigail and Willard inspecting a new housing development. The announcer's voice . . . "As Willard Jennings campaigned this afternoon for the seat to be made vacant by the retirement of his uncle, Congressman Porter Jennings, he pledged to continue the family tradition of service to the constituency."

There was an interview with Abigail. "How does it feel to spend your honeymoon campaigning?"

Abigail's reply: "I can't think of a better way than being at my husband's side helping him begin his career in public life."

There was a soft lilt in Abigail's voice, the unmistakable trace of a Southern accent. Pat did a rapid calculation. At that point Abigail had been in Virginia less than three months. She marked that segment for the program.

There were clips of five campaigns in all. As they progressed, Abigail increasingly played a major role in reelection efforts. Often her speech would begin "My husband is in Washington doing a job for you. Unlike many others, he is not taking time from the important work of the Congress to campaign for himself. I'm glad to be able to tell you just a few of his accomplishments."

The films of social events at the estate were hardest to watch. WILLARD'S 35TH BIRTHDAY. Two young couples posing with Abigail and Willard—Jack and Jackie Kennedy and Dean and Renée Adams . . . both recent newlyweds . . .

It was the first time Pat had seen a film of her mother. Renée was wearing a pale green gown; her dark hair fell loosely on her shoulders. There was a hesitancy about her, but when she smiled up at her husband, her expression was adoring. Pat found she could not bear to dwell on it. She was glad to let the film unwind. A few frames later, just the Kennedys and Jenningses were posing together. She made a note on her pad. That will be a wonderful clip for the program, she thought bitterly. The pre-Camelot days minus the

embarrassment of Congressman Dean Adams and the wife he murdered.

The last film she viewed was of Willard Jennings' funeral. In it was a newsreel clip that opened outside the National Cathedral. The announcer's voice was subdued. "The funeral cortege of Congressman Willard Jennings has just arrived. The great and the near-great are gathered inside to bid a final farewell to the Virginia legislator who died when his chartered plane crashed en route to a speaking engagement. Congressman Jennings and the pilot, George Graney, were killed instantly.

"The young widow is being escorted by Senator John Fitzgerald Kennedy of Massachusetts. Congressman Jennings' mother, Mrs. Stuart Jennings, is escorted by Congressman Dean Adams of Wisconsin. Senator Kennedy and Congressman Adams were Willard Jennings' closest friends."

Pat watched as Abigail emerged from the first car, her face composed, a black veil covering her blond hair. She wore a simply cut black silk suit and a string of pearls. The handsome young Senator from Massachusetts gravely offered her his arm.

The Congressman's mother was obviously grief-stricken. When she was assisted from the limousine, her eyes fell on the flag-draped casket. She clasped her hands together and shook her head slightly in a gesture of agonized rejection. As Pat watched, her father slid his arm under Mrs. Jennings' elbow and clasped her hand in his. Slowly the procession moved into the cathedral.

She had seen as much as she could absorb in one evening. Clearly the human interest material she had

been seeking was amply present in the old film clips. She turned out the lights in the library and went into the hall.

The hall was drafty. There had been no windows open in the library. She checked the dining room, kitchen and foyer. Everything was closed and locked.

But there was a draft.

A sense of apprehension made Pat's breath come faster. The door to the living room was closed. She put her hand on it. The space between the door and the frame was icy cold. Slowly she opened the door. A blast of cold air assaulted her. She reached for the chandelier switch.

The French doors to the patio were open. A pane of glass that had been cut from its frame was lying on the carpet.

And then she saw it.

Lolling against the fireplace, the right leg twisted under it, the white apron soaked with blood, was a Raggedy Ann doll. Sinking to her knees, Pat stared at it. A clever hand had painted downward curves on the stitched mouth, added tears to the cheeks and drawn lines on the forehead so that the typical Raggedy Ann smiling face had been transformed to a pain-filled weeping image.

She held her hand to her mouth to force back a shriek. Who had been here? Why? Half-hidden by the soiled apron was a sheet of paper pinned to the doll's dress. She reached for it; her fingers recoiling at the touch of the crusted blood. The same kind of cheap typing paper as the other note; the same small, slanted printing. *This is your last warning. There must not be a program glorifying Abigail Jennings.*

A creaking sound. One of the patio doors was moving. Was someone there? Pat jumped up. But it was the wind that was pushing the door back and forth. She ran across the room, yanked the doors together and turned the lock. But that was useless. The hand that had cut out the pane could reach through the empty frame, unlock the doors again. Maybe the intruder was still there, still hiding in the garden behind the evergreens.

Her hands shook as she dialed the police emergency number. The officer's voice was reassuring. "We'll send a squad car right away."

As she waited, Pat reread the note. This was the fourth time she'd been warned away from the program. Suddenly suspicious, she wondered if the threats were valid. Was it possible this was some kind of "dirty tricks" campaign to make the Senator's documentary a subject of gossip, to smear it with outlandish, distracting publicity?

What about the doll? Shocking to her because of the memory it evoked, but basically a Raggedy Ann with a garishly painted face. On closer examination, it seemed bizarre rather than frightening. Even the bloodied apron might be a crude attempt to horrify. If I were a reporter covering this story, I'd have a picture of that thing on the front page of tomorrow's newspaper, she thought.

The wail of the police siren decided her. Quickly she unpinned the note and left it on the mantelpiece. Rushing into the library, she dragged the carton from under the table and dropped the doll into it. The grisly apron sickened her. The doorbell was ringing—a steady, persistent peal. Impulsively she untied the

apron, pulled it off and buried it deep in the carton. Without it the doll resembled a hurt child.

She shoved the carton back under the table and hurried to admit the policemen.

12

Two police cars, their dome lights blazing, were in the driveway. A third car had followed them. Don't let it be the press, she prayed. But it was.

Photographs were taken of the broken pane; the grounds were searched, the living room dusted for fingerprints.

It was hard to explain the note. "It was pinned to something," a detective pointed out. "Where did you find it?"

"Right here by the fireplace." That was true enough.

The reporter was from the *Tribune*. He asked to see the note.

"I'd prefer not to have it made public," Pat urged. But he was allowed to read it.

"What does 'last warning' mean?" the detective asked. "Have you had other threats?"

Omitting the reference to "that house," she told them about the two phone calls, about the letter she'd found the first night.

"This one isn't signed," the detective pointed out. "Where's the other one?"

"I didn't keep it. It wasn't signed either."

"But on the phone he called himself an avenging angel?"

"He said something like 'I am an angel of mercy, of deliverance, an avenging angel.'"

"Sounds like a real screwball," the detective commented. He studied her keenly. "Funny he bothered to break in this time. Why not just slip an envelope under the door again?"

Dismayed, Pat watched the reporter scribbling in his notebook.

Finally the police were ready to go. The surfaces of all the living-room tables were smudged with fingerprint powder. The patio doors had been wired together so they couldn't be opened until the pane was replaced.

It was impossible to go to bed. Vacuuming the soot and grit from the living room, she decided, might help her unwind. As she worked, she couldn't forget the mutilated Raggedy Ann doll. *The child had run into the room . . . and tripped . . . the child fell over something soft, and its hands became wet and sticky . . . and the child looked up and saw . . .*

What did I see? Pat asked herself fiercely. What did I see?

Her hands worked unconsciously, vacuuming the worst of the greasy powder, then polishing the lovely old wooden tables with an oil-dampened chamois cloth, moving bric-a-brac, lifting and pushing furniture. The carpet had small clumps of slush and dirt from the policemen's shoes.

What did I see?

She began pushing the furniture back into place. No, not here; that table belongs on the short wall, that lamp on the piano, the slipper chair near the French doors.

It was only when she had finished that she understood what she had been doing.

The slipper chair. The movers had placed it too near the piano.

She'd run down the hall into the room. She'd screamed "Daddy, Daddy . . ." She'd tripped over her mother's body. Her mother was bleeding. She looked up, and then . . .

And then, only darkness . . .

It was nearly three o'clock. She couldn't think about it any more tonight. She was exhausted, and her leg ached. Her limp would have been obvious to anyone as she dragged the vacuum cleaner back to the storage closet and made her way upstairs.

At eight o'clock the telephone rang. The caller was Luther Pelham. Even coming out of the stupor of heavy sleep, Pat realized he was furious.

"Pat, I understand you had a break-in last night. Are you all right?"

She blinked, trying to force the sleep from her eyes and brain. "Yes."

"You made the front page of the *Tribune*. It's quite a caption. 'Anchorwoman's life threatened.' Let me read you the first paragraph:

" 'A break-in at her Georgetown home was the most recent in a series of bizarre threats received by television personality Patricia Traymore. The threats are tied to the documentary program "A Profile of Sena-

tor Abigail Jennings," which Miss Traymore will produce and narrate, to be aired next Wednesday night on
Potomac Cable Television.'

"That's just the kind of publicity Abigail needs!"

"I'm sorry," Pat stammered. "I tried to keep the
reporter away from the note."

"Did it ever occur to you to call *me*, instead of the
police? Frankly, I gave you credit for more brains than
you displayed last night. We could have had private
detectives watch your place. This is probably some
harmless nut, but the burning question in Washington
will be, Who hates Abigail so much?"

He was right. "I'm sorry," Pat repeated. Then she
added, "However, when you realize your home has
been broken into, and you're wondering if some nut
may be six feet away on the patio, I think it's a fairly
normal reaction to call the police."

"There's no use discussing it further until we can
assess the damage. Have you reviewed Abigail's
films?"

"Yes. I have some excellent material to edit."

"You didn't tell Abigail about being in Apple Junction?"

"No, I didn't."

"Well, if you're smart, you *won't!* That's all she
needs to hear now!"

Without saying goodbye, Luther hung up.

It was Arthur's habit to go to the bakery promptly at
eight for hot rolls and then pick up the morning paper.
Today he reversed the procedure. He was so eager to
see if the paper had anything about the break-in that
he went to the newsstand first.

There it was, right on the front page. He read the story through, relishing every word, then frowned. Nothing had been said about the Raggedy Ann doll. The doll had been his means of making them understand that violence had been committed in that house and might be again.

He purchased two seeded rolls and walked the three blocks back to the leaning frame house and up to the dreary apartment on the second floor. Only half a mile away King Street had expensive restaurants and shops, but the neighborhood here was run-down and shabby.

The door of Glory's bedroom was open, and he could see she was already dressed in a bright red sweater and jeans. Lately she'd gotten friendly with a girl in her office, a brazen type who was teaching Glory about makeup and had persuaded her to cut her hair.

She did not look up, even though she must have heard him coming in. He sighed. Glory's attitude toward him was becoming distant, even impatient. Like last night when he'd tried to tell her what a hard time old Mrs. Rodriguez had had swallowing her medicine and how he'd had to break up the pill and give her a little bread with it to hide the taste. Glory had interrupted him. "Father, can't we ever talk about anything except the nursing home?" And then she'd gone to a movie with some of the girls from work.

He put the rolls on plates and poured the coffee. "Soup's on," he called.

Glory hurried into the kitchen. She was wearing her coat and her purse was under her arm, as though she couldn't wait to leave.

"Hello," he said softly. "My little girl looks very pretty today."

Gloria didn't smile.

"How was the movie?" he asked.

"It was okay. Look, don't bother getting a roll or bun for me anymore. I'll have mine in the office with the others."

He felt crushed. He liked sharing breakfast with Glory before they left for work.

She must have sensed his disappointment, because she looked right at him and the expression in her eyes softened. "You're so good to me," she said, and her voice sounded a little sad.

For long minutes after she left, he sat staring into space. Last night had been exhausting. After all these years, to have been back in *that* house, in *that* room—to have placed Glory's doll on the exact spot where the child had lain . . . When he'd finished arranging it against the fireplace, the right leg crumpled under it, he had almost expected to turn around and see the bodies of the man and woman lying there again.

13

After Luther's call, Pat got up, made coffee and began editing the storyboards for the program. She had decided to plan two versions of the documentary, one including an opening segment about Abigail's early life in Apple Junction, the other starting at the wedding reception. The more she thought about it, the more she felt Luther's anger was justified. Abigail was skittish enough about the program without this upsetting publicity. At least I had the sense to hide the doll, she thought.

By nine o'clock she was in the library running off the rest of the films. Luther had already sent over edited segments of the Eleanor Brown case, showing Abigail leaving the courthouse after the Guilty verdict. Her regretful statement: "This is a very sad day for me. I only hope that now Eleanor will have the decency to tell where she has hidden that money. It may have been for my campaign fund, but far more important, it was the donations of people who believed in the goals I embrace."

A reporter asked: "Then, Senator, there is absolutely no truth to Eleanor's insistence that your chauffeur phoned her asking her to look for your diamond ring in the campaign-office safe?"

"My chauffeur was driving me that morning to a meeting in Richmond. The ring was on my finger."

And then the clip showed a picture of Eleanor Brown, a close-up that clearly revealed every feature of her small, colorless face, her timid mouth and shy eyes.

The reel ended with a scene of Abigail addressing college students. Her subject was Public Trust. Her theme was the absolute responsibility of a legislator to keep his or her own office and staff above reproach.

There was another segment Luther had already edited, a compilation of the Senator in airline-safety hearings, with excerpts from her speeches demanding more stringent regulations. Several times she referred to the fact that she had been widowed because her husband had entrusted his life to an inexperienced pilot in an ill-equipped plane.

At the end of each of those segments Luther had marked "*2-minute discussion between Senator J. and Pat T. on subject.*"

Pat bit her lip.

Both those segments were out of sync with what she was trying to do. What happened to my creative control of this project? she wondered. The whole thing is getting too rushed. No, the word is *botched.*

The phone rang as she began to go through Abigail's letters from constituents. It was Sam. "Pat, I read what happened. I've checked with the rental office for my place." Sam lived in the Watergate Towers.

"There are several sublets available. I want you to take one on a monthly basis until this character is caught."

"Sam, I can't. You know the kind of pressure I'm under. I have a locksmith coming. The police are going to keep a watch on the place. I have all my equipment set up here." She tried to change the subject. "My real problem is what to wear to the White House dinner."

"You always look lovely. Abigail is going to be there as well. I bumped into her this morning."

A short time later, the Senator phoned to express her shock at the break-in. Then she got to the point. "Unfortunately, the suggestion that you are being threatened because of this program is bound to lead to all sorts of speculation. I really want to get this thing wrapped up, Pat. Obviously, once it's completed and aired, the threats will end even if they are simply from some sort of crank. Have you reviewed the films I gave you?"

"Yes, I have," Pat replied. "There's wonderful material and I've got it marked off. But I'd like to borrow Toby. There are some places where I need names and more specific background."

They agreed that Toby would come over within the hour. When Pat hung up she had the feeling that in Abigail Jennings' estimation she had become an embarrassment.

Toby arrived forty-five minutes later, his leathery face creased in a smile. "I wish I'd been here when that joker tried to get in, Pat," he told her. "I'd've made mincemeat of him."

"I'll bet you would."

He sat at the library table while she ran the projec-

tor. "That's old Congressman Porter Jennings," Toby
answered at one point. "He was the one who said he
wouldn't retire if Willard didn't take over his seat. You
know that Virginia aristocracy. Think they own the
world. But I have to say that he bucked his sister-in-law
when he supported Abigail to succeed Willard. Willard's mother, that old she-devil, pulled out all the
stops to keep Abigail out of Congress. And between
us, she was a lot better Congressman than Willard. He
wasn't aggressive enough. You know what I mean?"

While waiting for Toby, Pat had reviewed the newspaper clippings about the Eleanor Brown case. The
case seemed almost too simple. Eleanor said that Toby
had phoned and sent her to the campaign office. Five
thousand dollars of the money had been recovered in
her storage area in the basement of her apartment
building.

"How do you think Eleanor Brown expected to get
away with such a flimsy story?" Pat now asked Toby.

Toby leaned back in the leather chair, crossing one
thick leg over the other, and shrugged. Pat noticed the
cigar in his breast pocket. Wincing inwardly, she invited him to smoke.

He beamed, sending his jowly face into a mass of
creases. "Thanks a lot. The Senator can't stand the
smell of cigar smoke. I don't dare have even a puff in
the car no matter how long I'm waiting for her."

He lit the cigar and puffed appreciatively.

"About Eleanor Brown," Pat suggested. She rested
her elbows on her knees, cupping her chin in her
hands.

"The way I figure it," Toby confided, "Eleanor
didn't think the money would be missed for a while.

They've kind of tightened up the law since then, but it really used to be that you could have big money sit in the campaign-office safe for a couple of weeks—even longer."

"But seventy-five thousand dollars in cash?"

"Miss Traymore . . . Pat, you gotta understand how many companies contribute to both sides in a campaign. They want to be sure to be with the winner. Now, of course you can't hand cash to a Senator in the office. *That's* against the law. So what the big shot does is visit the Senator, let him or her know he's planning to make a big donation, and then takes a walk with the Senator's aide on the Capitol grounds and turns over the money there. The Senator never touches it, but *knows* about it. It's put right in the campaign funds. But because it's in cash, if the competition gets elected it isn't so obvious. You know what I mean?"

"I see."

"Don't get me wrong. It's legal. But Phil had taken some big donations for Abigail, and of course Eleanor knew about them. Maybe she had some boyfriend who wanted to make a killing and only borrowed the money. Then when they looked for it so fast, she had to come up with an excuse."

"She just doesn't seem that sophisticated to me," Pat observed, thinking of the high school yearbook picture.

"Well, like the prosecutor said, still water runs deep. I hate to rush you, Pat, but the Senator will be needing me."

"There are just one or two more questions."

The phone rang. "I'll make this fast." Pat picked it up. "Pat Traymore."

"How are you, my dear?" She instantly recognized the precise, overly cultivated voice.

"Hello, Mr. Saunders." Too late she remembered that Toby knew Jeremy Saunders. Toby's head jerked up. Would he associate the name Saunders with the Jeremy Saunders he'd known in Apple Junction?

"I tried to get you several times early last evening," Saunders purred. He was not drunk this time. She was sure of it.

"You didn't leave your name."

"Recorded messages can be heard by the wrong ears. Don't you agree?"

"Just a moment, please." Pat looked at Toby. He was smoking his cigar thoughtfully and seemed indifferent to the call. Maybe he hadn't put together the name Saunders with a man he hadn't seen in thirty-five years.

"Toby, this is a private call. I wonder if . . ."

He stood up quickly before she could finish. "Want me to wait outside?"

"No, Toby. Just hang up when I get to the kitchen extension?" Deliberately she spoke his name again so that Jeremy would hear and not begin talking until he was sure only Pat was on the line.

Toby accepted the receiver casually, but he was certain it was Jeremy Saunders. Why was he calling Pat Traymore? Had she been in touch with him? Abigail would hit the ceiling. From the other end of the phone he heard the faint sound of breathing. That stinking phony, he thought. If he tries to smear Abby . . . !

Pat's voice came on. "Toby, would you mind hanging up?"

"Sure, Pat." He made his voice hearty. He hung up

the receiver with a definite click and didn't dare to try to ease it off the hook again.

"*Toby,*" Jeremy Saunders said, his voice incredulous. "Don't tell me you're hobnobbing with Toby Gorgone."

"He's helping me with some of the background material on the program," Pat replied. She kept her voice low.

"Of course. He's been there every step of the way with our stateswoman, hasn't he? Pat, I wanted to call because I realize that the combination of vodka and your sympathy made me rather indiscreet. I do insist that our conversation remain totally confidential. My wife and daughter would not enjoy having the shabby little tale of my involvement with Abigail aired on national television."

"I have no intention of quoting anything you told me," Pat replied. "The *Mirror* might be interested in gossipy personal material, but I assure you, I'm not."

"Very good. I'm greatly relieved." Saunders' voice became friendlier. "I saw Edwin Shepherd at the club. He tells me he gave you a copy of the newspaper showing Abby as the beauty queen. I'd forgotten about that. I do hope you plan to use the picture of Miss Apple Junction with her adoring mother. *That* one's worth a thousand words!"

"I really don't think so," Pat said coldly. His presumption had turned her off. "I'm afraid I'll have to get back to work, Mr. Saunders."

She hung up and went back into the library. Toby was sitting in the chair where she'd left him, but there was something different about him. The genial manner was gone. He seemed distracted and left almost immediately.

After he had gone, she flung open the window to get rid of the cigar smell. But the odor hung in the room. She realized that once again she felt acutely uneasy and jumped at every sound.

Back at the office, Toby went directly to Philip. "How's it going?"

Philip raised his eyes heavenward. "The Senator is in a state about the story. She just gave Luther Pelham hell for ever talking her into that documentary. She'd kill it in a minute if the publicity weren't already out. How did it go with Pat Traymore?"

Toby wasn't ready to talk about Apple Junction, but he did ask Philip to look into the question of the rental of the Adams house, which was also on his mind.

He knocked on the door of Abigail's office. She was quiet now—too quiet. That meant she was worried. She had the afternoon edition of the paper. "Look at this," she told him.

A famous Washington gossip column's lead item began:

Wags on Capitol Hill are placing bets on the identity of the person who threatened Patricia Traymore's life if she goes ahead with the documentary on Senator Jennings. Seems everyone has a candidate. The beautiful senior Senator from Virginia has a reputation among her colleagues as an abrasive perfectionist.

As Toby watched, Abigail Jennings, her face savage with fury, crumpled the paper in her hand and tossed it into a wastepaper basket.

14

Sam Kingsley snapped the last stud in his dress shirt and twisted his tie into a bow. He glanced at the clock on the mantel over his bedroom fireplace and decided he had more than enough time for a Scotch and soda.

His Watergate apartment commanded a sweeping view of the Potomac. From the side window of the living room he looked down at the Kennedy Center. Some evenings when he arrived late from the office, he'd go in and catch the second and third acts of a favorite opera.

After Janice died, there'd been no reason to keep the big house in Chevy Chase. Karen was living in San Francisco, and she and her husband spent their holidays with her in-laws in Palm Springs. Sam had given Karen her choice of dishes, silver, bric-a-brac and furniture and sold most of the rest. He had wanted to start with a clean slate in the hope that his pervading sense of weariness might subside.

Sam carried his glass to the window. The Potomac was shimmering from the lights of the apartment

building and the floodlights of Kennedy Center. Potomac fever. He had it. So did most of the people who came here. Would Pat catch it as well? he wondered.

He was damn worried about her. His FBI friend Jack Carlson had flatly told him: "First she gets a phone call, then a note under the door, then another phone call and finally a break-in with a warning note left in her home. You figure out what might happen next time.

"You've got a full-blown psycho who's about to explode. That slanted printing is a dead giveaway—and compare these notes. They're written only a few days apart. Some of the letters on the second one are practically illegible. His stress is building to a breaking point. And one way or another, that stress seems to be directed at your Pat Traymore."

His Pat Traymore. In those last months before Janice died, he'd managed to keep Pat from his thoughts. He'd always be grateful for that. He and Janice had managed to recapture something of their early closeness. She had died secure in his love.

Afterward, he had felt drained, exhausted, lifeless, *old.* Too old for a twenty-seven-year-old girl and all that a life with her would involve. He simply wanted peace.

Then he'd read that Pat was coming to work in Washington and he'd decided to phone and invite her to dinner. There was no way he could avoid her, or want to avoid her, and he did not intend their first meeting to be constrained by the presence of others. So he'd asked her out.

He had soon realized that whatever was between

them hadn't gone away, but was still simmering, waiting to blaze up—and that was what she wanted.

But what did *he* want?

"I don't know," Sam said aloud. Jack's warning rang in his ears: Suppose something happened to Pat?

The house phone rang. "Your car is here, Congressman," the doorman announced.

"Thank you. I'll be right down."

Sam put his half-empty glass on the bar and went into the bedroom to get his jacket and coat. His movements were brisk. In a few minutes he'd be with Pat.

Pat decided to wear an emerald satin gown with a beaded top to the White House dinner. It was an Oscar de la Renta that Veronica had insisted she purchase for the Boston Symphony Ball. Now she was glad she'd been talked into it. With it she wore her grandmother's emeralds.

"You don't look the part of the girl reporter," Sam commented when he picked her up.

"I don't know whether to take that as a compliment." Sam was wearing a navy blue cashmere coat and white silk scarf over his dinner jacket. What was it Abigail had called him? One of the most eligible bachelors in Washington?

"It was intended as one. No more phone calls or notes?" he asked.

"No." She had not yet told him about the doll and didn't want to bring it up now.

"Good. I'll feel better when that program is finished."

"*You'll* feel better."

In the limousine on the way to the White House, he asked her about her activities.

"Work," she said promptly. "Luther agreed with the film clips I selected and we've completed the storyboard. He's adamant about not crossing the Senator by including her early life. He's turning what's supposed to be a documentary into a paean of praise that's going to be journalistically unsound."

"And you can't do anything about it?"

"I could quit. But I didn't come down here to quit after the first week—not if I can help it."

They were at Eighteenth Street and Pennsylvania Avenue.

"Sam, was there ever a hotel on that corner?"

"Yes, the old Roger Smith. They tore it down about ten years ago."

When I was little I went to a Christmas party there. I wore a red velvet dress and white tights and black patent leather slippers. I spilled chocolate ice cream on the dress and cried and Daddy said, "It's not your fault, Kerry."

The limousine was drawing up to the northwest gate of the White House. They waited in line as each car stopped for the security check. When it was their turn, a respectful guard confirmed their names on the guest list.

Inside, the mansion was festive with holiday decorations. The Marine Band was playing in the marble foyer. Waiters were offering champagne. Pat recognized familiar faces among the assembled guests: film stars, Senators, Cabinet members, socialites, a grande dame of the theater.

"Have you ever been here before?" Sam asked.

"On a school trip when I was sixteen. We took the

tour and they told us that Abigail Adams used to hang her wash in what is now the East Room."

"You won't find any laundry there now. Come on. If you're going to have a career in Washington, you'd better get to know some people." A moment later he was introducing her to the President's press secretary.

Brian Salem was an amiable, rotund man. "Are you trying to push us off the front page, Miss Traymore?" he asked, smiling.

So even in the Oval Office the break-in had been discussed.

"Have the police any leads?"

"I'm not sure, but we all think it was just some sort of crank."

Penny Salem was a sharp-eyed, wiry woman in her early forties. "God knows Brian sees enough crank letters addressed to the President."

"I sure do," her husband agreed easily. "Anyone in public office is bound to step on toes. The more powerful you are, the madder somebody or some group gets at you. And Abigail Jennings takes positive stands on some mighty volatile issues. Oh, say, there's the lady now." He suddenly grinned. "Doesn't she look great?"

Abigail had just entered the East Room. This was one night she had not chosen to underplay her beauty. She was wearing an apricot satin gown with a bodice covered in pearls. A belled skirt complimented her small waist and slender frame. Her hair was loosely drawn back into a chignon. Soft waves framed her flawless features. Pale blue shadow accentuated the extraordinary eyes, and rose blush highlighted her

cheekbones. A deeper apricot shade outlined her perfectly shaped lips.

This was a different Abigail, laughing softly, laying a hand for just an extra moment on the arm of an octogenarian ambassador, accepting the tributes to her appearance as her due. Pat wondered if every other woman in the room felt as she did—suddenly colorless and insignificant.

Abigail had timed her arrival well. An instant later, the music from the Marine Band shifted to a stirring "Hail to the Chief." The President and First Lady were descending from their private quarters. With them were the new Prime Minister of Canada and his wife. As the last notes of "Hail to the Chief" died out, the opening chords of the Canadian national anthem began.

A receiving line was formed. When Pat and Sam approached the President and First Lady, Pat realized that her heart was pounding.

The First Lady was far more attractive in person than in her pictures. She had a long, tranquil face with a generous mouth and pale hazel eyes. Her hair was sandy with traces of gray. There was an air of total self-confidence about her. Her eyes crinkled when she smiled, and her lips parted to reveal strong, perfect teeth. She told Pat that when she was a girl her ambition had been to get a job in television. "And instead" —she laughed, looking up at her husband—"I had no sooner let go of the daisy chain at Vassar than I found myself married."

"I was smart enough to grab her before anyone else did," the President said. "Pat, I'm glad to meet you."

It was a palpable emotion to feel the solid handshake of the most powerful man in the world.

"They're good people," Sam commented as they accepted champagne. "And he's been a strong President. It's hard to believe he's completing his second term. He's young, not sixty yet. It'll be interesting to see what he does with the rest of his life."

Pat was studying the First Lady. "I'd love to do a program on her. She seems comfortable in her own skin."

"Her father was Ambassador to England; her grandfather was Vice President. Generations of breeding and money coupled with a diplomatic background do have a way of instilling self-confidence, Pat."

In the State Dining Room, the tables were set with Limoges china, an intricate green pattern, rimmed with gold. Pale green damask cloths and napkins with centerpieces of red roses and ferns in low crystal containers completed the effect. "Sorry we're not sitting together," Sam commented, "but you seem to have a good table. And please notice where Abigail has been placed."

She was at the President's table between the President and the guest of honor, the Prime Minister of Canada. "I wish I had this on camera," Pat murmured.

She glanced at the first few items on the menu: salmon in aspic, suprême of capon in flamed brandy sauce, wild rice.

Her dinner partner was the Chairman of the Joint Chiefs of Staff. The others at the table included a college president, a Pulitzer Prize-winning playwright, an Episcopal bishop, the director of Lincoln Center.

She glanced around to see where Sam had gone. He

was at the President's table directly across from Senator Jennings. They were smiling at each other. With a twinge of pain, Pat looked away.

Near the end of the dinner the President invited everyone to remember in prayer the Vice President, who was so seriously ill. He added, "More than any of us realized, he had been pursuing arduous fourteen-hour days without ever considering the toll they were taking on his health." When the tribute was completed, there was no doubt in anyone's mind that the Vice President would never resume his duties. As he sat down, the President smiled at Abigail. There was something of a public benediction in that glance.

"Well, did you enjoy yourself?" Sam asked on the way home. "That playwright at your table seemed quite taken with you. You danced with him three or four times, didn't you?"

"When you were dancing with the Senator. Sam, wasn't it quite an honor for you to be at the President's table?"

"It's always an honor to be placed there."

An odd constraint came over them. It seemed to Pat that suddenly the evening had gone flat. Was that the true reason Sam had gotten the invitation for her—so that she'd meet Washington people? Did he simply feel he had a certain obligation to help launch her before he withdrew from her life again?

He waited while she unlocked the door, but declined a nightcap. "I've got to get in a long day tomorrow. I'm leaving for Palm Springs on the six-o'clock flight to spend the holiday with Karen and Tom at his

family's place. Are you going to Concord for the holiday, Pat?"

She didn't want to tell him that Veronica and Charles had left for a Caribbean cruise. "This will be a working Christmas," she said.

"Let's have a belated celebration after the program is finished. And I'll give you your Christmas present then."

"That'll be fine." She hoped her voice sounded as casually friendly as his. She refused to reveal the emptiness she felt.

"You looked lovely, Pat. You'd be surprised at the number of people I heard commenting about you."

"I hope they were all my own age. Good night, Sam." She pushed the door open and went inside.

"Damn it, Pat!" Sam stepped into the foyer and spun her around. Her jacket fell from her shoulders as he pulled her to him.

Her hands slipped around his neck; her fingertips touched the collar of his coat, found the cool skin above it, twisted his thick, wavy hair. It was as she remembered—the faint good scent of his breath, the feel of his arms enveloping her, the absolute certainty that they belonged together. "Oh, my love," she whispered. "I've missed you so."

It was as if she had slapped him. In an involuntary movement, he straightened up and stepped back. Dumbfounded, Pat dropped her arms.

"Sam . . ."

"Pat, I'm, sorry . . ." He tried to smile. "You're just too damn attractive for your own good."

For a long minute they stared at each other. Then Sam grasped her shoulders. "Don't you think I'd like

nothing better than to pick up where we left off that day? I'm not going to do it to you, Pat. You're a beautiful young woman. Within six months you'll have your pick of half a dozen men who can give you the kind of life you should have. Pat, my time is past. I damn near lost my seat in the last election. And you know what my opponent said? He said it's time for new blood. Sam Kingsley's been around too long. He's in a rut. Let's give him the rest he needs."

"And you believed it?"

"I believe it because it's true. That last year and a half with Janice left me empty—empty and drained. Pat, it's hard for me to decide where I stand on any issue these days. Choosing what tie to wear is a big effort, for God's sake, but there is one decision I can stick to. I'm not going to foul up your life again."

"Have you ever stopped to think how much you'll foul it up by not coming back into it?"

Unhappily they stared at each other. "I'm simply not going to let myself believe that, Pat." Then he was gone.

15

Glory was different now. She had begun setting her hair in the morning. She had new clothes, more colorful. The blouses had high ruffled necks instead of button-down collars. And recently she had bought some earrings, a couple of pairs. He'd never seen her wear earrings before.

Every day now she told him not to make her a sandwich for lunch, that she would eat out.

"All by yourself?" he'd asked.

"No, Father."

"With Opal?"

"I'm just eating out"—and there was that unfamiliar note of impatience in her voice.

She didn't want to hear about his work at all anymore. He'd tried a couple of times to tell her how even with the respirator, old Mrs. Gillespie was rasping and coughing and in pain. Glory used to listen so sympathetically when he told her about his patients and agree when he said it would be a mercy if the angels

came for the very sick ones. Her agreement helped him carry out his mission.

He'd been so distracted with Glory that when he delivered Mrs. Gillespie to the Lord he'd been careless. He had thought she was asleep, but as he pulled out the respirator plug and prayed over her, she opened her eyes. She had understood what he was doing. Her chin had quivered, and she had whispered, "Please, please oh, . . . sweet Virgin, help me . . ." He'd watched the expression in her eyes change from terrified to glassy to vacant.

And Mrs. Harnick had seen him leaving Mrs. Gillespie's room.

Nurse Sheehan was the one who'd found Mrs. Gillespie. She hadn't accepted the old woman's death as the will of God. Instead she'd insisted that the respirator be checked to make sure it had been functioning properly. Later on he'd seen her with Mrs. Harnick. Mrs. Harnick was very much excited and pointing toward Mrs. Gillespie's room.

Everyone in the Home liked him except Nurse Sheehan. She was always reprimanding him, telling him that he was overstepping. "We have staff chaplains," she would say. "It's not your job to counsel people."

If he'd thought about Nurse Sheehan's being on duty today, he would never have gone near Mrs. Gillespie.

It was his worry over the Senator Jennings documentary that was consuming him, making it impossible for him to think straight. He had warned Patricia

Traymore four times that she must not continue to prepare that program.

There would be no fifth warning.

Pat simply wasn't sleepy. After an hour of restless tossing, she gave up and reached for a book. But her mind refused to become involved with the Churchill biography she had been looking forward to reading.

At one o'clock she shut her eyes. At three o'clock she went downstairs to heat a cup of milk. She had left the downstairs foyer light on, but even so, the staircase was dark and she had to reach for the railing where the steps curved.

She used to sit on this step just out of sight of the people in the foyer and watch company come. I had a blue nightgown with flowers on it. I was wearing it that night . . . I had been sitting here and then I was frightened and I went back up to bed. . . .

And then . . . "I don't know," she said aloud. "I don't know."

Even the hot milk did not induce sleep.

At four o'clock she went downstairs again and brought up the nearly completed storyboard.

The program would open with the Senator and Pat in the studio seated in front of an enlarged picture of Abigail and Willard Jennings in their wedding reception line. Mrs. Jennings senior had been edited out of the reel. While the film of the reception ran, the Senator would talk about meeting Willard while she was attending Radcliffe.

At least, that way I get something in about the Northeast, Pat thought.

Then they'd show a montage of Willard's Congres-

sional campaigns with Pat asking about Abigail's growing commitment to politics. Willard's thirty-fifth-birthday party would highlight the pre-Camelot years with the Kennedys.

Then would come the funeral, with Abigail escorted by Jack Kennedy. They'd eliminated the segment that showed her mother-in-law in a separate car. Then Abigail being sworn into Congress in black mourning attire, her face pale and grave.

Next came the footage about the embezzlement of the campaign funds and Abigail's commitment to airline safety. She sounds so strident and sanctimonious, Pat thought, and then you see the picture of that scared kid, Eleanor Brown. And it's one thing to be concerned about airline safety—another to keep pointing the finger at a pilot who also lost his life . . . But she knew she wouldn't be able to persuade Luther to change either segment.

The day after Christmas they would shoot Abigail in her office, with her staff and some carefully selected visitors. Congress had at last adjourned, and the shooting should go quickly.

At least Luther had agreed to a scene of Abigail in her own home with friends. Pat had suggested a Christmas supper party with shots of Abigail arranging the buffet table. The guests would be some distinguished Washington personalities as well as a few of her office staff who could not be with their families on the holiday.

The last scene would be the Senator returning home at dusk, a briefcase under her arm. And then the wrap-up: "Like many of the millions of single adults in the United States, Senator Abigail Jennings has found

her family, her vocation, her avocation in the work she loves."

Luther had written that line for Pat to deliver.

At eight o'clock Pat phoned Luther and asked him again to persuade the Senator to allow her early life to be included in the program. "What we have is dull," she said. "Except for those personal films, it's a thirty-minute campaign commercial."

Luther cut her off. "You've examined *all* the film?"

"Yes."

"How about photographs?"

"There were very few."

"Call and see if there are any more. No. I'll call. You're not very high on the Senator's list right now."

Forty-five minutes later she heard from Philip. Toby would be over around noon with photograph albums. The Senator believed Pat would find some interesting pictures in them.

Restlessly Pat wandered into the library. She had jammed the carton with the doll under the library table. She would use this time to go through more of her father's effects.

When she lifted the doll from the carton, she carried it to the window and examined it closely. A skillful pen had shaded the black button eyes, filled in the brows, given the mouth that mournful twist. In the daylight, it seemed even more pathetic. Was it supposed to represent her?

She put it aside and began to unpack the carton: the pictures of her mother and father; the packets of letters and papers; the photo albums. Her hands became soiled and dusty as she sorted the material into piles.

Then she sat cross-legged on the carpet and began to go through it.

Loving hands had kept the mementos of Dean Adams' boyhood. Report cards were neatly pasted in sequence. A-pluses, A's. The lowest mark a B-plus.

He had lived on a farm fifty miles from Milwaukee. The house was a medium-sized white frame with a small porch. There were pictures of him with his mother and father. My grandparents, Pat thought. She realized she didn't know their names. The back of one of the pictures was marked *Irene and Wilson with Dean, age 6 months.*

She picked up a packet of letters. The rubber band snapped and they scattered on the carpet. Quickly she gathered and glanced through them. One especially caught her eye.

Dear Mom,
Thank you. I guess those are the only words for all the years of sacrifice to put me through college and law school. I know all about the dresses you didn't buy, the outings you never attended with the other ladies in town. Long ago I promised I'd try to be just like Dad. I'll keep that promise. I love you. And remember to go to the doctor please. That cough sounded awfully deep.

　　　　　　　　　　　　　Your loving son,
　　　　　　　　　　　　　Dean

An obituary notice for Irene Wagner Adams was beneath the letter. It was dated six months later.

Tears blurred Pat's eyes for the young man who had not been ashamed to express his love for his mother. *She too had experienced that generous love. Her hand in his.*

Her screaming delight when he came home. Daddy. Daddy.
Swung high in the air and tossed up and strong hands catching
her. She was riding her tricycle down the driveway . . . her
knee scraping along gravel . . . his voice saying, "This won't
hurt much, Kerry. We have to make sure it's clean . . . What
kind of ice cream should we get? . . ."

The doorbell rang. Pat swept the pictures and letters together and stood up. Half of them spilled from
her arms as she tried to jam them into the carton. The
doorbell rang again, this time more insistently. She
scrambled to pick up the scattered photos and notes
and hide them with the others. She started from the
room and realized she'd forgotten to put away the
pictures of her parents and the Raggedy Ann doll.
Suppose Toby had come in here and seen them! She
dropped them into the carton and shoved it under the
table.

Toby was about to ring the bell again when she
yanked open the door. Involuntarily, she stepped back
as his bulky frame filled the doorway.

"I was just giving up on you!" His attempt to sound
genial didn't come off.

"Don't give up on me, Toby," she said coldly. Who
was he to be annoyed at having to wait a few seconds?
He seemed to be studying her. She glanced down and
realized how grimy her hands were and that she had
been rubbing her eyes. Her face was probably
smeared with dirt.

"You look like you were making mud pies." There
was a puzzled, suspicious expression on his face. She
didn't answer him. He shifted the package under his
arm, and the oversized onyx ring moved back and

forth on his finger. "Where do you want this stuff, Pat? In the library?"

"Yes."

He followed her so closely that she had the uneasy feeling he would crash into her if she stopped suddenly. Sitting cross-legged for so long had made her right leg numb, and she was favoring it.

"You limping, Pat? You didn't fall on the ice or anything, did you?"

You don't miss a trick, she thought. "Put the box on the table," she told him.

"Okay. I gotta get right back. The Senator wasn't happy about having to figure out where these albums were. I can see myself out."

She waited until she heard the front door close before she went to secure the bolt. As she reached the foyer, the door opened again. Toby seemed startled to see her standing there; then his face creased in an unpleasant smile. "That lock wouldn't keep out anyone who knew his way around, Pat," he said. "Be sure to use the dead bolt."

The Senator's additional material was a hodgepodge of newspaper clippings and fan letters. Most of the pictures were shots of her at political ceremonies, state dinners, ribbon-cutting ceremonies, inaugurations. As Pat turned the pages, several of them fluttered down to the floor.

The back pages of the album were more promising. She came upon an enlarged photo of a young Abigail and Willard seated on a blanket near a lake. He was reading to her. It was an idyllic setting; they looked like lovers on a Victorian cameo.

There were a few more snapshots that might fit into

a montage. At last she had gone through everything and bent down to retrieve the pictures that had fallen. Underneath one of them was a folded sheet of expensive notepaper. She opened it. It read:

Billy darling. You were splendid in the hearings this afternoon. I am so proud of you. I love you so and look forward to a lifetime of being with you, of working with you. Oh, my dearest we really are going to make a difference in this world.

A.

The letter was dated May 13. Willard Jennings had been on his way to deliver the commencement address when he met his death on May 20.

What a terrific wrap-up that would make! Pat exulted. It would quiet anyone who thinks of the Senator as cold and uncaring. If she could only persuade Luther to let her read the note on the program. How would it sound? "Billy darling," she read aloud. "I'm so sorry . . ."

Her voice broke. What is the matter with me? she thought impatiently. Firmly, she began again. "Billy darling. You were splendid. . . ."

16

On the twenty-third of December at 2 P.M. Senator Abigail Jennings sat in the library of her home with Toby and Philip and watched the telecast as the Vice President of the United States formally tendered his resignation to the Chief Executive.

Her lips dry, her fingernails digging into her palms, Abigail listened as the Vice President, propped on pillows in his hospital bed, ashen-faced and obviously dying, said in a surprisingly strong voice, "I had expected to withhold my decision until after the first of the year. However, I feel that it is my clear duty to vacate this office and have the line of succession to Chief Executive of this great country uncompromised. I am grateful for the confidence the President and my party expressed when I was twice chosen to be the Vice Presidential candidate. I am grateful to the people of the United States for having given me the opportunity to serve them."

With profound regret, the President accepted the resignation of his old friend and colleague. When

asked if he had decided on a replacement, he said, "I have a few ideas." But he declined to respond to the names suggested by the press.

Toby whistled. "Well, it's happened, Abby."

"Senator, mark my words . . ." Philip began.

"Be quiet and listen!" she snapped. As the scene in the hospital room ended, the camera focused on Luther Pelham in the newsroom of Potomac Cable.

"A historic moment," Luther began. With dignified reticence he recounted a brief history of the Vice Presidency and then came to the point. "The time has come for a woman to be selected for the high office . . . a woman with the necessary experience and proved expertise. Mr. President, choose *her* now."

Abigail laughed sharply. "Meaning me."

The phone began to ring. "That will be reporters. I'm not in," she said.

An hour later the press was still camped outside Abigail's home. Finally she agreed to an interview. Outwardly she was calm. She said that she was busy with preparations for a Christmas supper for friends. When asked if she expected to be appointed Vice President, she said in an amused tone, "Now, you really can't expect me to comment on that."

Once the door closed behind her, her expression and manner changed. Even Toby did not dare to cross the line.

Luther phoned to confirm the taping schedule. Abigail's raised voice could be heard throughout the house. "Yes, I saw it. You want to know something? I probably have this in the bag right now, without that damn program hanging over my head. I told you it was a rotten idea. Don't tell *me* you only wanted to help me.

You wanted to have me obligated to you, and we both know it."

Abigail's voice lowered, and Philip exchanged glances with Toby. "What did you find out?" he asked.

"Pat Traymore was up in Apple Junction last week. She stopped at the newspaper office and got some back issues. She visited Saunders, the guy who was sweet on Abby when she was a kid. He talked his head off to her. Then she saw the retired school principal who knew Abby. I was at Pat's house in Georgetown when Saunders phoned her."

"How much damage could any of those people do to the Senator?" Philip asked.

Toby shrugged. "It depends. Did you find out anything about the house?"

"Some," Philip told him. "We got to the realty company that has been renting it for years. They had a new tenant all lined up, but the bank handling the trust for the heirs said that someone in the family was planning to use it and it wouldn't be for rent again."

"Someone *in* the family?" Toby repeated. "*Who in* the family?"

"I would guess Pat Traymore," Philip said sarcastically.

"Don't get smart with me," Toby snapped. "I want to know *who* owns that place now, and *which* relative is using it."

With mixed emotions Pat watched Potomac Cable cover the Vice President's resignation. At the end of Luther's segment, the anchorman said that it was considered unlikely the President would name a successor before the New Year.

And we air the program on the twenty-seventh, Pat thought.

As Sam had predicted the first night she was in Washington, she might have a hand in the selection of the first woman Vice President.

Once again her sleep had been interrupted by troubled dreams. Did she really remember her mother and father so clearly, or was she confusing the films and pictures she had seen of them with reality? The memory of his bandaging her knee and taking her for ice cream was authentic. She was sure of that. But hadn't there also been times when she had pulled the pillow over her ears because of angry voices and hysterical weeping?

She was determined to finish reviewing her father's effects.

Doggedly she had examined the material and found herself increasingly concerned about the references to her mother. There were letters from her grandmother to Renée. One of them, dated six months before the tragedy, said: *"Renée, dear, the tone of your note troubles me. If you feel you are having onslaughts of depression again, please go into counseling immediately."*

It had been her grandmother, according to the newspaper articles, who had claimed that Dean Adams was an unstable personality.

She found a letter from her father to her mother written the year before their deaths:

Dear Renée,
I am pretty upset that you want to spend the entire summer in New Hampshire with Kerry. You must know how much I miss you both. It is absolutely necessary for

*me to go to Wisconsin. Why not give it a try? We can rent
a Steinway for you while you're there. I certainly understand that Mother's old spinet is hardly appropriate.
Please, dear. For my sake.*

Pat felt as though she were trying to remove bandages from a festering wound. The nearer she got to
the wound itself, the harder it was to pull the adhesive
from it. The sense of pain, emotional and even physical, was increasingly acute.

One of the cartons was filled with Christmas ornaments and strings of lights. They gave her an idea. She
would get a small Christmas tree. Why not? Where
were Veronica and Charles now? She consulted their
itinerary. Their ship would be putting in at St. John
tomorrow. She wondered if she could phone them on
Christmas Day.

The mail was a welcome respite. She had an abun-
dance of cards and invitations from her friends in Boston. *"Come up just for the day if you possibly can." "We're all
waiting for the program." "An Emmy for this one, Pat—not
just the nomination."*

One letter had been forwarded from Boston Cable.
The return-address sticker on the envelope read:
CATHERINE GRANEY, 22 BALSAM PLACE, RICHMOND,
VA.

Graney, Pat thought. That was the name of the pilot
who died with Willard Jennings.

The letter was brief:

*Dear Miss Traymore:
I have read that you are planning to prepare and narrate
a program about Senator Abigail Jennings. As one who*

*has had the opportunity to appreciate several of your fine
documentaries, I feel it imperative to notify you that the
program about Senator Abigail Jennings may become the
subject of a lawsuit. I warn you, do not give the Senator
the opportunity to discuss Willard Jennings' death. For
your own sake, don't let her assert that pilot error cost her
husband his life. That pilot, my husband, died too. And
believe me, it is a bitter joke that she dares to affect the
pose of a bereaved widow. If you wish to speak with me,
you may call me at this number: 804-555-6841.*

Pat went to the phone and dialed the number. It
rang many times. She was about to hang up when she
heard a hurried hello. It was Catherine Graney. The
background was noisy, as though a crowd of people
were there. Pat tried to make an appointment. "It will
have to be tomorrow," the woman told her. "I run an
antiques shop, and I'm having a sale today."

They agreed on a time, and she hurriedly gave Pat
directions.

That afternoon Pat went shopping. Her first stop
was an art shop. She left for reframing one of the old
sailing prints that had come from her father's office. It
would be her Christmas present to Sam.

"Have it for you in a week, Miss. That's a fine print.
Worth some money if you ever want to sell it."

"I don't want to sell it."

She stopped in the specialty market near the house
and ordered groceries, including a small turkey. At the
florist's she bought two poinsettias and a garland of
evergreen for the mantel. She found a Christmas tree
that stood as high as her shoulders. The pick of the
trees was gone, but this one was well enough shaped
and the pine needles had a luxurious sheen.

By early evening she had finished decorating. The tree was set near the patio doors. The mantel was draped with evergreen. One poinsettia was on the low round table next to the couch, the other on the cocktail table in front of the love seat.

She had hung all the paintings. She had had to guess at placing them, but even so, the living room was now complete. A fire, she thought. There was always a fire.

She laid one, ignited the papers and kindling, and positioned the screen. Then she fixed an omelette and salad and brought the tray to the living room. Tonight she would simply watch television and relax. She felt she had been pushing too hard, that she should let memory unfold in its own way. She had expected this room to be repugnant to her, but despite the terror of that last night, she found it warm and peaceful. Did it harbor happy memories as well?

She turned on the set. The President and First Lady flashed on the screen. They were boarding *Air Force One* en route to their family home for Christmas. Once again the President was being badgered about his choice. "I'll tell you who she or he is by the New Year," he called. "Merry Christmas."

She. Had that been a deliberate slip? Of course not.

Sam phoned a few minutes later. "Pat, how is it going?"

She wished her mouth would not go dry at the sound of his voice. "Fine. Did you see the President on TV just now?"

"Yes, I did. Well, we're surely down to two people. He's committed himself to selecting a woman. I'm going to give Abigail a call. She must be chewing her nails."

Pat raised her eyebrows. "I would be, in her place."
She twisted the tassel of her belt. "How's the
weather?"

"It's hot as hell. Frankly, I prefer Christmas in a
winter setting."

"Then you shouldn't have left. I was trooping
around buying a Christmas tree and it was cold
enough."

"What are your plans for Christmas Day? Will you
be at Abigail's for the supper party?"

"Yes. I'm surprised you weren't invited."

"I was. Pat, it's good to be with Karen and Tom, but
—well, this is Karen's family now, not mine. I had to
bite my tongue at lunch not to tell off some pompous
ass who had a laundry list of all the mistakes this Administration has made."

Pat couldn't resist. "Isn't Tom's mother fixing you
up with her available friends or cousins or whatever?"

Sam laughed. "I'm afraid so. I'm not staying till New
Year's. I'll be back a few days after Christmas. You
haven't had any more threats, have you?"

"Not even one breathless phone call. I miss you,
Sam," she added deliberately.

There was a pause. She could imagine his expression—worried, trying to find the right phrase. You
care every bit as much about me as you did two years
ago, she thought.

"Sam?"

His voice was constrained. "I miss you, too, Pat.
You're very important to me."

What a fantastic way to put it. "And you're one of
my very dearest friends."

Without waiting for his response, she hung up.

17

"Father, have you seen my Raggedy Ann doll?"

He smiled at Glory, hoping he didn't look nervous. "No, of course I haven't seen it. Didn't you have it in the closet in your bedroom?"

"Yes. I can't imagine . . . Father, are you sure you didn't throw it away?"

"Why would I throw it away?"

"I don't know." She got up from the table. "I'm going to do a little Christmas shopping. I won't be late." She looked worried, then asked, "Father, are you starting to feel sick again? You've been talking in your sleep the last few nights. I could hear you from my room. Is anything worrying you? You're not hearing those voices again, are you?"

He saw the fear in her eyes. He never should have told Glory about the voices. She hadn't understood. Worse, she had started to be nervous around him. "Oh, no. I was joking when I told you about them." He was sure she didn't believe him.

She put her hand on his arm. "You kept saying Mrs.

Gillespie's name in your sleep. Isn't she the woman who just died in the nursing home?"

After Glory went out, Arthur sat at the kitchen table, his thin legs wound around the rungs of the chair, thinking. Nurse Sheehan and the doctors had questioned him about Mrs. Gillespie: had he looked in on her?

"Yes," he'd admitted. "I just wanted to see if she was comfortable."

"How many times did you look in on her?"

"Once. She was asleep. She was fine."

"Mrs. Harnick and Mrs. Drury both thought they saw you. But Mrs. Drury said it was at five after three, and Mrs. Harnick was sure it was later."

"Mrs. Harnick is wrong. I only stopped in once."

They had to believe him. Half the time Mrs. Harnick was almost senile. *But the rest of the time she was very sharp.*

He suddenly picked up the newspaper again. He'd taken the Metro home. An old woman carrying a shopping bag and leaning on a cane had been on the platform. He'd been about to go over and offer to help her with her bag when the express roared into the station. The crowd had surged forward and a young fellow, his arms filled with schoolbooks, had nearly knocked the old lady over as he rushed to get a seat.

He recalled how he had helped her into the train just before the doors closed. "Are you all right?" he had asked.

"Oh, yes. My, I was afraid I'd fall. Young people are so careless. Not like in my day."

"They are cruel," he said softly.

The young man got off at Dupont Circle and crossed the platform. He had followed him, managed

to get next to him as he stood at the front of the crowd, right at the edge of the platform. As the train approached he had stepped behind him and jostled his arm so that one of the books began to slip. The young man grabbed for it. Off-balance as he was, it was easy to push him forward. The book and the young man landed on the tracks together.

The newspaper. Yes, here it was on page three: NINETEEN-YEAR-OLD STUDENT KILLED BY METRO. The account called the death an accident. A bystander had seen a book slip from the student's arm. He had bent forward to retrieve it and lost his balance.

The coffee cup in Arthur's hands had grown cold. He would make a fresh cup, then get to work.

There were so many helpless old people in the nursing home waiting for his attention. His mind had been on Patricia Traymore. That was why he hadn't been more careful about Mrs. Gillespie. Tomorrow he'd tell Glory he had to work late and he'd go back to Patricia Traymore's house.

He had to get in again.

Glory wanted her doll back.

At ten o'clock on the twenty-fourth Pat set off for Richmond. The sun had come out strong and golden, but the air was still very cold. It would be a frosty Christmas.

After leaving the highway she took three wrong turns and became thoroughly exasperated with herself. At last she found Balsam Place. It was a street of comfortable medium-sized Tudor-style houses. Number 22 was larger than its neighbors and had a carved sign ANTIQUES on the lawn.

Catherine Graney was waiting in the doorway. She was about fifty, with a square face, deep-set blue eyes and a sturdy, slim body. Her graying hair was straight and blunt-cut. She shook Pat's hand warmly. "I feel as though I know you. I go on buying trips to New England fairly often, and whenever I got the chance I watched your program."

The downstairs was used as a showroom. Chairs, couches, vases, lamps, paintings, Oriental carpets, china and fine glassware were all marked with tags. A Queen Anne breakfront held delicate figurines. A sleepy Irish setter, his dark red hair generously sprinkled with gray, was asleep in front of it.

"I live upstairs," Mrs. Graney explained. "Technically the shop is closed, but someone phoned and asked if she could stop in for a last-minute gift. You will have coffee, won't you?"

Pat took off her coat. She looked around, studying the contents of the room. "You have beautiful things."

"I like to think so." Mrs. Graney looked pleased. "I love searching out antiques and restoring them. My workshop is in the garage." She poured coffee from a Sheffield pot and handed a cup to Pat. "And I have the pleasure of being surrounded by beautiful things. With that auburn hair and gold blouse, you look as though you belong on that Chippendale couch."

"Thank you." Pat realized she liked this outspoken woman. There was something direct and honest about her. It made it possible to get right to the point of the visit. "Mrs. Graney, you can understand that your letter was quite startling. But will you tell me why you didn't contact the network directly, instead of writing to me?"

Catherine Graney took a sip of coffee. "As I told you, I've seen a number of your documentaries. I sense integrity in your work, and I didn't think you would willingly help to perpetuate a lie. That's why I'm appealing to you to make sure that George Graney's name is not mentioned on the Jennings program, and that Abigail Jennings does not refer to 'pilot error' in connection with Willard's death. My husband could fly anything that had wings."

Pat thought of the already-edited segments for the program. The Senator had denounced the pilot—but had she actually mentioned his name? Pat wasn't sure. But she did remember some of the details of the accident. "Didn't the investigation findings indicate that your husband was flying too low?" she asked.

"The *plane* was flying too low and went into the mountain. When Abigail Jennings started using that crash as a means for getting her name in the paper as a spokesperson for airline safety regulations, I should have objected immediately."

Pat watched as the Irish setter, seeming to sense the tension in his mistress' voice, got up, stretched, ambled across the room and settled at her feet. Catherine leaned over and patted him.

"Why *didn't* you speak up immediately?"

"Many reasons. I had a baby a few weeks after the accident. And I suppose I wanted to be considerate of Willard's mother."

"Willard's mother?"

"Yes. You see, George used to fly Willard Jennings quite often. They became good friends. Old Mrs. Jennings knew that, and she came to me after the crash had been sighted—to *me*, not to her daughter-in-law—

and we sat together and waited for the final word. She put a very generous sum of money in trust for my son's education. I didn't want to make her unhappy by using the weapon I could have used against Abigail Jennings. We both had our suspicions, but to her, scandal was anathema."

Three grandfather clocks simultaneously chimed the hour. It was one o'clock. The sun streamed into the room. Pat noticed that Catherine Graney twisted her gold wedding band as she spoke. Apparently, she had never remarried. "What weapon could you have used?" she asked.

"I could have destroyed Abigail's credibility. Willard was miserably unhappy with her and with politics. The day he died he was planning to announce that he was not seeking reelection and that he was accepting the presidency of a college. He wanted the academic life. The last morning he and Abigail had a terrible fight at the airport. She pleaded with him not to announce his resignation. And he told her, right in front of George and me—'Abigail, it won't make a damn bit of difference to you. We're finished.' "

"Abigail and Willard Jennings were on the verge of *divorce?*"

"This 'noble widow' business has always been a posture. My son, George Graney, Junior, is an Air Force pilot now. He never knew his dad. But I'm not going to have him embarrassed by any more of her lies. And whether I win the suit or not, I'll make the whole world realize what a phony she's always been."

Pat tried to choose her words carefully. "Mrs. Graney, I will certainly do what I can to see that your husband isn't referred to in a derogatory way. But I

must tell you, I've been going through the Senator's private files and everything I see suggests that Abigail and Willard Jennings were very much in love."

Catherine Graney looked scornful. "I'd like to see the expression on old Mrs. Jennings' face if she ever heard *that!* Tell you what: on your way back, drive an extra mile and pass Hillcrest. That's the Jennings estate. And imagine how strongly a woman must have felt not to leave it—or one red cent—to her own daughter-in-law."

Fifteen minutes later, Pat was looking through high iron gates at the lovely mansion set on the crest of the snow-covered grounds. As Willard's widow, Abigail had had every right to think she might inherit this estate as well as his seat in Congress. As his divorced wife, on the other hand, she would have been the outcast once again. If Catherine Graney was to be believed, the tragedy Abigail spoke so movingly about had, in fact, been the stroke of fortune that twenty-five years ago saved her from oblivion.

18

"It looks good, Abby," Toby said genially.

"It should photograph well," she agreed. They were admiring the Christmas tree in Abigail's living room. The dining-room table was already set for the Christmas buffet.

"There are bound to be reporters hanging around tomorrow morning," she said. "Find out what time the early services are at the Cathedral. I should be seen there."

She didn't plan to leave a stone unturned. Ever since the President had said, "I'll announce *her*," Abigail had been sick with nervousness.

"I'm the better candidate," she'd said a dozen times. "Claire is from his own region. That's not good. If only we weren't involved with the damn program."

"It might help you," he said soothingly, though secretly he was as worried as she.

"Toby, it might help if I were running for elective office in a big field of candidates. But I don't think the President is going to see the damn thing and jump up

and say '*She's* for me.' But he just might wait to see if there's negative reaction to it before he announces his decision."

He knew she was right. "Don't worry. Anyway, you can't pull out. The program's already in the listings."

She'd carefully selected the guests for the Christmas buffet supper. Among them she had two Senators, three Congressmen, a Supreme Court Justice and Luther Pelham. "I only wish Sam Kingsley weren't in California," she said.

By six o'clock, everything had been arranged. Abby had a goose cooking in the oven. She would serve it cold at the supper the next day. The warm, rich smell filled the house. It reminded Toby of being in the kitchen of the Saunders house when they were high school kids. That kitchen always smelled of good food roasting or baking. Francey Foster had been some cook. You had to give her that!

"Well, I guess I'll be on my way, Abby."

"Got a heavy date, Toby?"

"Not too heavy." The Steakburger waitress was beginning to bore him. Eventually they all did.

"I'll see you in the morning. Pick me up early."

"Right, Senator. Sleep well. You want to look your best tomorrow."

Toby left Abby fussing with some strands of tinsel that weren't hanging straight. He went back to his apartment, showered and put on slacks, a textured shirt and a sports jacket. The Steakburger kid had pretty definitely told him she didn't plan to cook tonight. He would take her out for a change and then they'd go back to her apartment for a nightcap.

Toby didn't enjoy spending his money on food—

not when the ponies were so interesting. He pulled on his dark green knitted tie and was looking at himself in the mirror when the phone rang. It was Abby.

"Go out and get me a copy of *The National Mirror*," she demanded.

"The *Mirror?*"

"You heard me—go out and get it. Philip just phoned. Miss Apple Junction and her elegant mother are on the front page. Who dug out that picture? Who?"

Toby gripped the phone. Pat Traymore had been in the newspaper office at Apple Junction. Jeremy Saunders had phoned Pat Traymore. "Senator, if someone is trying to put the screws on you, I'll make mincemeat of them."

Pat was home by three-thirty and looked forward to an hour's nap. As usual, the extra exertion of standing and climbing to hang the pictures the night before had taken its toll on her leg. The dull, steady ache had been persistent during the drive from Richmond. But she'd scarcely entered the house when the phone rang. It was Lila Thatcher.

"I'm so glad I've caught you, Pat. I've been watching for you. Are you free this evening?"

"As a matter of fact . . ." Caught off guard, Pat could not think of a reasonable excuse. You can't lie easily to a psychic, she thought.

Lila interrupted. "*Don't* be busy. The Ambassador is having people in for his usual Christmas Eve supper and I phoned and told him I'd like to bring you. After all, you are one of his neighbors now. He'd be delighted."

The octogenarian retired Ambassador was perhaps the most distinguished elder statesmen of the District. Few world leaders visiting Washington failed to stop at the Ambassador's home.

"I'd love to go," Pat said warmly. "Thank you for thinking of me."

When she hung up, Pat went up to the bedroom. The guests at the Ambassador's home would be a dressy crowd. She decided to wear a black velvet suit with sable-banded cuffs.

She still had time to soak in a hot tub for fifteen minutes and then to take a nap.

As she lay back in the tub, Pat noticed that a corner of the bland beige wallpaper was peeling. A swatch of Wedgwood blue could be seen underneath. Reaching up, she peeled back a large piece of the top layer of paper.

That was what she remembered—that lovely violet and Wedgwood blue. *And the bed had an ivory satin quilted spread,* she thought, *and we had a blue carpet on the floor.*

Mechanically she dried herself and pulled on a terry-cloth caftan. The bedroom was cool and already filled with late-afternoon shadows.

As a precaution, she set the alarm for four-thirty before drifting off to sleep.

The angry voices . . . the blankets pulled over her head . . . the loud noise . . . another loud noise . . . her bare feet silent on the stairs . . .

The insistent pealing of the alarm woke her. She rubbed her forehead trying to recall the shadowy dream. Had the wallpaper triggered something in her head? Oh, God, if only she hadn't set the alarm.

But it's coming closer, she thought. The truth comes closer each time. . . .

Slowly she got up and went to the vanity in the dressing room. Her face was strained and pale. A creaking sound down the hallway made her whirl around, her hand at her throat. But of course, it was just the house settling.

Promptly at five, Lila Thatcher rang the bell. She stood framed in the doorway, almost elfin with her rosy cheeks and white hair. She looked festive in an Autumn Haze mink coat with a Christmas corsage pinned on the wide collar.

"Have we time for a glass of sherry?" Pat asked.

"I think so." Lila glanced at the slender Carrara marble table and matching marble-framed mirror in the foyer. "I always loved those pieces. I'm glad to see them back."

"You know." It was a statement. "I thought so the other night."

She had set out a decanter of sherry and a plate of sweet biscuits on the cocktail table. Lila paused at the doorway of the living room. "Yes," she said, "you've done a very good job. Of course, it's been so long, but it is as I remember it. That wonderful carpet; that couch. Even the paintings," she murmured. "No wonder I've been troubled. Pat, are you sure this is wise?"

They sat down and Pat poured the sherry. "I don't know if it's wise. I *do* know it's necessary."

"How much do you remember?"

"Bits. Pieces. Nothing that hangs together."

"I used to call the hospital to inquire about you. You were unconscious for months. When you were moved, we were given to understand that if you did pull

through, you'd be permanently damaged. And then the death notice appeared."

"Veronica . . . my mother's sister and her husband adopted me. My grandmother didn't want the scandal following me . . . or them."

"And that's why they changed your first name as well?"

"My name is Patricia Kerry. I gather the Kerry was my father's idea. Patricia was my grandmother's name. They decided that as long as they were changing my last name they might as well start using my real first name too."

"So Kerry Adams became Patricia Traymore. What are you hoping to find here?" Lila took a sip of sherry and set down the glass.

Restlessly Pat got up and walked over to the piano. In a reflex action she reached toward the keyboard, then pulled her hands back.

Lila was watching her. "You play?"

"Only for pleasure."

"Your mother played constantly. You *know* that."

"Yes. Veronica has told me about her. You see, at first I only wanted to understand what happened here. Then I realized that ever since I can remember I've hated my father; hated him for hurting me so, for robbing me of my mother. I think I hoped to find some indication that he was sick, falling apart—I don't know what. But now, as I begin to remember little things, I realize it's more than that. I'm not the same person I would have become if . . ."

She gestured at the area where the bodies had been found. ". . . if all this hadn't happened. I need to link the child I was with the person I am. I've lost some part

of myself back there. I have so many preconceived ideas—my mother was an angel, my father a devil. Veronica hinted that my father destroyed my mother's musical career and then her life. But what about *him?* She married a politician and then refused to share his life. Was that fair? How much was I a catalyst of the trouble between them? Veronica told me once that this house was *too small.* When my mother tried to practice, I'd wake up and start crying."

"Catalyst," Lila said. "That's exactly what I'm afraid you are, Pat. You're setting things in motion that are best left alone." She studied her. "You seem to have recovered very well from your injuries."

"It took a long time. When I finally regained consciousness, I had to be taught everything all over again. I didn't understand words. I didn't know how to use a fork. I wore the brace on my leg till I was seven."

Lila realized she was very warm. Only a moment before she'd felt cool. She didn't want to examine the reason for the change. She knew only that this room had not yet completed its scenario of tragedy. She stood up. "We'd better not keep the Ambassador waiting," she said briskly.

She could see in Pat's face the cheekbones and sensitive mouth of Renée, the wide-spaced eyes and auburn hair of Dean.

"All right, Lila, you've studied me long enough," Pat said. "Which one of them do I resemble?"

"Both," Lila said honestly, "but I think you are more like your father."

"Not in every way, please, God." Pat's attempt at a smile was a forlorn failure.

19

Well-hidden in the shadows of the trees and shrubs, Arthur observed Pat and Lila through the patio doors. He had been bitterly disappointed to see the lighted house, the car in the driveway. Maybe he wouldn't be able to search for the doll tonight. And he desperately wanted Glory to have it in time for Christmas. He tried to hear what the women were saying but could not catch more than an occasional word. They were both dressed up. Could they be going out? He decided to wait. Avidly he studied Patricia Traymore's face. She was so serious, her expression so troubled. Had she begun to heed his warnings? For her sake he hoped so.

He had been watching only a few minutes when they stood up. They *were* going out. Silently he crept along the side of the house and in a moment heard the sound of the front door opening. They did not take the car. They could not be going too far, maybe to a neighbor's house or a nearby restaurant. He would have to hurry.

Quickly he made his way back to the patio. Patricia

Traymore had left the living-room lights on and he could see the strong new locks on the French doors. Even if he cut a pane he would not be able to get in. He had anticipated that and had planned what he would do. There was an elm tree next to the patio, one that would be easy to climb. A thick branch ran just under an upstairs window.

The night he left the doll he'd noticed that window was not completely closed at the top. It sagged as though it didn't hang properly. It would be easy to force it open.

A few minutes later he was stepping over the sill onto the floor. He listened intently. The room had a hollow feeling. Cautiously he turned on his flashlight. The room was empty and he opened the door to the hallway. He was sure he was alone in the house. Where should he begin searching?

He'd gone to so much trouble because of the doll. He'd almost been caught taking the vial of blood from the lab in the nursing home. He'd forgotten how much Glory loved her doll, how when he'd tiptoe into her room just to see if she was sleeping peacefully, she'd always had the doll clutched in her arms.

It was incredible to him that for the second time in a week he was inside this house again. The memory of that long ago morning was still so vivid: the ambulance, lights flashing, sirens blazing, tires screeching in the driveway. The sidewalk crowded with people, neighbors with coats thrown over expensive bathrobes; police cars barricading N Street; cops everywhere. A woman screaming. She was the housekeeper who'd found the bodies.

He and his fellow ambulance attendant from

Georgetown Hospital had rushed into the house. A young cop was on guard at the door. "Don't hurry. They don't need you."

The man lying on his back, the bullet in his temple, must have died instantly. The gun was between him and the woman. She had pitched forward and the blood from the chest wound stained the rug around her. Her eyes were still open, staring, unfocused, as though she'd wondered what had happened, how it had happened. She couldn't have been more than thirty. Her dark hair was scattered over her shoulders. Her thin face had delicate nostrils and high cheekbones. A yellow silk robe billowed around her like an evening gown.

He'd been the first to bend over the little girl. Her red hair was so matted with dried blood it had turned auburn; her right leg was jutting from the flowered nightdress, the bone sticking up in a pyramid.

He'd bent closer. "Alive," he'd whispered. Bedlam. I.V. hooked up. They'd hung a bottle of O negative; clamped an oxygen mask on the small, still face; splinted the shattered leg. He'd helped swathe the head, his fingers soothing her forehead, her hair curling around his fingers. Someone said her name was Kerry. "If it is God's will, I'll save you, Kerry," he'd whispered.

"She can't make it," the intern told him roughly, and pushed him out of the way. The police photographers snapped pictures of the little girl; of the corpses. Chalk marks on the carpet outlined the positions of the bodies.

Even then he'd felt the house was a place of sin and evil, a place where two innocent flowers, a young

woman and her little girl, had been willfully violated. He'd pointed out the house to Glory once and told her all about that morning.

Little Kerry had remained in an intensive-care unit at Georgetown Hospital for two months. He'd looked in on her as often as he could. She never woke up, just lay there, a sleeping doll. He had come to understand that she was not supposed to live and had tried to find a way to deliver her to the Lord. But before he could act, she was moved to a long-term-care facility near Boston, and after a while he read that she'd died.

His sister had had a doll. "Let me help take care of it," he'd pleaded. "We'll pretend it's sick and I'll make it well." His father's heavy, callused hand had slammed his face. Blood had gushed from his nose. "Make that well, you sissy."

He began to search for Glory's doll in Patricia Traymore's bedroom. Opening the closet, he examined the shelves and the floor, but it wasn't there. With sullen anger he observed the many expensive clothes. Silk blouses, and negligées, and gowns, and the kind of suits you see in magazine ads. Glory wore jeans and sweaters most of the time, and she bought them at K-Mart. The people in the nursing home were usually in flannel nightgowns and oversized robes that swaddled their shapeless bodies. One of Patricia Traymore's robes startled him. It was a brown wool tunic with a corded belt. It reminded him of a monk's habit. He took it out of the closet and held it against him. Next he investigated the deep bottom drawers of the dresser. The doll wasn't there either. If the doll was still in the house it was not in her bedroom. He couldn't waste so much time. He glanced into the closets of the empty bedrooms and went downstairs.

Patricia Traymore had left the vestibule light on, as well as a lamp in the library and others in the living room—she had even left on the lights on the Christmas tree. She was sinfully wasteful, he thought angrily. It was unfair to use so much energy, when old people couldn't even afford to heat their own homes. And the tree was already dry. *If a flame touched it, it would ignite and the branches would crackle and the ornaments melt.*

One of the ornaments had fallen from the tree. He picked it up and replaced it. There was really no hiding place in the living room.

The library was the last room he searched. The files were locked—that's where she had probably put it. Then he noticed the carton jammed far back under the library table. And somehow he *knew.* He had to tug hard to get the carton out but when he opened it his heart beat joyfully. There was Glory's precious doll.

The apron was gone, but he couldn't waste time looking for it. He walked through all the rooms, carefully examining them for signs of his presence. He hadn't turned a light on or off or touched a door. He had plenty of experience from his work in the nursing home. Of course if Patricia Traymore looked for the doll, she'd know that someone had come in. But that carton was pushed far under the table. Maybe she wouldn't miss the doll for a while.

He would go out the same way he'd come in—from the second story bedroom window. Patricia Traymore didn't use that bedroom; she probably didn't even glance in it for days at a time.

He had entered the house at five-fifteen. The chimes of the church near the college tolled six as he slid

down the tree, made his furtive way through the yard and disappeared into the night.

The Ambassador's house was immense. Stark white walls provided a vivid backdrop for his magnificent art collection. Comfortable, richly upholstered couches and antique Georgian tables caught Pat's eye. A huge Christmas tree decorated with silver ornaments stood in front of the patio doors.

The dining room table was set with an elaborate buffet: caviar and sturgeon, a Virginia ham, turkey en gelée, hot biscuits and salads. Two waiters discreetly refilled the guests' champagne glasses.

Ambassador Cardell, small, trim and whitehaired, welcomed Pat with courtly grace and introduced her to his sister Rowena Van Cleef, who now lived with him. "His baby sister," Mrs. Van Cleef told Pat, her eyes twinkling. "I'm only seventy-four; Edward is eighty-two."

There were some forty other people present. *Sotto voce*, Lila pointed out the most celebrated to Pat. "The British Ambassador and his wife, Sir John and Lady Clemens . . . the French Ambassador . . . Donald Arlen—he's about to be appointed head of the World Bank . . . General Wilkins is the tall man by the mantel—he's taking over the NATO command . . . Senator Whitlock—that's *not* his wife with him . . ."

She introduced Pat to the neighborhood people. Pat was surprised to discover she was the center of attention. Was there any indication of who might have been responsible for the break-in? Didn't it seem as though the President was going to appoint Senator Jennings

Vice President? Was the Senator easy to work with? Did they tape the entire program in advance?

Gina Butterfield, the columnist from *The Washington Tribune*, had drifted over and was listening avidly to what Pat was saying.

"It's so extraordinary that someone broke into your house and left a threatening note," the columnist observed. "Obviously you didn't take it seriously."

Pat tried to sound offhand. "We all feel it was the work of a crank. I'm sorry so much was made of it. It really is unfair to the Senator."

The columnist smiled. "My dear, this is Washington. Surely you don't believe that anything this newsy can be ignored. You seem very sanguine, but if I were in your shoes I'd be quite upset to find my home broken into and my life threatened."

"Especially in that house," another volunteered. "Were you told about the Adams murder-suicide there?"

Pat stared at the bubbles in her champagne glass. "Yes, I'd heard the story. But it was so long ago, wasn't it?"

"Must we discuss that subject?" Lila broke in. "It is Christmas Eve."

"Wait a minute," Gina Butterfield said quickly. *"Adams. Congressman Adams.* Do you mean that Pat is living in the house where he killed himself? How did the press miss that?"

"What possible connection does it have to the break-in?" Lila snapped.

Pat felt the older woman touch her arm in a warning gesture. Was her expression revealing too much?

The Ambassador stopped at their group. "Please, help yourselves to some supper," he urged.

Pat turned to follow him, but the columnist's question to another guest stopped her.

"You were living here in Georgetown at the time of the deaths?"

"Yes, indeed," the woman answered. "Just two houses down from them. My mother was alive then. We knew the Adams couple quite well."

"That was before I came to Washington," Gina Butterfield explained, "but of course I heard all the rumors. Is it true there was a lot more to the case than came out?"

"Of course it's true." The neighbor's lips parted in a crafty smile. "Renée's mother, Mrs. Schuyler, played the *grande dame* in Boston. She told the press that Renée had realized her marriage was a mistake and planned to divorce Dean Adams."

"Pat, shall we get something to eat?" Lila's arm urged her away.

"Wasn't she getting the divorce?" Gina asked.

"I doubt it," the other snapped. "She was insane about Dean, crazy jealous of him, resentful of his work. A real dud at parties. Never opened her mouth. And the way she'd practice that damn piano eight hours a day. In warm weather we all went wild listening to it. And believe me, she was no Myra Hess. Her playing was altogether pedestrian."

I won't believe this, Pat thought. I don't want to believe it. What was the columnist asking now? Something about Dean Adams having a reputation as a womanizer?

"He was so attractive that women always made a

play for him." The neighbor shrugged her shoulders. "I was only twenty-three then, and I had a huge crush on him. He used to walk with little Kerry in the evening. I made it my business to bump into them regularly, but it didn't do me any good. I think we'd better get on that buffet line. I'm starved."

"Was Congressman Adams visibly unstable?" Gina asked.

"Of course not. Renée's mother started that talk. She knew what she was doing. Remember, both their fingerprints were on the gun. My mother and I always thought that Renée was probably the one who flipped and shot up the place. And as far as what happened to Kerry . . . Listen, those bony pianist's hands were mighty powerful! I wouldn't have put it past her to have hit that poor child that night."

20

Sam sipped a light beer as he stared aimlessly across the crowd at the Palm Springs Racquet Club. Turning his head, he glanced at his daughter and smiled. Karen had inherited her mother's coloring; her deep tan only made her blond hair seem that much lighter. Her hand rested on her husband's arm. Thomas Walton Snow, Jr., was a very nice fellow, Sam thought. A good husband; a successful businessman. His family was too boringly social for Sam's taste, but he was happy that his daughter had married well.

Since his arrival, Sam had been introduced to several extremely attractive women in their early forties—widows, grass widows, career types, each ready to select a man for the rest of her life. All of this only caused Sam to feel a cumulative restlessness, an inability to settle down, an aching, pervasive sense of not belonging.

Where in the merry hell *did* he belong?

In Washington. That was where. It was good to be

with Karen, but he simply didn't give a damn about the rest of the people she found so intensely satisfying.

My child is twenty-four years old, he thought. She's happily married. She's expecting a baby. I don't want to be introduced to all the eligible forty-plus women in Palm Springs.

"Daddy, will you please stop scowling?"

Karen leaned across the table, kissed him and then settled back with Tom's arm around her. He surveyed the bright, expectant faces of Tom's family. In another day or so they'd start to get fed up. He'd become a difficult guest.

"Sweetheart," he said to Karen, making his voice confidential. "You asked me if you thought the President would appoint Senator Jennings Vice President, and I said I didn't know. I should be more honest. I think she'll get it."

All eyes were suddenly focused on him.

"Tomorrow night the Senator is having a Christmas supper party at her home; you'll see some of it on the television program. She'd like me to be there. If you don't mind, I think I should attend."

Everyone understood. Karen's father-in-law sent out for a timetable. If Sam left L.A. the next morning on the 8 A.M. flight, he'd be at National Airport by four-thirty East Coast time. How interesting to be a guest at the televised dinner party. Everyone was looking forward to the program.

Only Karen was quiet. Then, laughing, she said, "Daddy, cut the baloney. I've heard the rumors that Senator Jennings has her eye on you!"

21

At nine-fifteen, Pat and Lila walked silently together from the Ambassador's party. It was only when they were within reach of their own houses that Lila said quietly, "Pat, I can't tell you how sorry I am."

"How much of what that woman said was true and how much was exaggeration? I must know." Phrases kept running through her mind: neurotic . . . long, bony fingers . . . womanizer . . . We think she hit that poor kid . . . "I really need to know how much is true," she repeated.

"Pat, she's a vicious gossip. She knew perfectly well what she was doing when she started to talk about the background of the house with that woman from *The Washington Tribune.*"

"She was mistaken, of course," Pat said tonelessly.

"Mistaken?"

They were at Lila's gate. Pat looked across the street at her own house. Even though she'd left several lights burning downstairs, it still seemed remote and shadowy. "You see, there's one thing that I'm quite sure I

remember. When I ran through the foyer into the living room that night I tripped over my mother's body." She turned to Lila. "So you see what that gets me: a neurotic mother who apparently found me a nuisance and a father who went berserk and tried to kill me. Quite a heritage, isn't it?"

Lila didn't answer. The sense of foreboding that had been nagging at her was becoming acute. "Oh, Kerry, I want to help you."

Pat pressed her hand. "You are helping me, Lila," she said. "Good night."

In the library, the red button on the answering machine was flashing. Pat rewound the tape. There was a single call on the unit. "This is Luther Pelham. It is now seven-twenty. We have a crisis. No matter what time you get in, call me at Senator Jennings' home, 703/555-0143. It is imperative that we meet there tonight."

Her mouth suddenly dry, Pat phoned the number. It was busy. It took three more attempts before she got through. Toby answered.

"This is Pat Traymore, Toby. What's wrong?"

"Plenty. Where are you?"

"At home."

"All right. Mr. Pelham has a car standing by to pick you up. It should be there in ten minutes."

"Toby, what's wrong?"

"Miss Traymore, maybe that's something you're going to have to explain to the Senator."

He hung up.

A half-hour later the network staff car that Luther had sent pulled up in front of Senator Jennings' home

in McLean. On the drive over, Pat had worried herself
with endless suppositions, but all her thoughts led to
the same chilling conclusion: something had happened to further upset or embarrass the Senator, and
whatever it was, she was being blamed.

A grim-faced Toby opened the door and led her into
the library. Silent shapes were seated around the table
in a council of war, the atmosphere oddly at variance
with the poinsettia plants flanking the fireplace.

Senator Jennings, icy calm, her sphinxlike expression cast in marble, stared through Pat. Philip was to
the Senator's right, his long, thin strands of colorless
hair no longer combed carefully over his oval skull.

Luther Pelham's cheekbones were mottled purple.
He appeared to be on the verge of a stroke.

This isn't a trial, Pat thought. It's an inquisition. My
guilt has already been decided. But for what? Without
offering her a seat, Toby dropped his heavy bulk into
the last chair at the table.

"Senator," Pat said, "something is terribly wrong
and it's quite evident it has to do with me. Will someone please tell me what's going on?"

There was a newspaper in the middle of the table.
With one gesture, Philip flipped it over and pushed it
at Pat. "Where did they get that picture?" he asked
coldly.

Pat stared down at the cover of *The National Mirror*.
The headline read: "WILL MISS APPLE JUNCTION BE
THE FIRST WOMAN VEEP?" The picture, which took
up the entire cover, was of Abigail in her Miss Apple
Junction crown standing with her mother.

Enlarged, the picture revealed even more cruelly
the massive dimensions of Francey Foster. Bulging

flesh strained against the splotchy print of her badly cut dress. The arm around Abigail was dimpled with fat; the proud smile only emphasized the double-chinned face.

"You've seen this picture before," Philip snapped.

"Yes." How horrible for the Senator, she thought. She remembered Abigail's stern observation that she had spent more than thirty years trying to put Apple Junction behind her. Ignoring the others, Pat addressed the Senator directly. "Surely you can't believe I had anything to do with the *Mirror* getting this picture?"

"Listen, Miss Traymore," Toby answered, "don't bother lying. I found out that you were snooping around Apple Junction, including digging up back issues of the newspaper. I was at your place the day Saunders called." There was nothing deferential about Toby now.

"I have told the Senator you went to Apple Junction against my explicit orders," Luther thundered.

Pat understood the warning. She was not to let Abigail Jennings know that Luther had acceded to her trip to Abigail's birthplace. But that didn't matter now. What mattered was Abigail. "Senator," she began, "I understand how you must feel . . ."

The effect of her words was explosive. Abigail jumped to her feet. "Do you indeed? I thought I'd been plain enough, but let me start again. I hated every minute of my life in that stinking town. Luther and Toby have finally gotten around to letting me in on your activities up there, so I know you saw Jeremy Saunders. What did that useless leech tell you? That I

had to use the back door and that my mother was the cook? I'll *bet* he did.

"I believe you released that picture, Pat Traymore. And I know why. You're bound and determined you're going to profile me *your* way. You *like* Cinderella stories. In your letters to me you insinuated as much. And when I was bloody fool enough to let myself get talked into this program, you decided that it had to be done *your* way so everyone could talk about that poignant, moving Patricia Traymore touch. Never mind that it could cost me everything I've been working for all my life."

"You believe I would send out that picture to somehow further my own career?" Pat looked from one to the other. "Luther, has the Senator seen the storyboard yet?"

"Yes, she has."

"How about the alternative storyboard?"

"Forget that one."

"What alternative storyboard?" Philip demanded.

"The one I've been begging Luther to use—and I assure you it has no mention of the first beauty contest or picture from it. Senator, in a way you're right. I do want to see this production done my way. But for the best possible reason. I have admired you tremendously. When I wrote to you, I didn't know there was any chance that you might soon be appointed Vice President. I was looking ahead and hoping you would be a serious contender for the Presidential nomination next year."

Pat paused for breath, then rushed on. "I wish you'd dig out that first letter I sent you. I meant what I said. The one problem you have is that the American public

considers you cold and remote. That picture is a good example. Obviously you're ashamed of it. But look at the expression on your mother's face. She's so *proud* of you! She's fat—is that what bothers you? Millions of people are overweight, and in your mother's generation a lot more older people were. So if I were you, when you get inquiries, I'd tell whoever asked me that that was the first beauty contest and you entered because you knew how happy it would make your mother if you won. There isn't a mother in the world who won't like you for that. Luther can show you the rest of my suggestions for the show. But I can tell you this. If you're not appointed Vice President, it won't be because of this picture; it will be because of your reaction to it and your being ashamed of your background.

"I'll ask the driver to take me home," she said. Then, eyes blazing, she turned to Luther. "You can call me in the morning and let me know if you still want me on this program. Good night, Senator."

She turned to go. Luther's voice stopped her. "Toby, get your ass out of that chair and make some coffee. Pat, sit down and let's start fixing this mess."

It was one-thirty when Pat got home. She changed into a nightgown and robe, made tea, brought it into the living room and curled up on the couch.

Staring at the Christmas tree, she reflected on the day. If she accepted what Catherine Graney said, all the talk about the great love between Abigail and Willard Jennings was a lie. If she believed what she had heard at the Ambassador's party, her mother had been a neurotic. If she believed Senator Jennings, every-

thing Jeremy Saunders had told her was a twisted complaint.

It was he who must have sent the picture of Abigail to the *Mirror*. It was just the sort of mean-spirited thing he would do.

She swallowed the last sip of tea and got up. There was no use trying to think about it anymore. Walking over to the Christmas tree, she reached for the switch to turn off the lights, then paused. When she and Lila were having sherry, she thought she'd noticed that one of the ornaments had slipped from its branch and was lying on the floor. My mistake, she thought.

She shrugged and went to bed.

22

At nine-fifteen on Christmas morning, Toby was standing at the stove in Abigail Jennings' kitchen waiting for the coffee to perk. He hoped that he'd be able to have a cup himself before Abby appeared. True, he'd known her since they were kids, but this was one day he couldn't predict what her mood was likely to be. Last night had been some mess. There'd been only two other times he'd seen her so upset, and he never let himself think of either of them.

After Pat Traymore left, Abby and Pelham and Phil had sat around for another hour still trying to decide what to do. Or, rather, Abby had shouted at Pelham, telling him a dozen times that she still thought Pat Traymore was working for Claire Lawrence, that maybe Pelham was too.

Even for her, Abigail had gone pretty far, and Toby was amazed that Pelham had taken it. Later Phil supplied the answer: "Listen, he's the biggest TV news personality in the country. He's made millions. But he's sixty years old, and he's bored stiff. Now he wants

to be another Edward R. Murrow. Murrow capped his career as head of the U.S. Information Agency. Pelham wants that job so bad he can taste it. Tremendous prestige and no more competing for ratings. The Senator will deliver for him if he delivers for her. He knows she's got a right to scream about the way this program is going."

Toby had to agree with what Pelham said. Like it or not, the damage was done. Either the program was produced from the angle of including Apple Junction and the beauty contests or it would seem like a farce.

"You can't ignore the fact you're on the cover of *The National Mirror*," Pelham kept telling Abby. "It's read by four million people and handed away to God knows how many more. That picture is going to be reprinted by every sensational newspaper in this country. You've got to decide what you're going to tell them about it."

"Tell them?" Abby had stormed. "I'll tell them the truth: my father was a lush and the only decent thing he ever did was die when I was six. Then I can say that my fat mother had the viewpoint of a scullery maid and her highest ambition for me was that I'd be Miss Apple Junction and a good cook. Don't you think that's exactly the background a Vice President is supposed to have?" She had cried tears of rage. Abigail was no crybaby. Toby could remember only those few occasions. . . .

He had said his piece. "Abby, listen to me. You're stuck with Francey's picture, so get your act together and go along with Pat Traymore's suggestion."

That had calmed her down. She trusted him.

He heard Abby's steps in the hall. He was anxious to see what she'd be wearing. Pelham had agreed that she

should show up at Christmas services at the Cathedral and wear something photogenic but not too luxurious. "Leave your mink home," he'd said.

"Good morning, Toby. Merry Christmas." The tone was sarcastic but under control. Even before he turned around he knew Abby had recovered her cool.

"Merry Christmas, Senator." He swung around. "Hey, you look great."

She was wearing a double-breasted bright red walking suit. The coat came to her fingertips. The skirt was pleated.

"Like one of Santa's helpers," she snapped. But even though she sounded crabby, there was a sort of joke in her voice. She picked up her cup and held it out in a toast. "We're going to bring this one off too, aren't we, Toby?"

"You bet we are!"

They were waiting for her at the Cathedral. As soon as Abigail got out of the car, a television correspondent held up a microphone to her.

"Merry Christmas, Senator."

"Merry Christmas, Bob." Abby was smart, Toby reflected. She made it her business to know all the press and TV people, no matter how unimportant they were.

"Senator, you're about to go into Christmas services at the National Cathedral. Is there a special prayer you'll be offering?"

Abby hesitated just long enough. Then she said, "Bob, I guess we're all praying for world peace, aren't we? And after that my prayer is for the hungry. Wouldn't it be wonderful if we knew that every man,

woman and child on this earth would be eating a good dinner tonight?" She smiled and joined the people streaming through the portal of the Cathedral.

Toby got back into the car. Terrific, he thought. He reached under the driver's seat and pulled out the racing charts. The ponies hadn't been too good to him lately. It was about time his luck changed.

The service lasted an hour and fifteen minutes. When the Senator came out another reporter was waiting for her. This one had some hard questions to ask. "Senator, have you seen *The National Mirror* cover this week?"

Toby had just gotten around the car to open the door. He held his breath, waiting to see how she'd handle herself.

Abby smiled—a warm, happy smile. "Yes, indeed."

"What do you think of it, Senator?"

Abby laughed. "I was astonished. I must say I'm more used to being mentioned in the *Congressional Record* than in *The National Mirror.*"

"Did the appearance of that picture upset or anger you, Senator?"

"Of course not. Why should it? I suppose that, like most of us, on holidays I think about the people I loved who aren't with me anymore. That picture made me remember how happy my mother was when I won that contest. I entered it to please her. She was widowed, you know, and brought me up alone. We were very, very close."

Now her eyes became moist, her lips trembled. Quickly she bent her head and got into the car. With a decisive snap, Toby closed the door behind her.

The recorder light was blinking when Pat returned from the morning service. Automatically she pressed the rewind button until the tape screeched to a halt, then switched to playback.

The first three calls were disconnects. Then Sam came on, his voice edgy. "Pat, I've been trying to reach you. I'm just boarding a plane for D.C. See you at Abigail's this evening."

How loving can you get? Sam had planned to spend the week with Karen and her husband. And now he's rushing home. Abigail had obviously summoned him to be one of her close and intimate friends at her Christmas supper. There *was* something between them! Abigail was eight years older, but didn't look it. Plenty of men married older women.

Luther Pelham had also phoned. "Continue to work on the second version of the storyboard. Be at the Senator's home at four P.M. If you are called by newspapers about the *Mirror* picture, claim you haven't seen it."

The next message began in a soft, troubled voice: "Miss Traymore—er, Pat—you may not remember me. [A pause.] Of course you will; it's just you meet so many people, don't you? [Pause.] I must hurry. This is Margaret Langley. I am the principal . . . retired, of course . . . of Apple Junction High School."

The message time had run out. Exasperated, Pat bit her lip.

Miss Langley had called back. This time she said hurriedly, "To continue, please call me at 518/555-2460." There were sounds of tremulous breathing.

Then Miss Langley burst out, "Miss Traymore, I heard from Eleanor today."

The phone rang only once before Miss Langley answered. Pat identified herself and was interrupted immediately. "Miss Traymore, after all these years I've heard from Eleanor. Just as I came in from church the phone was ringing and she said hello in that sweet, shy voice and we both started to cry."

"Miss Langley, where is Eleanor? What is she doing?"

There was a pause; then Margaret Langley spoke carefully, as though trying to choose exactly the right words. "She didn't tell me where she is. She said she is much better and doesn't want to be hiding forever. She said she is thinking of turning herself in. She knows she'll go back to jail—she did violate her parole. She said that this time she'd like me to visit her."

"Turning herself in!" Pat thought of the stunned, helpless face of Eleanor Brown after her conviction. "What did you tell her?"

"I begged her to call you. I thought you might be able to get her parole reinstated." Now Margaret Langley's voice broke. "Miss Traymore, please don't let that girl go back to prison."

"I'll try," Pat promised. "I have a friend, a Congressman, who will help. Miss Langley, please, for Eleanor's sake, do you know where I can reach her?"

"No, honestly, I don't."

"If she calls back, beg her to contact me before she surrenders. Her bargaining position will be so much stronger."

"I knew you'd want to help. I knew you were a good person." Now Margaret Langley's tone changed. "I

want you to know how happy I am that that nice Mr. Pelham phoned and invited me to be on your program. Someone is coming to interview and tape me tomorrow morning."

So Luther had taken that suggestion too. "I'm so glad." Pat tried to sound enthusiastic. "Now, remember to tell Eleanor to call me."

She lowered the receiver slowly. If Eleanor Brown was the timid girl Miss Langley believed her to be, turning herself in would be a tremendous act of courage. But for Abigail Jennings, it could be mortally embarrassing if, in the next few days, a vulnerable young woman was marched back to prison still protesting her innocence of the theft from Abigail's office.

23

As he walked down the corridor of the nursing home, Arthur sensed the tension and was immediately on guard. The place seemed peaceful enough. Christmas trees and Hanukkah candles stood on card tables covered with felt and make-believe snow. All the doors of the patients' rooms had greeting cards taped to them. Christmas music was playing on the stereo in the recreation room. But something was wrong.

"Good morning, Mrs. Harnick. How are you feeling?" She was advancing slowly down the hall on her walker, her birdlike frame bent over, her hair scraggly around her ashen face. She looked up at him without raising her head. Just her eyes moved, sunken, watery, afraid.

"Stay away from me, Arthur," she said, her voice aquiver. "I told them you came out of Anita's room, and I know I'm right."

He touched Mrs. Harnick's arm, but she shrank away. "Of course I was in Mrs. Gillespie's room," he said. "She and I were friends."

"She wasn't your friend. She was afraid of you."

He tried not to show his anger. "Now, Mrs. Harnick . . ."

"I mean what I say. Anita wanted to stay alive. Her daughter, Anna Marie, was coming to see her. She hadn't been East for two years. Anita said she didn't care when she died as long as she saw her Anna Marie again. She didn't just stop breathing. I told them that."

The head nurse, Elizabeth Sheehan, sat at a desk halfway down the corridor. He hated her. She had a stern face, and blue-gray eyes that could turn steel gray when she was angry. "Arthur, before you make your rounds please come to the office."

He followed her into the business office of the nursing home, the place where families would come to make arrangements to jettison their old people. But today there weren't any relatives, only a baby-faced young man in a raincoat with shoes that needed a shine. He had a pleasant smile and a very warm manner, but Arthur wasn't fooled.

"I'm Detective Barrott," he said.

The superintendent of the home, Dr. Cole, was also there.

"Arthur, sit down," he said, trying to make his voice friendly. "Thank you, Nurse Sheehan; you needn't wait."

Arthur chose a straight chair and remembered to fold his hands in his lap and look just a little puzzled, as though he had no idea what was going on. He'd practiced that look in front of the mirror.

"Arthur, Mrs. Gillespie died last Thursday," Detective Barrott said.

Arthur nodded and made his expression regretful. He was suddenly glad he'd met Mrs. Harnick in the hall. "I know. I was so hoping she'd live just a little longer. Her daughter was coming to visit her and she hadn't seen her for two years."

"You knew that?" Dr. Cole asked.

"Of course. Mrs. Gillespie told me."

"I see. We didn't realize she'd discussed her daughter's visit."

"Doctor, you know how long it took to feed Mrs. Gillespie. Sometimes she'd need to rest and we'd just talk."

"Arthur, were you glad to see Mrs. Gillespie die?" Detective Barrott asked.

"I'm glad she died before that cancer got much worse. She would have been in terrible pain. Isn't that right, Doctor?" He looked at Dr. Cole now, making his eyes wide.

"It's possible, yes," Dr. Cole said unwillingly. "Of course one never knows. . . ."

"But I wish Mrs. Gillespie had lived to see Anna Marie. She and I used to pray over that. She used to ask me to read prayers from her *Saint Anthony Missal* for a special favor. That was her prayer."

Detective Barrott was studying him carefully. "Arthur, did you visit Mrs. Gillespie's room last Monday?"

"Oh, yes, I went in just before Nurse Krause made her rounds. But Mrs. Gillespie didn't want anything."

"Mrs. Harnick said she saw you coming out of Mrs. Gillespie's room at about five of four. Is that true?"

Arthur had figured out his answer. "No, I didn't go in her room. I *looked* in her room, but she was asleep.

She'd had a bad night and I was worried about her. Mrs. Harnick saw me look in."

Dr. Cole leaned back in his chair. He seemed relieved.

Detective Barrott's voice got softer. "But the other day you said Mrs. Harnick was wrong."

"No, somebody asked me if I'd *gone into* Mrs. Gillespie's room twice. I hadn't. But then, when I thought about it, I remembered I'd looked in. So Mrs. Harnick and I were both right, you see."

Dr. Cole was smiling now. "Arthur is one of our most caring helpers," he said. "I told you that, Mr. Barrott."

But Detective Barrott wasn't smiling. "Arthur, do many of the orderlies pray with the patients or is it just you?"

"Oh, I think it's just me. You see, I was in a seminary once. I was planning to become a priest but got sick and had to leave. In a way I think of myself as a clergyman."

Detective Barrott's eyes, soft and limpid, encouraged confidences. "How old were you when you went into that seminary, Arthur?" he asked kindly.

"I was twenty. And I stayed until I was twenty and a half."

"I see," Detective Barrott said. "Tell me, Arthur, what seminary were you in?"

"I was at Collegeville, Minnesota, with the Benedictine community."

Detective Barrott pulled out a notebook and wrote that down. Too late Arthur realized he had told too much. Suppose Detective Barrott got in touch with the

community and they told that after Father Damian's death, Arthur had been requested to leave.

Arthur worried about that all day. Even though Dr. Cole told him to go back to work, he could feel the suspicious glances from Nurse Sheehan. All the patients were looking at him in a peculiar way.

When he went to look in on old Mr. Thoman, his daughter was there and she said, "Arthur, you don't have to worry about my dad anymore. I've asked Nurse Sheehan to appoint another orderly to help him."

It was a slap in the face. Only last week Mr. Thoman had said, "I can't put up with feeling so sick much longer." Arthur had comforted him saying, "Maybe God won't ask you to, Mr. Thoman."

Arthur tried to keep his smile bright as he crossed the recreation room to help Mr. Whelan, who was struggling to his feet. As he walked Mr. Whelan down the hall to the lavatory and back, he realized that he was getting a headache, one of those blinding ones that made lights dance in front of his eyes. He knew what would happen next.

As he eased Mr. Whelan back into his chair, he glanced at the television set. The screen was all cloudy and then a face began to form, the face of Gabriel as he would look on Judgment Day. Gabriel spoke only to him. "Arthur, you are not safe here anymore."

"I understand." He didn't know he'd said the words out loud until Mr. Whelan said, "Shhh."

When he went down to his locker, Arthur carefully packed his personal effects but left his extra uniform and old shoes. He was off tomorrow and Wednesday, so they might not realize he wouldn't return on Thurs-

day morning unless for some reason they searched his locker and found it empty.

He put on his sports jacket, the brown-and-yellow one he'd bought at J. C. Penney's last year. He kept it here so that if he was meeting Glory for a movie or something, he could look nice.

In the pocket of his raincoat he put the pair of socks that had three hundred dollars stuffed in the toes. He always kept emergency money available, both here and at home, just in case he had to leave suddenly.

The locker room was cold and dingy. There was no one around. They'd given the day off to as many of the staff as possible. *He* had volunteered to work.

His hands were restless and dry; his nerves were screaming with resentment. They had no right to treat him like this. Restlessly his eyes roamed around the barren room. Most of the supplies were locked up in the big storage room, but there was a kind of catchall closet near the stairs. It was filled with opened bottles and cans of cleaning agents and unwashed dust rags. He thought of those people upstairs—Mrs. Harnick accusing him, Mr. Thoman's daughter telling him to stay away from her father, Nurse Sheehan. How dared they whisper about him, question him, reject him!

In the closet he found a half-empty can of turpentine. He loosened the cap, then turned the can on its side. Drops of turpentine began to drip onto the floor. He left the closet door open. Right next to it, a dozen bags of trash were piled together waiting to be carried out to the dump site.

Arthur didn't smoke, but when visitors left packs of cigarettes around the nursing home, he always picked them up for Glory. Now he took a Salem from his

pocket, lit it, puffed until he was sure it wouldn't go out, unfastened the tie on one of the trash bags and dropped it in.

It would not take long. The cigarette would smolder; then the whole bag would catch fire; then the other bags would go, and the dripping turpentine would cause the fire to burn out of control. The rags in the closet would cause dense smoke, and by the time the staff tried to get the old people out, the whole building would be gone. It would seem to be a careless accident—an ignited cigarette in the trash; a fire caused by an overturned can of turpentine that had dripped from the shelf—if the investigators could even piece that much together.

He retied the bag as the faint, good burning smell made his nostrils quiver and his loins tighten, then hurried from the building and down the lonely street toward the Metro.

Glory was on the couch in the living room reading a book when Arthur got home. She was wearing a very pretty blue wool housecoat, with a zipper that came up to her neck and long, full sleeves. The book she was reading was a novel on the best-seller list that had cost $15.95. Arthur had never in his life spent more than a dollar for a book. He and Glory would go to second-hand stores and browse and come home with six or seven titles. And it was their pleasure to sit companionably reading. But somehow the dog-eared volumes with the stained covers that they had delighted in purchasing seemed poor and shabby next to this book with the shiny jacket and crisp new pages. The girls in the office had given it to her.

Glory had fixed a roast chicken for him, and cranberry sauce and hot muffins. But it was no pleasure
eating Christmas dinner alone. She'd said she wasn't
hungry. She seemed to be thinking so deeply. Several
times he caught her staring at him, her eyes questioning and troubled. They reminded him of the way Mrs.
Harnick had looked at him. He didn't want Glory to be
afraid of him.

"I have a present for you," he told her. "I know
you'll like it." Yesterday, at the big discount store in
the mall, he'd bought a frilly white apron for the Raggedy Ann doll, and except for a few spots on the dress,
the doll looked just the same. And he'd bought Christmas paper and wrappings and made it look like a real
present.

"And I have a present for you, Father."

They exchanged the gifts solemnly. "You open
first," he said. He wanted to see her expression. She'd
be so happy.

"All right." She smiled, and he noticed that her hair
seemed lighter. Was she coloring it?

She untied the ribbon carefully, pushed back the
paper, and the frilly apron showed first. "What . . .
oh, Father." She was startled. "You found her. What a
pretty new apron." She looked pleased, but not as
exquisitely happy as he'd expected. Then her face became very thoughtful. "Look at that poor, sad face.
And that's the way I thought of myself. I remember the
day I painted it. I was so sick, wasn't I?"

"Will you take her to bed with you again?" he asked.
"That's why you wanted her, isn't it?"

"Oh, no. I just wanted to look at her. Open your
present. It will make you happy, I think."

It was a handsome blue-and-white wool sweater with a V-neck and long sleeves. "I knitted it for you, Father," Glory told him happily. "Would you believe I finally was able to stick with something and finish it? I guess I'm getting my act together. It's about time, don't you think?"

"I like you just as you are," he said. "I like taking care of you."

"But pretty soon it may be impossible," she said.

They both knew what she meant.

It was time to tell her. "Glory," he said carefully. "Today I was asked to do something very special. There are a number of nursing homes in Tennessee that are badly understaffed and need the kind of help I can give to very sick patients. They want me to go there right away and select one of them to work in."

"Move? Again?" She looked dismayed.

"Yes, Glory. I do God's work, and now it's my turn to ask for your help. You're a great comfort to me. We will leave Thursday morning."

He was sure he'd be safe until then. At the very least, the fire would have caused great confusion. At best, his personnel records might be destroyed. But even if the fire was put out before it burned the place down, it would probably be at least a few days before the police could check his references and find the long gaps between employment, or learn the reason he'd been asked to leave the seminary. By the time that detective wanted to question him again, he and Glory would be gone.

For a long time Glory was silent. Then she said, "Father, if my picture is on that program Wednesday night, I'm going to turn myself in. People all over the

country will see it, and I can't go on any longer wondering if someone is staring at me because he or she
knows who I am. Otherwise I will go with you to Tennessee." Her lip quivered, and he knew she was near
tears.

He went to her and patted her cheek. He could not
tell Glory that the only reason he was waiting until
Thursday to go away was because of that program.

"Father," Glory burst out, "I've started to be happy
here. I don't think it's fair the way they expect you to
just pick up and go all the time."

24

At 1:30 P.M. Lila rang Pat's doorbell. She was carrying
a small package. "Merry Christmas!"

"Merry Christmas. Come in." Pat was genuinely
pleased by the visit. She had been trying to decide
whether or not to confide in Luther that Eleanor might
turn herself in to the police. And how could she
broach the subject of Catherine Graney to him? The
prospect of a lawsuit would send him into orbit.

"I won't stay but a minute," Lila said. "I just wanted
to give you some fruitcake. It's a specialty of mine."

Pat hugged her impulsively. "I'm glad you did
come. It's terribly odd to be so quiet on Christmas
afternoon. How about a glass of sherry?"

Lila looked at her watch. "I'll be out of here by
quarter of two," she announced.

Pat led her back to the living room; got a plate, a
knife and glasses; poured the sherry and cut thin slices
of the cake. "Marvelous," she pronounced after sam-
pling it.

"It is good, isn't it?" Lila agreed. Her eyes darted

around the living room. "You've changed something in here."

"I switched a couple of paintings. I realized they were in the wrong place."

"How much is coming back to you?"

"Some." Pat admitted. "I was in the library working. Then something just made me come in here. As soon as I did, I knew that the still life and the landscape should be reversed."

"What else, Pat? There's more."

"I'm so darn edgy," Pat said simply. "And I don't know why."

"Pat, please don't stay here. Move to an apartment, a hotel." Lila clasped her hands imploringly.

"I can't," Pat said. "But help me now. Were you ever in here on Christmas Day? What was it like?"

"That last year, you were three and a half and able to really understand Christmas. They were both so delighted with you. It was a day of genuine happiness."

"I sometimes think I remember a little of that day. I had a walking doll and was trying to make it walk with me. Could that have been true?"

"You did have a walking doll that year, yes."

"My mother played the piano that afternoon, didn't she?"

"Yes."

Pat walked over to the piano, opened it. "Do you remember what she played that Christmas?"

"I'm sure it was her favorite Christmas carol. It's called 'Bells of Christmas.' "

"I know it. Veronica wanted me to learn it. She said

my grandmother loved it." Slowly her fingers began to run over the keys.

Lila watched and listened. When the last notes faded away, she said, "That was very much like your mother playing. I told you you resemble your father, but I never realized until this minute how startling the resemblance is. Somebody who knew him well is bound to make the connection."

At three o'clock the television crew from Potomac Cable Network arrived at Senator Jennings' house to tape her Christmas supper.

Toby watched them with a hawk's eye as they set up in the living and dining rooms, making it his business to be sure nothing got broken or scratched. He knew how much everything in the place meant to Abby.

Pat Traymore and Luther Pelham came within a minute or two of each other. Pat was wearing a white wool dress that showed off her figure. Her hair was twisted in a kind of bun. Toby had never seen her wear it like that. It made her look different and yet familiar. Who the hell did she remind him of? Toby wondered.

She seemed relaxed, but you could tell Pelham wasn't. As soon as he walked in, he started snapping at one of the cameramen. Abigail was uptight, and that didn't help either. Right away she tangled with Traymore. Pat wanted to set the food out on the buffet table and tape the Senator inspecting it and making little changes in the way it was placed. Abigail didn't want to put the food out so early.

"Senator, it takes time to get exactly the feeling we want," Pat told her. "It will be much easier to do now

than when your guests are standing around watching."

"I won't have my guests standing around like extras in a B movie," Abigail snapped.

"Then I suggest we photograph the table now."

Toby noticed that Pat didn't back down when she wanted something done. Luther remarked that Abigail had prepared all the food herself, and that was another hassle. Pat wanted a shot of her in the kitchen working.

"Senator, everybody thinks you just phone a caterer when you have a party. That you actually do everything yourself will endear you to all the women who are stuck preparing three meals a day, to say nothing of the men and women whose hobby is cooking."

Abigail flatly rejected the idea, but Pat kept insisting. "Senator, the whole purpose of our being here is to make people see you as a human being."

In the end it was Toby who persuaded Abigail to go along. "Come on, show them you're a regular Julia Child, Senator," he coaxed.

Abby refused to put an apron over her designer shirt and slacks, but when she began to put hors d'oeuvre together, she made it clear she was a gourmet cook. Toby watched as she rolled batter for pastry shells, chopped ham for quiche, seasoned crabmeat, those long, slender fingers working miraculously. No messy kitchen for Abby. Well, you had to give a tip of the hat to Francey Foster for that.

Once the crew started taping, Abigail began to relax. They had done only a couple of takes when Pat said, "Senator, thank you. I'm sure we have what we want. That came over very well. Now, if you don't

mind changing to whatever you're planning to wear at the party, we can get the footage at the table."

Toby was anxious to see what Abigail would wear. She's been hemming and hawing between a couple of outfits. He was pleased when she came back, wearing a yellow satin blouse that matched the yellow in her plaid taffeta skirt. Her hair was soft around her face and neck. Her eye makeup was heavier than usual. She looked stunning. Besides, she had a glow about her. Toby knew why. Sam Kingsley had phoned to say he'd be at the party.

There was no question Abby had set her cap for Sam Kingsley. Toby hadn't missed the way she'd suggested to her friends that they put Sam next to her at dinner parties. There was something about him that reminded Toby of Billy, and of course that was the big attraction for Abby. She'd put on a good show in public, but she'd been a basket case when Billy died.

Toby knew Sam didn't like him. But that wasn't a problem. Sam wouldn't last any longer than the others had. Abby was too domineering for most men. Either they got sick of adjusting to her schedule and moods, or if they knuckled under, she got sick of them. He, Toby, would be part of Abby's life until one or the other of them died. She'd be lost without him, and she knew it.

As he watched her posing at the buffet table, a tinge of regret made him swallow hard. Every once in a while he daydreamed about how it would have been if he'd been smart in school instead of just having the smarts; if he'd gone on to become an engineer instead of a jack-of-all-trades. And if he'd been good-looking like that wimp Jeremy Saunders, instead of rough-

faced and burly—well, who knew? Somewhere along the line, Abby might have fallen for him.

He dismissed the thought and got back to work.

Promptly at five the first car drove up. The retired Supreme Court Justice and his wife entered a minute or two later. "Merry Christmas, Madam Vice President," the Justice said.

Abigail returned his kiss warmly. "From your lips to God's ear," she laughed.

Other guests began to flow in. Hired waiters poured champagne and punch. "Keep the hard stuff for later," Luther had suggested. "The Bible Belt doesn't like to be reminded that its public officials serve booze."

Sam was the last to arrive. Abigail opened the door for him. Her kiss on his cheek was affectionate. Luther was directing the other camera toward them. Pat felt her heart sink. Sam and Abigail made a stunning couple—both tall, her ash blond hair contrasting with his dark head, the streaks of gray in his hair a subtle balance to the fine lines around her eyes.

Pat could see everyone clustering around Sam. I only think about him as *Sam*, she thought. I've never seen him in his professional element. Was that the way it had been with her mother and father? They'd met when they were both vacationing on Martha's Vineyard. They'd married within a month, never really knowing or understanding each other's worlds—and then the clash had begun.

Except I wouldn't clash with you, Sam. I like your world.

Abigail must have said something amusing; everyone laughed. Sam smiled at her.

"That's a nice shot, Pat," the cameraman said. "A little sexy—you know what I mean? You never see Senator Jennings with a guy. People *like* that." The cameraman was beaming.

"All the world loves a lover," Pat replied.

"We've got enough," Luther suddenly announced. "Let the Senator and her guests have some peace. Pat, you be at the Senator's office for the taping in the morning. I'll be in Apple Junction. You know what we need." He turned his back, dismissing her.

Did his attitude result from the picture in the *Mirror* or from her refusal to sleep with him? Only time would tell.

She slipped past the guests, down the hallway and into the den, where she'd left her coat.

"Pat."

She turned around. "Sam!" He was standing in the doorway, looking at her. "Ah, Congressman. Season's greetings." She reached for her coat.

"Pat, you're not leaving?"

"No one invited me to stay."

He came over, took the coat from her. "What's this about the *Mirror* cover?"

She told him. "And it seems the senior Senator from Virginia believes I slipped that picture to that rag just to get my way about this program."

He put his hand on her shoulder. "You didn't?"

"That sounds like a question!" Could he really believe she'd had anything to do with the *Mirror* cover? If so, he didn't know her at all. Or maybe it was time she

realized that the man she thought she knew didn't exist.

"Pat, I can't leave yet, but I should be able to get away in an hour. Are you going home?"

"Yes, I am. Why?"

"I'll be there as soon as I can. I'll take you to dinner."

"All the decent restaurants will be closed. Stay; enjoy yourself." She tried to pull away from him.

"Miss Traymore, if you give me your keys, I'll bring your car around."

They sprang apart, both embarrassed. "Toby, what the hell are *you* doing here?" Sam snapped.

Toby looked at him impassively. "The Senator is about to ask her guests in to supper, Congressman, and told me to round them up. She particularly told me to look for you."

Sam was still holding Pat's coat. She reached for it. "I can get my own car, Toby," she said. She looked at him directly. He was standing in the doorway, a large, dark mass. She tried to pass him, but he didn't move.

"*May* I?"

He was staring at her, his expression distracted. "Oh, sure. Sorry." He stepped aside, and unconsciously she shrank against the wall to avoid brushing against him.

Pat drove at breakneck speed trying to escape the memory of how warmly Abigail and Sam had greeted each other, of the subtle way in which the others seemed to treat them as a couple. It was a quarter to eight when she got home. Grateful that she'd had the foresight to cook the turkey, she made a sandwich and

poured a glass of wine. The house felt dark and empty. She turned on the lights in the foyer, library, dining room and living room, then plugged in the tree.

The other day the living room had somehow seemed warmer, more livable. Now, for some reason, it was uncomfortable, shadowy. Why? Her eye caught a strand of tinsel almost hidden on a brilliant apricot-hued section of the carpet. Yesterday when she and Lila were here, she thought she'd seen an ornament with a piece of tinsel lying on this area of the carpet. Perhaps it had been just the tinsel.

The television set was in the library. She carried the sandwich and the wine there. Potomac Cable had hourly news highlights. She wondered if they'd show Abigail at church.

They did. Pat watched dispassionately as Abigail stepped from the car, the bright red suit dramatic against her flawless skin and hair, her eyes soft as she voiced her prayer for the hungry. This was the woman Pat had revered. The newscaster announced, "Later Senator Jennings was questioned about her picture as a young beauty queen, which is on the cover of this week's *National Mirror*." A postage-stamp-size picture of the *Mirror* cover was shown. "With tears in her eyes the Senator recalled her mother's desire to have her enter that contest. Potomac Cable Network wishes Senator Abigail Jennings a very merry Christmas; and we're sure that her mother, were she aware of her success, would be terribly proud of her."

"Good Lord," Pat cried. Jumping up, she pushed the button that turned off the set. "And Luther has the gall to call that news! No wonder the media are criticized for bias."

Restlessly she began to jot down the conflicting statements she had been hearing all week:

Catherine Graney said that Abigail and Willard were about to divorce.
Senator Jennings claims she loved her husband very much.

Eleanor Brown stole $75,000 from Senator Jennings.
Eleanor Brown swears she did not steal that money.

George Graney was a master pilot; his plane was carefully inspected before takeoff.
Senator Jennings said George Graney was a careless pilot with second-rate equipment.

Nothing adds up, Pat thought, absolutely nothing!

It was nearly eleven o'clock before the door chimes signaled Sam's arrival. At ten-thirty, ready to give up on him, Pat had gone to her room, then told herself that if Sam were not coming, he would have called. She changed to silk pajamas that were comfortable for lounging but technically still suitable for receiving guests. She washed her face, then touched her eyelids lightly with shadow and her lips with gloss. No point looking like a mouse, she thought—not when he'd just left the beauty queen.

Swiftly she hung up the clothes she had left scattered over the room. Was Sam neat? I don't even know that, she thought. The one night they had stayed together certainly hadn't been any barometer of either of their personal habits. When they'd checked into the

motel she'd brushed her teeth with the folding tooth-brush she always carried in her cosmetic case. "I wish I had one of those," he'd said. She'd smiled up at his reflection in the mirror. "One of my favorite lines from *Random Harvest* was when the minister asks Smithy and Paula if they're so in love they use the same toothbrush." She ran hers under hot water, spread toothpaste across the bristles and handed it to him. "Be my guest."

That toothbrush was now in a velvet jeweler's box in the top drawer of the vanity. Some women press roses or tie ribbons around letters, Pat thought. I kept a toothbrush.

She had just come down the stairs when the chimes rang again. "Come in, come in, whoever you are," she said.

Sam's expression was contrite. "Pat, I'm sorry. I couldn't get away as fast as I'd hoped. And then I cabbed to my place, dropped my bags and picked up my car. Were you on your way to bed?"

"Not at all. If you mean this outfit, its technically called lounging pajamas and, according to the Saks brochure, is perfect for that evening at home when entertaining a few friends."

"Just be careful which friends you entertain," Sam suggested. "That's a pretty sexy-looking getup."

She took his coat; the fine wool was still cold from the icy wind.

He bent down to kiss her.

"Would you like a drink?" Without waiting for his answer, she led him into the library and silently pointed to the bar. He poured brandy into snifters and handed one to her. "I assume this is still your after-dinner choice?"

She nodded and deliberately chose the fan-back chair across from the couch.

Sam had changed when he stopped at his apartment. He was wearing an Argyle sweater with a predominantly blue-and-gray pattern that complemented the blueness of his eyes, the touches of gray in his dark brown hair. He settled on the couch, and it seemed to her there was a weariness in the way he moved and in the lines around his eyes.

"How did it go after I left?"

"About as you saw it. We did have one high point, however. The President phoned to wish Abigail a merry Christmas."

"*The President phoned!* Sam, does that mean . . . ?"

"My bet is he's milking this for all it's worth. He probably phoned Claire Lawrence as well."

"You mean he hasn't made his decision?"

"I think he's still sending up trial balloons. You saw the way he featured Abigail at the White House dinner last week. But he and the First Lady also went to a private supper in Claire's honor the next night."

"Sam, how badly did that *Mirror* cover hurt Senator Jennings?"

He shrugged. "Hard to say. Abigail has done the Southern-aristocracy scene a little too heavily for a lot of people around here. On the other hand, it just may make her sympathetic. Another problem: that publicity about the threats to you has made for a lot of locker-room jokes on Capitol Hill—and they're all on Abigail."

Pat stared at her untouched brandy. Her mouth suddenly felt dry and brackish. Last week Sam had been worried about *her* because of the break-in. Now he was

sharing Abigail's reaction to the publicity. Well, in a way it made things easier. "If this program causes any more unfavorable publicity to Senator Jennings, could it cost her the Vice Presidency?"

"Perhaps. No President, particularly one who's had a spotless administration, is going to risk having it tarnished."

"That's exactly what I was afraid you'd say." She told him about Eleanor Brown and Catherine Graney. "I don't know what to do," she concluded. "Should I warn Luther to keep away from those subjects on the program? If I do, he'll have to tell the Senator the reason."

"There's no way Abigail can take any more aggravation," Sam said flatly. "After the others left she was really wired."

"After the others left!" Pat raised an eyebrow. "You mean you stayed?"

"She asked me to."

"I see." She felt her heart sink. It confirmed everything she had been thinking. "Then I shouldn't tell Luther."

"Try it this way. If that girl . . ."

"Eleanor Brown."

"Yes—if she calls you, persuade her to wait until I see if we can plea-bargain on her parole. In that case there'd be no publicity, at least until the President announces his selection."

"And Catherine Graney."

"Let me look into the records of that crash. She probably doesn't have a leg to stand on. Do you think either one of these women might have made those threats to you?"

"I've never met Eleanor. I'm sure it wasn't Catherine Graney. And don't forget it was a man's voice."

"Of course. He hasn't called again?"

Her eyes fell on the carton under the table. She considered, then rejected, the idea of showing the Raggedy Ann doll to Sam. She did not want him concerning himself about her anymore. "No, he hasn't."

"That's good news." He finished the brandy and set the glass on the table. "I'd better be on my way. It's been a long day and you must be bushed."

It was the opening she was waiting for. "Sam, on the way home from the Senator's tonight, I did some hard thinking. Want to hear about it?"

"Certainly."

"I came to Washington with three specific and rather idealistic goals in mind. I was going to do an Emmy-winning documentary on a wonderful, noble woman. I was going to find an explanation for what my father did to my mother and me. And I was going to see you and it would be the reunion of the century. Well, none of these turned out as I expected. Abigail Jennings is a good politician and a strong leader, but she isn't a nice person. I was suckered into this program because my preconceived notions about Abigail suited Luther Pelham, and whatever reputation I've achieved in the industry gives credibility to what is essentially P.R. fluff. There's so much about that lady that doesn't hang together that it frightens me.

"I've also been here long enough to know that my mother wasn't a saint, as I'd been led to believe, and very possibly goaded my father into some form of temporary insanity that night. That's not the full story —not yet; but it's close.

"And as for us, Sam, I do owe you an apology. I certainly was terribly naive to think that I was anything more to you than a casual affair. The fact that you never called me after Janice died should have been the tip-off, but I guess I'm not a quick study. You can stop worrying now. I don't intend to embarrass you with any more declarations of love. It's very clear you've got something going with Abigail Jennings."

"I don't have anything going with Abigail!"

"Oh, yes, you do. Maybe you don't know it yet, but you do. That lady *wants* you, Sam. Anyone with half an eye can see that. And you didn't cut short your vacation and come rushing across the country at her summons without good reason. Just forget about having to let me down easy. Really, Sam, all that talk about being worn out and not able to make decisions isn't very becoming. You can drop it now."

"I told you that because it's *true.*"

"Then snap out of it. It doesn't become you. You're a handsome, virile man with twenty or thirty good years ahead of you." She managed a smile. "Maybe the prospect of becoming a grandfather is a little shocking to your ego."

"Are you finished?"

"Quite."

"Then if you don't mind, I've overstayed my welcome." He got up, his face flushed.

She reached out her hand. "There's no reason not to be friends. Washington is a small town. That *is* the reason you called me in the first place, isn't it?"

He didn't answer.

With a certain degree of satisfaction, Pat heard him slam the front door as he left.

25

"Senator, they'll probably want you to be anchorwoman on the *Today* show," Toby volunteered genially. He glanced into the rearview mirror to see Abby's reaction. They were on their way to the office. At 6:30 A.M. on December 26 it was still dark and bone-chilling.

"I have no desire to be anchorwoman on the *Today* show or any other show," Abigail snapped. "Toby, what the hell do I look like? I never closed an eye last night. Toby, the President *phoned* me . . . he *phoned* me personally. He said to have a good rest over the Christmas recess because it was going to be a busy year ahead. What could he have meant by that? . . . Toby, I can taste it. The Vice Presidency. Toby, *why* didn't I follow my instincts? *Why* did I let Luther Pelham talk me into this program? Where was my head?"

"Senator, listen. That picture may be the best thing that ever happened to you. It's for sure that wallflower Claire Lawrence never won any contests. Maybe Pat

Traymore is right. That kind of makes you more accessible . . . is that the word?"

They were going over the Roosevelt Bridge, and traffic was picking up. Toby concentrated on the driving. When he looked again into the rearview mirror, Abby's hands were still in her lap. "Toby, I've worked for this."

"I know you have, Abby."

"It isn't fair to lose it just because I've had to claw my way up."

"You're not going to lose it, Senator."

"I don't know. There's something about Pat Traymore that disturbs me. She's managed to give me two bouts of embarrassing publicity in one week. There's more to her than we know."

"Senator, Phil checked her out. She's been touting you since she was in college. She wrote an essay on you her senior year at Wellesley. She's on the level. She may be bad luck, but she's on the level."

"She's trouble. I warn you, there's something else about her."

The car swung past the Capitol and pulled up at the Russell Senate Office Building. "I'll be right up, Senator, and I promise you, I'll keep an eye on Pat Traymore. She won't get in your way." He hopped out of the car to open the door for Abby.

She accepted his hand, got out, then impulsively squeezed his fingers. "Toby, look at that girl's eyes. There's something about them . . . something secretive . . . as though . . ."

She didn't finish the sentence. But for Toby, it wasn't necessary.

At six o'clock Philip was waiting in the office to admit Pat and the network camera crew.

Sleepy-eyed guards and cleaning women with weary, patient faces were the only other people in evidence in the Russell building. In Abigail's office, Pat and the cameramen bent over the storyboard. "We'll only give three minutes to this segment," Pat said. "I want the feeling of the Senator arriving at an empty office and starting work before anyone shows up. Then Philip coming in to brief her . . . a shot of her daily calendar, but don't show the date . . . then office help arriving; the phones starting; a shot of the daily mail; the Senator greeting visitors from her state; the Senator talking to a constituent; Phil in and out with the messages. You know what we want—a sense of behind-the-scenes in a Senator's workday office."

When Abigail arrived, they were ready for her. Pat explained the first shot she wanted, and the Senator nodded and returned to the vestibule. Cameras rolled, and her key turned in the latch. Her expression was preoccupied and businesslike. She slipped off the gray cashmere cape that covered a well-cut but restrained pin-striped gray suit. Even the way she ran her fingers through her hair as she tossed off her hat was natural, the gesture of someone who cares about her appearance but is preoccupied with more important matters.

"Cut," Pat said. "Senator, that's fine, just the feeling I wanted." Her spontaneous praise sounded patronizing even to her own ears.

Senator Jennings' smile was enigmatic. "Thank you. Now what?"

Pat explained the scene with the mail, Phil and the constituent, Maggie Sayles.

The taping went smoothly. Pat quickly realized that Senator Jennings had a natural instinct for presenting herself at the best camera angle. The pin-striped suit gave her an executive, businesslike appearance that would be a nice contrast to the taffeta skirt at the Christmas supper party. Her earrings were silver; she wore a silver tie pin, stark and slim against the ascot of a soft gray silk blouse. It was the Senator's idea to photograph her office in a long shot showing the flags of both the United States and Virginia and then to have only the flag of the United States behind her in close-ups.

Pat watched the camera angle in as Abigail carefully selected a letter from the mound of mail on her desk—a letter in a childish handwriting. Another touch of theater, Pat thought. How smart of her. Then the constituent, Maggie, came in—the one whom Abigail had helped to find a nursing home for her mother. Abigail sprang up to meet her, kissed her affectionately, led her to a chair . . . all animation, warmth, concern.

She does mean the concern, Pat thought. I was here when she got that woman's mother into a home; but there's so much showmanship going on now. Are all politicians like this? Am I simply too damn naive?

By ten o'clock they had finished. Having reassured Abigail that they had everything they needed, Pat and the camera crew got ready to leave. "We'll do the first rough edit this afternoon," Pat told the director. "Then go over it with Luther tonight."

"I think it's going to turn out great," the cameraman volunteered.

"It's turning into a good show. That much I'll grant," Pat said.

26

Arthur's night had been filled with dreams of Mrs. Gillespie's eyes as they'd started to glaze over. In the morning he was heavy-eyed and tired. He got up and made coffee and would have gone out for rolls, but Glory asked him not to. "I won't have any, and after I go to work, you should get some rest. You didn't sleep well, did you?"

"How did you know?" He sat across from her at the table, watching as she perched at the edge of her chair.

"You kept calling out. Did Mrs. Gillespie's death worry you so much, Father? I know how often you used to talk about her."

A chill of fear went through him. Suppose they asked Glory about him? What would she say? Nothing ever to hurt him, but how would she know? He tried to choose his words carefully.

"It's just I'm so sad she didn't get to see her daughter before she died. We both wanted that."

Glory gulped her coffee and got up from the table.

"Father, I wish you would take some time off and rest. I think you're working too hard."

"I'm fine, Glory. What was I saying in my sleep?"

"You kept telling Mrs. Gillespie to close her eyes. What were you dreaming about her?"

Glory was looking at him as if she were almost frightened of him, he thought. What did she know, or guess? After she had gone, he stared into his cup, worried and suddenly tired. He was restless and decided to go out for a walk. It didn't help. After a few blocks he turned back.

He had reached the corner of his street when he noticed the excitement. A police car was stopped in front of his home. Instinctively he ducked into the doorway of a vacant house and watched from the foyer. Whom did they want? Glory? Himself?

He would have to warn her. He'd tell her to meet him somewhere and they'd go away again. He had the $300 in cash, and he had $622 in Baltimore in a savings account under a different name. They could make that last until he had a new job. It was easy to get work in a nursing home. They were all desperate for orderlies.

He slipped along the side of the house, cut through the adjacent yard, hurried to the corner and phoned Glory's office.

She was on another line. "Get her," he told the girl angrily. "It's important. Tell her Father says it's important."

When Glory got on the phone, she sounded impatient. "Father, what *is* it?"

He told her. He thought she'd cry or get upset, but

there was nothing from her—just silence. "Glory . . . ?"

"Yes, Father." Her voice was quiet, lifeless.

"Leave right now, don't say anything, act like you're going to the ladies' room. Meet me at Metro Central, the Twelfth and G exit. We'll be gone before they have a chance to put out an alert. We'll pick up the money at the bank in Baltimore and then go South."

"No, Father." Now Glory's voice sounded strong, sure. "I'm not running anymore. Thank you, Father. You don't have to run anymore for me. I'm going to the police."

"Glory. No. Wait. Maybe it will be all right. Promise me. *Not yet.*"

A police car was cruising slowly down the block. He could not lose another minute. As she whispered, "I promise," he hung up the phone and ducked into a doorway. When the squad car had passed, he shoved his hands into his pockets and with his stiff, unyielding gait made his way to the Metro station.

It was a subdued Abigail who returned to the car at ten-thirty. Toby started to speak, but something told him to keep his mouth shut. Let Abby be the one to decide if she wanted to get things off her chest.

"Toby, I don't feel like going home yet," Abigail said suddenly, "Take me over to Watergate. I can get a late breakfast there."

"Sure, Senator." He made his voice hearty, as though the request were not unusual. He knew why Abby had selected that place. Sam Kingsley lived in the same building as the restaurant. The next thing,

she'd probably phone upstairs and if Sam was in, ask him to join her for coffee.

Fine, but that hadn't been a casual chat in the den between Kingsley and Pat Traymore last night. There was something between those two. He didn't want to see Abby get hurt again. He wondered if he should tip her off.

Glancing over his shoulder, he noticed that Abigail was checking her makeup in her hand mirror. "You look fantastic, Senator," he said.

At the Watergate complex the doorman opened the car door, and Toby noticed the extra-large smile and respectful bow. Hell, there were one hundred Senators in Washington but only one Vice President. *I want it for you, Abby,* he thought. *Nothing will stand in your way if I have anything to say about it.*

He steered the car to where the other drivers were parked and got out to say hello. Today the talk was all about Abigail. He overheard a Cabinet member's driver say, "It's practically all sewed up for Senator Jennings."

Abby, you're almost there, girl, he thought exultantly.

Abby was gone more than an hour, so he had plenty of time to read the newspaper. Finally he opened the Style section to glance at the columns. Sometimes he could pick up useful tidbits to pass on to Abby. She was usually too busy to read gossip.

Gina Butterfield was the columnist everyone in Washington read. Today her column had a headline that ran across the two center pages of the section. Toby read it, then read it again, trying to deny what he was seeing. The headline was ADAMS DEATH HOUSE SCENE OF THREATS. SENATOR ABIGAIL JENNINGS IN-

VOLVED. The first couple of paragraphs of the story were in extra-large type:

Pat Traymore, the fast-rising young television newswoman hired by Potomac Cable to produce a documentary about Senator Jennings, has been harassed by letters, phone calls and a break-in threatening her life if she continues to work on the program.

A guest at the exclusive Christmas Eve supper of Ambassador Cardell, winsome Pat revealed that the house she is renting was the scene of the Adams murder-suicide twenty-four years ago. Pat claims not to be disturbed by the sinister history of the house, but other guests, long-time residents of the area, were not so complacent. . . .

The rest of the column was devoted to details of the Adams murder. On the pages were blown-up file photos of Dean and Renée Adams, the garish picture of the sacks in which their bodies were bundled, a close-up of their small daughter being carried out swathed in bloody bandages. "SIX MONTHS LATER KERRY ADAMS LOST HER VALIANT FIGHT FOR LIFE" was the caption under that picture.

The article hinted at a whitewash in the murder-suicide verdict:

Aristocratic Patricia Remington Schuyler, mother of the dead woman, insisted that Congressman Adams was unstable and about to be divorced by his socialite wife. But many old-tim-

ers in Washington think Dean Adams may have
been given a bum rap, that it was Renée Adams
who held the gun that night. "She was clearly
besotted by him," one friend told me, "and he
had a roving eye." Did her jealousy reach the
breaking point that night? *Who* may have triggered that tragic outburst? Twenty-four years
later, Washington still speculates.

Abigail's picture in her Miss Apple Junction crown was
prominent. The copy under it read:

Most specials profiling celebrities are ho-hum
material, rehashes of the old Ed Murrow format.
But the upcoming program on Senator Abigail
Jennings will probably win the Nielsen ratings
for the week. After all, the Senator may become
our first woman Vice President. The smart
money is on her. Now everyone's hoping that the
footage will include more pictures of the distinguished senior Senator from Virginia in the
rhinestone crown she picked up as a beauty
queen along the way. And on the serious side, no
one can agree on who hates Abigail Jennings
enough to threaten the life of the newswoman
who conceived the idea of the program.

Half of the right-hand page was subcaptioned THE
PRE-CAMELOT YEARS. It was filled with photographs,
most of them informal snapshots.

The accompanying text read:

In a bizarre coincidence, Senator Abigail Jennings was at one time a frequent guest at the Adams house. She and her late husband, Congressman Willard Jennings, were close friends of Dean and Renée Adams and the John Kennedys. The three stunning young couples could not have guessed that the dark shadow of fate was hovering over that house and all their lives.

There were pictures of the six together and in mixed groups in the garden of the Georgetown house, on the Jennings estate in Virginia and at the Hyannis Port compound. And there were a half-dozen photos of Abigail alone in the group after Willard's death.

Toby uttered a savage, angry growl. He started to crumple the paper between his hands, willing the sickening pages to disintegrate under his sheer physical strength, but it was no use. It wouldn't go away.

He would have to show this to Abby as soon as he got her home. God only knew what her reaction would be. She *had* to keep her cool. Everything depended on that.

When Toby pulled the car up to the curb, Abigail was there, Sam Kingsley at her side. He started to get out, but Kingsley quickly opened the door for Abigail and helped her into the car. "Thanks for holding my hand, Sam," she said. "I feel a lot better. I'm sorry you can't make dinner."

"You promised me a rain check."

Toby drove quickly, frantic to get Abigail home, as though he needed to insulate her from public view until he could nurse her through the first reaction to the article.

"Sam is special," Abby said suddenly, ending the heavy silence. "You know how it's been with me all these years—but Toby, in a crazy way he reminds me of Billy. I have this feeling—just a feeling, mind you—that there could be something developing between Sam and me. It would be like having a second chance."

It was the first time she'd ever talked like this. Toby looked into the rearview mirror. Abigail was leaning against the seat, her body relaxed, her face soft and with a half-smile.

And he was the son-of-a-bitch who was going to have to destroy that hope and confidence.

"Toby, did you buy the paper?"

There was no use lying. "Yes, I did, Senator."

"Let me see it, please."

He handed back the first section.

"No, I don't feel like the news. Where's the section with the columns?"

"Not now, Senator." The traffic was light; they were over Chain Bridge. In a few minutes, they'd be home.

"What do you mean, *not now?*"

He didn't answer, and there was a long pause. Then Abigail said, her tone cold and brittle, "Something bad in one of the columns . . . something that could hurt me?"

"Something you won't like, Senator."

They drove the rest of the way in silence.

27

Over the Christmas holiday official Washington was a ghost town. The President was in his private vacation residence in the Southwest; Congress was in recess; the universities were closed for vacation. Washington became a sleepy city, a city waiting for the burst of activity that signaled the return of its Chief Executive, lawmakers and students.

Pat drove home through the light traffic. She wasn't hungry. A few nibbles of turkey and a cup of tea were as much as she wanted. She wondered how Luther was making out in Apple Junction. Had he turned on the courtly charm he had once used to woo her? All of that seemed long ago.

Apropos of Apple Junction, she wondered if Eleanor Brown had ever called Miss Langley back. *Eleanor Brown.* The girl was a pivotal figure in Pat's growing doubt about the integrity of the television program. What were the facts? It was Eleanor's word against Toby's. *Had* he phoned and requested her to go to the campaign office to look for the Senator's ring? The

Senator supported Toby's claim that he had been driving her at the time of the supposed call. And part of the money had been found in Eleanor's storage area. How had she expected to get away with such a flimsy alibi?

I wish I had a transcript of the trial, she thought.

She opened her pad and studied the sentences she had written down the night before. They still didn't add up. On the next page she wrote *Eleanor Brown*. What had Margaret Langley said about the girl? Tapping her pen on the desk and frowning in concentration, she began to jot her impressions of their conversation:

> *Eleanor was timid . . . she never chewed gum in class or talked when the teacher was out of the room . . . she loved her job in the Senator's office . . . she had just been promoted . . . she was taking art classes . . . she was going to Baltimore that day to sketch. . . .*

Pat read and reread her notes. A girl doing well at a responsible job who had just been given a promotion, but so stupid she had hidden stolen money in her own storage room.

Some stolen money. The bulk of it—$70,000—was never found.

A girl as timid as that would be a poor witness in her own defense.

Eleanor had had a nervous breakdown in prison. She would have had to be a consummate actress to fake that. But she had violated her parole.

And what about Toby? He had been the witness who contradicted Eleanor's story. He had sworn he never

phoned her that morning. Senator Jennings had confirmed that Toby was driving her at the time of the alleged call.

Would Senator Jennings deliberately lie for Toby, deliberately allow an innocent girl to go to prison?

But suppose someone who *sounded* like Toby had phoned Eleanor? In that case all three—Eleanor, Toby and the Senator—had been telling the truth. Who else would have known about Eleanor's storage space in her apartment building? What about the person who had made the threats, broken in here, left the doll? Could he be the *x* factor in the disappearance of the campaign funds?

The doll. Pat pushed back her chair and reached for the carton jammed under the library table, then changed her mind. There was nothing to be gained by looking at the doll now. The sight of that weeping face was too unsettling. After the program was aired, if there were no more threats, she'd throw it away. If there were any more letters or phone calls or attempted break-ins, she'd have to show the doll to the police.

On the next page in her pad she wrote *Toby*, then fished through the desk drawer for the cassettes of her interviews.

She had recorded Toby in the car that first afternoon. He hadn't realized she was taping him, and his voice was somewhat muffled. She turned the sound as high as possible, pushed the "play" button and began to take notes.

Maybe Abby stuck her neck out for me . . . I was working for a bookie in New York and almost got in trouble

. . . I used to drive Abby and Willard Jennings to that house for parties . . . cute little kid, Kerry.

She was glad to switch to the interview with the waitress, Ethel Stubbins, and her husband, Ernie. They had said something about Toby. She found the segment, Ernie saying, "Say hello to him for me. Ask him if he's still losing money on the horses."

Jeremy Saunders had discussed Toby. She listened to his derisive remarks about the joyriding incident. his story about his father's buying off Abigail: "I always thought Toby had a hand in it."

After hearing the last of the cassettes, Pat read and reread her transcriptions. She knew what she had to do. If Eleanor turned herself in and was sent back to prison, Pat vowed she would stay with the case until she had satisfied herself as to Eleanor's guilt or innocence. And *if it turns out I believe her story,* Pat thought, *I'll do everything I can to help her.* Let the chips fall where they may—including Abigail Jennings' chips.

Pat wandered from the library into the foyer, and then to the staircase. She glanced up, then hesitated. *The step above the turn. That's where I used to sit.* Impulsively she hurried up the stairs, sat on that step, leaned her head against the baluster and closed her eyes.

Her father was in the foyer. She had shrunk deeper into the shadows, knowing that he was angry, that this time he would not joke about finding her here. She had run back to bed.

She hurried up the rest of the staircase. Her old room was past the guest room, across the back of the house, overlooking the garden. It was empty now.

She'd walked in here that first morning as the mov-

ing men were scurrying through the house, but it had evoked absolutely no memories. Now it seemed she could remember the bed with the frilly white canopy, the small rocking chair near the window with the music box, the shelves of toys.

I came back to bed that night. I was frightened because Daddy was so angry. The living room is right underneath this room. I could hear voices; they were shouting at each other. Then the loud noise and Mother screaming, "No . . . No!"

Mother screaming. After the loud noise. Had she been able to scream after she was shot or had she screamed when she realized she had shot her husband?

Pat felt her body begin to shake. She grasped the door for support, felt the dampness in her palms and forehead. Her breath was coming in short, hard gasps. She thought, I am afraid. But it's over. It was so long ago.

She turned and realized she was running down the hall; she was rushing down the staircase. I am back there, she thought. I am going to remember. *"Daddy, Daddy,"* she called softly. At the foot of the stairs, she turned and began to stumble through the foyer, her arms outstretched. *Daddy . . . Daddy!*

At the living-room door she crumpled to her knees. Vague shadows were around her but would not take form. Burying her face in her hands, she began to sob . . . "Mother, Daddy, come home."

She had awakened and there had been a strange baby-sitter. Mother. Daddy. I want my mother. I want my daddy. And they had come. Mother rocking her. Kerry, Kerry it's all right. Daddy patting her hair; his arms around both of them. Shhh, Kerry, we're here.

After a while Pat slid into a sitting position and leaned against the wall, staring into the room. Another memory had broken through. She was sure it was accurate. No matter which one was guilty that last night, she thought fiercely, I know that both of them loved me. . . .

28

There was a movie theater on Wisconsin Avenue that opened at ten. Arthur went into a cafeteria near it and dawdled over coffee, then walked around the neighborhood until the box office opened.

Whenever he was upset, he liked to go to the movies. He would choose a seat near the back and against the wall. And he'd buy the tallest bag of popcorn and sit and eat and watch unseeingly as the figures moved on the screen.

He liked the feeling of people near him but not conscious of him, the voices and music on the soundtrack, the anonymity of the darkened auditorium. It gave him a place to think. Now he settled in and stared blankly at the screen.

It had been a mistake to set the fire. There had been no mention of it in the newspaper. When he got off the Metro, he'd phoned the nursing home and the operator had answered at once. He'd muffled his voice: "I'm Mrs. Harnick's son. How serious was the fire?"

"Oh, sir, it was discovered almost at once. A smol-

dering cigarette in the trash bag. We didn't know any of the guests were even aware of it."

That meant they must have seen the overturned can of turpentine. No one would believe it had tipped accidentally.

If only he hadn't mentioned the monastery. Of course, the office there might simply say: "Yes, our records indicate Arthur Stevens was with us for a short time."

Suppose they were pressed for details? "He left at the suggestion of his spiritual director."

"May we speak to the spiritual director?"

"He died some years ago."

Would they tell why he had been asked to leave? Would they study the records of the nursing home and see which patients had died in these few years and how many of them he had helped to nurse? He was sure they wouldn't understand that he was only being kind, only alleviating suffering.

Twice before he'd been questioned when patients he had cared for had slipped away to the Lord.

"Were you glad to see them die, Arthur?"

"I was glad to see them at peace. I did everything possible to help them get well or at least be comfortable."

When there was no hope, no relief from pain, when old people became too weak to even whisper or moan, when the doctors and relatives agreed it would be a blessing if God took them, then, and only then, did he help them slip away.

If he had known that Anita Gillespie was looking forward to seeing her daughter, he would have waited.

It would have given him so much joy to know Mrs. Gillespie died happy.

That was the problem. She had been fighting death, not reconciled to it. That was why she had been too frightened to understand he was only trying to help her.

It was his concern for Glory that had made him so careless. He could remember the night the worry had begun. They were having dinner at home together, each reading a section of the newspaper, and Glory had cried, "Oh, dear God!" She was looking at the television page of the *Tribune* and had seen the announcement of the Senator Jennings program. It would include the highlights of her career. He had begged Glory not to be upset; he was sure it would be all right. But she hadn't listened. She'd started to sob. "Maybe it's better to face it," she'd said. "I don't want to live my life like this any longer."

Right then her attitude began to change. He stared ahead, heedlessly chewing on the popcorn. He had not been given the privilege of formally taking his vows. Instead, he had sworn them privately. Poverty, chastity, and obedience. Never once had he broken them—but he used to get so lonely. . . .

Then nine years ago he'd met Glory. She'd been sitting in the dreary waiting room of the clinic, clutching the Raggedy Ann doll and waiting her turn to see the psychiatrist. The doll was what had caught his attention. Something made him wait around outside for her.

They'd started walking toward the bus stop together. He'd explained he was a priest but had left parish work to work directly with the sick. She'd told

him all about herself, how she'd been in prison for a crime she didn't commit and she was on parole and lived in a furnished room. "I'm not allowed to smoke in my room," she told him, "or even have a hot plate so I can fix coffee or soup when I don't want to go out to the drugstore to eat."

They went for ice cream and it began to get dark. She said she was late and the woman where she lived would be angry. Then she started to cry and said she'd rather be dead than go back there. And he had taken her home with him. "You will be a child in my care," he'd told her. And she was like a helpless child. He gave her his bedroom and slept on the couch, and in the beginning she would just lie in bed and cry. For a few weeks the cops came around the clinic to see if she'd shown up again, but then they lost interest.

They'd gone to Baltimore. That was when he told her he was going to tell everyone that she was his daughter. "You call me Father anyhow," he said. And he had named her Gloria.

Slowly she had started to get better. But for nearly seven years she had left the apartment only at night; she was so sure that a policeman would recognize her.

He'd worked in different nursing homes around Baltimore, and then two years ago it was necessary to leave and they'd come to Alexandria. Glory loved being near Washington, but she was afraid she might run into people who knew her. He convinced her that was foolish. "None of the people from the Senator's office would ever come near this neighborhood." Even so, whenever Glory went out, she wore dark glasses. Gradually her spells of depression began to ease. She

needed less and less of the medicine he brought from the nursing home, and she'd gotten the typing job.

Arthur finished the popcorn. He would not leave Washington until tomorrow night, after he'd seen the program about Senator Jennings. He never helped people slip away until there was absolutely nothing the doctors could do for them, until his voices directed him that their time had come. Neither would he condemn Patricia Traymore without evidence. If she did not talk about Glory on the program or show her picture, Glory would be safe. He would arrange to meet her and they'd go away together.

But if Glory was exposed to the world as a thief, she would give herself up. This time she would die in prison. He was sure of it. He had seen enough people who had lost the will to live. But if it happened, Patricia Traymore would be punished for that terrible sin! He would go to the house where she lived and mete out justice to her.

Three Thousand N Street. Even the house where Patricia Traymore lived was a symbol of suffering and death.

The movie was ending. Where could he go now?

You must hide, Arthur.

"But where?" He realized he had spoken aloud. The woman in the seat ahead of him turned and glanced back.

Three Thousand N Street, the voices whispered. *Go there, Arthur. Go in the window again. Think about the closet.*

The image of the closet in the unused bedroom filled his mind. He would be warm and safe concealed behind the rows of shelves in that closet. The lights were on in the theater and he stood up quickly. He

must not draw attention to himself. He would go to another movie now and another after that. By then it would be dark. Where better to spend the hours until the broadcast tomorrow evening than in Patricia Traymore's own home? No one would dream of looking for him there.

She must have her chance to be exonerated, Arthur. You must not be too hasty. The words swirled in the air above his head. "I understand," he said. If there was no reference to Glory on the program, Patricia Traymore would never know that he had been staying with her. But if Glory was shown and identified, Patricia would be punished by the angels.

He would light the avenging torch.

29

At one o'clock Lila Thatcher's maid returned from grocery shopping. Lila was in her study working on a lecture she was planning to give the following week at the University of Maryland. The subject was "Harness Your Psychic Gift." Lila bent over the typewriter, her hands clasped.

The maid knocked on the door. "Miss Lila, you don't look too happy." The maid spoke with the comfortable familiarity of an employee who had become a trusted friend.

"I'm not, Ouida. For someone who's trying to teach people to use their psychic skills, my own are pretty scrambled today."

"I brought in the *Tribune*. Do you want to see it now?"

"Yes, I think so."

Five minutes later, in angry disbelief, Lila was reading the Gina Butterfield spread. Fifteen minutes later, she was ringing Pat's doorbell. With dismay she real-

ized Pat had been weeping. "There's something I have to show you," she explained.

They went into the library. Lila laid the paper on the table and opened it. She watched as Pat saw the headline and the color drained from her face.

Helplessly Pat skimmed the copy, glanced at the pictures. "My God, it makes me sound as though I was blabbing about the break-in, the Senator, this house, *everything*. Lila, I can't tell you how upset they'll all be. Luther Pelham had every single picture of my mother and father edited out of the old films. He didn't want any connection between the Senator and, I quote him, 'the Adams mess.' It's as though there's a force in action I can't stop. I don't know whether to try to explain, to resign or what." She tried to hold back angry tears.

Lila began to fold the newspaper. "I can't advise you about the job, but I can tell you that you must not look at this again, Kerry. I had to show it to you, but I'm taking it home with me. It's not wise for you to see yourself as you were that day, like a broken doll."

Pat grabbed the older woman's arm. "Why did you say that?"

"Say what? You mean why did I call you Kerry? That just slipped out."

"No, I mean why did you compare me to a broken doll?"

Lila stared at her and then looked down at the newspaper. "It's in here," she said. "I just read it. Look." In the lead column Gina Butterfield had reprinted some of the original *Tribune* story about the murder-suicide.

Police Chief Collins, commenting on the grisly
scene, said, "It's the worst I've ever come across.
When I saw that poor little kid like a broken doll,
I wondered why he hadn't shot her too. It would
have been easier for her."

"A broken doll," Pat whispered. "Whoever left it
knew me then."

"Left *what?* Pat, sit down. You look as though you're
going to faint. I'll get you a glass of water." Lila hurried from the room.

Pat leaned her head against the back of the couch
and closed her eyes. When she had looked up the
newspaper accounts of the tragedy, she had seen the
pictures of the bodies being carried out; of herself,
bandaged and bloody on the stretcher. But seeing
them juxtaposed against those of the smiling, apparently carefree young couples was worse. She didn't
remember reading that quote from the police chief.
Maybe she hadn't seen the issue in which it appeared.
But it proved that whoever had threatened her knew
who she was, had known her then.

Lila came back. She had filled a glass with cold water.

"I'm all right," Pat said. "Lila, the night someone
broke in here, he didn't just leave a note." She tugged
at the carton to try to get it out from under the library
table. It was wedged in so tightly that it wouldn't
budge. I can't believe I jammed it in like this, Pat
thought. As she struggled, she told Lila about finding
the doll.

Shocked, Lila absorbed what she was hearing. The
intruder had left a bloodied doll against the fireplace?

Pat was in danger here. She had sensed it all along. She was still in danger.

Pat freed the carton. She opened it, going through it rapidly. Lila watched as her expression changed from surprise to alarm. "Pat, what is it?"

"The doll. It's gone."

"Are you sure . . ."

"I put it here myself. I looked at it again just the other day. Lila, I took its apron off. It was sickening to look at. I shoved it way down. Maybe it's still here." Pat fished through the box. "Look, here it is."

Lila stared at the crumpled piece of white cotton, soiled with reddish-brown stains, the strings of the sash hanging limply from the sides.

"When was the last time you saw the doll?"

"Saturday afternoon. I had it out on the table. The Senator's chauffeur came with more of her photograph albums. I hid it in the carton again. I didn't want him to see it." Pat paused.

"Wait. There was something about Toby when he came in. He was brusque and kept eyeing everything in this room. I hadn't answered the bell right away and I think he wondered what I'd been up to. And then he said he'd let himself out. When I heard the door close, I decided to slide the bolt, and Lila, the door was opening again. Toby had something that looked like a credit card in his hand. He tried to pass it off by insinuating that he was just testing the lock for me, and that I should be sure to keep the bolt on.

"He knew me when I was little. Maybe he's the one who's been threatening me. But why?"

It was not yet midafternoon, but the day had turned gray and cloudy. The dark wood paneling and the

fading light made Pat seem small and vulnerable. "We must call the police immediately," Lila said. "They'll question the chauffeur."

"I can't do that. Can you imagine what the Senator would think? And it's only a possibility. But I do know someone who can have Toby investigated quietly." Pat saw the distress on Lila's face. "It's going to be all right," she assured her. "I'll keep the bolt on the door —and Lila, if everything that's happened is an attempt to stop the program, it's really too late. We're taping the Senator arriving home this evening. Tomorrow we do some in-studio scenes and tomorrow night it will be aired. After that there won't be any point in trying to scare me. And I'm beginning to think that's what this is about—just an attempt to scare me off."

Lila left a few minutes later. Pat had to be at the studio at four o'clock. She promised she would phone her Congressman friend—Sam Kingsley—and ask him to have the chauffeur investigated. To Lila's consternation, Pat insisted on keeping the newspaper. "I'll have to read it carefully and know exactly what it says. If you don't give me this, I'll go out and buy another one."

Lila's maid had the door open when she came up the steps. "I've been watching for you, Miss Lila," she explained. "You never finished your lunch and you looked real upset when you left."

"You've been watching for me, Ouida?" Lila went into the dining room and walked over to the windows facing the street. From there she could see the entire frontage and the right side of Pat's house and property. "It won't work," she murmured. "He broke in

through the patio doors and I can't see them from
here."

"What did you say, Miss Lila?"

"It's nothing. I'm going to keep a stillwatch and I
had thought of setting my typewriter on a table just
back from the windows."

"A stillwatch?"

"Yes, it's an expression that means if you believe
something is wrong, you keep a vigil."

"You think something is wrong at Miss Traymore's?
You think that prowler may come back again?"

Lila stared at the unnatural darkness surrounding
Pat's house. With an acute sense of foreboding she
answered somberly, "That's just what I think."

30

From the moment Father phoned her, Glory had been waiting for the police to come. At ten o'clock it happened. The door of the real estate office opened and a man in his mid-thirties came in. She looked up and saw a squad car parked out front. Her fingers dropped from the typewriter.

"Detective Barrott," the visitor said, and held up a badge. "I'd like to speak with Gloria Stevens. Is she here?"

Glory stood up. Already she could hear his questions: *Isn't your real name Eleanor Brown? Why did you violate parole? How long did you think you could get away with it?*

Detective Barrott came over to her. He had a frank, chubby face with sandy hair that curled around his ears. His eyes were inquisitive but not unfriendly. She realized he was about her own age, and somehow he seemed a little less frightening than the scornful detective who had questioned her after the money was found in her storage room.

"Miss Stevens? Don't be nervous. I wonder if I could speak to you privately?"

"We could go in here." She led the way into Mr. Schuller's small private office. There were two leather chairs in front of Mr. Schuller's desk. She sat in one of them and the detective settled in the other.

"You looked scared," he said kindly. "You have nothing to worry about. We just want to talk to your dad. Do you know where we can reach him?"

Talk to her dad. Father! She swallowed. "When I left for work he was home. He probably went to the bakery."

"He didn't come back. Maybe when he saw the police car in front of your house, he decided not to. Do you think he might be with some relatives or friends?"

"I . . . I don't know. Why do you want to talk to him?"

"Just to ask a few questions. By any chance has he called you this morning?"

This man thought Arthur was her father. He wasn't interested in her.

"He . . . he did call. But I was on the phone with my boss."

"What did he want?"

"He . . . wanted me to meet him and I said I couldn't."

"Where did he want you to meet him?"

Father's words rang in her ears. *Metro Central . . . Twelfth and G exit . . .* Was he there now? Was he in trouble? Father had taken care of her all these years. She could not hurt him now.

She chose her words carefully. "I couldn't stay on the phone. I . . . I just said I couldn't leave the office

and practically hung up on him. Why do you want to talk to him? What's wrong?"

"Well, maybe nothing." The detective's voice was kind. "Does your dad talk to you about his patients?"

"Yes." It was easy to answer that question. "He cares so much about them."

"Has he ever mentioned Mrs. Gillespie to you?"

"Yes. She died last week, didn't she? He felt so bad. Something about her daughter coming to visit her." She thought about the way he had cried out in his sleep, "Close your eyes, Mrs. Gillespie. Close your eyes." Maybe he had made a mistake when he was helping Mrs. Gillespie and they were blaming him for it.

"Has he seemed different lately—nervous or anything like that?"

"He is the kindest man I know. His whole life is devoted to helping people. In fact, they just asked him at the nursing home to go to Tennessee and help out there."

The detective smiled. "How old are you, Miss Stevens?"

"Thirty-four."

He looked surprised. "You don't look it. According to the employment records, Arthur Stevens is forty-nine." He paused, then in a friendly voice added, "He's not your real father, is he?"

Soon he would be pinning her down with questions. "He used to be a parish priest but decided to spend his whole life caring for the sick. When I was very ill and had no one, he took me in."

Now he would ask her real name. But he didn't.

"I see. Miss . . . Miss Stevens, we do want to talk

to, er . . . Father Stevens. If he calls you, will you contact me?" He gave her his card. DETECTIVE WILLIAM BARROTT. She could sense him studying her. Why wasn't he asking her more questions about herself, about her background?

He was gone. She sat alone in the private office until Opal came in.

"Gloria, is anything wrong?"

Opal was a good friend, the best friend she'd ever had. Opal had helped her think of herself as a woman again. Opal was always after her to go to parties, saying her boyfriend would fix her up with a blind date. She'd always refused.

"Gloria, what's wrong?" Opal repeated. "You look terrible."

"No, nothing's wrong. I have a headache. Do you think I could go home?"

"Sure; I'll finish your typing. Gloria, if there's anything I can do . . ."

Glory looked into her friend's troubled face. "Not anymore, but thank you for everything."

She walked home. The temperature was in the forties, but even so, the day was raw with a chill that penetrated her coat and gloves. The apartment, with its shabby, rented furniture, seemed strangely empty, as though it sensed they would not be returning. She went to the hall closet and found the battered black suitcase that Father had bought at a garage sale. She packed her meager supply of clothing, her cosmetics and the new book Opal had given her for Christmas. The suitcase wasn't large, and it was hard to force the locks to snap.

There was something else—her Raggedy Ann doll.

At the mental-health clinic the psychiatrist had asked her to draw a picture of how she felt about herself, but somehow she couldn't do that. The doll was with some others on a shelf, and he had given it to her. "Do you think you could show me how this doll would look if it were you?"

It hadn't been hard to paint the tears and to sketch in the frightened look about the eyes and to change the thrust of the mouth so that instead of smiling it seemed about to scream.

"That bad?" the doctor had said when she was finished.

"Worse."

Oh, Father, she thought, I wish I could stay here and wait until you call me. But they're going to find out about me. That detective is probably having me checked right now. I can't run away anymore. While I have the courage, I have to turn myself in. Maybe it will help me get a lighter sentence for breaking parole.

There was one promise she could keep. Miss Langley had begged her to call that television celebrity Patricia Traymore before she did anything. Now she made the call, told what she planned and listened impassively to Pat's emotional pleading.

Finally at three o'clock she left. A car was parked down the street. Two men were sitting in it. "That's the girl," one of them said. "She was lying about not planning to meet Stevens." He sounded regretful.

The other man pressed his foot on the pedal. "I told you she was holding back on you. Ten bucks she'll lead us to Stevens now."

31

Pat sped across town to the Lotus Inn Restaurant on Wisconsin Avenue. Desperately she tried to think of some way she could persuade Eleanor Brown not to surrender herself yet. Surely she could be persuaded to listen to reason.

She had tried to reach Sam, but after five rings had slammed down the phone and run out. Now as she rushed into the restaurant she wondered if she would recognize the girl from her high school picture. Was she using her own name? Probably not.

The hostess greeted her. "Are you Miss Traymore?"

"Yes, I am."

"Miss Brown is waiting for you."

She was sitting at a rear table sipping chablis. Pat slipped into the chair opposite her, trying to collect herself to know what to say. Eleanor Brown had not changed very much from her high school picture. She was obviously older, no longer painfully thin and prettier than Pat had expected, but there was no mistaking her.

She spoke softly. "Miss Traymore? Thank you for coming."

"Eleanor, please listen to me. We can get you a lawyer. You can be out on bail while we work something out. You were in the midst of a breakdown when you violated parole. There are so many angles a good lawyer can work."

The waiter came with an appetizer of butterfly shrimp. "I used to dream of these," Eleanor said. "Do you want to order something?"

"No. Nothing. Eleanor, did you understand what I said?"

"Yes, I did." Eleanor dipped one of the shrimp in the sweet sauce. "Oh, that's good." Her face was pale but determined. "Miss Traymore, I hope I can get my parole reinstated, but if I can't, I know I'm strong enough now to serve the time they gave me. I can sleep in a cell, and wear a prison uniform, and eat that slop they call food, and put up with the strip searches and the boredom. When I get out I won't have to hide anymore, and I'm going to spend the rest of my life trying to prove my innocence."

"Eleanor, wasn't the money found in your possession?"

"Miss Traymore, half the people in the office knew about that storeroom. When I moved from one apartment to the other, six or eight of them helped. We made a party of it. The furniture I couldn't use was carried down to the storage room. *Some* of the money was found there, but seventy thousand dollars went into someone else's pocket."

"Eleanor, you claim Toby phoned you and he said

he didn't. Didn't you think it unusual to be asked to go to the campaign office on Sunday?"

Eleanor pushed aside the shells on her plate. "No. You see the Senator was up for reelection. A lot of mailings were sent from the campaign office. She used to drop by and help just to make the volunteers feel important. When she did that she would take off her big diamond ring. It was a little loose and she really was careless with it. A couple of times she left without it."

"And Toby or someone sounding like Toby said she'd lost or mislaid it again."

"Yes. I knew she'd been in the campaign office on Saturday helping with the mailings, so it sounded perfectly natural that she might have forgotten it again and one of the senior aides might have put it in the safe for her.

"I believe Toby was driving the Senator at the time the call was made. The voice was muffled and whoever spoke to me didn't say much. It was something like, 'See if the Senator's ring is in the campaign safe and let her know.' I was annoyed because I wanted to go to Richmond to sketch and I even said something like 'she'll probably find it under her nose.' Whoever it was who phoned sort of laughed and hung up. If Abigail Jennings hadn't talked so much about the second chance she had given me, called me a convicted thief, I would have had a better chance of reasonable doubt. I've lost eleven years of my life for something I didn't do and I'm not losing another day." She stood up and laid money on the table. "That should cover everything." Bending down, she picked up her suitcase, then paused. "You know what's hardest for me now?

I'm breaking my promise to the man I've been living with, and he's been so good to me. He begged me not to go to the police yet. I wish I could explain to him, but I don't know where he is."

"Can I call him for you later? What's his name? Where does he work?"

"His name is Arthur Stevens. I think there's some problem at his job. He won't be there. There's nothing you can do. I hope your program is very successful, Miss Traymore. I was terribly upset when I read the announcement about it. I knew that if even one picture of me was shown I'd be in jail within twenty-four hours. But you know, that made me realize how tired I was of running. In a crazy way, it gave me the courage to face going back to prison so that someday I really will be free. Father, I mean Arthur Stevens, just couldn't accept that. And now I'd better go before I run out of courage."

Helplessly Pat watched her retreating back.

As Eleanor left the restaurant two men at a corner table got up and followed her out.

32

"Abby, it's not as bad as it could be." In the forty years he had known her, it was only the third time he had had his arms around her. She was sobbing helplessly.

"Why didn't you tell me she was staying in that house?"

"There was no reason to."

They were in Abigail's living room. He'd shown her the article when they arrived, then tried to calm the inevitable explosion.

"Abby, tomorrow this newspaper will be lining garbage cans."

"I don't want to line garbage cans!" she'd screamed.

He poured a straight Scotch and made her drink it. "Come on, Senator, pull yourself together. Maybe there's a photographer hiding in the bushes."

"Shut up, you bloody fool." But the suggestion had been enough to shock her. And after the drink, she'd started to cry. "Toby, it looks like the old penny-

dreadful scandal sheets. And that picture. Toby, *that picture.*" She didn't mean the one of her and Francey.

He put his arms around her, clumsily patted her back and realized with the dullness of a long-accepted pain that he was nothing more to her than a railing to grab when your feet gave way underneath you.

"If anyone really studies the pictures! Toby, look at *that* one."

"Nobody's going to bother."

"Toby, that girl—that Pat Traymore. How did she happen to lease that house? It can't be a coincidence."

"The house has been rented to twelve different tenants in the past twenty-four years. She's just another one of them." Toby tried to make his voice hearty. He didn't believe that; but on the other hand, Phil still hadn't been able to uncover the details of the rental. "Senator, you gotta hang in there. Whoever made those threats to Pat Traymore . . ."

"Toby, *how do we know there were threats?* How do we know this isn't a calculated attempt to embarrass me?"

He was so startled he stepped back. In a reflex action she pulled away from him, and they stared at each other. "God Almighty, Abby, do you think she *engineered* this?"

The ring of the telephone made them both jump. He looked at her. "You want me . . ."

"Yes." She held her hands up to her face. "I don't give a goddamn who's calling. I'm not here."

"Senator Jennings' residence." Toby put on his butler's voice. "May I take a message for the Senator? She's not available at the moment." He winked at Abby and was rewarded by the trace of a smile. "The President. . . . Oh, just a minute, sir." He held his

hand over the mouthpiece. "Abby, the President is calling you. . . ."

"Toby, don't you dare . . ."

"Abby, for chrissake, it's the *President!*"

She clasped her hands to her lips, then came over and took the phone from him. "If this is your idea of a joke . . ." She got on. "Abigail Jennings."

Toby watched as her expression changed. "Mr. President. I'm so sorry. . . . I'm sorry . . . Some reading . . . That's why I left word. . . . I'm sorry. . . . Yes, sir, of course. Yes, I can be at the White House tomorrow evening . . . eight-thirty, of course. Yes, we've been quite busy with this program. Frankly, I'm not comfortable being the subject of this sort of thing. . . . Why, how kind of you. . . . Sir, you mean . . . I simply don't know what to say. . . . Of course, I understand. . . . Thank you, sir."

She hung up. Dazed, she looked at Toby. "I'm not to tell a soul. He's announcing his appointment of me tomorrow night after the program. He said it isn't a bad idea the whole country gets to know me a little better. He laughed about the *Mirror* cover. He said his mother was a big gal too, but that I'm much prettier now than when I was seventeen. Toby, I'm going to be Vice President of the United States!" She laughed hysterically and flung herself at him.

"Abby, you *did* it!" He lifted her off her feet.

An instant later her face twisted with tension. "Toby, nothing can happen . . . Nothing must stop this. . . ."

He put her down and covered both her hands in his. "Abby, I *swear* nothing will keep this from you."

She started to laugh and then began to cry. "Toby,

I'm on a roller coaster. You and that damn Scotch. You know I can't drink. Toby—*Vice President!*"

He had to ease her down. His voice soothing, he said, "Later on we'll take a ride over and just kind of cruise past your new house, Abby. You're finally getting a mansion. Next stop Massachusetts Avenue."

"Toby, shut up. Just make me a cup of tea. I'm going to take a shower and try to collect myself. Vice President! My God, my God!"

He put the kettle on and then, not bothering with a coat, walked to the roadside mailbox and flipped it open. The usual collection of junk—coupons, contests, "You may have won two million dollars". . . . Ninety-nine percent of Abby's personal mail went through the office.

Then he saw it. The blue envelope with the handwritten address. A personal note to Abby. He looked at the upper left-hand corner and felt the blood drain from his face.

The note was from Catherine Graney.

33

Sam drove across town on 7th Street, already a little late for his noon appointment with Larry Saggiotes of the National Transportation Safety Board.

After he left Pat, he'd gone home and lain awake most of the night, his emotions shifting from anger to a sober examination of Pat's charges.

"Can I help you, sir?"

"What? Oh, sorry." Sheepishly Sam realized he'd been so deep in thought, he had arrived in the lobby of the FAA building without realizing he had come through the revolving door. The security guard was looking at him curiously.

He went up to the eighth floor and gave his name to the receptionist. "It will be just a few minutes," she said.

Sam settled into a chair. Had Abigail and Willard Jennings been having a violent argument that last day? he wondered. But that didn't have to mean anything. He remembered there were times when he'd threatened to quit Congress, to get a job that would provide

some of the luxuries that Janice deserved. She'd argued with him and stormed at him, and anyone who heard them would have thought they couldn't stand each other. Maybe the pilot's widow did hear Abigail arguing with Willard Jennings that day. Maybe Willard was disgusted about something and ready to give up politics and she didn't want him burning his bridges.

Sam had called his FBI friend Jack Carlson to trace the report of the crash.

"Twenty-seven years ago? That could be a tough one," Jack had said. "The National Transportation Safety Board handles investigations into crashes now, but that many years ago the Civil Aeronautics Administration was in charge. Let me call you back."

At nine-thirty Jack had phoned back. "You're in luck," he'd said laconically. "Most records are shredded after ten years, but when prominent people are involved, the investigation reports are stored in the Safety Board warehouse. They've got the data on accidents involving everyone from Amelia Earhart and Carole Lombard to Dag Hammarskjöld and Hale Boggs. My contact at the board is Larry Saggiotes. He'll get the report sent to his office, look it over. He suggests you come by about noon. He'll review it with you."

"Excuse me, sir. Mr. Saggiotes will see you now."

Sam looked up. He had a feeling the receptionist had been trying to get his attention. I'd better get with it, he thought. He followed her down the corridor.

Larry Saggiotes was a big man whose features and coloring reflected his Greek heritage. They exchanged greetings. Sam gave a carefully edited explanation of why he'd wanted to investigate the crash.

Larry settled back in his chair, frowning. "Nice day here, isn't it?" he commented. "But it's foggy in New York, icy in Minneapolis, pouring in Dallas. Yet in the next twenty-four hours one hundred twenty thousand commercial, military and private planes will take off and land in this country. And the odds against any of them crashing are astronomical. That's why when a plane that's been checked out by an expert mechanic and flown by a master pilot on a day with good visibility suddenly crashes into a mountain and is scattered over two square miles of rocky landscape, we're not happy."

"The Jennings plane!"

"The Jennings plane," Larry confirmed. "I've just read the report. What happened? We don't know. The last contact with George Graney was when he left traffic control in Richmond. There was no suggestion of trouble. It was a routine two-hour flight. And then he was overdue."

"And the verdict was pilot error?" Sam asked.

"*Probable* cause, pilot error. It always ends up like that when we can't come up with other answers. It was a fairly new Cessna twin-engine, so their engineers were around to prove the plane was in great shape. Willard Jennings' widow cried her eyes out about how she'd had a horror of small charter planes, that her husband had complained about rough landings with Graney."

"Did the possibility of foul play ever come up?"

"Congressman, the possibility of foul play is *always* investigated in a case like this. First we look for how it might have been done. Well, there are plenty of ways that are pretty hard to trace. For example, with all the

magnetic tape being used today, a strong magnet hidden in the cockpit could screw up all the instruments. Twenty-seven years ago that wouldn't have happened. But if anybody had fooled with the generator of Graney's plane, maybe, frayed or cut a wire, Graney would have had a complete loss of power right as he's flying over a mountain. The chances of recovering usable evidence would have been negligible.

"The fuel switch would be another possibility. That plane had two tanks. The pilot switched to the second tank when the first tank's needle indicated it was empty. Suppose the switch wasn't working? He wouldn't have had a chance to use the second tank. Then, of course, we have corrosive acid. Somebody who doesn't want a plane to make it safely could have put a leaky container of the stuff on board. It could be in the luggage area, under a seat—wouldn't matter. That would eat through the cables within half an hour and there'd be no controlling the plane. But that would be easier to discover."

"Did any of this come up at the hearing?" Sam asked.

"There weren't enough pieces of that plane recovered to play Pick Up Sticks. So the next thing we do is look for motive. And found absolutely none. Graney's charter line was doing well; he hadn't taken out any recent insurance. The Congressman was so poorly insured it was amazing, but when you have family dough, you don't need insurance, I guess. Incidentally, this is the second request I've had for a copy of the report. Mrs. George Graney came in for one last week."

"Larry, if it's at all possible, I'm trying to keep Sena-

tor Jennings from being embarrassed by having this rehashed—and of course I'll study the report myself, but let me get this straight: was there any suggestion that George Graney was an inexperienced or careless pilot?"

"Absolutely none. He had an impeccable record, Congressman. He had been in air combat through the Korean War, then worked for United for a couple of years. This kind of flying was child's play to him."

"How about his equipment?"

"Always in top shape. His mechanics were good."

"So the pilot's widow has a valid reason to be upset that the blame for the crash got laid at George Graney's doorstep."

Larry blew a smoke ring the size of a cruller. "You bet she does—*more* than valid."

34

At ten minutes past four, Pat managed to reach Sam from the lobby of the Potomac Cable Network building. Without mentioning their quarrel, she told him about Eleanor Brown. "I couldn't stop her. She was determined to turn herself in."

"Calm down, Pat. I'll send a lawyer to see her. How long will you be at the network?"

"I don't know. Have you seen the *Tribune* today?"

"Just the headlines."

"Read the second section. A columnist I met the other night heard where I lived and rehashed everything."

"Pat, I'll be here. Come over when you finish at the network."

Luther was waiting for her in his office. She had expected to be treated as a pariah. Instead, he was fairly restrained. "The Apple Junction shooting went well," he told her. "It snowed there yesterday and that whole cruddy backwoods looked like the American

dream. We caught the Saunders house, the high school with the crèche in front and Main Street with its Christmas tree. We put a sign in front of the town hall: 'Apple Junction, Birthplace of Senator Abigail Foster Jennings.' "

Luther puffed on a cigarette. "That old lady, Margaret Langley, was a good interview. Kind of classy-looking and quaint. Nice touch having her talk about what a dedicated student the Senator was and showing the yearbook."

Pat realized that somehow it had become *Luther's* idea to do background shots in Apple Junction. "Have you seen the footage from last night and this morning?" she asked.

"Yes. It's okay. You might have gotten a little more of Abigail actually working at her desk. The sequence at Christmas dinner was fine."

"Surely you've seen today's *Tribune?*"

"Yes." Luther ground his cigarette into the ashtray and reached for another one. His voice changed. Telltale red spots appeared in his cheeks. "Pat, would you mind laying your cards on the table and explaining why you gave out that story?"

"Why I *what?*"

Now the restraint in Luther's manner disappeared. "Maybe a lot of people would consider it coincidence that so much has happened this week to give the Senator sensational publicity. I happen not to believe in coincidence. I agree with what Abigail said after that first picture came out in the *Mirror*. You've been out from day one to force us to produce this program *your* way. And I think you've used every trick in the books to get personal publicity for yourself. There isn't any-

one in Washington who isn't talking about Pat Traymore."

"If you believe that, you ought to fire me."

"And give you more headlines? No way. But just as a
matter of curiosity, will you answer a few questions for
me?"

"Go ahead."

"The first day in this office, I told you to edit out any
reference to Congressman Adams and his wife. Did
you know you were renting their house?"

"Yes, I did."

"Wouldn't it have been natural to mention it?"

"I don't think so. I certainly edited out every single
picture of them from the Senator's material—and incidentally, I did a damn good job of it. Have you run
through all those films?"

"Yes. You did do a good job. Then suppose you tell
me your reasoning for the threats. Anyone who knows
the business would realize that whether or not you
worked on the program it was going to be completed."

Pat chose her words carefully. "I think the threats
were just that—*threats*. I don't think anyone ever
meant to harm me, just scare me off. I think that someone is afraid to have the program made and thought
that if I didn't do it the project would be dropped."
She paused, then added deliberately, "That person
couldn't know I'm just a figurehead in a campaign to
make Abigail Jennings Vice President."

"Are you trying to insinuate . . . ?"

"No, not insinuate: state. Look, I fell for it. I fell for
being hired so fast, for being rushed down here to do
three months' work in a week, for having the material
for the program spoon-fed to me by you and the Sena-

tor. The little claim this program will have to being an honest documentary is because of the segments I had to force down your throats. It's only because of the rotten publicity I've inadvertently caused Abigail Jennings that I'm going to do my best to make this program work for her. But I warn you, when it's over, there are some things I intend to investigate."

"Such as . . . ?"

"Such as Eleanor Brown, the girl who was convicted of embezzling the campaign funds. I saw her today. She was about to turn herself in to the police. And she swears she never touched that money."

"Eleanor Brown turned herself in?" Luther interrupted. "We can make a plus out of that. As a parole violater, she won't get bail."

"Congressman Kingsley is trying to have bail set."

"That's a mistake. I'll see that she stays put until the President makes his appointment. After that, who cares? She had a fair trial. We'll talk about the case on the program just as we've written it, only we'll add the fact that because of the program she turned herself in. That'll spike her guns if she wants to make trouble."

Pat felt that somehow she had betrayed her trust. "I happen to think that girl is innocent, and if she is, I'll fight to get her a new trial."

"She's guilty," Luther snapped. "Otherwise why did she break parole? She's probably gone through that seventy thousand bucks now and wants to be able to stop running. Don't forget: a panel of jurors convicted her unanimously. You still believe in the jury system, I hope? Now, is there anything else? Any single thing that you know that could reflect badly on the Senator?"

She told him about Catherine Graney.

"So she's talking about suing the network?" Luther looked immensely pleased. "And you're worried about that?"

"If she starts gossiping about the Jennings marriage . . . the very fact that the Senator wasn't left a penny by her mother-in-law. . . ."

"Abigail will have the wholehearted support of every woman in America who's put up with a miserable mother-in-law. As far as the Jennings marriage goes, it's this Graney woman's word against the Senator and Toby . . . don't forget he was a witness to their last time together. And what about the letter you gave me that the Senator wrote to her husband? That's dated only a few days before he died."

"We *assume* that. Someone else could point out that she never filled in the *year.*"

"She can fill it in now if necessary. Anything else?"

"To the best of my knowledge those are the only two places where the Senator might have unfavorable publicity. I'm prepared to give my word of honor on that."

"All right." Luther seemed appeased. "I'm taking a crew to tape the Senator going into her home this evening—that end-of-the-day working scene."

"Don't you want me at that taping?"

"I want you as far away from Abigail Jennings as you can get until she has time to calm down. Pat, have you read your contract with this network carefully?"

"I think so."

"Then you do realize we have the right to cancel your employment here for a specified cash settlement? Frankly, I don't buy the cock-and-bull story that some-

one is trying to keep this program from being made. But I almost admire you for having made yourself a household word in Washington, and you've done it by piggybacking onto a woman who's dedicated her whole life to public service."

"Have *you* read my contract?" Pat asked.

"I wrote it."

"Then you do know you gave me creative control of the projects to which I'm assigned. Do you think you've fulfilled my contract this week?" She opened the door of Luther's office, sure that everyone in the newsroom was listening to them.

Luther's last words echoed through the room: "By this time next week the terms of your contract will be moot."

It was one of the few times in her life that Pat slammed a door.

Fifteen minutes later she was giving her name to the desk clerk in Sam's apartment building.

Sam was waiting in the hallway when the elevator stopped at his floor. "Pat, you look bushed," he told her.

"I am." Wearily she looked up at him. He was wearing the same Argyle sweater he'd had on the night before. With a stab of pain she noted again how it brought out the blueness of his eyes. He took her arm and they walked down the long corridor.

Inside the apartment, her immediate impression was surprise at the decor. Charcoal gray sectional furniture was grouped in the center of the room. The walls had a number of good prints and a few first-class

paintings. The carpet was wall-to-wall in a tweedy gray-black-and-white combination.

Somehow in Sam's home she'd expected a more traditional look—a couch with arms, easy chairs, family pieces. An Oriental, however worn, would have been a distinct improvement over the carpet. He asked her what she thought of the place and she told him.

Sam's eyes crinkled. "You sure know how to get invited back, don't you? You're right, of course. I wanted to make a clean sweep, start over, and naturally outdid myself. I agree. This place does look like a motel lobby."

"Then why stay here? I gather you have other options."

"Oh, the apartment is fine," Sam said easily. "It's just the furniture that bugs me. I rang out the old but didn't know exactly what the new was supposed to be."

It was a half-joking statement that suddenly assumed too much weight. "By any chance, do you have a Scotch for a tired lady?" she asked.

"Sure do." He went over to the bar. "Lots of soda, one ice cube, twist of lemon if possible, but don't worry if you're out of lemon." He smiled.

"I'm sure I don't sound that wimpy."

"Not wimpy, just considerate." He mixed the drinks and placed them on the cocktail table. "Sit down and don't be so fidgety. How did the studio go?"

"By this time next week I probably won't have a job. You see, Luther really thinks I'm pulling all this as a publicity stunt and he rather admires my moxie for trying it."

"I think Abigail has somewhat the same view."

Pat raised an eyebrow. "I'm sure you'd be the first to know. Sam, I hardly expected to call you so quickly after last night. In fact, my guess would have been a nice three-month cooling-off period before we met as disinterested friends. But I do need some help fast, and I certainly can't look to Luther Pelham for it. So I'm afraid you're elected."

"Not exactly the reason I'd choose to hear from you, but I'm glad to be of service."

Sam was different today. She could feel it. It was as though that vacillating aimlessness were missing. "Sam, there was something else about the break-in." As calmly as possible, she told him about the Raggedy Ann doll. "And now the doll is gone."

"Pat, are you telling me that someone has been back in your house without you knowing it?"

"Yes."

"Then you're not going to spend another minute there."

Restlessly she got up and walked over to the window. "That isn't the answer. Sam, in a crazy way the fact that the doll is gone is almost reassuring. I don't think whoever has been threatening me really intends to hurt me. Otherwise he certainly would have done it. I think he's afraid of what the program might do to *him*. And I've got some ideas." Quickly she explained her analysis of the Eleanor Brown case. "If Eleanor Brown wasn't lying, Toby was. If Toby was lying, the Senator was covering up for him, and that seems incredible. But suppose another person was involved who could imitate Toby's voice, who knew about Eleanor's storeroom and planted just enough of the money to make her look guilty?"

"How do you explain the doll and the threats?"

"I think someone who knew me when I was little, and may have recognized me, is trying to scare me and stop this program. Sam, what do you make of this? *Toby* knew me when I was little. Toby has become truly hostile toward me. I thought at first it was because of the Senator and all the bad publicity, but the other day he kept eyeing the library as though he was casing it. And after he left, he let himself back in. He didn't realize I intended to follow him to slide the safety bolt. He tried to say he was just testing the lock and that anyone could get in and I should be careful. I fell for that—but Sam, I really am nervous about him. Could you have him checked out and see if he's ever been in trouble? I mean real trouble?"

"Yes, I can. I never liked that bird myself." He came up behind her, put his arms around her waist. In an instinctive reaction she leaned back against him. "I've missed you, Pat."

"Since last night?"

"No, since two years ago."

"You could have fooled me." For a moment she gave herself up to the sheer joy of being close to him; then she turned and faced him. "Sam, a little residual affection doesn't add up to what I want. So why don't you just . . ."

His arms were tight around her. His lips were no longer tentative. "I'm fresh out of residual affection."

For long moments they stood there, silhouetted against the window.

Finally Pat stepped back. Sam let her go. They looked at each other. "Pat," he said, "everything you said last night was true except one thing. There is

absolutely nothing between Abigail and me. Can you give me a little time to find myself again? I didn't know until I saw you this week that I've been functioning like a zombie."

She tried to smile. "You seem to forget, I need some time too. Memory Lane isn't as simple as I expected it to be."

"Do you think you're getting honest impressions of that night?"

"Honest, perhaps, but not particularly desirable. I'm beginning to believe my mother may have been the one who went crazy that night, and somehow that's harder."

"Why do you think that?"

"It's not why I *think* it, but why she may have snapped that interests me now. Well, one more day and 'The Life and Times of Abigail Jennings' will be presented to the world. And at that point I start doing some real investigating. I just wish to God this whole thing wasn't so rushed. Sam, there's too much that doesn't hang together. And I don't care what Luther Pelham thinks. That segment about the plane crash is going to blow up in Abigail's face. Catherine Graney means business."

She declined his invitation to dinner. "This has been a grueling day. I was up at four o'clock to get ready for the Senator's office, and tomorrow we finish taping. I'm going to fix a sandwich and be in bed by nine o'clock."

At the door, he held her once more. "When I'm seventy, you'll be forty-nine."

"And when you're one hundred and three, I'll be

eighty-two. You'll get a trace on Toby and you'll let me know when you hear anything about Eleanor Brown?"

"Of course."

When Pat left, Sam phoned Jack Carlson and quickly told him what Pat had confided.

Jack whistled. "You mean that guy's been back? Sam, you really have a loony. Sure we can check this Toby character, but do me a favor. Get me a sample of his handwriting, can you?"

35

Detective Barrott was kind. He believed she was telling the truth. But the older detective was hostile. Over and over Eleanor answered the same questions from him.

How could she tell them where she was keeping seventy thousand dollars that she'd never even seen?

Was she angry at Patricia Traymore for preparing the program that might force her out of hiding? No, of course not. At first she was afraid and then she knew she couldn't hide anymore, that she'd be glad if it were over.

Did she know where Patricia Traymore lived? Yes, Father had told her that Patricia Traymore lived in the Adams house in Georgetown. He'd shown her that house once. He'd been on the ambulance squad of Georgetown Hospital when that awful tragedy had happened. Break into that house? Of course not. How could she?

In the cell she sat on the edge of the bunk wondering how she could have thought she was strong

enough to go back into this world. The steel bars and the insulting intimacy of the open toilet, the sense of entrapment, the haunting depression that like a black fog was beginning to envelop her.

She lay on the bunk and wondered where Father had gone. It was impossible that they seemed to be suggesting he would deliberately hurt anyone. He was the kindest man she had ever known. But he had been terribly nervous after Mrs. Gillespie died.

She hoped he wouldn't be angry that she had given herself up. They would have arrested her anyway. She was sure Detective Barrott was planning to investigate her.

Had Father gone away? Probably. With growing concern Eleanor thought of the many times he had changed jobs. Where was he now?

Arthur had an early dinner in a cafeteria on 14th Street. He chose beef stew, lemon meringue pie and coffee. He ate slowly and carefully. It was important that he eat well now. It might be days before he had a hot meal again.

His plans were made. After dark he would go back to Patricia Traymore's house. He'd slip in through the upstairs window. He'd settle himself in the closet in the guest room. He'd bring cans of soda; he still had one of the Danish pastries and two of the rolls from this morning in his pocket. He'd better pick up some cans of juice too. And maybe he should get some peanut butter and rye bread. That would be enough to hold him over until he saw the program the next night.

He had to spend ninety of his precious dollars on a miniature black-and-white TV with a headset. That

way he could watch the program right in Patricia Traymore's house.

On the way to her house, he'd buy caffeine pills in the drugstore. He couldn't take the chance of crying out in his sleep. Oh, she'd probably never hear him from her room, but he couldn't risk it.

Forty minutes later he was in Georgetown, two streets from Patricia Traymore's home. The whole area was quiet, more quiet than he would have liked. Now that the Christmas shopping was over, a stranger was more likely to be noticed. The police might even be keeping a watch on Miss Traymore's house. But the fact that she had the corner property helped. The house behind hers was dark.

Arthur slipped into the yard of the unlighted house. The wooden fence that separated the backyards wasn't high. He dropped his shopping bag over the fence, making sure that it slid down onto a snowbank, and then easily climbed over.

He waited. There wasn't a sound. Miss Traymore's car wasn't in the driveway. Her house was totally dark.

It was awkward getting up the tree with the shopping bag. The trunk was icy and hard to grasp; he could feel its rough coldness through his gloves. Without the tiers of branches, he could not have made it. The window was stiff and hard to raise. When he stepped over the sill into the room, the floorboards creaked heavily.

For agonizing minutes he waited by the window, ready to bolt out again, to clamber down the tree and run across the yard. But there was only silence in the house. That and the occasional rumble of the furnace.

He began to organize his hiding place in the closet.

To his satisfaction he realized that the shelves were not attached to the walls. If he spread them out just a little, they would look as though they were touching the walls and no one would realize how much space he had in the triangular area behind him.

Carefully he began to set up his secret place. He selected a thick quilt and laid it on the floor. It was large enough to use as a sleeping bag. He set up his supplies of food and his television set. There were four king-size pillows on the lowest shelf.

In a few minutes he was settled. Now he needed to explore.

Unfortunately, she hadn't left any lights on. It meant he could move around only by holding his flashlight very low to the floor so no gleam could show out the window. Several times he practiced going back and forth between the guest bedroom and the master suite. He tested the floorboards and found the one that creaked.

It took him twelve seconds to make his way down the hall from his closet to Pat's room. He crept into her room and over to the vanity table. He had never seen such pretty objects. Her comb and mirror and brushes were all decorated with ornate silver. He took the stopper from the perfume bottle and inhaled the subtle fragrance.

Then he went into the bathroom, noticed her negligee on the back of the door and tentatively touched it. Angrily he thought that this was the kind of clothing Glory would enjoy.

Had the police gone to Glory's office to question her? She should be home now. He wanted to talk to her.

He made his way over to the bed, found the phone on the night table and dialed. After the fourth ring he began to frown. She had talked about turning herself in to the police, but she would never do that after having promised she'd wait. No, she was probably lying in bed, trembling, waiting to see if her picture was shown on the program tomorrow night.

He replaced the phone on the night table but sat crouched by Pat's bed. Already he missed Glory. He was keenly aware of the solitary quiet of the house. But he knew that soon his voices would come to join him.

36

"That was fine, Senator," Luther said. "Sorry I had to ask you to change. But we did want the look of a single working day, so you had to be wearing the same outfit coming home as going out."

"It's all right. I should have realized that," Abigail said shortly.

They were in her living room. The camera crew were packing their equipment. Toby could see that Abigail had no intention of offering Pelham a drink. She just wanted to be rid of him.

Luther was obviously getting the message. "Hurry up," he snapped at the crew. Then he smiled ingratiatingly. "I know it's been a long day for you, Abigail. Just one more session in the studio tomorrow morning and we'll wrap it up."

"That will be the happiest moment in my life."

Toby wished Abigail could relax. They'd gone for a drive and passed the Vice President's mansion a couple of times. Abby had even joked about it: "Can you imagine what the columnists would say if they saw me

casing the place?" But as soon as the camera crew arrived, she'd tensed up again.

Pelham was putting on his coat. "The President has called a news conference for nine P.M. in the East Room tomorrow night. Are you planning to be there, Abigail?"

"I believe I've been invited," she said.

"That makes our timing excellent. The program will run between six-thirty and seven, so there won't be a schedule conflict for the viewers."

"I'm sure all of Washington is fainting with anticipation," Abigail said. "Luther, I really am terribly tired."

"Of course. Forgive me. I'll see you in the morning. Nine o'clock, if that's all right."

"One minute more and I'd have gone mad," Abigail said when she and Toby were finally alone. "And when I think all this is absolutely unnecessary . . ."

"No, it's not unnecessary, Senator," Toby said soothingly. "You still have to be confirmed by Congress. Sure, you'll get a majority, but it would be nice if a lot of people sent telegrams cheering your nomination along. The program can do that for you."

"In that case it will be worth it."

"Abby, is there anything more you want me for tonight?"

"No, I'm going to bed early and read until I fall asleep. It's been a long day." She smiled, and he could see she was starting to unwind. "Which waitresses are you chasing now? Or is it a poker game?"

Pat got home at six-thirty. She switched on the foyer light, but the stairs past the turn remained in shadow.

Her father's angry words suddenly echoed in her ears: "You shouldn't have come."

That last night the bell had run insistently; her father had opened the door; someone had brushed past him; that person had been looking up—that is why she was so scared; Daddy was angry and she was afraid she'd been seen.

Her hand shook as she placed it on the banister. There's no use getting upset, she thought. It's just that I'm overtired and it's been a rough day. I'll get comfortable and fix some dinner.

In her bedroom she undressed quickly and reached for the robe on the back of the door, then decided she would wear the brown velour caftan instead. It was warm and comfortable.

At her dressing table she tied back her hair and began to cream her face. Mechanically her fingertips moved over her skin, rotating in the pattern the beautician had taught her, pressing for an instant against her temples, touching the faint scar near her hairline.

The furniture behind her was reflected in the mirror; the posts of the bed seemed like tall sentinels. She looked intently into the mirror. She had heard that if you picture an imaginary dot on your forehead and stare into it you can hypnotize yourself and retreat back into the past. For a full minute she concentrated on the imaginary dot, and had the odd sensation of watching herself walking backward into a tunnel . . . and it seemed she was not alone. She had a sense of another presence.

Ridiculous. She was getting lightheaded and fanciful.

Going downstairs to the kitchen, she fixed an omelette, coffee and toast and forced herself to eat.

The kitchen had a cozy, calming warmth. She and her mother and father must sometimes have eaten together here. Did she have a vague recollection of sitting on her father's lap at this table? Veronica had shown her their last Christmas card. It was signed Dean, Renée and Kerry. She said the names aloud, "Dean, Renée and Kerry" and wondered why the cadence seemed wrong.

Rinsing the dishes and putting them in the dishwasher was a reason for delaying what she knew must be done. She had to study that newspaper article and see if it divulged any new facts about Dean and Renée Adams.

The paper was still on the library table. Opening it to the center spread, she forced herself to read every line of the text. Much of it she already knew but that did not help to deaden the pain . . . "The gun smeared with both their fingerprints . . . Dean Adams had died instantly from the bullet wound in his forehead . . . Renée Adams might have lived a short time. . . ." One column emphasized the rumors her neighbors had gleefully picked up at the party: the marriage was clearly unhappy, Renée had urged her husband to leave Washington, she despised the constant round of receptions, she was jealous of the attention her husband attracted from other women. . . .

That quote from a neighbor: "She was clearly besotted with him—and *he* had a roving eye."

There were persistent rumors that Renée, not Dean, had fired the gun. At the inquest, Renée's mother had attempted to squelch that speculation. "It is not a mystery," she said, "it is a tragedy. Only a few days before she was murdered, my daughter told me she

was coming home with Kerry and would file for divorce and custody. I believe that her decision triggered his violence."

She could have been right, Pat thought. I remember tripping over a body. Why am I sure it was Mother's, not his? *She wasn't sure.*

She studied the informal snapshots that covered most of the second page. Willard Jennings was so scholarly-looking. Catherine Graney had said that he wanted to give up Congress and accept a college presidency. And Abigail had been an absolutely beautiful young woman. There was one rather blurred snapshot sandwiched in among the others. Pat glanced at it several times, then moved the paper so that the light shone directly on it.

It was a candid shot that had been taken on the beach. Her father, her mother and Abigail were in a group with two other people. Her mother was absorbed in a book. The two strangers were lying on blankets, their eyes closed. The camera had caught her father and Abigail looking at each other. There was no mistaking the air of intimacy.

There was a magnifying glass in the desk. Pat found it and held it over the picture. Magnified, Abigail's expression became rapturous. Her father's eyes were tender as they looked down at her. Their hands were touching.

Pat folded the newspaper. What did the pictures mean? A casual flirtation? Her father had been attractive to women, probably encouraged their attention. Abigail had been a beautiful young widow. Maybe that was all it amounted to.

As always when she was troubled, Pat turned to

music. In the living room she plugged in the Christmas-tree lights and impulsively switched off the chandelier. At the piano she let her fingers rove over the keys until she found the soft notes of Beethoven's *Pathétique*.

Sam had been himself again today, the way she'd remembered him, strong and confident. He needed time. Of course he did. So did she. Two years ago they'd felt so torn and guilty about their relationship. Now it could be different.

Her father and Abigail Jennings. Had they been involved? Had she just been one in a string of casual affairs? Her father might have been a ladies' man. Why not? He was certainly attractive, and it was the style among rising young politicians then—look at the Kennedys. . . .

Eleanor Brown. Had the lawyer been able to arrange bail for her? Sam hadn't phoned. Eleanor is innocent, Pat told herself—I am sure of it.

Liszt's *Liebestraum*. That was what she was playing now. And the Beethoven. She had unconsciously chosen both those pieces the other night as well. Had her mother played them here? The mood of both of them was the same, plaintive and lonely.

"Renée, listen to me. Stop playing and listen to me." "I can't. Let me alone." The voices—his troubled and urgent, hers despairing.

They quarreled so much, Pat thought. After the quarrels she would play for hours. But sometimes, when she was happy, she'd put me on the bench next to her. *"No, Kerry, this way. Put your fingers here. . . . She can pick out the notes when I hum them. She's a natural."*

Pat felt her hands beginning the opening notes of

Mendelsohn's *Opus 30, Number 3*, another piece that suggested pain. She stood up. There were too many ghosts in this room.

Sam phoned just as she was starting up the stairs again. "They won't release Eleanor Brown. They're afraid she'll jump bail. It seems the man she's living with is a suspect in some nursing-home deaths."

"Sam, I can't stand thinking of that girl in a cell."

"Frank Crowley, the lawyer I sent, thinks she's telling the truth. He's getting a transcript of her trial in the morning. We'll do what we can for her, Pat. It may not be much, I'm afraid. . . . How are you?"

"Just about to turn in."

"The place locked up?"

"Bolted tight."

"Good. Pat, it may be all over but the shouting. Quite a few of us have been invited to the White House tomorrow night. The President's making an important announcement. Your name is on the media list. I checked."

"Sam, do you think . . . ?"

"I just don't know. The money's on Abigail, but the President is really playing it close. None of the possible appointees has been given Secret Service protection yet. That's always a tip-off. I guess the President wants to keep everyone guessing until the last minute. But no matter who gets it, you and I will go out and celebrate."

"Suppose you don't agree with his choice?"

"At this point I don't give a damn whom he chooses. I've got other things in mind. I want to celebrate just being with you. I want to catch up on the last two years. After we stopped seeing each other, the only

way I could get over missing you was to tell myself why it wouldn't have worked even if I was free. After a while, I guess I started to believe my own lies."

Pat's laugh was shaky. She blinked back the sudden moisture in her eyes. "Apology accepted."

"Then I want to talk about not wasting any more of our lives."

"I thought you needed more time. . . ."

"Neither of us does." Even his voice was different—confident, strong, the way she had remembered it all those nights she had lain awake thinking about him. "Pat, I fell hopelessly in love with you that day on Cape Cod. Nothing will ever change that. I'm so damn grateful you waited for me."

"I had no choice. Oh, God, Sam, it's going to be marvelous. I love you so."

For minutes after they said goodbye, Pat stood with her hand resting on the telephone as though by touching it, she could hear again every single word Sam had uttered. Finally, still smiling softly, she started up the stairs. A sudden creaking sound overhead startled her. She knew what it was. That one board on the upstairs landing which always moved when she stepped on it.

Don't be ridiculous, she told herself.

The hallway was poorly lit by flame-shaped bulbs in wall sconces. She started to go into her bedroom, then impulsively turned and walked toward the back of the house. Deliberately she stepped on the loose board and listened as it responded with a distinct creaking. I'd swear that's the sound I heard. She went into her old bedroom. Her footsteps echoed on the uncarpeted floor. The room was stuffy and hot.

The door of the guest bedroom was not quite

closed. It was much cooler in there. She felt a draft and walked over to the window. The window was open from the top. She tried to close it, then realized the sash cord was broken. That's what it is, she thought; there's probably enough draft to make the door sway. Even so, she opened the closet and glanced at the shelves of bedding and linen.

In her room she undressed quickly and got into bed. It was ridiculous to still feel so jittery. Think about Sam; think about the life that they would have together.

Her last impression before she began to doze was the strange feeling that she was not alone. It didn't make sense, but she was too tired to think about it.

With a sigh of relief, Catherine Graney reversed the sign on the shop door from "OPEN" to "CLOSED." For the day after Christmas, business had been unexpectedly brisk. A buyer from Texas had bought the pair of Rudolstadt figura candelabra, the marquetry game tables and the Stouk carpet. It had been a most impressive sale.

Catherine turned off the lights in her shop and went upstairs to her apartment, Sligo at her heels. She had laid a fire that morning. Now she touched a match to the paper under the kindling. Sligo settled in his favorite spot.

Going into the kitchen, she began to fix dinner. Next week when young George was here she'd enjoy cooking big meals. But a chop and a salad were all she wanted now.

George had called her the day before to wish her a merry Christmas and to tell her the news. He'd been

promoted to major. "Twenty-seven years old and an oak leaf already!" she'd exclaimed. "By God, would your Dad be proud."

Catherine put her chop under the broiler. One more good reason not to let Abigail Jennings smear George senior's name any longer. She wondered what Abigail had thought of the letter. She had worked and reworked it before mailing it Christmas Eve.

I must insist you take the opportunity on the upcoming program to publicly acknowledge that there has never been a shred of proof to indicate that pilot error caused your husband's fatal accident. It is not enough to no longer smear George Graney's reputation: you must set the record straight. If you do not, I will sue you for libel and reveal your true relationship with Willard Jennings.

At eleven o'clock she watched the news. At eleven-thirty Sligo nuzzled her hand. "I know," she groaned. "Okay, get your leash."

The evening was dark. Earlier there'd been some stars, but now the sky was clouded over. The breeze was raw, and Catherine pulled up the collar of her coat. "This is going to be one quick walk," she told Sligo.

There was a path through the woods near her house. Usually she and Sligo cut through there and then walked back around the block. Now he strained at the leash, rushing her through the path to his favorite bushes and trees. Then he stopped abruptly and a low growl came from his throat.

"Come on," Catherine said impatiently. All that she'd need would be for him to go after a skunk.

Sligo leaped forward. Bewildered, Catherine watched as a hand shot out and grabbed the old animal in a lock around the neck. There was a sickening cracking sound, and Sligo's limp body dropped onto the hardened snow.

Catherine tried to scream, but no sound came. The hand that had snapped Sligo's neck was raised over her head, and in the instant before she died, Catherine Graney finally understood what had happened that long-ago day.

37

On the morning of December 27, Sam got up at seven, reread the transcript of the CAA investigation into the crash that had killed Congressman Willard Jennings, underlined a particular sentence and phoned Jack Carlson. "How are you coming with that report on Toby Gorgone?"

"I'll have it by eleven."

"Are you free for lunch? I have something to show you." It was the sentence from the transcript: *"Congressman Jennings' chauffeur, Toby Gorgone, placed his luggage on the plane."* Sam wanted to read the report on Toby before discussing it.

They agreed to meet at the Gangplank Restaurant at noon.

Next Sam phoned Frank Crowley, the attorney he'd hired to represent Eleanor Brown, and invited him to the same lunch. "Can you have the transcript of Eleanor Brown's trial with you?"

"I'll make sure I have it, Sam."

The coffee was perking. Sam poured a cup and

turned on the kitchen radio. Most of the nine-o'clock news was over. The weatherman was now promising a partly sunny day. The temperature would be in the low thirties. And then the headlines were recapped, including the fact that the body of a prominent antiques dealer, Mrs. Catherine Graney of Richmond, had been found in a wooded area near her home. Her dog's neck had been broken. Police believed the animal had died trying to defend her.

Catherine Graney dead! Just as she'd been about to blow open a potential scandal involving Abigail. "I don't believe in coincidence," Sam said aloud. "I just don't believe in it."

For the rest of the morning he agonized over his suspicions. Several times he reached for the phone to call the White House. Each time he withdrew his hand.

He had absolutely no proof that Toby Gorgone was anything but what he appeared to be, a devoted bodyguard-chauffeur for Abigail. Even if Toby was guilty of the crime, he had absolutely no proof that Abigail was aware of his activities.

The President would announce the appointment of Abigail that night. Sam was sure of it. But the confirmation hearings were several weeks away. There would be time to launch a thorough investigation. And this time I'll make sure there's no whitewash, he thought grimly.

Somehow Sam was sure that Toby was responsible for the threats to Pat. If he had anything to hide, he wouldn't want her digging into the past.

If he turned out to be the one who had threatened her . . .

Sam clenched his hands into fists. He was no longer thinking of himself as a grandfather-to-be.

Abigail twisted her hands nervously. "We should have left earlier," she said, "we're in all the traffic. Step on it."

"Don't worry, Senator," Toby said soothingly. "They can't start taping without you. How did you sleep?"

"I kept waking up. All I could think of was 'I am going to be Vice President of the United States.' Turn on the radio. Let's see what they're saying about me. . . ."

The eight-thirty CBS news was just beginning. "Rumors persist that the reason the President has called a news conference for this evening is to announce his choice of either Senator Abigail Jennings or Senator Claire Lawrence as Vice President of the United States, the first woman to be so honored." And then: "In a tragic coincidence, it has been learned that Mrs. Catherine Graney, the Richmond antiques dealer found murdered while walking her dog, is the widow of the pilot who died twenty-seven years ago in a plane crash with Congressman Willard Jennings. Abigail Jennings began her political career when she was appointed to complete her husband's term. . . ."

"Toby!"

He glanced into the rearview mirror. Abigail looked shocked. "Toby, how awful."

"Yeah, it's lousy." He watched as Abigail's expression hardened.

"I'll never forget how Willard's mother went to that

woman and sat with her when the plane was overdue. She never even called to see how *I* was."

"Well, they're together now, Abby. Look how fast the traffic is moving. We'll be at the studio right on time."

As they pulled into the private parking area, Abigail asked quietly, "What did you do last night, Toby—play poker or have a date?"

"I saw the little lady from Steakburger and spent the evening with her. Why? You checking on me? You want to talk to her, Senator?" Now his tone had an indignant edge.

"No, of course not. You're welcome to your cocktail waitresses, on your own time. I hope you enjoyed yourself."

"I did. I haven't been taking much personal time lately."

"I know. I've kept you awfully busy." Her voice was conciliatory. "It's just . . ."

"Just *what*, Senator?"

"Nothing . . . nothing at all."

At eight o'clock Eleanor was taken for a lie-detector test. She had slept surprisingly well. She remembered that first night in a cell eleven years ago when she had suddenly started to scream. "You expressed acute claustrophobia that night," a psychiatrist had told her after the breakdown. But now there was a curious peacefulness about not running anymore.

Could Father have hurt those old people? Eleanor racked her brain, trying to remember a single example of his being anything but kind and gentle. There was none.

"This door." The matron led her into a small room near the cellblock. Detective Barrott was reading the newspaper. She was glad he was there. He didn't treat her as though she were a liar. He looked up at her and smiled.

Even when another man came in and hooked her to the lie-detector machine, she didn't start to cry the way she had after her arrest for stealing from the Senator. Instead, she sat in the chair, held up her doll and a little embarrassed, asked if they'd mind if she kept it with her. They didn't act as though it were a crazy request. Frank Crowley, that nice fatherly-looking man who was her lawyer, came in. She had tried to explain to him yesterday that she couldn't pay him more than the nearly five hundred dollars she'd saved, but he told her not to worry about it.

"Eleanor, you can still refuse to take this test," he told her now, and she said that she understood.

At first the man who was giving her the test asked simple, even silly, questions about her age and education and her favorite food. Then he started asking the ones she'd been gearing herself to hear.

"Have you ever stolen anything?"

"No."

"Not even anything small, like a crayon or a piece of chalk when you were little?"

The last time she'd been asked that, she'd started sobbing, "I'm not a thief. I'm *not* a thief." But now it wasn't that hard. She pretended she was talking to Detective Barrott, not this brusque, impersonal stranger. "I've never, ever stolen anything in my life," she said earnestly. "Not even a crayon or a piece of

chalk. I couldn't take anything that belonged to anyone else."

"What about the bottle of perfume when you were in high school?"

"*I did not steal it.* I swear to you. I forgot to give it to the clerk!"

"How often do you drink? Every day?"

"Oh, no. I just have wine sometimes, and not very much. It makes me sleepy." She noticed that Detective Barrott smiled.

"Did you take the seventy-five thousand dollars from Senator Jennings' campaign office?"

Last time during the test, she'd gotten hysterical at that question. Now she simply said, "No, I did not."

"But you put five thousand dollars of that money in your storage room, didn't you?"

"No, I did not."

"Then how do you think it got there?"

The questions went on and on. "Did you lie when you claimed Toby Gorgone phoned?"

"No, I did not."

"You're sure it was Toby Gorgone?"

"I thought it was. If it wasn't, it sounded just like him."

Then the incredible questions began: "Did you know Arthur Stevens was a suspect in the death of one of his patients, a Mrs. Anita Gillespie?"

She almost lost control. "No, I did not. I can't believe that." Then she remembered the way he'd yelled in his sleep: "*Close your eyes, Mrs. Gillespie. Close your eyes!*"

"You do believe it's possible. It shows up right in this test."

"No," she whispered. "Father could never have hurt anyone, only help them. He takes it so to heart when one of his patients is in pain."

"Do you think he might try to stop the pain?"

"I don't know what you mean."

"I think you do. Eleanor, Arthur Stevens tried to set fire to the nursing home on Christmas Day."

"That's impossible."

The shock of what she was hearing made Eleanor blanch. Horrified, she stared at the interrogator as he asked his last question: "Did you ever have any reason to suspect that Arthur Stevens was a homicidal maniac?"

During the night Arthur swallowed caffeine pills every two hours. He could not risk falling asleep and calling out. Instead he sat crouched in the closet, too tense to lie down, staring into the dark.

He'd been so careless. When Patricia Traymore came home, he'd listened at the door of the closet to the sounds of her moving around the house. He'd heard the roar of the pipes when she showered; she'd gone back downstairs and he'd smelled coffee perking. Then she had begun playing the piano. Knowing it was safe to go out, he'd sat on the landing listening to the music.

That was when the voices started talking to him again, telling him that when this was over he must find a new nursing home where he could continue his mission. He'd been so deep in meditation that he hadn't realized that the music had stopped, hadn't thought about where he was until he heard Patricia Traymore's footsteps on the stairs.

In his rush to get to his hiding place he'd stepped on the loose board, and she had known something was wrong. He hadn't dared to breathe when she opened the door of the closet. But of course it never occurred to her to look behind the shelves.

And so he had kept watch all night, straining for the sounds of her awakening, glad when she finally left the house, but afraid to leave the closet for more than a few minutes at a time. A housekeeper might come in and hear him.

The long hours passed. Then the voices directed him to take the brown robe from Patricia Traymore's closet and put it on.

If she had betrayed Glory, he would be suitably clothed to mete out her punishment.

38

Pat arrived at the network building at nine thirty-five and decided to have coffee and an English muffin in the drugstore. She wasn't ready for the charged atmosphere, underlying irritability and explosive nerves that she knew would be waiting on this final day of taping and editing. Her head was vaguely throbbing, her whole body sore. She knew that she had slept restlessly and that her dreams had been troubled. At one point she had cried out, but she couldn't remember what she had said.

In the car she had turned on the news and learned about Catherine Graney's death. She couldn't put the image of the woman out of her mind. The way her face had brightened when she talked about her son; the affectionate pat she had given her aging Irish setter. Catherine Graney would have followed through on her threat to sue Senator Jennings and the network after the program was aired. Her death had ended that threat.

Had she been the random victim of a mugger? The

report had said she was walking her dog. What was his name? Sligo? It seemed unlikely that a criminal would choose to attack a woman with a large dog.

Pat pushed back the English muffin. She wasn't hungry. Only three days ago she had shared coffee with Catherine Graney. Now that attractive, vibrant woman was dead.

When she reached the studio, Luther was already on the set, his face mottled, his lips bloodless, his eyes constantly roving, hunting for flaws. "I said to get rid of those flowers!" he was shouting. "I don't give a damn whether they were just delivered or not. They look dead. Can't anybody do anything right around here? And that chair isn't high enough for the Senator. It looks like a goddamn milking stool." He spotted Pat. "I see you're finally here. You heard about that Graney woman? We'll have to redo the segment of Abigail talking about traffic safety. She comes across a little too heavy on the pilot. There's bound to be backlash when people find out his widow is a crime victim. We start taping in ten minutes."

Pat stared at Luther. Catherine Graney had been a good and decent person and all this man cared about was that her death had caused a setback in the taping. Wordlessly she turned and went into the dressing room.

Senator Jennings was seated in front of a mirror, a towel wrapped around her shoulders. The makeup artist was anxiously hovering over her, dabbing a touch of powder on her nose.

The Senator's fingers were tightly locked together. Her greeting was cordial enough. "This is it, Pat. Will you be as glad to be finished as I?"

"Yes, I think so, Senator."

The makeup girl picked up the can of hair spray and tested it.

"Don't use that stuff on me," the Senator snapped. "I don't want to look like a Barbie doll."

"I'm sorry." The girl's tone faltered. "Most people . . ." Her voice trailed off.

Aware that Abigail was watching her in the mirror, Pat deliberately avoided eye contact.

"There are a few points we should discuss." Now Abigail's tone was brisk and businesslike. "I'm just as glad we're redoing the air-safety segment, even though of course it's terrible about Mrs. Graney. But I want to come off more emphatically on the necessity for better facilities at small airports. And I've decided we should talk more about my mother. There's no use not meeting that *Mirror* picture and that spread in yesterday's *Tribune* head on. And we should certainly emphasize my role in foreign affairs. I've prepared some questions for you to ask me."

Pat put down the brush she was holding and turned to face the Senator. *"Have* you?"

Four hours later, over sandwiches and coffee, a small group sat in the projection room viewing the completed tape. Abigail was in the first row, Luther and Philip on either side of her. Pat sat several rows behind them with the assistant director. In the last row, Toby kept his solitary vigil.

The program opened with Pat, Luther and the Senator sitting in a semicircle. "Hello, and welcome to the first program in our series *Women in Government.* . . ." Pat studied herself critically. Her voice was huskier

than usual; there was something in the rigid way she was sitting that suggested tension. Luther was totally at ease, and on the whole, the opening sounded all right. She and Abigail complemented each other well. Abigail's blue silk dress had been a good choice; it expressed femininity without frills. Her smile was warm, her eyes crinkled. Her acknowledgment of the flattering introduction had no hint of coyness.

They discussed her position as senior Senator from Virginia. Abigail: "It's a tremendously demanding and satisfying job. . . ." The montage of shots of Apple Junction. The shot of Abigail with her mother. Pat watched the screen as Abigail's voice became tender. "My mother faced the same problem as so many working mothers today. She was widowed when I was six. She didn't want to leave me alone and so she took a job as a housekeeper. She sacrificed a hotel-management career so that she'd be there when I came home from school. We were very close. She was always embarrassed about her weight. She had a glandular problem. I guess a lot of people can understand. When I tried to get her to live with Willard and me, she'd laugh and say, 'No way is the mountain coming to Washington.' She was a funny, dear lady." At that point Abigail's voice trembled. And then Abigail explained the beauty contest: "Talk about win it for the Gipper . . . I won that for Mommy. . . ."

Pat found herself caught in the spell of Abigail's warmth. Even the scene in Abigail's den when the Senator had called her mother a fat tyrant seemed unreal now. But it *was* real, she thought. Abigail Jennings is a consummate actress. The clips of the reception and the first campaign. Pat's questions to Abigail:

"Senator, you were a young bride; you were completing your last year in college and you were helping your husband campaign for his first seat in Congress. Tell us how you felt about that." Abigail's answer: "It was wonderful. I was very much in love. I'd always pictured myself getting a job as an assistant to someone in public office. To be there right at the beginning was thrilling. You see, even though a Jennings had always held that seat, Willard's competition was stiff. The night we heard Willard had been elected—I can't describe it. Every election victory is exciting, but the first one is unforgettable."

The clip with the Kennedys at Willard Jennings' birthday party . . . Abigail said, "We were all so young. . . . There were three or four couples who used to get together regularly and we'd sit around for hours talking. We were all so sure we could help to change the world and make life better. Now those young statesmen are gone. I'm the only one left in government and I often think of the plans Willard and Jack and the others were making."

And my father was one of the "others," Pat reflected as she watched the screen.

There were several genuinely touching scenes. Maggie in the office with Abigail thanking her for finding her mother a place in the nursing home; a young mother tightly holding her three-year-old daughter and telling how her ex-husband had kidnapped the child. "No one would help me. No one. And then someone said, 'Call Senator Jennings. She gets things done.' "

Yes, she does, Pat agreed.

But then, with Luther interviewing her, Abigail dis-

cussed the embezzled campaign funds. "I'm so glad that Eleanor Brown has turned herself in to complete her debt to society. I only hope that she may also be honest enough to return whatever is left of that money, or tell who shared in spending it."

Something made Pat turn around. In the semi-darkness of the screening room, Toby's thick bulk loomed in his chair, his hands folded under his chin, the onyx ring gleaming on his finger. His head was nodding approval. Quickly she looked back at the screen, not wanting to meet his gaze.

Luther questioned Abigail about her commitment to airline safety. "Willard was constantly asked to speak at colleges and he accepted every possible date. He said that college was the time when young people were beginning to form mature judgments about the world, about government. We were living on a Congressman's salary and had to be very careful. I am a widow today because my husband chartered the cheapest plane he could find. . . . Do you know the statistics on how many army pilots bought a second-hand plane and tried to start a charter airline on a shoestring? Most of them went out of business. They hadn't the funds to keep the planes in proper condition. My husband died over twenty-five years ago and I've been fighting ever since to bar those small planes from busy fields. And I've always worked closely with the Airline Pilots Association to tighten and maintain rigid standards for pilots."

No mention of George Graney, but once again the implied reason for Willard Jennings' death. After all these years Abigail won't stop underscoring the blame for that accident, Pat thought. As she watched herself

on the screen, she realized that the documentary had turned out exactly as she had planned it; it portrayed Abigail Jennings as a sympathetic human being and a dedicated public servant. The realization brought no satisfaction.

The program ended with Abigail walking into her home in the near-dark and Pat's commentary that like so many single adults, Abigail was going home alone, and she would spend the evening at her desk studying proposed legislation.

The screen went dark, and as the room brightened, they all stood up. Pat watched for Abigail's reaction. The Senator turned to Toby. He nodded approvingly, and with a relaxed smile Abigail pronounced the program a success.

She glanced at Pat. "In spite of all the problems, you've done a very good job. And you were right about using my early background. I'm sorry I gave you so much grief. Luther, what do you think?"

"I think you come across terrific. Pat, what's your feeling?"

Pat considered. They were all satisfied, and the ending was technically all right. Then what was it that was forcing her to press for an additional scene? The letter. She wanted to read the letter Abigail had written to Willard Jennings. "I have one problem," she said. "The personal aspects of this program are what make it special. I wish we hadn't ended on a business note."

Abigail raised her eyes impatiently. Toby frowned. The atmosphere in the room suddenly became strained. The projectionist's voice came over the loudspeaker. "Is that a wrap?"

"No. Run the last scene again," Luther snapped.

The room darkened and an instant later the closing two minutes of the program were replayed.

They all watched intently. Luther was the first to comment. "We can leave it, but I think Pat may be right."

"That's wonderful," Abigail said. "What are you going to do about it? I've got to be at the White House in a few hours and I don't intend to arrive there at the last second."

Can I get her to go along with me? Pat wondered. For some reason she desperately wanted to read the "Billy darling" letter and she wanted the Senator's spontaneous reaction to it. But Abigail had insisted on seeing every inch of the storyboard before they taped. Pat tried to sound casual. "Senator, you've been very generous in opening your personal files to us. In the last batch Toby brought over I found a letter that might just give the final personal touch we want. Of course you can read it before we tape, but I think it would have a more natural quality if you don't. In any case, if it doesn't work, we'll go with the present close."

Abigail's eyes narrowed. She looked at Luther. "Have you read this letter?"

"Yes, I have. I agree with Pat. But it's up to you."

She turned to Philip and Toby. "You two went over everything you released for possible use on the program?"

"Everything, Senator."

She shrugged. "In that case . . . Just make sure you don't read a letter from someone saying she was Miss Apple Junction the year after me."

They all laughed. There is something changed about her, Pat thought. She's surer of herself.

"We'll shoot in ten minutes," Luther said.

Pat hurried into the dressing room. She dabbed fresh powder on the beads of perspiration that had formed on her forehead. What is the matter with me? she asked herself fiercely.

The door opened and Abigail came in. She opened her purse and pulled out a compact. "Pat, that program is pretty good, isn't it?"

"Yes, it is."

"I was so against it. I had such a bad feeling about it. You've done a great job making me look like a pretty nice person." She smiled. "Seeing the tape, I liked myself better than I have in a long time."

"I'm glad." Here again was the woman she had admired so much.

A few minutes later they were back on the set. With her hand, Pat was covering the letter she was about to read. Luther began to speak. "Senator, we want to thank you for sharing your time with us in this very personal way. What you have accomplished is certainly an inspiration to everyone and surely an example of how good can come from tragedy. When we were planning this program, you gave us many of your private papers. Among them we found a letter you wrote to your husband, Congressman Willard Jennings. I think this letter sums up the young woman you were and the woman you became. May I allow Pat to read it to you now?"

Abigail tilted her head, her expression questioning.

Pat unfolded the letter. Her voice husky, she read it slowly. "Billy, darling." Her throat tightened. She had

to force herself to go on. Again her mouth was hopelessly dry. She glanced up. Abigail was staring at her,
the color draining from her face. "You were splendid
in the hearings this afternoon. I am so proud of you. I
love you so and look forward to a lifetime of being with
you, of working with you. Oh, my dearest, we really are
going to make a difference in this world."

Luther interjected, "That note was written on May
thirteenth, and on May twentieth Congressman Willard Jennings died and you went on alone to make a
difference in this world. Senator Abigail Jennings,
thank you."

The Senator's eyes were shining. A tender half-
smile played at the corners of her mouth. She nodded
and her lips formed the words "Thank you."

"Cut," the director called.

Luther jumped up. "Senator, that was perfect. Everybody will . . ."

He stopped in mid-sentence as Abigail lunged forward and grabbed the letter from Pat's hand. "Where
did you *get* that?" she shrieked. "What are you trying
to *do* to me?"

"Senator, I told you, we don't have to use it," Luther protested.

Pat stared as Abigail's face twisted into a mask of
anger and pain. Where had she seen that expression,
on *that* face, once before?

A bulky figure rushed past her. Toby was shaking
the Senator, almost shouting at her: "Abby, get hold
of yourself. That was a great way to end the program.
*Abby, it's okay to let people know about your last letter to your
husband.*"

"My . . . last . . . letter?" Abigail raised one

hand to cover her face as though she were trying to remold her expression. "Of course . . . I'm sorry . . . It's just that Willard and I used to write little notes to each other all the time. . . . I'm so glad you found—the last one. . . ."

Pat sat immobilized. "Billy darling, Billy darling . . ." The words had a drumroll cadence, hammering in her mind. Gripping the arms of the chair, she looked up and met Toby's savage stare. She shrank back in mindless terror.

He turned back to Abigail and, with Luther and Phil assisting, escorted her from the studio. One by one the floodlights were turned off. "Hey, Pat," the cameraman called. "That's a wrap, isn't it?"

At last she was able to get up. "It's a wrap," she agreed.

39

Whenever Sam was wrestling with a problem, a long walk had a way of clearing his head and helping him think. That was why he elected to walk the several miles from his apartment to the Southwest section of the District. The Gangplank Restaurant was on the Washington Channel, and as he neared it, he studied the restless pattern of the whitecaps.

Cape Cod. Nauset Beach. Pat walking beside him, her hair tossed by the wind, her arm tucked in his, the incredible sense of freedom, as though it were just the two of them and sky and beach and ocean. Next summer we'll go back, he promised himself.

The restaurant resembled a ship moored to the dock. He hurried up the gangplank, enjoying the faint undulating feeling.

Jack Carlson was already seated at a window table. Several crushed cigarettes were in the ashtray in front of him, and he was sipping a Perrier. Sam apologized for being late.

"I'm early," Jack said simply. He was a trim, gray-

haired man with bright, inquisitive eyes. He and Sam had been friends for more than twenty years.

Sam ordered a gin martini. "Maybe that will quiet me down or pick me up," he explained with an attempt at a smile. He felt Jack's eyes studying him.

"I've seen you looking more cheerful," Jack commented. "Sam, what made you ask us to check on Toby Gorgone?"

"Only a hunch." Sam felt himself tense. "Did you come up with anything interesting?"

"I'd say so."

"Hello, Sam." Frank Crowley, his normally pale face ruddy from the cold, his heavy white hair somewhat disheveled, joined them. He introduced himself to Jack, adjusted his silver-rimmed glasses, opened his briefcase and pulled out a bulky envelope. "I'm lucky to be here," he announced. "I started going through the trial transcript and almost forgot the time." The waiter was at his elbow. "Vodka martini, very dry," he ordered. "Sam, you seem to be the only one I know who can still drink gin martinis."

Without waiting for a reply, he continued. *"United States* versus *Eleanor Brown.* Makes interesting reading and boils down to one simple issue: which member of Senator Jennings' official family was lying, Eleanor or Toby? Eleanor took the stand in her own defense. A big mistake. She started talking about the shoplifting connection and the prosecutor blew it up until you'd think she'd robbed Fort Knox. The Senator's testimony didn't help any. She talked too damn much about giving Eleanor a second chance. I've marked the most relevant pages." He handed Carlson the transcript.

Jack took an envelope from his pocket. "Here's the fact sheet you wanted on Gorgone, Sam."

Sam skimmed it, raised his eyebrows and reread it carefully.

Apple Junction: Suspect in car theft. Police chase resulted in death of three. No indictment.
Apple Junction: Suspect in bookmaking operation. No indictment.
New York City: Suspect in firebombing of car resulting in death of loan shark. No indictment. Thought to be on fringe of Mafia.
May have settled gambling debts by performing services for mob.
Other relevant fact: Exceptional mechanical aptitude.

"A perfectly clean record," he said sarcastically.

Over sliced-steak sandwiches they discussed, compared and evaluated the fact sheet on Toby Gorgone, Eleanor Brown's trial transcript, the CAA findings on the plane crash and the news of Catherine Graney's murder. By the time coffee was served, they had separately and jointly arrived at disturbing possibilities: Toby was a mechanical whiz who had left a suitcase on the Jennings plane minutes before takeoff and the plane had crashed under mysterious circumstances. Toby was a gambler who might have been in debt to bookies at the time the campaign funds disappeared.

"It seems to me that Senator Jennings and this character Toby take turns exchanging favors," Crowley commented. "She alibis for him and he pulls her chestnuts out of the fire."

"I can't believe Abigail Jennings would deliberately send a young girl to prison," Sam said flatly. "And I certainly don't believe she'd be party to the murder of her husband." He realized they were all whispering now. They were talking about a woman who in a few hours might become Vice President–designate of the United States.

The restaurant was starting to empty. The diners, most of them government people, were hurrying back to their jobs. Probably at one point during lunch every one of them had speculated about the President's conference tonight.

"Sam, I've seen dozens of characters like this Toby," Jack said. "Most of them in the mob. They're devoted to the head guy. They smooth his path—and take care of themselves at the same time. Perhaps Senator Jennings wasn't involved in Toby's activities. But look at it this way: Let's say Toby knew Willard Jennings wanted to give up his seat in Congress and get a divorce from Abigail. Jennings wasn't worth fifty thousand bucks in his own right. Mama held the purse strings. So Abigail would have been out of the political scene, dropped by Willard Jennings' circle of friends and back to being an ex-beauty queen from a hick town. And Toby decided not to let that happen."

"Are you suggesting she returned the favor by lying for him about the campaign money?" Sam asked.

"Not necessarily," Frank said. "Here—read the Senator's testimony on the stand. She admitted that they stopped at a gas station around the time Eleanor received the call. The engine had developed a knock and Toby wanted to check it. She swears he was never out of her sight. But she *was* on her way to deliver a

speech and probably studying her notes. One minute
she probably saw Toby in front of the car tinkering at
the engine; the next maybe he was behind it getting a
tool out of the trunk. How long does it take to scoot
around to the public phone, dial a number and leave a
two-second message? I'd have torn that testimony
apart. But even assuming we're right, I can't understand why Toby picked Eleanor."

"That's easy," Jack said. "He knew about her record. He knew how sensitive she was. Without that
open-and-shut case, there'd have been a full-blown
investigation into the missing funds. He'd have been a
suspect and his background investigated. He's smart
enough to have gotten away with another 'no indictment' on his fact sheet, but the Senator would have
been pressured by the party to get rid of him."

"If what we believe about Toby Gorgone checks
out," Sam concluded, "Catherine Graney's death becomes too timely, too convenient to be a case of random murder."

"If Abigail Jennings gets the nod from the President
tonight," Jack said, "and it comes out that her chauffeur murdered the Graney woman, those confirmation
hearings will be a worldwide scandal."

The three men sat at the table, each somberly reflecting on the possible embarrassment to the President. Sam finally broke the silence.

"One bright note is if we can prove Toby wrote
those threatening notes and arrest him, I can stop
worrying about Pat."

Frank Crowley nodded at Jack. "And if your people
get enough on him, Toby might be persuaded to tell
the truth about the campaign funds. I tell you, to see

that poor girl Eleanor Brown taking that lie-detector test this morning and swearing she'd never even stolen a piece of chalk would break your heart. She doesn't look eighteen, never mind thirty-four. That prison experience almost killed her. After her breakdown a shrink had her paint a doll's face to show how she felt. She still carries that doll around with her. The damn thing would give you the creeps. It looks like a battered child."

"A doll!" Sam exclaimed. "She has a *doll.* By any chance, is it a Raggedy Ann doll?"

At Frank's astonished nod, he signaled for more coffee. "I'm afraid we're barking up the wrong tree," he said wearily. "Let's start all over again."

40

Toby poured a Manhattan into the chilled cocktail glass and set it down in front of Abigail. "Drink this, Senator. You need it."

"Toby where did she get that letter? Where did she get it?"

"I don't know, Senator."

"It couldn't have been in anything you gave her. I never saw it again after I wrote it. *How much does she know?* Toby, if she could prove I was there that night . . ."

"She can't, Senator. No one can. And no matter what she may have dug up, she hasn't any proof. Come on, she did you a favor. That letter will clinch sympathy for you. Wait and see."

He finally appeased her the only way that worked. *"Trust* me! Don't worry about it. Have I ever let you down?" He calmed her a little, but even so, she was still a bundle of nerves. And in a few hours she was due at the White House.

"Listen, Abby," he said. "While I fix you something to eat, I want you to belt two Manhattans. After that

have a hot bath and sleep for an hour. Then get yourself in your best-looking outfit. This is the biggest
night of your life."

He meant it. She had reason to be uspet—plenty of
reason. The minute he heard the letter being read,
he'd been on his feet. But as soon as Pelham said,
"Your husband was lost a week later," he'd known it
would be all right.

Abby almost blew it. Once again he'd been there to
stop her from making a terrible mistake.

Abby reached for her glass. "Bottoms up," she said,
and a touch of a smile lingered around her lips. "Toby,
in a little while we'll have it."

The Vice Presidency. "That's right, Senator." He
was sitting on a hassock across from the couch.

"Ah, Toby," she said. "What would I have become
without you?"

"State assemblywoman from Apple Junction."

"Oh, sure." She tried to smile.

Her hair was loose around her face and she didn't
look more than thirty years old. She was so slim. Slim
the way a woman should be. Not a bag of bones, but
firm and sleek.

"Toby, you look as though you're thinking. That
would be a first."

He grinned at her, glad she was starting to loosen
up. "You're the smart one. I leave the thinking to
you."

She sipped the drink quickly. "The program turned
out all right?"

"I keep telling you . . . it wouldn't have made
sense for you to carry on about the letter. She did you
a favor."

"I know. . . . It's just . . ."

The Manhattan was hitting her. He had to get some food into her. "Senator, you relax. I'll fix a tray for you."

"Yes . . . that would be a good idea. Toby, do you realize that a few hours from now I'm going to be Vice President–designate of the United States?"

"I sure do, Abby."

"We all know how ceremonial the office is. But Toby, if I do a good job, they may not be able to deny me the top spot next year. That's what I intend to have happen."

"I know that, Senator." Toby refilled her glass. "I'm going to fix you an omelette. Then you're going to take a nap. This is your night."

Toby got up. He couldn't look anymore at the naked yearning on her face. He'd seen it the day she got the news that she wouldn't be eligible for a scholarship to Radcliffe. She'd come over to where he was mowing the lawn and shown him the letter, then sat on the porch steps, hugged her legs and dropped her head in her lap. She'd been eighteen years old. "Toby, I want to go there so bad. I can't rot in this stinking town. I can't. . . ."

And then he'd suggested she romance that jerk Jeremy Saunders. . . .

He'd helped her other times, helped her to find her destiny.

And now, once again, somebody was trying to ruin everything for her.

Toby went into the kitchen. As he prepared the dinner he tried to envision how interesting it would be

when Abby was one heartbeat away from the Presidency.

The phone rang. It was Phil. "The Senator okay?"

"She's fine. Look, I'm getting her dinner."

"I have a piece of information you wanted. Guess who owns Pat Traymore's house."

Toby waited.

"Pat Traymore, that's who. It's been in trust for her since she was four years old."

Toby whistled soundlessly. Those eyes, that hair, a certain look about her . . . Why hadn't he figured it out before this? He could have blown everything by being so dumb.

Phil's voice was querulous. "Did you hear me? I said . . ."

"I heard you. Just keep it under your hat. What the Senator don't know won't hurt her."

A short time later he went back to his apartment above the garage. Under his urging, Abigail decided to watch the program while resting in her room. At eight o'clock he would bring the car around and they'd leave for the White House.

He waited until the program had been on a few minutes, then quietly left his apartment. His car, a black Toyota, was in the driveway. He pushed it until he could roll it down to the street. He didn't want Abby to know he was going out. He had a little less than an hour and a half for the round trip to Pat Traymore's house.

It was enough to do what was needed.

41

Pat drove across Massachusetts Avenue, up Q Street, over the Buffalo Bridge and into Georgetown. Her head was aching now—a steady throbbing. She drove by rote, observing traffic lights subconsciously.

Presently she was on 31st Street, turning the corner, pulling into her driveway. She was on the steps, the slap of the wind on her face. Her fingers were fumbling in her purse for her key. The lock was clicking; she was pushing the door open, going into the shadowy quiet of the foyer.

In a reflex action, she closed the door and leaned against it. The coat was heavy on her shoulders. She shrugged it off, tossed it aside. She raised her head; her eyes became riveted on the step at the bend of the staircase. *There was a child sitting there. A child with long reddish-brown hair, her chin leaning on the palms of her hands; her expression curious.*

I wasn't asleep, she thought. I heard the doorbell ring and I wanted to see who was coming. *Daddy opened the door and someone pushed past him. He was angry. I ran*

back to bed. When I heard the first shot, I didn't come right down. I stayed in bed and screamed for Daddy.

But he didn't come. And I heard another loud bang and ran down the stairs to the living room. . . .

And then . . .

She realized she was trembling and light-headed. Going into the library, she poured brandy into a tumbler and sipped it quickly. Why had Senator Jennings been so devastated by that letter? She'd been panicky, furious, frightened.

Why?

It didn't make sense.

And why did I get so upset reading it? Why has it upset me every time I've read it?

The way Toby looked at me as though he hated me. The way he shouted at the Senator. He wasn't trying to calm her down. He was trying to warn her about something. But what?

She sat huddled in the corner of the sofa, her arms clasped around her knees. I used to sit in here like this when Daddy was working at his desk. "You can stay, Kerry, as long as you promise to be quiet." Why was her memory of him so vivid now? She could see him, not as he'd looked in the film clips but as he'd been here in this room, leaning back in the chair, tapping his fingers on the desk when he was concentrating.

The newspaper article was still open on the desk. On a sudden impulse she went over to it, reread it carefully. Her eyes kept coming back to the picture of her father and Abigail Jennings on the beach. There was an undeniably intimate quality there. A summer-afternoon flirtation or more? Suppose her mother had looked up and caught that glance between them?

Why was she so afraid? She'd slept so badly last
night. A hot bath and a brief rest would help calm her
down. Slowly she went upstairs to her room. Again she
had the eerie feeling she was being watched. She had
had the same sensation the night before, before she
fell asleep, but again she brushed it from her mind.

The phone rang just as she reached her room. It was
Lila.

"Pat, are you all right? I'm worried about you. I
don't want to alarm you, but I must. I sense danger
around you. Won't you please come over here now
and stay with me?"

"Lila, I think the impression you're getting is that
I'm really quite close to a breakthrough in remembering that night. Something happened today, during the
final taping, that seems to be triggering it. But don't
worry—no matter what it is, I can handle it."

"Pat, *listen* to me. You shouldn't be in that house
now!"

"It's the only way I'll be able to piece it together."

She's nervous because of the break-ins, Pat told herself as she lay in the tub. She's afraid I can't face the
truth. She slipped on her terry-cloth robe. Sitting at
the dressing table, she unpinned her hair and began to
brush it. She'd been wearing it in a chignon most of
the week. She knew Sam liked it best when it was loose.
Tonight she'd wear it that way.

She got into bed and turned the radio on low. She
hadn't expected to doze, but she soon drifted off. The
sound of Eleanor's name startled her into consciousness.

The bedside clock read six-fifteen. The program
would be on in fifteen minutes.

"Giving as her motive that she could no longer endure the fear of being recognized, Miss Brown has surrendered and was taken into custody. She still steadfastly maintains her innocence of the theft for which she was convicted. A police spokesman said that in the nine years since she violated parole, Miss Brown had been living with a paramedic Arthur Stevens. Stevens is a suspect in a series of nursing-home deaths and a warrant has been issued for his arrest. A religious fanatic, he has been dubbed the 'nursing home angel.'"

"The Nursing Home Angel!" The first time he phoned, the caller had referred to himself as an angel of mercy, of deliverance, of vengeance. Pat bolted up and grabbed the phone. Frantically she dialed Sam's number, let the phone ring ten, twelve, fourteen times before she finally replaced it. If only she had realized what Eleanor was saying when she talked about Arthur Stevens! *He had begged Eleanor not to give herself up. To save Eleanor he might have tried to stop the program.*

Could Eleanor have been aware of those threats? No, I'm sure she wasn't, Pat decided. Her lawyer should know about this before we tell the police.

It was twenty-five past six. She got out of bed, tightened the belt of her robe and put on her slippers. As she hurried down the stairs, she wondered where Arthur Stevens was now. Was he aware that Eleanor was under arrest? Would he see the program and blame her when Eleanor's picture was shown? Blame her because Eleanor had not kept her promise to wait before going to the police?

In the living room she turned the chandelier to the brightest setting and took a moment to light the

Christmas tree before switching on the set. Even so, the room had an oddly cheerless quality. Settling herself on the couch, she watched intently as the credits rolled after the six-o'clock news.

She had wanted the chance to watch the program alone. In the studio she'd been conscious of tuning into everyone else's reactions to it. Even so, she realized she was dreading seeing it again. It was much more than the usual apprehension of launching a new series.

The furnace rumbled and a hissing of air came from the heat risers. The sound made her jump. It's crazy what this place is doing to me, she thought.

The program was beginning. Critically Pat studied the three of them—the Senator, Luther and herself, sitting in the semicircle. The background was good. Luther had been right about changing the flowers. Abigail showed none of the tension she'd exhibited off-camera. The footage on Apple Junction was well chosen. Abigail's reminiscences about her early life had just the right touch of human interest. And it's all such a lie, Pat thought.

The films of Abigail and Willard Jennings at their wedding reception, at parties on the estate, during his campaigns. Abigail's tender memories of her husband as the clips were shown. "Willard and I . . . ," "My husband and I . . ." Funny she never once referred to him as Billy.

With growing awareness, Pat realized that the films of Abigail as a young woman had an oddly familiar quality. They were evoking memories that had nothing to do with her having viewed them so many times. Why was that happening now?

There was a commercial break.

The segment about Eleanor Brown and the embezzled funds would come next.

Arthur heard Patricia Traymore go down the stairs. Cautiously he tiptoed until he was sure he was listening to the faint sounds of the television broadcast coming from downstairs. He had been afraid that friends might join her to view the program. But she was alone.

For the first time in all these years he felt as though he were dressed in the garb God intended him to wear. With moist, open palms, he smoothed the fine wool against his body. This woman even defiled sacred garments. What right had she to wear the raiment of the chosen?

Returning to his secret place, he put on the earphones, turned on the set and adjusted the picture. He had tapped into the cable antenna, and the screen was remarkably clear. Kneeling as before an altar, his hands locked in the posture of prayer, Arthur began to watch the program.

Lila sat watching the documentary, her dinner on a tray before her. It was hard to make even a pretense of eating. Her absolute certainty that Pat was in serious danger only heightened as she saw Pat's image on the screen.

Cassandra's warnings, she thought bitterly. Pat won't listen to me. She simply has to get out of that house *or she will suffer a death more violent than her parents endured. She is running out of time.*

Lila had met Sam Kingsley just once and liked him

very much. She sensed that he was important to Pat.
Would it be of any use to try to talk to Congressman
Kingsley, share her apprehension with him? Could she
possibly persuade him to insist that Pat leave her
home until this dark aura around it dissolved?

She pushed the tray aside, got up and reached for
the green book. She would call him immediately.

Sam went directly to his office from the restaurant.
He had several meetings scheduled, but found it impossible to concentrate on any of them. His mind kept
returning to the luncheon discussions.

They had built a strong circumstantial case against
Toby Gorgone, but Sam had been a prosecutor long
enough to know that strong circumstantial evidence
can be upset like a house of cards. And the Raggedy
Ann doll was upsetting the case against Toby. If Toby
was innocent of involvement in the plane crash and
the embezzled funds, if Catherine Graney had been
the victim of a random mugging, then Abigail Jennings was what she seemed to be—above reproach
and a worthy candidate for the job most people expected her to get. But the more Sam thought about
Toby, the more uneasy he got.

At twenty after six he was finally free and immediately dialed Pat. Her phone was busy. Quickly he
locked his desk. He wanted to get home in time to
watch the documentary.

The sound of the telephone stopped him as he was
rushing out of the office. Some instinct warned him
not to ignore it.

It was Jack Carlson. "Sam, are you alone?"

"Yes."

"We have some new developments in the Catherine Graney case. Her son found a draft of a letter she wrote to Senator Jennings. A letter that probably arrived at the Senator's house yesterday. It's pretty strong stuff. Mrs. Graney intended to attack Senator Jennings' version of her relationship with her husband, and she was going to sue her for libel if she didn't retract her statements about pilot error on the program."

Sam whistled. "Are you saying that Abigail may have received that letter yesterday?"

"Exactly. But that isn't the half of it. Mrs. Graney's neighbors had a party last night. We got a list of the guests and checked them all out. One young couple who came late, about eleven-fifteen or so, had trouble locating the exact street. They'd asked directions from a guy who was getting in his car two blocks away. He brushed them off fast. The car was a black Toyota, with Virginia plates. They described someone who sounds like Gorgone. The girl even remembers he was wearing a heavy, dark ring. We're picking Toby up for questioning. Do you think you ought to phone the White House?"

Toby might have been seen near the site of Catherine Graney's murder. If he had killed Catherine Graney, everything else they suspected of him was possible, even logical. "Abigail has to know about this immediately," Sam said. "I'll go to her now. She should have the chance to withdraw her name from consideration. If she refuses, I'll call the President myself. Even if she had no idea of what Toby was up to, she's got to accept the moral responsibility."

"I don't think that lady has ever worried about

moral responsibility. If J. Edgar were alive, she wouldn't have gotten this far toward the Vice Presidency. You saw that article in the *Trib* the other day about what great pals she was with Congressman Adams and his wife."

"I saw it."

"Like the paper said, there was always a rumor that another woman was the direct cause of the fatal quarrel. I was new in the Bureau when that case broke, but when I read that article, something started bugging me. On a hunch I pulled the Adams file. We have a memo in it about a freshman Congresswoman named Abigail Jennings. All the indications were that *she* was that other woman."

Try as she would, Abigail couldn't rest. The knowledge that in a few hours she would be nominated to be Vice President of the United States was too exhilarating to bear.

Madam Vice President. *Air Force Two* and the mansion on the grounds of the old Naval Observatory. Presiding over the Senate and representing the President all over the world.

In two years the Presidential nomination. I'll win, she promised herself. Golda Meir. Indira Gandhi. Margaret Thatcher. Abigail Jennings.

The Senate had been a mighty step up. The night she was elected Luther had said, "Well, Abigail, you're a member of the world's most exclusive club."

Now another vast step was impending. No longer one of one hundred Senators, but the second-highest official in the land.

She had decided to wear a three-piece outfit, a silk

blouse and skirt with a knitted jacket, in tones of pink and gray. It would show up well on the television sets.

Vice President Abigail Jennings . . .

It was six-fifteen. She got up from the chaise, went over to her dressing table and brushed her hair. With deft strokes she applied a touch of eye shadow and mascara. Excitement had flushed her cheeks; she didn't need blush. She might as well get dressed now, watch the program and practice her acceptance speech until it was time to leave for the White House.

She slipped into the suit and fastened a gold-and-diamond sunburst pin to her jacket. The library television set had the biggest screen. She'd watch her program in there.

"Stay tuned for *Women in Government.*"

She had already seen everything but the last few minutes of the program. Even so, it was reassuring to watch it again. Apple Junction under a fresh coating of snow had a down-home country look that concealed its shabby dreariness. Thoughtfully she studied the Saunders home. She remembered when Mrs. Saunders had ordered her to retrace her steps and take the path to the service entrance. She'd made that miserable witch pay for that mistake.

If it weren't for Toby's figuring out how to get the money for Radcliffe, where would she be now?

The Saunderses *owed* me that money, she told herself. Twelve years of humiliations in that house!

She watched the clips of the wedding reception, the early campaigns, Willard's funeral. She remembered the exultation she had felt when in the funeral car Jack Kennedy had agreed to urge the Governor to appoint her to complete Willard's term.

The insistent ring of the doorbell startled her. No one ever dropped in. Could someone from the press be brazen enough to ring like that? She tried to ignore it. But the peal became a steady, unbroken intrusion. She hurried to the door. "Who is it?"

"Sam."

She pulled open the door. He stepped in, his face grim, but she barely glanced at him. "Sam, why aren't you watching *This Is Your Life?* Come on." Grabbing his hand, she ran ahead into the library. On the program, Luther was asking her about her commitment to airline safety.

"Abigail, I have to talk to you."

"Sam, for heaven's sake. Don't you want me to see my own program?"

"This won't wait." Against the background of the documentary, he told her why he had come. He watched the disbelief grow in her eyes.

"You're trying to say Toby may have killed the Graney woman? You're crazy."

"Am I?"

"He was out on a date. That waitress will vouch for him."

"Two people described him accurately. The letter Catherine Graney wrote you was the motive."

"What letter?"

They stared at each other, and her face paled.

"He picks up your mail, doesn't he, Abigail?"

"Yes."

"Did he get it yesterday?"

"Yes."

"And what did he bring in?"

"The usual junk. Wait a minute. You can't make these accusations about him. You make them *to* him."

"Then call him in here now. He's going to be picked up for questioning anyway."

Sam watched as Abigail dialed the phone. Dispassionately he observed the beautiful outfit she was wearing. She was dressed up to become Vice President, he thought.

Abigail held the receiver to her ear, listening to the bell ring. "He's probably just not answering. He certainly wouldn't expect me to be calling." Her voice trailed off, then became resolutely brisk. "Sam, you can't believe what you're saying. Pat Traymore put you up to this. She's been out to sabotage me from the beginning."

"Pat has nothing to do with the fact that Toby Gorgone was seen near Catherine Graney's home."

On the television screen Abigail was discussing her leadership in airline safety regulations. "I am a widow today because my husband chartered the cheapest plane he could find."

Sam pointed to the set. "That statement would have been enough to send Catherine Graney to the newspapers tomorrow morning, and Toby knew it. Abigail, if the President has called this news conference tonight to introduce you as Vice President—designate, you've got to ask him to postpone the announcement until this is cleared up."

"Have you taken leave of your senses? I don't care if Toby was two blocks from where that woman was killed. What does it prove? Maybe he has a girlfriend or a floating card game in Richmond. He's probably

just not answering the phone. I wish to God I hadn't bothered to answer the door."

A sense of urgency overwhelmed Sam. Yesterday Pat had told him that she felt Toby had become hostile to her; that she was becoming nervous when he was around. Only a few minutes ago Abigail had said that Pat was trying to sabotage her. Did Toby believe that? Sam grasped Abigail's shoulders. "Is there any reason that Toby might consider Pat a threat to you?"

"Sam, stop it! Let go of me! He was just as upset as I about the publicity she's caused, but even that turned out all right. In fact, he thinks that in the long run she did me a favor."

"Are you *sure?*"

"Sam, Toby never laid eyes on Pat Traymore before last week. You're not being rational."

He never laid eyes on her before last week? That wasn't true. Toby had known Pat well as a child. Could he have recognized her? Abigail had been involved with Pat's father. Was Pat becoming aware of that? Forgive me, Pat, he thought. I have to tell her. "Abigail, Pat Traymore is Dean Adams' daughter, Kerry."

"Pat Traymore is—Kerry?" Abigail's eyes widened with shock. Then she shook herself free. "You don't know what you're talking about. Kerry Adams is dead."

"I'm telling you Pat Traymore is Kerry Adams. I've been told that you were involved with her father, that you may have triggered that last quarrel. Pat is starting to remember bits and pieces of that night. Would Toby try to protect you or himself from anything she might find out?"

"No," Abigail said flatly. "I don't care if she remembers seeing me. Nothing that happened was my fault."

"*Toby*—what about *Toby?* Was he there?"

"She never saw him. When he went back for my purse he told me she was already unconscious."

The implications of what she had said burst upon both of them. Sam ran for the door, Abigail stumbling behind him.

Arthur watched the film clips of Glory in handcuffs being led from the courtroom after the Guilty verdict. There was one close-up of her. Her face was dazed and expressionless, but her pupils were enormous. The uncomprehending pain in her eyes brought tears to his own. He buried his face in his hands as Luther Pelham talked about Glory's nervous breakdown, her parole as a psychiatric outpatient, her disappearance nine years ago. And then, not wanting to believe what he was hearing, he listened as Pelham said, "Yesterday, citing her overwhelming fear of being recognized, Eleanor Brown surrendered to the police. She is now in custody and will be returned to federal prison to complete her sentence."

Glory had surrendered to the police. She had broken her promise to him.

No. She had been *driven* to break her promise—driven by the certainty that this program would expose her. He knew he would never see her again.

His voices, angry and vengeful, began speaking to him. Clenching his fists, he listened intently. When they were silent, he tore off the headset. Without bothering to push the shelves together to conceal his hid-

ing place, he hurried out to the landing and descended the stairs.

Pat sat motionless, studying the program. She watched herself begin to read the letter. "Billy, darling."

"Billy," she whispered. "Billy."

Raptly she studied Abigail Jennings' shocked expression, the involuntary clenching of her hands before she managed with iron control to assume a pleasant misty-eyed demeanor as the letter was read to her.

She had seen that anguished expression on Abigail's face before.

"Billy, darling. Billy, darling."

"You must not call Mommy 'Renée.'"

"But Daddy calls you 'Renée' . . ."

The way Abigail had lunged at her when the cameras stopped rolling. *"Where did you get that letter? What are you trying to do to me?"*

Toby's shout: "It's all right, Abby. It's all right to let people hear the last letter you wrote your husband." *"Your husband."* That's what he'd been trying to tell her.

The picture of Abigail and her father on the beach, their hands touching.

Abigail was the one who had rung the bell that night, who had pushed past her father, her face ravaged with grief and anger.

"You must not call me 'Renée,' and you must not call Daddy 'Billy.'"

Dean *Wilson* Adams. Her *father*—not Willard Jennings—was Billy!

The letter! She had found it on the floor in the

library the day she had tried to hide her father's personal papers from Toby. That letter must have fallen from *his* files, not Abigail's.

Abigail had been here that night. She and Dean Adams—*Billy* Adams—had been lovers. Had she precipitated that final quarrel?

A little girl was crouched in bed, her hands over her ears to drown out the angry voices.

The shot.

"Daddy! Daddy!"

Another loud bang.

And then I ran downstairs. I tripped over Mother's body. Someone else was there. Abigail? Oh, God, could Abigail Jennings have been there when I ran into the room?

The patio door had opened.

The phone began to ring, and in the same instant, the chandeliers went off. Pat jumped up and spun around. Illuminated by the twinkling lights of the Christmas tree an apparition was rushing toward her, the tall, gaunt figure of a monk with a vacant unlined face and silvery hair that fell forward over glittering china blue eyes.

Toby drove toward Georgetown, careful to keep his car below the speed limit. This was one night he didn't need a ticket. He'd waited until the documentary was on before he left. He knew Abby would be glued to the set for that half-hour. If she did phone him after the program, he could always say he'd been outside checking the car.

From the beginning he'd known there was something weirdly familiar about Pat Traymore. Years ago

he hadn't shed any tears when he'd read that Kerry Adams had "succumbed to her injuries." Not that anything a three-or-four-year-old kid said stood up in court; but even so, it wasn't the kind of grief he needed.

Abby had been right. Pat Traymore had been out to put the screws on them from the beginning. But she wasn't going to get away with it.

He was on M Street in Georgetown. He turned onto 31st Street and drove to N, then turned right. He knew where to park. He'd done it before.

The right side of the property extended halfway down the block. He left the car just around the next corner, walked back and ignoring the padlocked gate, easily scaled the fence. Silently he melted into the shadowy area beyond the patio.

It was impossible not to think about the other night in this place—dragging Abby out, holding his hand over her mouth to keep her from crying out, laying her on the back seat of the car, hearing her terrified moan, "My purse is in there" and going back.

Edging his way under cover of the tree trunks, Toby pressed against the back of the house until he was on the patio a few inches from the doors. Turning his head, he glanced cautiously inside.

His blood froze. Pat Traymore was lying on the couch, her hands and legs tied behind her. Her mouth was taped. A priest or monk, his back to the door, was kneeling beside her and lighting the candles in a silver candelabrum. What in hell was he up to? The man turned, and Toby had a better chance to see him. He wasn't a real priest. That wasn't a habit—it was some

sort of robe. The look on his face reminded Toby of a neighbor who years before had gone berserk.

The guy was yelling at Pat Traymore. Toby could barely make out the words. "You did not heed my warnings. You were given the choice."

Warnings. They thought Pat Traymore had made up that story about the phone calls and the break-in. But if she hadn't . . . As Toby watched, the man carried the candelabrum over to the Christmas tree and set it under the lowest branch.

He was setting fire to the place! Pat Traymore would be trapped in there. All he had to do was get back into the car and go home.

Toby flattened against the wall. The man was heading toward the patio doors. *Suppose he was found in there?* Everyone knew Pat Traymore had been getting threats. If this place burned and she was found with the guy who had been threatening her, that would be the end of it. No more investigations, no possibility that someone would talk about having seen a strange car parked in the neighborhood.

Toby listened for the click of the lock. The robed stranger pushed open the patio doors, then turned back to look into the room.

Silently Toby moved over and stood behind him.

As the closing credits of the program rolled onto the screen, Lila redialed Sam's number. But it was useless. There was still no answer. Again she tried to phone Pat. After a half-dozen rings she hung up and walked over to the window. Pat's car was still in the driveway. Lila was positive she was home. As Lila watched, it

seemed there was a reddish glow behind the dark aura surrounding the house.

Should she call the police? Suppose Pat was simply coming close to the memory of the tragedy; suppose the danger Lila was sensing was of an emotional not physical nature. Pat wanted so desperately to understand how one of her parents had hurt her so badly. Suppose the truth was even worse than she had envisioned?

What could the police do if Pat simply refused to answer the door? They would never break it down just because Lila had told them about her premonitions. Lila knew exactly how scornful of parapsychology the policemen could be.

Helplessly she stood at the window staring at the whirling clouds of blackness which were enveloping the house across the street.

The patio doors. They had opened that night. She had looked up and seen him and run to him, wrapping her arms around his legs. Toby, her friend who always gave her piggy-back rides. And he had picked her up and thrown her . . .

Toby . . . it had been *Toby*.

And he was there now, standing behind Arthur Stevens. . . .

Arthur sensed Toby's presence and whirled around. The blow from Toby's hand caught him directly on the throat, sending him reeling backward across the room. With a gasping, strangling cry he collapsed near the fireplace. His eyes closed; his head lolled to the side.

Toby came into the room. Pat shrank from the sight

of the thick legs in the dark trousers, the massive body, the powerful hands, the dark square of the onyx ring.

He bent over her. "You know, don't you, Kerry? As soon as I figured out who you were, I was sure you'd get around to doping it out. I'm sorry about what happened, but I had to take care of Abby. She was crazy about Billy. When she saw your mother shoot him, she fell apart. If I hadn't come back for her purse, I swear I wouldn't of touched you. I just wanted to shut you up for a while. But now you're out to get Abby, and that can't happen.

"You made it easy for me this time, Kerry. Everyone knows you've been getting threats. I didn't expect to be so lucky. Now this kook will be found with you and no more questions asked. You ask too many questions —you know that?"

The branches directly above the candelabrum suddenly ignited. They began to crackle, and gusts of smoke surged toward the ceiling. "The whole room will be gone in a few minutes, Kerry. I've got to get back now. It's a big night for Abby."

He patted her cheek. "Sorry."

The entire tree burst into flame. As she watched him closing the patio doors behind him, the carpet began to smolder. The pungent odor of evergreen mingled with the smoke. She tried to hold her breath. Her eyes stung so painfully that it was impossible to keep them open. She'd suffocate here. Rolling to the edge of the couch, she threw herself to the floor. Her forehead banged against the leg of the cocktail table. Gasping at the sudden pain, she began to wriggle toward the hall. With her hands tied behind her, she could barely move. She managed to flip over onto her back, brace

her hands under her and use them to propel herself forward. The heavy terry-cloth robe hampered her. Her bare feet slid helplessly over the carpet.

At the threshhold of the living room, she stopped. If she could manage to close the door, she'd keep the fire from spreading, at least for a few minutes. She dragged herself over the doorsill. The metal plate broke the skin on her hands. Squirming around the door, she propped herself against the wall, wedged her shoulder behind the door and leaned backward until she heard the latch click. The hallway was already filling with smoke. She couldn't tell any longer which way she was going. If she made a mistake and wandered into the library, she wouldn't have a chance.

Using the baseboard for guidance, she inched her way toward the front door.

42

Lila tried once again to reach Pat. This time she asked the operator to check the number. The phone was in working order.

She could not wait any longer. Something was terribly wrong. She dialed the police. She could ask them to check Pat's house, tell them she thought she had seen the prowler. But when the desk sergeant answered, she could not speak. Her throat closed as though she was choking. Her nostrils filled with the smell of acrid smoke. Pain shot through her wrists and ankles. Her body suffused with heat. The sergeant repeated his name impatiently. At last Lila found her voice.

"Three thousand N Street," she shrieked. "Patricia Traymore is dying! Patricia Traymore is dying!"

Sam drove at a frenzied pace, running red lights, hoping to pick up a police escort. Beside him Abigail sat, her clenched hands pressing against her lips.

"Abigail, I want the truth. What happened the night Dean and Renée Adams died?"

"Billy had promised he'd get a divorce. . . . That day he called me and said he couldn't do it. . . . That he had to make a go of his marriage . . . That he couldn't leave Kerry. I thought Renée was in Boston. I went there to plead with him. Renée went wild when she saw me. She had found out about us. Billy kept a gun in the desk. She turned it on herself. . . . He tried to get it from her . . . the gun went off. . . . Sam, it was a nightmare. He died before my eyes!"

"Then who killed *her?*" Sam demanded. "Who?"

"She killed herself," Abigail sobbed. "Toby knew there'd be trouble. He was watching from the patio. He dragged me out to the car. Sam, I was in shock. I didn't know what was happening. The last I saw was Renée standing there, holding the gun. Toby had to go back for my purse. Sam, I heard that second shot before he went back into the house. I swear it. He didn't tell me about Kerry until the next day. He said she must have come down right after we left, that Renée must have shoved her against the fireplace to get her out of the way. But he didn't realize she'd been seriously injured."

"Pat remembers tripping over her mother's body."

"No. That's impossible. She can't have."

The tires screeched as they turned onto Wisconsin Avenue.

"You've always believed Toby," he accused her, "because you *wanted* to believe him. It was better for you that way. Did you believe the plane crash was an accident, Abigail—a fortunate accident? Did you be-

lieve Toby when you alibied for him for the campaign funds?"

"Yes . . . yes. . . ."

The streets were packed with pedestrians. Wildly he honked the horn. The dinner crowd was drifting into the restaurants. He raced the car down M Street, across 31st Street to the corner of N and floored the brake pedal. They were both thrown forward.

"Oh, my God," Abigail whispered.

An elderly woman, screaming for help, was banging her fists against the front door of Pat's house. A police car, its siren wailing, was racing down the block.

The house was in flames.

Toby hurried through the yard toward the fence. It was all over now. No more loose ends. No pilot's widow to stir up trouble for Abigail. No Kerry Adams to remember what happened in the living room that night.

He'd have to hurry. Pretty soon Abby would be looking for him. She was due at the White House in an hour. *Someone was yelling for help. Someone must have spotted smoke.* He heard the police siren and he began to run.

He'd just reached the fence when a car roared past, spun around the corner and screeched to a stop. Car doors slammed and he heard a man shouting Pat Traymore's name. Sam Kingsley! He had to get out of here. The whole back of the house was starting to go. Someone would see him.

"Not the front door, Sam, back here, back here." Toby dropped from the fence. Abby. It was Abby. She was running along the side of the house, heading for

the patio. He ran to her, overtook her. "Abby, for Christ sake, stay away from there."

She looked at him wildeyed. The smell of smoke permeated the night air. A side window blew out and flames whooshed across the lawn.

"Toby, is Kerry in there?" Abby grabbed his lapels.

"I don't know what you're talking about."

"Toby, you were seen near the Graney woman's house last night."

"Abby, shut up! Last night I had dinner with my Steakburger friend. You saw me come in at ten-thirty."

"No I didn't."

"Yes, you did, Senator!"

"Then it's true. . . . What Sam told me . . ."

"Abby, don't pull that shit on me. I take care of you. You take care of me. It's always been like that, and you know it."

A second police car, its dome light blinking, sped past. "Abby, I've got to get out of here." There was no fear in his voice.

"Is Kerry in there?"

"I didn't start the fire. I didn't do a thing to her."

"Is she in there?"

"Yes."

"You oaf! You stupid, homicidal oaf! Get her *out* of there!" She pounded on his chest. "You heard me. Get her out of there." Flames shot through the roof. "Do as I say," she shouted.

For several seconds they stared at each other. Then Toby shrugged, giving in, and ran clumsily along the snow-covered side lawn, through the garden and onto the patio. The sound of fire engines wailed down the street as he kicked in the patio doors.

The heat inside was withering. Pulling off his coat, Toby wrapped it around his head and shoulders. She had been on the couch, somewhere to the right of the doors. It's because she's Billy's girl, he thought. It's all over for you, Abby. We can't pull this one off now. . . .

He was at the couch, running his hands along it. He couldn't see. She wasn't there.

He tried to feel the floor around the couch. A crackling sound exploded overhead. He had to get out of here—the whole place was going to cave in.

He stumbled toward the doors, guided only by the cold draft. Pieces of plaster fell on him and he lost his balance and fell. His hand touched human flesh. A face, but not a woman's face. It was the crazy.

Toby pulled himself up, felt himself shaking, felt the room shaking. A moment later the ceiling collapsed.

With his last breath he whispered, "Abby!" But he knew she couldn't help him this time. . . .

In a pushing, crawling motion, Pat moved inch by inch along the hallway. The tightly knotted rope had cut off the circulation in her right leg. She had to drag her legs, use only her fingers and palms to propel herself. The floorboards were becoming unbearably hot. The acrid smoke stung her eyes and skin. She couldn't feel the baseboard any longer. She was disoriented. It was hopeless. She was choking. She was going to burn to death.

Then it began . . . the pounding . . . the voice . . . Lila's voice shouting for help. . . . Pat twisted her body, tried to move toward the sound. A roar from the back of the house shook the floor. The whole

house was collapsing. She felt herself losing consciousness. . . . She had been meant to die in this house.

As blackness overwhelmed her, she heard a cacophony of hammering, splintering noises. They were trying to break the door down. She was so near it. A rush of cold air. Funnels of flames and smoke roaring toward the draft . . . Men's angry voices shouting, *"It's too late. You can't go in there."* Lila's screams: *"Help her, help her."* Sam's desperate, furious *"Let go of me."*

Sam . . . Sam . . . Footsteps running past her . . . Sam yelling her name. With the last of her strength, Pat lifted her legs and smashed them against the wall.

He turned. In the light of the flames, he saw her, scooped her up, and ran out of the house.

The street was crowded with fire engines and squad cars. Onlookers huddled together in shocked silence. Abigail stood statuelike as the ambulance attendants worked over Pat. Sam was kneeling at the side of the stretcher, his hands caressing Pat's arms, his face bleak with apprehension. A trembling, ashen-faced Lila was standing a few feet away, her eyes riveted on Pat's still body. Around them, hot sooty debris drifted from the wreckage of the house.

"Her pulsebeat is getting stronger," the attendant said.

Pat stirred, tried to push aside the oxygen mask. "Sam . . ."

"I'm here, darling." He looked up as Abigail touched his shoulder. Her face was smudged with grimy smoke. The suit she had planned to wear to the

White House was soiled and wrinkled. "I'm glad Kerry's all right, Sam. Take good care of her."

"I intend to."

"I'll get a policeman to drive me to a phone. I don't feel quite up to telling the President in person that I must resign from public life. Let me know what I need to do to help Eleanor Brown."

Slowly she began to walk to the nearest police car. Recognizing her, the onlookers broke into astonished comments and parted to open a path for her. Some of them began clapping. "Your program was great, Senator," someone yelled. "We love you." "We're rooting for you to be Vice President," another one shouted.

As she stepped into the car, Abigail Jennings turned, and with a tortured half-smile forced herself to acknowledge their greetings for the last time.

43

On December 29 at 9 P.M. the President strode into the East Room of the White House for the news conference he had summarily postponed two nights earlier. He walked to the lectern where the microphones had been placed. "I wonder why we're all here," he remarked. There was a burst of laughter.

The President expressed regret at the untimely resignation of the former Vice President. Then he continued, "There are many outstanding legislators who would fill the role with great distinction and could complete my second term in office if for any reason I were unable to. However, the person I have chosen to be Vice President, with the hearty approval of the leaders of all branches of the government and subject to confirmation by the Congress, is one who will fill a unique place in the history of this country. Ladies and gentlemen, it is my pleasure to present to you the first woman Vice President of the United States, Senator Claire Lawrence of Wisconsin."

A roar of applause erupted as the White House audience jumped to its feet.

Nestled together on the couch in his apartment, Sam and Pat watched the news conference. "I wonder if Abigail is seeing this," Pat said.

"I imagine she is."

"She never needed Toby's kind of help. She could have done it on her own."

"That's true. And it's the saddest part of it."

"What will happen to her?"

"She'll leave Washington. But don't count her out. Abigail's tough. She'll fight her way back. And this time without that goon in the background."

"She did so much good," Pat said sadly. "In so many ways, she *was* the woman I believed her to be."

They listened to Claire Lawrence's acceptance speech. Then Sam helped Pat to her feet. "With your eyebrows and lashes singed, you have the most incredible surprised look." He cupped her face in his hands. "Feel good to be out of the hospital?"

"You know it!"

He had come so close to losing her. Now she was looking up at him, her face trusting but troubled.

"What will happen to Eleanor?" she asked. "You haven't said anything and I've been afraid to ask."

"I didn't mean *not* to tell you. The revised statement from Abigail coupled with everything else we have on Toby will exonerate her. How about you? Now that you know the truth, how do you feel about your mother and father?"

"Happy that it wasn't my father who pulled the trigger. Sorry for my mother. Glad that neither one of

them hurt me that night. They were absolutely wrong for each other, but so much that happened was nobody's fault. Maybe I'm starting to understand people better. At least I hope so."

"Think about this. If your parents hadn't gotten together, you wouldn't be around, and I might be spending the rest of my life in a place that's decorated . . . how did you put it . . . like a motel lobby?"

"Something like that."

"Have you decided about the job?"

"I don't know. Luther does seem sincere about wanting me to stay. I guess for what it's worth the program was well received. He's asked me to start planning one on Claire Lawrence and thinks we might even be able to get the First Lady. It's mighty tempting. He swears this time I'll have creative control of my projects. And with you around, he certainly won't try any more passes at me."

"He'd better not!" Sam put his arm around her and saw the faint beginning of a smile. "Come on. You like a water view." They walked to the window and looked out. The night had clouded over but the Potomac gleamed in the lights of the Kennedy Center.

"I don't think I've ever experienced anything like seeing that house on fire, knowing you were inside," he said. His arm tightened around her. "I can't lose you, Pat, not now, not ever." He kissed her. "I'm dead serious about not wasting any more time. Would a honeymoon in Caneel Bay next week suit you?"

"Save your money. I'd rather go back to the Cape."

"And the Ebb Tide?"

"You guessed it. With just one change." She looked up at him and her smile became radiant. "This time when we leave we'll take the same plane home."

POCKET
B O O K S

WEEP NO MORE, MY LADY

MARY HIGGINS CLARK

Beautiful young Elizabeth Lange is haunted by the tragic loss of her beloved sister, Leila - a stage and screen star who plunged to her death form the balcony of her New York penthouse. But the circumstances are mysterious. Why would Leila take her own life at the height of her fame and success?

Invited to Cypress Point Spa by a friend, Elizabeth finds herself confronted by a cast of characters who all had motives for killing her sister - including Leila's lover, Ted Winters. And she quickly discovers her own life might also be under threat ...

PRICE £4.99

ISBN 0 671 85399 6

POCKET

B O O K S

REMEMBER ME

MARY HIGGINS CLARK

Unable to forgive herself for the death of her two-year-old son, Menley Nichol's marriage to Adam starts to fall apart - until the birth of their daughter Hannah promises to revitalize their relationship. Adam rents a house on Cape Cod, confident that the tranquillity of the place will be ideal for his young family.

But at Remember House, an eighteen-century landmark with a sinister past, strange incidents make Menley relive the horror of the accident in which she lost her son . . . incidents which make her fear for Hannah . . .

PRICE £4.99

ISBN 0671 85345 7

POCKET BOOKS

LET ME CALL YOU SWEETHEART

MARY HIGGINS CLARK

When Kerry McGrath - a smart, relentless prosecutor - takes her daughter to see a plastic surgeon following a car accident, she sees a woman in the surgery with a beautiful, hauntingly familiar face. On a subsequent visit, she sees the same face again - on a different woman . . .

Suddenly she remembers: both these women look startlingly like Suzanne Reardon, the 'Sweetheart Murder' victim whose husband, Skip, is now serving a life sentence for that murder.

When Kerry starts asking questions, she discovers that just about everyone wants to keep the case closed. Still she persists - but her puzzled queries have triggered a response and she finds herself in great, growing danger.

PRICE £5.99

ISBN 0 671 85347 3

POCKET
B O O K S

<u>ORDER FORM</u>

This book and other Mary Higgins Clark titles are available from your book shop or can be ordered direct from the publisher.

☐ Weep No More, My Lady 0671 853996 £4.99
☐ Remember Me 0671 853457 £4.99
☐ Let Me Call You Sweetheart 0671 853473 £5.99

Please send cheque or postal order for the value of the book, and add the following for postage and packing: UK inc. BFPO 75p per book; OVERSEAS Inc. EIRE £1 per book. OR: Please debit this amount from my:

VISA/ACCESS/MASTERCARD...
CARD NO...
EXPIRY DATE...
AMOUNT £..
NAME..
ADDRESS..
....

SIGNATURE..

Send orders to:
SIMON & SCHUSTER CASH SALES
PO Box 29, Douglas, Isle of Man, IM99 1BQ
Tel: 01624 675137, Fax 01624 670923
http://www.bookpost.co.uk
Please allow 28 days for delivery.
Prices and availability subject to change without notice.

SUNBURST

Mavis Thomas

Thelma Barrington's life was restricted to caring for her late parents. She feels old — like a maiden aunt — useful for babysitting and minding the family pet. When she's suddenly thrown together with Myron, a charming, younger man, he proposes marriage. This wonderful chance of a new life is shadowed by doubts: is it her bank balance that attracts him? And, when, following a tragedy, Thelma has to care for her two young nephews, will Myron stay — or just walk away?

MARRY IN HASTE

Moyra Tarling

'Marry me . . . ' Evan Mathieson had once whispered. But now Jade Adams's former dream groom has become a father to his 'nephew' Matt, and to keep him Evan needs a wife. Jade can't refuse the man she's always yearned for, or the little boy to whom she could be a mother. Now Jade dreams of becoming a true wife to her new husband. But can hopes of a new-found love survive the secret she'd locked in her heart long ago?

A PROMISE FOR TOMORROW

Gillian Villiers

When Hope has to close her beloved shop, she reluctantly accepts her godmother's suggestion and returns to her family's roots in southern Scotland. Although caring for Mr Jackson is challenging, surprisingly, it's fun to do, and gradually she is able to put her business disaster into perspective. She is drawn into village life, and wonders if she could grow particularly close to farmer's son Robbie. But first she must sort out some long-hidden family secrets . . .

DECEPTION

Fay Cunningham

When Alex bumps into Lucas Fairfax in Marbella all she wants is a story. So when she gets mistaken for his daughter's new nanny she jumps at the chance to see inside his sea-front villa. All's fair in love and journalism and a story about Lucas Fairfax, on holiday with his daughter, will be quite a scoop. But Alex didn't plan on falling in love, and now her deception is threatening to tear them apart.

THE AUDACIOUS HIGHWAYMAN

Beth James

When Sophie once again meets her childhood hero Julian, who's been sent home in disgrace, she feels that romance has made her life complete. However, her brother Tom and his friend Harry must confine Sophie to her home because highwaymen have been sighted in the area. Sophie, contemptuous of the highwayman rumours, finds that any secret assignation with Julian seems doomed to failure. Then — when she's involved in a frightening encounter with the highwayman — her life is changed for ever.

Other titles in the
Linford Romance Library:

WITHIN THESE WALLS

Susan Sarapuk

When Annie revisits Chattelcombe
Priory, it's inevitable that unwelcome
memories are stirred. It's where
she'd fallen in love with Edward,
and where Charlotte's accident, which
changed everything, had happened.
When Edward returns to buy the
Priory, he also attempts to win back
Annie. But Tim, the vicar, wants to
turn the Priory into a retreat centre,
and Annie finds herself torn between
the two men. Then, she discovers a
secret, which changes her perception
of the past . . .

To Julie

Prologue

40,000 BC – *Neander Valley, east of modern-day Düsseldorf, Germany*

HE HAD BEEN STARING OUT AT THE RAGING STORM FOR *days, hungrier than he could ever remember. The limestone cave was still warm thanks to the fire he had started as soon as he'd regained enough strength to collect wood. The flames were weaker now and his stockpile had run out. His skills with fire had always been a source of great pride, both for him and his mate. Now, his cave, his sanctuary, was also his prison.*

He knew, with a deep and intuitive certainty, that he was the last of his kind. It made him sad. And angry. He stood at the cave entrance, his furs wrapped tightly around his shoulders, and screamed in defiant rage at the world outside as though he could drown out the howling wind.

During the night of the last full moon his mate had been angry that he was too sick to go out with the other hunters to find food, so she had gone instead. She hadn't come back. When he had eventually grown strong enough to leave the cave he had gone looking for her. He hadn't found her, but had instead stumbled across the bodies of several

1

others of his tribe – not just the hunters, but their mates and a few of the young. They had been half-buried in the snow where the gorge opened into the wide river valley and he had puzzled over what had befallen them. Many of his people had already died, either from hunger or cold during the previous harsh winter – their already low numbers dwindling steadily as the winters became worse and powerful storms ravaged the landscape. They had found it difficult to adapt; familiar plants and animals had disappeared, and food supplies had become even scarcer.

None of the bodies he'd found showed any obvious signs of injury from attack by rival groups or wild animals and he attributed their red and blistered skin to frostbite, but was confused about why they had stayed out long enough to freeze to death, when they were so close to the shelter of their caves.

Overcome with grief he had struggled back to his cave. He had wanted to bury and mourn them properly but knew that would have to wait until his strength returned. His priority had been to find food and he'd been lucky to come across a skinny young deer lying dead against the base of a tree. He was so hungry and exhausted he didn't stop to question whether its death was related to those of his people.

He'd carried the carcass back to his cave high above the valley floor, where he cooked it over the fire and ate until he was fit to burst. Now, four days later, with the carcass cleaned to the bone, he used its hollowed-out skull to cook what little quantity of root vegetables and grasses he had been able to find before the storm set in. But his hunger was back again.

Two weeks later, with the storm showing no signs of abating, he too would die, but of starvation rather than the fatal radiation exposure from the powerful coronal mass

2

ejection that had taken the lives of the rest of his tribe, the shelter of his cave offering him the cruel protection that had pointlessly prolonged his life.

He died oblivious to how special he would become. Many millennia later, when his remains were found, no one would know that he had indeed been the last of his kind to survive in northern Eurasia. And yet, by one of those rare twists of fate, he was also the first of his kind to be identified by the Homo sapien *scholars who studied his bones. They named him Felhofer One, or Neanderthal One, and many of them would ponder what had caused so many of his species to disappear so suddenly.*

3

PART I

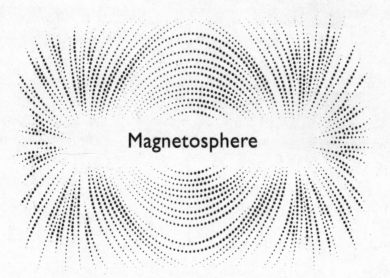

Magnetosphere

I

Saturday, 22 October 2039 – outside Fairbanks, Alaska

BRAD GROCHOWIAK WAS LOOKING FORWARD TO SPEND-
ing some holiday time with Laura and the kids. First,
though, he was looking forward to the end of this particular drive, to unloading and hitting the sack at the
Holiday Inn Express. To be fair, the regular 350-mile
route north from Anchorage to Fairbanks wasn't so bad,
even in late October, as long as the weather stayed clear.

The night had been uneventful and he had less than an
hour of his journey to go. Behind him, almost bumper to
bumper, were six other giant trucks, identical to his own
apart from their lack of a human occupant. Instead, all
were linked via their autonomous AI systems. Although
Brad had not had to do anything the entire journey, he
knew the trucking company felt reassured having a
human in the lead vehicle ready to take over manual control if necessary. After all, there was always the chance
that severe weather could close in unexpectedly, particularly at this time of year. While this was an unnecessary
regulation – the truck's AI system could see far better

7

than he ever could in bad weather and poor light – Brad wasn't complaining. It kept him in work. In the twelve years he had been working for the company he had yet to intervene on any journey.

He stretched his arms out, arching his back to loosen the stiffness, then, giving the stubble on his head a vigorous rub, he leaned forward and touched the windscreen where the movie he'd only half been paying attention to faded away and the glass reverted to its natural transparency, allowing him to take in the landscape outside. It was already late morning, but the sky was only just showing signs of changing colour, heralding the start of a new day. As the sky brightened, the blackness of the snowy landscape on either side of the road turned a deep blue, contrasting spectacularly with the fiery red band of light spreading across the peaks of the mountain range far to the west. Brad had witnessed this Alaskan alpenglow all his life and it never failed to take his breath away. This had always been his favourite time of day, just before the sun spilled its first rays over the opposite horizon.

It was only once the sun had dragged itself up into view, flooding the world with its winter light, that a tiny detail of colour caught his attention. Against the backdrop of dazzling white snow a smudge of orange and black stood out. At first Brad thought this was another vehicle far ahead on the road, or possibly a brightly coloured building in the distance, but then realized that it was a smear on the windscreen – most likely an insect that had, thanks to the unforgiving law of conservation of momentum, come off worse in its head-on collision with an object a hundred million times its mass.

In itself, the fate of one bug wouldn't have registered on Brad's consciousness, but he soon noticed there were marks of several more suicidal insects all over the windscreen. He surprised himself by recognizing what they were: monarch butterflies. Last spring he'd helped his daughter with a school project collecting butterflies in the garden. Grace had informed him, with the innocent sagacity that only a nine-year-old possesses, that they were called tiger swallowtails – even though, she explained seriously, they looked very similar in colouring to their more famous cousins the monarchs. Apparently, despite monarchs never venturing this far north, you could tell the two species apart by the shape of their wings. Leaning forward to examine one of the smudges decorating his windscreen more carefully, he decided that these ones were almost certainly monarchs. But Grace was a smart kid and if she said you didn't get monarchs in Alaska then you didn't. Besides, butterflies were pretty little things you saw fluttering about in summertime, not in late October and this far north where the temperature was well below freezing already.

With not much else to do with his time, he decided to investigate the matter further. His on-board computer was basic, but sufficient for his purposes. Brad didn't feel the need for the latest holographics or virtual reality surround displays – as long as he was online he was happy. And it was reassuring to know that, however isolated he might feel out in this desolate landscape, there were always dozens of solar-powered internet drones in the stratosphere miles above his head, instantly linking him to the rest of the world.

He cleared his throat, then spoke loudly enough to be heard above the hum of the truck's electric motor.

'Computer, show me a picture of a monarch butterfly.'

No sooner had he finished speaking than he was staring at an array of colourful images on one side of his windscreen.

Here is a selection of images of monarchs.

Yup, he had been right. The insects stuck to his windscreen were indeed monarchs. Grace would be proud of him.

'Tell me about monarch butterfly migrations.'

There was a brief pause before the computer answered. Brad knew this delay was deliberate. People didn't like the machines they communicated with responding instantly, which they were of course capable of, as though knowing in advance what they were going to be asked. Instead, all virtual-assistant AIs and chatbots these days had up to a second of built-in delay time to make them seem more humanlike in their interactions.

Monarchs undertake one of the world's great annual migratory journeys, when millions escape south-east Canada's harsh winters and fly south-west all the way to Mexico. Others, west of the Canadian Rockies, will migrate due south to California. Monarch butterflies are among the many species of animals, which include several migratory birds and marine creatures, that use an inner biological compass to find their way by following the Earth's magnetic field lines.

'When are monarch butterflies found in Alaska?'

Monarchs cannot be found in Alaska. It is too far north for them.

Brad conjured up in his mind an image of the map of North America. Wherever these insects had flown from, they had most certainly not been heading towards warmer climes. Clearly this group must have been hopelessly lost.

10

Did their squadron leader have such a bad sense of direction that it had led them north instead of south? And if so, how the hell had it landed such an important job? The thought amused him. No. Surely they obeyed some sort of collective swarm mentality. But was it possible that there had been some fault in their inner compasses, however the hell they worked? He would ask Grace when he got home. It would make for a good science project. He thought about sending her the AR footage of the butterflies he had recorded on his retinal display but decided it could wait. Anyway, it'd be more fun to chat to Grace about this face to face rather than just copying over an augmented reality clip of what he was seeing on his screen.

It never occurred to him that the fault might not lie with the butterflies at all. Absent-mindedly, he flicked on the wipers to clear the windscreen of the multi-coloured carnage.

2

Monday, 28 January 2041 – Rio de Janeiro

SARAH MAITLIN STARED AT HER DISPLAY AND TRIED TO clear her head, her third cafezinho of the evening cold and forgotten on her desk. She had always found coffee more effective at clearing niggling headaches than pills. Running both hands through her hair, she absent-mindedly gathered it up, twisting and tucking it into a self-sustaining bun. The coolness of the air-conditioning on her exposed neck caused a chill to run through her, despite the climate-controlled environment in the lab. She retrieved the sweater that had been hanging over the back of her chair all day, slipping it over her T-shirt, and had a sudden vision of her mother rebuking her for not caring enough about her wardrobe. 'Why do you still wear that horrible old thing?' she'd no doubt say. 'You're a very attractive woman, if you'd only make the effort.' She smiled wryly at the thought. Her mother back in England was desperate for grandchildren and kept a close eye on Sarah's biological clock – more than ever now that she was in her late thirties – and her multiple failed relationships.

She dragged her attention back to the holographic

display in front of her. Ordinarily, these images would have been of no more than academic interest, but this was different. As the physicist on duty at the Solar Science Institute in Rio, it was Sarah's responsibility to keep a close eye on the Sun's activity. Although the Institute had been set up twenty years ago to carry out basic astrophysics research, its main function over the past couple of years had been to provide early warning of any abnormal solar activity that might be of concern – the current situation being a case in point.

The centre of the holo filling her field of vision was dominated by a high-resolution 3D video feed of the Sun, captured by a group of satellites in orbit around it – a detailed image that was both beautiful and terrifying. It was so realistic she could almost feel the heat on her face. Staring at the slowly spinning three-dimensional projection, she focused her attention on one region of the Sun's churning and fiery surface. What she was looking at was more than a little concerning.

She'd hoped to knock off for the day a couple of hours ago, but now knew she wouldn't be leaving her desk just yet. Her cats would be hungry, so she made a mental note to call her neighbour in a few minutes and ask her to feed them.

It suddenly occurred to her that she hadn't eaten anything herself since breakfast. Working this hard wasn't doing her any good; there'd been no gym in a fortnight and her social life was a disaster. She couldn't remember the last time she'd been out for a drink or dinner.

A decent break was what she needed, just as soon as this latest crisis was over. Maybe a day or two down on Copacabana. Although given the recent increasing size and number of ozone holes being punched through the atmosphere, the UV-shielded zones on the beach would be packed. These days not even the most dedicated sun-worshipper would risk lying out in the unprotected open for long. In many parts of the world it was becoming so bad that some people were reluctant to venture outside their own homes at all these days, even at night, so as not to risk unnecessary exposure to the increasingly power-ful cosmic radiation. Many had micro sensors embedded under their skin to monitor the presence of high-energy particles and to alert them if it reached hazardous levels.

But when it came to dangerous radiation from space, nothing could compete with a well-aimed blast from a cor-onal mass ejection. Until a few years ago, these enormous bubbles of hot plasma spat out by the Sun were of interest only to solar physicists. Sarah recalled trying to explain to her father why she found the subject so fascinating.

'What's the worry?' he'd argued. 'After all, the Earth has survived just fine for the past however many gazillion years without the Sun frying us.' Ben Maitlin made no secret of his wish that his daughter had followed him into political journalism. 'That's how to change the world,' he'd told her, 'more effectively than any politician can.' But Sarah had chosen a career in science instead, dealing with concepts he often found difficult to get his head around. And yet she knew he was immensely proud of her, always insisting she send him a copy of each research paper she published. Her mother had told her how he would often pull out her most recent article at dinner parties when asked how his daughter was getting on, and proceed to read out its title with an extravagant flourish, without the faintest idea what it meant.

Ben Maitlin was an intelligent man who tried hard to keep abreast of scientific developments. Sarah sometimes found it frustrating that many other journalists, scientifi-cally illiterate hacks, now regarded themselves as experts

14

on coronal mass ejections. Their interest was certainly understandable given the very real threat CMEs were beginning to pose, and at least they were reporting on them. And that at least meant that the politicians might now finally do something.

Over the last two years, Sarah's work had taken on an urgency that was in stark contrast to the sedate, curiosity-driven research she had enjoyed ever since her PhD. The most recent measurement of the strength and distribution of the Earth's magnetic field was terrifying. It was now down to just half the strength it had been when she was born and the implications of this were only too clear to her.

Of course, governments around the world had avoided engendering widespread panic by simply downplaying the risks. This policy created its own problems for many scientists, who could see what was coming but found their warnings falling on deaf political ears, exactly as had happened a generation earlier with climate change. It was beyond short-sighted that there was *still* no coordinated international response to the crisis that was beginning to unfold. The science couldn't be any simpler: the Earth's magnetic field, which for billions of years had protected the planet's fragile biosphere from dangerous radiation from space, was now no longer up to the task. And that meant humanity had some serious problems.

She examined the images and streams of scrolling data hanging like ghosts in the air in front of her. Like the conductor of an orchestra, she manipulated the data, saving the information in a virtual folder. This coronal ejection would hit the Earth in less than forty-eight hours and it wasn't going to be pleasant.

'Hey, Miguel, come and take a look at this.'

Replacing the holo of the Sun with one of the Earth, she highlighted all the data collated on the CME – its energy, spread, and the all-important SAT, the Shock Arrival Time.

Miguel wandered across and peered over her shoulder. 'Well, that's going to knock out some power grids. Where will it hit?'

'Looks like the Indian Ocean mostly. Almost definitely central and south-east Asia too.'

'We might get lucky if it arrives a few hours early. Then most of the flux would hit—'

'—the South Pacific, yes. But, that's just wishful thinking. Anyway, I'm not sure it'd be much comfort. It's still going to knock out a stack of comm sats.'

Sarah closed her eyes and rubbed them with thumb and forefinger. She decided to run her simulations again. No need to panic the authorities in those countries unless she was sure. If she'd got her calculations wrong and the CME ended up missing the Earth entirely then she would be accused of crying wolf.

'Do me a quick favour, Miguel? Run a check on paths of all medium- and low-orbit sats above a five-thousand-kilometre radius centred on, um . . .' She stared at the slowly spinning globe. '. . . Centred on Nepal, I think.'

'Then correlate it with SAT, right?'

Sarah knew that the SAT was the big uncertainty. No one could accurately predict the variation in the speed of an approaching CME, or the extension of the pulse. 'Yes, and assume the usual eight- to ten-hour window.'

Feeling stiff, she extended her legs and arched her back, lifting her body off the seat, stretching cramped muscles. Another late night beckoned. In mid-stretch, she suddenly became aware that she hadn't heard Miguel walking back to his desk and that he was still standing behind her. She swivelled round in her chair rather more quickly than she intended.

16

'Well?'

Miguel grinned and ambled back to his corner of the lab. Once seated, he pulled his display visor down over his eyes and started to hum tunelessly as his fingers danced across the virtual display hanging in the air in front of him, gathering and manipulating the data from the thousands of registered satellites. He would rule out the ones that would definitely not be crossing the path of the high-energy cascade of electrons, protons and atomic nuclei, then feed all the information on the rest into his simulation codes.

Despite his irritating humming, Sarah felt a sense of admiration for the bright young Brazilian. He was smart and passionate about his work. She wondered whether his outward cheerfulness was genuine or whether he was just trying to hide his own apprehension.

3

MARC BRUCKNER WAS ENJOYING THE PEACE AND QUIET
of his favourite vineyard. When he'd arrived there late in
the afternoon there had been several other customers,
mainly elderly couples. He'd nodded greetings and then
found a secluded table at the far end of the courtyard
tucked under the shade of a large kauri tree. Its thick
brown trunk was full of carved romantic graffiti from
previous love-struck patrons. None of this registered on
Marc's consciousness, though; his own failed marriage
was still too raw. He'd initially felt self-conscious about
drinking alone while all around him people seemed to be
blissfully paired up. A few glasses of wine would soon
dispel any awkwardness. Alcohol seemed to be his only
faithful companion these days.

He remembered only too well the accusing look on his
daughter Evie's face when he had told her he needed to
move back to New Zealand for a while. 'How is running
away to the other side of the world going to make things
better?' she'd asked through angry tears.

18

It was true that he had come back to New Zealand with the genuine intention of 'getting his shit together' as his father had been fond of saying. Well, it had only been two weeks – surely he couldn't be expected to turn his life around as soon as he'd landed. After all, he'd been fighting his demons for a long time; he'd been diagnosed with depression and anxiety several years ago, which meant he'd received all the clinical help he'd needed, but he still found it hard to shake the feeling that his problems were no more than a failure of moral fibre and will-power and that he could somehow talk himself better.

It had been a warm and sticky afternoon, with the westering sun bringing out the best in the colours of the surrounding flora. The vineyard sat on top of a hill and afforded Marc a beautiful panoramic view of the island – from the well-manicured bushes and shrubs of the garden itself to the surrounding apricot, lime and plum trees further down the hill. Beyond was a lush rolling landscape, with more vineyards and farms dotted on adjacent hill-tops. In fact, if he strained his neck up over the nearest bush he could see all the way down to the westernmost point of the island and Matiatia Bay, where the ferries transported inhabitants and the tourists to and from Auckland twenty kilometres across the water.

Marc had sat pondering the mess of a life he'd left behind in America: his failed marriage, the broken relationship with his daughter, the car crash that his academic career had turned into, despite his success as one of the world's foremost physicists ... The only intrusion on his thoughts this afternoon had been the soft, competing sounds of insects and birds. Although he had not seen them, he knew an entire ecosystem existed hidden beneath the foliage, with grey warblers and fantails hopping from branch to twig searching for bugs, beetles and caterpillars.

19

That had been a few hours ago. Now that darkness had closed in, with the lights of the Auckland skyline sparkling in the distance, he decided that Waiheke Island had to be just about the most beautiful spot on Earth. Why hadn't he thought of spending more time here before? He recalled summer holidays on the island as a boy, swimming, fishing or messing around on his father's boat. But his parents had only bought their retirement home on the south side long after he had moved to the States. Now that they were gone, their home was his. But he refused to accept that he was ready to settle down here just yet. There was still a flickering hope that he could put his life and research career back on track.

Well into his second bottle of Syrah, he leaned carefully back in his chair to gaze up at the night sky, deciding to count shooting stars. He guessed he was probably the last customer still left at the vineyard. Faint music drifted across the courtyard from inside the building and he kept catching snatches of it, deciding it was Frank Sinatra, crooning about flying off to Jupiter and Mars – rather appropriately, thought Marc, as he tried to locate those two planets among the hundreds of twinkling stars.

Coming back to New Zealand had definitely been the right move. The stress of the divorce coinciding with the meltdown he'd suffered at Columbia University and the small-mindedness of academic colleagues he had thought he could count on as friends had all finally become too much to cope with.

Maybe he really should put his past behind him and settle down here. Was it really such a bad idea? There were plenty of projects he could think of that would occupy him. And if he got too stir-crazy he could always go back to New York and try to pick up where he'd left off. After all, he was still on the right side of fifty, so it wasn't like he was ready to retire any time soon.

He allowed his eyes to adjust to the dark so that he could pick out the very faintest dots of light. It was funny how people assumed that all physicists were familiar with every star, planet and constellation in the night sky. He'd lost count of the number of times he'd had to explain that he was not an astronomer and that his research involved looking down at mathematical equations, or getting buried in complex electronic kit, studying the world at the tiniest of scales, rather than looking up at the heavens. Thanks to his colour-blindness, he couldn't even tell Venus from Mars.

He'd taken out his augmented-reality lenses so as not to have the spectacle ruined by any unnecessary overlaid information. The night sky lost its aesthetic beauty and majesty when each bright dot had detailed statistics superimposed around it. Of course, it wasn't difficult to switch off his AR feed whenever he wanted, but there was something liberating about taking his contacts out – like walking barefoot on fresh grass.

And yet, like countless others, Marc found it hard to do without AR – its use had become so ubiquitous that it was now hard to remember a time when no one had access to instant information overlying their field of vision. He marvelled at humanity's ability to adapt to new technologies so quickly that it forgot how it had ever coped before. Born, as he was, just a few years after the dawn of the internet, and despite his scientific training, Marc was finding it increasingly hard to keep up with the pace of change, and when it came to the very latest fads he considered himself a bit of a dinosaur, preferring to wear the old-fashioned AR contact lenses rather than the liquid Nano-Gee retinal implants that had become all the rage in recent years.

21

The field had been revolutionized with breathtaking rapidity once it was discovered that AR no longer needed the user to wear glasses or contact lenses on which to superimpose text, images and video – a veil of data through which they could still see the physical world around them. Instead, if you chose to – and most people under the age of forty chose to – you could access everything you needed from the Cloud as an integrated part of your vision. In fact, if you closed your eyes to block out the external world, the AR world really came into its own.

It was a research team at Berkeley who had first discovered how to control the light-sensitive cryptochrome biomolecules covering the back of the retina. Several members of the team had quickly seen the potential of their breakthrough and within five years had become the world's first trillionaires. Once it was understood how these proteins could be switched on and off with tiny electromagnetic signals sent to the users' eyes from their Cloud-linked wristpads, rapid advances were made in the technology. Almost overnight, it seemed to Marc, everyone had access to double vision: reality and augmented reality, overlapping and yet, with a little practice, quite separate. So good had the AR projections onto the retina now become, that the technology's main teething problem came from the user confusing the projection with the physical universe beyond.

'Can I get you anything else, Professor Bruckner?'

The soft voice behind him that snapped him back from his reverie belonged to Melissa, the vineyard owners' daughter, who was waitressing at Stony Hill during the summer. She was doing a good job of hiding her impatience to knock off for the night.

'Thanks, Melissa, no. Just finishing this glass and I'm off.' Then he added, 'Sorry if you've been waiting to close.'

'That's all right,' she smiled. 'Dad pays by the hour.' She collected the small lamp from the adjacent table and pushed the four surrounding chairs in closer. Turning to go back inside she looked up at the night sky. 'It's so pretty up there, isn't it? All those swirling colours.'

Marc was puzzled and turned to look, following her gaze. 'Oh, my God, it's the aurora!' he gasped. 'It's so vivid!' The evening sky over the Pacific glowed majestically in green-white swirling patterns, constantly changing and stunningly beautiful.

Marc decided this was the perfect end to the evening. Together they gazed up at a curtain of light to the left of the vineyard roof that grew more intense, then spread slowly round behind them before fading, only to be replaced by an equally stunning pattern on the right side. He and Melissa watched in appreciative silence.

However, as the novelty of the spectacle began to wear off, Marc got a niggling feeling that he was missing something obvious. Something very important. The thought germinated and grew in his mind, despite the wine that was blunting his analytical skills. Then it suddenly hit him. He ran a quick mental check to make sure he'd got his bearings right. The impressive Aurora Australis he was looking at was in completely the wrong direction. It should have been in the southern sky, towards the Pole. But this display was to the north. How the hell was that even possible?

4

Thursday, 31 January – 05:30, New Delhi

FLIGHT AI-231 FROM STOCKHOLM WAS BEGINNING ITS descent into Delhi. Captain Joseph Rahman preferred these old-fashioned subsonic journeys even though they took all night. He just didn't feel comfortable doing too many hyperskips these days. Thanks to the weakening magnetic field of the Earth, they carried an increasingly high radiation risk. While he could understand the attraction of getting from Europe to India in forty-five minutes by skimming off the upper atmosphere at Mach 10, like a stone on the surface of a pond, he was determined to minimize his own exposure to the bombardment from cosmic rays.

He switched on the cabin's exterior projection, so that the feed from the hundreds of tiny cameras covering the outer surface of the plane mapped onto the interior of the windowless fuselage, making it appear entirely transparent to the passengers. But it was a pointless exercise. Ordinarily, the panoramic view this gave as the plane came in to land would have been a quite dramatic experience, with the lights of the mostly still sleeping megacity spread out below. Instead, they were greeted by a wall of white thanks to the thick fog that often engulfed Indira Gandhi Airport at this time of year. They'd been circling in a holding pattern at three thousand metres for forty minutes now, waiting their turn to land.

Suddenly several of his displays went blank.

It looked like an issue with the satnav system. He waited a few minutes for the aircraft's AI to resolve the matter. With nothing for him to do he flicked on the intercom to update his crew and passengers. Like all pilots for the past hundred years, Captain Rahman's tone was deep and rich, and, with twenty-five years of flight experience under his belt, exuded calm confidence.

'Sorry for this slight delay, ladies and gentlemen, we're still waiting to be given a slot to land. There might also be a further short delay as we look into a problem with the plane's AI. We hope to fix this quickly and I'll keep you posted.' Then, to avoid any unnecessary panic, he added, 'There's absolutely nothing to be alarmed about.'

Still, he now had to keep an eye on the battery gauge. A strong headwind for most of the journey from Stockholm, then this long hold above Indira Gandhi Airport, meant that the charge was lower than he would have liked.

While his two young co-pilots busied themselves trying to find the source of the satnav problem, he radioed air traffic control.

'Delhi, this is Air India two-three-one. We've lost satlink, so I guess we're entirely in your hands now. We're running low on batteries too.'

The response from the control tower was reassuringly immediate:

'Copy that, two-three-one. You now have clearance to land. Sit back and we'll take it from here.'

Rahman allowed himself a small sigh of relief. Most airports now had AI systems that would take control of all incoming flights if necessary, particularly in poor visibility, manoeuvring the planes remotely to the correct approach angle. However, thanks to the ubiquity of artificial intelligence in all complex systems, aircraft were generally more than capable of doing the job themselves, and international regulations stipulated that airports' air traffic control should only step in when absolutely necessary. Captain Rahman was more than happy to hand over his plane on this occasion: his aircraft's AI system, more powerful than old-fashioned autopilots, could not function without GPS. Still, he promised himself he'd get to the bottom of the problem once he was on the ground. GPS had only ever failed him on one previous occasion; and that time he'd at least been able to see outside and watch as the invisible hands of the airport's AI system had guided the plane down safely.

Then, just as suddenly as the satellite signal had dropped out, so now did the aircraft's entire communication system. There was a sudden jolt as it was released from the hold of the control tower.

OK, *now* he would have something to do. Shit, this was getting serious. Still, no need to panic. He turned to his co-pilots, who were both watching him intensely. He smiled at them reassuringly and tried to keep his voice steady. 'Come on, guys, let's stay professional here. It'll be a story to dine out on, right?' Without waiting for a response from either of them he turned his attention back to the job at hand.

'Delhi, this is Air India two-three-one. What the hell just happened there?'

'Sorry, two-three-one, seems we have a major electronics issue down here too. We—'

The voice in Rahman's earpiece was suddenly drowned out by static.

'I didn't catch that, Delhi, say again?'

Still nothing but static.

Joseph Rahman took a deep breath and checked his fuel gauge again. He no longer had enough juice to pull up and climb above the fog and wait for the issue to be resolved. He thought back to his early days of flying twenty years ago when an airport's instrument landing system would have allowed him to conduct a textbook instrument approach – particularly in this thick fog, which would have been a definite CAT 3. But hardly any airports had ILS systems any more – a technology involving a localizer antenna and a glide slope system that would between them provide the aircraft's computer with all the information it needed to land safely without the pilot's intervention. Nowadays, everything was reliant on AI minds and GPS. And neither looked like being of any help to Flight AI-231 right now.

Landing a modern aircraft manually was something of a novelty that he would normally have relished, but this was going to require considerable skill and a bucket-load of luck. He was confident that before they'd lost contact they were on the precise bearing to come in on the southeast runway. He also knew that his air speed was right and the glide slope indicator was still showing that he was approaching the runway at the correct angle: three degrees to the horizontal. That meant trying to land was a far less dangerous option than circling through the fog in the hope that the problem got fixed. For all he knew, the other dozen or so aircraft in the vicinity were also flying blind.

'OK, here we go,' he said, more to himself than anyone else. 'We just have to keep this bearing steady and descend smoothly, then hope to God we see those runway lights in time to tweak our approach.'

He flicked the comms button. 'Can I have your

attention again please, ladies and gentlemen? I am about to adjust your seats to cocoon mode as this might be a bumpy landing.'

He then quickly added, 'Cabin crew, please confirm all passengers secure then take your seats. Five minutes to landing.'

He could tell his co-pilots were now more than a little scared. They'd been chatting away in Hindi throughout the flight but were now silent. They were both sitting bolt upright in their seats looking out straight ahead, waiting to catch a glimpse of the runway lights through the fog. Rahman kept his eye on the altimeter, which now showed that they had dropped to four hundred metres and slowed to two-fifty knots. If he'd had more time to consider the situation he was in, as a detached observer, he might have remembered something he had been taught all those years ago in training – information that he'd never needed to consider or act upon. So, it never occurred to him that an altimeter can give a false reading of altitude in thick fog because pockets of cold air screw with the pressure reading.

He shot his two co-pilots a quick glance and winked. 'We've got this. Two minutes to landing, guys. Let's just hope we see those lights s—'

Captain Joseph Rahman wasn't used to being confronted with his own mortality so unexpectedly.

'What the *fuck*?'

Flight AI-231 slammed down into the airport carpark two kilometres short of the runway at a little over three hundred kilometres per hour.

Captain Rahman had just enough time to wonder why the ground had come up to greet his plane so early and to feel the searing heat of the explosion before everything went black.

5

Friday, 1 February – Waiheke Island, New Zealand

THE SUN HAD BEEN STREAMING IN THROUGH THE GAPS
in the blinds for hours and Marc had been trying, unsuccessfully, to block it out by draping one arm over his eyes.
Reluctantly, he rolled over in bed to check the time,
squinting and trying to raise his head as little as necessary off the pillow. It was already ten-thirty. He'd not got
to bed till just before dawn but knew the way he was feeling had little to do with the lack of sleep. It had been two
days since the strange aurora and it had bugged him all
day yesterday while he was out on a fishing trip. By early
evening, he'd been famished, so he'd returned, moored
the boat and headed up to the house. Of course he tried
to convince himself that the quickness in his step was
nothing more than a combination of hunger and a keen
scientific urge to investigate the aurora, but he knew the
deeper need was to get back to the unopened bottle of
Scotch calling out to him.

The most popular opinion on the various news feeds
regarded the strangely displaced aurora as just another
crazy consequence of the increasing influence of cosmic

rays on an ever more vulnerable planet. However, the beautiful magnetic display in the upper atmosphere above south-east Asia was a sideline to the big news: a plane crash-landing in Delhi and the loss of three hundred and twenty lives. Air disasters were extremely rare these days and this one appeared to have been caused by several communication satellites being fried. By the time he'd dragged himself off the sofa and stumbled to the kitchen to find something to eat it was past midnight and the bottle of Scotch was already more than half empty.

Well, he was most certainly paying the price this morning for his over-indulgence. Not that it bothered him so much any more. The dull ache above his eyes first thing in the morning had become such a familiar friend these past few months that he hardly gave it a second thought; he even welcomed the groggy feeling that did such a good job of numbing the ever-present wretchedness. He rolled out of bed and plodded unsteadily downstairs. Shuffling into the living room, he voice-activated the blinds across the French windows to open, then decided against it and closed them again. Instead, he activated the wall display and headed for the kitchen. But the news report he caught as he was leaving made him turn back to the large screen.

All the networks were reporting the same story: that at least six communication satellites had been damaged by a burst of high-energy particles from space. Authorities in India, China and Malaysia were saying how lucky they were to have escaped so lightly. Apart from the Air India passengers, the only other casualties being reported were three hospital patients on life-support machines in a remote Indian village, where the emergency generator had failed to kick in after a power-grid failure in the region, and a Bangladeshi construction worker who had been electrocuted while replacing components at the top

30

of a transmission tower. It saddened Marc to think that the economies of countries like Bangladesh, still counting the cost of climate change, continued to use humans rather than bots to carry out such dangerous work.

He checked what was currently trending on both the surface and dark web social media. But while most of the chatter was about whether this direct hit from a coronal ejection was just a one-off event or a warning that the Sun would be belching out more of its contents in the Earth's direction, the cacophony of noise made it hard to pick out anything sensible. Viewpoints ranging from enraged libertarians and conspiracy theorists disputing that anything had happened at all, to the even more vociferous end-of-the-world fanatics convinced this was finally the sign they had been waiting for, all competed for attention. The virtual-assistant system installed in the house, even running its highly sophisticated sorting algorithm, was proving unable to weed out the spam from the ham to build any reliable picture.

Marc sighed. As usual, you had to do a little digging to get to the truth. 'Select favourites only. Past twenty-four hours. Keywords: magnetic storm, solar flare, threat level.'

One thing he hadn't done yet was change the VA's settings, so it still spoke in the voice of the old British natural-history broadcaster Sir David Attenborough, a favourite of his mother's:

> The top hit discussion is whether the current event was due directly to the weakening of the Earth's magnetosphere – consensus rating 95.2 per cent – and how soon the Flip will happen and restore the planet's protective magnetic shield – consensus on when this will occur is in the range of six months to five years from now.

None of this was new. For several years now, many scientists had been debating the expected reversal of the Earth's field, when the north and south magnetic poles would switch over. But unless this was going to have a clear impact on their daily lives, most people were not interested. Now, it seemed, they were finally sitting up and taking notice.

At least he had an answer on the impressive aurora he'd witnessed at the vineyard that night, because this had to be more than coincidence. The solar ejection must have caused an impressive geomagnetic storm, screwing with what was left of the magnetic field and producing the colourful northern sky. Marc grunted and turned away from the wall screen. He wondered whether he should be more concerned about this latest crisis – indeed whether he should be showing more of an interest in the state of the planet generally. But he just found it too difficult to care much about anything these days.

A cool shower and two coffees later and his head began to clear. He popped a couple of painkillers anyway. He knew he could have avoided this hangover entirely if he'd taken an enzypill last night. He knew there was a supply in the house somewhere – and sure, they'd have guaranteed he woke up bright and fresh, thanks to their anti-diuretic hormones, ADH and ALDH enzyme enhancers and sugar-level controllers, but that defeated the object; why bother drinking in the first place if you were going to stop the alcohol from fucking up your brain's neurotransmitters? Marc sometimes wondered whether a wholesome hangover was penance for his over-indulgence.

Needing something to eat to settle his stomach, he padded barefoot into the kitchen in his boxer shorts and an old CERN T-shirt with its *Particle physics gives me a hadron* slogan now barely legible. Charlotte, his ex-wife, had always hated that T-shirt. But then, towards the end, it seemed there wasn't much about Marc that Charlotte *hadn't* hated. Not caring about the outside world was, he knew deep down, just another symptom of his illness, but he also knew that she was partly right when she would accuse him of just being selfish. In the Marc-centric universe, stuff happened elsewhere to other people and they would just have to deal with it. If it didn't impact on him then he preferred to mind his own business. Shaking his head, he wondered when that had started. Did it really coincide with the onset of his depression? He hadn't always felt like this; there had been a time when, as an idealist and brilliant young scientist, he'd thought he could change the world.

Ah, what the hell. What difference would it make anyway what he thought? Twenty-four hours from now the global media would have moved on to some other story. It had taken the world decades to acknowledge that anthropogenic climate change was a real threat to humanity, so why should this rare threat from space be anything more than a temporary distraction from the constant backdrop of terrorism and global cyber wars?

He took a bowl down from the cupboard – almost everything in the house was just as it was when his parents had died, within four months of each other three years ago, and he'd not got round to having a good clear-out.

He sat down at the breakfast bar with a bowl of cereal and forced himself to think more positively. Yesterday had been a good day out on the boat, with the sea breeze taking the edge off the warm sun. He'd felt physically lighter and the future didn't seem so dark. Today, he decided, he would be more productive. He'd get started on a few DIY projects around the house. There was plenty to do. He'd spent the past fortnight generally loafing about, but now it was time to get his arse in gear.

He'd just finished eating his breakfast when his wristpad buzzed. It was Charlotte. He did a quick mental calculation. It would be early evening now in New York and she would be just getting home from work. No doubt she would exaggerate how frazzled and tired she was feeling. And to be honest, who could blame her – considering that she was holding down a stressful job that she didn't particularly enjoy and was bringing up a teenage daughter singlehandedly, while he wallowed in his lazy self-indulgence on the other side of the world? He knew only too well that, like Evie, Charlotte was convinced he'd taken the coward's way out by escaping to New Zealand instead of continuing to get the professional help he needed in New York.

He tapped his wristpad and Charlotte's face appeared on the kitchen screen in front of him.

'You look like shit.'

He ran his fingers absent-mindedly through his drying hair in an attempt to tame it. He immediately regretted not sticking her on audio only. 'And hello to you too, Charlie. To what do I owe this honour?' He tried to sound as cheerful as he could manage.

Charlotte sighed. 'Hard as this might be for you to believe, I genuinely wanted to see how you're doing.' She looked tired, but to Marc it was still the same face he'd fallen in love with all those years ago. In fact, she looked more attractive than ever now – now that he'd lost her to someone else. And he had long since come to terms with the fact that he had no one to blame but himself.

'. . . and I see from the bags under your eyes that you're still not sleeping well.'

He chose to ignore the comment. The last thing he

wanted was another cycle of pointless argument: *No, this time I really will quit / I've heard that a thousand times before.* They'd been down that road too many times. Anyway, when he did drag himself back from the brink, and he would, it would be on his own terms and for Evie's sake.

'So, how're things? How's Evie?' Marc asked. If there was one light that had continued to shine throughout even his very darkest days, it was his daughter. 'Still mad with me? I've tried contacting her every day, but she won't respond.'

'What did you expect, Marc? She's fifteen; she's had to live with her father struggling with depression since she was ten, then watch her parents tearing their marriage apart; and finally, without any warning or explanation, her father disappears from her life.'

Marc didn't protest. His mood swings had driven a wedge between him and those he loved. After being kicked out of his faculty position because of the drinking, he knew he'd had to 'get away', just when Evie was getting used to the routine of spending weekends with him. He'd hoped she'd be able to understand that he needed, temporarily, to put some distance between himself and his old life. His relationship with his daughter had always been close. Sometimes it felt like she was the only human on Earth who understood his struggle with his inner demons. And despite the hormonal changes she was going through at the moment, it would still melt his heart when she gave him one of her tight, unconditional, almost urgent hugs.

He nodded slowly. 'I guess I had that coming. And it's not like I've ever had any illusions of winning Father of the Year, right? Anyway, and I was going to let you know, there's a conference in Princeton on dark-matter physics next week, which I plan to attend. Qiang is going and it would be good to catch up with him too. As soon as it's over I'll head up to see Evie. I'll stay at George Palmer's place.'

Charlotte raised an eyebrow and gave a wry smile. 'You mean you were going to let me know once you'd got here. Well, I'm sure Evie will be pleased to see you, I promise. She's just hurting and needs a bit of time. Try to spend more than a few hours with her, though. It would be good for both of you to try and mend some bridges.'

Marc heard the sound of a door slamming in the background behind Charlotte and detected a sudden stiffening of her features. She turned round and called out, 'Hi, honey, I'm in here, chatting to Marc.' Her boyfriend Jeremy had just got in. Jeremy Giles, the successful politician, was in so many ways the exact opposite of Marc. And OK, so 'boyfriend' was no longer the right term to use since he'd moved in with Charlie as soon as the ink had dried on the divorce settlement papers. Still, Marc didn't want to have to face his smarmy smile again any time soon.

Luckily, Charlotte didn't want to prolong their chat any more than he did. 'OK. Well, let me know your travel plans as soon as they're firmed up. And, believe it or not, it would still be good to see you.'

'You too. Love to Evie.'

The screen blinked off.

Maybe it was the thought of a fit and virile Jeremy Giles screwing his ex-wife; or maybe it was just the urge to blow off some of his pent-up frustration, but Marc decided he would go out for a long run – as if an hour's jog on the beach was all that was needed to put his life back together. For a man of forty-seven, he was in remarkably good health and had at least avoided the expanding waistline of so many of his contemporaries.

Before he went upstairs to change, he decided to take one final look for any serious reporting on the geomagnetic storm and what had caused it. He thought about searching for any announcements from NASA, ESA or CNSA, but he knew the space agencies of America, Europe and China could no longer be relied on to give the whole story – the old secrecy and rivalries of the space race of the 1960s and '70s were back stronger than ever as the competition for resources on the Moon and Mars became ever fiercer. He sat down in front of his kitchen screen. If anyone knew, it would be the team at the Rio Solar Science Institute. Last year, he'd sat on a US grant-funding committee and reviewed a research proposal from the SSI. His conclusion was that they did solid science and that it would be crazy not to support them in the current climate.

'Search past twenty-four hours. Filter. Coronal mass ejection. Solar Science Institute. Statement.' The results came back quickly. There were over two million internet sites reporting on an interview given by a Dr Sarah Maitlin from the SSI on a morning show on Globo in Brazil. A further search on the name returned forty-eight million hits, all in the past ten hours. It seemed that Dr Maitlin was something of a news sensation. Marc was intrigued enough to watch the Globo interview in full, then did a quick search on Maitlin's scientific work. She was a British solar physicist in her late thirties whose most cited research papers had been over ten years ago, on sunspots. He started watching another interview she'd given, this time with a BBC journalist whom she appeared to know. Her slightly more relaxed demeanour, compared with her somewhat nervous Globo performance, meant that she smiled when he introduced her, revealing just how attractive she was – no wonder the shallow news networks all wanted a piece of her – although in this particular instance her academic credentials spoke for themselves.

Despite the potential levels of radiation that, according to Sarah Maitlin, were now getting through more easily than ever, especially here in New Zealand, which was sitting under a massive hole in the ozone layer, Marc decided to go out for his run anyway. As it was, the mid-day sun was going to make it unpleasantly warm, and he hadn't yet acclimatized since arriving from a freezing New York. His headache now receding, he bounded up the stairs two at a time to grab his running shoes.

Whatever Dr Maitlin had to say about the fate of the world could wait.

6

Wednesday, 6 February – New York

HER HEAD WAS BUZZING. SARAH SAT ALONE IN THE back of the Manhattan taxi as it raced across town. She could have got a drone cab, but the street traffic this time of the evening was no busier than the air above it.

So much had happened to her since first detecting the coronal ejection back at the Institute that she really hadn't had time to take stock. It felt as though she had talked herself dry to the press; surely there wasn't any more she could possibly say about solar cycles, solar storms, solar flares, sunspots, solar wind or coronal mass ejections. The media attention was finally waning now after a whirlwind few days and she felt drained, but she was still a long way from being able to get back to her research at the SSI, or any semblance of normality.

Sitting back, she closed her eyes, overcome by an unexpected feeling of loneliness. There was no one she felt close enough to and on whom she could offload, or simply unwind with – and not just here in New York, but anywhere. Sure, there were plenty of academic colleagues around the world she knew well enough to socialize with when their paths crossed, but none were close friends. And, as her mother would all too often point out, many women her age had found partners to share their lives with and even settled down to start families.

She smiled to herself. Much as she loved her mother and enjoyed spending time with her back in England when she could, she had long since stopped taking advice from her. In any case, she enjoyed her own company . . . most of the time. And, heaven knows, she certainly didn't need a man in her life right now. After two mistakes, there was no way she was prepared to get involved in another relationship just yet. She would readily admit that both failures had partly been her fault. She had been accused by Simon during a big row in Rio last summer of being too preoccupied with her work, which was true. But she certainly didn't regret that. The truth was she really loved her research, and Simon just hadn't been important enough for her to be prepared to make the room for him in her life that he had expected.

But now her work was being put on temporary hold. First had come the phone calls from the local media in Rio; within an hour of the Delhi plane crash, still late Wednesday evening, Rio local time, reports were emerging that the accident had not been due to any fault with the aircraft, pilot error or even extreme weather conditions. It had been a severe and catastrophic comms failure. Once the Indian news agencies had pinned the accident on the exotic explanation of particles from space knocking out the communications, the hunt had been on for someone to explain the science.

It began when a local TV news researcher had called, sounding overly cheerful given the graveness of the news. Like many news networks around the world, he had traced the sequence of events back and found a report of

Sarah having warned the authorities of the arrival of a serious cosmic-ray storm. The Globo News journalist had struck lucky by being the first to get hold of Sarah's private contact details. It was gone 11 p.m. when she'd taken that first call just as she was getting ready for bed. By one in the morning, she had given seven other online interviews to various news agencies.

Following three hours' sleep and a quick shower, she had been driven to a nearby helipad where a team from Globo had been waiting to fly her to the downtown media hub for a live slot on the morning news.

After the interview, an excited young analyst working for the station told her that the regular twenty million Brazilian viewers of the programme had been joined by hundreds of millions watching online around the world. The interview had started smoothly, and Sarah had felt surprisingly calm. The TV anchor who interviewed her was absurdly glamorous and immaculately dressed, making Sarah feel self-consciously scruffy alongside her. But the woman was a consummate professional and seemed to show a genuine interest in what Sarah had to say. She had explained in very careful, non-technical terms how the weakening magnetic field of the Earth could no longer deflect the high-energy particles from space, and that while this particular energetic solar burst would normally have been treated as an isolated and freak incident, the world could expect more violent events in the future as the planet's defence weakened further. She'd felt on safe ground explaining this and was confident with the science. Most people knew about the growing number of holes in the ozone layer in the upper atmosphere and the general heightened levels of radiation exposure, but a direct hit from coronal mass ejections was something new to many, and the fact that this one seemed to have been directly responsible for bringing down Flight AI-231 had captured the world's attention.

But just when she thought the interview was winding up, the woman began asking questions she felt she couldn't offer a confident opinion on. She knew that being a scientist meant she was expected to be an expert on everything, but what had annoyed her was that the woman could clearly see her discomfort and yet carried on pressing for answers. She had wanted to know when Sarah expected the Flip to happen and how quickly the strength of the field would be restored once magnetic north and south had switched over. She then asked how satellites or electricity grids could be protected before this happened and things settled down, and even what could be done to protect people from the harm cosmic rays could cause them directly. Had Sarah been lulled into a false sense of security by being first asked about the stuff she knew? Was this a trap? Did the network or the producers of this particular news programme have any political agenda? She had forced herself to remain calm.

She explained how, once the poles had flipped and the field had regained its strength, everything would slowly return to normal, but until it did, and that could take decades, the surface of the planet was highly exposed.

But her reluctance to be drawn in to speculating about these issues and her mumbled protests about not being qualified to comment were all instantly dubbed into fifty languages by software that even picked up, and mimicked, the frustrated tone of her voice.

By the time the interview was over she felt drained. The syrupy smile and exaggerated fake gratitude of her interviewer had only made her more resentful of the woman. She'd been eager to get back to her apartment.

Maybe if she'd had the chance to discuss all this with her boss, Philipe Santos, he could have advised her on what she should and shouldn't comment on. But, as director of the SSI, he had been just as inundated as her with media enquiries and had brushed off her concerns, saying he had full confidence in her. He had then flown to Brasília to talk politics. No doubt he would be looking for ways of turning his institute's early detection of the CME to his advantage by talking up the role the SSI could play in providing an advance-warning system which could help avert any future such tragedies, naturally only by securing significantly larger funding.

The following day she'd received a message from Santos telling her to set up a VR meeting with the SSI's counterpart research organization in London, the Helios Institute, to see if there was any mileage in collaborating more closely on a CME early-warning system. Although she knew it was a long shot, she asked him if it would be possible for her to fly to London to speak to them in person. These days, the convenience of a VR visor meant no one had to travel to conferences any more. Sarah knew full well that her avatar could meet up with the avatars of the Helios Institute scientists at a computer-simulated location of their choice, but she was also aware that she hadn't visited her parents in almost a year. So she had argued the case for needing to be physically in London in order to properly discuss the latest solar data face to face. Santos was no fool and knew her real reason for wanting to go, but he was also a reasonable man.

By early Thursday evening she was flying across the Atlantic to the country of her birth and the chance for some brief respite, and maybe even a relaxing weekend at her parents' house on the south coast of England.

In fact, visiting them had highlighted just how long it

43

had been since she'd last been over. She had been sensible enough not to try and adjust her body clock for the three short days of her trip, knowing she'd be flying back across the Atlantic soon enough.

Her parents had both been following her Globo interview. 'You sounded very confident and self-assured, darling,' remarked her mother, 'and, do you know, for the first time I think I now understand what your work is about. I know you've tried explaining it many times to me but, well, you know me.'

Her father had suggested they go out for a pub lunch at one of their old haunts; one that held fond memories for Sarah too, from what seemed like many lifetimes ago.

During the relatively short drive along the coastal road from her parents' home in Southsea, she had only half listened to her mother's animated monologue updating her on the latest news of family friends and relatives she hadn't seen or spoken to in years. She stared out at the soggy world outside through the rivulets of rain running down the window. She recalled vividly, as though it were just yesterday, the childhood frustration both she and her brother would feel during the family's regular summer drive to the sandy expanse of West Wittering beach; frustration at losing valuable beach time before the tide came in as the car crawled slowly along with the rest of the summer traffic towards the popular resort. But on this particular Sunday three decades later, the roads were nearly empty. With the pitter-patter of the rain on the car roof making more noise than the hum of its electric engine, her father had informed her in his typical matter-of-fact way that these days this coast road wasn't much busier even during the height of the summer season. West Wittering beach and much of the surrounding low-lying marshlands were now permanently underwater, part of the changing coastline of the British Isles thanks to the rising sea levels.

But the dismal weather notwithstanding, the day had been wonderful. After eating Brazilian cuisine for so long, a proper English Sunday roast with 'all the trimmings' had really hit the spot. The Lamb Inn down by the seafront in the Witterings was a family favourite and they were lucky to have got a table when booking so late. The entire day had felt soaked in nostalgia, just as it did every time she came back to visit her parents. As she always did on such visits, it made her question why she had moved so far away from all these childhood memories.

That day now seemed like a parallel reality in which time ran at a different pace – a temporary haven of sanity in the eye of a storm. But there had been yet more surprises in store. On Sunday evening, she'd received a message from the prime minister's office and a summons to attend Whitehall first thing on Monday morning to brief the UK government's crisis response committee, COBRA.

Sarah was intrigued as to why they would feel it necessary, or even useful, to speak to her. After all, if they had just wanted reliable scientific advice, then surely any number of solar physicists at the Helios Institute in London could have briefed them. She figured that political aides and civil servants were no less lazy than many in the media when it came to looking for expert opinion. You just checked to see who everyone else had been talking to.

Her meeting with the PM, along with several ministers and aides, had been a somewhat surreal experience. The British government had been debating recently whether to fund a joint Sino-British ten-year project to build a new early-warning satellite system and couldn't decide whether it would be worth the multi-billion-pound outlay, given the nature of the new threat posed by solar particles. The prime minister and several faceless civil servants had all been pleasant enough – in fact, the PM had positively oozed an obsequious charm that was mildly unsettling. Having been out of the country for so long, she didn't really have a strong opinion on his true political views. Like the previous few populist governments, these people seemed keen, and short-sighted enough, to insist on knowing the views of any British scientists who they felt could give them technological insider knowledge that they could use to negotiate a deal with China.

But what on earth she could tell them that they didn't already know, she had no idea. Maybe they were crediting her with deeper insights than she could offer. She had simply repeated what she had said already countless times about the uncertainties of even the most sophisticated solar model. Why couldn't they understand that space weather was just as unpredictable as terrestrial weather?

But if Sarah had thought she'd now be able to head home and get back to her research, then she had underestimated the impact of her sudden fame. The day after her Whitehall meeting, and while immersed in discussions at Helios in London, she'd received a further unexpected message. This time her presence was requested in New York, by the UN Secretary-General Abelli herself. She had made her excuses to the Helios scientists and looked around for somewhere she could make a call in private. In the end she decided to play it safe and headed for a rear exit from the building. Although she had not been told that her invitation to the UN was a secret, she still thought it prudent to have some privacy.

She'd stepped out into the chilly late afternoon air and

the deserted backstreet and immediately wished she'd remembered her coat. The steady hum of hundreds of drones in the air above her head filled her ears: delivery drones, window-cleaning drones, surveillance and monitoring drones, all going about their business, choreographed by the London Transport AI so that they zipped past each other in every possible direction in three dimensions, never colliding or getting in the way of the much larger taxi drones that buzzed through the swarm.

Sarah tapped her wristpad and called her father. As a retired political correspondent, he would have as good an idea as anyone what this all meant.

For all the justifiable criticism of the UN's ineffectiveness, especially since the epicentre of global power had shifted to east Asia, it still had considerable influence. And in any case, it remained the only body that even came close to being neutral on the world stage.

His smiling face filled the screen on her wrist, although she could see that he was speaking to her from his study.

'Hi, Dad. Listen, I'm afraid I'm flying out again tomorrow so I'm not going to get the chance to get back down to see you and Mum after all. I'm really sorry.'

'What? Already? But sweetheart, you've only been in the country a few days.'

'Yeah, I know. I'm sorry. And I need some advice.'

'That's what dads are for, right?' His features took on a more serious look, which amused her. Sometimes he acted as though she was still eight years old rather than thirty-eight. She smiled. 'Well, you know I had my Downing Street meeting yesterday? The PM seemed a nice enough guy. Wouldn't trust him as far as I could spit, of course.' This was exactly the sort of thing her father would say, for she knew full well what he thought of the current government.

47

True to form, he grunted his disapproval. 'Well, yes, I could have told you that for nothing. So, how did it go? Assuming you're allowed to tell me anything.'

'Well, we'll probably both get shot for treason if we're caught,' she said in mock trepidation. Her father had retired seven years ago, but still wrote the odd stingingly critical article on the government's unpopular and draconian robot ethics and drone surveillance laws. She recounted her hour-long meeting the day before. 'Nothing much to report, really. I went over the usual science and the risks of a coronal ejection hitting the UK. It's all stuff they know already, Dad. They really didn't need to hear it from me. Anyway, I called because of something else that's just come up that's even more important and I wanted to pick your brains.'

His eyebrows shot up and he sat back in his chair in mock astonishment. 'Really? Even more important than explaining basic science to a philistine like our prime minister? What could possibly be more pressing?'

Sarah chuckled. Then, without thinking, she quickly glanced up and down the street to make sure she was still alone. 'I've been invited to join some crack UN committee looking into the solar threat. To be honest, the whole thing is nuts. The committee seems to be full of government ministers, ambassadors and other high-profile characters. I mean, people with real power. I keep wondering why they suddenly want the advice of a mid-career scientist like me who has not had any real experience in science policy or politics.'

'Don't knock it. You're an excellent solar physicist and they would do well to listen to what you have to say. And as for this committee, it sounds like another one of those intergovernmental panels to me – you know, like the IPCC. What bloody good this new one would do I don't know, but I guess it's about time some action, any action, was taken.'

Sarah knew only too well that it was largely thanks to the efforts of the IPCC over the past forty years that the worst effects of climate change had been averted. And the same was true for the panel on antimicrobial resistance. The controversy these days was with the Intergovernmental Panel on Population Displacement, which had its work cut out and was hugely unpopular. But then the mass migrations forced by sea-level rises were still going on.

'Well, anyway, I hope I'm not the only scientist on this panel and it's not just a bunch of megalomaniac politicians with their own vested interests. I mean, how do these things work?'

'I'm happy that you think I'm the fount of all knowledge and wisdom. But I'm just a retired hack keeping his head down while watching others try to sort out the planet. But since you ask, I'm not catching any whiff of conspiracy theories here.'

Sarah had wondered whether those who held the reins of power really did have the planet's interests at heart, or if that was an outdated and naively optimistic view. In any case, did her father still have his finger on the pulse of world politics any longer? Well, she'd find out soon enough.

'OK, Dad, I'll try to keep you posted. Give my love to Mum.'

'I will. And try to get some sleep, you look tired.'

'Don't worry, Dad, I'll get a decent night's sleep before I head out.'

'Good. Saving the world can be exhausting, you know. And remember, your mother and I are very proud of you.'

*

49

That had been twenty-four hours ago. Here she was now on the other side of the Atlantic, in a driverless cab weaving its way across a vibrant Manhattan on a bitterly cold evening. She still wasn't sure what she felt about having been thrust into the limelight like this.

The truth was that she wasn't cut out for this world of politics and public relations. In fact, rather than feeling flattered by all the attention, she'd felt a growing insecurity – a nagging anxiety that her shortcomings and the many gaps in her knowledge would, sooner or later, be exposed. She kept telling herself this was classic imposter syndrome. She was easily as highly qualified and knowledgeable as anyone else in her field, and she'd worked hard to get to the position she was in. Still, returning home briefly had meant she could hide away for a couple of days and hope that everyone forgot about her as the world moved on to another story.

As the taxi pulled up outside her hotel, a cheerful electronic voice said, 'Have a nice day, Dr Maitlin. Thank you for using New York Autocabs,' and the door of the car slid open as her fare registered. The place she was staying at was a small but comfortable hotel ideally situated in downtown Manhattan between 5th and Park Avenues. There was a welcoming aroma of coffee in the lobby. Nodding a hello in the direction of the bored-looking receptionist, she poured herself a mug and headed up to her room.

She felt relieved to finally have some time to recuperate, catch up on some work and maybe look up an old friend from university days who now lived and worked in New York, before her Saturday morning meeting at the UN. Walking into her room, she was greeted by a gust of warm air and absent-mindedly commanded the heating to be turned down a few degrees. As she turned to close the door she spotted an envelope on the floor.

Who delivered paper notes any more? And who slipped them under hotel-room doors, for Christ's sake? Intrigued, she picked it up and pulled out a neatly folded sheet of paper. The words were quaintly hand-written on UN headed notepaper.

Dear Dr Maitlin

My name is Professor Gabriel Aguda, a geologist at the University of Lagos, but mostly these days I act as an Advisor on Earth Sciences to the UN here in New York. Like you, I have been recruited onto the new UN committee. I must say it's a relief to have another scientist on board and as you can imagine I'm looking forward to meeting you. If possible, would you like to get together for breakfast first? I can try to bring you up to speed on what this is all about. If so, I can meet you in your hotel lobby at 7.30 on Saturday morning.

If I don't hear from you, then I'll assume this is the plan. But if for any reason we cannot touch base before the meeting itself then do ping me at any time in the coming days.

Yours truly,
Gabriel Aguda

The note had a charm to it. Presumably, Aguda was some-one who didn't trust cybersecurity systems enough to leave her a message online. She blinked to activate her augmented reality and her field of vision was filled with her favourite 3D search engine intervening semi-transparently in front of her view of the hotel-room surroundings. She said, 'Search Gabriel Aguda United Nations.'

It seemed the geologist had been a powerful mover and shaker in the academic world and had written a number of influential and highly cited papers on earthquake prediction early in his career. Recently, though, he seemed to have operated more as a politician than a scientist, although he still spent part of his time back in his home country of Nigeria as well as teaching as an adjunct professor at the University of Rochester.

Since she had no UN allies yet, breakfast with Gabriel Aguda sounded like a good place to start.

7

Thursday, 7 February – Tehran

TWENTY-YEAR-OLD COMPUTER SCIENCE STUDENT SHIREEN Darvish was certain her mother cooked the very best *fesen-joon* in the world and she would take on anyone who claimed otherwise. When the rich aroma of the pomegranate stew wafted up to her bedroom, seeping beneath her closed door, she realized how hungry she was.

Although she was physically in her room, which was so crammed with electronic equipment it resembled a space mission control centre, Shireen's mind was some-where else entirely. Inside her virtual reality helmet was a universe of data and lines of machine code – an electronic landscape of pure information. And it was a world Shireen had always found more familiar and reassuring than the real one.

She'd been working hard for several hours but was still reluctant to leave her computer even for a moment. She was at last closing in on something big. The last few months had been spent testing and re-testing her Tro-jan horse hacking software; she'd almost been badly burned on a couple of occasions when she'd been sure the authorities were on to her, but finally she felt that all the bases were covered.

Which was just as well, because she had important end-of-year examinations in the summer and didn't want to fall behind in her classes. She justified the time spent on her extracurricular interests because they were so closely aligned with the courses she was taking at Tehran University. Still, she found that her thoughts were increasingly drifting towards her secret project, even during lectures. The only person who knew that her mind was elsewhere was her close friend Majid. And even he didn't know the half of it.

Shireen was well aware she was far from alone, for there were millions like her around the world – though few were as smart – all obsessed with finding ways of cracking uncrackable codes, infiltrating the most secret recesses of cyberspace, whether by stealth or in the open. She hated the generic term 'cyberterrorism', which was used by the authorities to include anyone who preferred the anonymity of the dark web. At least it meant that cybersecurity remained a lucrative career of choice for many young computer science graduates around the world. But while Shireen acknowledged that there were people who wished to use cyberattacks to harm humanity because of some ideology they had bought into, she felt she was part of a more benign and altruistic movement of cyberhackers. She was a cyb, and she was proud of it. She saw the aim of the cyb movement as exposing injustices committed in the very name of global cybersecurity. Not that the authorities would see it that way if she were ever caught. She smiled to herself. *I'm too clever to be caught.*

Born in the early 2020s, Shireen had not known a time when quantum key distribution was not the standard means of securing online data. She knew from her cryptography classes at university that until the mid-twenties data had been protected online using public key cryptosystems like RSA. Several months ago, while staying with her elderly great-aunt Pirween in Isfahan, she had tried explaining encryption to her. 'If I asked you to multiply two big numbers together, Auntie, say one hundred and ninety-three times five hundred and sixty-nine, could you give me the answer?'

'Not in my head, dear, but I can do it easily enough on my tablet,' her aunt had replied, holding up the old-fashioned device close to her mouth. It amused Shireen that the elderly woman, like many of her generation, still didn't trust the technology of augmented reality, preferring archaic handheld tablets – there was even still a market for early-twenties smartphones.

Her aunt began speaking into her device. 'Tablet, multiply one hundred and—'

'—you'll find it's a hundred and nine thousand, eight hundred and seventeen.'

'Did you just do that in your head? If so, I'm very impressed.'

'Actually, no, Auntie, I've used this example before, so I just remember the answer. Now, what if I asked you to work out the only two numbers which, when multiplied together, give a hundred and nine thousand, eight hundred and seventeen? Could you do that?'

'Isn't that what you just asked me?' said her aunt, looking genuinely puzzled.

'No!' said Shireen, feeling a little exasperated. 'The first time I gave you two numbers to multiply and asked for the answer, which is straightforward. But now I've given you the answer and I'm asking you to do it in reverse.'

'Well, it's five hundred and something-something times . . . I mean, if I had a pen and paper—'

'Please, Auntie, I meant if I'd started the conversation just with the big number . . .'

The old woman had laughed. 'I know, dear, I'm teasing.'

'OK, bear with me. You see, the first problem: multiplying two numbers together, however big they are, can be done on any calculator. Lots of people can even multiply two three-digit numbers in their heads easily enough. But the reverse used to be an almost impossible task. It's called finding the prime factors of a number. When you were young, that would have been how your credit-card details were stored securely online.'

'Public key encryption. I remember it well. And I remember the panic when the first quantum computers came along, and nothing was secure online any more.'

'Yup, they could do what no other computer had been able to do before, however powerful, and crack the problem of factorizing big numbers. So, quantum key distribution came along and was much more secure because—'

'Because,' her aunt chipped in '. . . because . . . wait, I know this. It's because of quantum entanglement. If you try to spy on something you disturb it, however careful you are, and you set off the quantum alarm.'

This time it was Shireen's turn to laugh. 'That's a pretty good summary, yes. The "observer effect".'

Having grown up with it, Shireen felt completely at home immersed in the world of fuzzy quantum bits of information, a strange digital reality in which the binary certainty of zeros or ones is replaced by a ghostly existence of both at the same time.

Hers was a world within a world, the vast cyberspace – a universe made up not of physical particles, but of pure information, flowing, interacting and constantly evolving within its own dimensions. Shireen's talents of course ran in the family. She was very proud of the fact that both her parents had been among the early whizz-kids of the Invisible Internet Project, the underground network that sat below the surface of the web and which had originally been used for secret surfing and information exchange. Her father had even worked on the anonymous communication software project, Tor, at MIT before returning to Iran to join the underground dark web movement of the early 2020s that toppled the Islamic regime. This meant he knew more than most about cybersecurity, anonymized communication, multi-layer encryption and so-called onion routing. Her mother had pioneered techniques for hacking public key crypto-systems with home-made quantum computers running codes that made use of Shor's algorithm to factorize large numbers.

But Shireen was a child of the new world order, which was dominated by the code war. When pervasive computing took off in the early twenties, when she was a young child, it still had a name: it was referred to as the Internet of Things; but it was soon clear that it no longer needed to be called anything. In a world where everything was connected to everything else, only her grandparents' generation still used phrases like 'look online' instead of just 'look'. It had begun with home and office appliances linked wirelessly to handheld devices, but eventually everything was networked; sensors, cameras, embedded nano servers and energy harvesters were all ubiquitous and built into the infrastructure of the modern world, from buildings and transport to clothing and household items.

Eventually world governments and multinationals woke up to the desperate need for advanced cybersecurity systems, but not before the anonymous hacking of international cryptocurrency banking had brought the world markets crashing down in 2028, followed by the devastating cyberattack six months later on the AI system controlling London, one of the world's first 'smart cities'. That onslaught had infected many of the algorithms controlling the city's transport, commerce and environmental infrastructures, sending ten million people back into the Stone Age for three weeks.

These events prompted action and led to the development of the Sentinels, cybersecurity artificial intelligences that would continuously patrol the Cloud, hunting for anomalies, viruses and leaks. They became the guardians of the larger AIs, or Minds, that ran everything from air traffic control and defence systems to power plants and financial institutions. And despite the cyberattack on London in '28, most large cities were now run entirely by Minds. Since the mid 2030s, a constant battle had been raging between the Sentinels and the rogue AIs developed by cyberterrorist groups, sent into the Cloud to test them.

Shireen didn't feel she truly belonged in either camp, but the code war fascinated her nevertheless. She rated her talents high, far exceeding those of her parents, which was why she had avoided any mention of her latest project – not because they wouldn't understand the technical details, but because she knew they would have warned her off. In any case, she was now playing in the big league and it wasn't just her own safety she had to think about; her parents would also be in jeopardy if the authorities ever tracked her down.

There was a knock on her bedroom door. 'Come on down and eat, darling; it's time you took a break from your studies.' Wearing her VR visor, Shireen couldn't see her mother, but knew she wouldn't set foot in the room for fear of disturbing her daughter's concentration.

'It's OK, Mum, you *can* come in, you know.' Shireen had to smile. Her mother was the sweetest person in the world but could be so naive. She felt a pang of guilt, as she always did, that her mother had mistakenly assumed she was hard at work behind her visor. She blinked several times in rapid succession to turn down the volume of the music she was listening to. She was everything her mother wasn't: brash, self-confident and subversive. On the walls around the house there were old hard-copy photos in picture frames, of her mother when she was a young student, around Shireen's age, showing her still wearing a headscarf – the strict Islamic dress code that had been enforced in Iran for half a century. And here was Shireen in her shorts and T-shirt, with VR headset wrapped around her bright-pink cropped hair, and tattoos covering more than half her body. This played to her advantage: the more her parents focused on their daughter's rebellious fashion sense the less they were likely to notice her cyberhacking projects. Of course, they knew she wasn't spending all that time in her room on her studies, but they would have been mortified to discover what she was really working on.

She waved her haptic-gloved hands elegantly in front of her face and wiggled her fingers, touch-typing in a 3D virtual-reality space that only she could see, to iconize the multitude of windows and applications. She then removed her visor and stretched. Her mother was still standing smiling in the doorway. She cut an elegant figure – slim and considerably taller than her daughter. Shireen wondered if she herself would look that good thirty years from now. Her life was so much more comfortable than her mother's had been at her age. The pace of cultural change in Persian society during Shireen's lifetime had been nothing short of remarkable. In the space of less than twenty years, their country had gone from a conservative religious state to a liberal democracy with all the excesses and corruptions of any mid-twenty-first-century capitalist state. Many older Persians could even remember the time under the Shah seventy years ago and so had seen the country come full circle. Did being able to dye her hair, dress outrageously and be open about her sexuality mean that life was really any better now? But then she hadn't lived through the Iran of her parents.

Even though they were only three, her mother always insisted on laying the table as though for a banquet. Even the large dish of rice at the centre of the table was a work of art, with saffron-coloured grains piled in a neat spiral over plain white rice, and raisins and almonds sprinkled on top. Then there was the *fesenjoon*. She was again suddenly conscious of how hungry she felt. But, as usual, she knew that by the end of the meal she'd be so full she'd struggle to get up.

Her father, already seated at the table, looked up when she came in. 'Ah, she's back in the real world. Still busy trying to hack through the great firewall of China?'

To an outsider, Reza Darvish's casual attitude towards his daughter's hobby might have appeared at best cavalier and at worst shockingly reckless. But Shireen had gone to considerable lengths to ensure that, as far as her parents were concerned, she was indulging in nothing more than an innocent pastime.

'*Trying* to hack through? I'm unstoppable, Dad,' she replied light-heartedly as she shovelled a large portion of rice onto her plate. The smile disappeared from her father's face and his voice took on a more sombre tone.

'It's a dangerous game, Reenie. A lot of cybs who get too close to secrets simply go missing. I'd hate to think you're mixing with that crowd.' He sighed. 'And I should know,' he added for good measure.

She hoped the meal wasn't going to be accompanied by one of her father's well-rehearsed lectures on cybersecurity. He could sometimes be infuriatingly old-fashioned in his views.

Her mother walked into the dining room with a large bowl of salad and caught the last few words. 'Come on, Reza, Shireen's smarter than that.' She ruffled her daughter's spiky hair affectionately as she sat down next to her. Shireen waved her mother's hand away in mock annoyance.

'Well, as long as you're keeping on top of your studies, I suppose,' said her father, his voice softening again. 'I just wish you had other interests beyond your bedroom walls. You do know there's a big world out there, full of art and music and literature and science?'

'Plenty of time for all that, Dad,' she said through a mouthful of food. 'I'm only twenty and I have cyberspace at my feet. Once I've conquered that, I'll explore the real world.'

Her mother laughed, tilting her head back as she did so. The sound had a purity about it that made her look even more beautiful. Shireen caught her father looking over, smiling. It was clear in his eyes just how deeply he still loved his wife. Her mother turned to her. 'If this were twenty years ago we'd have been looking for a husband for you by now,' she joked.

For all their middle-class, left-leaning liberal secularism, her parents still identified with their Muslim culture. Shireen found this poignant and somehow comforting. Persians were stubbornly proud of their rich history, sometimes infuriatingly so. But then they did have five thousand years of history to call upon. Anyway, Shireen had not found the right time to tell them that they should give up any hope of having a son-in-law. One day, Iran would truly catch up with the rest of the twenty-first century and then her parents might get themselves a daughter-in-law.

'If it's OK with you, I'd like to pop out later. I need to talk to Majid about a coursework assignment for next week.' The part about meeting Majid, at least, was true.

'What time is your first lecture tomorrow?' her father asked. 'It'd do you good to have an early night for a change.'

'I don't have a class until my advanced algorithms at eleven.' The new maglev meant her daily commute from Ray on the outskirts of Tehran to the campus in the centre of the city took less than twenty minutes. She could afford a lie-in tomorrow.

She saw her parents exchange exasperated looks and decided it was best to change the subject. For the rest of the meal they discussed the growing concerns about the threat from the Sun and whether governments were keeping any information back.

After dinner, Shireen helped her mother carry the dishes through to the kitchen, stepping over the cleaner bots heading in the opposite direction to suck up any stray grains of rice on the floor underneath the table. Her mother could see she was eager to escape and waved her away. 'Go, go. Say hello to Majid for us.'

Majid had been Shireen's friend since childhood, and since they were now both studying on the same course, he was one of the very few people – no, wait, scratch that: the only person – whom she could trust entirely. And even then, she didn't feel able to share her latest project with him completely – mostly for his own safety. Plus, he'd probably tell her not to be so foolish. So, she would have to be careful how she elicited his help. Majid didn't have her intuitive feel for navigating through the dark web, nor her brilliance in quantum information theory. He certainly lacked her sixth sense when it came to knowing how to probe for weaknesses in multi-layered encrypted data.

It was a clear, chilly evening when she left the house. She felt a thrill at the thought of how close she was getting to a real breakthrough. Her small car was parked in the drive. She jumped in and voice-activated the destination. 'Majid's house' was all it needed to know. Slumped back in her seat while it reversed itself onto the road, she wondered how much she could confide in Majid.

The car weaved its way silently and unerringly through the early-evening Tehran traffic and Shireen stared out of the window, impatient to get to her friend's apartment, not taking much notice of the familiar sights and sounds of the city rushing by outside. Soon, the car turned off the highway and travelled along quieter tree-lined avenues. Shireen ran through in her head how she should tackle Majid without alarming him, or insulting him. It wasn't his views or advice that she was interested in eliciting, but the use of the quantum computer he had recently acquired – or rather that his father had bought for him. Strictly speaking, she didn't actually need a quantum computer to hack into a quantum key distribution repeater system, but the firewalls around it were impregnable. There was no way they could be watching her watching them – whoever 'they' might be.

She felt confident that running her algorithm on his machine would be the final phase, when she would at last gain access to files that had been better protected than anything she had encountered before. She still had no idea what those files contained, but the way they had been encrypted and hidden bore all the hallmarks of ultra-sensitive government secrets, probably Chinese in origin – red rag to a bull for any self-respecting cyb. Now, after months of effort, she was approaching the endgame, even though she hadn't given any thought to what she would do with the information once she had it.

For Shireen, being a cyb was more than a hobby. She sometimes tried to convince herself that hacking was just an intellectual challenge, like solving a maths problem or completing a tough jigsaw puzzle. But the truth was that she was addicted to it – her desire to break an unbreakable code was no different to the obsession of an old-fashioned safe-cracker. And the dangers of getting caught were just as real.

With her thoughts already on abstract lines of coding, Shireen watched the world go by – couples wrapped up against the chilly evening air, out for an after-dinner stroll, and late office workers eager to get home after a long day, overtaken by joggers in colourful kit preferring the fresh evening air to their virtual-reality treadmills.

She didn't ping Majid until her car pulled up outside his apartment. That way he couldn't make any excuses about wanting an early night or being too busy.

'Hey, Hajji. I'm outside. Can I pop up for an hour? I need the use of your new toy . . . and you know how you just live to make me happy.' 'Hajji' was her term of endearment for her friend, who had been on a pilgrimage to Mecca with his grandfather when he was ten. He hated the nickname, which was why Shireen enjoyed using it.

'Yeah, OK. But not for long. I've got a class in the morning.' She heard the sigh of resignation in his voice. He buzzed her in. 'Thanks. I promise I won't outstay my welcome.'

When Shireen got to his floor, the door was already open. She breezed into the apartment to find her friend standing in the hallway. He had a slight frame and was no taller than Shireen. His carefully barbered goatee beard, which he was convinced added gravitas and compensated for what he lacked in physical stature, was a source of constant teasing by Shireen.

She gave him a tight hug. 'And don't you dare give me that "class in the morning" shit. You forget: I know our timetable.'

'Whatever. I could still do with an early night. What was it you wanted? Don't tell me it's to do with your Trojan horse attack algorithm, whatever the hell that is, because if it is, I really don't think I can help much.'

Shireen gave him a wink. 'Don't worry, it's not your acute intellectual powers I need right now; it's your hardware.' Majid's recently acquired solid-state giga-qubit quantum computer – a matt-black cube the size of a shoebox that now had pride of place in the middle of his desk by the large window overlooking the street – had, in theory at least, the processing capacity of a human brain, but until someone figured out how to write the software to get it to think for itself it was still just a dumb machine.

Majid's apartment unashamedly betrayed his family's wealth. It was an interesting mix of old and new, decorated with luxurious drapes and classic, almost gaudy furnishing. But to the expert eye, the trappings of mid-century technology were integrated everywhere, with sensors and microchips in every appliance and fixture, communicating with each other and ready to adjust or go into action on command. Shireen often joked that a man who even needed his socks to have their own IP address, so they could remind him when they needed washing, wouldn't last five minutes in a post-apocalyptic world. 'And don't expect me to be there to help you survive,' she would say. 'You know you'd only slow me down.'

Majid went over to his desk and placed the ball of his

thumb on its black glass surface. There was a hum and ripple of light as a keyboard and colourful array of function keys appeared. Shireen stood behind him, rested her chin on his shoulder and murmured in his ear. 'Thank you, Hajji.'

Majid looked like he had resigned himself to letting her do whatever she needed to because he walked away from the desk in silence and collapsed onto the sofa to watch. But no sooner had he sat down than he bounced back up again and said, 'OK, before you get too lost in code, would you like me to order pizza?'

'No thanks, I've eaten,' she replied without even turning to him. 'But you go ahead. I'm hoping this won't take too long anyway.' Her fingers darted around the smooth surface as she tapped the keys, then she spoke a few commands into her wristpad to allow the computer to identify her. When she was satisfied she was connected, she wandered over to a chair, picked up the hololens visor and haptic gloves she'd brought with her and put them on. Sitting down, she tucked her feet underneath her body like a meditating Buddha.

After the briefest of pauses while the computer connected with the new hardware, her vision was filled with a glowing display screen and her retinal AR was relegated to a tiny icon in the bottom left corner. Using her gloved hands to control the display, she quickly accessed her files and, within seconds, was floating in the reassuringly familiar three-dimensional virtual reality of her darkweb space.

Right then, this is it. She felt a surge of adrenalin as she contemplated what she was about to do. As she always did when she was concentrating, she began to talk through the steps she needed to follow, providing herself with a running commentary as she worked.

'You're mumbling again,' she heard Majid say.

'Hmm?' She was no longer really paying attention to the real world outside.

'I said you're doing that thing again ... you know, where you talk to yourself.'

Then, after a brief pause, he added, 'Reenie, I don't *need* to know what you're up to, but can I just check that whatever it is won't be traced back here?'

It hadn't occurred to her just how much she was asking of her best friend, but something in his voice betrayed his nervousness and she suddenly realized that she wasn't the only one taking a risk. Of course, she would make sure all traces of having used Majid's computer would be thoroughly erased, but maybe she did owe him some explanation.

Her concentration broken, she paused to think about what she should do. How much could she afford to tell him? Wasn't it more sensible, and safe, to keep him as much in the dark as possible? No, that wasn't fair.

She tried to push away what she realized were her true motives for revealing what she was doing to Majid. If she was honest, it was really more about her. Opening up would be a mixture of a boast and a confession.

She felt full of nervous energy at the prospect of sharing her ideas with another person, even though she guessed he would struggle to follow all the details. She took off her visor, untucked her legs again and turned to face him. He was staring at her like an affectionate puppy. Under all her bravado and tattoos, Shireen was well aware, because she had been told so on many occasions, that she was elfishly attractive; and she also knew that Majid had feelings for her that went beyond friendship. But they had an understanding, and he knew those feelings would never be reciprocated.

'OK, Majid, I'm going to let you in on my little project.' She pulled off her gloves to signal that she was going to devote all her attention to him for the next few minutes. 'You know I've been trying for ages to find a way through those new encryption protocols I told you about?'

'Yes, but just last week you said—'

'I know . . .' interrupted Shireen eagerly. 'Last week I said that was impossible, right? Because the Chinese had increased the number of their Sentinels protecting the repeater stations.' She knew that Majid was familiar with the basic science, but unlike her he was less than comfortable with the whole subject of quantum key distribution. He sometimes confessed to her that he should never have chosen computer science as his major at university. Why couldn't he just have opted for a simpler subject – basically anything that didn't involve the counterintuitive ideas of quantum physics.

'Well, that was last week. I think I may have found a back door,' Shireen continued. 'There's been some rather busy traffic recently between the Chinese authorities and other governments, and all the communications have been locked with unusually high levels of encryption, so I'm pretty sure there's something big going down that is being kept very hush-hush.'

' "*Something big*"?' Majid almost shouted. 'Are we talking international espionage? Or just your crazy conspiracy theory shit?' He chewed his top lip and ran both hands over the back of his shaven head. Two years ago, they had both been arrested during the student anti-corruption riots. Luckily his father had sufficient influence to get the charges against them dropped. But the incident meant they had needed to be more careful. Shireen tried to reassure her friend. 'Don't look so worried. You know that I know what I'm doing, right?'

'I know you *think* you know what you're doing. And OK, I don't know any cyb smarter than you. But how can you be so sure you're not biting off more than you can chew this time?'

'Because . . .' Shireen jumped out of her chair with renewed excitement and onto the sofa next to Majid. 'Because . . . I think I've found two weaknesses. The first, which I've suspected for a while, is a vulnerability in the repeater control system that allows me to hack in to it. The second – and this really is quite beautiful – is a weakness in the cloning algorithm in the repeater, which means I can make a copy of the quantum key without it affecting what's sent on to the genuine recipient.'

Majid was gaping at her.

'All I need is for a window to open up for a few seconds. I can get in, copy the key and get the hell out again.' She sat back and looked at Majid's reaction, then looked over at the black box on his desk containing the quantum computer. 'And that's why I need your new toy.'

However, Majid looked anything but reassured. He leaned forward and grabbed her by the shoulders. For a brief moment she wondered whether he was going to try and *shake* some sense into her. Instead, he said, 'But the whole point of quantum key distribution is that you *can't* eavesdrop without giving yourself away! I may not be as smart as you, Reenie, but I know enough from my quantum cryptography classes that this is the whole fucking point of the system. Any attempt to break the code disturbs the delicate quantum entangled state and sends an alert to the source, which then immediately switches to a different encryption key. Wasn't that the subject of last week's lecture – something about the Ekert 91 protocol?'

Shireen grinned, suddenly feeling even more pleased with herself. 'I know, foolproof, right? And you know as well as I do that every cyb in the world is looking for new attack strategies that target vulnerabilities in the system. And if you ask any of them they'll tell you that the obvious man-in-the-middle attacks and the photon number splitting attacks don't work. In fact, government and corporation sites don't even bother following up on these cyber alerts any more. And that's the beauty of it; they're so cocksure their encryptions can't be broken that no one is watching me.'

'And that's what you think you've done, is it? You've found a way of getting hold of a quantum encryption key without detection . . . a window where the laws of physics are no longer in control?' Majid's curiosity had now seemingly got the better of his nerves. He leapt to his feet and paced around the room. 'OK, how?'

'This, my dear Hajji, is why I will one day rule the world, while you will simply exist to wait on me hand and foot and serve me *bastani* and *faloodeh* until I get so big I explode. You see, I've found the one weakness in the system that plays them at their own quantum game: my very own Trojan horse code. It's so quiet, so imperceptible, that no one will ever know I've been snooping.'

'OK, your majesty,' he said, placing both hands on his chest and bowing, 'but . . . surely if—'

Shireen interrupted him, realizing she would have to try harder to explain. 'OK, listen. Quantum Information Theory one-oh-one – well, more correctly, basic communications engineering – says it's not possible to completely eliminate errors in electronic communications because of factors like noise and signal degradation, right? Well, early quantum encryption systems allowed for key exchanges where the error rate could be as high as twenty per cent. They felt that was acceptable since any eavesdropper would be too loud and clumsy and so give themselves away. But then ten years ago those new phase-remapping "intercept and resend" attacks meant things had to tighten up.'

'OK, please stop patronizing me, Shireen.' She could tell by the impatient look on his face that he still hadn't heard anything he didn't know already. 'I know that when cyberattacks suddenly grew a few years ago it was because eavesdroppers got so good they could intercept a tiny fraction of the signal sent during a quantum key exchange while never pushing the error rate over the twenty per cent threshold. So, their attacks were hidden in the noise. But once the authorities discovered this, they worked to bring that error threshold down.' He then added for good measure, 'Correct me if I'm being too slow-witted for you.'

Shireen ignored her friend's indignation. 'Exactly. So now only error rates below three per cent are accepted as noise and ignored. Anything above that and you're screwed. The problem has been that no one can eavesdrop quietly enough not to trigger much higher error rates than three per cent.'

Shireen left a dramatic pause to maximize the impact of what she was about to say. 'Well, no one, that is, until it was figured out by yours truly.' She grinned broadly. 'You see, I've found a crucial chink in the armour. It's a weakness in the quantum cloning algorithm. If it wasn't so cool, I'd be thinking of writing a paper on it. But why tell the rest of the world when I can have a bit of fun first?'

But instead of the unadulterated admiration she had expected, he just stared at her.

'How can you possibly call this fun? Who else knows about it?'

'Just you and me, of course, you idiot. And it's going to

71

stay that way.' *For now*, she thought to herself. It all depended what the files contained.

'Well, now I really wish you hadn't shared any of this with me, Reenie. It's too much of a responsibility. I mean, if this works then you've most likely just put both our lives in danger.'

'Oh, don't be such a drama queen, Hajji. When I'm finished, I'll make sure I erase every last qubit of data and code from your system. I'll be out of your hair – if you had any – and you can go get your beauty sleep.' She pulled down the visor again and put on the gloves. 'Now, this should only take a few minutes.' She compiled the cloning code and, after a quick run through her checklist, set it running.

Five minutes later she sat bolt upright and let out a whoop of triumph. She couldn't quite believe she'd done it. She now had stored deep in her dark-web file system the passwords that would unlock data no human other than a chosen few was meant to see. She recognized that whatever was in those files was so sensitive that she dreaded to think what might happen to her if she was ever found out. For the time being she had no intention of accessing the files. So, she spent the next few minutes covering her tracks and deleting all trace of her evening's activities.

Finally satisfied, she ripped off her visor and gloves and stretched her legs out. She glanced over at Majid. He looked like he was still sulking. 'I have a really bad feeling about this,' he muttered.

She stood up, suddenly feeling exhausted. 'Thanks for this, Hajji. I'll see you tomorrow morning, OK?' And then she added, 'It's going to be fine, I promise.' She leaned over and kissed her friend on the top of his head. He looked up at her and smiled weakly.

She walked out of the apartment without waiting for a reply and closed the door behind her.

Stepping out into the late-evening air, she felt elated and full of nervous excitement. She would open the files as soon as she got home. She just hoped that whatever they contained wouldn't stop her getting to sleep. Tomorrow, she would have to go to her classes as normal, as though nothing was any different.

She got in her car, told it to take her home, then began humming to herself.

Within minutes of Shireen's departure, a black van pulled up outside Majid's apartment. Oblivious to the chain of events that were already unfolding, Shireen could not know that her life, and her friend's, were about to be turned upside down.

8

Thursday, 7 February – Cat Island, Bahamas

FRANK PEDERSEN HAD BEEN CHECKING THE WEATHER updates since he'd woken at six. He'd been following the news of the storm that was building in the Atlantic and which was heading his way. It certainly didn't look very pretty out there. After half an hour working up a sweat in his gym, he'd eaten a large bowl of muesli and had a cold shower. It was such a warm and muggy morning he was soon sweating again through his T-shirt. He now prowled from room to room like a caged cat, not able to settle or take his mind off the approaching storm.

Frank Pedersen wasn't the sort of man to feel anxious. He'd pretty much always got what he'd wanted in life, and on those few occasions when there was worrying to be done, he'd left it to others. In fact, it could be said that one of his skills was to surround himself with professional worry absorbers. Over the years, people had debated whether his success was due to serendipity, brilliance or sheer perseverance – the truth being a combination of all three. He'd made his first million by the age of nineteen and his first billion by twenty-six. He hadn't achieved this by being particularly ruthless either; just by being . . . well . . . lucky, brilliant and hard-working. Even before he went to California, his entrepreneurial skills, combined with his keen eye for the next big thing in computing, had attracted lucrative job offers from several up-and-coming tech companies. That was at the turn of the millennium when a lot of smart, computer-savvy young people were beginning to shape the course of history. But even though he was eager to get over to Silicon Valley to be part of the IT revolution, Frank wanted to do things his way, which he duly did. Much to his parents' initial disappointment, he'd left Aarhus for San Francisco and never looked back. Throughout his career, he never deliberately courted or achieved the fame or star quality of others of his generation, such as Zuckerberg, Dorsey, Page and Brin, but then his self-belief meant he had only ever needed to impress one person: himself.

Now, with two marriages behind him, a business empire that pretty much ran itself and no more mountains left to climb, he had taken early semi-retirement to enjoy the quiet solitude of his own company and his two German shepherds in a secluded villa on top of a hill on a remote Caribbean island. The villa had originally been a hermitage, built by a Roman Catholic priest just before the Second World War, which he had instantly fallen in love with. Although he had spent millions converting the old building into a twenty-first-century fortress, he had refused to invest in a decent road up from the small town of New Bight, a few kilometres away on the west coast of the island, deciding that he preferred the isolation afforded by the steep rocky climb to reach him. Not that Frank Pedersen thought of himself as a recluse – forty-five years of keeping his finger on the technological pulse of the planet wasn't an addiction he wished to be cured of. Anyway, who was ever truly alone these days?

But he was feeling pretty cut off and alone this morning. This storm was looking increasingly ugly. Truth be told, it had been a pretty unremarkable hurricane season, with fewer than the average number of tropical cyclones being promoted to hurricane status. One of the consequences of the changes to the Earth's climate over the previous two decades had been the extension of the traditional autumn Atlantic hurricane season well into December, and even January. However, this new one, quickly dubbed Hurricane Jerome, was late by any standards. Not only that, but it had skipped several stages in the usual life-cycle of such storms, which would typically build up from depression, through tropical storm, to full-blown hurricane within a matter of several days. Instead, it had jumped from nothing to a category five in just a few hours.

Yesterday evening, when he first heard the news of the storm, he'd been advised by friends and associates back in California to get the hell out. After all, it was their job to worry about him. His heli had been flown over to the island and sat waiting on the tarmac six kilometres away. A quick call from him and it could have been at the Hermitage in a matter of minutes to whisk him away to safety. However, he insisted this was an unnecessary precaution and had instead ordered it to fly back to Florida, five hundred kilometres away, without him. He'd experienced six hurricane seasons on Cat Island and had never seen the need to flee, preferring to stick it out here just like he always did. After all, the Hermitage was designed to withstand anything nature might throw at it, particularly since he'd had its walls reinforced with criss-cross beams of a steel–graphene alloy, making it no more likely to blow over than the hill itself. And its situation at the top of Como Hill meant that, unlike the town below, it was safely above the high-point of even the most formidable tsunami. Nevertheless, this morning he was starting to feel that his decision to stay might have been somewhat imprudent. And Frank Pedersen never made imprudent decisions.

The dogs were showing signs of anxiety too. It might have been something they could smell in the air or just that they were feeding off Frank's unease. Unusually for her, Beth was curled up quietly beneath the living-room table with her nose tucked under her tail and just one brown eye following Frank around the room. Sheba paced around after him wanting to be made a fuss of all the time.

He turned around to look at them and, hands on hips in mock exasperation, spoke in a stern voice. 'You're being such babies. Go on outside and run around a bit while the weather's still OK.' Christ knows how long they were all going to be cooped indoors once the storm hit. He opened the door for them, but they just sat where they were and looked at him suspiciously. 'Suit yourselves.' Before closing the door, he stepped outside himself. The world seemed so quiet, but not in a peaceful way. Unusually for his hilltop, he noticed there was no wind at all, nor, rather more surreally, any of the usual chirping of birds or buzzing of insects in the bushes around the Hermitage. The thick grey cloud above him seemed almost solid in texture, and so low he could almost jump up and touch it. The air felt heavy and suspenseful. It was as if the world was full of pent-up energy, like a compressed spring waiting to be released.

He wandered back in, closed the door and went to the kitchen for a beer. Ten o'clock in the morning wasn't too early, was it? Of course it wasn't. And it might help cure him of his stupid jitters.

He'd bought the Hermitage eleven years ago and it had taken him five years to renovate it – essentially to transform it from a crumbling stone shell to a high-tech luxury villa. For years before he'd bought it, it had served as no more than a tourist destination, mainly on account of it being situated at the highest point in all of the Bahamas – or rather, of what was left of the Bahamas, since the rising sea level had consumed almost three quarters of the islands' land. Frank had always enjoyed his holidays in the Caribbean and had happily donated hundreds of millions of dollars of his personal wealth to relief funds over the years. In fact, Cat Island, where he had decided to settle, had emerged remarkably unscathed by virtue of protruding a few tens of metres higher above the water than the other islands.

He took out a bottle of Kalik from the fridge and twisted off the cap, then wandered back to check yet again for a weather update. The centre of the living room was taken up with a real-time, high-resolution, three-dimensional hologram of Hurricane Jerome. Frank stood in front of it and took a deep swig from the bottle. The swirling mass of cloud was spinning slowly and dragging its spiral arms like tentacles around its edges. It certainly looked like one mean motherfucker. There were interspersed flashes of light at the bottom where lightning discharged the storm's huge electrical energy into the sea. He found it interesting that the hurricane's name was the same as that of the priest who'd built his hermitage; the Right Reverend Monsignor John Hawes had also been known locally on the island as Father Jerome.

Meteorologists were already claiming that Jerome should be designated a category seven. When he'd first settled on Cat Island, Frank had taken a serious interest in hurricane classification and was aware that a new category six had recently been added beyond the previous highest five, which had been deemed insufficient to describe hurricanes with wind speeds over 280 kilometres per hour, as had been recorded with increasing regularity in recent years. This morning, drones and satellites tracking Jerome had recorded sustained wind speeds of well over 350 kilometres per hour.

He flicked through the different networks on his holo display and stopped at the BBC News Channel. Frank stood and watched as a young meteorologist explained in a very excited voice what was so special about this particular superhurricane:

'Scientists have known for over a century that galactic cosmic rays – subatomic particles reaching us from deep space – could adversely affect the weather on Earth, but they were mostly of academic interest only. After all, the Earth's magnetic field has always done its job of deflecting most of these particles before they got too close to the Earth's surface.

'The only other group of people they had been of any concern to were satellite manufacturers who had to build in appropriate shielding to avoid their sensitive electronics being fried. But now, the conjunction of two occurrences is having a dramatic effect never experienced before by humankind.'

Frank was well aware that his own business empire relied critically on the reliability of communication satellites, and while none of his own had been affected by the CME that had struck over India last week, he was becoming increasingly worried about the potential risks of the weakened magnetic field. The meteorologist meanwhile was now in full explainer mode.

'Firstly, the Sun happens to be going through its solar minimum right now, the low-activity stage of its eleven-year cycle, which means that its own magnetic field, the Heliosphere, is much weaker, so the number of galactic cosmic rays that can now reach the Earth is higher.

'Secondly, the dramatic weakening of the Earth's field itself, which we have been hearing a lot about of late, means that these cosmic rays can penetrate to much lower levels of the atmosphere, ionizing the air, which in turn seeds thick, giant clouds.

'This increased ionization also causes the electrical conduction of the lower atmosphere to increase dramatically, creating exceptional temperature and pressure gradients over heights of just a few kilometres. Our models predict that already violent storms are able to feed off this electrical energy. To make matters worse, over this past week astronomers have observed a sharp spike in the intensity of cosmic rays hitting the Earth, and are busy trying to locate the source. I'm told, and this is of course not my area, that a powerful supernova, an exploding star in a nearby galaxy, may be responsible.'

Frank was beginning to feel a little incredulous. Having to cope with higher levels of radiation, even hurricanes, was one thing, but 'exploding stars in nearby galaxies'? Come on. Seriously?

'In any case, this sudden surge in cosmic ray intensity is giving us some interesting, to say the least, weather conditions. And this is now evident over the mid-Atlantic, where dramatic changes in atmospheric conditions are having a profound effect on the hurricane season. The warming ocean has already resulted in more severe, and frequent, storms, but it appears that Hurricane Jerome is the first true superstorm to draw on this vast new source of energy from space. It's basically plugging into the *power source of distant exploding stars. And as we can see, the results are quite stunning.'*

'Stunning' might be an adjective appropriate for someone safely watching from the other side of the world, but when you were in the hurricane's path . . .

'If anything, Hurricane Jerome is just getting started. Thousands of metres above the sea, more and more storm clouds are now coalescing and joining its giant swirling vortex. The winds in its outer wall are at this moment sweeping across the ocean in a circle twelve hundred kilometres in diameter, at well over a hundred and sixty kilometres per hour, whipping it up; and this is combined with exceptionally low atmospheric pressure just above the surface of the water. This means . . .'

Frank had heard enough. He turned away, commanding the holo off as he did so. Normally so rational and logical, he decided that discretion was the better part of valour and that it was probably time to head for the safety of the wine cellar. He wandered around the villa collecting together the few essential supplies he'd need for a day or two underground: bedding, food and water for him and the dogs, several LED lamps, the portable holo, an induction charger and a couple of e-pads. He hadn't been confident that his net drones would be safe enough above the storm and had already commanded them back to the mainland. This, of course, meant that his connectivity to the outside world was going to be patchy, particularly underneath several metres of rock.

So confident had he been in the past about the solidity of the Hermitage that he had never felt the need for a dedicated storm shelter. In any case, unlike the stone buildings above it, the wine cellar was carved out of the rock of the hill itself. But he had also never felt it necessary to stock the cellar up with emergency supplies on the off-chance he ever had to use it. Well, now he did.

What he missed right now was Maisie, his assistant, on whom he relied increasingly these days to organize his life and ensure that the 'little things' were taken care of. During the lengthy periods that he now spent out here at the Hermitage, Maisie would come over for a full day every week to make sure he wasn't entirely neglecting his businesses and that he wasn't in need of anything. Now, she was hundreds of kilometres away and Frank was having to think for himself. But he felt confident that he had everything he needed for what might be a couple of days. The wine cellar, true to its primary purpose, was as perfect a place as anywhere to spend some time.

It had originally been a crypt, though Frank had no idea whether anyone had been entombed there, nor what had become of the bodies if they had – although it still had the words 'Blessed are the Dead Who Die in the Lord' carved on a large block of granite above the entrance. To reach it involved going outside, crossing the courtyard and descending several roughly chiselled steps to approach from the side of the rocky outcrop on which the Hermitage was built. Frank had had a thick oak door put in to replace the metal gate that had previously blocked the entrance. So, his wine collection, last valued at well over a million dollars, was safe within the crypt's cool and dry conditions.

The dogs had initially been reluctant to abandon the safety of the house and had taken some coaxing. Then, when he had left them in the cellar to return to the house for a few more bits and pieces, they had started howling, clearly spooked by the approaching storm.

Finally secure, with vault door safely closed, Frank could hear that it had started raining heavily. The wind had suddenly picked up too and was now howling around the building above his head. He mentally ran through his checklist to make sure he'd not forgotten any crucial items he might need. Although if he had, it was too late anyway – there was no way he would be going back up now.

He decided it was as good a time as any to sample one of his prize wines and he strolled down the dimly lit passageways past arrays of dusty wine bottles stacked from floor to ceiling – which was only one and a half metres high at the sides, but arched up to three metres down the middle of the passages. The place had a strange smell. It was more than just a dry, stale mustiness and Frank had always found it slightly unnerving. It was an imperceptibly faint, sweet stench of rot, as though the place wanted to cling to its original role as a resting place for the decaying flesh of long-dead inhabitants of the island, and that Frank and his precious wine collection were merely temporary intruders.

He settled on a modest Malbec and, wrapping it in the bottom of his T-shirt, he twisted it round to wipe it clean, transferring its filthy film of dust to his clothes. He then wandered back to the deeper end of the cellar, where the lighting was better and the noise from outside fainter.

The dogs, sitting side by side a few feet away, were watching him intensely. 'You two girls OK? Come on, this is fun.'

They both jumped up eagerly and trotted over to him to be made a fuss of, reassured that, despite his earlier tension, their master now appeared more relaxed and calm. Frank knew they would hate not being able to go outside to do their business. Come to think of it, he wasn't particularly delighted by the prospect of shitting in a bucket either. He hoped it wouldn't come to that. Fuck. Toilet paper! Oh, well, too late now.

The storm raged outside. The noise was now deafening. Suddenly, without any warning flicker, the lights went out. The solar-powered generator must have been knocked out. He reached down in the pitch black to the floor by his feet where he remembered he'd left the LED lamps and felt around for the nearest one. He picked it up and switched it on. He left the others off but still within reach – no need to use up their charge unnecessarily.

Beth and Sheba settled down again, now that they knew Frank wasn't abandoning them, and both curled up on the filthy floor under the old wooden bench. He opened the bottle of red, feeling pleased with himself for remembering to bring down a wine glass. Making himself as comfortable as possible on the bench, he tried to distract himself with a book. For the first time that day he started to feel less tense. Let the storm do its worst. Frank Pedersen was going nowhere.

After several hours during which the storm raged with increasing ferocity, he must have fallen asleep, because he was slowly dragged back to wakefulness by the sound of Beth whining by the cellar door at the far end, scratching it to go out. It took several seconds of disorientation before it struck him what had changed. He could only hear the dog whining because there was no competing noise from the other side of the oak door. After the deafening racket of the storm outside, the contrast was eerie. He checked his watch. It was late afternoon, and his first thought was that the hurricane had passed, allowing himself a moment of self-congratulatory triumph. But his relief was short-lived; a quick mental calculation told him this was impossible. When he'd last checked, just before coming down to the cellar, the storm had been over a thousand kilometres across. At the speed the forecasters had said it was moving, it could not have covered a distance equal to its entire diameter in the time that had elapsed. In fact, by his reckoning, it should only be halfway across. The silence must mean that the eye of the hurricane was now directly overhead.

He went over to the door and released the catch. Something outside was stopping it from swinging open, but with a firmer push he managed to dislodge the tree branch that had been blown across it. Before he could stop them, the dogs scampered out from behind him. Sheba came to a halt just outside the door and sniffed the air, while Beth trotted down the steps and disappeared into a bush. Frank stood and stared. *'Jesus Christ!'*

The scene that greeted him was astonishing. The villa above him was blocked from view at this angle, but he could see out right across the island. There was a very light breeze and the sky overhead was clear, but a few kilometres out to sea was a sight he knew he would never forget: a wall of dark churning clouds that extended all the way around him, stretching up into the sky. That the sun was peeking through the hole in the roof of the hurricane only added to the dreamlike scenario. He looked down towards the coast – or rather, where he expected the coast to be. The sea now extended almost a kilometre further inland than it had done yesterday, only stopping where the land began to rise. New Bight had disappeared. All that remained of the town above water was the church steeple.

Venturing further out, Frank walked down a few steps to get a better view of his home behind him. The first thing that struck him was the missing Hermitage tower. The thirty-foot bell tower had been the only part of the old building not reinforced along with the rest of the property. The storm had brought it down, reducing it to a mound of rubble – large chunks of brickwork and stone were now strewn across the courtyard. He needed to have a quick scout around to assess any further damage.

He walked briskly up the path that led round to the top of the hill. A wave of relief washed over him as he saw that, apart from the bell tower, the rest of the Hermitage was relatively undamaged. Luckily, it appeared that the back of the building had taken the brunt of, and survived, the full force of the winds. He scrambled over the scattered bricks knowing he didn't have long before he had to get back to the cellar. Looking back the way he'd come he caught a glimpse of both dogs trotting back inside.

Relieved at his animals' good sense, he started back across the courtyard himself. It occurred to him that if the first half of the hurricane had battered the back of his home then it would now be the turn of the front to bear the brunt. Oh well, if he had to rebuild the place, then so be it.

Zigzagging his way across the courtyard around the ruins of the collapsed tower, he was about ten metres from the steps when he felt the winds suddenly pick up. Puzzled, he turned round. The approaching wall of the storm had been over to his right and so he hadn't seen how close it was. Now, it was patently obvious that he had utterly misjudged how fast it was moving towards him. With a renewed sense of urgency, he hurried on, his progress slowed by the large chunks of masonry.

In the space of those few seconds it took him to cover the short distance to safety, the winds sweeping across Como Hill picked up from a gentle breeze to the full force of Hurricane Jerome: over three hundred and eighty kilometres an hour. Frank Pedersen was running now.

Or at least he went through the motions of running, for he was suddenly plucked up off the ground, as though he were no more than a dry leaf caught in an autumn breeze, along with pieces of the Hermitage roof and an assortment of tree branches and bushes. Tumbling through the air like a rag-doll, Frank didn't have time to feel afraid or to make sense of what was happening to him, because the logic circuits in his brain that had served him so well all his life now simply ceased to function. Instead of terror, he felt a strange sense of exhilaration, as a child might when tossed into the air by a parent. But unlike the child's relief as it fell back down to the safety of strong adult arms, Frank had no such reprieve. Hurricane Jerome was no respecter of Newtonian gravity.

Any feelings of anxiety or exhilaration he might have had ended the moment a passing oak tree slammed into him, snapping his neck instantly.

9

SIX HUNDRED KILOMETRES SOUTH-EAST OF CAT ISLAND, and while a still alive but edgy Frank Pedersen was about to open a bottle of beer, the rain had been steadily falling all morning and was getting heavier. The sea was becoming choppier too – more irritable than tempestuous, but it was clear to anyone who knew the sea that nothing but raw rage lay ahead. Joseph Smith knew the sea. He'd been a fisherman all his life and had a pretty good idea what was coming, but for the time being his small fishing trawler trudged along happily enough. Given the recent meagre hauls, Joseph knew that he couldn't afford not to go out these days, whatever the weather. So, against the wishes of his wife, he had left the village with his son Zain before dawn to ensure a good few hours for a semi-decent catch before they had to turn back. Joseph figured that if there was a sudden change, then they'd need fifteen minutes to reel in the nets, then another hour to get back to shore, if he opened the engine all the way up.

On the other hand, why take any unnecessary risks?

Maybe it had been foolish to come out at all. Joseph had always trusted his instincts, and his instincts were now telling him to call it a day, albeit a very short one, and head back. It was still only ten-thirty in the morning and they had been out for just over three hours. But then no other fool was even out on the water today.

'Start the winches, boy, I'm calling it,' he shouted across the deck to his son.

'Why, Pa? It don't look too bad to me yet,' laughed Zain with the bravado of youth.

'Just do it. I'm not in your mother's good books as it is, so it's best we get back before things get too interesting out here.'

Joseph ducked inside the wheelhouse to work out the most efficient bearing to take if the wind suddenly started picking up in the next hour or so.

Zain was sixteen and, Joseph was sure, would be happy enough to get back home as soon as possible too. The boy had recently developed a serious crush on their neighbour's daughter, Aliya. A year younger than him, he'd known her all his life, but this past year she had blossomed into a beautiful young woman. The two had been spending a lot of time together.

Joseph stared at the screen in front of him and tried to make sense of the live weather map it was showing, when it struck him why it had looked so odd. A sudden chill ran through him. When he'd last checked the satellite data, just under half an hour ago, the centre of Hurricane Jerome had been seven hundred and twenty kilometres to the east and heading towards them at about twenty knots. Given its size, this meant that the outer edges, where the wind and rain really picked up and the sea turned brutal, would not reach them for another couple of hours – plenty of time to get back to shore. But that had changed. His mouth suddenly felt dry. He licked his lips. The storm had just doubled in size in the space of thirty minutes. It was such a ridiculous notion that Joseph assumed it had to be a mistake in the readings. But if the current data were correct then the outer wall of the hurricane was far closer than he'd thought.

He rushed back out on deck. It seemed to him that even in these few minutes conditions had worsened, and the rain was now pouring down. His son was standing at the stern, his legs braced against the roll of the boat, next to the boom holding the power block that fed the nets out behind. Joseph shouted out to Zain, but the boy couldn't hear him. Holding on to the rail, he made his way to the stern and grabbed his son by the shoulders. 'Zain,' he yelled into the storm, 'we're going to have to cut the nets free and get the hell out of here.'

Joseph tried his best to appear calm and relaxed, but Zain read the nervousness in his eyes. 'Cut the nets? Why don't we reel them in?' his son shouted.

Joseph didn't want to lose his nets, but he knew it would take at least twenty minutes for the hydraulic pump to winch them in – time he now calculated he didn't have. In any case the pump ran off the main engines and he needed all the power he could get if he was going to outrun the approaching hurricane.

'The storm's a lot closer than I thought. We really don't have a choice,' he shouted above the increasing roar of the rain and wind.

Zain didn't question him any further and instead hurried back to the wheelhouse where they kept the tools. Joseph tried to rationalize that this wasn't a decision he was taking lightly. They would struggle to afford new nets to replace these ones. He watched as his son came back with the large cable cutters and Joseph left him to it,

90

struggling against the driving rain back to the wheel-house. They were twenty-two kilometres away from the coast. At full throttle, in this weather, they would get back to port in about forty minutes. Although the hurricane to their east was moving in the same direction, the circling winds at its outer edges, if it caught up with them, would be slamming into the port side of the boat.

Joseph wrestled the boat around against the angry sea and began the race for home. A few minutes later, the door slammed open as Zain stumbled in accompanied by an angry gust of salty spray. He leaned his weight against the door and forced it shut. 'The nets are gone,' he said breathlessly and reached for an old towel to dry his face. Joseph cursed himself for thinking that coming out this morning was ever a good idea. There would most definitely be all hell to pay when he got back home and had to admit his folly. Still, he would worry about that later.

Joseph Smith knew the sea and still felt confident. With the nets cut and the boat heading home, he had done all he could. It was now a straight race between him and the storm.

The wipers skidded ineffectively back and forth across the windshield as the rain lashed down. Joseph couldn't see much beyond the bow of the boat through the curtain of rain, just the deep charcoal-grey hue of the stormy sky. It seemed to him as though the thunder clouds extended all the way down to the sea.

Then a sudden flash of lightning briefly lit up the world outside, and Joseph froze.

'Oh, dear God, no.'

The dark sky he'd been staring at wasn't sky at all, but a giant wall of water bearing down on his small boat.

His knuckles whitened as he gripped the wheel with a futile intensity. Had he been able to articulate any

91

semblance of rational thought at that moment he might have admitted that this was no longer a fair struggle between man and nature – that his puny little fishing boat was but an insignificant toy at the mercy of the rolling mountainous waves.

'Forgive me, Elsa,' he sobbed, thinking of his wife back home. He could hear his son screaming somewhere behind him.

For a second or two, the world outside went quiet as the wind dropped, as though in respectful anticipation, and the boat began to tilt up.

10

Thursday, 7 February – San Juan, Puerto Rico

CAMILA HAD LIVED THROUGH HER FAIR SHARE OF HUR-
ricanes during her eighty-five years in San Juan and knew
the drill. She'd spent the morning calling family and
friends, making them promise that they would stay safely
indoors with sufficient supplies to keep them going for a
few days until the storm had passed. She'd been busy baking and cooking since hearing the weather forecasts two
days ago. Wiping her hands on her apron she took out several Tupperware boxes from the cupboard. The rich aroma
of chorizo and shellfish in her large pot of *asopao* permeated the whole of her ground-floor apartment. She'd now
cooked enough food to feed a platoon for a week and
began portioning up the thick soup. She'd keep most of it
in her fridge but decided to take a couple of portions up to
Grace Morales on the fifth floor.

Camila was feeling rejuvenated after the recent stem-
cell injections had cleared up the arthritis in her knees,
and was keen to impress her friend with her newfound
vigour. Besides, she wanted to have a better view out to
sea than she had from her own flat on the ground floor.

It had been an exceptionally warm and sticky week, and now the rain had started. The wind had been building all morning and was currently strong enough to blow the lids off garbage bins, sending them rolling down the street with an assortment of autumn leaves, paper, plastic and anything else not firmly secured. Counting the cost of the damage wrought by storms was a fact of life for Camila, and she was sure it would be much worse than just a bin lid that needed replacing. Last year her two sons had clubbed together to replace her old windows with graphene-toughened glass that could withstand the brute force of the far stronger winds – something she was even more grateful for today.

Picking up the soup, she left her apartment. She thought about getting in the lift, but then decided she'd like to see the look on Grace's face after telling her she'd climbed five flights of stairs.

Grace was indeed impressed by her old friend's regained mobility, though at first she'd been startled by Camila's breathlessness.

'Well, there's no need to show off on my account, my dear,' she scolded. 'What's the use of healthy knees if your heart gives out?'

Camila still managed to chuckle as she caught her breath. 'I can see how jealous you are, Grace. No point trying to hide it. Now put the kettle on.' She barged past her friend into the apartment.

To Camila's relief, Grace seemed just as unconcerned as she was by the approaching storm. They would keep each other calm.

After catching up on family gossip the two women settled down by the front window with a coffee and a piece of cake. It was a beautiful view to the north, overlooking the Laguna to the picturesque district of Condado, an affluent tree-lined neighbourhood with hotels and apartment blocks that, in turn, overlooked the Atlantic. To the west was the hundred-and-thirty-year-old Dos Hermanos bridge that linked Condado with the entrance to old San Juan.

That is, it would have been a beautiful view. But not today.

Over the next hour, they watched as the storm continued to build outside. From their vantage point they could see the palm trees below them swaying ever more dramatically in the strengthening winds. And as the hurricane approached, their unease began to build. Camila had lived through hundreds of storms in her life, but there was something different about this one that she didn't like. And yet she couldn't quite put her finger on why she felt a growing sense of foreboding.

Had visibility been better they would have seen the first of the storm surges approaching from out at sea. As it was, Camila could just make out the other side of the lagoon. Through the driving rain she saw a few foolish motorists still out on the roads, despite the tsunami warnings that had been broadcast all morning, including several cars crossing the Dos Hermanos bridge spanning the lagoon, trying to reach safety as quickly as they could.

Arriving about a minute apart, it seemed that each tidal surge was bigger than the previous one.

Then, as though tiring of playing games, Hurricane Jerome decided to show Camila what it was truly capable of. She sat transfixed, her coffee cup slipping, unnoticed, from her fingers onto the floor. She watched as first the roads and then the bridge itself disappeared underneath the giant wave. Her heart began pounding in her chest, this time with terror rather than physical exertion. She could just about make out a few cars being carried along by the water as it advanced across the lagoon towards them. The scene looked like something from one of those badly made disaster movies she remembered watching as a young girl.

'Oh, sweet Lord. Those poor souls,' cried Grace.

An almost forgotten memory from Camila's childhood rose unbidden, of a summer's day on the beach with her two sisters when they had built an elaborate sand castle. After hours of painstaking work, sculpting turrets, battlements, walls and moat, they had then watched as the tide came in, quickly washing away their creation until the sand was flat and featureless once more.

As the wall of water continued across the lagoon towards them, looming ever larger, she instinctively reached across and grabbed hold of Grace's hand. Their apartment window was thankfully higher than the top of the wave, so they were able to watch from their prime location as it slammed into their building, causing it to shudder. She heard screams from downstairs followed by what sounded like several explosions. Maybe those newly reinforced windows weren't a match for a million-ton tsunami.

The wave had reached as high as the floor below them when it hit but had now subsided so that only the first two floors of the building were underwater. The realization that her trip upstairs had most likely saved her life left Camila shaken. How many hundreds of lives were, at this very moment, coming to an end, trapped in their homes underneath the water? She looked across at her friend. Tears were running down Grace's cheeks as she let out an anguished whimpering sound.

Camila felt too numb to speak. She still hadn't moved when, less than a minute later, the next, even larger surge hit land. This time, the wave seemed to have one purpose only. Reluctant to give up its immense store of energy until the final moment, it came for Camila.

II

Saturday, 9 February – New York

SARAH HAD SPENT THE HOUR SINCE WAKING UP IN HER hotel room following the awful news of the devastation wreaked by Hurricane Jerome. The casualty count already stood at well over thirty thousand, and would no doubt rise further. Now, two days after it had reached maximum strength, it had been downscaled to a category four, but was still strong enough to pose a threat to life. It had switched direction and was moving north, still out at sea, which meant it would miss the US eastern seaboard. Sarah had been brooding over whether its extraordinary strength was indeed correlated with the weakened magnetic field, as many commentators were now claiming.

She showered, dressed and headed down to meet Gabriel Aguda. She found him sitting on a sofa in the hotel lobby. He smiled and stood up to greet her. He was a giant of a man, in his mid-sixties, and clearly carrying more weight than even his almost two-metre-tall frame justified. What also struck her was the garishly coloured cotton shirt he was wearing under a faded brown corduroy jacket. He might move in high-powered political circles, but he nevertheless maintained a typical academic dress sense.

'Dr Maitlin . . . Sarah, if I may, it's good to meet you at last.' He extended an enormous hand.

Sarah shook it. There was something else about him that didn't fit the mental image she'd formed from his profile and the photos she'd found online. But she couldn't put her finger on it. 'Well, it's kind of you to come and meet me like this, but I wasn't sure—'

'I hope you haven't had breakfast,' Aguda interrupted. 'There's a nice pancake place just across the road. And we have a lot to discuss before this morning's meeting. And do please call me Gabriel.'

They stepped outside.

The cold air stung her face and she yanked her woolly hat from a coat pocket, quickly pulling it over her head. All around her were signs that the normally stoical New Yorkers were nervous and preoccupied. Most of the people she passed wore the familiar glazed look of attention being focused on retinal displays, presumably following reports on Hurricane Jerome and its progress. Her own attention was snapped rudely back by Aguda's booming voice alongside her. And she wasn't the only one, as several passing pedestrians were startled out of their reverie and gave him a wide berth.

'I hope you don't mind if we start talking shop right away . . .' he said, as he stepped off the kerb and strode across the busy street without a moment's hesitation. He appeared oblivious to the dozen or more driverless cabs that had to brake suddenly, jolting their passengers. Sarah rushed to keep up with him. 'It's just that you and I are the only two scientists on the committee, and there are certainly others on there who don't quite appreciate the magnitude of the danger our planet is facing.'

On the other side of the road, she quickened her pace to draw level with the giant Nigerian. 'These people are politicians, Sarah,' he continued. 'They only listen to us when they think they have to, and they cherry-pick evidence if it suits their purposes and ambitions.'

Where was he going with this? Was he about to reveal something important to her? Was there some conflict of interest on the committee such that he needed friends?

Aguda seemed unconcerned that anyone else might overhear him as he continued in his loud, deep voice. 'At the moment, governments are in panic mode,' he thundered. 'Despite the months of warnings that something like the Air India incident was bound to happen it's only now that they're taking it seriously; of course, you and I know the situation is only going to get worse. We've seen the destruction that Hurricane Jerome has caused. You know as well as I do that these events are connected.'

Sarah made a mental note to get him to explain this connection further. But a more immediate question popped into her head.

'OK, so if governments are now finally listening to the scientists and putting contingency plans into place, why is this committee necessary at all?'

Aguda gave her an indulgent smile. 'You have a lot to learn, Sarah. It's not so much *having* contingency plans, but rather who chooses *which* ones to put in place, and then who pays for them. Oh, and even more crucially of course, who pays to replace all the communication satellites that get damaged in any future event like the recent CME. We have to have a solid international consensus. As for us, well, I guess you and I are there to give the committee scientific legitimacy.

'Don't get me wrong, I'd like to think we still have a vital role to play. But the fact is, Sarah, while the UN is pretty toothless, and not exactly untouched by corruption, it is still the only organization that can claim to stand up to China. And if we – you and I, that is – don't press home the seriousness of the current threat facing the world, then China will just act in its own interests, as it always does.' He gave a rueful grunt.

They had reached a busy intersection and Sarah lost Aguda for a few seconds as they fought their way through a crowd waiting at a crossing. She hoped this breakfast was worth all the effort and wondered whether it wouldn't have been more sensible just to grab a snack at the hotel before heading to the meeting. She drew up alongside him again.

None of what he'd said so far was news. Sarah knew full well that the UN had struggled for many years to ensure that its voice was heard on the world stage. But she had detected an urgency in Aguda's voice that hinted at something more – something he wasn't telling her. It felt as though he was rather too keen to win her over to his side. But if so, what or who were the opposition? Before she could quiz him further, they arrived at the diner.

The place was packed, but the warmth provided a welcome respite from the sharp cold outside. The smell of coffee and baked pastries pervading the air was enticing, and the general hubbub of conversation was so loud that Sarah almost had to shout to be heard.

'OK, so my next question is: why me? Why would a committee as high-powered as you say it is recruit someone like me, with no experience of dealing with politicians, and all just because I made it onto some news networks?' She wasn't quite sure what she wanted to hear. 'I hope they're not just looking for someone to be the scientific spokesperson for the committee, wheeled out to face the media every time there's a crisis.' She had no intention of acting as a mouthpiece for governments wishing to tell the world that everything would be fine.

Aguda's guffaw coincided with a lull in the buzz of the diner, startling a passing waitress, who dropped the handful of cutlery she'd been carrying. Sarah watched as two bots glided over and helped the girl pick it up.

Aguda didn't seem to have even noticed and simply carried on where he'd left off. 'On the contrary, my dear, your credentials as a researcher have been thoroughly vetted and, believe me, you come with the very highest recommendations.'

Sarah bit her lip and let his patronizing tone pass. Aguda had clearly mistaken her misgivings for insecurity. She certainly didn't need his approbation.

He continued, 'We needed someone to tell us, not only just how bad things are likely to get in the coming months, but how reliably and how far in advance we can predict these sorts of geomagnetic storms. Of course, just as importantly, we did indeed want someone without the baggage of vested interest or political ambitions.'

Aguda's lecture – because that was what it was beginning to feel like to her – was interrupted by one of the bots that had been helping the waitress. Gliding up to them, it informed them in its singsong voice that a table was now available. Sarah noted absent-mindedly that it was a model popular these days, both in homes and in the service industry, mainly for its versatility. It didn't have the processing ability and machine-learning skills of the new companion bots, which were able to react to human emotions almost as well as dogs, but then there really wasn't much call for empathy in a New York diner. In fact, dispassionate and efficient service was ideal.

She followed Aguda and the bot to a corner table near

the back of the diner. After a moment checking the menu screen, they each tapped out their orders of coffee and pancakes. Sarah checked the time on her retinal clock; they had less than an hour before they had to report at the UN building across town.

Luckily, Gabriel also appeared mindful of their limited time and his demeanour suddenly became more serious. He leaned forward across the table towards her. 'OK, Sarah, how much do you know about geomagnetism?' His breath smelled of peppermint and stale cigars.

Was this going to be an interview, or was he just gauging her level of knowledge before he continued his lecture? 'Well, I'm a solar physicist – my expertise is in the magnetic field of the Sun, not the Earth. So, if you're asking me how much I know about the weakening strength of the magnetosphere and the approaching Flip then, no, it's not really my area.'

'Good, because it is *my* area.' Gabriel smiled. 'Please stop me if I'm telling you anything that's too basic, OK?'

'OK.' Sarah nodded. The shoe was on the other foot for a change, she thought wryly to herself – she'd spent the past few days saying the same thing to journalists and politicians.

'Well, as I'm sure you know,' began Aguda, 'the location of the Earth's magnetic north has been on the move for the past few centuries, but in recent years it's been speeding up. It used to be in North America; now it's in Asia.' Sarah was shocked by this revelation, and equally by the fact that she hadn't known about it before. She was aware the pole had been shifting, but she clearly hadn't been keeping up to date.

'That in itself, of course, is not the issue,' continued Aguda. 'Unlike the Sun's magnetic polarity, which reverses every decade or so, the Earth's magnetic field only flips over a few times in a million years, but each geomagnetic reversal takes thousands of years to complete. And in any case, the next one is now long overdue – by about half a million years, in fact.

'But a long-standing problem is that we don't fully understand what triggers such a reversal. I mean, we know that the Earth's molten core is disrupted in some way, but—'

'—But what's happening now isn't one of those slow reversals, right?'

'No, the speed at which the field is changing suggests a quite different mechanism. And it's one that we geologists have seen before, in the relatively recent geological history.'

Gabriel paused theatrically just as their coffee and pancakes arrived and he lowered his voice to a conspiratorial whisper.

'Have you ever come across something called the Laschamp excursion?'

'Can't say that I have, no,' she replied, unwrapping her knife and fork from their napkin and immediately tucking in to her breakfast. 'Tell me.'

Gabriel grew animated, his own pancakes forgotten. 'Well, in the 1960s, geologists found strong evidence in the ancient lava near the village of Laschamp in central France showing that there'd been a temporary, and geologically very brief, reversal of the Earth's magnetic field. This happened about forty thousand years ago. In fact, the magnetic poles switched over for such a short time before flipping back again that we call it an "excursion", rather than a "reversal".'

Again, Sarah was surprised she hadn't come across this information before. The scientist in her was intrigued and she looked up from her plate, fork with skewered piece of pancake frozen halfway to her mouth. 'Forty thousand years ago; that would put it during the last ice age, right?'

'Correct. And guess what else is of significance forty thousand years ago.'

Sarah took an educated guess. 'Um, isn't that round about the time that modern humans arrived in Europe?'

'Yes, that's partly correct.' Aguda was clearly getting into his stride now, his own pancakes still untouched. '*Homo sapiens* migrated to Europe from both Africa and Asia in several waves, many tens of thousands of years ago. But forty thousand years ago was also when Neanderthals disappeared from Europe.'

'Wait a minute. Isn't that the same thing? Didn't *Homo sapiens* replace Neanderthals in Europe? And where they overlapped, they even interbred, but Neanderthals gradually became extinct because they couldn't compete . . .' Sarah recalled a lecture by a highly regarded palaeontologist in which he'd argued that Neanderthals hadn't gone extinct at all but were simply lost in the noise as they interbred with the much larger *Homo sapien* numbers.

Aguda smiled. 'Your knowledge of palaeontology isn't bad for a physicist.' Not for the first time, Sarah wondered where this was all going. She checked the time. They would need to be on their way soon if they were to make the start of the meeting, and she still wasn't sure what point Gabriel was trying to make. But the geologist continued with his lecture.

'Certainly, there were pockets of Neanderthals hanging around southern Europe for another ten thousand years, but the majority disappeared rather suddenly – we think this is because of some cataclysmic event. And most geologists now believe it was the Laschamp excursion.'

104

Sarah felt a growing sense of foreboding as the implications of what she was hearing began to sink in. 'Hang on – you're saying that what's happening with the Earth's magnetic field *now* is like an event that happened forty thousand years ago – and that it was so awful it caused the near extinction of an entire species of humans? Fuck! And this was all down to a weakening of the magnetic field?'

'That's exactly what I am saying. The geological data suggest that during those few hundred years that the field was temporarily reversed it had just one tenth of its normal strength.'

'So, considerably weaker than now.'

Aguda nodded. 'But that's not even the most interesting thing. During the few months of actual transition, while the field was doing the flipping, it disappeared almost entirely. So, you can imagine what that would have meant. The potential disintegration of the ozone layer in the atmosphere leading to lethal levels of radiation streaming in from space as well as a serious and very sudden disruption of the Earth's climate.'

Sarah had by now lost her appetite. She thought about Hurricane Jerome, a thousand kilometres out to sea from where she was sitting, with a trail of death and destruction in its wake. Maybe it was just her imagination, but the diner seemed a lot quieter now – perhaps her senses were just blocking out the surrounding sights and sounds as she focused on processing all the new information. She turned back to Aguda. 'I guess it makes sense that the reason Jerome was so powerful may be because the high cosmic ray flux is playing havoc with atmospheric conditions . . .'

Aguda finished her train of logic. '. . . And the reason that radiation is so high? Because the weakened magnetic field can't block it. So, the energy of the cosmic rays that are already getting through the atmosphere is being absorbed to transform hurricanes into deadly superhurricanes.'

Sarah had spent the past two weeks concerned about geomagnetic storms wiping out telecommunication systems. But this was all far more terrifying.

She ran her fingers through her hair and tried to clear her head, her half-eaten plate of pancakes forgotten. She needed to remain rational. And, yes, maybe this was all getting a little far-fetched. 'But this Laschamp event . . . you're talking about climatic conditions that brought about the end of an entire species . . . and if they were that severe why didn't they cause a mass extinction of lots of other life on Earth at the same time?'

'You have to remember that the climate in northern Europe during the ice age was already harsh enough. So, any further disruption would have tipped the balance from unforgiving to intolerable as far as the Neanderthals and many other animals and plants were concerned.'

'Okaay . . . I'll buy that,' she said, still not entirely persuaded. 'But why would it be the Neanderthals who were affected and not *Homo sapiens*? I thought the Neanderthals were a hardy species.'

Aguda leaned back in his chair and spoke through a mouthful of pancake – the end of the world seemingly not affecting his appetite. 'It's simple geography, Sarah. The further north you go, the harsher the climate and the narrower the margin for comfort if things get worse. So, southern Europe and Africa, where most modern humans had settled, didn't fare so badly. Also, Neanderthals tended to be fair-skinned and redheaded, which suggests that, in the almost complete absence of an ozone layer, they would have been especially susceptible to ultraviolet B damage.'

Well, that certainly seemed to make sense, thought Sarah. The ozone layer was already depleted dramatically in several regions around the globe and presumably with further weakening of the field it would be one of the first casualties under the bombardment of solar particles. Still, was Gabriel Aguda pushing a controversial theory that the rest of the scientific community wasn't ready to accept, one based on an overly dramatic interpretation of meagre data? It was one thing to be speculating about an event that took place in the last ice age, quite another to suggest it might be happening again.

Gabriel must have sensed her scepticism because his demeanour changed, and he leaned forward again. 'All the evidence we have points to it: the dramatic cosmic ray activity getting through the ionosphere and the resulting increased concentration of long-lived cosmogenic isotopes like beryllium-10 and chlorine-36 in the atmosphere, the sudden changing weather patterns. What we've got to hope for is a quick transition to the Flip so that the field can pick up strength again in a few months.'

'And in the meantime?'

'In the meantime, we have to do what we can to minimize its impact. After all, we should surely be better placed to protect ourselves than those poor Neanderthals, right?'

Sarah wasn't so sure. It wasn't the continuous bombardment of cosmic rays from deep space that worried her as much as the sudden unpredictable bursts of activity from the Sun. The UN committee weren't going to like what she would tell them about the potential impact of any future large coronal ejections. Of course, a lot depended on how much weaker the Earth's field got. But there was something bugging her about all this and she suddenly realized what it was. 'OK, tell me this. How can you be confident the transition will be over quickly so the field can recover its strength? I thought geologists only worked on timescales of millions of years. Surely, even the forty thousand years since the Laschamp excursion is just a blink of an eye for you.'

Aguda went quiet for a few seconds, as though gathering his thoughts. 'Well, in a sense you're right. But our computer simulations of the way the Earth's magnetic field evolves are pretty sophisticated. A geomagnetic reversal isn't like a planet-sized bar magnet swinging around a hundred and eighty degrees. Instead, you tend to get a brief, messy stage when it's all over the place, as though there are multiple magnets inside the liquid centre of the planet all acting in different directions. These different fields *should* then coalesce into just one, in which the magnetic north pole ends up near the geographic south pole, in Antarctica.

'In fact, the satellites currently mapping the magnetic field intensity have already picked up regions over the Pacific and South America where the field strength is actually increasing. All our computer simulations using these data predict that the transition will be over before the end of the year, by which time full recovery should be quick.'

The diner customers were beginning to thin out now and Aguda, noticing that Sarah had put down her knife and fork and wasn't making any attempt to finish her pancakes, tapped his wristpad onto the interactive table display to pay the bill.

'But things are going to get worse before then, right? The coming months are going to be tough.' Sarah tried to fight back the strong sense of despair.

Aguda nodded. 'That's where you come in, Sarah. We need to know how bad things will get if the field intensity drops much further – maybe to just a few per cent of its full capacity. And if we get another direct hit from a coronal mass ejection.'

'And *if* we get through this?'

'Once the field has flipped, things should recover quickly, and everything will be business as usual. Of course, it'll be a huge boon for compass manufacturers, since all compass needles would then be pointing the wrong way!'

Sarah made a half-hearted attempt to smile. Deep in thought, she stood up and reached for her coat hanging on the back of her chair. She looked around the diner at the preoccupied New Yorkers getting on with their lives despite the growing threat from space. We take so much for granted in our thin biosphere, she thought, that we forget just how fragile it – and we – really are.

12

Saturday, 9 February – New York

SARAH FOLLOWED AGUDA THROUGH THE HUGE REVOLV-
ing glass doors with their built-in biometric scanners, into
the vast hallway of the United Nations building. The time
on her retinal display showed 08:45. The Nigerian geologist
towered over her as they waited at the reception desk. Like
many others, she had often wondered why the United
Nations still carried its old name. It barely made sense
now that many multinational companies had seats at the
table. Yet everyone knew that the UN, however ineffective
it had become, still endeavoured to present itself as a
benign global organization. She looked up at one of the
huge black granite walls. Above the United Nations symbol of a circular world map between two olive branches,
were emblazoned the words:

Security Without Liberty is Oppression.

Liberty Without Security is Delusion.

The motto had been adopted soon after the signing of
the Geneva Convention on Privacy eleven years ago, in

110

2030, which had been required to cope with the rise in cyberterrorism, cyber espionage and the weaponization of code. Sarah contemplated how the twentieth-century 'cold war' had turned into the twenty-first-century 'code war'.

The desk bot directed them to a security gate on the far side of the hallway. There, she followed Gabriel through a sophisticated retinal scanner. Once through, she was asked by a disembodied voice to stand still with her arms outstretched. A robotic arm with an oval-shaped black pad extended itself and skimmed around her body. The process took seconds.

Once through, she turned to Aguda. 'Is that it? Don't we get issued with electronic passes?'

He grinned at her. 'Oh, but we have been. The retinal scan you just had has other functions beyond mere identification. Your normal AR capability has been temporarily deactivated and replaced with an internal one that'll allow you to identify committee members and access documentation. You've also been tagged with a retinal ID code that not only gives you access to those restricted areas you have clearance for, but tracks your movements all the time you're in the building.'

'And that body scanner?'

'Ah, that's a recent addition. It's a full-body B-Mouse scanner – sorry, a Blümich portable MRI scanner combined with an ultrasound transducer. Basically, nothing can be hidden from it.'

Aguda must have seen the blank look on her face and smiled. 'Been standard issue here for a few months now. I'm surprised you haven't come across one before.'

She shrugged. 'I guess I've never been this close to real political power and such high-level security.'

'Well, the UN now has a detailed 3D scan of your

111

anatomy that even your doctor would envy. And if you happened to be carrying on, or in, your person any form of electronic or chemical device, right down to the nanoscale, they'd know about it.' Sarah wondered how long it would take for someone with the know-how and determination to beat this technology.

They were joined by a smartly dressed man in his mid-twenties, who escorted them across a large, bland hallway to the elevators and up to the fifteenth floor. When they emerged, she noted that the corridors here were brighter and the whole place buzzed with activity. They reached a frosted-glass door with a sign saying HCR1. 'Here it is, sir, madam: Holographic Chamber Room One,' said their young guide. 'The senator and the rest of the committee are waiting for you.' Sarah guessed that sensors throughout the building would have been tracking their progress from the moment they passed security, constantly reconfirming their identity, because the sturdy aluminium oxynitride door swished open as they approached it. She noted the one-way mirrored windows of the room: opaque from the outside, but transparent when viewed from inside, so the occupants of the room had already witnessed their arrival.

The room was smaller than she had anticipated and dominated by a large white oval table covered by interactive display glass, with seating space for about twenty people around it. Only half that number were present. Apart from two empty chairs for the new arrivals, the remainder of the places were taken up with sleek black holotubes instead of chairs, each about two metres high. The cylinders' entire outer surfaces were covered with thousands of nano-devices, each of which in turn contained a tiny solid-state laser. When activated, these would beam out light in all directions to create a high-resolution holographic real-time image of any remote committee member not able to be physically present at the meeting. The result, always impressive, was an illusion so realistic it was easy to forget that the person wasn't actually in the room. For now, the eight tubes sat dormant.

A man with cropped light brown hair and an expensive-looking suit stood up as they came in. He was tall and athletic-looking, though still dwarfed by the Nigerian geologist. 'Ah, Gabriel. And Dr Maitlin. Good morning to you both.' He approached, hand outstretched.

'Sarah,' said Aguda, 'this is Senator Hogan, our committee chair.' The man's grip was firmer than it needed to be and his dark eyes pierced hers as though he were probing her soul more thoroughly than any retinal scanning device. It was unsettling. 'Pleased to meet you, Senator.' She managed to keep her voice steady and hold his gaze.

'We're all very pleased to have you on board.' His smile had all the warmth of a great white shark. Sarah knew very little about the senator from Indiana other than what she had read online: that he was a highly skilled and ambitious politician and one of the youngest on Capitol Hill. Aguda had briefed her during their cab ride, filling in some of the gaps about Hogan, as well as a few of the other committee members.

She saw her name glowing on a prism-shaped LED display on the table, adjacent to an empty seat, and walked over to it. Aguda's seat was to her left. To her right was a younger man she recognized as the president of Aramco-Sol, the world's largest company. His name was Jassim Othman, and he was a renowned playboy. It was widely known that his company, built by his father, had risen phoenix-like from the smouldering ashes of the dramatic collapse of the once wealthy Gulf States, whose economies had been destroyed by the twin catastrophes of climate change and the abandonment of fossil fuels as a resource. AramcoSol had seen this coming and had invested heavily in perovskite-crystal technology for solar power as soon as it became clear that this was the material of choice for cheap, efficient photovoltaic cells. At the same time, it had shaken off its historical allegiances to the Kingdom of Saudi Arabia. Jassim Othman saw that Sarah had recognized him and gave her what she presumed was his most alluring smile.

She suddenly became aware of a low hum from the holotubes around the table. Within a few seconds their black solidity faded and was replaced by full-sized holograms of the remaining committee members. Once they had all materialized there followed a brief buzz of conversation as the remote members exchanged pleasantries with those physically present and with each other. Everyone seemed to know everyone else, Sarah noted, and some exchanges were warmer than others. She looked round the table at each person in turn, scanning the rudimentary information provided on her AR feed. Several of them were not politicians but CEOs of multinational companies. She reflected on how world politics had been transformed during her lifetime. Even before the mass migrations forced by rising sea levels in the early thirties, physical country borders had been getting increasingly blurred. The world was now more noticeably split along economic rather than geographical boundaries and was defined as much by online firewalls set up by multinational companies operating in the Cloud and the movement of cryptocurrencies between them as it was by the old national borders.

The hubbub of conversation was cut short by Hogan, who called the meeting to order. 'Welcome, everybody,' he said, looking around the table. 'We will dispense with personal introductions; most of you know everyone already. But of course I want to extend a special welcome to our new member, Dr Sarah Maitlin, a scientist whose expertise is, I am sure, going to be invaluable to us.' A few looked at her and nodded. 'In any case,' continued Hogan, 'you all have AR info about each other. I'm sorry it's so sparse, but it seems some of you still don't trust the security measures here and are being somewhat reticent.' He looked across and smiled thinly at one of the holos. Sarah's AR informed her that this was Xu Furong, the Chinese ambassador to the US, and that he was speaking from his office in Washington.

Ambassador Xu responded sombrely – Sarah's universal translator implant converting his Cantonese into English while at the same time mimicking the deep, gravelly tone of his voice. 'That remains to be seen. Let us hope that the young English scientist can give us some encouraging news.'

The illusion that the man was physically in the room was made complete as he appeared to look straight at Sarah as he spoke.

'Indeed,' said Hogan. 'Well, you'll all be aware that our business for today centres around what Dr Maitlin can tell us about the recent solar activity.' Hogan turned to Sarah.

'So, "*young English scientist*" –' He said it in a tone obviously intended to be light-hearted, but which came across to Sarah as patronizing. She let the comment pass but decided she most certainly did not like Hogan. '– let me give you a brief summary of why our committee exists. You may recognize one or two of the people around this table, but others you will not. We come from a wide mix of backgrounds. As I'm sure you're aware, geopolitics has been on the rise again in recent years. And even though the movement of displaced populations has blurred state borders further, it has also led to a rise in the powers of governments as the world has experienced renewed competition for space and resources. And yet many multinationals –' He glanced over and smiled at Jassim Othman, who nodded curtly back. '– remain larger and more powerful than all but the richest countries.

'This, um, welcome desire for international cooperation means that there is still a need for an umbrella organization like the United Nations that can provide a forum for global decision-making. Now, you might argue that the UN is a beast that has long since lost its teeth, but it is once again being called upon to act as arbiter and overseer of humankind's affairs. And that's why you see seated around you representatives from several large multinational companies, which of course have as much right to have their say as any nation state.'

Sarah tried to give the impression that she was grateful for this tutorial. Did Hogan think she'd just woken up from a decade-long suspended animation? Thankfully, it sounded like he was finally getting round to business.

'And you will know that the reason you have been invited onto our committee is because of your unrivalled knowledge of these solar events and how to model and predict them. We're informed that the most recent model you've been working on in your institute in Brazil is the most advanced yet.'

'We believe it is, yes,' replied Sarah without trying to hide her sense of pride in the work, even though, if she were honest, it was mostly done by a powerful AI. The computer simulations of the Sun no longer existed as thousands of lines of code written by human programmers. Like almost everything in the modern world that required the analysis and processing of huge amounts of data, pattern recognition and predicting how those patterns would evolve in time, it was really the job of deep neural networks rather than humans.

She suddenly realized that Hogan and the other committee members were looking at her expectantly, waiting for her to say something more. Hogan broke the brief silence. 'Well . . . we need to know what it tells us about the predictability and impact of any future events like the one that caused the recent geomagnetic storm that brought that plane down and, more importantly in my view, fried a quarter of the commsats over the Indian Ocean. We also need to know what effect they may have on our weather systems and if we should expect more extreme events like Hurricane Jerome.'

It surprised Sarah that Hogan would be more concerned with damage to global communication systems than the loss of human life, and she wondered what political causes this committee had been set up to serve. She decided that full disclosure as soon as possible was the safest course of action and butted in. 'Can I make clear that, as a solar physicist, my expertise doesn't extend to geomagnetic storms and their effects on the climate.'

Hogan shot her a quick glance, suggesting he was not used to being interrupted. But his features softened almost immediately as though a switch controlling them had been flicked. 'I perfectly understand. So rather than detain our distinguished members, or indeed you, any longer than necessary, maybe you can give us an update on your work; in lay terms, of course.' He laughed and looked around the table. Several others laughed too.

What a bunch of patronizing fools, thought Sarah. While she couldn't assume that they knew much about her research, she wasn't naive enough to think that they wouldn't all have been thoroughly briefed by their science advisors.

'Thank you, Senator,' she said. 'Yes, of course, I'll try to keep this, ah, simple.' She placed her left hand on the table and tapped her wristpad, transferring the holographic presentation she'd prepared the day before to the room's system. Then, taking a deep breath, she began. 'I'm relieved to hear that you don't want me to comment on whether cosmic rays were linked to Hurricane Jerome – not until we've made further analyses. But hard though this might be for you to accept, I believe we have an even bigger problem to worry about.' She had rehearsed this part of her speech several times in her head and felt her confidence return.

'As most of you will probably know already, coronal ejections – giant bubbles of electrified gas thrown out from the surface of the Sun – take place on average several times a day. And since they can be ejected at any angle in three dimensions, the chance of one heading directly towards Earth is low, typically once every fortnight.' As she spoke she activated the presentation. A holographic animation of the Solar System appeared hovering above the centre of the conference table at head height. The Sun was a football-sized, glowing and dynamic orange sphere, exquisite in its detail, with Earth and the inner planets orbiting slowly around it. Every now and then it spat out a tiny diffuse ball of fire that travelled radially outwards, spreading and fading slowly as it did so.

'A typical CME carries a total amount of energy *one hundred times greater* than that produced by the giant asteroid impact that wiped out the dinosaurs sixty-five million years ago.'

Several people stared at her incredulously as this statistic sank in.

118

'So, how have we managed to survive so long under this onslaught from our sun? Well, throughout its history, our planet has always had its magnetic field to cushion the impact of coronal ejections – think of it as planet-sized bubble-wrap. But . . . if that magnetic field is severely weakened then . . . well . . . well, no one really knows what the implications are.'

An immaculately dressed, grey-haired man with a trim beard sitting across the table from her cut in. 'Ah, come now, Dr Maitlin, please do not lecture us.' He had addressed her in English, she realized; her United Nations-issue AR informed her that he was Ashraf al-Magribi, the Egyptian Minister of the Interior. He spoke in a clear, confident voice, as though accustomed to being listened to. 'We already know all we need to about these coronal ejections and how and why they are formed. That is not why you have been asked onto this committee.'

Sarah felt momentarily winded, not quite knowing how to respond to this sudden hostility. A woman sitting next to the Egyptian turned to admonish him. She looked about the same age as Sarah, but even from across the table Sarah could tell that she'd had extensive tissue-engineering work and skin nano-implants. However, it was her voice that betrayed the decades her face was hiding. 'There's no need for such an insulting tone, Mr Magribi. We have invited Dr Maitlin to join our committee, so at least do her the courtesy of listening without interrupting.' Her voice was soft, yet commanded immediate respect and al-Magribi sniffed and stroked his beard, trying not to look as though he'd just been put in his place.

Sarah's AR informed her that the woman was Filomena Crespo, the immensely powerful Brazilian vice-president of Samsung, and she wondered whether her representing a multinational company rather than a nation state meant she was less encumbered by politics and thus more likely to be sympathetic. Maybe she just felt it necessary to defend a fellow woman – after all, Ms Crespo would have started her career back at a time when women needed to work twice as hard to prove their worth in reaching the very top of the career ladder. Whatever the reason, Sarah was grateful.

She guessed that an Egyptian representing a population of a hundred and twenty million would be particularly keen to have some reassurances. After all, his country's agricultural infrastructure was in tatters since the disappearance of much of the Nile Delta a decade ago, one of the first regions to fall victim to the rising sea levels, which had put an almost unbearable strain on an already fragile economy.

She resumed her presentation: 'Of course, not all Earth-bound CMEs are dangerous. We think about one in five would cause us major concern. The issue is that everyone is probably looking in the wrong place.'

Now she had their full attention. *This is it. This is where I get to shake them from their smug complacency.* 'You see, you've been worried about the coronal ejection's impact on the magnetic field itself, causing a geomagnetic storm.'

'You're still not telling us anything new, Dr Maitlin,' the Chinese ambassador said coldly.

Sarah felt her face get hot as anger suddenly rose inside her again. *For fuck's sake, it's not like I asked to come onto this bloody committee. What would they do if I just stood up and walked out?* She took a deep breath and composed herself. 'My *point*, Ambassador, is that geomagnetic storms are not necessarily what should be concerning us right now. The communication satellites taken out last week that caused the crash of Flight AI-231 were fried by the direct impact of high-energy particles in the ejection itself and *not*, as everyone seems to think, by a geomagnetic storm.

'Catastrophic though they can be, our focus now should not be on the more predictable problems of disruption to power grids or disturbance to radio signals that we've had to worry about during geomagnetic storms in the past, but rather the threat of *direct* exposure to the burst of CME radiation hitting the Earth.'

She flicked on to the next holo image. It showed an animation of the Earth with its surrounding magnetic field, which was represented by flux lines emanating from the Earth's poles and curving round in ever larger loops. The shape of the field was shown compressed on the Earth's Sunward side to a distance of about ten Earth radii. 'The reason the side of the Earth's magnetosphere – its magnetic field – facing the Sun is squashed is the pressure of the solar wind. But on the night side of the Earth you can see how the field lines are stretched out so that the magnetosphere extends like a tail behind us.

'But . . . this is what the magnetosphere *should* look like at full strength. Now watch what happens in the event of a direct hit from a CME.' As she spoke, the animation showed an approaching coronal mass ejection, a colourful cloud of plasma far larger than the Earth. When it slammed into the magnetosphere it caused the field lines to distort and stretch, compressing even more on the side that took the full impact. 'The high-energy particles in the CME are deflected around the Earth by the field, like water parting around a rock in the middle of a fast-moving stream.

'Even though the majority of these particles don't get through to us, the highly charged plasma of the CME

sets off a geomagnetic storm – a disturbance in the magnetosphere that causes powerful electromagnetic currents
to flow around the planet.

'Now then, you might expect that a *weaker* magnetic
field would mean less violent geomagnetic storms. And
you'd be right. But . . .' She ran the animation again, but
this time there were fewer field lines surrounding the
Earth. '. . . a weaker field is also less effective at stopping
the high-energy bombardment of the subatomic particles.
So, instead of them being deflected around the Earth by
the magnetosphere, more of them can punch through it.'

She paused briefly to see the reaction on the committee's
faces. Yes, she certainly had their complete attention now.

She added, 'Maybe *this* is something new, or does
everyone know this already? In which case, I really don't
know what my role is here today.'

She realized that she had probably raised her voice a
little too much, but so what? They wanted the truth, and
they'd got it, with no sugar coating.

The room suddenly erupted in a hubbub of questions,
mostly directly to her, and Senator Hogan needed to call
the meeting to order. 'I think, ladies and gentlemen, that
the point Dr Maitlin makes is very important, and can
potentially be seen as encouraging news.'

'Encouraging? In what possible way can it be encouraging? Or have I just completely misheard Dr Maitlin?'
said the Finnish delegate, a slim woman with cropped
white hair sitting off to Sarah's left.

Hogan smiled. 'The reason we asked Dr Maitlin onto
this committee was so that she could tell us just how precisely she and her team could forecast the arrival time of
a CME, so that the world can take the necessary precau-
tions. If the main threat is therefore from the initial CME
impact, then I would guess that is a far more reliable

thing to predict than any subsequent geomagnetic storm it might cause. Am I right, Dr Maitlin?'

Sarah had a sinking feeling. OK, here it comes. Clearly, she had already not endeared herself to most of the committee, and they sure as hell weren't going to like what she had to tell them next.

She decided to just give them the facts as calmly as she could. She took a deep breath. 'Ejections aimed at the Earth are called "halo events" because of the way they look to us. As the approaching cloud of an ejection looms larger and larger it appears to envelop the Sun, forming a halo around it. This means that, unlike with one heading off, say, at right angles to the line between the Sun and the Earth, predicting its speed is difficult, because we can't see it moving from a side-on view. With something coming straight at us, we just *can't* predict precisely when it will hit us.'

It was Aguda's turn to interrupt her. 'But don't we have solar orbiting satellites that can give us enough of a side-on view? They'd be beyond the path of the ejection – outside of the line of fire – and therefore safe from being fried. They can track the ejection and give us an accurate approach velocity.' To illustrate his point, he extended his arms, pointing his two index fingers towards a point in front of him, and brought them together.

On cue, Sarah clicked to the next image, which showed the Earth in its orbit around the Sun and the location of two satellites in the same orbit, one ahead of Earth and the other lagging behind. 'That's true,' she said. 'We have the STEREO2 spacecraft that give us just this view, but by the time the CME is close enough for this to be useful, it's too late and the ejection is almost upon us.'

Even though she was having to relay unpalatable news, she nevertheless felt on much firmer ground now, science she'd spent her entire career working on.

'So, instead, we have to make predictions based on simulations. These can take into account everything our AIs can learn about an ejection, from the Sun's own magnetic field to the solar wind, to the size and strength of the ejection itself. All this just so we can get one number out at the end: the SAT, or Shock Arrival Time.'

The Chinese ambassador interrupted her again. 'But of course, the number we all want from you, Dr Maitlin, is a different one, and is based on the accuracy of this prediction. How wide is the arrival-time window? How much advance warning do we get?'

Sarah took another deep breath. 'Since CMEs can travel at a wide range of speeds – anything from a few hundred to several thousand kilometres per second – our best estimate, based on a combination of computer predictions and satellite data . . . is a window of eight hours.'

Everyone stared at Sarah. Al-Magribi broke the silence. 'Do you mean to tell us we will know we're *going* to be hit, but not *when*? This means it could hit anywhere?'

'That's correct, I'm afraid. We must face up to the fact that the population of entire continents will need to stay indoors if they are to avoid a potentially fatal dose of radiation. And that's not to mention the damage done to animal and plant life. No single country will know if it'll be hit until it is too late to act. And this is something that is likely to happen again and again in the coming months.' Once again, everyone started talking at once. Her uncompromising assessment had clearly been both unexpected and unwelcome.

'But I still don't understand,' cut in the Finnish delegate loudly. 'How does this eight-hour uncertainty come in?'

Sarah manipulated her fingers on the touch-sensitive section of the table in front of her to retrieve the very first holo image she had shown of the Earth slowly rotating about its axis. 'Our planet takes twenty-four hours to complete a full revolution, right? So, over the space of eight hours one whole third of the planet's surface could be exposed to the impact.'

An uneasy ripple of conversation spread around the table. This was as good a time as any to hit them with the *coup de grâce*.

'And I'm afraid there's one more thing.' She had to raise her voice to be heard. 'Before the CME even reaches Earth, we'll be bombarded by a stream of high-energy protons, the vanguard of the pulse. Because these particles will be travelling at near light speed, they'll reach us about ten minutes after the CME is ejected by the Sun. Normally, they'd be deflected by the magnetosphere, but in its weakened state some will get through and pose a serious radiation risk.'

This new revelation left everyone stunned. After a few seconds, Hogan was the first to speak. 'None of this really changes anything. We already knew we would have to put in place various emergency strategies and procedures in the event of a direct hit. All this means is that more individual governments are going to have to do this than we thought.'

'And even if there is a strong chance a CME will miss us,' continued Aguda. There were a few reluctant nods around the table.

'But,' continued the senator, 'we still need to write our report and agree on a united plan of action.'

Sarah felt a wave of relief that she'd finally got this off her chest. The world was in peril, but at least it was no longer just her worry.

PART II

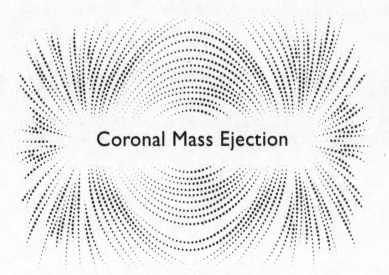

Coronal Mass Ejection

13

QIANG LEE HAD ARRIVED EARLY AT McCOSH HALL ON Princeton University Campus, where the dark-matter conference was being held. He felt relieved to have made it at all as so many flights into New York had been cancelled due to fears of what Hurricane Jerome might do next. The superstorm was all anyone seemed to be talking about at the moment and was certainly the only topic on all the AR news feeds.

His name badge read 'Prof. Lee, Qiang (IHEP)', which made him smile. The Institute for High Energy Physics in Beijing now had a strong enough international reputation that its rather generic acronym was sufficient to place the wearer. After turning away from the registration desk with his conference bag, he took a look inside it. There was a time when it would have been filled with useless pieces of paper: maps, leaflets listing the best pizza restaurants in town and glossy brochures of 'Things to do while in Princeton' – mostly open markets, art exhibitions and community amateur dramatics events. By contrast this one was almost empty, but he was pleased to see that

129

along with a folded plastic e-pad containing the pro-gramme and the rest of the conference information there was a pad of notepaper and pen. Hardly any delegates used such pads any more, but Qiang liked to doodle or work on dense algebraic derivations while only half listen-ing to the talks.

Strolling back outside the building, he wondered how his old friend and collaborator would be. He'd heard about Marc Bruckner's marriage breakdown, and how he'd fallen out with several people in the Physics Depart-ment at Columbia and had finally escaped to his late parents' summer home in New Zealand for some much-needed convalescence. Having spoken to him last night, Qiang decided he did look and sound a lot better than he had dared to expect. Was that just an act for his benefit? Could sufferers from depression recover so quickly? He doubted it. Maybe it was more to do with the anticipa-tion of seeing his daughter Evie after the conference.

Their brief online exchange had brought back mem-ories of those heady days in the late twenties when the two men had made the biggest breakthrough in particle physics research since the discovery of the Higgs boson, that dark matter self-interacts, creating normal matter in a burst of high energy.

He spotted Marc striding purposefully across the grass towards him and waved. Marc waved back and grinned broadly. As soon as he was close enough Qiang extended his hand, but Marc pulled him into a bear hug.

Qiang smiled, feeling a little awkward. 'It's good to see you. And I'm glad you could make this meeting. We've got a lot of catching up to do.'

Both men had long since given up on the idea that a scientific conference was about listening to the talks. They could find out about other people's research any time and from anywhere. No, conferences were about renewing acquaintances, discussing the politics of academia and, of course, knocking around new ideas in the bar. Qiang wondered whether Marc could still outdrink everyone else.

The two men walked into the building where thirty or more delegates were milling around greeting each other. There was an audible drop in the level of background chatter as Marc was spotted. He didn't seem to care and Qiang was relieved, although he felt certain that had it been him on the receiving end, he'd have been devastated. Maybe Marc was just good at hiding his feelings.

They picked up coffees and wandered into the lecture theatre to claim their seats – not too close to the front or the rear, but always to one side in case they needed an early escape if a talk was particularly boring.

As soon as they were seated, Marc turned to Qiang. 'So, how's Chyou doing? And the kids . . . they must be school age now?'

'Yup, the boys are both at school and doing well. And Chyou is fine. Although I think she still misses New York.'

'What? Are you crazy? What's to miss?'

'When were you last in Beijing, Marc?' chided Qiang. 'Chyou says she misses Manhattan's clean air and provincial feel.' They both laughed.

'How about you? When you said that you'd moved back to New Zealand I expected you to turn into a hermit and shut yourself away from the world.'

Marc sighed. 'Yes, I did think about leading a life of solitude and focusing full-time on feeling sorry for myself . . .' His eyes took on a distant, glazed look. Then he shrugged and smiled. 'But, you know what? Fuck it. Life is only as bleak as the lens you look at it through, right? Anyway, did you know Evie turns sixteen next week?'

'Wow, sweet little Evie? I remember babysitting her when she was the same age as my boys are now.' Qiang thought back to those times when Marc and Charlotte seemed to have the perfect marriage and family life with their young daughter. He looked closely at his old friend.

Marc smiled self-consciously under Qiang's scrutiny. 'Time marches on, my friend,' he said. 'I see you've got the odd grey hair yourself now.'

Qiang shrugged. 'That's just Chinese bureaucracy for you, and the never-ending writing of grant proposals. Not something I guess you're too worried about these days.' As soon as he'd said it, he regretted it and started to apologize. Marc cut him off.

'Hey, don't be silly; it's true, I don't. Anyway, I haven't decided what to do next. I haven't entirely ruled out getting back into academia.'

Other delegates were starting to filter into the hall. 'So, what's new with you, Qiang? I saw your last paper before Christmas. What are you working on now?'

Qiang couldn't hide his change in demeanour and it was clear Marc had picked up on it. There was no point keeping what he knew to himself any longer, so he dropped his voice to a whisper. 'That's why I was so relieved when you told me you'd be here. If you hadn't come I would have flown down to New Zealand to speak to you.'

He wondered what Marc would think of his crazy idea.

132

14

MARC WAS INTRIGUED. IT TOOK A LOT FOR QIANG TO openly show emotion in this way. Looking down at the programme of talks for the morning he groaned inwardly. 'Look,' he said, 'this session is basically welcoming speeches and a couple of plenary overview talks – nothing we don't already know. Come on.' He stood up and ushered his friend out into the aisle and up the steps at the side of the lecture theatre.

The two men strolled out of the building, now walking against the stream of delegates entering through the glass doors. Once outside in the crisp morning sunshine again, Marc said, 'Well, it seems my rehabilitation into the dark-matter community didn't last long. But then I'm really not ready to sit through all that drivel just yet, especially not forty-five minutes of crusty old Goldstein telling us how everything we know about the subject is down to him; and certainly not when you've got something important to tell me. So, come on, spill the beans.'

Qiang shook his head and watched in silence as a few late-running delegates hurried past them, nodding their greetings as they went. Marc thrust his hands into the pockets of his coat, hunching his shoulders against the chill air, and waited for Qiang to talk. When they were finally alone, Marc turned to his friend, puzzled at the apparent need for secrecy. 'Well?'

Qiang had pulled his collar up against the cold, which made him look even more conspiratorial, like an old-fashioned spy. Marc suppressed a smile.

'OK, but I must first ask you to promise to keep what I say confidential.'

Marc shrugged his shoulders and frowned. What could be so important? 'Of course, but why do you even need to ask me that? How can you worry that I would ever talk about your work before you'd published?'

'It's not something that will *ever* get published.' Qiang looked around nervously as though he feared they were being watched. 'Several weeks ago, I was invited to Shanghai with a group of other scientists – mostly geologists, but still a surprising spread of expertise. Anyway, we had a couple of meetings with some high-level government officials. It was clear they wanted us to put our heads together to address the implications of the weakening magnetic field.'

Marc raised his eyebrows. 'What? Oh . . . I see. Well, you know you've really made it in the world of science when your government asks you to solve a problem you're no more qualified to tackle than my plumber,' he chuckled. Qiang frowned. Whatever he was involved in, it was obviously something that concerned him. Marc gripped his arm and looked his friend in the eyes.

'Sorry, Qiang, I didn't mean to suggest that you— OK, look, this doesn't sound too sinister to me. I mean, everyone's talking about the Flip and when it's going to happen. They're saying later this year. And after this horrific hurricane, which may or may not be linked to the weakening field, not to mention the CME that brought down the Air India plane . . . well, it can't happen soon enough, I guess.'

He now saw something in Qiang's eyes that unsettled him. There was a wild excitement that looked somewhat out of place. Qiang grew suddenly animated and started walking more briskly. 'And *that's* the issue,' he almost shouted. Then, as though remembering what a risk he was taking, suddenly dropped his voice back to a whisper. 'What I learned from these meetings is that they believe the Flip may not happen as soon as we hope.'

'What do you mean? Are there new data?'

'No one is saying as much, but . . . Well, let me just say that the secrecy we've all been sworn to would suggest that we're not being told everything.'

Marc tried to suppress his impatience. 'OK, look, I know what the Chinese authorities are like with secrecy and I can understand that you feel you're taking a huge risk by talking about it, even to someone I hope you feel you can trust. But I'm also guessing you have good reason for wanting to confide in me. So come on, what the fuck *is* it you're trying to tell me?'

Qiang drew in a deep breath of the cold morning air and slumped his shoulders in resignation. 'Well, I don't know what they are basing their information on, but they've been looking at putting plans in place to cope with a drastically weakened magnetosphere over a three- to five-year period.'

Marc stopped abruptly in his tracks. 'Sorry, did you just say three to five *years*?' He stared incredulously at his friend.

Qiang gave him a grim nod. 'I know. This dramatically conflicts with the official line, which is that we just need to ride this out for a few months before the Flip and the field rights itself, not several *years*.'

Marc rubbed his hand slowly against his stubbly cheek. Why would the world be told things would start returning to normal in a few months if it was really going to take years? And what further damage could be caused if the field continued to weaken? Would life be fried by cosmic radiation? Would the ozone layer be stripped away? He stood gazing out across the campus, contemplating the ramifications of what he was hearing.

Qiang had carried on walking without slowing and Marc hurried after him, falling into step with him just as he began talking again. 'They encouraged us to come up with various proposals, from protective shields in orbit, to excavating vast underground bunkers. I didn't really have much to offer. But on my return to Beijing, I started thinking. What if, for the sake of argument, we *had* to do something about the magnetic field itself? What if we simply couldn't wait around for the planet to right itself?'

Up ahead, jogging towards them, was a young couple, probably lost in music only they could hear. But Qiang nevertheless waited until they had passed and were a safe distance away before he continued.

'I've been doing some digging around in the scientific literature. Did you know it's only in the last ten years or so, thanks to advances in neutrino imaging, that we've properly understood how the Earth's magnetic field is generated?'

He didn't wait for an answer. 'Well, the liquid metal core of the Earth is basically a giant dynamo. As it swirls around it generates electric currents and magnetic fields, which push more conducting liquid metal around to create even stronger currents, and so stronger fields, and so on. It's a gigantic feedback loop.'

Despite the seriousness of the subject, Marc couldn't help but feel a little amused. Qiang's deep expertise in particle physics was so specialized, so niche, that, brilliant scientist though he was, he was only now discovering basic high-school geomagnetism. He was animatedly waving his arms around and wiggling his fingers to simulate various circular motions. His enthusiasm reminded Marc of those early years when he would pop into his office at Columbia first thing in the morning with a new idea and start scrawling Feynman diagrams on the board, while Marc tried desperately to keep up. But the subject matter now was far more important than a theoretical curiosity about the structure of dark matter.

'But,' continued Qiang, 'if this liquid core gets disturbed, the magnetic field gets weaker. And right now, turbulent vortices thousands of kilometres below our feet are disrupting its smooth circular flow.

'So, my question is this: if we really had to, is there a way of kick-starting the core again? How could we deliver a massive boost of energy to the right spots at the right time to push the liquid metal in the right direction?'

Marc was intrigued. 'I guess it's a bit like sticking your finger into emptying bathwater above the plughole and stirring it to recover the steady circular vortex after it has been messed up.'

'Exactly,' said Qiang with a small smile. 'Only it's not so easy to stick a giant finger into our planet. So, the problem is how to deliver that energy. In the old Hollywood movies, there'd be an expedition to the centre of the Earth, in which some kind of manned subterranean craft would blast its way to the core with a laser beam. Of course it's a fun idea, but you and I both know it's quite unrealistic. I mean, even today, the deepest boreholes in the Earth's crust don't penetrate beyond about twenty kilometres.

Compared with the six and a half thousand kilometres to the centre, that's barely a pinprick.'

They had left the large academic buildings behind and were now walking through rows of student apartments. They passed a Starbucks, busy with university staff and students picking up breakfast on their way to offices, labs and classes.

Qiang stopped again and looked around, as though only now noticing how far they had walked. He turned to face Marc and put a conspiratorial hand on his arm. 'Maybe we should start heading back.' Marc shrugged, and they turned to retrace their route. Qiang continued. 'So, if you wanted to deliver energy to the centre of the Earth without it being lost en route, what would you use?'

'You mean like proton beam therapy to treat tumours?'

'Exactly. Deliver energy into living tissue without obstruction, then dump it exactly where it's needed inside the body at a precise location. What if, instead of a human patient, you were dealing with the entire planet?'

Marc was puzzled. He was clearly missing something obvious. 'OK, we already use neutrino beams for imaging the interior of the Earth, but that wouldn't work here. Hardly any energy loss. Most of the particles in those beams pass straight through.'

He sensed that Qiang was waiting patiently for the penny to drop. And it suddenly hit him like a bombshell. 'Of course!' he shouted. 'Fucking hell, Qiang . . .'

A woman walking her dog on the other side of the road stopped to look over at the two men. Qiang gave her a friendly wave.

Marc was oblivious, finally realizing what Qiang was getting at. Of course there was a way to reach the Earth's core. But it would involve a beam of particles trillions of times heavier and yet far more elusive than neutrinos.

More to the point, they were the particles to which the two men had devoted their research careers.

'Neutralinos!'

Qiang stared up at him, bright-eyed. Expectant. Knowing he no longer needed to say any more.

For the past twenty years, the two physicists had dedicated their lives to studying dark matter – more specifically, seeing what would happen when beams of neutralinos, the particles of dark matter, smashed together at high energy. Like their tiny cousins the neutrinos, these particles hardly interact with normal matter at all and so would pass through the Earth unobstructed. But, cross two beams of neutralinos together . . . Marc liked to quote Spengler, the character from the old movie *Ghostbusters*: *'Don't cross the streams.'*

His mind was racing. What if you aimed multiple beams of neutralinos down into the ground from different locations around the planet, all meeting at one point deep in the core? They would each travel through the Earth as though it were completely transparent, but if they met . . . He tried to do the calculations in his head to determine how big a bang that would make. Big enough to kick-start the Earth's core again? He couldn't tell whether the idea was even feasible; he knew too little about geophysics. It was certainly a daring idea. Actually, scratch that, it was a crazy idea. Even if it worked, it would take years to put it into practice.

He realized Qiang was still staring at him, waiting for him to say something. He exhaled noisily. 'I'm assuming you've not shared this ridiculous suggestion with anyone else.'

'Of course not. But what if we had no choice but to try it?'

Marc felt a strange mix of terror and excitement. All thoughts of going back to New Zealand were gone for now.

15

Monday, 11 February – Tehran

SHIREEN HAD BEEN ON THE RUN FOR THREE DAYS. Savak, the recently resurrected and feared Iranian secret service, had been on her tail and getting closer all the time. It hadn't taken her much effort to hack into surveillance cameras to monitor locations around the city that she had passed through and watch as they clumsily followed clues she had deliberately left as bait to throw them off course. So far, it had worked, and she had managed to stay one crucial step ahead of them. But unless everything went according to plan, which she admitted was a long shot, especially since the plan itself was still so hazy, it would only be a matter of time before they caught up with her.

Her world had started caving in when Majid hadn't shown up for class on Friday, the morning after her successful hacking session in his apartment. But it wasn't until lunchtime that a mutual friend on the dark web informed her that Majid had been arrested after receiving a visit from Savak late on Thursday evening. How close had she been to getting caught too? They must have very

140

quickly traced the security breach to his computer. Poor, innocent Majid. She felt wretched about getting him mixed up in all this, and at the same time terrified by the speed with which the authorities had reacted. Clearly, she hadn't been quite as careful as she'd thought.

Majid must have tried to cover for her, otherwise she'd have been picked up too, but he had bought her a few precious hours – enough for her to put a rough plan of action in place with the help of several cybs on the dark web whom she felt she could trust. By Friday evening she had yet to look at the files she'd obtained, now buried deep in her little corner of the dark web where even the most sophisticated AIs wouldn't find them. Or so she hoped. After all, *she'd* managed to acquire them, hadn't she? But she hadn't allowed her paranoia to get the better of her. One of the advantages of the dark web was its sheer size – layer upon layer, world upon world, like a multiverse of realities coexisting in the same cyberspace yet never interacting, allowing millions to hide their secrets away from prying eyes.

She hadn't gone back home on Friday. Savak agents would be there waiting for her, she was sure of it. Of course, her parents would have been sick with worry, but for now, the less they knew the better. Instead, she'd headed for the most secure place she could think of: an internet café called Nine Nights – a typically geeky play on the '1001 Nights' stories, but with the number interpreted in binary. It was a popular haunt of the Tehran cyb community, run by a retired coder by the name of Hashimi who in an earlier life had been an associate of her father's.

Hashimi was a tall, thin man, with a grizzled grey beard that used to scare her as a young girl when he would come round to their house. The beard had always made him look much older than his years. Even now, she figured, he had to be only around sixty. But he had kind eyes that shone with a deep wisdom she found reassuring. A few years ago, he and her father had fallen out over Hashimi's shady dark-web activities and she hated to think how disappointed her father would be if he knew she had come to Hashimi for help instead of confiding in him.

She had no choice now but to trust the man. He had been very pleased to see her when she had turned up just as he was closing the café. But his mood changed to one of concern when he'd seen the look in her eyes. He'd ushered her inside, locked up the café and sat her down. She had told him about the files without giving him too much detail about exactly how she had acquired them. Although he'd been initially reluctant to get involved, the look in his eyes gave away his palpable admiration for what she had achieved, and he was clearly as intrigued as she was by what the files might contain. Nevertheless, it had taken all her powers of persuasion to stop him from contacting her father. He'd led her through a dimly lit corridor to a door at the back of the building that required biometric access. The room they entered looked like a cross between a junkyard and NASA's Mission Control Center. It was filled with an array of old computers with old-fashioned physical display screens and cables covering the floor. She could swear that much of the hardware looked older than she was. And yet the familiar electronic hum and glowing LEDs left her in no doubt that this was a working environment. Every square centimetre of surface area was filled with a mix of electronic gadgetry, empty food cartons, beer bottles and coffee cups. Along one wall was stacked a bewildering mountain of defunct hardware that presumably Hashimi couldn't bring himself to get rid of. On the other side of the room was an unmade bed and a small sink. Shireen had wondered under what circumstances he might have needed to spend the night in this electronic bunker when his own apartment was just upstairs.

She'd felt overwhelmingly grateful when Hashimi left her alone to read the contents of the files in privacy. But he'd insisted she come and get him if and when she needed his help.

It had taken her about an hour to access and scan through all the files. Among them was high-resolution satellite footage, magnetic-field data, graphs and tables, scientific papers in preprint form, emails, internal memos and confidential reports. By the end, she had been left in no doubt what she had. Nor did it take her long to work out why people at the very top of the food chain wouldn't want this information to get out.

The facts were simple enough. Here was solid evidence that powerful individuals, and possibly entire governments, had been hiding the truth about the Earth's weakening magnetic field: it was not about to flip, but was instead slowly dying, probably permanently. The official line to the public seemed to be that quite the opposite was taking place: that pockets of the magnetic field in the southern hemisphere were recovering fast and that the crisis would be over by the end of the year. These files told a very different story, however, and it terrified Shireen. She had sat staring into space for a long time, trying to clear her head and calm her nerves. She didn't understand all of the science, but it didn't take much effort to piece together what this implied: without a magnetosphere, all life on Earth would eventually be wiped out.

Shireen had lived her entire life in a world struggling to cope with the severe consequences of climate change, and humankind was finally winning the battle to turn things around. Was it now about to face an even greater challenge to its survival? What she had not been able to find was the source of the cover-up. Who had ordered it, and why?

She had to form a rational plan of action. But she didn't have much time. For a few minutes she had even seriously contemplated turning herself in and handing over the files. She was clearly out of her depth. But she doubted she'd have got away with a simple reprimand. After all, she couldn't now un-know the contents of the files, nor could the authorities be sure she hadn't already released them on the dark web. No, that wasn't ever really an option.

The only alternative was to make the files public and hope that there were still people in power uncorrupted by this secret and who could protect her.

What would happen next, she had no idea, but the world needed to know. Later that evening she had confided in Hashimi and showed him the contents of the files. He had agreed it would be naive to think she could simply make them public by releasing them online. Their contents would be instantly discredited and branded as fraudulent – just another attempt by cyberterrorists to embarrass the global order alongside the millions of other conspiracy theories, fake 'leaks' and elaborate hoaxes that were part and parcel of the online world these days. And disseminating them across the dark web, which would have been very easy, was an even worse idea. No one would take it seriously. It would just be lost in the noise. No, the only way was for the files to be leaked by a source of utmost reliability – someone in a position of power who was beyond reproach.

But finding the right person wasn't even the difficult part. The files would have to be delivered *in person*. She couldn't risk simply emailing them and hope they would be taken seriously. Besides, that would involve retrieving the files from the safe depths of the dark web and sending them across the surface web where they would certainly be tracked and intercepted by monitor AIs before they reached their destination.

She couldn't risk getting in touch with her parents herself, so she had asked Hashimi if he could do so as surreptitiously as possible, letting them know she was OK and warning them to go dark. She knew full well that they would have been watched very closely by Savak, but the one thing she was confident of was that her parents were more than capable of disappearing off-grid for a few days. She guessed they would know how to shake off Savak surveillance and head up to the mountains north of the city where they had friends they could rely on to hide them. She had begged Hashimi to share with them only the sketchiest of information – enough for them to take the matter seriously. The less they knew, the safer they would be.

After a little digging, Hashimi had informed her that Majid had been released, causing fresh waves of relief and guilt to wash through her. Poor Majid. It wouldn't have taken Savak long to get the truth out of him, or what little he knew of it. And they wouldn't have needed to use force: a simple chemical relaxant that affected his higher cognitive functions, followed by an fMRI scan, would allow them to read his thoughts like an open book. It was hardly telepathy – all they had to do was to see which parts of his brain lit up in answer to yes/no questions. They'd have learned quickly enough that he was an innocent accomplice who knew nothing about the content of the secret files. She just hoped he would escape serious punishment.

Now, she hoped, she had only herself to worry about.

Almost anyone else would have been picked up within the hour: hooking up to the Cloud for anything as simple as purchasing a bus ticket or a sandwich would instantly reveal their location. It wouldn't help much staying off-line either; the thousands of miniature cameras hidden throughout the infrastructure of the city could locate anyone within seconds.

But Shireen wasn't just anyone.

She would need to keep on the move, and to stay hidden from prying cameras. A simple disguise wouldn't be enough to hide her – pattern-recognition software running Grover algorithms would sift through a CCTV database of twenty million people going about their daily business throughout the city to find her just by the way she walked.

No, she needed a squelch jammer, an illegal electronic device that could disrupt the video-feed signal from any cameras close enough to biometrically identify the person possessing it. As a favour to her father and knowing how damaging her information could be for the hated Savak, Hashimi had provided her with his own jammer. But he had warned her that even being constantly on the move was risky – it wouldn't take long for the trail of signal interference to be traced and extrapolated. The jammer needed to be used sparingly.

He had persuaded her to get a night's sleep first and had made up the bed in the back room, then cooked her a late supper.

The following morning was the closest that Savak had yet come to catching up with her. She was awoken by raised voices at 5 a.m. The café couldn't be open yet, which could only mean that they had found her already. She didn't stop to think about how. Scrambling out of bed, she stood in the middle of the room among the stacks of cardboard boxes and tried to make out the conversation outside. Her eyes darted about the room for an escape route. Grabbing her shoes and the rucksack containing the jammer along with the few personal belongings she had with her, she ran for the small back window. It didn't look locked, but still resisted her attempts to open it. She considered breaking the glass, but finally managed to prise it free of the rust and layers of paint that had kept it closed for what must have been years, and swung it part-way open. She couldn't make out much in the darkness beyond other than that it gave onto a narrow alleyway.

The voices outside were growing louder and suddenly the door to the room flew open. Leaping up onto the window sill, she squeezed her waiflike body through the narrow gap and out into the cold early-morning air in one clumsy motion and jumped down into the alleyway.

She hit the ground running, stumbling over several garbage bags and just managing to stay on her feet, her arms cartwheeling about wildly as she ran, trying to regain her balance. Her surroundings took on a dreamlike quality, but this was no immersive VR game – it was really happening. Pure animal instinct took over and she kept running. The panic she felt made her chest constrict and she found it harder to breathe than the physical exertion of the running would account for. As soon as she had covered several blocks, she stopped to slip on her shoes, then pulled the rucksack off her back, reached in and flicked on the jammer.

She then continued at a brisk walking pace. She needed to put as much distance as she could between herself and her pursuers.

The last thing Hashimi had done the previous evening was give her a contact he said might be willing to help get her out of the city, so when she reached a local park, she had found a bench hidden within high shrubbery and sat down to gather her thoughts. She could no longer risk using her wristpad and AR – that would instantly give her location away. Instead, she had to do this the old-fashioned way. She pulled out the small tablet that Hashimi had given her and fired it up. She knew she wouldn't be able to hide her position for long, so she simply displaced it. It was an old trick – a simple case of electronic ventriloquism: suggesting that she was access-ing the Cloud from several kilometres away. For now, the best she could do was keep them at arm's length and guessing what her next move would be.

That had been Saturday morning.

Now, forty-eight hours later, it seemed like a lifetime ago. She had hardly slept since then and was feeling cold, hungry and in desperate need of a shower, but she had so far stayed out of Savak's reach. And she was at last about to meet the cyb whom Hashimi had recommended and who had thankfully agreed to help her. Her contact was a legend on the dark web and, despite her exhaustion and anxiety, Shireen felt excited to be meeting her. Known only as Mother, she never stayed in one place long and had evaded the authorities for over a decade, so Shireen had no idea whether the meeting would be face-to-face. Contact had been established on Saturday morning but they had exchanged very little information. Although Shireen hadn't told her about the files, she'd got the impression that Mother knew more than she was letting on. What she had told her was that she needed to get out of the country and across to America. What she hadn't told her was why.

Shireen had chosen her target carefully, using Hashi-mi's tablet to carry out a search of potential candidates around the world. It had to be someone she could entrust with the files, but also someone who fulfilled certain other criteria. A scientific training was vital, or they wouldn't understand the implications of the satellite data. But it also had to be someone who couldn't have been part of the cover-up in the first place, someone she might have a half-decent chance of convincing that the files were genuine, who could be then trusted to do the right thing and, most importantly, who would be listened to by the world's media.

If this was a worldwide cover-up then she couldn't go to any one government since she didn't know who was involved. No, it had to be the United Nations. She had discovered a new UN committee set up to tackle the weakening-field crisis, but it had only two scientists – the rest of its members being politicians. And it hadn't taken her long to settle on the younger of the two: a British solar physicist by the name of Sarah Maitlin who, until a fortnight ago, had been an anonymous academic working at a research institute in Brazil modelling coronal mass ejections, who had been suddenly plunged into the media spotlight after the Air India plane crash and now seemed to have been recruited onto the UN committee that was examining future threats. The other scientist, a geologist by the name of Aguda, seemed to have the more relevant credentials, but he appeared to have been involved in UN work for several years, which meant he could conceivably also be part of the cover-up. Anyway, Shireen would trust a woman over a man any day. Had she had more time, she was sure she could have come up with a more foolproof plan than simply betting everything on someone she had never met, but this was the best she could do with her limited time and resources.

Now, two days after establishing contact with Mother,

149

it seemed half the global cyb community already knew Shireen very well. News spreads fast. The dark web was awash with stories about the young Iranian cyb who'd achieved what no one had believed possible: cracking a high-security quantum-encrypted website and gaining access to secret files, with speculation and rumours about their contents growing ever more outlandish.

For her part, Shireen knew very little about Mother other than that the woman was Turkish in origin and was currently in Tehran – something that Hashimi must have known. The rest was a mix of mythology, rumours and conspiracy theories.

Mother had agreed to meet her at a secret location – which was on the other side of the vast metropolis, but Shireen had managed to make it there on foot, resting overnight on park benches, mingling with the city's homeless, always keeping her hood pulled up to hide her face and avoid any prying surveillance cameras.

She arrived at the address just before dawn. It was an old apartment block on the corner of two quiet roads. Pausing for a moment at the bottom of the steps, she scanned her surroundings. There was no one in sight. The narrow door's paint was peeling and the large brass knocker had seen better days. Just as she was wondering whether to knock, the door buzzed and she heard a lock click, so she pushed it open and ventured nervously inside.

The hallway was in semi-darkness and she peered around her. Suddenly a man stepped forward out of the shadows, startling her.

He was tall and spindly with a thick beard and shaven head. In the dim hall light he looked to be in his late twenties. He spoke softly. 'You are Shireen?'

She nodded. 'Then please follow me. We must not keep Mother waiting.'

Without waiting for her, the man started up the chipped marble staircase, taking the stairs three at a time, his footsteps echoing around the quiet hallway. Two floors up, at the end of a gloomy corridor, he stopped and unlocked a shabby-looking door.

She followed him into a sparsely furnished apartment. There were no curtains at the window and the room was lit only by a street lamp outside. In the centre was a flimsy-looking table laden with electronics. The man directed Shireen to a chair next to it. 'Please, sit down and put on the visor.' She spotted the VR helmet and suddenly understood what this implied. Of course she would not be meeting Mother physically – how naive of her ever to have thought that. The cyb could be anywhere in the world. She felt an odd mix of disappointment and relief.

Her guide then turned and left the room without saying any more, closing the door softly behind him.

Picking up the visor, Shireen sat down on the edge of the chair and placed the helmet carefully over her head. It instantly moulded itself to the shape of her face, blocking out the light from outside and plunging her into darkness. She activated the switch beneath her left ear and her field of vision suddenly lit up. At first, she could only make out a kaleidoscope of colours, but they quickly resolved themselves and a virtual world came into sharp focus. She recognized the rudimentary details in the surrounding landscape. It looked like thousands of other generic virtual reality worlds both on the dark and surface webs and there was something reassuring and comforting about its familiarity.

In fact, this one looked more basic than most. It was a bright, sunny day and she was standing in the middle of an empty courtyard surrounded by imposing grey buildings that could have represented just about anything, anywhere. A door in the building to her right opened, through which a woman appeared and walked briskly towards her. She was wearing a splendidly colourful long robe, a traditional Turkish *entari*, with gold buttons done up from the waist to the throat. Below the waist was an equally bright and patterned long skirt covering leather boots. Shireen knew better than to project a person's avatar onto their real-life persona, but this woman was tall, elegant and handsome-looking – everything Shireen had imagined 'Mother' to be.

The woman smiled and greeted Shireen in perfect Farsi, the software translating whatever language Mother was physically speaking in. 'Hello, Shireen, I'm Evren Olgun. Well done for making it this far, but you are far from out of the woods yet.' Shireen didn't need to be told this. But at least she now stood a fighting chance of completing her task.

'Thank you for agreeing to help me. It's a real honour to meet you, Mother ... er ... I mean Evren.'

Evren's avatar tipped her head back and laughed. 'Well, Shireen, I am sure you're smart enough to know that my motives are not purely altruistic. You have achieved something many of our smartest cybs across the world have failed to do – you've found a way to break through the tightest quantum encryption security. And, while I am certainly intrigued by whatever is in those files, I know that if everything goes according to plan then I, along with the rest of the world, will know about it soon enough. So, for now, what is of far more interest to me is *how* you did it.'

Shireen had guessed all along that the price to pay for getting Mother's help would be to share with her the details of the Trojan horse software. It made sense that Mother would want to make as much use of the quantum hacking trick as she could before the authorities discovered the weakness in the system Shireen had exposed and closed the door for good. But to do that they would have to catch her first. That was why she hoped she could trust Mother not to double-cross her. It was in her interests to keep Shireen from being captured for as long as possible.

Evren continued. 'You must know that we have very little time. After all, it's not just Savak, or even Interpol, that you should be worrying about. At this moment there are many other special-interest groups and cyber cells trying to track you down too. Word will have quickly spread that you have a way of cracking encrypted secrets and everyone wants to get their hands on it. So, here's the deal. I will get you out of the country and safely to America if you hand over the code. But it has to happen now.'

The sudden insistence in Evren's voice sent another wave of panic through Shireen. What if she told her everything she knew and then was kept prisoner in this room, a sure-fire way to guarantee her not getting caught. But she had no choice now other than to trust the older cyb. What other option did she have?

A large transparent display screen appeared, hovering in the space between the two avatars. 'So, show me,' said Evren.

It took just a few minutes for Shireen to access her Trojan horse software on the virtual screen within the virtual world. Line upon line of code scrolled down the screen as she explained, proudly, what she had done. When she finished, the older woman was silent for a few moments. When she finally spoke, Shireen detected more than an undertone of admiration in her voice, which had taken on an excited fervour.

'This is astonishing! And you can be sure we will put

it to good use, and it will help our cause immeasurably. There are too many secrets these days that are being kept from the people.'

Shireen wondered what Mother would say if she knew the contents of the files she had uncovered – the biggest secret of them all.

Evren's voice suddenly softened. 'You know, you really are a quite remarkable young woman and I'm sorry that you are in this situation. Maybe, if you succeed in getting the files' contents out, we may one day be able to work together. For now, I must go, as there is much work to be done.'

'Wait! What am I supposed to do now?'

The point of the deal with Evren had been to receive help in getting to New York to meet Sarah Maitlin. Evren couldn't just leave her now.

As if reading her mind, the older cyb said: 'Don't worry. Lambros, the young man waiting outside, will give you a small gift from me that will help you get out of the country. You can trust him.'

Without further explanation, Evren spun round, her robe twirling rather more impressively than it would in the physical world. Shireen watched the woman walk away, and she was suddenly consumed with doubt, and feeling more alone than at any time in her life. She lifted the VR visor off her head and allowed herself a few seconds for her eyes to readjust to the gloomy room.

She walked to the door, half expecting it to be locked. It wasn't.

Lambros was standing just outside and nodded to her. Before she had a chance to say anything, he said, 'She is quite something, isn't she?' The awe in his voice was obvious. 'Now hold out your wristpad.'

What did he need it for? Had she just made a huge

154

mistake trusting these people? A new wave of panic swept through her. Lambros must have caught the look on her face because he smiled broadly. 'You do want your ticket to America, don't you?'

Shireen was astonished. He must have been there during her VR meeting with Evren. But, surely, he couldn't have set this up so quickly?

'How could you have known . . .'

'. . . that you need to get to New York? To meet Dr Sarah Maitlin? But we've known all along. We've been monitoring all activity on Hashimi's pad since you first started researching Dr Maitlin's background and we guessed, correctly as it turns out, that she would be the one you would reach out to with your, um, new revelations.

'Oh, don't worry,' he added when Shireen recoiled in horror, 'Savak have no idea. And as far as we can tell, neither do Interpol. They don't have the sort of access to the activities of our community on the dark web that we do. Nor do they have loyal friends like Hashimi. If they did, we wouldn't survive for long.'

Reluctantly, Shireen held out her arm and he held his wristpad above hers for a couple of seconds.

'There you are. Your new ID and flight ticket to New York. Now then, there's something else you're going to need if you're to stand a chance.'

He was holding a tiny capsule between his thumb and forefinger, which he now held out to her. She felt a surge of excitement as she carefully took the small metal cylinder from him. Following his mimed instruction, she twisted open the top to reveal a grey sphere smaller than a garden pea, which she tipped into her palm.

She'd heard rumours of such e-pills. Their micro-SD cards had a storage capacity of half a zettabyte, equivalent to the capacity of the entire internet thirty years ago. But this was the first time she had seen one. So, this was her reward, the piece of nanotechnology that was to help her deliver the files. Evren must have been very confident she would tell her everything she wanted.

'You must swallow it now,' said Lambros. 'It has micro-grappling hooks that will activate when it hits the lining of your stomach to anchor it. It then sits there, drawing power from your body heat, for forty-eight hours before detaching itself.

'As you know, wherever you are, biometrical scanners are in constant operation – facial recognition, iris identification, gait, everything. The pill detects the scanners and sends them fake information. This technology will be much more effective than that squelch jammer you've been using.'

Shireen let the remark slide. She still had Hashimi's jammer in the rucksack and was hoping to be able to keep hold of it. She stared at the tiny device in her hand. 'What you're saying is that it essentially makes me invisible?'

'Not quite. What it cannot do, of course, is help you if you undergo a DNA g-scan, so let's hope that isn't necessary.' Shireen knew full well that a physical DNA sample could not be faked; if she had to go through one at the airport then the game was up.

'But surely, getting through security means I'll need to pass through a scanner. Won't the pill itself show up?' Shireen guessed that the pill's developers would have thought of this but wasn't expecting the answer she got.

'Don't worry, the pill itself is completely undetectable.'

Shireen shook her head in disbelief. 'But ... ultrasound scanners are *designed* to look for just this sort of thing. They'd see it even if it was the size of a grain of sand. It's—'

Lambros held up his hand, interrupting her. 'The pill is coated with a metamaterial layer.'

Shireen had heard of the new smart materials that could be used as cloaking devices. Their optical properties meant they could bend light around them and make themselves invisible. 'But ... the scanners I'll have to go through at the airport are not electromagnetic. The pill may be invisible to light, but not to high-frequency ultrasound.'

Lambros grinned, his white teeth gleaming in the dimly lit corridor. 'You ask too many questions. The pill is coated with a tuneable metapaint that reacts to soundwaves rather than light. Its properties are altered as soon as it detects the high-frequency signal hitting it and it takes less than a microsecond for it to adjust and react to that wavelength. Then ... well, for all intents and purposes, it simply disappears.

'Your flight is in four hours, but the e-pill won't activate for another hour or two, so you'll still need your quaint jammer to get you to the airport, I'm afraid.'

Shireen stared at him while her brain processed this information. Neither of them had moved from outside the door of the room she had exited. Lambros was still looking down at her expectantly. When she couldn't think of a reason to stall any longer, she placed the pill on her tongue and swallowed.

16

Monday, 11 February – Tehran

THERE THEY WERE AGAIN – THE TWO SAVAK AGENTS, A man and a woman, that she had spotted earlier. They were getting uncomfortably close. Luckily, they hadn't actually seen her yet, having, she hoped, only tracked her to the busy shopping mall from the trail of blocked CCTV cameras where she'd used her jammer. Pulling her hood up to hide her face, Shireen kept walking as briskly as she dared, out of the mall and across the street, following the signs to the maglev station. She hardly noticed the driving rain.

At the station, she was relieved to see there were no biometric scanners and she was able to purchase a ticket with her new ID while keeping her face hidden under the hood. Boarding the maglev train, she found a seat – near the door just in case a hasty exit was required. Wiping the rain from her eyes, she took off her rucksack. For all her tiredness, it felt as if every nerve in her body was on high alert. Only when the doors closed and the train started to move did she begin to relax. As they picked up speed, gliding smoothly above the busy Tehran streets,

Shireen closed her eyes and thought back over the events of the past few days.

Her hope was that Savak would fail to anticipate that she'd try to leave the country, that they'd assume she was smart enough not to attempt something so preposterous. She looked around the maglev carriage again. She'd have to change seats soon since jamming any camera for more than a minute or two would raise alarms. Luckily the fifty-kilometre journey out to the airport wouldn't take long. She turned to look out the window. Rivulets of water ran horizontally on the outside of the glass as the maglev skimmed silently along its monorail track at three hundred kilometres per hour.

She was snapped back to reality when a shrill shout behind her pierced the hubbub of conversation in the carriage. 'SHIREEN DARVISH, STAND UP AND TURN AROUND SLOWLY.'

Turning, she saw the female Savak agent standing a few metres away, stun gun aimed directly at her. Fuck. What a fool she'd been. Raising her arms slowly, she stood and faced the agent.

She heard a woman behind her scream and was aware of several other passengers in her peripheral vision slowly and silently edging away from their seats and moving to the far end of the carriage. A sudden, unexpected calm washed over her and the analytical part of her brain immediately began to rationalize why this might be. Was it relief that this was finally Game Over? Or was it just her way of coping with extreme stress? After all, the situation was so ridiculous that it didn't seem real. Yes, that was it. It just didn't feel like any of this was really happening. In fact, she had encountered scenarios like this on numerous occasions while immersed in VR gaming simulations.

159

She contemplated the stun gun pointing at her chest and ran through her options. What would she do if this really were a computer game? An urgent voice in her head told her that the only sensible option was to surrender, then this whole futile adventure would be over.

She surprised herself by deciding to ignore the voice. Had she really come this far just to give up now? But what were the alternatives? Maybe feigning docile compliance before suddenly striking? No. Ridiculous. This was the real world and she was just a computer nerd, not a highly trained assassin with special skills or hidden weapons. The woman was small and stocky, not much taller than Shireen, and Shireen didn't fancy her chances in a fight, even without a gun pointing at her.

However, the choice was made for her. The train suddenly decelerated as it approached its stop. Shireen grabbed the side of the seat to steady herself, but the agent, holding the stun gun up with both arms, lost her balance and fell forward. It was all Shireen needed and instinct took over. Bending forward, she charged, her leading left shoulder connecting with the agent's chin with a crunch. The agent gasped and stumbled backward, hitting her head hard on a handrail in the middle of the carriage and landing on the floor with Shireen on top of her.

Shireen sat up, astride the dazed agent's midriff, and looked around. The train had now stopped, and the carriage doors slid open. Most of the passengers were scrambling to leave, and the few standing on the platform ready to board took one look at the scene in the carriage and hesitated. However, a handful had decided to gather round and enjoy the action, gawping at the two women on the floor, by their glazed stares each making a retinal recording, no doubt for immediate uploading on social media. But thankfully, no one tried to intervene.

Shireen spied the agent's gun lying on the floor a metre away and smiled to herself. She'd wasted countless hours playing 'shoot 'em up' video games and regarded herself as something of an expert on all types of firearms, whether standard issue or illegal. This was a Leyden Taser. It fired two tiny needles, delivering a painful electric shock, instantly incapacitating the victim for a few minutes.

The doors closed, and the train began to move again. The agent let out a groan and lifted her hand to her head. Shireen rolled off her and reached for the gun just as the agent opened her eyes and sat up. Without thinking, she pointed it and pulled the trigger. The stun gun fizzed, and the darts embedded themselves in the agent's neck.

The agent jolted and arched her back as the electro-magnetic pulse shot through her body, then quickly slumped back into unconsciousness. Shireen stood and turned to face the other passengers. She felt trapped. Even though the gun would need reloading, she held it up, arms outstretched, and swivelled round, taking it through 360 degrees. Most of the passengers took a step back, but a couple simply held their ground. She knew she wouldn't be able to stop them uploading their footage immediately, each one trying to be the first to report the incident in the hope of it going viral. So, she had very little time to do what she needed. Her mind was racing. One more stop before the airport: Rahahan Square and the Central Station where intercity trains left for Qom, Isfahan and Shiraz in the south, Mashhad in the east and Tabriz in the west. Could she still pull this off? She had to try. 'You all saw what happened. I'm not a criminal, but I need to get away to clear my name. Please don't stop me getting off at Rahahan. I have to catch my train out of the city.'

To her astonishment, several people began to applaud. Others nodded approval. Of course. People hated Savak.

Those of her grandparents' generation had many stories to tell, but even they admitted that the agency had gained further notoriety in recent years, as though trying to make up the lost forty-five years of Islamic state rule during which it had been disbanded. She walked slowly towards the doors as people backed away, opening up a route for her. She never once lowered the gun. After all, she had not spotted the second agent yet. He must by now know what had happened.

The two minutes to the next stop were the longest of her life. Police at Rahahan station would surely have been alerted by now – would there be a welcoming committee on the platform already? At least no one on the train seemed interested in trying to overpower her; they were a passive audience eager to see how the incident played out.

Just as the train began to slow, a crazy idea popped into her head. It could make all the difference and it might just work. She returned quickly to the unconscious agent. The woman was far heavier than she'd expected, but she summoned up all her energy reserves and slowly pulled her up into a sitting position against a seat where she would have a clear view of the maglev doors. However, she needed the agent conscious for what she had in mind. She slapped her across the face. No response. She slapped her again, harder this time, and the agent's eyes slowly flickered open. Good. She was pinning her hopes on the woman not being able to move very quickly just yet, while her muscles recovered from the electric shock, but she would hopefully be conscious enough to activate her AR and record the next few seconds.

Shireen grabbed her rucksack from the seat and rushed towards the doors just as they swished open. Moments ago, she had felt utterly exhausted – now, she was buzzing. Without looking back, she squeezed through the

throng of passengers trying to board. No welcome committee, thank God. Once on the platform, she pushed her
way past the crowds towards the exit, ignoring their
curses and angry shouts. Looking back, she caught a
momentary glimpse of the Savak agent stumbling from
the carriage before she was hidden from view. Shireen
had no time left. If the agent managed to keep the train
at the station it would be all over. She felt a wave of relief
on hearing the warning bleeps signalling departure. At
the last moment, she dived back onto the train through
the doors of the last carriage just as they were sliding
shut. The train began to move again, and she turned to
hide her face from the platform side.

Had she done enough? The agent had seen her get off
and the passengers would corroborate her stated intention to catch a train out of Tehran. If all went to plan, the
authorities would be hunting for her in and around the
vast Central Station for long enough to buy her the time
she needed to board her flight. She chose a seat towards
the back of the carriage and, for the second time in the
space of a few minutes, slumped down exhausted, grateful that the other passengers were ignoring her.

The squelch jammer could still do the trick of disrupting the airport security cameras, but she should now
assume the new identity that Evren had provided for her.
There would surely be heightened security at the airport,
but if the e-pill she'd taken did what it was meant to then
any cameras and scanners running surveillance software
would register her fake ID. She sighed inwardly: it was a
big *if*. She just hoped that there were no Savak agents at
the airport, as they wouldn't need to rely on biometric
software to identify her.

On arrival, she made her way through the airport terminal without further incident. Reluctantly, she dropped

the jammer into a bin as she passed. It had taken her this far, but she couldn't afford to be caught with it at security. Next hurdle: the departures gate. Ahead of her, just as she'd anticipated, were the ultrasound scanners. Crunch time. The e-pill should have activated by now, but would it get picked up in the scanner? She had no choice but to keep going. She stepped into the pod, and the reinforced glass screen swished closed behind her as she followed the pictorial instructions and raised both arms above her head. Time stood still. The scan took only a few seconds, but it seemed to last for ever. Lowering her arms, she turned to wait for the exit door to slide open. Instead, a disembodied voice above her head announced: 'Scan inconclusive. Please turn around, placing your feet on the marked spots again, and raise your arms over your head.'

She resumed the position. Her heart was pounding. *Stay calm. Stay calm.*

Finally, the door swished open and she was through, her panic replaced with euphoria. That clever little pill had come through after all.

Her flight had already begun boarding by the time she reached the gate. Joining the back of the queue, she shuffled along with the other passengers, most of whom looked like businessmen and -women, and all seemed preoccupied with their retinal feeds. She wondered why boarding was so slow.

It was only when she got to within a few metres of the gate that she saw the reason for the delay: a security guard holding a DNA g-scanner, taking micro skin samples from each passenger.

Fuck. Fuck. Fuck.

So near, and yet so far. She was overcome with a sense of despair and felt close to tears. Was the genetic scanner a recent addition? Was it there for her? Turning around as casually as she dared, she started heading back the way she'd come. She just needed a few moments to think and regain her composure. She hadn't come this far only to fail now.

She had reached the end of the queue and was almost back in the open departure area again when she felt a firm hand on her shoulder.

'Excuse me, miss, could you come with me?' The burly security guard towered over her. He was in his thirties and looked to be wearing a uniform several sizes too small for him. His cap, pulled down over his eyes, covered a mop of long, unruly hair.

Panicking, she jerked away from him, trying to twist her body free, but the hand on her shoulder tightened with a steely grip, his fingers digging into her painfully. 'I wouldn't try that if I were you,' he hissed, 'you really wouldn't get very far.' Several passengers turned to stare. She looked up at the guard and nodded weakly. With his hand still firmly gripping her shoulder he led her away from the gate.

As they walked, he said quietly: 'You are Shireen Darvish, aren't you?'

She looked at him silently. So the game was up.

'That g-scan would have revealed your identity, so you panicked, right?'

You were clearly picked for this job because of your astonishingly sharp intellect. Shireen no longer had the stomach for her usual defiance. 'Did I look that guilty?'

The guard grinned. 'No, I knew what you looked like because Mother Cyb described you to me. I've been expecting you.' He took his hand away from her shoulder.

Shireen recoiled in shock. How could Evren betray her? *Why* would she betray her now? Why let her get this far? It didn't make sense.

165

The guard saw the shock on her face and his grin grew even wider, showing several crooked teeth. 'Hey, stop panicking. My job was to ensure you boarded this flight safely, which means bypassing the g-scan. To be honest, we weren't expecting this level of security just yet, but you must have triggered something.' Then he added, somewhat sheepishly, 'You know, I'm a big admirer of what you've done, as are all of us in the cyb community.'

Shireen opened and closed her mouth in utter bemusement but couldn't think of anything to say. The guard was clearly not expecting a response because he had already turned away and was looking around to check if the coast was clear. 'Come on. Let's get you on board before anyone gets even more suspicious.'

When she finally managed to get words out, all she could say was, 'Thank you.'

He led her through an adjacent gate, which he accessed with a security pass, and down a deserted corridor that led on to the walkway to the plane. A minute later, she was in her seat on the flight to New York.

She sat still, hardly daring to breathe. She knew that all the time the e-pill was working, she could remain anonymous. What happened after its forty-eight-hour lifetime she had no idea. She hoped that by then she would have achieved what she'd set out to do. For the first time in a couple of days, she wondered how her parents were doing. Had they remained out of sight? She wondered who else would now be looking for her. Maybe she'd even made it onto Interpol's most-wanted list. *I guess I'm now officially an international cyberterrorist. Mum and Dad will be so proud.*

Sighing, she turned to look out of the window as the plane taxied towards the runway. She half-expected to see Savak agents sprinting towards her across the tarmac to stop the plane. Suddenly she was pressed back in her seat as the plane accelerated. The relief of take-off was so overwhelming that she at last began to cry. No one was watching so she let the tears flow freely, silently. Then, without warning, exhaustion overcame her and she fell into a deep, dreamless sleep.

17

Sunday, 10 February – New York

THE SUNDAY AFTERNOON THAT MARC HAD BEEN SO looking forward to, spending time with his daughter, started badly. How could he have been so deluded as to think that Evie would rush into his arms, all forgiveness and smiles, as soon as she saw him? He'd picked her up at midday from the smart terraced address that had been, until a few months ago, his home for seven years. Instead, all he received was a brief, perfunctory hug.

And yet he was determined to try and lift her mood from this brooding, standoffish resentment to at least get a glimpse of the bubbly, ebullient Evie he knew was somewhere underneath.

'I thought we'd spend the afternoon in Bryant Park. You know how much you used to enjoy our Sunday afternoons there.'

'That was when I was five years old, Dad. Maybe you hadn't noticed, but I'm not a kid any more.'

He tried desperately to work out the last time they had actually spent time together as a family and realized he couldn't recall it. Instead he said, 'Well, you'll always be my little—'

'—Don't, Dad. Please,' she said in a pleading voice, and he sighed. They walked in silence for the next couple of minutes.

When they reached the junction, he had to stop himself from instinctively grabbing hold of her hand to cross the road. *Shit, she's right. I still think of her as a young child.* He decided to tackle full on the issue that was such a barrier between them.

'Look, I know what a disappointment I must be to you, and I know it'll take time for you to fully forgive me. But you will, when you see I'm not such an arsehole any more.'

'Dad, you're not a disappointment, honest. And I know more than you probably think I do about depression and how it can control people. But . . . well, can't you see that your leaving us – well, leaving me – and going off like that was taking the coward's way out? Running away from your problems won't make them disappear, or suddenly make you well again.'

She was right. Of course she was. His little girl was now a mature young woman with her own blossoming wisdom. He felt a mixture of shame, as her words hit home, and pride in this wonderful person walking alongside him. He resisted the temptation to put his arm around her and instead he tried to make light of the situation. 'Well, if you really wanted to help make me feel better, you'd let me buy you pizza for lunch and then allow me to spend an afternoon with my favourite human being on the planet.'

Evie finally smiled. 'Oh, planning on spending the afternoon alone then, are you?'

'Yeah, yeah. OK.'

After pizza they went for a walk around Bryant Park. Despite a promising start to the weather that morning – the first blue skies seen since the remnants of Hurricane Jerome had drifted back out into the Atlantic – things were now taking a turn for the worse. The wind was picking up and the sky had turned grey. Marc hoped the rain would hold off for a few hours. At least Evie's mood had thawed considerably.

'You know it's glorious summer weather down in Waiheke at the moment. I've been doing a lot of work on Grandma and Grandpa's house, and the boat. I'd love it if you could come over to visit.'

'Dad, you do know I go to school, right? And by the time we break for summer it'll be turning colder down there. Geography isn't my strongest subject, but I know that much.'

Marc shrugged. 'Still, you'll love it. I bet you can't remember too much from your only trip to NZ. You'd have been . . . um . . .'

'I was seven. Don't you remember, Dad, we celebrated my seventh birthday at Grandma and Grandpa's house? They held a party and there was no one my age and you got drunk and got into an argument with Grandpa and—'

'—OK, yes, I remember. Sorry.'

'I miss them, you know: Grandma and Grandpa. Even though I didn't see that much of them.'

'Yeah, me too,' he said quietly.

Time to change the subject. 'So, anyway, how're you getting on with Jeremy Golden Balls these days?'

Evie giggled. 'He's fine, Dad, honest. He can be a bit overbearing at times, but mostly he's OK. And Mum seems happy. She's very tired, but . . .'

Marc looked at his daughter, wondering what it was she was reluctant to spit out. 'But, what?'

Evie looked down at her feet. 'Well, the house is a lot quieter these days, that's all.'

Ah, yes, of course. He and Charlie had done a lot of shouting in the last few months before he'd moved out. But he'd been locked too deeply in his own dark world to think much about how it might have affected Evie. The truth was he did feel better knowing that Evie, and Charlie for that matter, were happier now.

Bryant Park was still Marc's favourite place in Manhattan. There were so many memories of happier family times spent there, picnicking on the grass during the summer. After feeding the pigeons, he'd queue for ice cream while Charlie took Evie for a ride on the carousel. That still seemed like yesterday and he felt a sudden wave of melancholia at the thought of how much his, and Evie's, life had changed in recent months. He managed to push it away.

Today the park looked very different. Although still full of joggers and dog-walkers, it now looked bleak under the leaden sky. The cold wind whistled through the bare branches of the tall trees on the outer edges of the park. During the summer months, they blocked out the surrounding skyscrapers, but their leafless skeletons exposed the glass and concrete buildings beyond. They walked slowly around the park, twice, with Evie starting to do more of the talking.

By the time they made it back to the apartment, the skies had begun to clear again, and the threat of rain had receded.

'Do you want to come in for a bit? Say hi to Mum? Jeremy isn't around.'

'Probably not a good idea, Evie.'

'No, probably not.' She gave him a hug, this time for a little longer. He didn't kid himself that all was well again

171

between them, but today had been a good start. She turned and ran up the steps to the front door.

'I'll stop by on Tuesday if that's OK,' he shouted after her. 'And I expect you to have some idea what you'd like for your birthday.' He made a mental note to ask Charlie what she had got her.

She waved without looking back. A moment later she was inside with the door closed behind her.

It must have been the familiarity of the street and the house, and the near-normality of the time he'd just spent with his daughter, but Marc just stood there outside his old apartment for several minutes feeling flat. It seemed the girl who'd laughed at his jokes, and who'd announced gleefully on every occasion: 'You're *so* weird, Dad', which had been a default reaction to almost anything he said or did, was growing into an independent young woman who no longer needed him. He thought about going up the steps and knocking on the door. What would he say? Would he apologize again, ask for things to go back to the way they were? Too late for that.

He sighed, wondering what to do with himself for twenty-four hours. He'd decided against the offer to stay with an old friend while in town and had checked into a hotel instead. But he was starting to have serious misgivings about what Qiang had roped him in for the following evening. His younger colleague had been invited to a reception held by the Chinese ambassador, and Marc was his plus-one. Whoopie-fucking-doo. All that banal small talk with politicians and diplomats. He wondered what the protocol was at events like that regarding sloping off early.

Still, it was great that Qiang was moving up in the world. His involvement with the Chinese investigation into the Earth's magnetic field had obviously got him

172

fast-tracked along the corridors of power. And if Marc could help him in any way – then it was the very least he owed him. He was also desperate to discuss further with Qiang his idea about neutralino beams. It was all too crazy to be taken seriously, of course, but it was an interesting hypothetical problem to consider.

18

Monday, 11 February – New York

IT HAD BEEN JUST 48 HOURS SINCE SARAH'S UN MEET-
ing, and she already had several high-level meetings lined
up in her diary, mostly about what sort of contingency
plans to put in place to cope with a whole range of scary
scenarios. She found it infuriating that the politicians she
spoke to were still more worried about what the geo-
storm after a direct hit from a CME might do to global
electronics networks and telecommunication satellites
than they were about a potentially catastrophic exposure
of entire populations to the radiation itself. At least they
acknowledged the very real danger of secondary threats
like hurricanes and tsunamis, and it was a relief to see so
many other scientists being drafted in.

What she hadn't been prepared for was the secrecy.
While her warnings about the heightened danger of coronal mass ejections hitting the Earth were being taken very
seriously within the corridors of power, both at the UN
and elsewhere, in public and across the networks politicians were actively downplaying the threat. Not that this
seemed to have much influence either way – most people

were immune to what they read or heard on their AR feeds and were cynical about anything politicians said, preferring to just get on with their own lives.

That was something Sarah could identify with. Right now, all she wanted was to curl up in her hotel room with a book and glass of wine and pretend this was all a bad dream. But that wasn't going to happen this evening. Spending an afternoon shopping for something to wear to a fancy cocktail party, as she had just done, was the last thing she'd felt in the mood for and it all seemed rather surreal. But a last-minute invitation to Ambassador Xu's reception this evening meant a necessary trip into town.

She'd been a little surprised to receive the invitation, but assumed it was Aguda's doing. After all, she hadn't exactly endeared herself to the Chinese ambassador so far. Hopefully, Aguda and one or two of the other scientists she'd met at the UN would also be there.

Her frustratingly extended stay in New York was at least more comfortable now that she had been upgraded to the Plaza Hotel on Fifth Avenue. She estimated she would need another two weeks to finish writing her section of the report the committee had been asked to produce. She had been checking every day with her young research colleague Miguel in Rio and was itching to get back to her own research again. The sooner she could escape from the political machinations of the UN, the better.

She tapped her wristpad and checked the invitation on her AR. The Chinese Embassy was sending a car at seven, so she had just under an hour to kill.

Suddenly her wristpad pinged as a text message came through. Odd. It was on her private account, and only her parents had access to that. It must be her father. She hoped everything was OK. She quickly focused her eyes on the AR display in the top right of her field of vision, but the message wasn't from her parents.

It was short, as though composed in a hurry:

My name is Shireen Darvish. I wish you no harm. I know you are leaving the hotel at seven. Meet me downstairs in the female bathroom near the lobby at 6.50. I have information you have to see.

Please. I have no one else to turn to.

She squeezed her eyes shut and took a few deep breaths. Alarm and anxiety quickly morphed into curiosity and she read the message again. *OK, think. Someone has got hold of your private contact details. Fine – there are plenty of smart hackers out there. But this all sounds very cloak and dagger.*

Of course she wouldn't be able to resist this. Anyway, what's the worst that could happen in a hotel bathroom with people coming in and out all the time? She spent a few minutes online trying to learn a little more about this Shireen Darvish, but drew a blank. Very strange. It was unheard of for an individual to leave not a single footprint on the net.

At a quarter to seven, she grabbed her coat and bag and left the room.

The hotel lobby was busy and noisy, with a number of new guests arriving, leaving their islands of suitcases clustered around the reception desk as they checked in. Other guests were heading out into the early New York evening. Sarah stopped to look around. She couldn't see anyone who looked remotely suspicious or who might be watching her. She glanced at the time. 6:50. She turned and strolled as casually as she could to the door marked 'Ladies'.

176

A well-dressed middle-aged woman was coming out just as Sarah entered.

Once inside and the door closed, she looked around. She couldn't see anyone, but two of the cubicle doors were shut. She whispered, 'Hello? Ms . . . Ms Darvish? Are you in here?'

Silence.

Puzzled, she waited a few seconds before turning back towards the door.

Suddenly she heard the click of a lock and the far cubicle door opened slowly. A diminutive girl, in her late teens or early twenties, stepped out very cautiously. She had an unruly crop of bright pink hair and several nose rings. Sarah's first impression was that she looked exhausted and very, very scared. She watched her carefully while at the same time making sure she could make a run for the exit if she needed to.

'Please. We don't have much time.' The girl spoke in a soft, halting voice in perfect English with what sounded like a Turkish or Persian accent. She sounded, and looked, on edge, her eyes darting around nervously. She quickly ducked down to look under the only closed cubicle door and, presumably satisfied that it was empty and that they were alone, gestured to Sarah to approach her. 'My name is Shireen Darvish and I'm a computer science student from Tehran. You must believe what I am about to tell you.'

Sarah remained rooted to the spot.

The girl took a step towards her and began to speak faster, as though reciting a prepared speech. 'I have in my possession highly secret documents that I have gained access to. I don't have time to explain how, but you need to see them. The world needs to see them before the information is erased for good.'

Sarah must have looked incredulous, but what the young woman said next sounded even more preposterous.

'I know how this must look to you but believe me when I say I am not crazy. It's possible that the fate of humanity depends on you getting this information out and using your reputation to back up its authenticity.'

Yup, that sounds exactly that. Crazy. As though humanity wasn't in enough trouble already. And yet there was something about this woman: a desperate, haunted look in her eyes. She might be deluded or unstable, but Sarah was willing to bet she genuinely believed what she was saying. Her AR was giving her no information at all as she stared at the young lady. She was clearly being very careful at keeping her identity a secret.

Sarah took a deep breath, her curiosity stronger than ever now. 'OK, tell me a few things first. Who do you work for?'

'No one. I told you, I'm a student at Tehran University.'

Sarah realized she had not made herself clear. 'No, I mean who else is involved in this?'

'I am working alone.'

Sarah stiffened in surprise. 'You mean you were able to gain access to such highly sensitive information without help?'

Shireen looked at her quietly, her big brown eyes now shining in defiance.

'Oh, come on, I wasn't born yesterday. If this information is as sensitive as you say it is, then the firewalls would be so impregnable that even Google and SonyIntel would struggle to get past them, so who's backing you?' Sarah wondered what sort of organization could be behind such a high-risk operation. Did this young woman belong to one of the many global cyberterrorist cells or could she really be an exceptionally talented cyb acting alone? In any case, in today's world with its ubiquitous electronic surveillance, it would have been almost impossible for a fugitive from the law, as she must be with all this cloak and dagger secrecy, to travel halfway across the world without being caught. So, either she had help from powerful people or she was in possession of superpowers. Either way . . .

Just then the bathroom door opened, and two elderly women walked in. One went into a cubicle while the other looked at Sarah and smiled, then headed to a large mirror to check her makeup. Sarah walked over to the far corner of the bathroom and began washing her hands. The young Iranian followed her and turned on an adjacent tap.

When Sarah felt confident they couldn't be overheard she whispered, 'Do you really expect me to believe you travelled thousands of kilometres, risking so much, to meet me *physically* when you could have just contacted me from Iran?'

Shireen answered quickly, as though she had been expecting the question. 'And would you have believed me if my avatar had popped up in your AR space? Hi, I'm Shireen and I'm a cyberhacker who has a secret to share?' When Sarah didn't reply she continued. 'Can't you see? Anyone could have done that. You'd have thought it was fake and ignored me. And I couldn't risk just sending you the files in case they got intercepted. I had to come in person, to deliver the files to you physically. And, yes, since you mention it, I've risked everything to get here.'

'But why me? If you were so desperate for this information to get out, why not simply release it?'

'And what do you think would have happened then? It would have made no difference if it had gone viral and been seen by a billion people. Whoever is behind this is powerful enough to have immediately discredited the story as fake and replaced it with a watertight counter-narrative. So, I needed someone who would be believed – someone who couldn't be silenced. Someone who cared as much about the truth as I do.'

'But you don't even *know* me,' whispered Sarah loudly, and jerked her head around quickly, realizing she could have been overheard. But the woman by the mirror had now left and the other was still in a cubicle. 'How dare you presume what my motives might be and try to involve me in whatever this is about.'

The second woman emerged from the cubicle and walked over to wash her hands. Sarah waited silently until she had left and they were alone again, then turned to Shireen and sighed. 'OK, give me something to go on. What's in these files?'

Shireen began to speak quickly, picking up her well-rehearsed speech where she'd left off. 'I follow the news. I know about the threat of the weakening field. I know you sit on a powerful UN committee that's looking into it. But as far as I can tell you're not a politician and you don't serve any political interests. So, you're the only person I can hope to trust to get this information out. The data I've sent you show that the recent measurements of the Earth's magnetic field have been tampered with. I don't know who's behind it, but there's been some cover-up.'

Sarah stared at her. What the hell was that supposed to mean? 'If this is some sort of ridiculous conspiracy theory bullshit—'

Shireen tapped her wristpad. 'You need to see the files. Please, Dr Maitlin. I have them here—'

'Wait a minute.' Sarah felt a rising panic. 'Before you implicate me in this, this . . . whatever it is, I'll ask you again. You mentioned the UN committee I'm on, but there are plenty of people who are more powerful and better placed than me to go public with your information. Dr Gabriel Aguda for one – he's a geologist after all and he understands a lot more about the magnetic field measurements. So, why me?'

Shireen was nodding vigorously, as if she had anticipated Sarah's response. 'A mixture of gut instinct and logic. I needed someone who couldn't possibly have been involved in the cover-up. I'm not saying that Aguda is part of this – it's just that, well, you've just joined that committee, so I knew you would be, um, clean.' After the briefest of hesitations, she added, 'Also, I feel I can trust . . . another woman.'

Sarah wasn't sure how to respond. But Shireen hadn't finished. 'The files can only be accessed by me biometrically. But I'm now copying them over to your Cloud space. I had to do it this way – only by meeting you physically could I get them over to you directly. Any other route would risk interception. Now please, I beg you, look at them. You will understand why they need to be released to every organization, media outlet and scientist you can think of, as quickly as possible. I don't know how much more time we have before it's too late and I'm silenced.'

Sarah tapped her wristpad and saw that several folders had been downloaded. Each looked like it contained many files.

She was aware that Shireen was still staring at her intensely, but knew she didn't have time to look at the files now. She quickly checked the time. 'OK, I have to go. But how will I be able to get in touch with you?'

'You can't. But, maybe you can help secure my release from custody. As soon as this goes public it will be clear that I am in New York.' Then she added, almost too quietly for Sarah to hear, 'And I am too tired to keep running.' All the intensity in the girl's manner just a minute ago now drained away, as though a fire had just gone out in her eyes. That scared Sarah more than anything Shireen had told her – that she must have risked so much coming this far to entrust her with information, while knowing for certain that she would be arrested for doing so. What the hell was in those files?

Sarah didn't know what else to say. She nodded at Shireen, turned quickly and walked out.

Her car was waiting outside the hotel entrance. As she walked out to it she ran through the strange encounter again. The young cyb had clearly been through a lot just to get these files to her. She might well be a completely deluded conspiracy theorist convinced about yet another ridiculous global cover-up, but there was something about her that Sarah recognized: an intelligence and defiance in the girl's eyes that reminded her of her own young self.

As soon as she was alone in the car and it had pulled away from the kerb, Sarah opened the files and began to scan them. There were three separate folders, each containing hundreds of documents. Some of these were data files, some were graphs, some were images showing colour-coded maps of magnetic field strengths around the Earth, and some were reports, in both Chinese and English. But only half a dozen or so were marked as priority. They had been flagged by Shireen and gathered together in a bundle under the heading 'READ THESE FIRST'. She worked her way through them with growing shock, trying to digest the information as quickly as she could.

As she did so, she started running through her options. Of course, this might all be completely fabricated. It would be a simple matter to concoct such a story, with bogus data and fictional reports, something a cyber group intent on causing disruption would be more than capable of doing.

But what if this was the real deal?

No, she decided, what she was looking at was genuine: these were raw satellite data stretching back over the past two years and they flew in the face of what Aguda had told her a week ago in the diner. Equally shockingly, there were reports making it clear how the data should be changed so that the officially released statistics gave quite the opposite result: that field measurements in the southern hemisphere showed regions where the magnetic field was *gaining* in strength, rather than weakening, in readiness for a pole reversal, probably sometime later this year – something these files suggested wasn't going to happen.

Well, whoever was behind this – and she guessed it had to go far up the chain of command – had lied to Aguda and the rest of the world.

Damn it, Aguda, are you in on this too? Oh, what the fuck have I got myself mixed up in?

She looked out of the car window to get her bearings. She was passing Central Park on her left. It was beginning to snow but she was too deep in thought to notice.

She went over the 'facts' again. The satellite data had been tampered with, that much seemed clear. In fact, it seemed that the original measurements contained in these files showed unequivocally that the field was getting weaker ... *everywhere*. But that was just crazy. If the Earth's magnetic field was really dying ... No, that was too horrifying to contemplate.

As a scientist and now a member of a highly influential UN committee, she knew it would be utterly irresponsible, not to mention dangerous, to make this information public without checking its validity carefully first. On its own, of course, the data would not have meant much to

183

a non-scientist. But there were other documents and emails, from anonymous senders to equally anonymous recipients, demanding emphatically that the original data be buried.

She knew she had to do something, to trust someone. The obvious choice was Aguda. He would, she hoped, know what to do, and who else she could trust.

She attached a few of the files to a brief voice message, explaining her meeting with Shireen, and pinged it to Gabriel. She was taking a huge risk with this and couldn't be certain about Aguda's trustworthiness. Nor could she be sure the files wouldn't be intercepted on the way to him. After everything Shireen must have gone through to get the files to her . . . But what else could she do? Who else could she turn to? She slumped back in her seat and waited for a response. While she did so, her mind drifted. There had been just two occasions in her life when she had experienced this deep feeling of foreboding. One was nine years ago, when her mother had been diagnosed with advanced Hodgkin's lymphoma. The other was when she was fourteen and had been called into the headmistress's office at school to be told that her brother Matt had been in a road accident. On both occasions, her anxiety had eventually turned to relief. Somehow, this time she didn't believe there would be a happy ending.

A thousand questions tumbled over each other in her head. How widely did this conspiracy stretch? Who knew about it? How many countries had been colluding to keep this information from getting out? And, most importantly, why? What possible good would come of hiding the truth? Was it simply to avert mass panic while the authorities dealt with the crisis? *I have to think sensibly about this. I'm part of the establishment now, not some disillusioned cyber anarchist trying to bring down corrupt global powers. Shit.*

The car glided along silently. She rested her head against the window pane, briefly enjoying the refreshing coolness of the glass against her temple. Her heart was racing and her stomach was churning. She thought about scanning the web for more information, but quickly dismissed that idea as a waste of time.

Just then, her wristpad pinged and Aguda appeared on her AR feed. He was dressed in a tuxedo and at first she hardly recognized him. So, he was going to the reception too, or most likely he was already there. He looked more solemn than she had ever seen him. She tapped her pad to connect and instantly the cameras in the car picked her up and linked with her feed.

'Hello, Sarah. I see from your surroundings that you are on your way here. Please don't do anything until you arrive. I will meet you and we can discuss this in private properly.'

'No, just tell me please, did you know about this?'

There were a few seconds of silence, as though he were weighing up different options. Then he said, 'Yes, Sarah, I did know. I'm afraid I lied when I told you the field was regaining its strength. But please, can this wait until you get here when I can explain more carefully?'

Sarah felt sick. 'Damn it, Gabriel, if you're in on this, what's to stop me from just sending this information out, right now, before I get to you and you talk me out of it, or, or God knows what? I mean, does everyone else on our committee apart from me know the truth – that the Earth's magnetic field is fucking dying and not getting ready for the Flip at all?'

'No, Sarah, not everyone. And please try to stay calm and not do anything you'll regret.'

But she couldn't help herself, her indignation and fury growing by the second. 'How could you deliberately keep this from me? Everything we're putting in our report is to do with temporary measures to deal with the consequences of a weakened field for a few months. Not this – not the end of the fucking world!'

Aguda nodded sympathetically. 'Look, I know what you must be thinking right now. But I'm asking you not to do anything rash. Please.'

Sarah took a deep breath. She would be at the reception in ten minutes. Maybe this was the sensible, measured thing to do. After all, what could 'they' do to her?

She didn't register the two jet-black vans that sped past her in the opposite direction.

Still furious, she didn't know what else to say to Aguda, so she disconnected. It occurred to her that the Chinese government, as the dominant player on the global stage, would be in on it for sure. It was unthinkable that the world's last remaining superpower wasn't at the heart of this cover-up. In which case, she was now heading straight into the lion's den.

19

Monday, 11 February – New York

SHIREEN FELT DRAINED, AS THOUGH EVERY LAST DROP
of strength and will-power that had sustained her over the
past few days had finally been used up. The e-pill inside her
still had a day to go, but she almost didn't care any more.
She was no longer concerned whether she was caught
now – her fate was in someone else's hands. She just prayed
Sarah would do the right thing.

Wondering what to do next, she decided she would find
a quiet corner in the hotel lobby and check the news outlets. If Sarah had released the files, it would only be a matter
of minutes before someone picked it up and reported it.

She found a wide sofa hidden away behind a couple of
large potted plants to the side of the hotel's grand staircase. Sitting down, she tapped on her AR feed and started
scanning various networks. To make herself more comfortable, she rested her head on the soft cushions and
quickly felt herself drifting off. She didn't resist.

Almost immediately, she was pulled sharply out of her
doze by loud shouts. She jerked upright to be confronted
by four armed FBI agents. It couldn't have been more

than ten minutes since Sarah had left. So, she must have released the files almost immediately. Or had she just betrayed her? But her head was too foggy to try and think anything through. She looked at the men in front of her passively, feeling numb.

'Stay exactly where you are and don't move a muscle,' said one of the agents, holding a stun gun directly at her chest. She had no intention of moving, so she stared back at the man. Two others approached her and pulled her roughly to her feet. She didn't put up any resistance as her arms were yanked painfully behind her back and her wrists cuffed.

The fact that she had been found so quickly meant one of two things: either Sarah Maitlin had indeed released the files and her movements had been traced back to the hotel where its cameras had identified Shireen ... or Sarah had sold her out and just informed the authorities. She hoped her instincts had been right and that she had chosen Sarah wisely.

Of course, there was a third possibility: that Sarah had been naive enough to hold back from releasing the files just yet, or, worse still, to put her trust in people who would try to stop her. Whatever had happened, it was too late to worry about it now, and she wouldn't have long to find out. She wondered whether her backup plan had been needed and, if so, whether it had worked. She allowed herself to be led off through the hotel lobby and out to a waiting black van.

20

IN THE GATHERING DARKNESS OUTSIDE, THE SNOW WAS
coming down a little heavier now and the traffic was moving slowly. Sarah was looking out, deep in thought, at the
early-evening Manhattan lights, a glistening kaleidoscope
of colours diffracted and reflected by a thousand drifting
snowflakes, when she suddenly caught sight of a tiny drone
through the falling curtain of snowflakes. It had appeared
from nowhere and was now hovering about a metre from
the window, level with her eyes and keeping pace with the
car's slow progress. No sooner had she identified it as a
media drone than she spotted several others joining it and
hovering alongside the car, all with their miniature cameras focused on her. Confused, she touched the window to
opaque, hiding herself away from their prying eyes.

What on earth would they be following her for? She
checked her AR. What she saw was astonishing. Her
mouth went dry and she felt a tightness in her chest as the
horrid truth of what was unfolding hit home. Her entire
conversation with Aguda just a few minutes earlier was
being relayed live across the net and was spreading like

wildfire. The information that Shireen Darvish had been so desperate to release to the world was now well and truly out there, for better or worse, and the world was reacting. But it was Sarah's face and name, not Shireen's, that was spreading exponentially across both the official and social media networks. No doubt it wouldn't take very long for AIs to analyse the footage and determine that it was a genuine exchange between two scientists working for the United Nations.

She'd been played. Presumably by Shireen. Had that been the young cyb's intention all along? And anyway, how could she have known that Sarah would confide in someone rather than release the files? It certainly wouldn't have been difficult for someone of Shireen's obvious ability to copy a spyware code over with the files – one that would activate as soon as she made contact with anyone, sending the footage to a site that linked to major hubs around the world. The decision on what to do with the files had been taken out of Sarah's hands. *But no one has the files themselves yet, unless of course Shireen has released them, now that their authenticity has been endorsed by my outburst to Aguda and his admission. No. Wait. Shireen wouldn't need to do anything. If my conversation has been leaked out then the files could also have been released, from* my *account. Oh, this is all just fucking great.*

Sitting back, she closed her eyes. Shit. Too late to do anything about it now. Maybe the world did need to know the truth. After all, if a patient is diagnosed with a terminal illness, doctors have no right to hide it from them.

It certainly hadn't taken the media long to locate her. She checked her feed and saw that she was already being pinged to respond to a growing cacophony of requests for statements. Any attention she'd received over the past two weeks was going to look pretty lame compared to what she was going to have to face now.

Clear of the heavy traffic, her chauffeurless limo suddenly picked up speed as it headed northwards along First Avenue to the reception in Manhattan's Upper East Side.

21

SENATOR PETER HOGAN STOOD IN FRONT OF THE FULL-
length mirror and adjusted his bow tie. He smiled, liking
what he saw. These days he felt an inner strength and
tranquillity in knowing he was in complete control of his
own destiny. He flicked a speck of dust off the shiny silk
lapel of his dinner jacket.

Looking back, he had to admit that his career had gone
exceptionally well. He was intelligent and ambitious and
had used both traits well to build up his power base. But,
despite appearances, he was still very much a loner. His
only true friends were his three dogs. Animals understood
him. They asked nothing of him other than to provide
them with food and shelter and, in return, granted him
obedience and loyalty. Humans were different. Too many
of them failed in life because they allowed emotions to
cloud their judgement. To him, traits such as compassion
and empathy served no purpose when it came to survival
of the species. Sure, altruism could be found among many
creatures, like bees and termites, but that was simple kin
selection: ensuring the propagation of an individual's

genes by helping those closest to it genetically to survive. But human culture had tried to push this idea too far. And that was always going to be its downfall. Selflessness was overrated.

By any measure, his career in politics had been meteoric. After graduating from the University of Notre Dame back in '26 he'd started out by serving on the Indiana State Election Board before working as an attorney in practice, mainly dealing with environmental cases pushing for the closure of the State's remaining coal-fired power plants, the last of which shut its gates in '34. He ran for the US Senate as a Democrat in '37 on an anti-corruption ticket, sweeping to victory to become the youngest member of Congress at that time at the age of thirty-two.

While it seemed that just about everyone in politics now considered themselves to be an environmentalist, they had different ways of showing it. In a state like Indiana, which along with West Virginia had been at the bottom of the Green League Table of America for many years, standing for election as a champion of the environment was now a good political move. But Peter Hogan was smart enough to know that he could not reveal his true feelings. A passion to protect the biosphere from further destruction by humankind was one thing, but to let slip his contempt for humanity itself would not have been a particularly wise move. Instead, he made sure that his green credentials were just what the administration, desperate for allies in Congress, were looking for: someone who could help lift the country out of the doldrums after the failure of The Walls project, which of course he had opposed from the outset. That two-trillion-dollar, overly ambitious scheme to build five-metre-high sea walls to protect the country's coastal cities was doomed before it got started. He had spoken out vociferously against it, when other politicians saw it as the only solution. Now, of course, southern states such as Louisiana and Mississippi were bankrupt and unable to fund their huge repopulation programmes to deal with the displaced inhabitants of lost coastal cities like New Orleans and Gulfport.

People who had never met him thought Hogan came across as charming; smart and ambitious, but likeable and warm. Those who did know him would have agreed with the first three attributes but would have struggled to apply the last two to him. Senator Peter Hogan was anything but likeable and warm.

In recent months, he'd felt particularly good about life. In fact, the charm button was so much easier to switch on now that the fate of humankind was sealed. It would certainly serve no purpose for the public to know the truth about the dying magnetic field. What would be the point of panicking billions of people? After all, nothing could be done about it now. Far better for everyone if the world remained in its innocent ignorant slumber, hoping as always that things would eventually turn out for the best.

Well, amen to that.

He left the bedroom and walked downstairs, checking the time as he went: seven-fifteen. Time to leave. He didn't like to be too late, but always enjoyed a grand entrance. He uttered a command as he entered the kitchen and the French windows slid silently open. His dogs, who had been sitting patiently out on the patio, ran in. They were hungry.

As he walked out of the front door of his luxury apartment, just ten minutes' walk away from Ambassador Xu's mansion, his wristpad buzzed. It was Gabriel Aguda. The man looked highly agitated.

22

DESPITE THE CHILL, MARC WAS FEELING UNCOMFORT-ably warm under the tightly buttoned collar of his dress shirt as he walked up the mansion steps with Qiang. He'd struggled to find a dinner jacket at short notice and had ended up borrowing the whole outfit from a former Columbia University colleague. Now he wished he'd just worn the old grey suit he'd packed back in Auckland. After all, he wasn't planning on impressing anyone this evening.

Qiang also appeared out of place and awkward, despite looking the part, complete with a resplendent bright red bow tie. The Chinese physicist must have seen the amused look on his face.

'I really do prefer the familiarity of a traditional scientific conference dinner, you know, where all I have to do to smarten up is to put on a jacket and tie—'

'—Yup, preferably one with a science-themed image on it, like a Feynman diagram or the periodic table,' laughed Marc.

Qiang nodded in fake seriousness. 'That's the beauty

of ties like that, they're so terrible, they go with whatever shirt you've been wearing during the day.'

They joined the throng of well-heeled guests arriving at the reception, all of whom seemed to exude that same casual air of confidence and entitlement that always marked out the wealthy and powerful.

The Chinese ambassador's mansion was an impressive building. Technically a townhouse, it had been built in 1911 in neo-French Renaissance style by an American billionaire whose family had finally sold it to the Chinese government ten years ago, just one example of so much of America's prime real estate these days that was now owned by the East. Its imposing steps led up to the main entrance, where an equally imposing doorway was set back from a stone arch. Spotlights high on the roof of the building bathed everything in an insipid bluish hue.

Marc and Qiang presented themselves for retinal scans by the two muscle mountains at the door and then had to pass through a security scanner. Once inside the ornately decorated grand hallway they were accosted by half a dozen bots carrying trays of drinks. Picking up a glass of champagne, Marc surveyed his surroundings. His eyes were first drawn to the fabulously colourful floor, which was covered in beautiful and intricate mosaic tiles. All around him were symbols of wealth and power. There was also no shortage of antique Chinese art on show: colourful Qing Dynasty paintings, Ming vases on pedestals and glazed ceramics of Chinese warriors on horseback. All this ostentation made Marc feel angry, although he couldn't figure out why.

He looked over to see Qiang already chatting to several other guests. Marc knew the protocol at occasions such as these. He would be expected to use face-recognition software in his retinal AR to find people he should be introducing himself to and, glancing around, he was amused to see that most people were doing just that. With a tinge of nostalgia, he thought back to the time, not so many years ago, when you could walk up to a stranger at a party and ask them how they knew the host or what they did for a living. Better still, if conference delegates were wearing name tags, you could try to sneak a glance down at it without appearing to break eye contact with the person, especially if you felt it was someone you should know. He had a secret and reluctant admiration for the younger generation, for whom the skill of simultaneously scanning their AR while seemingly engaging directly with the person in front of them came so naturally.

Qiang must have noticed him watching and walked over. Marc put his hand on the younger man's shoulder. 'It's OK, you know. You go and do the necessary schmoozing. Just don't leave me alone all evening – I haven't got to perform any social niceties at this party, but don't forget I am supposed to be your date for the night.' Qiang grinned and wandered off into the main reception room where most of the guests were gathering.

Marc wandered over to one of the pictures on the wall to take a closer look. It depicted a Chinese man sitting at the base of a crooked tree. He guessed it was an original and probably worth a fortune. His thoughts drifted back to his afternoon with Evie and how long it would take to fix their relationship. Still feeling flat, he strolled among the guests. Everywhere he heard the usual sycophantic and nauseatingly forced greetings and exchanges of pleasantries – always necessary to establish the social order at such occasions. But apart from the odd polite nod or smile from a few guests who either didn't know who he was or didn't feel inclined to chat to him, he was invisible. He maintained a faint smile frozen on his face that, he hoped, gave him the air of someone at ease with his surroundings and who attended such functions all the time. And he hated himself for doing it.

One or two of the guests were now starting to raise their voices in more animated conversation and a number of them were standing still to focus on their AR feeds. Was some piece of news breaking?

He decided he wasn't interested enough to check right now and drifted back outside to get some fresh air. As he stood at the top of the steps, a limo pulled up with another VIP guest. An elegantly dressed woman in a knee-length black cocktail dress got out. She was carrying her coat over her arm, clearly not feeling the cold. Her blonde shoulder-length hair looked silvery under the building spotlights. She was surrounded by a flurry of tiny skeeter drones hovering over her head, mechanical dragonflies recording her every move and presumably beaming their feed to news networks. Marc watched as several security guards ushered her quickly up the steps towards him. She looked vaguely familiar, but he couldn't quite place her. Was she an internet star? A politician? There was something about her body language and defiant expression, however, that didn't quite fit. She gave off a sense of aloofness that was less self-importance, and more nervous resolve.

As she reached the top of the stairs she passed within a metre of where he was standing, and he saw a steeliness to her posture – her head held high. She had been looking straight ahead, not speaking, not smiling, but for the briefest of moments, their eyes met. It seemed to Marc to last an embarrassingly long time but couldn't have been more than a second. She had a glazed look suggesting her thoughts were very far from her immediate surroundings.

After she was swept inside, he followed her back in, just

catching her being led up the grand staircase, which had only a few minutes earlier been roped off. Many of the guests around him were now talking in excited voices and Marc tapped a passing man's shoulder. The man turned, his eyes clearly more than half focused on his AR feed.

'Sorry, but could you tell me what's going on? Who is this woman?'

'Check your feed, pal. That's Sarah Maitlin, one of the scientists involved in some scandal.'

At first, it didn't register, but then it hit him. Of course! She was the British scientist who'd been in the news a couple of weeks ago talking about the geomagnetic storm. But what was she doing at a reception held by the Chinese ambassador to the United States? And why was she the belle of the ball? Surely her media appearances hadn't earned her such A-lister status? And anyway, what fucking scandal?

He walked into the main reception room, where he spotted Qiang in conversation with an elderly couple on the far side. His friend broke off when Marc approached, and introduced the pair as the Portuguese ambassador and her husband. They nodded to Marc but were clearly not in the mood for small talk.

Qiang sounded agitated and excited. He'd already removed his bow tie, as though whatever was now unfolding trumped any pretence of the formal occasion this was meant to be. 'Have you been following the news, Marc? If true, this is huge.'

'What? You mean in the few minutes since I last spoke to you? No, of course I've bloody not. I've been too preoccupied wondering why I am the only bloody person here who seems to be clueless.'

He watched as Qiang pulled out and unfolded a plastic e-pad and activated it with his wristpad. He moved his fingers over it and brought up a live news feed, then passed it to Marc. At the bottom of the screen, alongside the words 'Breaking News', was the scrolling headline:

*SECRET FILES REVEAL STARTLING COVER-UP.
IS THE EARTH'S MAGNETIC FIELD DYING?
HAS THERE BEEN A CONSPIRACY TO HIDE THE TRUTH?
NEURAL NETS REVEAL AUTHENTICITY OF SCIENTISTS AT CENTRE OF SCANDAL.*

The footage was of Sarah Maitlin in an online video chat with a man, and they were arguing about what to do with new revelations about the Earth's magnetic field. Marc noticed that Sarah was wearing the dress he'd just seen her in, so this footage must have been from earlier this evening.

It was followed by live footage of a reporter standing outside the Plaza Hotel in downtown Manhattan talking excitedly about a cyberterrorist group that had obtained top-secret files containing highly sensitive information. He claimed this group's plot had been foiled and arrests had been made.

On the one hand, this sort of thing wasn't unusual; the networks supplied a steady stream of conspiracy stories and devastating cyber threats, but this time it seemed different, as though people could sense this was the real deal. As far as Marc could tell, as he quickly tapped and scanned his way through various news outlets on Qiang's e-pad, it appeared that Sarah Maitlin had been at the Plaza Hotel too, but it wasn't clear what her connection was. The reporter he'd seen first had claimed that she was some sort of whistle-blower, a hero, but there were other reports that she was in fact part of the cyberterrorist cell itself. Marc tried to dismiss all this speculation as the sort of rubbish that news networks would come out with at the start of a breaking story, in the frenetic skirmish to secure the lead coverage spot, with the billions of advertising revenue that would bring. At this very moment, network producers were probably frantically talking to their bosses, who were talking to their lawyers about what their position should be. After all, everyone in the news had to be either hero or villain. It didn't really matter which, as long as a choice was made quickly.

Marc was aware that all around him the sound of conversation was dropping away as more people stood around like zombies reading their feeds.

He exchanged a look with Qiang. If this was true and the Earth's magnetic field really was dying, then the cover-up was far worse than the prospect of a mere *delay* to the Flip that Qiang had been so concerned about during their conversation in Princeton two days earlier. Marc turned to the Portuguese ambassador, who had just finished speaking on her phone in a low, urgent voice. 'Is there any more you can tell us, Madam Ambassador? The news seems pretty confused right now.'

'I'm afraid we are all confused, Professor Bruckner. In fact, I'm needed back in my Washington office immediately.' She turned to speak to her husband and they both excused themselves and left. The room did indeed look like it was thinning out as politicians and dignitaries were recalled to their posts to deal with the inevitable shit-storm. Perhaps he and Qiang ought to be taking their idea a little more seriously. Perhaps, despite the utter outlandishness of the very notion of firing beams of dark matter into the Earth's core, it might turn out to be the only way to save the planet.

23

Monday, 11 February – New York

THE YOUNG WOMAN IN THE SMART BLUE SUIT WHO HAD
met Sarah at the entrance of the ambassador's residence
had insisted she follow her upstairs to a private conference room immediately. She had said it was for Sarah's
own safety, given the 'sensitivity of the current situation'.
Sarah's first instinct was to turn and run, but where
would she go? Who could she turn to for help or moral
support? She thought about asking for a lawyer to be
present, but decided she would just have to cope with
whatever was coming. After all, what could they possibly
do to her? She had done nothing wrong.

She was led into an empty conference room on the
second floor of the residence. The woman walked half a
pace ahead of her and didn't speak a word. Instead she
exuded cold efficiency. Was she embassy staff, FBI, Home-
land Security or something more sinister? The room Sarah
entered was cavernous and felt somewhat out of place in a
large stately home like this. It exuded power and efficiency,
less of a traditional boardroom and more of a high-tech
command centre, similar to the room at the UN where she

had first met Hogan and his committee, but larger and with portraits of important-looking figures in a range of power-stance poses adorning the walls. An interactive conference table took up more than half the room. She guessed it would normally have been lit up with an array of vid displays, e-docs and overlaying colourful graphics, but its graphene coating was now jet black. The woman pulled out a chair and gestured to her to sit down. 'Can I get you a drink, Dr Maitlin?'

'A glass of water, please.' She hoped her voice didn't betray the nervousness she was feeling. It felt like she was back at school and being hauled into the head's office for a reprimand. The woman went over to the sideboard. Sarah heard the chink of ice in a glass and moments later was handed her drink in silence. 'Thank you,' she said.

'Please wait here. Someone will be along shortly.'

The woman then turned and walked briskly out of the room, closing the door softly behind her.

Well, so much for the new cocktail dress. This is turning into one fun party. Sarah couldn't have felt more inappropriately dressed had she turned up at a funeral in a clown's outfit. She checked the time. It was seven-thirty – probably long enough for the world's media to have gone into meltdown over the satellite data revelations. Or maybe not. Maybe whoever had been behind burying this in the first place was also more than capable of putting a new spin on it, or even discrediting it. She took a deep breath to calm her nerves and wondered who she would be meeting. Was this to be a discussion among equals or were they going to blame her for the leak?

After a few minutes alone with her thoughts, she summoned up the courage to check her feed. Sure enough, all across the net no one was talking about anything else. Some commentators were claiming that this was the biggest international cover-up since the Vatican scandal of 2029. And Dr Sarah Maitlin was the main protagonist in this drama. Just fucking great.

It seemed like an age before the door to the conference room finally opened and two men walked in: Senator Hogan and the party host, Ambassador Xu. There was no sign of Aguda. Whatever was going on, this meeting was clearly meant to be far from the ears and eyes of journalists and other politicians.

So, what was this going to be? A debriefing or an interrogation?

Hogan paused and looked across the table, before sitting down. 'Good evening, Sarah.' The intensity of his reptilian stare made her skin crawl and it took every bit of her will-power to meet his gaze, but she was determined not to be cowed by him. When he spoke, his voice was flat and toneless, his tight grin more a rictus than a smile. 'It would appear that we have something of a crisis on our hands.'

She decided to say nothing for now. *Let's see how this plays out.* Hogan certainly didn't look like a man who'd just discovered that the world was about to end. Nor indeed did Xu Furong, whose face betrayed no emotion whatsoever. Like Hogan, his eyes never left Sarah. If they were deliberately trying to intimidate her, they were wasting their time.

After a pause, it was the ambassador who broke the silence. He spoke in perfect English. 'We are giving you the benefit of the doubt in assuming that it wasn't you who deliberately recorded and transmitted your conversation with Gabriel a few minutes ago.'

Sarah frowned, suddenly realizing how that might be one interpretation. 'Of course you bloody assume correctly. If I had wanted it leaked I'd have done it myself. I chose to speak with Aguda first because . . . well, because I needed to know the truth for certain before the rest of the world did.'

Hogan raised a hand towards the ambassador and smiled. 'Come on, Furong, we know full well that Dr Maitlin didn't do this. Besides, it will be easy enough to see if there was any spyware downloaded with the files placed there by the cyb.' He turned to smile at Sarah again. 'Something this big, this, ah, *scandalous* – the cyb couldn't possibly take the chance that you might betray her, and so it appears she's dropped you in it. And I have to say that Gabriel doesn't come out smelling of roses.'

The ambassador stared at Sarah, stone-faced.

Hogan continued. 'Still, Dr Maitlin the scientist, the seeker of truth and objectivity, not corrupted by the lies and deceits of the world of politics like the rest of us – you must surely be quietly relieved by this outcome. After all, the secret is out, and you presumably see yourself as playing the role of an innocent and blameless participant – the hero, even.'

The sarcasm in his voice was nauseating and she glared at him. So this was how it was going to be, was it? His tone suggested that Hogan most certainly did not see her as an innocent and blameless participant. He sat back in his chair. Was he deliberately trying to goad her?

She tried hard to keep her voice steady as she spoke through gritted teeth. 'Are you accusing me of wrongdoing, Senator? Seriously? You invite me onto your committee to provide my scientific expertise, and for what? This whole business has been a sham from the start. I'm the one to demand answers here, not you two. And where the hell is Aguda?'

'Gabriel will be joining us shortly. He's currently engaged elsewhere. In fact,' added Hogan, 'we are all going to be rather busy tonight, as you can imagine. Of course, we hope to count on you too.'

'What? You expect me to cooperate with you? To smooth this over? Damn it, we've been discussing recommendations to world governments about how to cope with potential CMEs *until the Earth recovers*, and yet it seems you knew the whole situation was futile? Tell me which bit I've got wrong.' Anger and indignation welled up inside her, threatening to overflow.

Then she added, before either man could respond, 'And in any case, just so we're clear, this is absolutely *not* about me. You're damn right I've done nothing wrong. But you . . . I mean, how dare you fabricate scientific data and lie to the world? And just how far does this lie stretch? What else are you hiding?'

'Oh, come on, Sarah,' said Hogan. He sounded almost amused by her outburst. 'I gave you more credit than that. Firstly, yes, of course we knew. But, you're playing in the grown-up world now, so save that touching moral outrage of yours for your pathetic world of liberal academia.'

Sarah felt an overwhelming urge to reach across and punch his conceited, supercilious face, but instead she sat back in her chair and closed her eyes. Her opportunity would come, she was sure of it.

Hogan lowered his voice and spoke softly. 'Listen to me carefully, Sarah. You are going to help us put this mess right. You're smart, and so I have no doubt that you will understand what I have to say. There are people around the world, people in positions of stupendous power, working within, and even above, world governments, who have been trying to ensure that nine billion people don't descend into collective mass hysteria. Tell me, what did you expect to happen – what is no doubt already happening – when those nine billion people found out what was being kept from them? That before this century is halfway through, the Earth will witness the fastest and most dramatic mass extinction since life first began four billion years ago? Please, do tell me what you expected them to do? At this very moment, I predict there will be potentially hundreds of extremist groups and cults springing up and promoting their own version of how to avoid the apocalypse or how to punish the authorities for bringing it on.'

Xu added, 'Not to mention how this news will be received by the Purifiers. If they are persuaded that the Sun is taking care of things for them, they may lose their *raison d'être*. On the other hand, this might embolden them and things could get far worse.'

Like most people, Sarah was familiar with the terrorist organization generally known as the Purifiers, although many people still referred to them by their original Arabic name of Almutahirun. In their basic ideology they were not so different from many other radical groups and end-of-days cults that had come and gone since the dawn of civilization, inasmuch as their central message was beautifully simple: humankind was destroying the planet, and the world was approaching *Yawm ad-Dīn* (the Day of Judgement) and *Yawm al-Qiyāmah* (the Day of Resurrection). Many world religions shared this belief that there would be a final assessment of humanity by God, which would begin with the annihilation of all life, followed by resurrection and judgement. But the Purifiers were impatient. They believed their role was to hasten the arrival of the Day of Judgement by whatever means necessary. The revelations about the Earth's magnetic field would only lend strength to their cause. Sarah wondered whether it would give them fresh impetus. Would they want to find some way to hurry things along? After all, their fatalistic philosophy was based on all hope in this

207

life being abandoned and instead looking to a plentiful afterlife that awaited the faithful.

Hogan's cold voice cut through her thoughts. 'So, I guess we now need to know. Can we still count on you?'

'*Count* on me?' she burst out. 'To do what, exactly?'

As she was debating whether she could trust any answer Hogan gave, he leaned forward across the table, his arms folded, and rested his chin on them. 'To clear up this mess you've been duped into creating, of course. Jesus, Sarah, are you really so naive?' He turned to Xu and gave him a quick look, which was meant to be one of innocent exasperation. He sighed, then said, 'OK, Sarah, you ask us what the truth of the situation is. Well, here's the truth. Yes, of course a plan to save the planet is in place.'

She noted that his demeanour had now changed to one of intense sincerity, like a parent dishing out important advice to an errant child, something he must have practised on the campaign trail to get elected to the Senate. 'We still want you to be part of that plan, Sarah.'

Again, he held her gaze for a few seconds before releasing her from his hypnotic stare. He sat back in his chair and, again, his personality switched. This time the chill was back in his voice. 'In return, you are going to help us clean up this mess. You see, between us, we will be going on a charm offensive to try to calm the world down. There will no doubt be unrest. Some governments that are, shall we say, less than well prepared will topple. And yes, people are going to die. Our job now is to sell a prettier, more optimistic future to the media, to calm nerves and to play down the consequences. People across the globe are going to need time to digest this. And they will be looking to those of us in charge to tell them everything will be OK. A statement is being carefully prepared as we speak.'

He paused to let his words sink in. Then, 'Of course, it

will naturally be more convincing coming from you. You will see that what is being developed is a quite ambitious rescue plan – one that would benefit from your expertise as a solar physicist. It goes without saying that you don't have to agree to this. So, we'll give you a minute or two to think the matter over.'

But Sarah knew she wasn't going to get the chance to mull it over, sleep on it or 'phone a friend', as her mother was fond of saying. In the end, her cold rationalism and survival instincts took over. Maybe she could be of more use working on the inside. Hogan was almost certainly right about the mass hysteria these revelations would now cause. He might be a cold-hearted bastard, driven by blind political ambition, but he certainly wasn't stupid. In the end none of these ethical questions were what decided it for her – it was her elemental scientific curiosity about the plan Hogan had hinted at. But she couldn't admit to that. It would be as though she had just rolled over and surrendered to these two bullies, and she was still angry at their arrogance. Suddenly, she saw a faint glimmer of salvation and clutched at it with the desperation of a drowning person grasping a lifebelt. 'OK, but on one condition.'

Hogan snorted in amusement. 'Bless you. Did you really think you were in a position to barter?'

Xu raised a hand. 'Wait a minute, Senator. I'm intrigued. Please continue, Dr Maitlin.'

Sarah sat upright and stared Hogan in the eye, hoping that she sounded and looked braver than she felt. 'The young cyb, Shireen – she was only doing what she believed was the right thing to do – and, for what it's worth, what I still believe was the right thing to do. I assume you have her in custody. I want her released, and all charges against her dropped.'

Hogan's laugh was that of someone who'd never in his life found anything funny. It was cold and unnervingly high-pitched, like the bark of a fox.

'I can see why that would play on your conscience. Again, you're not thinking this through. This cyb is going to be hailed as a hero. We wouldn't be able to keep her locked away for long anyway. So, yes, that sounds like a reasonable request, especially if you feel it will buy your redemption . . .' He laughed again, then sat back and kicked his chair away from the table. 'Well, we have work to do, don't we?' He pinched his thumb and forefinger together to activate a nano-mike on his nail, which he spoke into. 'Gabriel, you should join us.'

A few seconds later, Aguda came into the room, followed by the young woman Sarah had seen earlier and several other aides who had been waiting outside.

Sarah and the Nigerian geologist exchanged a glance. She didn't know what to say. She just knew she could never trust him again.

24

Saturday, 16 February – New York

SARAH STARED OUT OF THE WINDOW OF THE FBI LILIUM E-Jet as it came in to land at JFK. Across the aisle from her, Shireen had been sleeping soundly for the duration of the one-hour flight from DC. A few minutes earlier Sarah had needed to pull down her blind to block out the bright mid-morning sun as the aircraft banked at the start of its descent. But, now that it had dropped down through the thick grey cloud cover, the scene outside, and her mood, suddenly turned gloomier. She was looking across to where the Manhattan skyline should have been visible in the distance. Instead, she was greeted by a thick blanket of falling snow that dramatically reduced visibility.

She wondered what the weather was like in Rio, realizing how desperate she was to get back to the Institute and her research.

It had been a week during which her life had been turned upside down: not content with finding out that the fate of humanity hung in the balance, she'd had to make a public statement, with Aguda by her side, aimed at calming the nerves of billions of people around the

211

world. Governments in many countries had put their military on high alert, but that hadn't prevented the inevitable unrest and widespread rioting that had broken out. There'd been a large number of deaths reported in both Nairobi and Istanbul and huge demonstrations in most large cities. People were demanding to know what was being done to avert catastrophe. And Sarah felt personally responsible. Maybe Hogan had been right – wouldn't it have been better for the world to have remained in blissful ignorance of its fate? She looked over at the sleeping Iranian cyb. *You thought you were doing the right thing, didn't you? Well, for better or worse, it's out now.*

Sarah didn't blame Shireen for transmitting her conversation with Aguda to the world. She understood the girl's motives. But then Shireen wasn't the one who'd been getting death threats. Sarah had been shocked to the core by the first one she'd received, less than two hours after her broadcast statement late Monday evening. Someone had managed to hack through her security firewall to send her a colourful personal message about what they would do to her. And while she had immediately demanded heightened security, it hadn't prevented several other nasty threats getting through in the following couple of days. Thankfully, they seemed to have stopped now.

There had been frantic debates among world leaders as to whether they should continue to deny the truth – in fact, the official news networks in some countries were still maintaining the whole thing was fake. But from what Sarah had managed to learn from Aguda and Hogan, and to pick up on the more in-depth newscasts, most governments now knew that the genie was out of the bottle. Researchers in South America and Australia were analysing data from independent satellites over the

212

South Pacific, confirming the continuing weakening of the magnetic field.

But over the past few days she'd had bigger issues on her mind than the leaked documents or her own safety. Her thoughts drifted back to the 'rescue' plan she was now a part of. Now that the world knew about the dying field, the authorities saw no reason to keep their mission to save the world a secret either. Indeed, it was now vital that the public had some hope to cling to. The plan was audacious in scope.

The ambitious idea, as first explained to her by Aguda, was to perfect the design of a giant magnetic pulse device that could generate a powerful magnetic punch, strong enough to block a coronal ejection. Aguda had given her the MPD report and had even asked her to comment on it.

The following day she'd met up with him in his UN office. She had expected the atmosphere to be frosty when she walked in and had been taken aback by Aguda's friendly demeanour.

'Ah, Sarah, good morning. Please come in.'

She'd tried to clear her head of the multitude of emotions still swirling around: exhaustion from lack of sleep, worry about the ramifications of the Pandora's box she had played a part in opening, anger at Aguda for keeping the truth from her, and above all a deep-seated feeling of foreboding about the fate of the world. She had nevertheless tried hard to be professional and objective. He had been sitting behind a desk so impressive it made even his frame seem diminutive.

'I know I'm coming to this late, Gabriel, but I've read the report and, well, I just don't see how the sums stack up.'

Aguda had nodded sagely. Was this still an act, or could she finally trust him? 'I know it seems preposterous. But I'm proud of the progress that we've made so far,

213

and I think you will be too when you see more. As you will have seen in that report, work on the device is already advancing on several fronts.'

'By "several fronts" I suppose you mean where it would be built.'

'Yes, that's still the main sticking point. There's still no agreement on whether it should be based on Earth or in space, or whether it would be one device, or many scattered around the globe.'

'And is that a technical or an economic issue?' she'd asked, certain that no one could possibly be thinking about putting a price on the only hope to save humankind.

'Oh, it's definitely the engineering challenges that are proving the issue. You see, while I'm personally against it, the front runner for a working MPD is to build it in space.'

'But the report says nothing about *how* we get the components for such a large structure out to . . .'

'. . . four times the distance to the Moon and then assembling and testing it there, all in the space of a year. Exactly.' Aguda sat back, as though pleased that he had an ally. 'It's technologically possible, of course,' he continued. 'The best suggestion seems to be to get the components to the Moon in multiple trips and then assemble most of them at the Chinese moonbase, which has the necessary construction equipment and heavy industry already in place from their mining operation.'

Sarah had been astonished by the sheer scale of the proposal. 'So, why not just build an Earth-based device?'

'Oh, a number of countries are pushing for this, believe me. The problem here is that the magnetic pulses they would be aiming out into space would damage any satellites flying overhead at the time.'

Sarah felt she didn't know enough about the technical

specifications yet to comment on this. But, 'Surely knocking out a few satellites is the least of our problems?'

Aguda said nothing.

This had been the point when Sarah had voiced her central misgivings about the entire plan. No one appreciated the sheer strength of the punch that a massive coronal mass ejection could deliver better than she did. Were they really naive enough to think they could stop one?

'I know you aren't expecting me to comment on the engineering challenges. But I simply don't believe the basic physics.'

'Well, Sarah, this is something we do need your input on. The computer simulations that have been run so far suggest that if a magnetic pulse powerful enough and timed just right could be aimed at an incoming CME then it could slow it down, and even disperse it.'

Sarah shook her head in frustration. 'But that's not the issue. Your scenario will only work if the CME is moving in a straight line from the Sun, but if it spirals in from a slight angle, as it can do, then an e.m. pulse would be much less effective.'

Deep down she felt the whole enterprise was futile. Defending Earth against a really powerful CME with electromagnetic pulses would be like standing in torrential rain and trying to stay dry under a cocktail-stick umbrella.

The CME that caused the great solar storm of 1859 or the near miss of 2012, which – had it been ejected nine days earlier – would have met the Earth full on, frying the world's electronics and bringing much of human civilization to a halt, would both, if they struck today, be catastrophic. With the magnetosphere in its current sorry state, civilization on Earth wouldn't stand a chance.

Yet no one seemed to want to listen to her. Over the following days she had tried to get this point across, but there seemed to be no political will to take her warnings seriously, while the scientists and engineers working on the project were too busy trying to solve the thousand and one other technical problems they were facing. No one wanted to accept that the plan was doomed to failure from the outset.

What no one wanted to admit either was that dealing with CMEs was just the start. Even if this particular threat could be averted, it didn't stop the slow but constant bombardment of the atmosphere by cosmic-ray particles from deep space, coming from all directions, which would inexorably erode the atmosphere until the Earth eventually resembled its sister planet Mars: dead and lifeless. With no atmosphere, even the oceans would quickly evaporate. Apparently, that was a longer-term problem to worry about at a later date.

Her thoughts were now interrupted as Shireen stirred and opened her eyes. She looked a little embarrassed and self-conscious at having slept through the flight. Even though they had only met on three occasions, the two women had begun to develop a mutual bond, born out of a sense of 'us against the world'. Sarah was still impressed with the cyb's strength of character and unbending, principled determination, which had made her feel even more wretched about the way she had folded so compliantly to Hogan and Xu's demands.

Shireen had spent the past few days at a facility outside Washington, DC, run by the National Security Branch of the FBI. She had initially been questioned about her Trojan horse code, so they could shore up security loopholes before cyberhackers unearthed any more awkward revelations. Sarah had persuaded her to tell them everything as a condition for her release, and Shireen hadn't needed too much convincing. She seemed genuinely proud of what she had accomplished, and her main concern now seemed to be ensuring her parents' safety back in Iran. On some level, she even appeared to enjoy the admiration of her interrogators – one of them, a nerdy computer scientist, had been unable to hide his approbation.

Sarah had been relieved to hear that Shireen was to be released without charge and that while she wouldn't be able to fly back to Tehran just yet, she could at least come and go as she pleased. Shireen had requested that she be released into Sarah's care for the time being.

Shireen grinned at Sarah and she smiled back weakly, not that she had much to smile about at the moment.

25

DESPITE FRANK EGELHOF'S EXHAUSTION, HIS MIND WAS buzzing. It was late. Had his simulation not just finished running he'd have called it a night anyway. The drive home from the Max Planck Computing and Data Facility would probably take a further hour, even around the A99 Munich ring road. At least the traffic would be relatively light on a Saturday evening.

The computer simulations of the magnetic pulse device he'd been working on for the past seven weeks were finally running reliably, and his results looked conclusive. He was one of a number of scientists at the Max Planck involved with the MPD project, but his simulations were bound by a level of secrecy above those of his colleagues, a situation he found exhausting. He hated that he couldn't even talk about it to his wife, Rachel. But he could see why this was necessary – his job was to determine whether the space-based device was even feasible in principle, and there were, as far as he could tell, a lot of political careers, scientific reputations and investors' fortunes riding on his results. Removing his glasses, he stood and rubbed his eyes. He only used the glasses for desk work and didn't feel the need to have the routine surgery. Besides, he was very squeamish about that sort of thing.

He tapped the plasma screen to black and walked out of his office, remembering to touch the thumb pad on the handle; hearing the reassuring click of the lock, he wandered off down the corridor to the bathroom. Even though it was the weekend and very few people were around, particularly this late in the evening, he couldn't be too careful with security.

For days, he'd been hoping against hope that his results wouldn't confirm what he had suspected deep down all along. But finally he knew the project was doomed to failure. He'd had his doubts from the beginning but hadn't been allowed to voice them. Now he just felt flat. Of course, his paymasters still wouldn't want to hear what he had to tell them, but what could he do? His simulations were unequivocal. More than ever, he was aware of the need for discretion – bad enough that the world knew that the magnetic field was dying, but how much worse would things be if people were told that one of the two hyped plans to avert disaster wouldn't work? He just prayed that the Earth-based MPD project was still a viable alternative to the one he'd been working on.

The basic physics behind the project was simple enough, and on paper it had initially looked to Frank like it might actually work: gigantic toroidal superconducting magnets out in space that would send out intense electromagnetic pulses timed to meet any incoming coronal mass ejections and deflect them, just as the Earth's natural magnetic field had done for billions of years. The advantages of having the device in space were clear, and putting it at the first Lagrange point made obvious sense.

Situated a million miles from Earth on a straight line

between the Earth and the Sun, the L1 point has a very special geometric property. Normally, any body closer to the Sun than the Earth would orbit it faster – basic Newtonian dynamics – but this ignores the effect of the Earth's own gravity. If the body is sitting directly between the Earth and the Sun, then the Earth's gravitational pull in the opposite direction weakens the Sun's attraction on the body and so slows down its orbital speed. At the L1 point, the orbital period of the body exactly matches that of the Earth and so it remains always sitting on the direct line between the Earth and the Sun throughout the orbit.

Placing the MPD at the L1 point would mean it provided a permanent protective shield for any incoming CMEs from the Sun. It also had the added advantage over an Earth-based MPD that its magnetic pulses would always be directed away from the Earth so would not damage any Earth-orbiting satellites.

His computer models were meant to show the effects of bombardment of cosmic radiation on the ceramic material of the superconducting magnets, and it didn't look good. It was a catch-22 situation. Without substantial shielding, the magnets wouldn't survive very long in the harsh environment of the solar wind. But the necessary protective shielding would itself then prevent the magnetic pulses from getting out with sufficient strength to stop an incoming CME. Basically, the device wouldn't work out in space, and that was that.

Hurrying down the flight of stairs, he looked forward to getting home. When he returned to his office he would have to send a secure email to his bosses with these latest results, then encrypt all his codes and output data files before he could leave for the night. He was one of a team of twenty computer scientists working on the MPD simulations, but right now it seemed he was the only one still in the building after 9 p.m. on a Saturday. He wondered whether Rachel would be asleep when he got home. She had been very patient with him these past few weeks as he spent increasingly long hours at work. He pushed open the door to the bathroom and walked in as the lights flicked on. The place smelled of disinfectant and was sparklingly clean. The evening janitor bots must have just finished their cleaning round.

Despite the quietness of the building, he didn't hear the man who had followed him in until it was too late. He'd unbuttoned his flies by the urinal and begun relieving himself when he was suddenly aware of a shuffle of footsteps behind him. Surprised, he turned his head to look and in so doing ensured that the first bullet entered his right cheek, exiting the front of his face and leaving behind the remains of what used to be his nose and jaw. Egelhof fell back against the urinal, gurgling with pain as blood filled his throat. This was cut short by another bullet, which passed through his left eye and into his brain. The third bullet to his head as he fell was unnecessary. He crumpled to the ground in a pool of blood and piss. The sounds of his brief cry and the three silenced gunshots were heard by no one else.

The simple message scrawled on the note that was then pinned to his body, and which was found by the security guard doing his rounds later that evening, was a mix of English and German:

Delaying the inevitable is pointless.
Die Welt wird der Menschheit gereinigt werden.
The Purifiers.
[Delaying the inevitable is pointless. The world will be cleansed of the human disease.]

It is one of those sad ironies that had the assassin waited just another twenty-four hours, his own sources would have been able to inform him that there was no need for this mission to sabotage humanity's last chance of survival – that neither Frank Egelhof nor the MPD project posed any threat to their dream of letting nature take its course.

The murder of a respected German computer scientist hardly made the news the following day. Besides, far more interesting to those at the top were the demoralizing revelations discovered on Frank Egelhof's computer – and these were kept quiet.

26

Monday, 18 February – New York

MARC PUSHED THE CHAIR BACK FROM THE DESK IN HIS hotel room, stood, stretched and yawned. He was in desperate need of a decent night's sleep. Evie's birthday celebrations on Friday had been a welcome distraction from the anxiety and stress that so many were feeling these days, although it was clear that everyone was putting on an act, pretending that life was continuing as normal. The afternoon had indeed seemed a little surreal at first, especially so for Marc. For a start it felt a little weird to be just another guest – along with twenty of Evie's friends, a few family friends and his ex-wife Charlotte's elderly parents – in the house he'd called home for so many years. Thankfully, Charlie had been gracious and friendly towards him and he'd even managed to have a civil conversation with her partner, Jeremy, the smarmy politician.

Most importantly, Evie had seemed genuinely pleased to see him, although he couldn't help but notice the slightly surprised look on her face when he'd walked in, as though she hadn't expected him to keep his promise and show up. At least the birthday present he'd bought her, an elegant gold locket on a chain, had been a success.

'Oh, Dad, it's beautiful.'

'I thought I wouldn't risk getting you anything techie or anything within VR as I know I'd probably get it wrong. And that's despite your mum's detailed suggestions.'

'Yes, you would definitely have screwed up. But this is lovely – real Old School.'

'I'm pleased you like it, not to say bloody relieved.'

He'd hardly had the chance to chat to Evie after that for the rest of the afternoon, but the highlight of the day had been when he was leaving, one of the last to do so: Evie had given him a tight hug and had told him she loved him. He'd walked the twenty blocks back to his hotel with a spring in his step he'd not felt for many months. All too briefly, the world seemed a little brighter. But by the time he'd reached his room the usual concerns had returned, and his thoughts drifted inevitably to the plan he and Qiang were putting together.

Qiang had arrived early the following morning and they had started their mini-research project to save the world.

Now, over forty-eight hours later, he surveyed his surroundings. The hotel room looked chaotic. The large entertainment screen occupying one wall had been turned into an interactive display with diagrams, graphs and colourful graphics packed together and overlying each other; his king-sized bed was buried under a patchwork of sheets of paper full of algebraic symbols written in his illegible scrawl. He preferred to see his calculations laid out the old-fashioned way: writing his equations down in longhand, which of course had meant finding a store that sold paper.

In the middle of the floor sat Qiang, immersed in his own calculations, wearing his VR visor and haptic gloves, manipulating virtual screens in mid-air, which he controlled with deft fingers. The two physicists had settled back into their old research routine, bouncing ideas around, each setting up hypotheses or mathematical arguments to be knocked down by the other – only this time they weren't just being driven by intellectual curiosity; this time the fate of the planet was at stake. They had spent all weekend running through their equations and computer codes, only leaving the room for food or fresh air.

Marc was relieved that Qiang hadn't needed much persuading to keep their idea a secret until they were completely satisfied it was at least scientifically feasible. But he also knew they were in a race against time, and after the most intense and sustained effort that either man had experienced in his life, their wild plan was finally coming together – maybe even getting close enough to something fully workable. But exhausting though it was, Marc was feeling invigorated by the intellectual effort he was putting into the work. And while he couldn't admit as much to Qiang, he was guiltily aware of a lightness of spirit and renewed sense of purpose he hadn't had for years, despite the magnitude of the project and the grim consequences if it failed.

He'd kept the 'Do Not Disturb' sign hanging outside his door because he didn't want any of the sheets of handwritten calculations touched until he was confident that his final numbers were correct. The previous night, after Qiang had left around midnight, he'd slept on the sofa to avoid having to disturb the bed.

Someone must have reported the three-day-long sign, however, because he'd received a visit from the hotel manager earlier in the day. He'd had to let him into the room to show him that he wasn't engaged in anything illegal and promised that it would be ready for cleaning by the following morning.

Marc knelt down beside Qiang and groaned at the stiffness in his knees. 'How's it going in there? I don't know about you, but I am ready for a coffee.'

Qiang, blind to the outside world, waved him away. 'Almost finished. I promise. I'm just recompiling this fluid-dynamics code. One of the subroutines kept returning floating point errors, but I think I've fixed it.'

Marc stood up again. He needed to get out, get some fresh air, maybe even go for a run. Above all, he needed some coffee. Things had finally calmed down on the streets of New York and the city was slowly returning to a semblance of normality after the demonstrations and riots of the previous week.

Marc wandered over to the interactive screen on the wall, pretty sure it had never been used for anything like this before. He stared at the dense combination of graphs and equations. Were they ready to unveil their scheme to the world? He hoped they wouldn't have to reopen the heated argument they'd had last night about who they would tell first.

'Marc, we have to be realistic. Why do you still have issues with approaching the Chinese?' Qiang had wanted to know.

'Come on, Qiang. It has nothing to do with that and you know it.'

'But my contacts in Shanghai recruited me to look into exactly this sort of idea. So, they are very unlikely to dismiss it out of hand.'

'I understand that, Qiang. But please, let's take things slowly. Let's see if there's even an appetite for something as outrageous as this. We need to talk to other scientists before we approach the politicians.'

'And you are convinced it has to be this Sarah Maitlin. Why? Neither of us has even met her. How do you know we can trust her?'

'I don't. But who can we really trust these days anyway?' Certainly, as a physicist, she would understand the merits of their plan and the urgency of getting it off the ground, but more crucially, of course, she was a UN insider who would know who to take it to.

'Listen, you agree that timing is crucial, right? So, I just don't think we can afford for this to go through all the levels of bureaucracy that would mean it possibly taking months before anything even gets started. No, we need a shortcut. Someone who has the ear of those who can make a fast decision.

'Why don't we at least set up a meeting with her? If she doesn't think she can fast-track this through her UN committee then it's your Shanghai boys.'

Qiang had finally been worn down rather than won over. He sighed. 'OK then, Marc, but only provided she's still in New York. We would need to meet her face to face. Any other way would be too risky at this stage.'

And so, it had been settled.

Marc wondered what Sarah thought of the MPD proposal that everyone was talking about. As far as he could see, it would, even if successful, be at best just a temporary fix – deflecting coronal mass ejections was not a permanent solution to the loss of the magnetosphere. The planet's atmosphere would continue to be gradually eroded by the solar wind. Over time, the entire biosphere would suffocate and die. No, the only hope for humanity was to kick-start the Earth's core again and bring the magnetosphere back to life.

It was then that Qiang let out a quiet whoop of triumph, snapping Marc out of his reverie. He turned back from the screen. 'OK, I'm happy with the numbers,' Qiang said, deftly touching and swiping to one side the virtual displays floating around his head, then removed his visor and gloves. He stood up, stretched his arms over his head and turned to Marc. 'It checks out, just like you predicted. Correcting for relativistic kinematics for the energy pulse in the core isn't necessary.'

Marc grinned at his friend, whose hair, following the removal of his visor, was in a state of dishevelment impressive even by his high standards. 'I fucking knew it,' he said, clenching his fist and punching the air. 'Then we're all set, right? We can't take this any further without carrying out full simulations. And we're going to need help with that.' Qiang grinned back and nodded enthusiastically. He looked tired, with dark bags under his eyes from the lack of sleep, but his eyes were shining with an inner fire.

Marc rubbed his chin, feeling the three days' growth of beard. 'I don't suppose you could do a coffee run, could you?' he asked. 'I feel I need a shave and a shower before I do anything else.'

Qiang smiled. 'Yeah, OK.' He headed for the door.

'And close the door carefully behind you. Last time it slammed, and the breeze blew a couple of pages off the bed.'

Qiang grinned and nodded slowly. When he'd gone, Marc stared down at the mass of paperwork spread out on his bed and tried to summon the energy to move to the bathroom. This was a rewarding kind of exhaustion, though, the type that followed a long and sustained period of creativity, just like the old days, when nothing got in the way of his research once he was on to something big.

He'd tried hard not to allow himself the luxury of believing their plan might actually work, but now he couldn't help but think of Evie again. Maybe this would give her back a future she probably wouldn't otherwise have.

But if he were truly honest with himself, Marc would have to admit that these past three days hadn't really been about saving the world, or even saving his daughter – but rather more selfish motives. This had always been where he felt happiest: waist-deep in mathematics. And once he was 'in the zone' the outside world faded away, leaving just him and his equations. He was in an abstract, enchanted world, rich with symbols and beautiful in its logic. The creativity he experienced at such times was not so different from that of a sculptor, poet or musician, and his sense of achievement no less than that of an explorer or mountaineer.

He began to gather the sheets of paper carefully together. *I really need to number these pages, or I'll regret it.* He thought about what he and Qiang had achieved. Strangely, the particle physics aspects, which he knew best, were the easy part. What was tricky was figuring out how to set the whole thing up: there would need to be a suite of dark-matter accelerators, all producing beams of neutralinos and firing them straight down into the ground from different locations around the globe. The mathematical problem was twofold: what was the minimum number needed and where should they be located?

Of course, whatever the answer, it would make the project stupendously expensive. Several new particle accelerators would have to be built from scratch, and ridiculously quickly. The sheer audacity of the plan made it sound crazy.

He knew the physics would work, and he knew it wouldn't take long to convince other scientists of its feasibility. The more pressing issue was whether there was the political will to do it, and to have it up and running in a matter of months.

For some reason, an image from his childhood obsession with *Star Trek* floated into his consciousness as he pictured the Starship *Enterprise* with her shields up. If they weakened, it would leave her exposed to a Klingon attack. Now, the Earth was the *Enterprise* with her shields down and the Sun was the Klingon ship waiting to strike.

Once he'd finished stacking the papers neatly on the desk, he headed for the bathroom. Staring into the mirror, it occurred to him that they needed an appropriate acronym – something the politicians and media could latch on to. After all, every great scientific project, space mission, telescope or particle accelerator had to have a name. But he felt too tired for any more creativity just now. He finished shaving and jumped in the shower, welcoming the sensation of the hot water as it washed away his aches and tiredness, only half thinking about a name for their project.

Qiang had calculated that eight different neutralino accelerators would be needed, spread across the globe, all firing their beams into the centre of the planet to deliver enough energy to set off a seismic shock wave that would kick-start the flow of the molten core. However, Marc could think of only three laboratories that could currently do that job: CERN in Switzerland, Fermilab in the US and J-PARC in Japan. Their locations were ideal, but it was almost inconceivable to think that five new accelerators could be built, in under a year. And yet it was even more inconceivable to think that humanity wouldn't come together to try.

As he stepped out of the shower it finally hit him. He

ran naked and dripping to the desk and found a pen and scrap of paper. That was it. They would call it the Odin Project.

Marc had read a lot of Germanic and Norse mythology and his favourite deity had always been the god Odin who, with his staff and broad hat, reminded Marc of Gandalf in *The Lord of the Rings*. And Odin, the god of death, knowledge and healing, was the perfect choice for an experiment that, through physics knowledge, could heal the planet and pull it back from the brink of death.

He scribbled down a list of relevant words beginning with each of the four letters and quickly came up with a winning combination: The O.D.I.N. Project would stand for Octangular Directional Ignition with Neutralinos. It was perfect.

He then scampered back to the bathroom to finish drying himself off. He didn't want to give his young friend a scare.

The one thing that Marc had only privately contemplated, and suspected Qiang had too, was the possibility that the project would go ahead, but still fail. Because there would be no second chance. For example, what happened if any one of the eight neutralino beams misfired or missed the central collision point thousands of kilometres deep within the Earth's core, even by a single millimetre? The eight beams had to come together, each from a different direction, and meet simultaneously at precisely the same point to create a burst of pure energy that would be directed around the molten core. But without this careful balancing act from their combined momentum, a shock wave would instead be sent outward towards the planet's surface. It would be like firing a bullet up at a glass roof: the Earth's crust would be shattered, bringing about the end of most life on the planet far more efficiently than the dying field could do.

The question is whether the rest of the world can be persuaded that this is a risk we have to take.

Dressed and feeling half human again, he decided to look up Sarah Maitlin while he waited for Qiang to get back. He sat down on the bed and activated his AR. It took him just a few seconds to locate her, and he sent a brief message.

> *Dr Maitlin, my name is Marc Bruckner, a particle physicist. I apologize for getting in touch with you out of the blue and hope you don't dismiss me as a nutter. Please check my academic credentials. I have strong reservations about the MPD project, and suspect you might do too, although of course I have nothing to base this on. But, there may be another solution. I think you may currently be in New York, as am I, and I wondered if you might agree to a brief meeting. Please contact me as a matter of some urgency so I can tell you a little more.*
>
> *Best wishes, Professor Marc Bruckner.*

As soon as he'd sent the message he lay back on his bed and closed his eyes.

He was awoken from sleep by his wristpad pinging. He tapped it and Sarah Maitlin's face appeared. He sat bolt upright and self-consciously rubbed his eyes. How long had he been asleep? And where was Qiang?

'Professor Bruckner, hello. You wanted to talk to me,' Sarah said in her British accent. He noticed she had activated surround block to ensure that all he saw was her face and not where she was. She looked distracted and sombre.

'Ah, Dr Maitlin. Thank you for getting back to me. I appreciate that this is all a little unconventional, but then we live in, um, interesting times.'

Sarah didn't answer, so he decided this wasn't the time for pleasantries or small talk and ploughed ahead. He hadn't rehearsed what to say and realized he needed to tread carefully, both because he didn't want to scare her off and because he didn't know who else might be listening in.

'My colleague Professor Qiang Lee and I have a scientific proposal to put to you. We feel that your research field, your public profile and your position in the UN all mean you're the ideal person to make things happen.'

'I see. Of course, firstly, let me say I know of your work, Professor Bruckner, so I'm satisfied you're genuine, despite your recent personal problems.'

So, she had checked up on him and clearly wasn't going to be pulling any punches. But then her voice softened a little. 'In fact, I attended a talk you gave on dark matter when I was a grad student in Cambridge about fifteen years ago.'

Way to go to make me feel old. 'Wow, OK, so—' He tried to recall what the occasion might have been but gave up.

'Sarah, if I may, listen, I don't want to say any more at the moment. Is it possible to meet with you in person to discuss this matter? And, yes, I know how this must sound.'

There was a pause. Then, 'OK, but give me something to go on first.'

'Well, we – that is, Qiang Lee and I – think that—'

233

Even as he searched for the words to say, he realized how ludicrous it all sounded. 'Look, I really would prefer it if you heard the details from both of us.' Then he added, 'Let's just say you can't afford *not* to hear us out.'

In his mind, Marc heard her say, *Oh, but I most certainly can, Professor Bruckner*, but she didn't. Maybe it was something in his voice she had picked up, or maybe she just sensed his desperation, because her face grew larger on the screen as she lifted her wristpad closer to it and at the same time dropped her voice a little – an interesting conspiratorial gesture, although quite pointless if anyone was indeed listening in. Then she said, 'There's a diner on the corner of Madison and East Twenty-Seventh. They do great pancakes. It'll be busy, so I can guarantee anonymity and privacy. How about tomorrow morning at eight?'

'Sounds perfect. See you tomorrow . . . And thank you.' Marc resisted the temptation to say anything else.

Her face disappeared from the screen.

Two minutes later, there was a knock on the door and he opened it to Qiang, who was holding two large paper cups of coffee.

'Ah, the wanderer returns,' he said. 'You took your time.'

'Sorry, I couldn't find anything open. It seems that with all the unrest of the past few days, a lot of the shops haven't reopened yet.'

Marc seized one of the cups from his friend and took a deep sip. It tasted wonderful, despite being only luke-warm. He wondered whether the place Sarah had suggested they meet tomorrow would also be closed. Then he realized he'd have to break the news to Qiang that he'd gone ahead and set up the meeting without consulting his friend. He decided to stall.

'So, the "Odin" Project. Whaddaya think?'

Qiang shot him a puzzled look.

'That's what we're going to call it,' said Marc, taking a second sip of coffee and wandering back to his bed. 'Oh, and we get to discuss it with Sarah Maitlin over breakfast tomorrow morning.'

27

Tuesday, 19 February – New York

QIANG LEE APPEARED LESS ENTHUSIASTIC THAN HIS older colleague about talking openly to Sarah. Maybe he was just naturally shy. At first, she thought it might be because he had reservations about their audacious plan, but soon realized he was just uneasy about trusting her. And why should he? She'd had to learn herself not to trust anyone these days.

Marc Bruckner, on the other hand, was far more candid. 'I know how this sounds,' he said after they had ordered breakfast. 'A stupid plot from an old Hollywood disaster movie. But we really believe it can work.'

'Firstly, why me?' she asked, recalling the number of times she had asked that question over the past few weeks: of the world's media obsessed with hearing her views, of the British government, of Aguda when she had been recruited onto the UN committee, of Shireen who had singled her out with the revelations about the dying field . . . How lovely that people seemed so naturally drawn to her. 'Why not go further up the chain of command to people who can actually make things happen?'

Qiang grunted, but Marc was clear about his motives. 'Look, you're a physicist too, so we felt—' He gave Qiang a quick sideways glance. '—*I* felt that you would at least see it as feasible in principle. Plus, of course, we think the magnetic pulse plan is useless – even if successful, it's nothing more than a temporary measure, and we can't just sit around waiting for the planet to die. If we do nothing, the Earth will end up a dead planet like Mars. But, hey, I'm not telling you anything you don't know.'

Sarah didn't reply. She pondered how she had so quickly morphed from innocent ingénue to influential figure in world politics. What was it that people saw in her that made her the target of such attention, and trust?

They were sitting at a table not far from the one she'd shared with Aguda ten days earlier, but the diner was much quieter this morning. In fact, she'd noticed far fewer people out on the streets these past few days; the civil unrest – which had been particularly bad in New York – triggered by the satellite data revelations, and further exacerbated by the ensuing political uncertainty and turmoil, meant that many people were either anxious about leaving the safety of their homes or simply too dispirited to go to work. Trouble had erupted hard on the heels of her leaked conversation with Aguda and their subsequent network appearance, and had got so bad in various parts of the city that the National Guard had had to be called in.

Marc began to give her the full sales pitch and seemed unashamed to do so, waxing lyrical about high-energy beams of dark-matter particles produced by accelerators around the globe, $E=mc^2$, seismic waves and liquid metal cores.

Sarah listened as they described the Odin Project. No one in the world knew more about dark matter than

Bruckner and Lee – hell, they were still in the running for the Nobel Prize – but the idea of firing beams of high-energy particles into the Earth's core made the MPD proposal sound almost reasonable. This plan was nothing short of crazy. And when had the ability to do world-class research ruled out the possibility of pushing a crackpot theory later in life? There were plenty of examples of geniuses going off the rails . . .

Having read the stories of Marc's broken marriage and his long struggle with depression, she was quite surprised by his disarming charm and openness. But it was clear that behind the breezy façade lay a complex character that he kept carefully locked away. And yet, there was something in his eyes that made her want to believe him – a fiery zeal that he couldn't quite hide. He was good-looking, in a rough-round-the-edges way, as though he couldn't be bothered to put in the effort any more. She tried to work out how old he must be – probably mid-forties. She also knew he had a teenage daughter and wondered what part she played in stoking his desire to make this plan work.

In the end, what persuaded her to take their idea seriously wasn't so much the science – that was for others to assess – but the fact that she knew better than Marc how ineffectual the MPD project really was. She had seen the negative results from the simulations of the space-based MPD produced by the murdered German computer scientist.

So she promised to take their proposal, with her own endorsement for what that was worth, to Peter Hogan and the committee, in the hope that they would agree for Marc and Qiang to give a more formal presentation at the UN.

'But please don't get your hopes up. They could well

dismiss it out of hand as being too outlandish, too risky and too expensive to take seriously.'

Qiang leaned forward, slamming his fist on the table. 'But how could they *not* listen to us? What's the point of worrying about cost, if the world is coming to an end?' Marc rested his hand on the younger man's shoulder to calm him. But Sarah understood his frustration.

'Look, I didn't say they won't listen, just that you have to prepare yourselves for disappointment.'

'We have other options, you know,' said Qiang. 'It may be that the Chinese government is more receptive than your UN committee.'

Sarah shrugged. 'Possibly. But just remember that the current international stance is that the MPD project is still the only official solution, whether space-based or terrestrial.'

But for how much longer, she wondered. Would there come a time when the MPD option was shelved for good and Marc and Qiang's Odin Project would be seriously considered?

28

Wednesday, 13 March – Rio de Janeiro

SARAH HAD BEEN WOKEN UP BY HER TWO CATS – ONE
scratching at the open bedroom door, knowing this would
eventually prompt a response from her, and the other
purring loudly in her ear as it curled up on the pillow
between her head and the back wall.

No, it's too early, you little rascals. Leave me alone.

She pushed the cat off the bed and lay staring up at the
ceiling, letting her vision swim into focus. It had been
over three weeks since she had first met with Marc and
Qiang in New York and there still hadn't been any progress in getting their plan heard by the right people. It
had been extremely frustrating. Although other scientists
had acknowledged that it was theoretically feasible, most
governments simply didn't have the appetite to switch
from the MPD plan to what Peter Hogan had referred to
as science fiction.

She promised Marc that she would keep pushing for it
but she had been needed back in Rio to monitor and gather
data on the latest, unusually high, solar activity. She had
left Shireen to stay on in her New York apartment. The

240

FBI were still watching the young Iranian closely, but it seemed unnecessary for Sarah to act as a full-time chaperone. Now, back in her own apartment, she at least felt a semblance of familiar routine returning to her life after the past anything-but-routine weeks. But the deep-seated sense of dread and impending catastrophe never left her. If anything, it was worse now, invading her dreams most nights. On several occasions she had woken up in a sweat from a nightmare of a dystopian post-apocalyptic world, helpless to do anything about saving humanity. She had found herself talking to her parents more regularly too, with each of them hiding their anxiety and keeping up the pretence of normality.

Even though there was no reason why she should be held personally responsible for saving the world, she still felt frustrated by her helplessness. But all she could do was what was asked of her, to provide information about potential CMEs, which she fed back to the UN task group working on the magnetic pulse devices.

She crawled out of bed and plodded to the bathroom. The photovoltaic glass of her large bedroom windows had already reacted to her movements and changed from opaque to clear, allowing the early-morning sun to stream in, and she guessed it was already about six-thirty. 'Coffee on. Latest solar update,' she croaked. Reassuringly, her home AI had no problem recognizing her voice and responded with a breezy Good morning, Sarah, and she heard the reassuring sound of the coffee machine clicking on in the kitchen. The cats wouldn't even let her sit on the toilet in peace and were now both weaving in and out of her legs. *Serves me right, being away for so long. They've got used to being fed at this ungodly hour by Mrs Azevedo.* That reminded her: she made a note to check that her upgraded house bot was ready for collection, although

241

she had to admit she'd been enjoying getting back to her old household chores, away from the media spotlight and polluted UN politics.

She tapped the big bathroom mirror and its interactive screen burst to life, showing her several images of the latest solar activity. The European Space Agency's Solar Orbiter satellite, the closest man-made object to the Sun, was revealing an even higher flare activity than yesterday, which meant an increased risk of CMEs. Even more worrying was the fact that several CMEs over the past couple of days had been ejected from a region close to the Sun's central disc and were being sprayed out in the plane of the inner planets' orbits, although so far none towards Earth. She had stressed in her report to Hogan that few CMEs ever scored a direct hit on Earth. And the seriously disruptive and dangerous ones occurred on average once a century.

She tapped off the interactive screen on the mirror and the technical display was replaced by her half-awake and dishevelled reflection staring back at her. She turned away and headed for the shower. It was going to be another warm and sticky day and she enjoyed the invigorating coldness of the water. Then, dressing in an old pair of jeans and T-shirt – it was a relief to be back in her normal scruffy clothes again – she headed into the kitchen to grab a coffee. She'd pick up breakfast when she got to the Institute.

Five minutes later she was ready to leave. The traffic shouldn't be too bad this time of the morning, especially since she was able to weave around the cars on her bike. Besides, the roads were significantly quieter these days. The Rio riots had been particularly violent, with vehicles set on fire and shops ransacked. So, many people were still afraid to go out. She picked up her crash helmet and two lithium-air batteries from the induction pad they had been charging on. 'Leaving apartment. Back this evening,' she said hastily, and her AI system responded with a warm, Thank you, Sarah. Enjoy your day. She hurried down the two flights of stairs, and then thumb-activated the door down to the small basement carpark. It was seven-fifteen.

In the basement, she walked over to the dimly lit far corner where she kept her motorbike. The 100bhp Yamaha was her pride and joy and probably the thing she had missed the most while in the States.

Just then she heard a familiar voice behind her. 'Hi, Sarah, when did you get back?'

She turned to see Luca Aumann, the Austrian journalist from the ground-floor apartment, who was with his young daughter. 'Oh, morning . . . Luca. Yes, I got back a couple of days ago.' She smiled at the girl, whose name came to her just in time. 'Hello, Laura. Ooh, I like your hair.'

Laura smiled back shyly and held her blonde pigtails one in each hand. 'Papa helped me do them,' she said in a soft voice. Sarah recalled that the girl spent half her time with her father and the other half presumably with her mother somewhere.

She turned back to meet Luca's eyes and was instantly lost for words. Luca Aumann always made her feel like an awkward teenager and she was suddenly conscious of how scruffy she must appear to him in his expensive-looking jacket and open-neck shirt. How did he stay so cool in this humidity?

She suddenly realized she had been staring at him without saying anything and felt her cheeks begin to flush. But Luca put an end to her discomfort. 'Well, it's good to see you again. Laura and I are off to the park to feed the ducks before school, aren't we, Laura?' The girl nodded and showed Sarah the paper bag she was holding. 'Anyway, now that you're back, Sarah, you should come down and have dinner with us one evening.'

'That'd be lovely, thank you. Say hello to the ducks for me, Laura.' Sarah gave the little girl a brief wave before turning to her motorbike. She heard their car door close as she clicked the batteries into position. She put on her helmet, swung her leg over and fired up the engine, relieved that it started on first go. She sat for a moment enjoying the artificially generated rumble of a fossil-fuel internal combustion engine. Reversing quickly, she headed up the ramp, out onto the road and into the morning traffic.

Interlude

Wednesday, 13 March – STEREO2 spacecraft

At 10:28 Coordinate Universal Time – 07:28 in Rio de Janeiro – *the two Solar Terrestrial Relations Observatory spacecraft moving in separated heliocentric orbits, one far ahead of the Earth and the other lagging behind, recorded the approach of a large coronal ejection which, a few minutes earlier, had been expelled by the Sun and then immediately picked up speed as it travelled through space. Their combined data placed the CME on a trajectory that would almost perfectly rendezvous with Earth.*

At about the same time that the two spacecraft first detected the ejection, which was just over eight minutes after it had actually left the Sun's surface, high-energy photons, both ultraviolet and X-ray, hit the Earth's upper atmosphere, ionizing its gases. In itself, this caused no harm to the biosphere, but the levels of ionization were so severe that over half the world's radio communications were temporarily wiped out, disrupting the information flow from many satellites. And with much of the global internet connectivity now using dual laser–radio technology, with data being sent and received between thousands of drones that filled the sky at an altitude of 20 km, the disruption to radio signals was enough to shut down large parts of the internet too.

This meant that when the warning signals sent by both STEREO2 spacecraft that a CME was on its way arrived at the near-Earth satellites thirty seconds later, they went no further. So, no one knew that just eleven minutes after that, the CME's vanguard of high-energy particles – protons moving at close to the speed of light – would hit the Earth. Many of these protons would collide with molecules of air in the upper atmosphere, causing a shower of new particles, such as muons, to rain down to the surface. But with Earth's depleted magnetic field unable to deflect them, many of the original protons from the Sun would themselves also make their way to the ground. They would be deadly.

For many years, several strategies had been in place to cope with a CME-induced geomagnetic storm. These had been reviewed and revised in the light of the Earth's weakening magnetic field. The Hogan committee had then recommended further strategies following the Air India disaster, including a shut-down of all non-essential communications and switching from large electricity grids to local generators. Cloud communications and data transfer would also switch from a combination of laser and radio transmission to laser only, since drone–drone and drone–Earth radio signals would be dramatically compromised by any large geomagnetic disturbance. None of this was implemented, since no one knew this particular coronal mass ejection was coming. Until it was too late.

29

Wednesday, 13 March – Rio de Janeiro

Joining the orderly AI-controlled morning traffic, Sarah enjoyed the freedom of being, almost, in complete control of the bike. She turned off her AR feed as she focused on the road – the chances of the Sun misbehaving during her half-hour journey seemed slim. As in most big cities, Rio de Janeiro's entire transportation system was run by an AI Mind that linked together and coordinated all the autonomous traffic on its roads, as well as all the traffic lights, which were needed for those vehicles still under the control of their human drivers. And the Mind would not allow her to exceed the speed limit or jump any lights even if she had wanted to: it would take over her bike's computer, commanding it to activate the brakes and slow down.

The traffic was light as she sped north up Rua de Santana, passing the abandoned and burnt-out vehicles on the side of the road – a reminder of the civil unrest the city had endured over the past few weeks. But she would soon hit the commuter rush hour when she reached Avenida Presidente Vargas, which ran into the city from the

247

west. As she reached the intersection she dropped the revs on the bike's throttle in anticipation of the Mind taking over control of her brakes. She still found this mix of manual and remote control of her bike disconcerting and preferred open country roads away from AI control, where she could manually apply her own brakes if and when necessary.

The first sign that something was wrong was when her brakes failed to activate automatically as she approached the busy intersection that got her onto the freeway. Strange. She was always stopped here by the Mind, even if for just a few seconds. Dropping down to a lower gear, she edged forward carefully. There was heavy traffic on the four lanes of the eastbound side of the road, which she had to cross, and it was completely stationary. It had been a long time since she had witnessed such an old-fashioned traffic jam – it just wasn't the sort of thing that happened in large cities any more. It occurred to her that, not so many years ago, this sort of scene would have been accompanied by a cacophony of revving internal combustion engines and car horns honking impatiently while drivers leaned out of their windows to shout at each other. This morning, everything was eerily quiet. People had quickly got used to relying on their cars' computers to do all the driving while they sat in comfort within their air-conditioned environment.

Weaving her way carefully around the stationary cars blocking her path, she noted the bemused looks on the faces of the passengers, suggesting that whatever had stopped the traffic had only happened recently. None of the cars on the westbound side were moving either, so it had to be a problem with the city's AI. But the Minds that ran the very largest megacities around the world simply didn't go down. Ever. She felt a creeping unease.

Pulling over, she dismounted and blinked on her AR. The feed was dead.

No reason to freak out just yet, girl – just because the entire net is down!

She steadied her breathing. *Logic before panic.* After all, she'd spent the last few days worrying about the Sun's abnormal activity, but that did *not* mean that this internet blackout was in any way related.

OK, think. If a solar blast really has knocked out radio-wave connectivity, then maybe I can still use my wristpad. Like her computer back in the apartment, it had a direct lasercom link to the STEREO2 spacecraft, which meant it didn't have to route through any Earth-orbit commsat. She quickly established a link and scanned recent solar activity.

Fuck.

She examined the data streaming across her vision and gasped. The incoming CME was a monster. Its size, speed and energy density were off the charts. Could it be a mistake? No, the stats would have been cross-correlated between the STEREO2 spacecraft. Her heart was now pounding as she did a quick mental calculation, trying to suppress her growing panic. The spacecraft had first detected the CME and begun sending their alert to Earth a few minutes ago, which would also have been when the electromagnetic pulse that must have brought down the net had hit.

Oh, shit . . . this is really, really bad. It means we've got at best ten to fifteen minutes before the proton blast. She knew that others at her institute and elsewhere who had direct links to STEREO2 would also be aware of the incoming CME, but they'd have little time to do much.

Under normal conditions, with a healthy magnetosphere, the proton shower that preceded the arrival of a

CME would not be cause for concern. But in its weakened state, the field would not provide an adequate shield. She estimated that it could potentially be worse than the radiation fallout from a thermonuclear blast. And that was before the main ejection hit the Earth in a day or two. Worst of all, with the net down there was no way to warn people. It was the stuff of nightmares.

She surveyed her surroundings on the highway. Everywhere, people were getting out of their cars. *They have no idea what's about to happen. And they can't stay here, exposed. Even in their cars they'll be like sitting ducks.* It would be like hiding inside a cardboard box on a firing range.

She ran to the nearest group of half a dozen well-dressed businessmen and -women and, instead of speaking in English and relying on their universal translators, she started to explain as best she could in her broken Portuguese that she was a scientist and she knew what had caused the blackout. Things were about to get very bad and they needed to find shelter – anywhere that could give them protection from the radiation from the sky.

They just stared at her as though she were mad. She switched to English in the hope that some of them would understand, either directly or through their UTs, and could pass on what she was saying.

'Please. I work at the Solar Science Institute. We're about to be hit by dangerous radiation from the Sun and we only have a few minutes. Everyone needs to get off the road.'

One young man turned to the woman next to him and muttered something that caused her to raise one hand to her mouth and conceal her laughter. An overweight middle-aged man who was already starting to sweat in the warm morning sun spat an impatient insult at Sarah in Portuguese, which she understood perfectly well and chose to ignore. She knew how she must sound; these days the world was full of doom-mongers preaching that the end of the world was nigh, some more wildly than others. But these people *had* to listen. She grabbed a well-dressed middle-aged woman firmly by the shoulders and spoke as clearly as she could. 'Listen to me. The internet blackout is because of the Sun. And it's going to get worse . . . and if you're exposed to it you could die. Please . . . *please*. Everyone needs to find some shelter. *Now.*'

She realized she was ranting, and the look on the woman's face confirmed how crazy she must sound.

She felt a hand on her own shoulder pulling her away and she let go of the woman. She stumbled backwards, losing her balance, and fell heavily, grazing her hands as she reached down to break her fall.

More people had gathered to check what the commotion was. A few, who had heard part of what she'd said, were now in animated conversation. A mother pulled her two young children from a car and, holding their hands firmly, began pushing her way through the crowd to the side of the road. Sarah sat, dazed, on the ground as a circle gathered around her and stared, while others lost interest and returned to their air-conditioned cars. A few people were looking up at the sky, shielding their eyes from the sun's glare.

She was helped to her feet by an embarrassed-looking young couple. Feeling both humiliated and enraged in equal measure, she began to explain to them, 'Please, you have to listen—', but they smiled awkwardly and retreated back down the road.

Time was running out. What more was she supposed to do?

Instead, a primal survival instinct kicked in, snuffing out any feelings of moral obligation. *Well, fuck you then. Stay out and enjoy your suntan.* She picked up her helmet and ran back to her bike. She knew where she needed to get to.

She swung her leg over the bike, hit ignition and revved the engine, ignoring the soreness in her right hand from her stumble. She turned the bike around and looked frantically for a route to get across the multiple lanes of traffic. She needed to head back the way she'd come, back to the Santa Barbara tunnel, but by now traffic was backed up in both directions along Rua de Santana, which had been so comparatively empty a few minutes ago.

People were standing around in the road ahead of her but, realizing that she had no intention of slowing down as she sped between the stationary cars, they scattered as she bore down on them. She left a tirade of obscenities in her wake. Tough. No time for pleasantries.

Suddenly, a car door swung open in front of her without warning and she had to slam on her brakes and swerve, still clipping the door sharply with her back wheel. The young occupant of the car jumped out and looked for a second like he was going to pull her from her bike. She ignored him and weaved her way onwards.

Up ahead of her several cars had tried, unsuccessfully, to turn around, causing utter chaos. Already voices were being raised and the first punches thrown. How quickly the rule of law broke down – how volatile the public mood was at the moment. The road looked completely blocked. She let out a scream of frustration.

With less than ten minutes before she needed to get to safety she knew she had to get off the highway. The narrow winding lanes of the Santa Teresa district were above her and she gunned the bike onto the pavement, up a steep grass slope and across flower beds. Suddenly, she was on a quiet residential road.

As the crow flies, the tunnel was less than a kilometre away, but would she have enough time to make it along the twisting steep roads on the Santa Teresa hill? She had to try. Revving the engine with renewed purpose, she sped off.

Twice her bike skidded as she wrestled to keep it on the winding road. Adrenalin was now surging through her, the single-minded determination to reach the tunnel blocking out all other emotions. She braked hard approaching another sharp U-bend, then gunned the throttle again with a twist of her right wrist even before she had straightened up. Too late to react, she saw a group of young boys playing football in the middle of the road. She slammed on her brakes again. Too hard. The tyres screeched as the bike swerved one way then the other. There was nothing she could as she lost her balance, still travelling at speed, and fell onto the road with the bike on top of her.

The bike slid along the road with her leg trapped underneath, ripping her jeans and cutting into her leg. Miraculously, the boys somehow managed to jump out of the way fractions of a second before woman and machine ploughed through them. She felt a sharp pain in her elbow as her arm displaced a brick that had been acting as a makeshift goalpost. Finally, Sarah and motorbike came to a stop in a shallow ditch by the side of the road. Dazed, she was vaguely aware that the boys were gathering around her. One or two were shouting, asking if she was OK, but a few were laughing. With her head pounding, she dragged her bloodied leg out from beneath the bike and forced herself to stand up. Lifting the machine up caused a spasm of pain to shoot up her left arm. She was pretty sure her elbow was fractured.

She turned to look at the boys. She wanted to scream at them, to tell them to get home, to find shelter, but they were already going back to their game. Ignoring the intense pain in her arm and leg, she heaved the bike back up and somehow managed to get back on. The engine was still running. Twisting the throttle, she flicked into gear and took off down the road again.

How long did she have? No time to check now. Just keep going.

Suddenly, there was a flash of light in her left eye, followed by two more in quick succession in her right eye. Please no, not yet.

For three quarters of a century astronauts had reported these flashes: high-energy particles from space travelling through the eyeball and hitting the back of the retina. So, this was it – the first and fastest particles from the Sun were arriving now, like the first few drops of rain before a downpour.

She turned a corner and felt a wave of relief as she saw the tunnel entrance on the road below her. The flashes were arriving more regularly. She gunned the throttle of the bike yet again, joining the road just a hundred metres from the tunnel entrance. The tailback of traffic now extended all the way into the tunnel. Without coming to a complete stop, she leapt from the bike, falling again and rolling over on the verge. She struggled to her feet and ripped off her helmet. Ignoring the searing pain in her leg, she half ran, half hobbled as fast as she could manage along the side of the road, pushing her way past commuters who had abandoned their cars. Many were rubbing their eyes, while some turned to stare at this wild woman in the torn and bloody jeans with dishevelled hair and panic in her eyes.

Consumed with pain and frustration, her breathing

loud and laboured, she ran. She shouted to people to follow her towards the shelter of the tunnel. No one did. In a week, two weeks, maybe more if they were particularly unlucky, many of these people would be dead from radiation exposure.

She could see the tunnel entrance looming larger. Almost there. The spots in her eyes were coming thick and fast now.

At last, she had made it. Plunging into the cool darkness, she kept on moving deeper inside, until she was sure that the mass of rock above her head was sufficient to provide enough shielding. She finally slumped back against the tunnel wall, gasping for air. She wondered what the occupants of the cars stuck in the jam here would think when they discovered how lucky they were.

Later that night, lying in hospital along with hundreds of people who, unlike her, appeared sick from radiation exposure, she drifted in and out of a fitful sleep. Her dreams were haunted by the memory of those young Brazilian boys playing football in the street and how they would probably have all died painfully and horribly of radiation exposure soon after. They had laughed at her and she had left them to die.

And she dreamed too about how much worse things were going to get.

Interlude

THE CORONAL MASS EJECTION HAD BEEN HEADING TOWARDS Earth for twenty-one hours. As it passed the first Lagrange point, a million miles from Earth, it washed over the Chinese Kuafu satellite. The satellite dutifully carried out the task it had been put there for and sent back data on the CME – to a mostly deaf humankind. Less than a minute before the CME reached Earth it began to feel the effects of the magnetosphere. Yet it hardly slowed down at all. Instead, it compressed the field ahead of it as though it were a car air-bag with not enough air in.

The CME blasted through the weakened outer Van Allen belt tens of thousands of kilometres above the Earth's surface, destroying it. Charged cosmic-ray particles – protons and electrons – trapped by the magnetosphere in this radiation shell for millennia, were now set free and quickly scattered into space like autumn leaves whipped up in a storm.

With the magnetosphere squashed so thin ahead of the CME, many of the thousands of satellites in orbit were left exposed to its full force, and their electronic circuitry was instantly fried.

Although the particles making up the CME were lower in

energy than the initial wave of protons that had arrived the day before, their sheer intensity meant they were just as deadly. There would have been an even greater number of fatalities had populations not been warned in time following the initial proton blast, but nothing could stop crops from being destroyed and livestock wiped out in many parts of the world.

Happening so close to the March equinox, the effects of the blast were felt most strongly around the equator. In South America, the final tally would reach two hundred thousand dead, mostly in eastern Brazil, where it coincided with the morning rush hour, with many people simply ignoring the warning messages. Luckily for those further west, it was too early in the day for many people to be outside their houses, which mostly offered them adequate protection. The same could not be said for sub-Saharan and southern Africa, where the radiation blast hit in the middle of the day. It was estimated that up to seven million people across forty countries suffered fatal exposure – dying either from lethal radiation poisoning in the immediate aftermath of the event or from cancers brought about by the ionizing radiation, over the following months, making it the world's worst natural disaster in recorded history.

A taste of things to come.

PART III

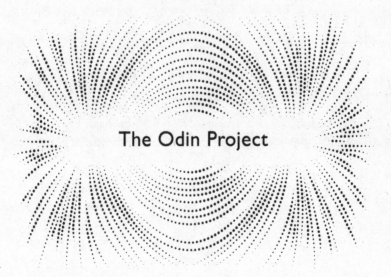

The Odin Project

30

MARC MADE HIS WAY PAST FAMILIAR BUILDINGS THROUGH the site of the vast laboratory complex of the Conseil européen pour la recherche nucléaire, where he had spent much of his early career, and considered how much had changed in his life over the past three months. In fact, it struck him that he felt pretty good about himself right now, in part due to his work on the Odin Project, but also because of his growing feelings towards Sarah and his continuing rehabilitation in the eyes of Evie – who seemed to be revelling in her father's new-found fame.

Things had moved rapidly in the days that followed the events of 13 and 14 March. With the world reeling from the shock of such a cataclysmic loss of life, rumours spread fast that this was not a freak event – that unless the magnetosphere recovered, more devastation was inevitable. Across the world, the sense of unease grew stronger. Fresh riots broke out; looting became so widespread that many governments were powerless to stop it; and few people were prepared to believe the official line, that the March CME really was a once-in-a-century event.

261

It quickly became clear that the magnetic pulse devices still being worked on would not offer the protection needed from any future threat from the Sun of similar magnitude. At best, an Earth-based device would provide a temporary preventative measure – a local shield protecting the lucky few beneath it – but never a permanent global solution.

One group revelling in all this chaos was the Purifiers. The end-of-the-world prophecy they held by was coming true, and they rejoiced. But that didn't dampen their enthusiasm for giving nature a helping hand. They upped the ambition and frequency of their attacks on government facilities and research labs working on potential solutions to the dying field, always driven and cajoled by their spiritual leader, Maksoob. Little was known of this shadowy figure, a man who had kindled a warped passion among his growing band of followers. He had recruited them carefully from around the world, mainly from among the disaffected and disillusioned in poverty-stricken areas: those in the once oil-rich nations of the Middle East and the millions displaced from coastal homes in southern Asia lost to the rising seas.

For several weeks after the Event, as it was now being referred to, Sarah had remained in Rio, in part to recover from her injuries – a fractured elbow, a sprained ankle and deep gashes in her leg – but also, as Marc had discovered when he'd visited her, because of her crushing feelings of guilt that she hadn't done enough to warn people about the deadly radiation from the sky on that fateful morning.

Despite her pleas to be discharged, she had been kept under observation in hospital for a week to ensure that she wasn't suffering from any radiation effects. Amid the chaos and disruption to travel in the days following the

Event, Marc had somehow managed to get on a flight down to Rio, in part out of a genuine desire to see Sarah and check up on her, but also in the hope that he might discuss the possibility of resurrecting the Odin Project.

Within minutes of seeing her sitting up in bed, he could tell that her physical injuries would heal quickly enough, but her mental state was a different matter. In contrast to the zest and determination he'd admired in the woman he'd got to know on the few occasions they'd spent time together in New York over the previous weeks, Sarah was now quiet and withdrawn. It was as though she'd put up an impregnable wall around her to block the outside world out while she battled her inner demons.

No one knew better than Marc Bruckner about the futility of trying to talk someone out of depression. But he had tried.

'Anyone would have done what you did. How could you possibly convince people in the few minutes you had out on the streets? And why risk fatally exposing yourself too?'

Sarah hadn't answered. Instead, she'd cried a lot that day.

The day after he'd arrived in Rio, Marc had received a call from Qiang.

'We've been asked to attend a briefing meeting at the UN tomorrow. It sounds like our idea is back on the table.'

'Says who?'

'Says . . . Well, I don't know who's made the decision. All I know is that they are now ready to listen to us, properly.'

Marc wasn't sure how he felt. 'Well, yes, I suppose desperate measures require desperate solutions, right?'

Qiang was quiet for a second, then he said, 'You know, that's exactly what they said to me!'

Marc had promised Sarah he'd come back to see her as soon as he could.

One week after the Event, news of the new plan to save the world had gone viral. Within days, everyone was talking about how dark matter was going to rescue humanity. The Odin Project had been born. It hadn't taken long for the feasibility of the science to be checked and confirmed. The official view was that it *could* work, in theory at least. And that was enough. It had brought governments together in a way never seen before. Marc had been astonished by the speed at which consensus had been reached. Not since the Second World War had so many nations rapidly invested so much time and resource into a single objective – but this time they were all working on the same side. The scale of the task made mid-twentieth-century technical achievements like the Manhattan Project and the space race seem like amateur diversions.

It was a warm June morning in Geneva and, despite what was at stake, Marc felt excited. He found it hard to believe just how rapidly the Odin Project had evolved from crazy speculations about firing beams of neutralinos into the core of the Earth to serious discussions about how this might be achieved and where facilities would need to be built, to designing and carrying out the first feasibility tests. Today, the results of the first real tests of his and Qiang's idea were being presented.

People were already taking their seats in the main auditorium as Marc made his way down towards the front. He quickly spotted Qiang in animated discussion with Gabriel Aguda and noticed the dramatic contrast in size between the two men. Aguda had consistently voiced his reservations about the Odin Project. Unlike the

MPDs, which he claimed at least gave the world a stay of execution, he'd argued strongly that this was too expensive, too uncertain, could not be achieved in time and, most importantly, diverted attention from the more 'reliable' MPDs option. Marc found it hard to read what the man was thinking.

Scanning the hall to see if Sarah had arrived, he soon spotted her sitting by the middle aisle on the far side. She mouthed, 'Good luck.'

As he navigated his way down to the stage area through the throngs of delegates standing around in the aisle, the irony of how his fortunes, and mood, had improved as a consequence of the situation that was sinking the rest of humanity into pessimism and anxiety was not lost on him.

Qiang had admitted that he too felt the same sense of purpose about the Odin Project – and argued that it was OK for Marc to feel positive. 'After all,' he'd said, 'if we don't have faith in the science, then we've lost.' Marc didn't buy this cheap psychology, but knew what Qiang had meant. They were, after all, leading the most ambitious and important scientific undertaking the world had ever known, one that would determine the future of the planet, which was, by any measure, pretty fucking awesome. If nothing else, it put his own demons into perspective.

He had been somewhat surprised at the speed of his reacceptance among the international community of high-energy physicists as soon as the Odin Project had taken off. The reputation of a research scientist was a fragile thing which, like one's virginity, could only be lost once. He'd certainly lost his. But here he was again, back at CERN where he'd spent the first fifteen years of his research career and the centre of attention for the world's leading scientists once more, and realizing that he still enjoyed it. He adjusted his tie as he walked. This was probably the first time ever he had given a physics talk in a jacket and tie, but he felt the occasion merited some sort of formality.

Of course, there was a dark backdrop to all this sanguine enthusiasm. Marc knew better than anyone just how outrageously ambitious the Odin Project truly was. There were simply too many unknowns, too many challenges, and too little margin for error.

And it was now clear that security was an even bigger problem than the science. As soon as the Odin Project was announced the Purifiers had issued a statement outlining their intent to sabotage it. So, they had begun to target the new facilities being built and the scientists and engineers working on the Project. In the past week alone, two accelerator physicists in Paris had been murdered and a research lab outside Tokyo had been extensively damaged by a bomb. Worst of all was the devastating destruction of the half-built Dark Matter Facility in Texas, which had been expected to play a central role in the Project. The vast underground lab had been obliterated by a huge blast, which the Purifiers claimed responsibility for, and which had buried alive three hundred workers and technicians. The depth of the facility underground meant that even in the unlikely event of there being any survivors, all hopes of rescue were futile.

Now, global security had been ramped up to near preposterous levels, almost doubling the cost of the Project. Armies had been mobilized and all travel restricted. The distribution of the financial burden had yet to be settled, but governments understood that they couldn't afford to delay.

Marc sat down in the front row of the auditorium next to Qiang, sweeping aside the sheet of paper with the words 'Reserved. Professor Bruckner' on it. The atmosphere of anticipation in the big hall was palpable, and Marc knew that the world outside was also holding its collective breath. The talks were being streamed live to billions.

He turned to his friend. 'Morning, Qiang. All set?'

Qiang merely nodded nervously, but Aguda, one seat along, said, 'It's OK for you two, Marc, you get to promise to save the world. I'm just the guy who has to make sure as few people as possible find out about the catastrophic consequences if you boys get anything wrong.'

'Well, so far, so good, right?' Marc had been more relieved than excited by the results from the recent Antarctica test.

Qiang turned to him. 'But there wasn't so much at stake, was there? We can afford to get it wrong for the test, but when we do the real thing . . .'

Mark said nothing. Qiang was right; they'd only have one shot at this. He turned to survey the audience behind them. The four hundred seats were all occupied now, and there were people still streaming in, packing the aisles and filling up the rear of the auditorium. Most were CERN scientists and engineers working on the Odin Project, but there were also groups representing various governments and media bodies. Marc had already met many of the movers and shakers the previous evening at dinner – including, for the first time, the leader of the American delegation, Senator Hogan, who he saw was now seated just two rows behind them and deep in conversation with CERN's director-general. Sarah had been right – there was something unsettling about Hogan's manner, a cold detachment that Marc had found disturbing. He'd taken an instant dislike to the man.

267

The noise began to subside in anticipation of the start of proceedings.

Qiang was fidgeting, cracking his knuckles as he always did when nervous. His task today was straightforward: he was to report on the first successful test in which the only three operating dark-matter accelerator labs – here at CERN, Fermilab near Chicago and J-PARC north of Tokyo – had all successfully fired their invisible beams down through the Earth. Everything had gone exactly to plan with three synchronized neutralino bursts, each passing unhindered through ten thousand kilometres of solid planet, converging just before they emerged at a point one hundred metres below the surface of the Antarctic ice.

Marc and Qiang had flown out to Antarctica to witness the experiment at first hand. It was the most nervous Marc had felt in his life. If this test had failed that would most likely have spelled the end of the Project.

The chosen spot for the dark-matter beams to converge, just south of the Kraul Mountains in the Norwegian dependency of Queen Maud Land, was a remote enough site, yet close enough to the British Halley Research Station eighty kilometres away to be carefully monitored from a safe distance.

After a twenty-four-hour delay due to a security breach at J-PARC, the three labs had fired their dark-matter bursts into the ground. When the pulses met, a split second later and thousands of kilometres away, they created a burst of energy so great it vaporized a volume of the remaining Antarctic ice, leaving behind a lake of hot, but rapidly cooling water three kilometres wide and two hundred metres deep. Under normal circumstances, such devastation would have horrified environmentalists, but these were not normal circumstances. Marc found himself wondering whether Oppenheimer, Fermi and the rest of the gang on the Manhattan Project had experienced the same feelings of awe and dread at such pure, unleashed power, as they gazed out at the first mushroom cloud in the New Mexico desert a century ago. The difference now was that, unlike the Manhattan Project, this test was meant to save humankind rather than incinerate it.

And yet he had to remind himself that this test had been with just three dark-matter beams rather than the eight he and Qiang were proposing, not to mention the fact that they had been operating at a fraction of the intensity that could be achieved, and which would ultimately be needed when the time came.

Marc's thoughts were interrupted when the lights dimmed, and he heard a familiar voice over the PA system. Despite the importance of the event, proceedings began just as all CERN conferences had done for some years past: with a welcoming address from the lab's Mind. The holographic human avatar representing the AI that controlled every aspect of the vast laboratory complex was, in contrast, simple and understated. The original programmers had created it in the stately image of a woman with white hair tied efficiently in a bun at the back of her head. Those listening to her without the use of the universal translators would hear her speak softly in English with a hint of an Italian accent. It was said that this was a deliberate nod by the programmers to the laboratory's first female director, Fabiola Gianotti. They had even given it her name. The real Dr Gianotti had retired several years ago but still came to the lab regularly. Marc had once asked her what she thought of the avatar created in her image.

'I'm very flattered,' she'd replied. 'If only it had been around when I was director. I could have taken longer holidays and left it in charge. It knows far more about how to run CERN than I ever did.'

Like everyone else in the room, Marc now saw the Mind's avatar in augmented reality and listened as Fabiola gave a brief introduction to the lab.

'Many of you will know that CERN was conceived in the late 1940s as a laboratory to be shared by many nations when particle physics research became too expensive for any one country to pursue alone. So, it is fitting that today it is the centre of operations for a new type of experiment – one that involves a truly worldwide collaboration between eight laboratories spread around the globe. Many of you will know that we have this type of connectivity in science already, with our largest radio telescopes linked together to effectively act as a single Earth-sized telescope to look deeper into space, but humankind has never attempted something as audacious as Project Odin.'

As the Mind went on to introduce Qiang and invite him to present the latest test results, Marc's attention drifted once again. The great human technological achievements of the past, such as the space exploration programmes to the Moon in the 1960s and Mars in the 2030s, had been driven by nothing more than national pride and economic supremacy; this current race against time was different. Unlike with the Moon and Mars programmes, failure now quite literally wasn't an option.

Sitting there, only half listening to Qiang describing the results of the Antarctic test, he felt a sudden unexpected surge of panic. This entire project really was quite insane. He tried to recall the confidence and excitement he'd experienced during that weekend of feverish activity in his New York hotel room, when the two men had conceived the plan. But despite their calculations being checked and verified by hundreds of other scientists, he now felt more nervous than ever.

Still, what choice did the world have? Secretly, a small part of him was hoping that someone else would come up with a better plan – one for which the chances of success were higher and where failure would not mean the end of the world. At least if something went wrong and one of the beams did in fact miss the intended rendezvous spot deep in the Earth's molten core, he wouldn't have too long to blame himself for destroying the planet.

Loud applause dragged him back to the here and now. Qiang had finished his short presentation and was returning to his seat. It was time. Standing, Marc waited for a second or two, trying to calm himself and collect his thoughts. He was conscious of hundreds of pairs of eyes burning into the back of his skull as he made his way to the stage. Pausing at the lectern to pick up the holo-control pad, Professor Marc Bruckner turned to face his audience and smiled.

'Ladies and gentlemen,' he began, 'I'm aware that many of you are not scientists and will therefore not appreciate the subtler details of dark-matter physics, particle decay pathways and the role of superconducting bending magnets. In any case, the documentation you have all been given lays this out in clearer detail than I am able to do.'

A murmur of light-hearted approval rippled through the audience, which would have come mainly from the non-scientists.

'As you know, ODIN stands for Octangular Directional Ignition with Neutralinos. This means eight beams of neutralinos, the particles of dark matter, all directed into the core of the planet from different points on the surface. But as you have just heard from Professor Lee, we currently have only three accelerator laboratories capable of producing these particles at sufficiently high energy and intensity.'

He wondered how what he was about to say would be received. After the tragedy in Texas, they had needed to come up with a revised plan. Many in the audience would now be hearing the new details for the first time.

He clicked the pad in his hand and a giant three-dimensional globe appeared suspended in the air in front of him, slowly rotating. Created by several holo-projectors around the stage, the bottom of the sphere hovered a metre above the ground, but its top almost reached the roof of the auditorium seven metres above the stage.

Marc walked across from the podium to stand in the centre of the projection, so that the globe's South Pole cut through his midriff. And because his eyeline coincided with the southern oceans, as the Earth spun he looked out at the audience through a blue translucent wall. He was aware that his actions might seem overly theatrical, but he had a practical reason for positioning himself inside the hologram. With a click of the pad in his hand, three bright lights lit up at the appropriate locations on the surface of the globe, depicting the sites of the only three labs capable of producing beams of dark matter.

He continued, 'The challenge is how to turn three beams into eight, each one aimed into the Earth's core from a different location.

'Those further five locations have now been identified. They were chosen for two reasons. The first is of course their strategic location on the surface of the planet. The second is that they all have much of the infrastructure that is needed already. You see, we won't be building five new dark-matter accelerators. Instead, we're using the beams from the three we already have, only we're splitting them up.'

As he spoke, he clicked his pad and five new lights appeared on the globe.

'All we need . . .' He paused to give the audience the chance to realize he'd meant those three words sardonically. This time the ripple of laughter came from the other physicists, who knew only too well the immense scale of the task. '. . . All we need . . . are giant superconducting magnets to bend the particle beams fired from the three main labs downward into the ground.'

A subdued buzz spread around the auditorium as people leaned in to each other, whispering, pointing at the globe. Marc began warming to his task.

'For example, the beam produced here at CERN will be split into three: one heading to the north coast of Norway in the Arctic Circle . . .' A red line lit up, joining the light that marked Geneva to another in the far north. It traced a perfect straight path that passed below the surface of the Earth instead of following its curvature above ground. '. . . a second to the deserts of Jordan just outside Amman, and a third to Cape Town in South Africa.' Two more bright lines appeared, radiating out from CERN.

A few people clapped enthusiastically, and then, feeling self-conscious, stopped again.

'Across in America, the Fermilab beam will be split in two: one heading straight down to the core directly beneath the lab and the other sent south to the Andean Plateau in Peru.

'Finally, the Japanese beam will also split into three, one directly down and the other two to facilities located on Big Island, Hawaii, and Dunedin in the south of New Zealand.

'Once the beams from the labs reach the six remote

locations, powerful magnets will bend them downwards, aiming them into the ground.'

As he spoke new red lines appeared around him pointing radially inwards from each location, to meet at the centre of the hologram at a point high above his head.

He now stepped back out of the holo image. 'As you can see, the eight beams,' he indicated back to the red spokes of light inside the sphere, 'two from the existing facilities and the other six from the new locations, all meet in a single spot in the Earth's core.'

Marc paused to join the audience in admiring the image. 'I could stop here and just ask you to wish us luck. But since I have you as a captive audience I feel I should share with you the *really* cool stuff.'

He looked out across the auditorium. There was a mixture of admiration and concentration on the sea of faces in front of him. His own earlier anxiety and pessimism about the Project had evaporated and his missionary zeal was filling him with a reassuring belief that this could really work. Marc Bruckner had spent his entire adult life testing and prodding the laws of nature. Now was the chance to put his years of study and research to the ultimate test.

He caught sight of Aguda sitting in the front row. The geologist's stony expression contrasted with the animated features of those around him.

Oh well, can't please everyone. For some reason his eyes drifted across to where Peter Hogan was sitting, but he found it impossible to read the man's blank expression, which he found somewhat unnerving. To counter his unease, he quickly glanced up at Sarah, who gave him a reassuring nod of encouragement. He took a deep breath.

'You see, ladies and gentlemen, for the magnets to bend

the trajectories of our beams from their original direction so that they enter the ground, the particles need to know the magnets are there and react to them, right?

'Yes, I know that sounds obvious. But, as I hope you all know by now, dark matter doesn't feel the presence of normal matter, by which I mean it's not affected by the electromagnetic force. So, just as dark matter passes through normal matter as if it weren't there, it will also be oblivious to the presence of the magnets, regardless of how powerful those magnets are.'

The background murmuring began afresh as many in the audience suddenly understood what seemed to be a fundamental flaw in the scheme.

Marc took a couple of steps closer to the front of the stage. 'So, here's the plan. We don't make beams of neutralinos, the usual dark-matter particles, to begin with, but heavier versions of them. These are called, somewhat unimaginatively I'm afraid, *heavy* neutralinos. Think of them as the normal neutralinos' overweight and short-lived cousins. Beams of these heavy particles will be created in all three accelerators, surviving just long enough, if produced at the right energy, to travel out to the six magnets.

'Then, just as they arrive at the magnets, and rather like Cinderella's coach at midnight, each of them transforms into yet another type of particle called a chargino.'

There was a smattering of laughter at this and Marc acknowledged it with good grace. 'Yes, I know, it sounds like I'm just making this stuff up as I go along, but I promise you I didn't invent these names.

'What's important,' he continued after the audience had settled, 'is that these charginos, as their name suggests, have an electric charge, which means they will be bent downwards by the magnets, but they too live for such a short time that they will almost immediately transform – we say decay – into the light neutralinos that we want. This step is crucial.'

Marc knew that the better the job he made of explaining things now, the easier his life would be in the press conference later. So, he ploughed on. 'The point is that the solid ground will appear to the charginos as just that: *solid*. If they don't transform in time to neutralinos they will be stopped dead in their tracks. This is because their electric charge interacts with the atoms that make up the stuff of the planet. Luckily for us, these charginos transform very quickly back into neutralinos. Once they do, it will be as though the Earth suddenly becomes transparent again and they continue on their path unobstructed, but this time in their new direction towards the core.

'The eight neutralino beams travel downwards until they meet, slamming together in the mother of all bangs. The energy this produces in the planet's liquid core will be a hundred million times greater than the burst that melted that chunk of Antarctica. We've calculated – that is, Professor Lee and I have calculated . . .' Marc nodded towards Qiang. '. . . that this would be enough to create a seismic pulse that kick-starts the Earth's inner dynamo, and switches the magnetosphere back on.'

As an afterthought he added, with a theatrical wave of his hands, 'And that's how we're going to save the world.'

There was wild and enthusiastic applause, even from colleagues who knew the science inside out. A few were standing, and he noticed that Sarah was among them.

He waited patiently for the applause to die down. When it was quiet again he asked, 'Right, does anyone have any questions?'

'Excuse me, Professor Bruckner.' A man in the second row was leaning towards the microphone by his seat.

Marc recognized him as a Swiss journalist from *Le Temps* who had interviewed him a couple of years ago. 'Could you please explain something to us lesser mortals? How can you know precisely when these different particles transform from one type to the other? From my basic understanding of quantum physics, this is not something you can control.'

Marc nodded. Unbidden, a famous quote came to him. He had a feeling it was from a Kurt Vonnegut novel, but couldn't remember the character or what the story was about. It was along the lines of: any scientist who couldn't explain to an eight-year-old what he was doing was a charlatan.

'You are right, of course, that particles decay according to the rules of quantum mechanics, which state that this takes place at an indeterminate moment. This is not to say that quantum mechanics is an imprecise theory, but rather that Nature herself hasn't decided when such individual quantum events will happen.'

The sage-like slow nodding from the journalist suggested to Marc that he was still following, or at least pretending to, so he ploughed on. 'Quantum mechanics tells us that the world of subatomic particles is a fuzzy one ruled by probability and uncertainty. So, while we cannot control or predict when any *given* particle will decay, we do know the *average* lifetime when we have lots of them. So, we produce very many heavy neutralinos in a tight bunch, all travelling at just the right speed, such that *most* of them will decay just before arrival at the magnet. Of course, some won't decay until it's too late and they'll overshoot the magnet. Those are lost. Others will decay too soon and won't even reach the magnet because they will interact with other atoms in the ground or the air and be knocked off their course. But most will make it, transforming just in time for the magnets to do their bending job on them.

'They enter the facilities as a pulse of dark-matter particles travelling through the air, which passes into a sealed beam pipe kept under high vacuum. Only once isolated inside this do they transform into charginos that get bent by the magnets, following an arc within the enclosed, curved pipe that carries them down to the ground.

'And because we know the speed and lifetime of these charginos we can calculate how far they will travel, on average, before they transform back into neutralinos, and so we just have to make sure the beam pipe and the surrounding magnets are high enough above the ground. We've calculated that raising them by about a hundred metres would be enough to give most charginos the chance to decay. Only then do they decay back to dark matter again and the pulse passes through the other end of the beam pipe like a phantom and continues down into the Earth.'

He paused to let the information sink in.

The journalist interjected: 'But isn't that quite a tough engineering challenge?'

Marc laughed. 'The whole project is something of an engineering challenge.' A number of people laughed too. 'But you're right. And so, there's an alternative plan that might be easier. The magnets are kept at ground level, but instead we bore a vertical tunnel into the ground, down which the beam pipe of charginos is directed, to give them that extra breathing space. Again, some longer-lived charginos won't have decayed in time. They hit the sealed end of the beam pipe and are lost.'

Marc wished he'd been able to give a more traditional seminar to an audience of physicists alone. That way he wouldn't have had to choose his language carefully and skip so much of the interesting technical detail. For example, he'd conveniently left out the fact that the heavy neutralino beams would decay into a host of other particles besides charginos, like W and Z bosons, which in turn would quickly decay into other more familiar particles like quarks and electrons, all of which would be slamming into the magnets at incredible energy. Hopefully they wouldn't destroy the electronics before the magnets had served their purpose.

All the other questions he fielded over the next fifteen minutes were easier to deal with, mainly because he was unable to give definitive answers. He could not say what the Odin Project's chances of success were, when it would be completed, and the beams fired for real, or whether he knew of other ways of getting energy to the Earth's core. He batted away the other obvious questions: yes, he was confident the Project could be kept secure; no, there had been no political pressure on the choice of the magnets' locations – the decision had been entirely scientific. And he also stressed that the original idea of using neutralino beams had been Qiang Lee's, not his.

The question he dreaded being asked didn't come up and he was relieved when the session ended. The one major detail he had deliberately left out of his talk was what happened if anything went wrong. If just one of the eight beams misfired, or missed the central collision point, then the energy pulse produced by the other seven would be out of kilter and . . . well, he tried not to think about that.

31

Monday, 17 June – CERN, Geneva

As the audience filtered out of the lecture theatre, Marc excused himself from the throng who had come down to talk to him. Qiang was engrossed in a spirited technical discussion with several CERN physicists, so he wandered out into the concourse where people were gathering and headed for the long coffee table on the far side. A serving bot glided towards him on the other side of the table.

What would you like to drink, Professor Bruckner? it asked in a singsong voice.

The bot was little more than a white plastic cube, the size of a human torso, with arms. It reminded Marc of a headless Bender, the robot from the animated TV series *Futurama* that he'd enjoyed as a teenager. These days, he'd got so used to the wide range of humanoid bots that worked behind bars and shop counters around the world that he'd forgotten how little CERN cared about anthropomorphizing their service robots, opting instead for minimalism and practicality.

'Black coffee, please,' he said to the cube.

Taking a sip of the strong brew, he wandered around in search of Sarah, quickly finding her in conversation with a group of younger men and women whom he recognized as local CERN scientists. Sarah was holding her coffee mug in both hands, laughing at something one of them was saying. He sensed an inner self-assurance and resolve about her that was in stark contrast to her feelings of helplessness and worthlessness in the weeks following the Event. He also noted as he approached that, despite the plainness of her clothes – a pale blue blouse over comfortable-looking black trousers and flat shoes – and her hair pulled back in a ponytail, she looked stunningly beautiful.

Just before he reached the group he was intercepted by an eager-looking young man who grabbed his hand and shook it enthusiastically. 'That was a great presentation you gave, Professor Bruckner. Do you really think it can work? I mean, will we get the necessary luminosity if we need a double in-flight decay?'

'You mean, are we sure we will still have enough neutralinos after the losses in the beam before and after the bending magnets?'

The young scientist nodded earnestly.

'At each stage there will inevitably be some loss, so we need to build in some redundancy when we generate our initial beams. But in answer to your first question, yes, I do believe it will work. All the simulations say it is possible . . . just. In any case, it *has* to work. What other choice do we have?'

With a parting nod, Marc retreated before the man could ask him anything else. When he joined the cluster around Sarah he noted that three of the group had adopted the familiar expression of people focusing on their retinal AR feeds. Then, almost in unison, several pulled out pocket pads and tapped a few commands on them. Marc looked over at Sarah, but she was watching the physicists expectantly.

'Excuse us . . .' said a man Marc recognized as a senior CERN technician called Carlo '. . . but it looks like the beam is about to be turned on shortly for today's run and we need to get back to the VENICE control room.'

Sarah looked perplexed. 'Venice?'

'Sorry,' said Carlo with a wry smile, 'VENICE is the name of our dark-matter detector. It stands for Very Energetic Neutralino-Ion Collider Experiment – basically a giant underground camera the size of a fifteen-storey building.' He saw the amused look on Sarah's face and added, 'Yes, I know. Sometimes it seems like we spend as much time inventing acronyms for our experiments and equipment as we do carrying out the science itself.'

'Huh, that's nothing,' said Sarah, 'you should hear some of the names of our space missions.'

Marc turned to her. 'They're colliding a beam of dark matter onto an iron target and analysing those highly rare collisions when they take place.'

'And how is this related to the Odin Project?' she asked.

'Well, we still need to understand how the unstable, heavier dark-matter particles decay, so this sort of routine experiment is a vital part of the Project.'

Carlo nodded at them. 'Why don't you come along? You can see for yourself.'

'OK,' replied Marc. 'Let me first go and let Qiang know I'm disappearing for a bit.'

The dazzling sunshine contrasted with the dim lighting inside the lecture theatre complex and the polarizers on Marc's contact lenses kicked in within seconds.

'The VENICE building is about a klick away, so we'll

take the buggies,' said Carlo, leading Marc and Sarah across the quad to where several of the CERN vehicles were parked. The three of them climbed into the first one. Carlo tapped the destination on a small display screen on the dashboard and the car moved off silently.

As they joined the CERN perimeter road Carlo pointed to a large grey structure in the distance that looked more like an aircraft hangar than a science laboratory. 'The VENICE complex is housed inside that building over there.'

'Presumably we won't see much of the detector itself,' said Sarah, 'since all the action is deep underground.'

Carlo nodded. 'Afraid so. You'll have to make do with the inside of the control room. Definitely not advisable to go down to the guts of the accelerator since this is the dangerous form of dark matter, the stuff that decays into nasty products that will do a lot of damage to living tissue.'

The rest of the short drive was covered in silence. Marc looked over at Sarah, who was staring out of the window lost in thought. He followed her line of sight – patterns of colourful lilies lined the roadside – and he wondered what was going through her mind. He had hoped to be able to spend more time with her, to get to know her, but they had both been incredibly busy recently.

They arrived at the VENICE building and followed Carlo inside. Marc enjoyed telling visitors that the aircraft hangar-sized structure was just the tip of the iceberg – the top bit of the VENICE complex that was above ground and which housed the all-important control room. And it was to this centre of operations that Carlo led them, their footsteps echoing around the building. Once inside the air-conditioned room, Carlo excused himself and went over to talk to several scientists who were staring up at two large screens displaying a myriad of scrolling numbers, graphs and colourful diagrams, showing the status of the experiment. Marc and Sarah stood and watched as about twenty other scientists busied themselves with their computer screens. Several turned and nodded to Marc then quickly returned to concentrate on their tasks.

'This is all just official protocol, you know,' Marc whispered to Sarah. 'Because Fabiola, the CERN Mind, will have everything under control. She always does.'

Sarah nodded. 'Not surprising really. An AI, plugged in and networked to millions of electronic components, is much better placed to fix any technical problems herself rather than rely on us flawed humans.'

On a whim, Marc grabbed Sarah's hand. 'Come with me. I want to show you something.' She looked puzzled and amused but didn't resist. He escorted her back out of the control room, down a ramp and across the cavernous building past an area filled with cranes and other heavy lifting equipment. He knew the perfect spot to get a closer look at the VENICE detector. Anyway, they would just be in the way in the control room. Their route eventually led them across a twisting metal gangway where they had to duck under pipework and tread carefully over hundreds of thick cables on the ground.

As they walked, Marc talked about the CERN Mind. 'As you can probably guess, Fabiola isn't networked to the Cloud, so there's little chance of cyberterrorists or hackers getting into her systems.'

'I think Fabiola is brilliant,' said Sarah. 'There's an air of confidence and control about her that's reassuring.'

Marc grinned. 'Well, that's the idea, of course,' he said. 'The human-looking avatar's appearance and voice were designed to exude complete competence. In fact, I sometimes think of her as supernaturally omnipresent.'

They climbed up a metal staircase and onto a walkway that stretched across a vast concrete chasm in the centre of the building. After a few metres, the walkway widened out to a viewing platform. They had arrived at one of the twenty holo stations scattered around the lab. 'Watch this,' he said, touching a wall display, and two overhead projectors began to hum. Like a phantom materializing in between them, the CERN Mind suddenly appeared as a human-sized holographic projection, startling Sarah, who stumbled back a step.

'Hello, Marc. Hello, Sarah. What can I do for you?' said Fabiola in her gentle voice with its unmistakable Italian accent.

Sarah looked delighted with this party trick. 'I know I shouldn't be surprised. She's running the entire CERN complex and so can identify everyone who's on site, but it's still nice. Hello, Fabiola.' Fabiola smiled. She'd always looked to Marc so much like the real person on whom she was based, and whom he knew so well, that he sometimes had to remind himself that he was talking to a computer and not a human being. But for people who had never met the real Fabiola Gianotti, the avatar looked like a kind, elderly aunt from some fairy tale.

He addressed the hologram. 'Fabiola, can you tell us what's happening here today?'

'Certainly, Marc. We're carrying out a routine experiment. In ten minutes, I'll be generating a neutralino beam at a luminosity of ten to the power of eleven particles per pulse and directing it onto atoms of iron in a target at the centre of the VENICE detector located beneath us.'

'Thank you, Fabiola. Well, in that case we won't take up any more of your time as we know how busy you are.'

'On the contrary, Marc, I am happy to discuss this with you, if you like. Unlike humans, I am able to multitask.'

Marc winked at Sarah. 'I know, Fabiola. That was a joke.'

Just then they heard a loud metallic ring, as though something heavy had been dropped. Its echo resonated around the giant building. Marc quickly tapped the hologram off and they both leaned over the railings of the walkway and peered into the large concrete cavern, twenty metres below.

'Was that the dark-matter beam hitting the iron target?' joked Sarah.

'Oh, very good. You solar physicists are so droll,' chuckled Marc, but he continued to concentrate on the floor far below them. Although he hadn't ever been down there, he knew it formed the roof of the shielding above the giant particle detector itself. He could see several manhole covers that would provide ways down into the bowels of the colossal instrument, deep underground. *Hmm . . . probably nothing. Just strange that there would be anyone down there right now—* Just then, he caught a glimpse of movement over on the far side. Someone – it looked like a man – disappeared into an open hole in the floor.

What the fuck? . . . Who would be crazy enough . . . no, stupid enough . . . to go down there just as a run is about to start? If the beam was switched on now that would be a suicide mission.

He felt Sarah touch him lightly on the shoulder. 'Hey, you OK? You look like you've seen a ghost.'

He shook his head. 'Not a ghost, no. A real live idiot climbing down into the detector.' He kept staring over at the open manhole through which the man had disappeared, hoping he would emerge again.

As he watched, another thought bubbled up to the surface of his consciousness, and now it hit him like a freight train. Fabiola had said that the beam of neutralinos had a luminosity of ten to the power of eleven. What to mere mortals would be just numbers with lots of zeroes, was for Marc Bruckner a world of mathematical symbols, colliding particles, heat and light. Such a high luminosity was one hell of a lot of dark matter concentrated onto one spot – in fact, a million times more 'punch' than there should be. It had to be a mistake. Yet that's what Fabiola had said, and Fabiola was a powerful AI that wouldn't just make a mistake like this. What the hell was going on?

He turned to look at Sarah. 'I know for sure he shouldn't be down there. But I think something else is very wrong. I have a horrible feeling *we* shouldn't be here either.'

Sarah stared back at him. 'What is it?'

He took a deep breath. 'The intensity of the neutralino beam is too high. It's even higher than the beams we used in the Antarctic test, and they caused one hell of a bang. The information Fabiola gave us can't be right.'

He spun back to the wall and tapped the pad to reactivate the holo. When the avatar of the CERN Mind materialized again, he said, 'Fabiola, why is the beam intensity so high?'

The silver-haired avatar smiled again. 'This luminosity is required to achieve optimum results for the current run.'

'What fucking optimum results?' Marc shouted. He was starting to panic. 'You do know what sort of energy would be produced with a ten to the eleven luminosity, right?'

'Yes, Marc. When the first pulse hits the target, it will release an energy equivalent of twenty-three kilotons of TNT – the power of a small thermonuclear warhead. I have estimated with 99.97 per cent certainty that this will happen. No other pulses will be necessary.'

His mouth suddenly went dry and tasted acidic. Was he going mad? Did the CERN Mind just say she was about to generate a dark-matter beam that would destroy CERN? For a moment, he was lost for words. Then, 'You bet your digital ass there won't be any more pulses.

287

Because there won't be any more CERN! Fabiola, switch off the beam, now. I command you.'

'I'm sorry, Marc, you don't have the authority.' The hologram smiled sweetly, like a mother telling her small child he couldn't have another cookie.

He looked over at Sarah, who was just staring at the holo. She now turned to him. 'We should get back to the control room and warn people.'

'This is quicker,' he said and, keeping his voice as steady as he could, he addressed the Mind: 'Fabiola, patch me through to the control room.'

Instantly, an image of the control room appeared on a screen on the wall behind the hologram. He knew at once that he wouldn't be telling them something they didn't already know. All around the room, people were shouting. Some were relaying data, others barking orders. One or two were just sitting back helplessly staring at computer screens no longer under their control. Carlo suddenly appeared in close-up, sounding frantic and scared. 'Marc, sorry, can't talk now. We have a crisis.'

'I know, Carlo. Some fucker has just hacked Fabiola! Look, I'm closest to the detector, so I'll see what I can do.'

'Hang on,' replied Carlo. 'We're trying to get back into the system, but it seems Fabiola has locked us out. None of the standard override protocols seem to be working. We're sending a team over. You should stay where you are.'

'Sod that, Carlo. Anyway, someone's already down there now. You do know that, right? Just tell me this: how long do we have until the beam comes on?'

'Just under eight minutes. Marc, if we can't get in and stop the run in the next two or three minutes we will have to evacuate.'

'Evacuate to where?' screamed Marc. 'If this is the

work of the Purifiers and they destroy CERN then that's curtains for the Project, and humanity.'

He turned back to Sarah. 'I'm going to try to switch off the beam manually. You need to get the hell out of here, quick.' He wondered whether the man he'd seen had realized what was about to happen and was already a step ahead of him. Or was he part of whatever was going on?

'The hell I am. You might need my help,' said Sarah. 'Besides, if this thing goes off where did you think I was supposed to go?'

Marc didn't stop to argue. Nodding, he said, 'Shit, Sarah, I'm sorry I've got you mixed up in this. OK, come down after me.'

He opened a gate in the railings, turned around and started to climb down a metal ladder bolted to the wall. He could hear Sarah's feet just above him. His hands were sweating, and he almost lost his grip. It didn't help that he was shaking too. He didn't like heights at the best of times, but he managed to push aside the thought of how far he would fall if he slipped.

He jumped the last five rungs and landed awkwardly. But he was up and running straight away across the featureless expanse of concrete towards the manhole cover. Without looking back, he heard Sarah running a few paces behind him. Their footsteps echoed off the walls of the chamber. Marc reached the opening where the man had disappeared and knelt down to peer into the blackness.

'Hello? Who's down there?'

No response. Shit, they'd have to go down into the detector – there was no way back now and the seconds were ticking by. He spun round and dropped his right leg in, feeling with his foot for the ladder rung. As soon as he found it, he lowered the rest of his body into the blackness and started the climb down. No time to act the gallant gentleman and wait for Sarah.

Three metres later he hit the ground and gave himself a few seconds to get accustomed to the dark. The room was crowded with instruments blinking their coloured tell-tales, and the minimal lighting lent everything an eerie alien glow. He was accosted by a dozen different sounds, from the hissing of vacuum pumps and the hum of magnets to the beeps of detectors, sensors and alarms. It seemed every bit of space was being used. He was fighting off his feelings of claustrophobia as Sarah joined him.

They quickly followed signs pointing to an elevator. When they reached its wide metal doors, Marc pushed the button and heard the whirring of a distant motor. It seemed to take for ever for it to arrive, but at last the doors slid open and they stepped into its spacious interior. It was clearly designed to transport many people at once, or large pieces of kit, in contrast to the narrow entrance in the roof they had just used.

'Where does this take us?' Sarah asked as they began to descend.

'Down six storeys to the core of the detector. The dark-matter beams haven't been generated yet, but the energy of the protons circling in the main ring is already being ramped up. A siren goes off when the dark-matter beam is on, and if we're still down here then— I don't know how long we've got or even what we can do, but we have to try.'

'Well, given what Fabiola just told us, I don't suppose it matters whether we're down here or back in the control room. We'll be vaporized either way,' said Sarah in a cold, flat voice.

The elevator doors rumbled open, and they were greeted with the sight of a vast underground cavern. On any other occasion it should have taken their breath away, but Marc wasn't in the mood to admire feats of technology. The hum of the electronics here was even louder than it was at the top. Sweeping his gaze around the chamber, he suddenly caught sight of movement over on one side. It looked like there were two people, a man and a woman, with their backs to him. They were crouched down in front of a piece of equipment and hadn't heard the arrival of the elevator over the background noise. Marc's initial reaction was one of relief, that someone was already here dealing with the situation.

'Hey,' he shouted, hurrying over to them, 'how's it going? Can you override things from here?' But they still seemingly couldn't hear him.

'Hey!' he shouted, louder this time.

The pair twisted their heads around. They appeared startled by the interruption. Marc could see clearly now that they had been working on what looked like an old-fashioned laptop perched on a wooden stool.

The man – who had a wiry frame and pale face beneath lank dark hair and who looked like he could be any other regular accelerator scientist – suddenly jumped up to face him and, with a cry of rage, picked up a metal bar lying on the ground next to him, then rushed at him like a wild animal protecting its domain.

'What the—?' Marc watched, hypnotized, too stunned to move.

As he ran towards Marc, the man twisted his body, lifting the bar above his head with both hands like a medieval knight wielding a longsword. By the time Marc came to his senses it was too late and his attacker was upon him.

The man's mistake was not to slow down as he approached. As he began to swing the heavy bar towards

Marc's head, it didn't respond quickly enough. The split second it took for it to arc round was all Sarah needed. She crashed into him from the side, sending them both sprawling, and the bar clattered across the floor.

Marc didn't hesitate. He ran towards them, picking up the bar on his way. 'Right, you're going to tell me what the fuck you're—'

But the man had already scrambled to his feet and was sprinting towards the still open elevator doors. Marc thought about giving chase, but decided he had a more pressing issue to deal with. He turned to Sarah, who was getting to her feet and rubbing the side of her head.

'Thanks for that. Are you OK?'

'I'm fine. Look, the woman's gone too.' She pointed to the abandoned laptop a few metres away.

They ran over to it and stared at the still open command windows on the screen.

Marc's heart was pounding, and he tried to clear his head. He couldn't afford to panic now, in what little time they had left. 'Right, we have to assume that whatever they were doing is connected with hacking into Fabiola. But I don't get this. It's all just so low-tech. Why would sophisticated cyberterrorists use decades-old technology . . . and why would they need to be down here in person, knowing that they would be caught up in the blast if they succeeded?'

'I think I can guess,' said Sarah, still breathless. 'Fabiola can't be accessed from the outside world, so the only way to hack her would be to get into her base-level machine code, from the inside.'

Marc nodded. 'And they would have assumed there'd be no interruptions down here.' He knelt down by the laptop and stared at the screen filled with lines of code.

'Ah, shit. What the hell are we supposed to do? We

don't have network access down here inside all this shielding, so we can't get help.' Marc's mind was racing. But maybe he could still shut Fabiola down. Their only hope was if the laptop was indeed plugged deep into her command level.

He began to type and executed various Unix commands, but nothing he did seemed to have any effect.

Behind him, Sarah suddenly stood up and shouted, 'Look, I'm no use to you here, so I'm heading back to let the guys in the control room know where you are. We need their help.' Without waiting for a response, she turned and ran towards the elevator. For a split second Marc thought about stopping her. What if she bumped into the terrorists? What good would it do if she made it back to the control room in time? How many more minutes, possibly just seconds, did they have, anyway? He pushed the thoughts away and turned his attention back to the screen.

Suddenly, he heard Fabiola's voice, loud and echoing above the background noise. It had the same gentle, almost reassuring quality as ever, which made it all the more chilling.

'You are accessing forbidden code, Marc. Please desist now.'

Good, he thought to himself, *I'm getting under her skin.*

Fabiola's repeated warnings reverberated with increasing urgency around the chamber. He tried to ignore them. He knew he just needed to find the correct reboot commands. His fingers danced around the keyboard as he tried to recall his almost forgotten programming knowhow.

Then, just as suddenly as it had started, the AI's voice went silent, and the computer screen went completely blank. Marc's fingers hovered above the keyboard, waiting. Had he done it? Had he really reset an AI Mind? Suddenly, two words popped up in the top left corner of the screen. He recognized them as the two best-known words in computer science, representing the output of the most basic program anyone could write – two words that became famous decades before he was born, but which still carried significance for anyone with coding knowledge. They said simply:

```
hello, world.
```

Marc stared at the screen for a few seconds. Of course, even a sophisticated AI like Fabiola would operate fundamentally on deep neural net architectures using reinforcement learning. Rebooting her really did mean wiping her memory clean.

His hands were now shaking uncontrollably, and he felt beads of sweat running down his temples. The deafening noise had stopped, as though a number of the machines had shut down. It had to be the scientists back in the control room. They had taken over manual control and stopped the run. Euphoric relief washed through him and he started to stand up, aware that his knees felt stiff. But he didn't get very far. He felt a sudden bolt of excruciating pain in the back of his head and everything went black.

For a few seconds after he came to, Marc couldn't figure out where he was. All he knew was that he had a splitting headache and the bright lights above him were not helping. As his surroundings swam into focus he made out a sea of concerned faces hovering over him. He recognized Carlo and tried to sit up, to speak, but a wave of dizziness overwhelmed him, and he flopped back down again. 'Don't try to move, Marc,' said Carlo. 'Enough heroics for one day, eh? You've been out cold for an hour.'

He tried to recall what had happened. He'd been down in the bowels of the VENICE detector. And he'd shut down the CERN Mind.

'Is the beam shut off?' he croaked. 'Is everything OK?'

'Yes. Thanks to you. We had less than fifty seconds to spare before we'd all have been vaporized.'

It came back to him now. 'What about those two who tried to sabotage the experiment? Were they Purifiers? I guess one of them hit me.'

'We don't know. There's no sign of them yet. But lab security and Geneva police are searching the lab. In fact, they would like to speak to you as soon as possible to get an ident.'

Marc tried to sit up again, more slowly this time. 'Where's Sarah? Is she OK?'

He saw her pushing her way in to him. 'I'm here, Marc. I'm fine. These guys showed up just in time, but not before one of the two we interrupted had hit you over the head.'

Marc grunted. 'Out of sheer bloody spite because we'd ruined their party.' He was relieved Sarah was safe. Hell, he was relieved CERN was safe. Those Judgement Day nutters seemed keen to sabotage any plans that would rescue humanity. If this was the work of the Purifiers, then maybe they had yet to realize that there was an option B – that the best way to ensure a quick and decisive end to humanity would be to wait for the endgame when the Odin Project was ready, then strike. Maybe they weren't as smart as people thought. Hacking a Mind with a museum-piece laptop and hitting people over the head – presumably with that fucking iron bar – didn't sound like the work of sophisticated cyberterrorists. But they'd still come close to succeeding. Too close.

By attempting to destroy one of the three labs capable of producing beams of dark matter they were clearly still aiming to prevent the Odin Project from getting off the ground in the first place. But it wouldn't take long for them, and the rest of the world, to realize just what a risk this entire venture was.

32

Wednesday, 3 July – Juliaca, Peru

DESPITE THE EVEN TIGHTER SECURITY AFTER THE CERN attack, the Project continued to move forward rapidly. But with only two months to go now to the planned Ignition, there was still so much to do. Sarah was relieved not to be directly involved with operational matters, or the messy world of politics, any longer. She had, however, found herself inescapably grouped with Marc and Qiang as one of the talismanic global representatives of the Project. She still loathed all the media attention this entailed, but she knew she really had no choice. Anyway, Marc and Qiang were good company. She continued to work hard at not falling for Marc's charms, but she sensed deeper feelings for him growing inside her that had nothing to do with any superficial physical attraction. Still, she had kept them locked away. These were no times for starting up a relationship, particularly with someone she had to work with professionally.

Having dealt with the world's press at CERN following the failed attack, their attention was now focused on Mag-4, under construction high on the Andean Plateau in southern Peru, one of six facilities around the world housing the giant magnets that would bend the beams down into the ground. The three physicists had come to the site to witness the next test: to see if a pulse of heavy neutralinos would indeed behave in the way Marc and Qiang had proposed – that the particles would decay at just the right moment to be bent by the magnets. Their official brief was to offer encouragement, discuss the science with the locals and generally provide the media with the charm offensive so vital in the face of continuing public opposition and widespread, but understandable, fear. Along with the other countries on the Pacific coast of South America, Peru had got off relatively lightly during the CME back in March. The initial devastating radiation burst had hit before 6 a.m. local time and most of the population had still been in bed, not out in the open.

As soon as she got off the plane at Juliaca Airport, Sarah could sense that the atmosphere was thinner. And despite the coolness of the air inside the bustling terminal, once out in the harsh sunlight she felt its warmth. They'd been warned of the discomfort they were likely to feel at such altitude – four thousand metres above sea level – and not to exert themselves for the first few days until they had acclimatized. So, she was grateful that a couple of bots took their luggage on ahead, weaving smoothly on their treads through the crowds entering and leaving the terminal building.

She didn't feel tired. The one-hour, ten-thousand-kilometre hyperskip from Geneva to Lima had been uneventful, as indeed had the much shorter heli flight across to Juliaca.

The city of Juliaca, in the Puno region of southern Peru, lay to the northwest of Lake Titicaca. It was a sprawling metropolis of over a million inhabitants and a thriving trade centre, forming the hub that linked Peru's three largest urban areas of Lima, Arequipa and Cusco to La Paz across the border in Bolivia.

A man in dark sunglasses was waving to them from across the road outside the terminal. Sarah noted that, in contrast to the three scientists' casual attire, he was wearing a three-piece grey suit, its buttoned-up jacket straining against his waistline and the fabric so shiny it glinted in the bright sunshine. She assumed this was their host, Dr Arnau Diaz-Torres, the Mag-4 chief engineer. He stood beaming at them as they approached, his thick, well-groomed moustache speckled with grey.

'Welcome. Welcome to Peru,' he said in his heavy Spanish accent, extending a hand to Sarah. 'Dr Maitlin, it is a pleasure to meet you. I have watched you on the news so much in recent months that I feel I know you.' He turned to Marc and Qiang. 'And, of course, you two gentlemen are my physics heroes. You are true giants of science.'

'It's a pleasure to be here,' replied Sarah. 'I hadn't quite expected it to be so warm, given this is your winter and we are so high up.'

'Oh, just wait until the sun goes down. The contrast in temperature between day and night up here is greater than in any desert.'

The doors of the car waiting alongside slid open and Sarah was a little surprised to see a driver inside. Diaz-Torres saw the look on her face. 'Because of the heightened security, we have decided that a human driver is the safer option. Humans are less likely to be hacked.' He laughed. 'Especially when we have such important visitors. We will of course have an army escort too.'

Sarah noticed for the first time the two jeeps on either side of their car, each one containing several heavily armed soldiers. They only slightly reassured her. She hadn't truly felt safe in a while, despite her round-the-clock protection. If the Purifiers wanted to strike, she was sure they'd find a way. Since the failed attempt to destroy CERN, they had been quiet, but no one believed they had given up. And yet the authorities were no closer to defeating them.

As they pulled away, Diaz-Torres said, 'You will be staying in accommodation within the high-security Mag-4 compound. But if you don't mind, we will go straight to the facility and I can show you how the Peruvian sector of the Odin Project is progressing.'

She detected more than a hint of pride in the man's voice. He then reached into the satchel on the seat beside him and took out various items and passed them around. 'I have taken the liberty of providing you all with sun hats and sun-block pills. These days the dangers of UV radiation are even greater than usual so far above sea level.' Sarah accepted her provisions and thanked the Peruvian, but when he turned his attention to Qiang, she exchanged a quick glance with Marc. They didn't have the heart to tell Diaz-Torres that they had everything they needed already in their rucksacks. Still, it was a sweet gesture.

They drove out of the airport and along the busy roads that skirted around the city centre. She stared out of the bullet-proof glass window, only half listening to Diaz-Torres as he explained how life had changed in Juliaca over the past few weeks. 'The city's population has been swelled by many thousands. And it isn't just all the scientists, engineers, technicians and the three thousand Mag-4 construction workers. We have bus-loads of tourists arriving each day, as well as many traders from around the region.'

300

It also looked to Sarah that a large fraction of the Peruvian army was making its presence felt. Groups of armed soldiers stood on every street corner and army vehicles rumbled up and down the main streets.

After about twenty minutes, they were on the winding highway north of the city. Sarah had visited the astronomical observatories in Chile, high in the Atacama Desert, but this landscape was even more spectacular. The Altiplano, or 'high plain', was more commonly known throughout the world as the Andean Plateau, where the seven-thousand-kilometre-long Andes mountain range was at its widest. On both sides, beyond the barren hills bulging up indiscriminately over the otherwise flat ground, were impressive peaks: to her left, like an array of giant shark's teeth, was a chain of majestic-looking volcanoes, and to her right, in their dramatic, serrated, snow-capped splendour, rose the Andes mountains themselves. The only vegetation she could see, stretching into the distance, was highland grass. Diaz-Torres explained that this was the *ichu*, the staple grazing food for the herds of llamas and alpacas.

They passed a picturesque lake and surrounding marshland almost entirely covered by a vast flock of pink flamingos, a sight Sarah found enchanting. Then, without warning, they were there. The view that greeted her around the next bend was impressive: a wide, flat plain surrounded on three sides by fierce-looking mountain ranges. At first, it was difficult to appreciate its scale, but she estimated it was about five to six kilometres deep and three kilometres wide. Along the entire length of the road, an imposing high fence had been erected, isolating the area from the outside world.

The car slowed down as the driver negotiated the dense traffic of other vehicles and people surrounding the compound. It looked as though an entire town had suddenly sprung up outside. Sarah's senses were bombarded with a sea of colour, sound and activity. There seemed to be everyone from tourists, well-wishers and curious onlookers to demonstrators and religious fanatics – including a group of end-of-the-world doomsayers in their long grey gowns and shaven heads, who were being watched carefully by the soldiers lining the fence. All these people mixed with the locals, and all seemed curious to witness the wonder of engineering in the distance that was part of the plan to save the world.

She watched as street traders tried to catch the eye of anyone venturing close enough to their colourful displays of traditional Peruvian hats, ponchos and pan pipes alongside hastily manufactured miniature models of the giant magnet and other Project-related souvenirs, all laid out on makeshift tables. The tourist industry seemed to be thriving, and it gave her an odd sense of faith in humanity. She even spotted tourists paying locals to take their picture posing with docile and cute-looking llamas. Even during such uncertain times, some things don't change.

Qiang laughed. 'The circus has come to town.'

'The biggest circus South America has ever seen,' agreed Diaz-Torres. 'And over there is the main attraction.'

Sarah followed his gaze beyond the crowds and the high-security fence towards a giant grey dome in the distance, inside which Mag-4 was being built.

'If this is a circus, then that is the Big Top, yes?' said Diaz-Torres. 'Did you know the locals already have a name for Mag-4? In our native Aymaran and Quechuan languages, they call this place *Ukhupacha waka*, which means "Temple of the Inner Earth".'

Sarah watched Qiang practise the words under his

breath; then, turning to Diaz-Torres, he said, 'I'm afraid the only words I know in Quechuan are *Machu Picchu.*'

The Peruvian smiled. 'We are still proud of our Incan heritage, you know. Locals have great affection for Pachamama, the Earth Mother, our ancient deity, and many in my country believe the dying of the Earth's magnetic field is due to mankind's misuse of Nature, which has been an affront to Pachamama.'

'They're not the only ones,' agreed Sarah. 'Everywhere you look, new and old religions are gaining followers. We've raped and pillaged our planet; we've changed our climate; we've destroyed so much. You'd think people would be *losing* faith.' Then, after a moment's hesitation, she added, 'I suppose it's only natural, given the threat we're facing right now. People want to trust the science, but if there's a chance that a higher power can lend a hand . . .' She turned back to look out of the window.

Driving through several gates with increasing levels of security, including biometric checks and sniffer bots, they finally entered the vast compound and a wide, newly tar-macked road that led in a straight line to the Mag-4 facility. From this distance, its scale was deceptive since it was dwarfed by the mountains behind it, but Sarah realized that it must be further away, and therefore much larger, than she had first estimated. As if reading her mind, Diaz-Torres said, 'The reason it has to be so big is because of all the shielding.'

Sarah nodded. 'And at the risk of sounding naive, that's presumably to block all the synchrotron radiation produced when the charged particles are bent by the magnets, right?'

'Precisely,' enthused Diaz-Torres. 'This is basically the world's biggest X-ray machine, but it has nothing to image. The X-rays are an unavoidable by-product when

303

the charginos are forced to change direction. But we still need to stop this radiation from zapping everything in its path.'

They pulled up outside the front of the dome. Sarah stepped out of the car into the bright sunshine and quickly reached for the sunglasses in her pocket. She looked back along the road they had come, to the perimeter fence and the crowds outside it. They were too far away for their sounds to carry and all she could hear was the faint whistle of wind around the dome and a deep hum of machinery coming from within. She arched her neck back to look up at the structure and, despite her sunglasses, still needed to squint. It was huge.

She turned to see Marc and Qiang already following Diaz-Torres towards the entrance and hurried to catch up with them. Just outside the door they were met by a young man who handed them hard hats.

Sarah donned hers and removed her sunglasses. 'Hard hats suit you,' smiled Marc as he adjusted the strap on his. 'You look like you mean business.'

'I always mean business, Bruckner. And don't you forget it.'

They followed Diaz-Torres in. Sarah had expected to walk into semi-darkness after the bright daylight outside, but it was quite the opposite – the centrepiece of the vast chamber was illuminated by powerful LED floodlights from all angles, giving it an almost supernaturally bright aura.

'Oh, my God . . .' she whispered. Her two companions also stopped suddenly in their tracks, speechless.

A hundred different sounds assaulted their ears. A huge drilling rig at the centre of the dome was the loudest, but backing support was provided by the hum of other machinery, the throb of electric currents, the shouts

304

of the workers, and the incessant sirens and alarms of equipment – ranging from low-frequency horns to high-pitched, ear-piercing bleeps.

Sarah realized Diaz-Torres was smiling broadly as he watched them, clearly happy with their reaction. He had to raise his voice to be heard above the cacophony of sound. 'The roof of the dome is as high as a thirty-storey building,' he shouted, 'just over a hundred metres. As you can see, the concrete shielding is not yet in place, but you get to see the magnets for now. There are twelve dipole magnets, each one forty-two metres in length and five metres in diameter.'

It felt to Sarah almost like a spiritual experience, here inside this vast cathedral to science. The magnets, suspended high above their heads, resembled black missiles arranged along three separate arcs, one above the other, each arc consisting of four magnets, and all held in place by high-tensile carbon nanotube scaffolding.

Sarah put her mouth close to Marc's ear and shouted, 'It looks like some crazy art installation.' He grinned at her.

'As you can see,' continued Diaz-Torres proudly, leading them further in towards the magnets, 'the beam, which will have travelled here from Fermilab in Chicago, comes in from over there.' He waved his hand vaguely.

Sarah and Marc had followed him, but Qiang remained rooted to his spot near the entrance, staring up as though hypnotized by the structure.

Diaz-Torres, now in full flow, continued his lecture. 'And the beam, as it comes in, has three opportunities to be bent. The neutralinos that decay quickly into charginos will get bent by the first set of four magnets in sequence, with each one in turn deflecting the particles by thirty degrees, until they are travelling downwards towards the centre of the Earth. For those neutralinos that

305

decay a little later and which pass straight through the first array of magnets, the second and third set provide further opportunities to catch and bend them. And so—'

Sarah interrupted him. 'Sorry, I thought you said each magnet bends the beam by thirty degrees,' she shouted. 'There are *four* magnets, and four times thirty makes a hundred and twenty degrees. But don't you need to bend the beam by a right angle: just ninety degrees? So why use four magnets when only three should be enough?'

'You are correct, Dr Maitlin, but don't forget the curvature of the Earth. The beam coming from Fermilab is actually travelling along the shortest path to get here – a perfect straight line – and since it does not have to follow the curvature of the Earth's surface it can tunnel straight through the ground. This means it arrives here from underneath us at an angle of just under thirty degrees to the horizontal. So, it has to be bent back by the magnets by more than a right angle – in fact, by a hundred and twenty degrees, which makes our job even harder.'

With the impromptu geometry seminar ended, Sarah excused herself and wandered over to the giant drilling rig positioned directly below the magnets at the very centre of the dome. A circular barrier stopped her from getting too close, but she could see the hole it was boring into the ground. It looked to be about a metre in diameter. So, this was where the beams from all three sets of magnets would be focused and combined as they began the vertical leg of their journey. She recalled the latest Project plans: the early estimates of a one-hundred-metre borehole had been deemed too conservative. Unless the charginos decayed back to neutralinos quickly, they wouldn't get very far once they hit solid matter. So, to be safe, it was decided that five-hundred-metre-deep vertical shafts would be created at each of the eight facilities to accommodate the beam pipes, which would be maintained under vacuum as empty as interstellar space, so as not to disturb the beams. Then once the charginos decayed back to neutralinos the world would suddenly become invisible to them again. Sarah felt she was getting the hang of all this dark-matter physics.

She heard Marc, Qiang and Diaz-Torres come up behind her. Diaz-Torres was still proudly explaining the workings of the facility to Marc and Qiang. He had to shout even louder over the noise of the drilling. 'All the shielding, along the quadrupole focusing magnets, goes in next week, and once that is calibrated we can start our first test run.

'Eventually, when we have to synchronize with the other seven beams we will need to control the pulse energy very carefully. Did you know we are twenty kilometres further from the centre of the Earth here than Mag-5 in Norway?'

Sarah watched Marc's carefully modulated reaction. Of course they knew. He and Qiang must have been through the geometry a thousand time, so it was sweet of him not to wish to hurt Diaz-Torres's feelings. 'Ah yes, of course, we are on the bulge of the equator here,' he shouted back, nodding his head gravely.

'As well as being at high altitude,' said Diaz-Torres, 'which means our beam heading into the Earth must travel further, so we must give it an extra boost of energy to make sure it arrives at Point Zero at the same time as the other pulses.'

Then he added with a flourish, 'In fact, even the tidal forces due to the Moon's gravity are included.'

He stood back, hands on hips, seemingly taking a personal pride in having surmounted so many difficulties.

Sarah was keen to find out what the next stage in

testing was. As a solar physicist used to studying whatever the Sun deemed fit to produce and send Earthwards, she wasn't accustomed to designing this sort of experiment and found it fascinating to be reminded of the many problems that had to be overcome. She walked closer to Diaz-Torres, so he could hear her. 'What is this first test designed to check?'

'Ah,' replied the Peruvian enthusiastically, 'if all goes to plan, a pulse of heavy neutralinos fired from Fermilab will be sent here to see if the magnets can do their job. Of course, with just the one beam, it should travel straight through the Earth to the other side, coming out in the South China Sea.'

Qiang nodded vigorously. 'Of course. And that's where Darklab will be waiting!' he shouted. Sarah now remembered why he was so excited. His institute in China had been developing a mini dark-matter accelerator for the past five years and he'd been heavily involved in getting it funded. Now it seemed that it would play its part in the latest test of the Odin Project. It was to be placed on-board a ship that would float above the point where this beam would emerge on the other side of the planet. Darklab would itself produce a small amount of dark matter and fire it down into the sea to meet the Mag-4 pulse head-on. The tiny energy created would then be picked up by the vessel's detectors.

She turned to Qiang. 'But if it's just to see if two colliding dark-matter beams can create energy inside the Earth, wasn't that what the Antarctic tests confirmed last month?'

As soon as she said it, she realized she knew the answer. She held up her hand to Qiang, indicating she didn't need him to respond. Of course, this test was to do two things: firstly, to make sure the magnets were doing their job of bending the beam and that neutralinos were indeed being created; and secondly, to check that they were being sent in precisely the right direction through the Earth.

Unbidden, the sheer scale, complexity and downright conceit of the entire Odin Project hit her, sending her mind reeling. *Is humankind truly capable of pulling this off? Maybe we're kidding ourselves if we think we can play God with our planet.* It was an unexpected notion. She came from a long line of agnostics and atheists and had always dismissed the term 'playing God' as nonsense. And yet, and yet . . . All the time the Project had been just an idea in Marc Bruckner and Qiang Lee's heads – a set of equations and computer simulations – she'd been fine, but seeing it take shape like this now suddenly unsettled her. A billion things could go wrong, a malfunction in a small component somewhere, one simple miscalculation, a bug in a line of code – and it would be curtains. She looked up at the giant magnets suspended high above her head. *What the hell were we thinking?*

33

A FAINT BREEZE RUFFLED THE TOPS OF THE TREES LIN-
ing the cycle path, but the sky was clear and blue. It was
going to be another hot day. The temperature in western
Europe had broken all records this summer and had
nudged above 40°C in Britain for the third year running.
Now, the country was in the middle of an early-autumn
heatwave. As she cycled to her new job, Shireen wondered what Majid would say if he saw her now, working
at one of the world's top cybersecurity organizations. Her
old friend had gone back to his university studies after
his release. They constantly chatted, but everything they
said was now closely monitored and she couldn't tell him
any details about where she was or what she was working on.

While she wouldn't go so far as saying she was happy –
no one ever talked about being 'happy' these days – her
life had become increasingly interesting. She still missed
home terribly, of course, and had even managed to visit
her parents over the summer. It had been wonderful,

310

despite being accompanied throughout by Savak agents. Even her mother and father didn't know what she was really working on, and although relieved that all charges against their daughter had been dropped, it still puzzled them. All she could do was reassure them that everything was fine. The official line was that she was simply helping the UN on a cybersecurity project.

She didn't mind that her university studies had been put on the back burner for now; it was the same for most people these days – all plans, hopes and dreams were currently on hold. It was as though nine billion humans were holding their collective breath, waiting to see whether there even was a future.

And the world didn't have long to wait. The Odin Project was nearing completion, and the moment when the dark-matter beams would be switched on for real, Ignition, was drawing nearer. Now it was just one week away and no one could see beyond that moment.

For her part, Shireen had made little progress of note so far. And time was running out. Whoever the Purifiers were, they appeared to be both well organized and well funded, and her attempts at hacking into their communications network on the dark web had so far proved unsuccessful.

After the CERN incident she had been one of an army of cyber experts assigned the job of uncovering who had been behind it. The Purifiers had not claimed responsibility, but then what group *would* claim credit for a botched attempt? But now, as Ignition approached, security was being ramped up to feverish levels. And work at Bletchley Park was no different. It suited Shireen just fine being able to come and go relatively freely, even though she knew that every move she made was being monitored and scrutinized. At least she'd been allowed to block out the intrusion into her augmented reality feed and get some privacy back.

She overtook a couple of joggers. It was only a fifteen-minute cycle ride from her apartment, but she was already feeling uncomfortably warm. She wondered what the rest of the cyb community would think if they knew what she had been doing these past few months: working for 'the enemy' to root out cyberterrorism – poacher turned gamekeeper. But then the rules of the game had changed.

Here at the CICT, Shireen almost felt at home. The work at the Centre for Intelligence on Cyberterrorism was in a high-security compound just outside the city of Milton Keynes, north of London, where she was part of a team of frighteningly brilliant young coders, mathematicians and cyber espionage specialists. Of course, no one ever used the organization's unflattering acronym and the place was known locally by its more popular name of Bletchley.

Everyone here, as far as she could tell, was doing pretty much what Bletchley Park had been famous for one hundred years ago when it was home to an equally brilliant group of young British cryptanalysts and codebreakers led by Alan Turing. Today, Bletchley was a United Nations of geeks, all working together to monitor worldwide cyberterrorist activities.

Most of the people seemed friendly enough. A few, like Koji, a Japanese mathematical prodigy who sat at the desk next to her, were her own age and quite fun to be around. But she seemed to have very little time for socializing.

Arriving at the front gate, she jumped off her bike and wheeled it through the biometric scanner. She locked it alongside dozens of others in the yard, then entered the cool, air-conditioned building. She nodded a greeting to an older man who'd come in just ahead of her. All she knew about him was what Koji had told her in the staff canteen the day she'd arrived, that he had been one of the original MIT team behind the first AI Sentinel.

For the first couple of weeks in June, after the UN had recruited her to work on protecting the Project, Shireen had been something of a celebrity herself. It seemed everyone had heard about her Trojan horse code, and everyone had ideas about how to improve it.

But here at Bletchley she was just another cyb prodigy. The remit of the scientists at Bletchley was clear. In fact, the need for their existence had been starkly highlighted by Shireen herself: that while the AI Minds around the world that ran and protected the infrastructure of society, from transport and financial systems to defence and security, were themselves mostly adequately protected by the Sentinels, there was still a place for human ingenuity to work alongside them.

Most of the time, of course, the Sentinels did a far better job at cybersecurity than any human ever could, since they were able to carry out tasks billions, and often trillions, of times faster, as well as being in constant communication with each other, exchanging the information content of an entire library of books in less than a nanosecond.

She still vividly remembered with nostalgic fondness a hiking trip with her father in the Alborz Mountains when she was thirteen. She recalled being cold and tired, but the scenery had been stunning. They had spent hours discussing AI and the way the world was changing. Her father explained to her that the notion of artificial general intelligence, when machines could do everything humans could, required AIs to be sentient, to develop self-awareness. Otherwise, they would stay just very clever zombies, with no true understanding of what they were doing. All the time this remained the case, humans could keep one step ahead of them. True machine consciousness, he'd said – she recalled this was the first time she'd heard the term 'the singularity' – would not be achieved for many decades.

Since that hiking trip just seven years ago the line between artificial and human intelligence had become increasingly blurred. Passing the Turing test had not meant that computers were now sentient, but it had highlighted instead that what most people thought of as consciousness was no longer so clear-cut. Sure, AIs now had very crude emotional states, but these had mostly been programmed in rather than learned. At best, the most powerful Minds were more like benign yet extreme psychopaths (those scoring close to the maximum of 40 on the Hare psychopathy checklist), in that they lacked the ability to feel basic emotions such as compassion, or to empathize with the emotional states of humans.

But Shireen's job was not to protect or monitor the AIs. She had been given a quite specific task: to infiltrate the Purifiers' network. She knew she wasn't the only one at Bletchley working on this and it was a little frustrating that she couldn't discuss anything with others. Surely pooling their mental resources would be more effective? But she also understood that it was probably safer for her to be doing this alone, following her instincts as she navigated her way through the vast dark web.

Later that morning, just as she was thinking of taking a short break, she received notification of a message sent to her dark web account. It was one that she only used very rarely and which few people had access to.

It was from Sarah. Shireen had suggested she contact her that way if she ever wanted to say something in private. This was the first time Sarah had used it.

She stared at her screen and her heart started beating faster. The message was brief and obscure:

Shireen, we have to meet today. Covent Garden
3 p.m. Tell no one.

She hadn't even known Sarah was in London, but thanks to her own past experience in avoiding the prying eyes and ears of drones and sensors Shireen immediately understood Sarah's choice of venue. Covent Garden was one of the busiest places in London – ideal if you didn't want to be spotted easily. But what might warrant such secrecy? She quickly sent back a reply.

OK. I can be there. What's going on?

She waited a couple of minutes for a response, but nothing came back. What the hell? Sarah would have sensitive information about all sorts of details relating to the Project, but the only reason she might want to contact Shireen at this point was if she knew something about the Purifiers and their plans.

For her own part, if she was going to get to Covent Garden without raising suspicion, Shireen decided the best course of action was to keep her story as simple and as close to the truth as possible. All staff at Bletchley were on call twenty-four hours a day and had been working around the clock for several weeks now as Ignition drew closer. And while officially everyone was still being positive about the outcome of the Project, it was also understood that many would want to have short visits to see family and loved ones to say their goodbyes, just in case. Everyone therefore was allowed a few hours off each week on compassionate grounds. Shireen had an aunt who lived in Soho, just a few minutes' walk from Covent Garden, whom she had been meaning to visit for several weeks past. It was the perfect cover.

Within half an hour she was on the high-speed shuttle from Milton Keynes to central London. Staring out of the window and lost deep in her thoughts, she didn't register the city's suburbs flying past. If required, she could go dark – disappear for a few hours so that she was untraceable – but there was nothing to suggest that was necessary yet. Not having any idea what Sarah wanted was frustrating. Anyway, for now let them keep track of her movements. Someone would no doubt have already checked out her cover story, but that was in hand. Her aunt had been delighted when she'd called her to say she would be dropping in.

The train slowed as it approached Euston Station and she checked the time. Midday. She could spend a couple of hours at her aunt's swapping family stories before she had to leave to meet Sarah. Every minute was going to feel like an hour.

34

Tuesday, 10 September – London

WITH ONE WEEK TO GO TILL IGNITION, MARC HAD BEEN in Geneva with Sarah to discuss final arrangements with the rest of the international task force. Although their relationship had remained platonic so far, Marc had been finding it increasingly difficult to hide his feelings for Sarah. He still wasn't entirely sure whether she felt the same but hadn't wanted to jeopardize their friendship by suddenly coming on strong. On the one hand, now really was not the time for romance, but then, if the Project failed and the world was destroyed, he wouldn't want anything to be left unsaid.

He'd been looking forward to the coming weekend when he planned to catch up with Evie in London. His daughter was over in Europe for a week with her high-school art class visiting museums and galleries in several capitals. Last night, he'd spent an enjoyable hour sharing in her delight as he watched the retinal video feed she had posted of her day at the Tate and National Portrait Galleries. He was amazed not only at the resilience and relaxed attitude of the young towards the Project, but that most schools around the world continued to function normally during these times.

It was then that his world had come crashing down.

First came the news from the London police that Evie had gone missing from her hotel. The alarm had been raised by her school party earlier that evening when her roommate had returned to the hotel from a shopping trip to find her not there. But, as the officers were very keen to stress, she could well have just gone out for a walk without telling anyone, although they acknowledged it was strange that she had also gone off-grid.

Within an hour of talking to the police he was back in his Geneva hotel making arrangements to fly to London – Sarah had insisted on accompanying him and the two of them had packed as quickly as they could. He'd clung to the hope that Evie would return, that she had just gone for a walk and got lost. But his wristpad had pinged as they were about to leave the hotel room. He'd stopped halfway out of the door to look at it.

Professor Bruckner, congratulations on cheating death in CERN. But now you will help us ensure that Mother Earth cleanses herself of the plague of humankind. If you want your daughter to live long enough to witness Mother Earth's glorious rebirth you will do exactly what we ask. If you inform the authorities about this message she will not live to see another sunrise.

Further instructions to follow. Acknowledge.

Marc had felt his world begin to swim and he'd stumbled against the door, then slumped to the floor. Sarah's voice, asking him what was wrong, had sounded as though it was coming from a great distance. He'd read through the message again. What did they want? What did the message even mean? The mention of Mother Earth indicated that this was from the Purifiers, or someone trying to pass as the Purifiers.

In a shaky voice, he'd spoken into his wristpad. 'Acknowledged.'

He didn't remember much more of that evening, or the flight to London. He had received a call from Charlotte in New York and had tried his best to hold himself together as he spoke to her. She had been hysterical with worry, wanting to catch the next flight over herself. She told him the police in London had spoken to her too and were keen to know if Evie was having any friendship problems, whether there were any girls on the school trip with whom she might have fallen out and which might have prompted her disappearance. Of course not, she had told them. Evie was popular and as well-balanced and sensible as any teenage girl could be. He'd managed to persuade his ex-wife that, for now, there would be absolutely no point in her coming over to London. Evie was bound to show up soon. Maybe her wristpad had been stolen and she couldn't find her way back to the hotel or contact anyone. He knew he hadn't sounded very convincing, but until he had more information he just couldn't risk telling her any more.

'Listen, Charlie, I'll be in London in a few hours and will call you as soon as I hear something.' He hoped he'd sounded calm enough.

So, here they were, sitting outside a café in one of the busiest locations in the crowded metropolis. Waiting. But not just for contact from the terrorists. Sarah had persuaded him that he . . . they . . . should enlist the help of her young cyb friend, Shireen; that if anyone could infiltrate the group and find his daughter, she could.

319

Marc had taken a lot of convincing. 'Sarah, we don't know what their demands are yet. All we do know is that the Purifiers will stop at nothing to get what they want.'

But Sarah had won the argument. 'Shireen is one of the world's smartest cyberhackers.' She lowered her voice to a conspiratorial whisper. 'I'm sure you know she's working for UN intelligence to infiltrate the Purifiers' network, so no one on the planet is better placed than she is to find Evie. And you know as well as I do that the vital thing now is time. The longer we wait the harder it will be to trace them.'

And so they waited for Shireen. And they waited for instructions from the kidnappers. Marc stared down at his wristpad willing a message to arrive – anything, just as long as he knew Evie was still alive. After a few minutes, he stood up. 'I'm going to get another coffee. You want one?'

'No, thanks,' said Sarah. 'I'll try to eat some of this salad. It's already looking a bit sorry for itself.'

Marc disappeared into the café. He'd been standing in the queue for no more than a minute when his wristpad buzzed. He looked down at it and what he saw made his blood run cold.

You really should eat some lunch, Professor. We
need you at your sharpest.
Stand by . . .

They were watching him.

That meant they would see him meeting Shireen too. He rushed back out again, his heart pounding. Several people turned to stare as he pushed his way through the crowded café entrance. Were the kidnappers among them? And how long had they been tracking him?

320

The look on his face must have betrayed the panic he felt, because Sarah froze. 'What is it?'

He showed her the message then slumped down in his chair and put his head in his hands. None of this seemed real.

Sarah put her hand gently on his arm and whispered, 'They can see us, but I don't think they can hear us. Remember, we chose this table ourselves, so it couldn't have been bugged in advance, and all the noise around us means no drone mike could pick up what we say if we speak softly.'

Marc looked up at her. She was right, but it didn't reassure him in the least. 'You know we won't be meeting your friend now. It's too risky. You can see that, right?'

Sarah held his gaze for a couple of seconds, then nodded.

Suddenly, his wristpad pinged again. He forced himself to look down at the new message.

Professor Bruckner, your Odin Project is an abomination and it will not succeed. As its architect, you will now become its destroyer. You will do exactly what we, the Purifiers, tell you, because you love your daughter. If you do then she will come to no harm, but you will only see her again once we are satisfied your task is complete.

The stomach-churning dread and anxiety he was feeling about Evie was now supplemented by an even deeper sense of foreboding. He tasted bile rising up in his throat. What was it they needed from him? It was clearly something they were confident he would agree to. Until recently, he would have said that a group as ruthless and resourceful as the Purifiers would have had a thousand

321

ways of stopping the Project, but not any more. Since their failed attempt to reduce CERN to a giant crater, the eight Project sites had become physically impenetrable fortresses and surveillance within and around them was bordering on the omniscient, while the security clearances necessary to access any aspect of the Project were becoming so tight that many of the scientists and engineers involved now found it difficult to do their jobs properly. Every conceivable weakness, from cracking quantum encrypted data files to hacking the Minds themselves, had now been addressed.

And yet . . . Had the Purifiers just found the Odin Project's Achilles heel: one of its two creators?

When the third message came through a minute later, he didn't know what to make of it at first.

> *In exchange for your daughter's life, we ask for a simple thing from you. You must give us access to your REAPER-9 code.*
>
> *It would be a shame if you allow some misplaced sense of moral duty to humanity to cloud your judgement. Your daughter's death will not be pleasant.*
>
> *You have 24 hours.*

He stared at it for a few seconds, his mind in turmoil. Then he understood.

When he raised his eyes to meet Sarah's, all he could feel was a numbing sense of hopelessness – it was an experience he knew well, only this time the demons were all too real.

She had read the message too because now she spoke softly and calmly. 'Take a deep breath, Marc, and tell me about the REAPER-9 program.'

He gathered his thoughts as best he could.

'It's a computer code that Qiang and I developed about fifteen years ago. It calculates dark-matter particle properties – their lifetimes, decay schemes and so on. It's a big code – over twenty thousand lines. It's what we used in the work that led to our breakthrough prediction.'

'Your discovery that dark matter self-interacts?' Sarah asked. 'But what's that got to do with the Project? I mean, that's all established science now, right? It's out there in the public domain.'

'It's not as simple as that.' He sighed, still trying to work out how the Purifiers had found this weakness. There were now hundreds of research teams around the globe working day and night on the Project; thousands of engineers were building the giant superconducting magnets, several in some of the remotest parts of the world; accelerator physicists, geologists and engineers were teaming up to finalize the finer details of the dark-matter beams to ensure that each pulse was aimed in precisely the right direction for all eight to meet within a single nanosecond at 'point zero', a volume the size of a peppercorn deep within the molten core of the planet. And yet, the Purifiers had still known exactly what, or rather whom, to target . . .

'You know, their plan is quite beautiful in its simplicity,' he said finally. 'The REAPER-9 program is still a vital part of the calibrations. And they want me to give them access to it. And I can guess why. All they'd need to do is change one line of code – a single line out of over twenty thousand.'

He saw the shocked look on Sarah's face. 'Many years ago,' he continued, 'I was involved in the calculations that first predicted the lifetime of the chargino, the particle that has to be bent by the magnets. The relevant

323

subroutine in the code deals with something called R-parity conservation and it's my numbers that feed into the main program. Changing that line of code would make our estimate of the chargino lifetime wrong.'

'And? What are the implications? I mean, you seem to be talking about lines of code – a simulation – but we will have real beams of particles doing what they do and the entire mission has been set up to make sure nothing goes wrong. What am I missing?'

Marc chewed his lip and shook his head. 'No, the REAPER-9 code is much more than a simulation. If it is altered so as to predict that the charginos will decay back into neutralinos more quickly than is really the case then the energy of the beams, the speed of the particles, will be adjusted to suit the prediction, and the beam will still consist of charged particles when it hits the ground.'

Sarah shook her head. 'I still don't get it. Why calculate lifetimes during the run itself? Why not hardwire these numbers into the accelerator design in advance?'

'Because then we would have no control. The energy and luminosity of the beams will always have tiny error bars and so all parameters have to be constantly adjusted. Remember, for the run to work, all eight beams need to coincide, and these particles are travelling at close to the speed of light. There is no margin for error.'

'OK, so it doesn't work. We'd just try again, right? Once we know, it can be corrected again.'

'Ah, but I know now what they will do. Or at least I can guess. They only want to tamper with the code controlling the CERN beams. They know I still have the access passwords to the codes being run at CERN. The beams from the other two labs would be unaffected.'

Sarah jerked back in her seat. 'What?' She had said it too loudly and a few people seated nearby turned to look at her. She leaned forward and lowered her voice again. 'But if not all eight beams meet at point zero then the perfect balance is destroyed, and the energy pulse gets sent back out again – to the Earth's crust.'

Marc nodded. 'If the CERN beams don't get through then that's three of the eight that are knocked out. The remaining five wouldn't cause a catastrophic event, but there would still be serious seismic activity: earthquakes and tsunamis wherever it emerges. But it's survivable.'

He saw the blood drain from Sarah's face. 'You mean "just" millions might die, rather than billions?'

Marc felt a sense of despair. 'That's what they seem prepared to risk – and, more to the point, that's what they seem confident *I* would be prepared to risk in order to save Evie.'

But now that he had explained what he thought their plan would be, he realized there was something bugging him. At first, he couldn't quite articulate it. Then it came to him. 'What I don't understand is why do it this way? Why not knock out just one of the eight beams and bring about the quick annihilation of the entire planet? Why three?'

'Maybe because this is easier,' replied Sarah. 'And it still ensures the failure of the Odin Project. Maybe they don't want humankind to bring about its own, sudden demise. Maybe the Purifiers themselves want to survive long enough to see their mission through, to be a part of the slow suffocation of all life as the planet loses its atmosphere. I don't know, Marc. It's all so fucking sick.'

Marc felt he was grasping at straws. 'But this way, we *would* try again. We would have to.'

'No, Marc, we wouldn't. Global opinion would swing away from the Odin Project, maybe back to the MPDs, and that would be that. You know how hard it was to make the case for the Project in the first place. Do you really believe they would sanction a second attempt? Besides, how can you even contemplate signing the death warrant of millions of innocent people? I know I can never forgive myself for not doing more in Rio back in March. I watched so many people die and just saved myself. This is different. You would be knowingly committing genocide.'

Marc felt anger rise up to the surface. What was she saying? That he would instead sacrifice his own daughter?

'Please spare me the moral philosophy, Sarah. I can't think beyond Evie for the moment. Can't you see that?'

They sat in silence. Finally, Sarah whispered, 'You know we can still find Evie, if you allow Shireen to help. Don't be fooled by her age – that young woman is astonishingly resourceful.'

Marc felt broken and emotionally drained. 'I have to, now, don't I? Otherwise, if I do as they say I will be buying my daughter's life with the blood of millions of others . . . other Evies and their families – people I will never meet. And you know what gets me most? It's that the kidnappers are so sure I would make that choice.'

Suddenly his wristpad buzzed again. But this time instead of a message it showed a grainy-looking video feed. It was very dark and hard to make out, so Marc cupped his hand around it to block out the harsh sunlight. His mouth went dry and he let out a quiet whimper. 'Oh, Jesus, no!' It was her. It was Evie. His daughter was lying unconscious on a rug on a filthy brick floor. Or was she just sleeping? He hoped she was sleeping. The lighting was just good enough for him to make out the gentle rise and fall of her chest. At least she was alive! Behind her, a stained brick wall and curved archway led into

326

darkness. It looked to Marc like a cellar. Or a dungeon. Then, without warning, the screen went blank.

'Oh, my God, Marc, where *is* that?' said Sarah softly.

He was too shocked to answer. Seeing his daughter like that had brought the full, horrible reality of the situation clearly into focus. Finally, he looked up at Sarah, a fire burning in his eyes. 'What time is it? We need to meet your friend.'

As if on cue, Sarah received a message. It was Shireen. She showed it to Marc.

Go dark. Turn off your devices and disconnect your AR feeds. Then leave your table and walk around to the other side of the piazza. It's busier there and we can lose whoever it is that seems to be watching you.

Sarah looked at Marc. 'I told you she was good. She's been watching us too. Come on, it's time we fought back.'

35

Tuesday, 10 September – London

GAINING ACCESS TO SEVERAL COVENT GARDEN SURVEIL-
lance cameras had been straightforward enough. Now,
standing in the shadows on one side of the bustling
piazza, Shireen studied her retinal feed carefully. On one
side of the split screen she had a bird's-eye view of Sarah
and Marc sitting at their café table, while on the other
half she could see the two men who were watching them.
One was an older man with a shaven head who seemed to
be in charge; the other, younger with a wispy beard,
looked like the tech guy. She smiled to herself. The watch-
ers were now the watched. She had no idea what they
wanted, but whatever the issue, it was serious. Marc and
Sarah seemed tense and animated. She'd hopefully find
out soon enough.

She'd realized as soon as she arrived that she wasn't the
only one using the camera aimed at the two scientists'
table and had tracked down the source of the other hack
to a bar on the south side of the piazza – far enough away
for what she had in mind. But the timing had to be right.
Having sent Sarah the message to go dark she waited

until the very last moment before she and Marc stood up to kill the feed from the café camera. She watched as the two men, after a moment's blank shock, broke into an animated discussion, presumably about why they no longer had eyes on their quarry. Shireen smiled to herself. *Not so clever now, are you, boys?* Suddenly, they both jumped up from their table and made their way out of the bar in a hurry, but it would take them a couple of minutes to reach the café – ample time, she hoped, for Sarah and Marc to lose them.

Making sure her baseball cap was pulled down to hide her face, she came out of the shadows into the harsh sunshine. She briefly caught sight of Sarah and Marc and made a beeline for them through the crowd. As she brushed past them she spoke under her breath without slowing or looking up. 'Follow me.'

A minute later, she was standing near the back of a throng of people gathered around a street performer. She couldn't see him clearly through the crowd but whatever he was doing – some conjuring trick, most likely – his patter was so infectiously enthusiastic that he had drawn a large audience. She had flicked on the squelch jammer in her rucksack as soon as she'd arrived. It was more sophisticated than the one Hashimi had given her in Tehran and she was now invisible to any drones or satellites overhead. She hoped it would also shield Sarah and Marc from being spotted once they were within range. Hopefully, it would give her enough time to find out what was going on.

It was just after 5 p.m. by the time Shireen arrived back at Bletchley and she was eager to get started. There were at least ten people still working at their desks, but no one had noticed her come in, their VR visors locking each of them away in a world only they could see.

329

Back at her desk, she pulled on her visor and accessed the vast repository of information she had built up on the Purifiers' network. For the first time, she now had a real lead to follow, only she had hours rather than days to infiltrate their cyberspace.

Her first task was relatively easy. Before she could find where Evie was being held, she needed to locate the kidnappers, and it didn't take long for her to trace the IP source of the original message sent to Marc the day before. She wasn't surprised to find that the kidnappers had put in place clever diversions, trapdoors and firewalls, but there was nothing she hadn't negotiated a gazillion times before. It appeared that whoever these people were, they had covered their tracks in a hurry, and that meant they would have been sloppy somewhere along the line. If she kept prodding and probing, she knew she would find what she was looking for. The Trojan horse spyware she was currently using had been modified significantly by the team at Bletchley. It was now more powerful than the original code she'd created.

Humming along to music as she worked, she let it guide her movements until she was swaying and manipulating her virtual displays in sync with the beat. She had recently become a fan of fusion punk, a synthesis of West African rock and angry Asian K-pop, and she found the urgency of the beats just what she needed to stimulate her thought processes when immersed in the dark web. Despite the magnitude of her task, Shireen felt happy, at one with cyberspace. Almost omniscient.

And while she worked, her spyware code flowed silently through the dark web, a digital ninja searching and probing for weaknesses, following leads, building up correlations, looking for patterns.

By 5:45, she had pinned down the origin of the messages

to Marc. They had come from somewhere inside the British Library on Euston Road in the centre of London. And, whereas cyberhackers would normally build in a delay to make it hard for anyone to determine the exact timing of the hack, in this case, the messages had been created and sent in real time. There. That was very sloppy. It took her less than two minutes to access the library's computer system and locate the record of everyone who had used it during the one-hour window between 2 p.m. and 3 p.m., which was when the final messages had been sent to Marc.

Of the one hundred or so people who'd used the library's computers, only seven had blocked their idents. Of those, five had left several minutes before the final message was sent, which meant there were just two suspects. Both had left the library just after 3 p.m.

All she had to do now was hack into the data from street cameras in the neighbourhood of the library to catch them leaving. Simple. Sure enough, they had left the library separately: a man and a woman, both in their early to mid-thirties. She now had sufficient biometric data to search for them.

The search for a match among the more than ten million Londoners captured on the city's many thousands of cameras took just a few seconds; she found the woman first, in a coffee shop across the road from the British Library. She was sitting in a corner with a milkshake, reading a book and looking like every other customer in there. Nothing suspicious. Shireen was almost certain she could rule her out as a kidnapper.

In contrast, the man was on the move. Each time-coded feed showed him at a different location, enabling her to plot his route across London. The most recent footage was just ten minutes ago when he'd entered the site of what looked like an old warehouse. The satellite data she accessed allowed her to survey the area and a quick search told her that it was near Tower Bridge, south of the Thames, a neighbourhood that had been among the worst flooded in London ten years earlier. Much of it was apparently still abandoned. Very private. Very convenient. She quickly accessed and commandeered a high-flying surveillance drone and zoomed in as tightly as she could onto the derelict building. Was this where they were holding Evie?

Piecing together a sketchy profile of the man from the information she could find on the dark web wasn't so easy. But while she couldn't yet link him to anyone or anything to do with the Purifiers, there was enough to suggest he had much to hide.

Removing her visor, she sat back in her chair and rubbed her eyes. It was almost 7 p.m. and there were five or six other people still working in the office. It occurred to her that she hadn't had anything to eat since the slice of cake at her aunt's apartment at lunchtime. But food could wait; like a lioness, she was closing in on her prey and couldn't afford to stop now. She slipped the visor back over her eyes, leaving the physical world behind again.

36

Tuesday, 10 September – London

ENTRUSTING HIS DAUGHTER'S LIFE TO A STRANGER – A girl barely five years older than Evie herself – terrified Marc. But what choice did he have? This past twenty-four hours had been a living nightmare.

Shireen had told them to avoid going back to the hotel, which was most likely being watched by the kidnappers. They needed to find somewhere with no surveillance cameras and wait for her call. Sarah suggested they take refuge at the Helios Institute, the solar research laboratory in the grounds of University College London where she was a regular guest and could gain access with her visitor's pass.

They had walked the two kilometres from Covent Garden to the Institute in silence. Marc couldn't get the image of Evie lying on that filthy mat out of his mind and was grateful to Sarah for leaving him alone with his thoughts. They didn't meet anyone on their way in. Sarah led him up to the fourth floor then heaved a sigh of relief when her thumbprint was recognized and the door of the office she had used on her last visit clicked open. The office was empty, and Sarah quickly closed and locked the door behind them.

Marc slumped onto a chair by the window and stared down at his wristpad. Shireen had done something to their devices to make sure they were secure. But he kept expecting at any moment to get a message from the kidnappers telling him they knew what he was up to. Within minutes, he was on his feet again, pacing around the small office, stopping every few minutes at the window to stare out at the city bathed in late afternoon sunlight. *Evie is out there somewhere, frightened and alone, and I'm stuck in here. Or maybe she isn't even in London any more?*

Sarah was sitting at the desk, nursing a mug of coffee and staring into the distance, clearly not knowing quite what to say to make him feel any better. He shouldn't have dragged her into all this, but not for the first time he felt grateful that she was with him.

It was just after eight and getting dark outside when he got the message from Shireen via the secure route she'd set up. His heart missed a beat as he read it. 'My God, Sarah. She's found her! Shireen's found Evie already.'

'I told you she was good,' said Sarah, rushing over to him.

He showed her the message.

Marc, I think they're keeping Evie in an abandoned warehouse south of the river. I've sent you the coordinates.

Sarah looked up at Marc. 'So, what do we do now?'

There really wasn't much to discuss and he hoped Sarah would understand. '*We* aren't going to do anything. I am.'

'Come on, I know she's your kid, but we're a team now. And I'm not your dutiful fucking sidekick—'

334

'Don't do this, please, Sarah. You must know I would readily sacrifice my life if it meant saving Evie, but I can't ask you to do the same. I need to see this through. Alone.'

'Let me guess, I stay here where it's safe, while you do your Indiana Jones routine and go beat up the bad guys?'

'It's not like that,' said Marc, with no hint of a smile. 'I know you can take care of yourself . . . It's just—'

'Fuck you, Marc Bruckner.'

'Look,' he said, holding her shoulders gently. He pulled her closer to him and looked into her eyes pleadingly. 'She's my baby girl. And I know you want to help, but if they even get a whiff of what we're up to I don't know what they'll do. And I can't risk that. Not even to spare your pride. I'm sorry.'

Sarah seemed to relax a little and sighed. 'So, what's your plan, Indi? You haven't got a gun or a whip. Dammit, you don't even have a hat.'

Marc smiled weakly. 'Look, if Shireen is right, then I can make it there by myself. At least I have the element of surprise on my side. If I find the odds are stacked against me then we can think of calling in the cavalry.'

Sarah suddenly reached up and kissed him gently on the lips. Somewhere deep inside him was a thrill that Sarah felt the same way about him as he did about her, but right now he was consumed by his fear for Evie. Sarah grinned at him as she pulled away.

'For luck,' she said. 'Please don't try anything stupid.'

I'm about to go after a bunch of maniacs who are holding my daughter captive, unarmed and with no plan. Define stupid.

He did his best to give her a wry smile and hurried out of the door.

*

335

It was a warm and sticky evening and beyond the Institute's courtyard the roads and skies were busy with traffic. It suddenly occurred to him that he couldn't risk getting a road or air cab in case the kidnappers traced him when he paid the fare. He had to stay as inconspicuous as possible. He looked around the courtyard until he found an unlocked bicycle, which he commandeered and wheeled out as quickly as he could, hoping the jammer Shireen had given him did its job. This would take him longer, but he couldn't take any risks. And it meant he could arrive unannounced. He hoped he wouldn't live to regret the delay.

He quickly worked up a sweat as he cycled in the evening humidity. He tried to stay as focused as he could, but the image of Evie locked away in the dark warehouse somewhere kept resurfacing. What did he expect to find when he got there? What would he do if the place was guarded, or if there were several people?

The traffic had thinned out dramatically by the time he reached Tower Bridge. He'd not been south of the Thames before and was shocked by the wasteland of abandoned office buildings, warehouses, and tower blocks. The rising sea levels had overwhelmed the Thames estuary, now five times larger than just a few decades ago, with much of the surrounding countryside in southeast England now underwater. London's flood defences had done a reasonable job of minimizing the impact on the capital, but large swathes of land south of the river had been sacrificed. He checked his surroundings against the map on his lenses, trusting Shireen that, like his wristpad, it was now safe to use his AR without being detected.

Many of the roads in this part of the city had become shallow waterways – a poor man's Venice – and he needed to negotiate a route through the few streets remaining accessible to road traffic. The area was deserted and appeared devoid of surveillance cameras, the ideal location to hide someone.

Just then, he heard Shireen's voice in his earphone.

'Marc, I'm tracking you and I can see you're nearly there. I'm still monitoring the warehouse and there's no sign of activity yet. I think you're safe to approach.'

His AR told him that the warehouse was just up ahead. Abandoning the bike against a wall, he ran the rest of the way. Keeping as close as he could to the buildings as he approached, he almost tripped over someone sleeping in a doorway. The man sat up, grunted and waved a large kitchen knife in Marc's direction. Already on edge, the incident gave Marc a scare. He didn't slow down.

The warehouse was in the middle of a fenced-off derelict site. He stood by the open gate for a few seconds to catch his breath. There were no windows on this side of the building, so he sprinted across the open yard to the nearest wall and waited to make sure he hadn't been spotted. Shireen's voice came through again.

'Marc, I can see you at the building. I have no idea what's waiting inside. Please be careful.'

He didn't reply. Instead, he peered around the corner, spotting a small window at about shoulder height just a few paces away. With his back tight up against the wall, he edged towards it and peered inside.

At first, the place looked empty, but then a flicker of artificial light caught his eye. There, in the gloom in the far corner, sat a fair-haired man in a T-shirt. He had his back to Marc and seemed to be staring intently at a computer monitor. On the floor around him was a haphazard array of electronic equipment. Marc couldn't be certain, but it looked to him like surveillance kit. It all seemed very makeshift. If this was their centre of operations, then they were clearly either moving in or moving out.

A surge of anger rippled through him. The man appeared to be alone. But where was Evie? Was there a basement? All thoughts of the folly of what he was about to do now evaporated. He threw caution to the wind and sprinted round the building to find a way in.

Right, then, dickhead, it's showtime.

The entrance was a large metal door and he eased it open until the gap was wide enough to squeeze through, relieved that it made no sound. Once inside, he stood still and tried to control his breathing. It took him a few seconds to adjust to the gloom. He was in a narrow entrance hall with what looked like a small kitchen off to his left. To his right was a corridor leading through to the main warehouse. He searched around for a weapon, realizing too late just how unprepared he was for this rescue mission. A filthy plank of wood leaning against the kitchen door looked sturdy enough to do some damage. He picked it up quietly, satisfied with its reassuring solidity, and crept slowly across the hallway. Detritus and broken glass, hard to avoid in the dim light, crunched as he walked and he cursed under his breath as he tried to cross it on tiptoe.

When he emerged into the main open space of the warehouse, he stood still in the shadows while his eyes darted around, searching for any sign of Evie, but he could see no obvious route down to a cellar. At least the man at the computer screen, who was still unaware of Marc's presence, appeared to be alone.

But the element of surprise didn't last.

Without warning, the man suddenly swivelled around in his chair and looked directly towards where Marc stood. Marc had no time to think. Luckily, shock had

338

temporarily immobilized his antagonist and it was all Marc needed. With a howl of rage, he charged.

The world took on a dreamlike quality as everything seemed to slow down. He had halved the distance between them when the man snapped to his senses and reached across the table for a gun. There wasn't enough time to cover the remaining ground and instinct took over. With an underarm swing, he propelled the plank of wood at the man with all his strength. It arced upwards through the air, catching him with a loud crack under the chin, throwing him backwards against the chair behind him and leaving him crumpled in a motionless heap.

Marc was by now on top of him. Snatching the gun off the table, he held it ready to fire, but his caution wasn't necessary. The man was out cold. His mouth was bleeding and hanging open at an unnatural angle – a broken jaw. Marc stood over him for a few seconds then swung round to examine the warehouse space once again, consumed by the need to find his daughter.

'EVIE. EVIE. CAN YOU HEAR ME? IT'S DAD.'

Silence.

After several minutes of desperate searching he gave up. Had he just come on a wild-goose chase? He tapped his wristpad and contacted Shireen. 'Shireen, I'm OK. But there's no sign of Evie here.'

'Shit. Tell me how I can help.'

'OK, stay with me.'

He considered reviving the still unconscious man and beating the information out of him, but instead turned his attention to the computer on the table. There had to be some clues there. The screen showed several windows of live video feed. The one that caught his attention first was a view of the interior of the warehouse itself. He was looking down on himself from above. He craned his neck back and, sure enough, hovering silently a few feet above his head was a tiny skeeter drone recording his every move. *That's how the man knew I was here.*

He looked back at the screen. Another window showed a view of Evie's prison: the rug she had been lying on and the stained brickwork behind it. But there was no sign of Evie. In the top left of the window were the words 'St Pancras'.

His heart sank. 'Shireen, I'm in the wrong place. I'm looking at what appears to be live footage of where Evie is, or was, being held, but I can't see any sign of her. It's definitely the same place as that video footage of her they sent me and it just says, "St Pancras".'

'OK, I am accessing that computer through your wrist-pad so that I can trace the origin of the feed. Give me a minute.'

Marc felt helpless. The man he'd overpowered was clearly one of the kidnappers, but if Evie wasn't here, what was this place? Some kind of safe house? Was Evie being kept captive in a temporary location and set to be moved here later? A sudden tiredness overwhelmed him as the adrenalin that had been surging through his body just a few minutes earlier, and which had sharpened his senses, now drained away. Had he missed his only chance of finding Evie?

Suddenly a woman's face appeared in a corner of the screen and she was staring straight at Marc. *And they know I'm here. Great.*

He jumped from the chair, not quite knowing what to do with himself. He couldn't stay here, that's for sure. Had he just signed his daughter's death warrant?

But where am I supposed to go? St Pancras Station? Is that where Evie is, or at least where she was? Stay calm and think, dammit. Think!

340

Then Shireen's voice again. 'Marc, I've found it. It's not St Pancras Station, it's St Pancras Church. She's being held captive in the crypt beneath it.'

'And where the hell is that?'

'There was a reason why Evie's captors contacted you from the British Library. The church is just across the road from it.'

'Oh, no,' moaned Marc. 'And that's just a couple of blocks away from the Institute, where Sarah is, where I just spent the past few hours. I've just been on a wild goose chase.' He stumbled out to the road. But Shireen hadn't finished.

'Marc, listen. Firstly, we wouldn't have found the place had you not gone to the warehouse. But there's something else. There wasn't just one of the kidnappers in the library this afternoon. There was a woman too. But I had stupidly discounted her.'

'How do you know this?' He was suddenly finding it hard to breathe and his head began pounding.

'Because I just hacked into her wristpad and put in an autotrack. She's just left the coffee shop where she's been all afternoon. It's up the road from the church. She must have been hanging around to keep an eye on things, and now it looks like she's heading there.'

It was the same woman he'd seen just now and who'd seen him too, he was sure of it. He'd run out of time. He couldn't get there before the kidnappers.

But Sarah could.

'Shireen, tell Sarah. Tell her—' He didn't know what he expected Sarah to do. He would be putting her directly in danger, and in some corner of his brain a warning voice told him this was a grave mistake, that it was not fair to ask her to do this. But what other choice did he have?

341

'Tell her to get to the church, but to stay out of sight. And if she sees anyone, not to do anything. I'll be there as quickly as I can. And Shireen, call the police. Our cover's blown now so there's no point in being careful any more.'

'OK,' said Shireen, 'I'll get eyes on the church too.' She disconnected.

Never in his life had Marc Bruckner felt so powerless.

37

Tuesday, 10 September – London

SARAH WAS OUT OF THE HELIOS INSTITUTE BUILDING and running before Shireen had finished briefing her, the information continuing to feed through to her retinal AR as she ran. In one corner of her field of vision was a map of the block between University College and the church; in another, she watched a live feed from a drone hovering above the church. She could be there in less than a minute.

The church was on a quiet, tree-lined avenue at its junction with the busy Euston Road. She slowed to a walk as she emerged from a side-street opposite, and approached the church more cautiously. She'd seen no one on the drone feed, so with luck she'd beaten the kidnappers back here. The churchyard was blocked off from the road by an imposing metal fence and a padlocked gate looked like the only entrance point. She rushed along the fence and around the side in search of another way in while Shireen told her what she could about the place.

'There's a crypt beneath the church. And images of it online show that its walls match those in that footage. It seems it was originally used as a catacomb and there are still over five hundred bodies entombed down there! But it's been abandoned for the past ten years, the perfect prison. Evie was down there, I'm sure, but I don't know if she still is.'

'Thanks,' panted Sarah. She stood still for a moment to take stock. Staring through the railings it struck her that there was something forsaken, sempiternal, about the place that she found deeply unsettling. All she could hear was her own heavy breathing.

Just then, Shireen spoke in her ear. 'Sarah, it looks like you've got company. You'd better hide.'

She ducked behind a tree just in time, because a second later she heard the sound of an engine. Peering from the shadows she saw a large anonymous black van pull up alongside the fence. A man jumped out and unlocked the gate, pushing it inwards. The entrance was wide enough for the van to drive into the churchyard and out of her line of sight. Were they about to move Evie to another location now that they knew Marc was on to them?

'Sarah, I've taken the drone up to two hundred metres in case they hear it, and its camera resolution isn't good enough to make out details, so it's just your eyes now.'

Sarah looked up and down the street. It was deserted. She edged her way back round to the front gate. There was no one visible in the yard and the van looked empty, so its occupants must have gone inside, down to the crypt presumably. She took a deep breath. Her heart was still racing from her run and was showing no sign of slowing down. Had it been just one person, maybe the woman from the coffee shop that Shireen had mentioned, she might have stood a chance. After all, she still had the element of surprise on her side. But she had no idea how many kidnappers there were.

'Sarah, I can just about make you out at the gate. Please be careful. There's nothing you can do right now so get back out of sight. The police are on their way.'

Shireen was right. But the decision was made for her. One of the kidnappers suddenly appeared from behind the van and pulled open the sliding door on its side. She realized all too late that she was caught in no man's land and in plain sight. He had spotted her. For what seemed like an eternity, neither of them moved, and the spell was only broken when two more of Evie's captors appeared – the man who had unlocked the gate and a woman. They were half carrying, half dragging Evie between them. Her clothing was dishevelled, and her face and hair smeared with dirt. At first, Sarah almost didn't recognize her. The girl looked dazed, as though drugged.

The sight snapped Sarah back to her senses. She was within arm's length of the gate and the open padlock was still dangling from the bolt.

Sprinting forward, she reached out and pulled the gate shut, slipping the padlock off the bolt as she did so. The driver, seeing what she was doing, started running too. She had no more than a couple of seconds. The gate clanged shut and she pushed the bolt across. Despite her fingers fumbling, she managed to slip the padlock back onto the bolt and click it shut just as the man reached the other side of the gate. He snarled and thrust both arms through the bars to grab at her, but she had already stepped out of his reach. She now watched transfixed as he pulled out a key from his pocket and tried to manipulate his hands through the bars to reach the padlock, but thankfully the angle was too awkward to allow him to get the key into it from inside.

The second man now released Evie from his grip and the girl dropped heavily to her knees. Sarah stood rooted to the spot in horror as he walked calmly around behind Evie and pointed a gun at the back of her head.

'That was a very stupid thing to do, Dr Maitlin,' he called over to her. 'My associate is going to pass you the key to that padlock and you will unlock it again, or your boyfriend may find it hard to forgive you with his daughter's blood on your hands.'

What choice did she have? What on earth had she been thinking anyway? That they would just sit around, imprisoned in the churchyard until the cavalry arrived? She slowly walked up to the gate again, her whole body shaking with anger. The man on the other side smiled cruelly at her as he stuck out his hand through the bars, offering her the key.

Just as he did so, she heard a sudden buzzing sound overhead. At first, she thought it must be the surveillance drone Shireen had commandeered. Looking up, she saw instead a weaponized police drone skim over the fence. Without slowing, it fired twice at the armed man standing behind Evie. He was thrown backwards in a spray of red, gun flying from his hand. The driver lunged at Sarah through the bars, but she stumbled backwards out of his reach once again and his hand snatched at thin air. Within seconds, more police drones dropped out of the sky and a cold mechanized voice ordered the two remaining kidnappers to lie down on the ground with their hands over their heads.

Sarah stood frozen to the spot. A robotic voice from one of the police helis above her head boomed out, 'Dr Maitlin, step back from the gate now.'

It snapped her out of her stupor, but instead of obeying, she without thinking rushed over to the gate and unlocked it, then dashed past the dead man to Evie. The girl just stared up at her, eyes wide in shock.

'Come on, Evie, let's get you out of here. You're safe now. I'm Sarah. Your dad has told me so much about you.' Helping the girl gently to her feet, she supported her limp frame and guided her back out to the street.

They hurried across to the other side and sat down on the kerb. The police had now physically arrived on the scene and were pouring into the churchyard. A small crowd of onlookers was beginning to gather outside.

Sarah watched numbly and hugged Evie tight. She could feel the girl shivering as she sobbed silently against her chest.

It was almost midnight by the time Sarah and Marc got to the hospital to be with Evie. Marc had understandably not wanted to leave his daughter's side but had to endure a thorough debriefing at Scotland Yard. Sarah had told them everything she knew and was confident that her story would tally with both Marc's and Shireen's, who were each being interviewed in separate rooms.

Now, perched next to Marc on the edge of Evie's hospital bed, Sarah watched the heavily sedated girl as she slept.

Marc spoke softly. 'One way or another this will all be over in a week.' His attempt at a smile was no doubt meant to be reassuring. Was he trying to convince her, or himself?

'A week suddenly seems an awfully long time, though, doesn't it?'

Marc rubbed his eyes and nodded. 'You know they'll keep trying, don't you?'

Sarah wondered whether the arrest of several of the Purifiers in London would provide enough intel to bring down their entire network. She doubted that very much.

38

MARC AWOKE JUST BEFORE DAWN AND LAY STILL FOR A few minutes. He thought about the trauma the terrifying ordeal of the previous week would have inflicted on his daughter. Charlotte had told him that Evie hadn't been sleeping well, even under mild sedation, and was waking up regularly from disturbing nightmares. Not surprising really, considering what she had been through. But given the current situation so close to Ignition, they had not been able to arrange any counselling for her. Still, she was a tough kid and if they got through all this, then there'd be time to worry about any lasting psychological scars. He had to keep telling himself that this was not his fault and that at least she was safe now. It had been quickly decided that families and loved ones of all key personnel connected with the Odin Project would be taken off-grid and moved into secret protective custody until after Ignition. But he missed Evie, now more than ever.

He listened to Sarah's soft breathing in bed next to him and turned to face her. She looked even more beautiful when she was sleeping. Had they just spent the night together because they might never get another chance? Or was it the only way they had of dealing with the stress they were under? Maybe it would have happened anyway at some point, under more normal circumstances. For him it was probably a combination of all three reasons.

He thought about going for a run to ease the tension he was feeling but knew that was no longer possible – the hotel was under heavy guard to protect the assembled scientists, journalists and politicians staying there and no one could leave or enter without good reason and without ridiculously tight security. Instead, he climbed quietly out of bed and padded across the cool marble floor to the window. Pulling up the blind, he opened the casement wide and took a deep breath, instantly feeling the contrast in temperature between the air-conditioned room and the warmth outside. He gazed out across the ancient city bathed in sepia early-morning light. After the heavy thunderstorm overnight, the sun was now rising above the distant desert skyline with its usual intensity and belligerence, signalling another sweleringly hot Middle Eastern day. Ignition had almost arrived: thirty-three hours to go. He wondered whether tomorrow's sunrise would be his last, and quickly pushed the thought away. *No, the Project will work.* He'd spent his career trying to tease out the secrets of dark matter and hadn't come this far for his life's work to count for nothing. He closed the window and wandered off to the shower. As he did so, he heard Sarah stirring and turned towards her.

'Hey.'

'Hey to you too.' Sarah stretched and smiled sleepily, the sheet that had been covering her now slipping down.

I'd better make that a cold shower.

Seeing him looking at her, Sarah grinned as she pulled the sheet back up. 'What time is it?'

'Early enough. Don't forget, we're meeting Qiang for breakfast before we head off.'

For both political and practical reasons, Mag-8 in Jordan had been chosen as the main centre of operations for the entire Project as the final countdown got under way. There was nothing more that could be done at this point. All the tests and checks were complete, and security was now so tight that nothing barring a major incident was going to stop Ignition going ahead. But the world could not afford for anything to go wrong, so it had been agreed that *if* any of the eight facilities was compromised or developed an unforeseen last-minute glitch, the entire run would be called off.

The threat of a strike of some kind by the Purifiers was uppermost in everyone's minds. But Marc also worried about another aspect of the Project. Tomorrow, control would pass over to the eight AI Minds, one at each facility around the globe. At T-minus three hours, the entire operation would go into Lockdown, meaning that while the Minds could communicate with each other, to raise any last-minute problems that might trigger a postponement, there would be no means whatsoever to intervene from outside. It was a radical decision. But the very real threat of cyberattack by the Purifiers meant that this was deemed to be the safest option.

And so, the fate of *Homo sapiens* would for the first time be in the hands, metaphorically speaking, of artificial intelligences. Marc would never have believed that such a day would come during his lifetime.

For a few days last week there had been a real possibility of delay to Ignition. First Mag-6 on New Zealand's South Island and then Mag-7 on Hawaii's Big Island had had to deal with mild earth tremors. Neither site was geologically ideal, but they were the only two

350

locations in the vast Pacific Ocean that could host the bending magnets. The tremors hadn't persisted, and they didn't seem to be precursors of more serious seismic activity that could have disrupted the alignment of the bending magnets, so the decision was taken not to postpone.

Then, just three days ago, Marc heard that J-PARC Laboratory, the site of one of the primary dark-matter accelerators, had problems with one of the superconducting magnets in its proton beam booster ring. Sections of a fifty-kilometre-long niobium cable wound around its central solenoid seemed to have degraded and had had to be replaced. The problem was quickly fixed, with the only damage being to the pride of the Japanese accelerator engineers.

And now everything appeared to be on track. After months of intense worldwide activity, the most ambitious, and certainly the most consequential enterprise ever attempted by humankind was ready. He hoped.

It all came down to this now. The waiting.

Over breakfast, Qiang looked agitated and irritable. 'I can't understand why so many VIPs have come to Jordan,' he said. 'I know Mag-8 is the designated epicentre of the whole operation and I can understand the need for the world's media to be here to report on it, but everyone else . . .?'

Marc didn't respond. Qiang was right, of course.

'. . . I mean, either the ground opens up under our feet, and that will be that, or nothing happens, and we won't know if it's been successful for months.'

Marc nodded. 'True. But a lot of people want to be part of history. They will be able to say they were there when the world was saved. Anyway, don't forget that most people have chosen the sensible option of spending what might be their last days at home with their loved ones.' Again, he thought about Evie.

It was Sarah who asked: 'For that matter, why are *we* even here? It's not like we can do anything now.' She had been intending to return to England to be with her family, until she realized she'd left it too late to travel.

Marc sighed. 'I guess it's our moral obligation to see this through. Well, mine and Qiang's anyway. But, hey, we'll all be global heroes when we save the world! And besides, if I'm going to be witness to the *end* of the world then what two better people to share the experience with.'

He'd meant it as a light-hearted joke, but it fell flat.

The decision to choose Mag-8 as the focal point of the operation had been made carefully. It was agreed that giving just one of the eight Minds, the one here in Jordan, override control was the only way to ensure the run couldn't be compromised. Every decision made by any one of the other seven Minds had to be passed through the Mag-8 Mind. The isolated location of the SESAME facility in the Jordanian desert also made security easier.

And meanwhile, the rest of the world became ever more nervous. All transport had now come to a virtual standstill; banks, offices and schools had closed; in many countries, the military had assumed control. All but essential emergency services had ground to a halt as entire communities gathered together for comfort. Old scores were settled, and differences resolved, sometimes peacefully, sometimes violently. Some people partied, some prayed, while others couldn't shake off an overwhelming sense of nihilism and futility. The number of suicides, by those not willing to wait around to witness the destruction of the planet, soared. A few hid themselves away in underground bunkers in the misguided hope that they would be protected if the Project failed.

Most people, however, remained resolutely optimistic about the success of the Project, unable to contemplate failure. Marc regularly heard the 'hope for the best, prepare for the worst' philosophy, where in this case the superlative 'worst' really meant that. No one could see beyond 12:45 Coordinate Universal Time on Tuesday, 17 September: the moment when all the waiting, all the preparation, all the testing and checking of formulae and calibration of instruments, was over. The moment of reckoning. Salvation or Armageddon.

It would be 15:45 here at Mag-8.

Two Jordanian military approached their table. The younger one, a soldier in army fatigues holding an impressive-looking semi-automatic M26 gun against his chest, stood just behind the senior officer, a man in his forties, immaculately dressed in khakis and sporting a magnificent thick black moustache. He spoke to them in perfect English. 'Excuse me for interrupting your breakfast, but we're about to depart for SESAME in a few minutes and we need all guests accounted for in the lobby.'

Marc and the others nodded their thanks, finished their coffee and readied themselves.

Situated an hour's drive outside Amman, the SESAME facility had begun its scientific life as a synchrotron source, with its first beams produced in early 2020 after many delays and huge political stumbling blocks. Now a major high-energy facility and the largest in the Middle East, it was still one of the few places in the world where Israeli, Saudi and Iranian scientists worked in close collaboration. So, if there ever was a place that symbolized humankind's ability to come together in the face of global adversity, this was it. What also made it an ideal location was that it already had the necessary infrastructure in place to build one of the giant bending magnets.

Marc, Sarah and Qiang arrived together with an army of other dignitaries, politicians and journalists in a large convoy of military vehicles and were ushered inside the building by nervous-looking soldiers. The main reception hall resembled the entrance to a grand palace. Marc marvelled at the high sheen of the luxurious patterned tiles on the floor and could smell the walls had been freshly painted in readiness for the eyes of the world.

As they shuffled along with the other guests he noticed Sarah stiffen. He followed her line of sight: on the far side of the room stood Senator Hogan, talking to a group of men and women. Marc touched her arm gently, making her jump. 'Ignore him, Sarah. I know he can be an unpleasant bully, but as soon as this is over you won't need to have any more to do with him.'

Sarah didn't respond.

They were led through to the main conference centre and asked to take their seats while 3D visors were handed out. They were to be given a virtual tour through each of the eight facilities. Marc had seen this several times before but placed his visor over his head anyway. He found it hard to believe that it was only seven months ago that Qiang had outlined his crazy idea of firing beams of dark matter into the Earth. And yet here they were. It had become a reality. He sat in his seat while he was transported around the world. At each of the eight sites, the local Mind in human avatar form acted as their guide, explaining the physics involved. Right now, any distraction that helped eat up the remaining hours was welcome. He reached out to Sarah, who was sitting next to him and, finding her hand, gave it a squeeze.

39

WHILE THE WORLD HELD ITS COLLECTIVE BREATH IN the final hours before Ignition, Shireen had been busier than ever. The cybercrime centre in Washington, DC, was larger and far busier than Bletchley. No more sedate cycling into work for her. She hadn't left the building in days and hadn't slept for forty-eight hours. Nor could she afford to – not now that she had finally found a way into the Purifiers' network.

Following the events in London the previous week, she had been informed that her unique skills were needed now more than ever. The authorities were certain the Purifiers would try something again, but when, where and how? Frustratingly, there had been no major breakthroughs following the arrests in London. The kidnappers had obeyed instructions without any knowledge of their chain of command. Now, a whole army of cybs had been recruited to try to break into their network using what meagre leads they had.

Since Shireen's role at Bletchley had been leaked

355

following Evie's kidnapping, she'd been informed she could no longer continue to work there and had instead been flown to Washington. She had desperately wanted to get back home to Tehran to be with her parents before Ignition, but all commercial flights had been suspended. She'd had a long and, she admitted, tearful chat to them two nights ago. Yes, she'd assured them, she was being looked after and treated well.

She estimated there had to be hundreds of international cybersecurity organizations now working alongside the Sentinels to ensure that both the hardware and the software of the Project were secure from attack. Many wanted to believe that the threat from the Purifiers had lessened – that the Project was safe.

But Shireen knew better. She had learned early on that this cult was not one to boast about its ideology or one that felt the need to spread its propaganda. After all, its whole *raison d'être* was to bring about the end of humankind, not to recruit new followers. Not any more. And whatever they planned to do, it would already be in place.

Paradoxically, as Ignition Day drew nearer the task of hacking into the Purifiers' network had become easier. As security surrounding all aspects of the Project tightened, the options available to the Purifiers narrowed. Shireen thought of it as a game of chess in which her opponent was losing pieces from the board, limiting the moves available to them.

It was quite clear to her, along with almost everyone else here in DC, what the Purifiers hoped to achieve. Their mission was simple. They saw the dying field as a fulfilment, a vindication, of their ideology. To start with they had tried everything they could to stop the Odin Project from getting off the ground. The slow, certain death of the *entire* human race had been their safest option. But now, with time running out to stop the Project, the quick, albeit incomplete annihilation of life brought about by a catastrophic malfunction if one of the eight beams failed was far more appealing. And with just a few hours left before Lockdown, when all eight facilities would be completely isolated from the outside world, Shireen knew that time was running out for the Purifiers – by deliberate design, no human intervention or interference would be possible after Lockdown.

But that also meant time was running out for her.

Then, just before midnight, she had her first real break. It was so unexpected that, at first, she thought it was a hoax. She'd found an obscure dark-web forum whose members displayed all the right ideological views. By hacking into the account of one of its members, a Texan white supremacist who believed that God was about to destroy everyone apart from the chosen few, of whom he of course was one, she was able to read all the postings. That was when the message came through. It appeared to have been distributed throughout the Purifiers' network, and it was all she'd needed to track it back to its source. Within minutes she'd found it. She stood and raised her visor. She needed a drink of water, needed to clear her head and try and make sense of it.

Shireen returned to her desk. She couldn't speak to anyone here. Not yet. She tried to calm down, hoping no one had noticed her excitement. But all the other cybs in the vast open-plan space had their visors on. The air-conditioned office suddenly struck her as very cold and she shivered. Feeling both elated and horrified in equal measure, she had to decide, quickly, what to do with the information. She needed to speak to Sarah and Marc. Her eyes flicked to the display on her visor. It would be early morning now in Jordan. The morning of the day of Ignition.

She pinged Sarah, and moments later the solar physicist's face appeared in the top right quarter of her visor display. The picture quality was poor, but all but essential communication drones had been switched off to limit net traffic, so the secure line she was using didn't have the necessary bandwidth. But she could still make out dark shadows under Sarah's bloodshot eyes. Shireen wasn't the only one unable to sleep, then.

Not having given any prior thought to how she was going to break the news, she decided to take it slowly.

She spoke softly so as not to be overheard. 'Hello, Sarah. Is Marc with you too?'

'Hi, Shireen. We haven't got you in vision. Are you contacting us through a visor?'

'Yes. Sorry it's a bit rude, but I'm, you know, still working.'

'Ah, OK. Of course, it must be gone midnight for you. But yes, Marc's here too.' The picture shifted as Sarah lifted up her wristpad so that Shireen could see Marc behind her. He smiled weakly and gave a little wave.

Suddenly aware of those around her, she took a deep breath.

'OK, listen. I've found something. The Purifiers are definitely planning some sort of attack.'

Sarah gasped, and Marc's face loomed large on Shireen's display as he leaned closer to Sarah's wristpad. '*What?*'

'I don't know any details yet, but I'm working on it. I picked up a brief message that suggests they have something in place.' She paused, gathering her thoughts. 'You're the first people I'm telling about this. I mean, it's not so much what the message says as who it's from. Let

358

me read it out to you.' She slid the window containing the message up her display alongside the video link so she could see it clearly. 'It says: "To all those who seek to purify Mother Earth of the scourge of *Homo sapiens*: Rejoice. The Day of Judgement is almost upon us. Tomorrow, we witness humanity's destruction by our own hands." And it's signed "Maksoob".'

Marc spoke first, his voice echoing. 'OK, it's from their top dog. But it doesn't really say anything. For all we know, this is just propaganda. There's nothing there to suggest they actually have a plan in place.'

'I agree. But that's not why I've contacted you,' Shireen said, a little too loudly. She pulled her visor up and quickly scanned the room to make sure she hadn't been heard. She'd got away with it. She lowered the visor, and her voice. 'It's who the message comes from! Everyone knows that Maksoob is this near-mythical leader, right? The man behind the Purifiers who is most likely much more than just a talismanic figurehead.'

She paused, her heart pounding. 'This is why you both needed to know. You see, I've found the source of the message. I know who he is now. Maksoob . . . it's Gabriel Aguda!'

Sarah and Marc seemed to freeze. They were aghast. Then Sarah spluttered, 'Aguda? It can't be. Surely that's ridiculous?'

Marc was frowning. He looked as if he was puzzling over a particularly difficult equation. 'Come on, Shireen, seriously? This sounds like some weird conspiracy-theory bullshit. What's the link between a respected academic geologist and a genocidal maniac terrorist? I mean, I've had my doubts about Aguda ever since the satellite data episode, and everyone knows he prefers the MPD option over Odin, but this . . . It's ludicrous.'

Shireen tried to control her frustration. She hadn't expected this reaction. 'Well, you're wrong, Marc. I know it.'

'OK, Shireen,' Sarah interjected. 'The question is what do we do about it? No one knows about this apart from the three of us, right? So, tell us, what evidence do you have?'

'I know this sounds crazy, but I traced the message back to Aguda's personal account—'

'Hang on, Shireen,' interrupted Sarah again. 'If he is Maksoob, why would Aguda be so stupid as to send an incriminating message from his personal account? Is this message enough to arrest and interrogate him?' Then after a pause, she added, 'It would of course mean postponing Ignition, until we could find out what they planned to do.'

Once again Marc's face loomed large on her screen. 'Another thing. Don't we need to consider the possibility that the Purifiers *want* you to think Aguda is Maksoob by constructing a bogus link? That they want to, you know, sow the seeds of doubt, just to postpone Ignition? That may be the best they can hope for now.'

Shireen couldn't understand what seemed to her like a defence of Aguda. Of course, they knew him better than she did and so might have been prepared to give him the benefit of the doubt, but . . . She tried again.

'Even if there's the slightest possibility Aguda is behind this and there is a sabotage plan in place, we have to let the authorities know. You know that, right? If Ignition is postponed, then so be it – at least we would be sure.'

Sarah shook her head slowly. 'Two problems with that. Firstly, if we go to the authorities now and demand that Aguda is arrested and interrogated, who are they going to believe? It's his word against ours. And we need to remember that Gabriel Aguda is vice chair of the Odin Project Committee. All we have is an inflammatory statement traced to the account of one of the world's most influential scientists by a young cyb who came to prominence when she hacked into government secret files. I'm sorry, Shireen, but that's what people will think. And we simply *don't have time before Lockdown* to persuade the right people, whoever the hell they might be.

'Secondly, and more crucially, if the Purifiers are indeed planning something then we still have hope, and a few precious hours, to find out what it might be *without* raising their suspicions. As soon as Aguda is arrested, and assuming he *is* Maksoob, then the game may be up. They will almost certainly have planned for that eventuality.'

Shireen couldn't believe what she was hearing, but Sarah hadn't finished her train of thought. 'Besides, we just need to keep the Project safe until Lockdown. The whole point of the Lockdown is that they would have to do something *before* then. After Lockdown, *no one* can interfere.'

Shireen had already considered this. It was what scared her more than anything else. She tried to keep the desperation out of her voice. 'But . . . what if they have something in place, some virus maybe, that only activates *after* Lockdown? And what if the Mag-8 Mind is infected or compromised, like the CERN Mind in the summer? Then there'd be nothing to stop it and we'd be helpless.'

This time Marc shook his head. 'Even if we could stop Ignition after Lockdown,' he said, 'and I have no idea what would be needed to do that, short of ordering a missile strike against Mag-8, then even that wouldn't be enough.'

Sarah turned around to face him, so the angle of her wristpad meant they were both out of vision now, seemingly having forgotten about Shireen. But she could still hear them. 'What do you mean?' asked Sarah.

'I mean we would have to knock out the other sites too. Think about it – if the Purifiers are capable of sabotaging Mag-8 in some way then we must assume they're capable of overriding any instruction to the other seven Minds to abort in the event of only Mag-8 being destroyed. Stopping just one of the eight beams is the nightmare scenario, remember. And even if we could avoid Ignition with such drastic measures then the Purifiers will still have won. The Project would be over.' He sounded exhausted.

'Jesus. So we lose either way.'

'There may be another way,' Shireen interjected. The idea had been swirling around in the back of her mind ever since she'd decided to contact Sarah and Marc. 'What if you could get something out of Aguda? I don't mean a full confession, just something incriminating enough to convince the world to listen to us and stop Ignition. He's there with you in Mag-8, after all.' They didn't reply, so she added, 'But you have less than six hours.'

40

SARAH KNEW THAT SHIREEN WAS RIGHT. THEY HAD TO find a way of confronting Aguda. And even if she was wrong about him, they couldn't afford to do nothing. It had taken her and Marc almost two hours of arguing before they settled on a plan, and Sarah could tell that he was unhappier than her by far. But they were running out of time discussing it, and she knew he could see the sense in her line of reasoning. It was the only card they had left to play.

The only way to entrap Aguda, she had argued, was if he felt safe and unthreatened. For that, she had to be the one to meet him, alone. Playing to his self-confidence, his *amour-propre*, might just force him to let slip something they could use. But to get him to meet in the first place was trickier. How could she do that without raising suspicion?

'He has to think I know more than I do – that I am a threat—'

'A threat he will want to deal with,' Marc reminded her.

'Marc, we've been through this.'

He didn't respond. Instead, he drew her close and held

363

her. She knew how uncomfortable he was feeling about the plan: allowing someone else he cared for to put themselves directly in danger like this. He'd just been through a major trauma in which he'd almost lost the person he loved most in the world. But Sarah wasn't Evie. And a father's love for his daughter was hardly the same as this ill-timed and misplaced chivalry.

Sarah knew Aguda had arrived at the Mag-8 facility an hour after them, along with Peter Hogan and an entourage of high-ranking officials. Most people were gathering in the vast viewing hall that overlooked the central chamber itself. The giant magnets loomed high above them like an alien space fleet hovering silently and menacingly; and below were the aluminium beam tubes, glistening under the bright lights that were suspended on the walls and roof of the chamber. All three tubes, each with its surrounding bending magnets, split off in sequence from the main cylinder whose sealed front end faced the northwest, ready to allow in the beam of heavy neutralinos arriving from CERN. The other ends of the three tubes pointed vertically down into the focusing chamber, where they merged again into a single cylinder, down which the beam of charginos would pass into the ground. The entire construct was an exact replica of the Mag-4 facility she'd seen before completion in Peru.

There were six hours to go before Ignition and three hours before Lockdown. The atmosphere was tense. People huddled in groups talking in hushed tones, as though even a raised voice might jeopardize the mission. The occasional laughter she heard sounded forced. Technicians and engineers went about their business carrying out final checks while they still could before Lockdown. Marc had found Qiang and taken him outside to talk to him away from prying eyes and ears. He'd insisted that since his colleague was the only other person they could really trust he needed to be brought up to speed.

Sarah hadn't wanted to confront Aguda in public in case he detected something in her manner that scared him off. So, they agreed she should stay out of his sight and send him a brief message instead. She found an empty meeting room to hide away in and composed the message:

> *Gabriel, I don't know who else to turn to, but I need to speak to someone urgently. There's a plot to sabotage Mag-8 that we've uncovered, and we have to warn people. Can we talk privately?*

Waiting for Aguda's response was almost unbearable. The minutes ticked by and she wondered whether he was deliberately ignoring the message. Did he suspect anything? Possibly. Would he be considering the possibility that they were trying to entrap him? Marc and Qiang joined her in the room.

'Damn it, Marc, it's been almost twenty minutes. He's not responded. Have we just made a terrible mistake?'

Marc began pacing up and down. 'Right, if we haven't heard from Aguda in another ten minutes, we'll have to go to security and insist he's arrested. They'd be crazy to ignore us.'

And then Sarah received a message:

> *Meet me in the old electron booster ring building. Fifteen minutes.*

Relief mixed with fear washed through her. This was it. The game was on.

The booster hall was situated within the old SESAME

building – an artefact of a bygone era despite its microtron accelerator still being used to produce the electrons that were injected into the much larger storage rings of the new accelerator. But from the start of the Project several months earlier, these experimental buildings had been sitting dormant and deserted, with all the large superconducting magnets being appropriated for Mag-8's construction.

The building was quiet when Sarah walked in, and the air smelled stale and suffocating. She could see the central area of the hall, the site of the accelerator ring, a circular tube forty metres in circumference and threaded through multiple magnets like a necklace. Hidden within high concentric shielding walls, it was accessed by following a winding corridor, like walking around the outer layers of a circular garden maze, but with two-metre-thick concrete walls instead of green hedges. Aguda obviously knew his way around the SESAME complex – the hall was certainly far from prying eyes and ears.

Despite feeling terrified, Sarah made her way to the experimental area. She rehearsed her lines. She couldn't afford to let her guard slip and nervously checked her AR feed to make sure it was recording everything she saw and heard. She wasn't surprised to see the network signal drop out as she walked deeper into the building. Marc and Shireen would by now have lost contact with her. Had Aguda chosen the location so that no one outside could eavesdrop? Did he suspect something? Did he even have any intention of letting her go? She knew the risk she was taking, but it had seemed the only way.

She wondered if Gabriel was already there. The shielding corridor opened up into a large hall. Looking about her, the only accessible floor space was a narrow walkway squeezed between the outer wall and the accelerator ring itself, which was situated about waist high all the way around. The chamber was crowded with instrumentation: stacks of shelving overflowing with electronic equipment connected by a multi-coloured spaghetti of wires and cables. Nothing seemed to be switched on. There was none of the usual comforting hum or the colourful glow of LEDs. There were tables on which lay abandoned tools and dormant computer displays.

The only sounds Sarah could hear were her own footsteps and the blood rushing in her ears. The lighting was poor on this side of the ring and, at first, she thought she was alone. Gabriel hadn't arrived yet. Maybe he wouldn't come. Maybe he planned to imprison her here until after Lockdown. No, he wouldn't be foolish enough to believe she was the only one who knew about the plan.

Then she saw a figure moving out from the shadows.

'Ah, Sarah. You came.'

She stopped dead in her tracks. At first, she was confused. Confusion that was quickly followed by a dreadful dawning realization. She felt a strange, prickly tingling as though electrodes had been attached to every part of her body.

It was Hogan. Senator Peter Hogan. And he was smiling his broadest smile.

He was wearing a stylish cream suit and was studying what looked to be a small display pad.

'I hope you're not too disappointed to see me instead of Gabriel. He felt this was just too important for him to deal with, and so he asked me.' He winked at her conspiratorially. Every nerve in her body yelled at her to run, but she knew she had to hear him out.

Resting the display gently on the table, Hogan walked slowly towards her. 'OK, Sarah, here we are, just the two of us.' He held his hands out to either side of him.

'So, I think we can be frank with each other, yes?' He didn't wait for an answer. 'Now then, you believe there's been some sort of security breach here at Mag-8 and that the Project is in jeopardy? This, just a few hours before the most portentous moment in human history. Don't you think you're leaving it rather late in the day to be worrying about monsters under the bed?'

To her relief, he stopped a couple of metres from her.

She managed to find her voice and to her surprise it sounded steadier than she could have hoped. 'Please don't be facetious, Senator. I needed to speak to Gabriel urgently because—'

'—because he's the person you go to when you dig up secrets, right? Just like you did with those files about the satellite data?'

He smiled again, flashing his shark's teeth. 'Well, I don't think Gabriel is in any position to help you right now. Poor Gabriel, a man always aiming higher than his limited intellect would allow. A man without the imagination to be anything other than a foot soldier.'

At first, Sarah wasn't quite sure what he'd meant. Then it hit her like a juggernaut. She didn't know how she knew, she just knew – as sure as she had been of anything in her life. *Oh, shit. Aguda isn't our man. He never was. I'm looking at Maksoob right now.*

She didn't need to rationalize how or why a successful American politician was also the leader of a terrorist organization intent on wiping humankind off the face of the Earth. A fresh rush of adrenalin coursed through her body. And it gave her courage. *I have to hold it together. Otherwise we'll have nothing.* Somehow, she managed to compose herself. She refocused her eyes to check her retinal feed was still recording. *OK, let's see what you've got, you bastard.*

368

'Then maybe you can help instead, Senator. After all, you're clearly the one with the real influence. A man people will listen to.'

When he didn't answer, she carried on. 'Of course, we don't want to trigger an unnecessary postponement of Ignition, because that would mean weeks of delay before we could try again, and I saw what happened in Rio. We can't risk waiting around for a catastrophic event like that to happen again.'

'Ah, of course, you were in Rio during the March Event. How awful for you. All that *tragic* loss of life you weren't able to stop . . .'

You bastard. White-hot anger rose up in her and she had to use all her resolve to keep it from bubbling over.

He smiled again. 'And tell me, Sarah. How, may I ask, has this information come to your attention? Given that the entire world's cybersecurity effort is at this very moment focused on ensuring today goes smoothly.'

She breathed deeply. 'I have reason to believe the Purifiers are here at Mag-8 and are planning some sort of act of sabotage.'

'Oh? And this is something *you* have discovered? That neither the Sentinels nor the rest of humanity seem to have picked up?'

Did she detect a slight rise in the level of his voice, as though he were becoming excited by this game? Good. And he hadn't yet asked her what the nature of her suspicions were. Was this an acknowledgement that there really was a plan in place?

'It would appear so, yes,' she prodded. 'Although Marc Bruckner believes the Purifiers know they've failed and that it's too late to stop Ignition now.'

'And what do you think, Sarah?' His eyes glittered.

Right, this is it. It doesn't matter that it's Hogan, not

369

Aguda. This was what she had rehearsed. She needed to get under his skin. 'I'm not so sure,' she replied as calmly as she could. 'Personally, I just don't think we can take that chance. They've shown themselves to be very ... resourceful. But then their failure so far also suggests they don't have the knowhow, intellect or imagination to strike the killer blow. Their acts seem too clumsy and random, too uncoordinated.'

Hogan's pale blue eyes drilled into hers. He seemed to be enjoying this. She had to keep going. She had just switched tack from claiming to have uncovered a plot, to arguing that the Purifiers weren't capable of carrying it out. And she didn't think Hogan had noticed.

'Personally, I wonder whether their supposed leader, Maksoob, really exists. He sounds more like a concept, invented by a group of desperate individuals. Of course, if he does exist and is planning something, then I would expect him to want to reveal himself at the end, to bathe in the glory of achieving his ultimate aim.'

For the first time in their conversation, Hogan didn't respond immediately. He appeared to be mulling over what she'd said. Aware of his own hesitation, he suddenly straightened himself and took a casual step closer. She called upon every ounce of determination not to back away from him and somehow managed to keep her feet rooted to the spot.

'This is getting boring, Sarah, and frankly I don't have the time for it. So, please stop playing the tiresome amateur psychologist.'

This was her chance.

'Oh, I'm not playing. I'm deadly serious. Strange that you haven't yet asked me what it is I know – what I may have uncovered – Senator Hogan. Or perhaps you would prefer to be addressed as "Maksoob"?'

It was as if a switch had been flipped. His smile evaporated to be replaced by a look of pure malevolence.

'Oh, Sarah,' he snarled, 'how very clever of you. And yet you were expecting to meet Gabriel. Did you find his message to the Purifiers? It's a little insulting that you fell for it so quickly – to think that Gabriel Aguda could control the destiny of the entire planet. Although of course I'm rather pleased you realize your mistake now.' His expression suddenly softened, and he turned his gaze upwards as though recalling a fond memory. 'Poor Gabriel, he's been useful in so many ways – always eager to play with the big boys, and oh so desperate to make his mark on the world.'

She had to think fast. *If Hogan sent the message out from Aguda's account to deflect attention, why do it at all? Why risk exposure at the last minute? Wait. Maybe it's obvious. Maybe he had to reach out to his followers – a last rallying cry from their prophet. His ego was too big not to.*

Then the cold psychopathic stare was back. She felt his eyes bore into her. 'So, tell me, Sarah, what's your plan? Is your knight in shining armour going to dash in and rescue you from my evil clutches?' He shook his head again as though reprimanding an errant child. 'I should inform you that I took the liberty of locking the door remotely as soon as I heard you enter. After all, we wouldn't want anyone disturbing our friendly chat. So, I'm afraid no one will be able to come in or out. It's just you and me until after Ignition.'

Despite her terror, she found the strength from somewhere to blurt out, 'Why? What is it you plan to do?'

He laughed. It was a blood-curdling laugh, devoid of human emotion. 'Oh, Sarah, is this where the good guy convinces the bad guy to reveal his master plan now that he thinks he's got away with it? How sweet. But that wouldn't be so much fun.'

Somehow, he was now just an arm's length away and she took an involuntary step back, feeling the cold metal of the accelerator ring against her back. She was trapped. And like a wolf moving in for the kill, Hogan sensed her panic. 'Sweet, innocent Dr Sarah Maitlin. You are so out of your depth right now. Did you really think that you could stop the inevitable?'

She needed to stall for time. She needed to find out what the inevitable was. She could worry about escape later. She couldn't give up now.

41

WHEN SHIREEN LOST CONTACT WITH SARAH, SHE FIRST assumed it was just the net being taken down for added security, but Sarah's retinal feed had dropped out as soon as she had entered the booster hall, so it had to be because of some sort of shielding inside the building. Had Aguda chosen to meet her there because he knew any transmissions to and from the outside world would be blocked? Marc didn't sound surprised when he contacted her a few seconds later. 'Shireen, I have no signal from Sarah – I assume you don't either.'

'No, I've lost signal too. What happened?'

'I could kick myself for not seeing this sooner. The radio frequency generated by the particle accelerator in there, when it's running, means that the whole building must have been acting as a giant Faraday cage to stop any radio waves escaping and interfering with the electronic instruments outside.'

'So Sarah's in there, alone with Aguda, and we can't see or hear what's happening.'

'You don't need to tell me that. I've got to go in after her.'

'No, wait!' She felt her voice rise. 'I mean you can't. If he sees you before Sarah can learn anything, it's all over.'

'It may be all over already, Shireen. If Aguda chose the location so as not to be heard, then maybe he knows we're on to him. And that means Sarah's life is in danger. I can't risk it.'

She knew she couldn't stop him. She switched her display to Marc's retinal feed, even though she knew it would be pointless as soon as he too went inside the building.

So, she saw the closed doors of the booster ring building at the same time that he did.

'Fuck. I'm locked out.' Marc's voice crackled through her earpiece. 'And Sarah's trapped in there with that monster. Shireen, is there anything you can do from your end?'

She didn't answer right away. A thought had suddenly occurred to her. If the doors were locked, then Aguda was definitely on to them. In which case, wouldn't he have simply locked Sarah inside, alone? She quickly traced his whereabouts from his wristpad.

Yup, she was right.

'Marc, Aguda's not in there with her. He's still somewhere in the main building, but I can't pinpoint his location any better than that.'

'You mean he's locked her in there alone? To keep her out of the way until Ignition? That doesn't make sense. Wouldn't he want to know what she knew?'

Marc was right. Aguda couldn't be sure who else knew.

She watched through Marc's eyes as he turned away from the doors and made his way back to the Mag-8 building. He said, 'OK, see if you can get those doors unlocked. I'm going to track down Aguda.'

'OK,' said Shireen, 'I'm sending through a map of the site with his location to your AR feed. But you're on your own after that. I have another idea. Contact me if you need to.'

Shireen knew trying to get Sarah out would be a waste of time. Hacking into the central control system at SES-AME in order to release those doors wouldn't work. Even before they went into Lockdown, the Mag-8 Mind or its Sentinels would be on to her instantly. Sarah was locked in there – alone but, as far as Shireen could tell, safe. And with just a few hours to go, they were getting nowhere. Still, maybe there was something she could try. It would be the most outrageous and foolish thing she'd ever attempted in her life. She shivered. Indeed, it might well mean the end of her life, but she had no other option. And she couldn't do it without help. First, she had to get across town to the FBI's National Security Facility.

She slipped out of the building in which she'd spent the past five days and into the cool night air. The streets were eerily quiet. The entire population of the city seemed to have decided to wait it out and watch events unfold on the few official media networks still operating. There were hardly any cars around either, but she found one that seemed to have been abandoned in a hurry near a charging pod. She climbed in, hacked its computer and headed for the Facility. On the way, she called the one person who might be willing to help her.

Zak Boardman picked up almost immediately. Like everyone, he sounded on edge, and was certainly surprised to hear from her. But he was also prepared to listen. Shireen smiled when she heard the young FBI man's voice. They had quite a bit in common. A few years older, Boardman had shown an almost embarrassing degree of admiration for her during the two days of interrogation after her arrest back in February. Of all the FBI team who had questioned her, he had been the most impressed with the Trojan horse code. She saw him as a kindred spirit and was now thankful that she'd kept in touch with him.

She pinged him the message from Maksoob and gave him a brief outline of what she knew.

'We can safely assume that *if* the Purifiers have done something as crude as planting a bomb inside Mag-8, then the Mind or its Sentinels would have found it by now, right?'

'Of course. So then what exactly *are* you suggesting they could do?'

Shireen hesitated. How much should she divulge? Too much, and he would try to talk her out of what she had in mind. More likely still, he would just think she was mad.

She took a deep breath. She had to take the chance. 'Zak, how much do you know about swarm technology?'

'Huh? Um . . . well, not my area but I know we have a lot of people working on it. So do the Chinese and Indians. It's no big secret. But why are you asking me this now? We're just hours away from Lockdown after all, and—'

'I know, Zak,' she interrupted. 'And I know anyone can look up the details online: flying nanomachines, manufactured in huge numbers, probably up to a billion in a single "swarm" – independent entities, acting in unison, but each obeying remarkably simple rules—'

'You mean like staying at a constant distance from their surrounding neighbours, which gives the illusion of choreographed motion?'

'Exactly. Like a murmuration of starlings weaving those stunning patterns in the sky.'

As she spoke, she only half registered the outside world. The car sped along its programmed route, manoeuvring around hastily parked, probably abandoned vehicles. The scene on the deserted Washington streets was like something from a post-apocalyptic horror movie.

'But that's wrong,' said Zak. 'A nanoswarm is much more like a single artificial organism, a cloud of programmable matter. Each nanobot processor has the storage capacity and power of an insect's brain. And yet, because it doesn't need any of this brain power for keeping itself "alive", or hunting for food or finding mates, its entire focus can be on its mission.'

It was what Shireen had feared. 'So, a swarm would be more like an army of a billion *telepathic* killer bees acting as a single unit?'

'Yes, but wait a minute, Shireen. Are you suggesting the Purifiers could have got their hands on a nanoswarm to send into Mag-8?'

When Zak said out loud what she had only toyed with in her mind, it made it sound both terrifying and so much more real.

'I don't know, Zak. I just think that, logically, it's the only option available to them if they want to evade detection by the Mind.'

'I still don't understand. How would that be possible?'

'I'll explain later. But I need to get into your TID Lab, and you're going to help me.' She knew she sounded more bright-eyed than she felt.

He was silent for a few seconds, then, 'OK, I'm listening.'

She checked the on-board map. She'd be with Zak in just over thirty minutes, enough time for her to outline what she had in mind and convince him that she wasn't completely crazy.

She got the car to drop her about fifty metres from the front gate of the NSF compound. Shireen had decided to walk the rest of the way. No need to spook the guards. As she approached, she spotted the skinny figure of the young agent standing in the glare from the harsh arc lights above the security gates.

Zak Boardman walked towards her, flanked by the two heavily armed sentries, both of whom looked like they'd rather be anywhere but here, tonight.

'That's far enough, Ms Darvish,' said one of them, who stood back, levelling his gun at her while the other approached. He held a biometric scanner in front of her face. He nodded as though satisfied and turned to Zak. 'OK, Agent Boardman, she's cleared to come in, but she stays with you at all times, understood?'

Zak thanked him and signalled to Shireen to follow him through the barriers into the compound.

Shireen fell in behind him, checking the time as she went. It had taken her longer than she'd expected to get here. Less than ninety minutes till Lockdown. Looking across at the imposing building, she could see a lot of activity inside. But Zak led her along a diagonal path that took them away from the main entrance towards the far side of the grounds. As they approached, she could make out the sleek glass and steel frame of a newer, smaller structure, half hidden by sycamore trees. This was it, the FBI's TID Lab. She knew enough about Total Immersive Displacement to understand that it was still a highly experimental technology. But it was her only chance.

She could tell Zak was nervous, but hoped he was smart enough to understand the ramifying consequences of not helping her. At first, he had tried to argue that *he* should be the one to displace. But she had persuaded him that it had to be her – because if anything went wrong she would need him to bring her back.

Total Immersive Displacement had been feasible for many years, ever since the early days of virtual reality. Shireen remembered her father talking to her about it when she was younger. She had grown up in a world where virtual reality was a given, but it had been mainly used in the entertainment industry, first for fully immersive gaming experiences and then, with widespread use of 360-degree stereoscopic cameras and binaural audio, in movie-making.

TID was very different. Full displacement technology, whereby one could, in the most real sense imaginable, experience being in a different physical location, remained a tightly controlled technology because of its security and ethical implications. Yet, it was an open secret that many countries' militaries had perfected true TID some years ago.

Zak hadn't said a word as they had made their way to the laboratory building. Now he presented his eyes and palm to the scanner and the doors slid open. As they entered the deserted building, the lights flicked on. Shireen hoped that their presence wouldn't attract attention. They walked along the corridor towards the lab, accompanied by the echo of their footsteps; as they went Zak outlined what the procedure involved. 'The subject is injected with nanobots directly into their bloodstream, which navigate their way to the brain.' Shireen felt him look at her as he continued. 'There they take over control of the neurons responsible for visual, auditory and other senses.'

Even though he wasn't telling her anything she didn't know already, she let him talk as it seemed to relax him. TID had been something of an obsession of hers ever since she'd heard about it. But she never imagined she would be able to experience it herself, and certainly not when the stakes were so high.

The idea itself was, she thought, technologically beautiful. The nanobots received their data from the remote location, transferring it directly to the subject and so giving him – or her – a total immersive experience: seeing, hearing, feeling, even smelling the location they were 'transported to' as though they were physically there. She felt her heartbeat quicken at the enormity of what she was about to do.

They reached the lab and, again, Zak had to be biometrically scanned in order to gain access. Shireen followed him into a large, brightly lit research lab. Everything looked pristine, as though no human had ever set foot in the place. One wall was covered with a bank of electronic instrumentation on which a few multi-coloured LED lights were blinking. The rest of the windowless lab was bare, gleaming white plastic. The only piece of furniture seemed to be a black leather reclining seat in the centre. It reminded Shireen of a dentist's chair.

She started to walk towards it when she noticed that Zak wasn't following her. She turned. He stood there, hovering just inside the lab entrance and looking more nervous than ever. She tried to control her frustration and smiled at him. 'Look, I know what I'm getting into here.'

He didn't reply but moved slowly to the bank of electronics and began switching on the instruments.

As the lab's background hum grew noticeably louder, Shireen suddenly acknowledged just what she was asking of the FBI agent. She went over to him and reached out to rest a hand on his arm. 'Look, Zak, I know this is mad. And I know it's dangerous. And the best we can hope for is that my worries are unfounded, the Project will go smoothly, and we'll both be arrested. But then if I don't—'

Zak's eyes suddenly flashed in anger. 'Don't you think I know that? Would you have got this far if I didn't?' He turned back to the instruments.

'I'm sorry.' Her voice was barely a whisper. She walked back to the chair in the middle of the room. Of course, there was every good reason to be nervous. What she was planning on doing had never been done before.

She ran her fingers along the smooth leather of the TID chair. It had a certain hypnotic quality about it, beautiful, yet terrifying in equal measure. She had dreamed of a moment like this. But now that it was a reality, all the excitement and romance had vanished. All that was left was a sense of foreboding.

The low electronic hum rose in pitch as the system booted up. Zak walked over to her. He was carrying a metal tray on which there was a very ordinary-looking syringe. 'Look, Shireen, TID technology is perfectly safe as long as you displace somewhere alone. But you want to put yourself *inside* the Mag-8 facility. That's sheer lunacy.' Damn it, he was still trying to talk her out of this. 'There's a Mind in there that is on high alert for *anything* out of the ordinary . . . anything at all.'

'I know that, Zak, and I know the risk I'm taking, but I need to do this. Whatever the Purifiers *may* have planned, I think it will only become evident *after* Lockdown. If I displace too early, then I'll be detected and kicked out by the human controllers. But it's crucial I'm inside when Lockdown happens. I just hope that the Mind gives me a chance to explain.'

She hoped she sounded more confident than she felt. Zak looked far from convinced, trying to appeal to her common sense. 'Listen, you know as well as I do that a Mind can assimilate new information and learn new tricks a million times faster than any human. So don't tell me you can outwit it.'

'I'm not. And I don't want to get into a pointless argument about machine consciousness.' She paused and looked at him. 'It's just that I don't think an AI Mind is capable of recognizing a *psychopathic* human mind, one willing to destroy the world. Which is why I have to help it.'

Without waiting for his response, Shireen eased herself into the chair. It felt cold where it met her skin. 'Can we just get on with this please, Zak? We don't have long and have to time this just right.'

He nodded, reached around to the back of the chair and produced a jet black, full head-and-face helmet. 'Put this on. It has several thousand sensors and probes on the inside that pick up your brain's activity and transmit your thoughts to the remote location. At the same time, it'll be sending data back in the opposite direction.' He paused, as though he was worried he'd spooked her too much, before adding, 'But it should feel quite comfortable.'

Shireen gingerly pulled the helmet over her head and let out a gasp of surprise. The front visor, which had looked black from the outside, projected bright, pale blue light on the inside. She felt as if she was staring up into a clear summer sky.

She could hear Zak hooking her up to various machines – monitors that would record her vital signs and allow him to instantly kill the power to the nanobots and bring her back. She felt her nervousness rise a notch. She thought about her parents at home in Tehran. She knew they'd be worrying whether the world would be around for them to ever see her again. She thought about Majid. She missed him more than ever. And she wondered what Sarah must be going through right now, imprisoned and helpless.

Zak snapped her out of her reverie. 'OK, Shireen. Are you ready?'

Her mouth felt dry. The Sentinels protecting the Mag-8 Mind, and even the Mind itself, would fry her brain if they saw her as a hostile presence and rejected the merge.

'OK, let's get on with this,' she whispered, almost to herself.

'Right, relax your arm. I hope this doesn't hurt too much. I've never done it before.' Then there was a sharp sensation of pressure in her forearm. She sucked in a deep breath. So, this was it. No turning back now. Zak had injected her with the nanobots. Suddenly this didn't seem like such a great idea. Within seconds she was floating, her body no longer belonging to her. She experienced a brief sense of panic. As a child, she had suffered from sleep paralysis: being fully awake and yet unable to move or speak. This felt like that – and then the sensation fell away . . .

Slowly the monochromatic blue light changed, and Shireen could pick out features. As her surroundings swam into focus she saw that she was standing in a garden, a place she guessed was a virtual-reality holding area for her to become familiar with the sensation of controlling her avatar body before she was displaced. She looked down to see that she was standing barefooted on a manicured lawn. All around her were thick bushes rich in colourful flowers. She could 'feel' the grass beneath her feet and smell the sweet scent of jasmines and roses. She tried lifting her hand up to her face and found it very easy. She told herself that what she was looking at was a computer-generated hand. It wasn't hers. She knew that back in the lab her own hand would not be moving. Her brain had sent a signal to the muscles to raise an arm, but the nanobots had intercepted it and translated it into the sensation of lifting the imaginary avatar limb.

Shireen had spent her life playing immersive VR games and was perfectly at ease experiencing the sensation of moving around and interacting in a computer-generated world. Wearing her gaming helmet, haptic suit and gloves, it was easy to fool the brain into believing you were in some fantasy world of aliens and monsters – but you still had to swivel your head to look around you, and you still had to physically move your arms, or manipulate your fingers, for your actions to be translated into the virtual world.

This was different. Every one of her senses was confirming to her that she was physically standing in the garden and the illusion was utterly impossible to shake, however hard she tried to convince herself otherwise. She fought back her panic and forced herself to relax, to accept it.

And when Zak spoke softly to her, she realized that it was a subtly different experience from the usual sensation of hearing, as though his voice was being generated inside her head: *OK, Shireen, listen to me because this is very important: there isn't any way the outside world can make contact with the Mag-8 Mind once Lockdown has been initiated, so it'll be up to the Mind to find you, not the other way round.*

I'm ready. Shireen could hear her own voice 'in her head' but wasn't sure if her lips had moved in the lab. However, her thought had clearly been transmitted to Zak because he immediately responded. *Good. Everything seems in order from this end. Now we just wait.*

42

SARAH COULDN'T JUST GIVE UP NOW. SHE MIGHT BE locked in with this monster, but she was still recording his confession. She needed to know what he had planned. *I have to play for time. Keep him talking. Let him think he's won.*

'So, tell me, Senator. Make me understand. What would motivate you to want to do this?'

'There's that amateur psychologist again,' laughed Hogan. He seemed to relax a little and stepped back from her, as though he felt he had all the time in the world and was having second thoughts about terminating their conversation just yet. 'Maybe I need to lie down on a couch if we're going to do this properly. OK then, Dr Maitlin, it's only a few hours till the end of the world, so why not? In any case, I don't plan for you personally to even live *that* long. Let's see if you have the intellectual capacity to understand.'

Jesus, he's going to confess his entire warped ideology to me. Then he's going to kill me. Her back was pressed hard against the electron beam pipe. The metal felt cold.

385

She stole a quick glance behind her to see if there was anything she could use as a weapon, hoping he hadn't noticed. *What if he does? He must know I'm not going down without a fight.* There was nothing. But she needed to keep him talking, get him to reveal something.

'Any evolutionary psychologist will tell you that your feelings of altruism – your empathy and compassion towards fellow human beings – is an evolved trait. You're not nice because you choose to be – it was in our ancestors' interests, going back a hundred thousand years, to show kindness, to cooperate. Or maybe you try to be good because some holy book says you had better be, otherwise you'll incur the displeasure of some Divine Creator. But on an individual basis, what use do we have for altruism other than to make us feel better about ourselves? What if you could turn off that switch? You would be liberated. Free from the desire – the need – to make others happy.'

'And you feel liberated, do you, Hogan? Is that it? But that's not enough for you, is it? Being ambivalent towards fellow humans is one thing, but your empty, psychopathic antipathy ... I mean, that takes a special kind of insanity.'

Hogan didn't look remotely unsettled.

'The truth is I can't really remember when my feelings towards my fellow man ... and, ah, woman ... sorry ... actually began. Did you know I read the work of Immanuel Kant as a student? Back then I thought I understood who I was – what I was – no different from a million other young men. A misanthrope. Only the more I read, the more I came to realize that men like Kant, or writers like Gustave Flaubert, or even geniuses like Michelangelo and Newton, all supposedly famous misanthropes, were just loners who didn't like being around other people – nothing more than a social phobia that led them to dislike everyone around them. They were weak, pathetic sociopaths, Sarah, and I grew to despise them even more than the rest of humanity.' He smiled that smile again. The dead smile that made her want to retch.

'You know, I really did try to rationalize my feelings, to understand my nihilism. And I think I did, in the end.' He paused, and looked away, as though trying to invoke human emotions. But he quickly snapped his attention back to Sarah and the cold sharp focus was back in his eyes.

'You do know we've brought this all on ourselves, don't you?' His voice was suddenly louder. 'How long have we been destroying our planet? And how long did you think it would be before the planet fought back? We changed its climate, we plundered its resources, we poisoned the land, the oceans and the atmosphere. Finally, Mother Earth has had enough. Is that so difficult to comprehend?' Flecks of spittle had appeared around the corners of his mouth.

My God, he really is totally, utterly mad. She tried to keep her face expressionless. In this new spirit of openness, would he finally reveal what she needed?

'It wasn't so difficult to take on the persona of Maksoob, either. People find the notion of a respected US senator leading such a double life so unlikely as to be laughable. And Maksoob is such a comic-book villain, isn't he? In my late twenties—' He paused, tilting his head to one side. 'By the way, you don't mind me telling you all this, do you? I mean, I hope you didn't have anywhere else you needed to be? Any other "pressing" engagements? Only, it's so lovely to be able to chat so candidly. And so close to the end of days. Anyway, as I was saying, in my late twenties, I was spending a lot of time in the Arabian Gulf advising governments on a proposed new clean

387

energy programme. One day, I was driven out to the Eastern Desert, where I met with disaffected Bedouin tribesmen. Many of them had grown up in the wealthiest countries in the world, with every conceivable luxury at their disposal. But with the oil crash of '28 coinciding with the new breakthroughs in solar energy tech it became clear that the world had lost its appetite for fossil fuels. Almost overnight, once-rich Gulf nations were plunged into deep poverty. It's not surprising they became bitter and angry.

'Easy pickings. I began recruiting on the dark web, first from the Middle East and gradually from every corner of the globe. But I was given an Arabic name, Maksoob, which I believe means "Recruited One". Bless them for thinking *they* had recruited *me* to their cause. I *gave* them the cause.'

He sighed. 'And there you have it, Sarah, now you know me. But I still don't suppose you can see why this is all necessary, can you?'

There was a madness in his eyes now that she hadn't seen before. As though he'd spent his life suppressing it in order to appear normal, to appear human. And now he could afford to let the mask slip, to reveal the monster beneath.

'Why *what* is necessary, Hogan?'

'Oh, I'm quite enjoying this. You want me to tell you what I have planned. Well, let's just say that it is deliciously simple – a basic oversight that everyone will be kicking themselves for missing, for the entire remainder of their lives, which I believe will be around ten minutes after Ignition.'

The table next to him was littered with an array of electronic detritus – discarded tools, components and dust-covered display pads. Hogan looked down and selected an ugly-looking spanner, testing its heft by moving it from one hand to the other and back again.

Shit. Was this it? Sarah felt a chill ripple through her. Hogan was bigger and physically stronger, and he was about to bludgeon her to death as if this was a nightmarish game of Cluedo. A whimper of fear escaped her lips and he grinned. It seemed to please him. He stepped towards her. Incredibly, she heard him humming to himself.

His sheer arrogance and over-confidence meant that he was still looking down at the spanner when she struck. With a war cry of rage, she leapt at him, channelling all her fear, her rage into her right arm. She punched forward, locking it just before impact. '*FUCK YOU, HOGAN,*' she screamed as the palm of her hand connected hard with his nose. She heard the crunch of breaking cartilage and the look of surprise on his face became a rictus of pain as his nose exploded in a fountain of blood. He was thrown backwards, tripping over thick cables, arms scrabbling to find a handhold as his head thudded against the edge of a steel casing protruding from the side of the booster ring.

He was unconscious before he hit the ground.

Adrenalin pumping, Sarah turned and ran back towards the winding corridor that led to the exit. She had no idea how she would get out. Hogan had said he'd locked the door remotely from within so presumably it could be opened from the inside. Reaching the steel door, she slammed her hand against the large EXIT button on the wall. Nothing happened.

Letting out a feral scream of frustration and rage that echoed around her, Sarah began hammering on the door. She had the proof that they so desperately needed that the Purifiers were planning something, but couldn't do anything with it. What were Marc and Shireen doing? Less than two hours till Lockdown and she had no connection with the outside world.

Pushing back a growing panic, Sarah wondered whether there was another way out, then remembered the e-pad that Hogan had been looking at when he'd stepped out of the shadows. Of course, that had to be how he had locked the door remotely.

She retraced her steps to the accelerator hall.

A streak of blood glittered wetly on the floor, but Hogan was nowhere to be seen. And neither was the e-pad he'd left on the table.

43

MARC SPRINTED BACK TO THE MAIN MAG-8 BUILDING.
No time to formulate a plan. If Aguda had locked Sarah
inside the electron booster hall then surely that was evidence not only of his guilt, but that he was planning
something and wanted her out of the way. But would he
be stupid enough to think that she was working alone?
This wasn't a scenario they had contemplated.

All he knew was that he had no choice now but to confront the geologist.

Shireen had said that Gabriel Aguda was somewhere in
the main building, but he wasn't among the rest of the dignitaries in the main viewing gallery. Trying to appear calm
and not draw attention to himself, Marc ran through his
options. He didn't have many. Well, this was it, no more
cloak and dagger heroics. He needed to alert security.

Marc couldn't claim to know General Hussain Hassan, a retired army general, well but he knew enough to
suggest that Hassan was the sort of man used to dishing
out orders, not taking them. And Marc had no reason
not to trust him.

He took the stairs down to the ground floor three at a time. Outside the general's office, he flashed his ID at the two guards who moved to block him. Too late: the door was open and the general waved him in.

The head of security at Mag-8 sat behind a large mahogany desk and in front of an even larger framed photograph of the King of Jordan. There were several others present, including a couple of UN officials Marc recognized, all engaged in an animated conversation.

Marc didn't have time for pleasantries and launched straight in.

'General, apologies for interrupting things but what I am about to tell you is critical, and you must believe me because we don't have much time.'

The general stared at him, his face unreadable.

'I have reason to believe that Dr Aguda is a dangerous man,' Marc continued, 'and we need to speak with him urgently.'

'Why do you say that, Professor?' The general's voice betrayed no emotion and, Marc thought, he didn't look particularly surprised. Did he already know about Aguda? If so, why wasn't Ignition being aborted?

Hassan didn't wait for a response from Marc. Instead he continued, 'You're late to the party, Professor Bruckner. We have this in hand.'

Marc was stunned. What the fuck was going on?

'Listen to me, goddammit, the Project itself is in jeopardy.' He slammed his fist on the desk and leaned towards the general. 'Gabriel Aguda is not who you think he is. He's plotting something, and we need to find him pretty damn quickly.'

'And I just told you,' Hassan said, his voice measured, 'that we have it under control.'

Kicking back his chair, the general stood and walked

392

round from behind his desk. He nodded at the others in the room. 'Excuse me, everyone. Come with me, Professor.'

Baffled, Marc was led out of the office and down the corridor to the far end of the building. A pair of Jordanian soldiers stood guard outside what Marc assumed must have been one of the many administrative offices. He could hear murmured conversation coming from within.

The soldiers jumped to attention, one opening the door.

Whatever it was that Marc expected to see, it wasn't this. A group of men and women parted to let the general and Marc through. That's when Marc saw Gabriel Aguda. In the far corner of the room, he sat at a terminal table, his head thrown forward and resting in a pool of slowly congealing blood. His glassy stare seemed to be directed straight at Marc. In his hand, hanging limply to one side, was a gun. He looked quite dead.

As he approached, Marc could see a neat hole above Aguda's ear where the bullet must have entered.

He felt bile rise up in his gorge. The general was speaking, and he forced himself to look away, to focus.

'We found out about Dr Aguda's involvement in a plot here at Mag-8 just under an hour ago. Within minutes, we found him here. We were warned that he would try something. The man was clearly unhinged and desperate to sabotage the Project.'

'But . . . what happened here?' muttered Marc, gesturing in the direction of the geologist's corpse. 'This looks like a suicide.'

'It would indeed appear so. Especially since he has conveniently left us a message.' The general raised a bushy eyebrow.

393

Was this Aguda's parting shot? Set whatever plan he had in motion, then, because he knew his cover had been blown, take his own life to keep it secret?

'So why have you not stopped Ignition?' Marc shouted.

'As I said, Professor, we have it in hand. Aguda was planning to set off an explosive device timed for the moment of Ignition. It would have destroyed Mag-8 just as the dark-matter beam arrived from CERN.'

Marc stared at the general. 'And how do you know all this?'

'Because, Professor Bruckner, we were tipped off, by the same source who alerted us to Aguda. The information was indeed reliable. We found the device hidden in the basement, just where we were told it would be, and defused it.'

Marc's mind was reeling. There was something not quite right here.

'But ... How? ... I thought security around all the sites was meant to be so tight you couldn't smuggle in a cheese sandwich without it raising the threat level. So, who ... who told you all this?'

'If you must know, it came from the very top. Senator Hogan himself had been alerted and he informed me. Now if you'll excuse me, Professor, I need to find the Senator, who also seems to have gone missing.'

The general turned to leave the conference room, then slowed down and turned back to Marc.

'Actually, Professor Bruckner, I meant to ask you, how did *you* come by this information? Have you spoken to the Senator today?'

'What?' Marc tried to make sense of all this. Somehow Hogan must have received his own intelligence at the same time as Shireen. Was that coincidence? He doubted it.

'I'll explain in a few minutes. But if you're sure the danger is over, I need a few of your men to come with me to help open the locked door of the booster hall. Aguda has locked Dr Maitlin in there.'

The general stared at Marc for a few seconds, then signalled to the two armed guards to go with him.

As Marc hurried across the compound flanked by the two silent soldiers, he tried to piece things together. Something was bugging him. The timing was all wrong. He checked the time as he ran. It had been forty-five minutes since he'd lost contact with Sarah. She'd been locked inside just after that. But if Hassan was right and Aguda had shot himself an hour ago, then he couldn't have been the one who had locked Sarah in.

It took just a few minutes for the soldiers to deactivate the electronic locking device hidden behind a wall panel and pull the large steel door open manually. As soon as there was enough of a gap, Marc pushed past them before they could stop him. As his eyes adjusted to the dim light inside he saw Sarah running towards him, shielding her eyes from the harsh glare of sunlight as she did so. He threw his arms around her. She was shaking.

'Marc, thank God,' she sobbed, but then suddenly pushed herself away from him. 'We don't have much time left.'

'It's OK, Sarah. They've found a device. And Aguda's dead. Shot himself.'

'Aguda's dead? Yes, that figures. Marc, it's not Aguda. It never was. It's Hogan. He's Maksoob. And he's completely crazy.' Then she added, 'And it's not over. Not by a long shot.'

Everything suddenly dropped into place. Of course it was Hogan. How could he have been so slow? This whole charade was set up by Hogan. Did he have Aguda killed? Did he do it himself?

'Marc, Hogan's in there somewhere.' Sarah turned and pointed back into the darkness. 'He was going to—' Her voice cracked and she paused, composing herself. 'He's hurt. I hit him and he fell but now I can't find him. We need to get to the control room and abort Ignition, now!'

Seeing the look of desperation in her face, he didn't ask any more questions.

'OK, we need to go. Tell me what you know on the way.'

But as he turned to go, he came face to face with the two soldiers, weapons aimed straight at him and Sarah.

'We are sorry, Professor,' said one. He looked almost apologetic. They were the first words he'd spoken. 'But General Hassan has ordered us to keep you and Dr Maitlin here until Lockdown.'

'What the fuck?' Sarah moved towards the door. 'This is insane. Did you not just hear us? Senator Hogan is the one you should be worried about, and he's somewhere in there and planning something that will kill you and everyone you love.'

The other, older soldier stepped forward and shoved Sarah back. Marc tensed, and grabbed Sarah's hand before she could retaliate. The younger man continued: 'General Hassan said you would accuse the American, Hogan. Now please, step back from this entrance. We have orders to shoot if you do not comply.'

As if to emphasize his point, he moved his gun from Sarah to Marc. For a brief second, Marc contemplated rushing them, but this wasn't a fight he could win.

Holding their guns level, the two guards backed out

into the sunlight. As the doors began to slide shut, the younger soldier repeated, 'We are sorry. We will be outside. You will be released as soon as Lockdown has been safely initiated.'

The doors closed and Marc heard the click of the electronic lock.

44

A DIGITAL CLOCK HOVERED IN THE TOP LEFT OF Shireen's field of vision. Zak had set it to countdown and she had been watching it for over an hour. With minimal sensory inputs for so long, she was beginning to hallucinate – drifting in and out of a vivid dream world so that she was finding it hard to remember where she was and what she was about to do. Once again, she forced herself to focus. She was still standing in the garden, and while she could move her arms and head, she seemed unable to move her feet away from the spot.

At last, she heard Zak's voice in her head. It sounded clear, but faint, as though coming to her from a great distance. *OK, Shireen. The countdown to Lockdown has begun and I'm sending you in.* Eight seconds to go and the garden began to dissolve away. A sudden bolt of excitement surged through her. It was working. She was inside the Mag-8 facility.

Her first sensation was that of a hundred different sounds. After the quiet of the TID Lab and then the peacefulness of the garden, now a cacophony of hums

398

and drones of machines and electronics greeted her. It all sounded so real; and the illusion that she was physically inside Mag-8 was remarkable. There above her head were the huge black superconducting magnets fixed in place on vast steel and graphene girders, with a multitude of cables, instruments and multi-coloured lights everywhere. The air against her skin felt warm and dry. She could almost taste the dust of the desert.

And her hunch had been correct: Lockdown hadn't severed the link. It was supposed to mean that all communication between the Mind and the outside world was now blocked, and yet the nanobots in her body were still receiving data from within Mag-8 and feeding it to her brain. Would she be able to send her thoughts back, through the mouth of her avatar standing in Mag-8, to communicate with the Mind?

Now that Lockdown was in place, the link made just moments earlier between her body in Washington and the Mag-8 Mind ten thousand kilometres away wasn't via the Cloud at all. It couldn't be. That was the point of Lockdown. Instead, the information exchange seemed to be being maintained purely by long-range quantum correlations. The nanobots were sufficiently quantum entangled with the molecules of air inside Mag-8 for quantum information to be exchanged. This TID technology was almost like magic, and it seemed – incredibly – to be working. Shireen felt a surge of pure elation.

This is the ultimate out-of-body experience. Einstein hated the idea of quantum entanglement, calling it 'spooky action at a distance', and yet here I am, my thoughts teleported halfway across the world from my physical body.

She was standing on a gantry high above the ground within a large enclosure. Looking about her she noted that she was close to one of the huge bending magnets. It hummed as though it were a living thing. In front of her was a waist-high safety bar. She reached a hand towards it. It felt cold and solid to the touch, pushing back against her fingers. How could that be when none of this was real? *No, wait, that's wrong. All of this . . . it is real. I'm the one who's not real. I'm actually still in Washington, DC. What's being reconstructed in my brain is whatever is being recorded by all the cameras and sensors inside the facility.*

Shireen's avatar peered down over the railings. The gantry she was on was about ten metres above the ground. The magnet closest to her was the uppermost one of the first level. Down on the ground directly below was a cubic structure, which she guessed housed the focusing magnet – the place where the dark-matter beams would come together and head vertically down. Shireen leaned out further still and looked up. The other two levels of magnets towered majestically and vertiginously far above her.

She now needed to make contact with the Mind and to persuade it to look for something, anything, that was out of the ordinary – something that would have become apparent only *after* Lockdown.

And first she had to earn its trust.

The dilemma she was acutely aware of was that her own presence here wasn't physical. In fact, she was no more 'real' than the Mind itself. They were both mere data. And to communicate and cooperate they would need to merge into one – a unique combination, a human– AI consciousness.

Shireen didn't have long to wait. Without warning she was plunged into blackness. Was this the work of the Sentinels protecting the Mag-8 Mind? They were less powerful AIs than the Mind itself, but their role was a simple one: to ensure that no alien software could penetrate and infect the Mind. That had to be it: they would have detected data flowing from the lab in Washington and were attempting to block it.

No, please don't let this be the end of it – that all this was for nothing. Shireen felt time running away from her. She had to reach out.

My name is Shireen Darvish and I am using TID to communicate with you. I am not a threat. I want to help.

Nothing. Sentinels would have figured this out anyway, but she wasn't sure what else to say. Suddenly the enormity of what had happened to her over the past few months crowded into her consciousness and for the first time in her life Shireen Darvish began to understand the true meaning of despair.

And it was then that she received a reply. She couldn't describe it. It wasn't a response transmitted in words as such but more of a feeling, a sense of meaning. Yes, that was it! And it was neither friendly nor aggressive, simply a statement of fact.

Shireen Darvish. You are not permitted to interact. Lockdown has been initiated.

A wave of relief crashed through her. Any communication suggested that they didn't see her as an immediate threat and that meant there was still hope.

I understand. But you require my help. Ignition may have been compromised. Give me access to the Mind.

The Mind cannot be accessed. No compromise has been detected. Lockdown is in place.

OK, maybe a different tack was needed. These guardian AIs were simply doing what they were programmed

401

to do. Hell, *they* were no more than sophisticated software programs. Now was probably a good time for her to stop thinking of them as living entities.

She felt a buzzing sensation in her head, which grew louder and more urgent, only it wasn't a sound – more like a vibration inside her skull, a hundred billion neurons trying to break free of their moorings. She was suddenly overcome by an indescribable giddiness, as though she were tumbling through space. The spinning sensation was horrible. There was no up or down, no anchor. She was lost in the void and her head was about to explode.

Let me off this ride. It's scary. Mama, can you tell them to stop? I don't like it . . . It's going too fast. I'm going to fall off . . .

A presence.

Get out. Get out of my head. I don't want you here.

Then . . . Empty. Silence. Nothingness.

She floated and observed and waited . . . and existed, without any feeling, purpose or sense of self. She couldn't think, or rationalize, had just a dim awareness that she had lost her mind.

Then, just as quickly as it had started, it was over, and she was back in control of her own thoughts. *What the hell had just happened?* She'd felt a dislocation, as though she were nothing more than a detached presence observing the functioning of her mind from afar. It felt as if her corporeal self had been pushed aside while her thoughts, dreams and memories were ransacked.

Could that be the Mind? Yes, it had to be.

Rather than observe the exchange between her and the Sentinels, it had decided to find out who the intruder was for itself and had merged with the intruder's thoughts! Shireen tried to rationalize how it could have done this. It

402

must have sent sophisticated spyware into her head via the nanobots in order to read her thoughts. She felt as though she had been violated, exposed, laid bare.

More importantly, though, contact had been made. She tried again.

I hope you now believe me when I say I wish no malice.

Suddenly, the lights came back on inside the facility and she heard a deep, rich, soft, unmistakably female voice.

You are Shireen Darvish. You believe Mag-8 to be compromised. Yet I do not detect any anomalies. I do not understand the nature of the possible attack. Your thoughts are confused. Please explain.

There are those who do not wish for the Odin Project to succeed. They want Mag-8 to fail.

Many do not want the Odin Project to go ahead. I under-stand this. They calculate the risks to be too high. But you are speaking of those who suffer from a corruption of human reasoning. Those who wish Ignition to go ahead, but for it to fail.

That's right. And I believe they've planted something inside Mag-8. Something you have not, and would not detect, unless you knew what to look for.

Had her hunch been correct? A nanoswarm could indeed be lurking inside Mag-8. Each bot would have specialized pincers to destroy almost anything in its path. A swarm could slice through matter like a knife through butter, dissolve reinforced armour, or get inside secure buildings through the tiniest of cracks.

She shuddered as she thought about it, or rather she would have done if she'd had control of her physical body. She was jerked back from her thoughts by the voice in her head.

You believe a swarm may have infiltrated the facility. You believe that if it is running autonomous software off-grid then I would only be aware of its presence if it interacted physically with anything within the facility. This is correct.

This wasn't proof that there really was a swarm floating somewhere in here, waiting, biding its time until the last moment to attack, but if it *were* present then the Mind would not necessarily know about it. A swarm could hover indefinitely like an invisible cloud, powered by artificial photosynthesis from surrounding electromagnetic radiation. The Mind could only see and feel what the sensors and cameras built into the facility could detect.

Is there a way to expose it if it is in here somewhere?

Yes.

The next second everything went completely dark. Had the Mind just turned off all the lights? Why? Before she could puzzle over it any further, the facility was suddenly bathed in a low-level blue-violet colour that gave the place a dreamlike quality. At the bottom of her field of vision Shireen saw the words:

MONOCHROMATIC UV LIGHT. 280 nm. 4.43 eV.

The interior of Mag-8 was being bathed in ultraviolet light. The Mind had squeezed the wavelength of the light produced by all the facility's LEDs down to 280 nanometres.

While she waited, it occurred to her that had she been truly physically present here, she would have remained in total darkness. Pure, monochromatic UV light is invisible to the human eye. But she wasn't looking through her physical eyes. The nanobots floating inside her body back in Washington had received the data and helpfully rendered it as visible violet light for her benefit.

Then, without the colour of the light she was seeing changing much, the numbers on her AR display altered. The light's wavelength had become shorter, while the second number, which she guessed was the corresponding energy of the light, had increased:

HIGH ENERGY UVC LIGHT. 100 nm. 12.4 eV.

What did this mean? She cursed as she struggled to remember her first-year introductory physics course on quantum theory. Something about the energy of light connected to its wavelength ... What was it? Come on, think. OK, high-energy radiation, like X-rays and gamma rays, had very short wavelength. That meant the shorter the wavelength the more energy the light carried. So, the Mind had just turned up the energy dial on the light. Had she been physically inside the facility at this moment, not only would she not see anything, but she would have been killed by the ionizing radiation too. What was the Mind up to? As though reading her thoughts, it spoke again.

If a nanobot swarm is present, it will react to high-energy ultraviolet light. Damaging to all life forms.

But nanobots are not living things.

You are correct. Living biomolecules are damaged by ultraviolet light. But although nanobots contain biological components, DNA building blocks, this UV frequency will not harm them. They have more rigid molecular bonds than living biological matter, which vibrate in the extreme UV range. Shining light of the correct colour on them pumps these bonds full of energy and they vibrate, emitting the energy as light again. Look below you.

Then it hit her what the Mind was doing. It was tuning the frequency of the light in Mag-8 until the swarm became visible. She leaned over the gantry railings and peered down at the ground beneath her.

What she saw made her gasp – or at least the sensation in her chest was as if she had taken a sharp intake of breath. Hovering in the air close to the large apparatus was a swirling cloud of bright sparkling lights that surrounded the focusing magnet near the entrance point in the ground where the dark-matter beam would disappear. It was hypnotically beautiful – like the twilight bioluminescence of a swarm of fireflies, only here she could not quite make out individual dots of light, but rather smeared-out clumps. The cloud was changing shape slowly and hovering in the same location.

The swarm is re-emitting the UV light that it is absorbing, betraying its presence. This will make it angry.

Shireen found that a very strange way to describe unthinking machines. What did the Mind mean? The swarm could not show emotions such as anger, but if it was programmed to remain hidden and then it was threatened . . .

This UV light is not destroying them, is it?

No. I cannot increase the energy of the light any higher or it will damage the instruments.

As if to confirm that the swarm now knew it had been exposed, it suddenly changed shape from a nebulous cloud into a concentrated snake-like formation that circled around a few times, sparkling as it did so. Then, without warning, it darted upwards, almost too fast for Shireen's avatar eyes to follow, slicing through one of the graphene girders supporting the magnet structure. It did this several times, back and forth, until Shireen felt a jolt as the platform she was standing on moved slightly.

Had it detected her presence? Was this an attack on her? And if so, how? She wasn't physically there. Could it be somehow sensing her as mere information? Something alien within Mag-8? Maybe cutting through the girder had nothing to do with her. Maybe once it was exposed, its task was to create havoc.

But the swarm now regrouped and was hovering, still sparkling, almost at eye level with where Shireen was standing. It seemed to be waiting for something. Maybe the brief act of destruction was a warning. Maybe it was being petulant, like an indignant toddler.

But she was wrong.

The swarm started to move slowly towards her. *Oh, no. This is crazy. The swarm can't 'see' me.*

And still the swarm came closer. The shimmering lights of the nanobots were now blocking her entire field of vision as it loomed in front of her. Shireen felt terrified.

I'm not really here. I'm not really here. To prove to herself that it couldn't physically harm her, she slowly reached out her hand to touch the front edge of the swarm. A searing pain shot through her fingers and up her arm, jerking her backwards.

Of course. For the same reason she could feel the solidity of the metal gantry beneath her feet, or the cold metal barrier in front of her, she could touch the nanobots. And if they were able to do to her what they did to that graphene girder . . . *But I'm not even here! The pain I felt is just an illusion. They can't physically harm me. It's all in my head.* And yet her hand and arm were now throbbing with pain. She backed away from the swarm, panic rising, until she came up against the cold metal casing of the magnet wall behind her. She had nowhere else to go.

And still the swarm approached her. It was as though it was contemplating how best to deal with this annoying presence.

Zak, Zak, pull me back! I don't think I can take the pain if they attack my face! Where the hell was he?

She felt as though she was experiencing a dreadful nightmare, while knowing it was only a dream. No, this was worse than that. The whole point of total immersive displacement was that the pain she would feel would be as real as anything her physical body could experience. The swarm was now centimetres from her face. It was then that Shireen knew she was going to die. She closed her eyes and waited.

The cold, when it came, penetrated her inner core. She gasped and froze for a few seconds, feeling icier than she had ever felt before, but just as quickly the sensation was gone. She opened her eyes. The swarm was still there, writhing in front of her, but it didn't seem as bright. At first, she didn't understand. It looked almost as though it was evaporating. Then, suddenly, without warning, the entire swarm snapped out of existence. Shireen hardly dared breathe. She waited, trying to make sense of what she had just witnessed.

Mind, what just happened there? Where's it gone?

The swarm has been neutralized. The danger is gone, Shireen Darvish.

Around her, the blue light gently returned to the normal LED white.

She remembered the display on her AR. It had changed. It now just read:

TEMPERATURE: 210 KELVIN.

She stared at the words. 210 Kelvin translated to a chilly 63 degrees Celsius below zero. No wonder she had felt cold. The nanobots in her brain must have readjusted the temperature just as they had changed the wavelength of the light. Would they also have protected her from the pain of the swarm if it had attacked? Shireen gave an involuntary shudder.

Mind. Please explain. Have you just done what I think you've done and frozen the swarm? How could it be that easy? Help me to understand.

The soothing, almost maternal voice replied.

The bio-molecular building blocks of the nanobots cannot function below 230 Kelvin. All other instrumentation and electronics in the facility is able to operate at optimum levels down to 200 Kelvin. I will maintain this temperature until after Ignition. I have run full diagnostics checks again. All systems and instruments are operational. Damaged graphene girder will complete self-healing in twelve minutes. Misaligned magnet now back in position.

The run will proceed.

Thank you, Shireen Darvish. This has been an interesting experience.

And with a jolt, Shireen was back in the VR garden. The Mind had said its piece and simply ejected her. The transition was so abrupt that for a moment she felt confused. She couldn't make sense of the sudden tranquillity of the garden after the noise inside Mag-8. The near-omniscient presence of the Mind, along with the threat of the swarm, had gone. She felt strangely alone.

Bring me back please, Zak.

Gradually, she became aware of a different sensation, one not of standing up, but of lying horizontally. And there was Zak, gently removing her helmet with a worried look on his face. 'Shireen? Shireen. You're back now.' His voice sounded distant, as if he was at the other end of a long tunnel.

Shireen knew she should smile but suddenly felt her stomach heave. Pushing herself up and away from the FBI man, she was violently sick.

She felt his hand on her shoulder. 'I'm so sorry, Zak,' she slurred. She was shivering uncontrollably, and she noticed that she was drenched in sweat. Every inch of her body ached. It felt as though she was one big bruise and her head pounded with a sickly headache.

She could see the concern in Zak's eyes but didn't yet have the strength to stay sitting up and instead flopped back on the chair. Then she looked at him and mumbled, her voice a croak, 'I was right, Zak, there was a swarm inside Mag-8. It . . . it . . . it was horrible. It would have destroyed everything.' She shuddered and wiped her mouth with the back of her hand.

The look of horror on Zak's face impelled her to continue quickly. 'But I think it's OK now. The Mind ... it spoke to me, Zak ... and it neutralized the swarm ... Ignition will go ahead.'

Again she tried to smile, because she felt the situation warranted it. She couldn't believe she had done it. Or rather, the Mind had done it.

And she couldn't stop shivering.

It was one hundred and sixty minutes to Ignition.

45

MARC AND SARAH WERE RELEASED FROM THE BOOSTER hall a few minutes after Lockdown. They persuaded the younger of the two soldiers guarding the block to lock the door behind them and to remain stationed outside. They had tried and failed to find Hogan inside the labyrinthine building – there were just too many places he could hide – but they were certain he was going nowhere.

It was too late to stop Ignition now, but they still hurried back to the Mag-8 building. Marc attempted to contact Shireen. She wasn't responding.

Inside the facility it was a hive of frantic activity. With a brusque 'C'mon, we need to find Hassan', Marc grabbed Sarah's hand and headed for the control room. They pushed their way through the milling scientists, technicians and officials, but there was no sign of the security chief. Marc recognized one of the younger accelerator physicists and stopped him as he was dashing past. 'Wait. You. What the hell is going on in there?'

'We don't know for sure. No one can make sense of it,' he replied breathlessly. 'The Mind is behaving irrationally.

412

First it went completely dark in there, then the temperature suddenly dropped to colder than a deep-freeze. We've no idea what it's up to.'

'And the Mind hasn't told you anything?'

'No, we're in Lockdown. All we can do is guess at what the issue has been.'

Everything seemed to be falling apart. This was the nightmare scenario. 'So, has it aborted Ignition?'

'No, it seems it's still going ahead. But something is very wrong.' The young man was close to tears. The dismaying conclusion had to be that after everything they had gone through, a Mind had been hacked, again. This was the end of the road.

Qiang now appeared by Marc's side. 'Where've you been? Have you heard? The order has just been given to evacuate both CERN and J-PARC.' He had a wild pleading look in his eyes, as though sure his older colleague could figure out a way to make things right. 'Marc, they say that's all we can do now. That if we can't abort and have to assume Mag-8 has failed then we have to destroy two of the dark-matter labs before Ignition.'

Marc just stared at Qiang. If those labs were destroyed that would knock out six of the eight beams. Yes, they would avert an immediate catastrophe, but it would signal the end of the Odin Project. He was turning to Sarah when his wristpad pinged. Shireen. He didn't really want to talk to the young cyb, but there was an urgency in her voice that focused his mind. She breathlessly recounted what she'd experienced with the Mind.

'Hold on, Shireen, I need to stop you there. I'm going to patch you through to everyone here. They need to hear this from you.' He jabbed at his wristpad, patching her in to the main control-room network. Her face suddenly appeared, multiple times, on the screens in both the control room and the viewing gallery. There were gasps as the young Iranian told her story. Beside him Sarah mouthed, 'Oh, my God,' and held her hands to her mouth. Disbelief quickly turned to amazement and awe as Shireen's account was corroborated by the young FBI cybersecurity officer who stood at her side.

Shireen appeared dazed by what she'd been through. Dark bags shrouded her eyes, her normally olive-coloured skin looked pale and sickly. And yet at that moment, for Marc at least, she was the most beautiful person in the world. It seemed she had just, single-handedly, averted the destruction of all life on Earth.

A tide of relief and excitement was quickly spreading through Mag-8. Surely, thought Marc, the order to destroy those two labs would be rescinded once these new revelations were communicated.

He was snapped out of his reverie by the sudden arrival of General Hassan, who pulled him and Sarah to one side.

'These are extraordinary times, so I will dispense with any apologies for what occurred earlier.'

He didn't look like a man expressing regret and Marc studied him dispassionately. Would he listen to them now?

The officer continued: 'And I admit that I appear not to have had it "all in hand" as I indicated earlier. Your friends in Washington have done something that I do not fully understand, but my scientists inform me that it was both foolish and brave and may indeed have just saved the Project.'

'So, has the order been given to stand down those missiles aimed at CERN and J-PARC?' Marc glanced at Sarah.

'Not yet. That would be foolish. But all the labs around the world have just watched that extraordinary message

414

from Washington. So, the fingers are, shall we say, no longer hovering over the buttons.' He let out a snort that Marc assumed was meant to indicate amusement.

'Good. Because Dr Maitlin has something she needs to tell you.'

Marc nodded to Sarah and then left her to bring the general up to speed on what she had learned from Hogan. He checked the time. 15:05. T-minus 40 minutes. He turned back to Qiang, who appeared to be in a daze.

'How are you holding up, mate?' he asked.

'I'm not sure. I don't think I can cope with much more of this. Anyway, you look pretty terrible yourself.'

'Thanks,' Marc grunted. 'Listen, can we just run through what we know?' Qiang nodded. 'OK . . . So, as far as we can tell, the swarm hasn't caused any irreparable damage, right? But is there any way that it, or something else, could have infected the Mind itself?'

'I doubt it. I think we just have to trust the Mind now.' Qiang neither sounded nor looked in the least bit reassuring.

'So, tell me, why do I still have this nagging feeling we're missing something?'

Just then Sarah touched him gently on the shoulder. He turned to her.

'A security team have been dispatched to the booster hall to find Hogan,' Sarah said with grim satisfaction.

The general nodded. 'If he's in there, we'll find him. We have to get some answers out of him and we don't have much more time. Now, will you please excuse me?'

Sarah said, 'Marc, Shireen wants to connect up with you, and Qiang too. She can't do much more from her end, but we could use her brain on this.'

'Sure,' said Marc. Everyone else seemed to think that they now had a clear run to Ignition. A bomb had been defused and the swarm had been neutralized. So, why was he still feeling so uneasy? It didn't help that both Qiang and Sarah seemed similarly anxious.

Shireen's voice popped into Marc's ear. She sounded nearly back to her old self. Good. 'Actually, Marc, though of course I'll do anything to help, I really think you and Qiang are best placed to know what could possibly still go wrong. Hopefully nothing, of course. But you two understand the science better than anyone.' Marc looked at Qiang. He couldn't think of anything to contribute.

'Maybe this will help.' Sarah frowned. 'When he thought he'd trapped me, Hogan boasted it would be something *simple*, something that could be easily overlooked. That doesn't sound like he was referring to the nanoswarm. But if not, what could he mean?'

Marc shook his head slowly. 'The Mind should be able to check every tiny component, and if it finds anything wrong it can either correct it or abort Ignition.'

'But what if the swarm has indeed been successful?' suggested Qiang.

Marc and Sarah looked at him. It was Sarah who completed his train of logic. 'Jesus. You mean, when it attacked and sliced through those girders, that was just a distraction? We were meant to think that it had been caught *before* it could carry out its plan—'

'—when in fact, it had already caused the damage it was meant to,' finished Qiang.

The enormity – and implications – of Qiang's suggestion was beginning to sink in when they were distracted by a sudden commotion. Several soldiers had entered and with them a restrained Senator Peter Hogan. Dried blood covered his face and the front of his shirt. He didn't seem to be resisting.

General Hassan turned and screamed at his men. 'Get him out of here! Now!'

One of the soldiers blurted out, 'But, sir, you said to bring him to you as soon as—'

'NOW! *Ibnil kelb!* Take him down to my office.' With that, Hassan marched off behind them out of the control room.

As he was being led away Hogan pulled back for a second and turned to look at Marc and Sarah. And he winked.

Could he sense their worry? Did he know they had thwarted the nanoswarm? And if he did, was there something else? Something so simple that it had occurred to no one?

Marc rubbed his eyes – God, he was tired – and turned to the others. He wasn't an experimentalist. He dealt with equations and lines of computer code, not real magnets and electronic instruments. But it was Shireen he addressed. 'Shireen, are you still hearing all this? OK, you said you first saw the swarm down by the focusing magnet, just above the vertical shaft where the beam disappears. What could—?'

Then it hit him. 'Of course. The shutter! We need to check the shutter,' he shouted. Qiang and Sarah, along with many of the technicians in the room, just stared at him.

'What do you mean?' said Qiang. 'What about the shutter?'

'Think about it. What's the simplest component that could go wrong? I mean, short of flicking a switch that turns off the electricity to the superconducting magnets. Isn't it the shutter that blocks off the beam path?'

'But why would the beam path ever need to be blocked off?' Sarah jumped in. 'That doesn't make sense, Marc.'

But he was no longer listening. He could feel the adrenalin beginning to kick in as he looked around the control room. 'Where's Maher? I need to see Maher.' He hurried

417

to the nearest Mag-8 technician, a young woman sitting at a terminal desk. 'Where is Maher?'

'Who?' she blurted, looking nervous.

'Maher bloody Haydar. Your boss! The chief fucking accelerator engineer. Where is he?'

'Oh, I . . . I—'

'Never mind. I'll find him.' Marc knew he should stop and explain, but never had time been more precious.

'Wait there,' he yelled over his shoulder at Sarah and Qiang as he barged out of the control room. 'I'll be back in a minute.'

He ran down the metal steps to ground level. The Project's engineer was talking to a couple of technicians by one of the giant steel doors that secured the interior of the Mag-8 hall from the outside world.

'Haydar!' Marc yelled. The man looked up, a concerned expression on his face.

'What is it, Professor Bruckner? You look like you've seen a jinn.'

'The shutter on the focusing magnet,' Marc began. 'You told me it was both the simplest and the most important component in the whole place, correct?'

'It is, yes.' The engineer smiled. 'If that shutter is closed when the chargino pulse reaches the quadrupole, then it will be blocked entirely.' He paused, a frown crossing his face. 'Why do you ask?'

'And you'd know if it was closed, right?'

Maher Haydar, a man fiercely proud of SESAME and what had been achieved with Mag-8, looked at him as if he had lost his mind. 'But *of course* it is open. We made sure it's open and the Mind will have done so too.'

'Yes, yes, but is there a way of checking now?'

Haydar looked bewildered, then relaxed a little. 'Professor, of all the things we have to be concerned with, believe me, the focusing-magnet shutter is not one of them. Even if it, somehow, got closed again – say from a sudden wind blowing off the desert, through some foul miraculous trickery of Iblis himself – then it would trigger a warning and the Mind would know about it.'

Out of the corner of his eye, Marc noticed that the two engineers Maher had been talking to were shaking their heads as though he were a fool. He ignored them.

'Damn it, tell me if I'm wrong—' He paused, to gather his thoughts. He had to get this right. No room for any mistakes now. 'Every one of the thousands of components within the Mag-8 facility has a multitude of instruments and sensors, monitoring and calibrating constantly, making sure everything is running smoothly, and ready to warn the Mind about any anomaly, yes?'

'That is correct.'

'Everything, apart from the shutter in the beam line just below the quadrupole magnet. That's the one component that relies on old technology. We joked about this a couple of days ago. It's so that it can be operated manually. It has a safety override that allows human intervention.'

'Again, correct, Professor. I don't understand where—'

'So how does the Mind know if it is open or closed?'

'Well, of course there is a sensor there that tells it—'

'—but just the one sensor, right? Not like every other component in Mag-8.'

'Just the one, yes. We build in redundancies, but in some cases that really isn't necessary.'

Marc grabbed the Jordanian by the shoulders. 'And what if that were damaged somehow – say its electronics had been fried, so the Mind still thought it was open when it wasn't?'

Maher stared at him in stunned silence for a couple of seconds, then he looked down at the pad he was holding

419

and tapped it. As he did so he said, 'There is a camera inside the magnet casing pointing directly at the shutter, that is not currently in use. It is not linked to the main network controlled by the Mind, so I may be able to turn it on remotely.'

Suddenly, the engineer let out a horrified whimper. He looked up at Marc and turned the pad towards him so he could see the screen. Marc felt a chill run through him. There was the shutter – a ten-centimetre-thick lead disc the diameter of a dinner plate – and it was sitting across the opening through which the chargino beam was due to pass in a few minutes' time.

He looked up at the engineer. 'Is there any way of getting inside Mag-8 and manually opening that shutter?'

Haydar had a glazed look on his face. The man was in complete shock. 'Maher!' Marc shouted. 'Please!'

The Jordanian's eyes refocused. 'There is a way, yes. But to use it . . . it would be suicide.'

Marc checked the time: five minutes to Ignition. 'Where? How? Talk to me, damn it.'

Haydar's eyes brimmed with tears. He nodded. 'Follow me,' he said, his voice no more than a whisper. He turned, his colleagues seemingly forgotten, and walked quickly away, with Marc at his shoulder.

'There's a way in around the other side. Few people know about it. The Mind certainly doesn't. There are no sensors there and the entrance is made entirely from basic non-smart materials, so it's totally off-grid.'

As they made their way round the building, Marc went over what he knew. If the shutter was closed, all the charginos would be stopped before they transformed back into neutralinos. There would be no contribution from Mag-8 to provide the precise balance required in the core when the other seven beams met, and that would

420

be that. He cursed under his breath. He couldn't believe it, after all these months. This was the nightmare scenario everyone had worked so hard to avoid. They had to open that shutter, and they had less than five minutes to do it. They were now in a quiet corridor that skirted the concrete shielding dome that housed the giant bending magnets. On the far side of Mag-8, Haydar stopped at a large, nondescript grey metal door. He stared at it for a moment as though he'd forgotten why he was there.

'Maher. Now open it, please!'

Haydar turned to him, an expression of desperate sadness on his face. 'But, Professor Bruckner, it won't do any good. We've got no time to send a bot in there. And even if we did, the Mind wouldn't let it get very far.'

Marc paused and took a deep breath. 'I know,' he said. 'We're not sending a bot in. *I'm* going in. Now open the goddam door!'

'It's four minutes to Ignition, Professor. You don't have time. And if you are in there when the beam arrives . . . the radiation burst . . . Also, it's sixty degrees below zero in there at the moment. You won't last four minutes without proper—'

Marc sighed. 'Just open the door, Maher. What other choice do we have?'

Haydar must have sensed something in his voice, because he turned and punched a multiple-digit number into a keypad by the door, and it clicked open. Marc pushed past him.

And he was running – running through a narrow alleyway that zigzagged between concrete shielding walls that towered like smooth white cliffs metres above him. He could feel the air getting colder. It was beginning to hurt his chest, so he tried to take shorter breaths. It occurred to him that he hadn't got around to calling Evie.

Damn it. She'd be so cross with him. And now he was letting her down again. He thought about Sarah and Qiang. He didn't think they could see him from the control room. Just as well. He knew he had to do this. It was the only way. The Odin Project was his greatest achievement and he wasn't prepared for it to fail now. Not when they were so close. The earlier panic and stress seemed to fall away. He had a job to do.

He emerged in the large open chamber. Above him rose the array of giant magnets, their superconducting coils humming a deep monotonous tone that he could feel in his bones. Ahead, at the very centre of the hall, was the quadrupole magnet itself, suspended above the borehole down which the dark-matter beam would travel to the Earth's core. If it could.

As he hurried towards it, he was stopped in his tracks by a sound that reverberated around the dome. It was the Mind, and it sounded like the voice of God.

Marc Bruckner. You should not be here. I cannot allow you to compromise the run.

Even though he had been expecting it, and knew it was nothing more than a synthetic voice generated by an artificial intelligence, it still filled him with awe. Yet he couldn't allow it to distract him. As he ran, he shouted out, 'Listen to me. I have been speaking with Shireen Darvish. The swarm you destroyed has already compromised the run. The shutter on the quadrupole magnet is closed.'

This cannot be so. My diagnostics would have alerted me.

He stopped briefly. The cold felt like sandpaper on the back of his throat. Where was the entrance to the central chamber? He looked up. 'The shutter sensor was destroyed by the swarm. You can't rely on what it's telling you. You must be able to check a different way. I mean, you're a fucking Mind.'

The cold was seeping through to his core and every breath he took in was like a sharp knife in his chest.

There was the briefest of pauses before the Mind responded.

You are correct. The shutter is closed. I am unable to open it.

'Then abort the run. Now.'

I can do that. But there is a risk.

'Oh, my God. Why?'

It is T-minus one hundred and twenty seconds. All three accelerators now have their proton-beam energies ramped up. The only way to abort now is to close six of the other seven shutters too and block the beams.

Marc tried to understand what he was hearing, but the cold seemed to be seeping into his brain, slowing it down. Why six shutters? Why not all seven? Yes, because they could afford to have one beam pass through, because it would simply carry on uninterrupted through the Earth and out the other side.

The Mind was still talking.

I have just communicated with the other Minds and determined that there is a non-negligible probability that one or more of them will not comply with my decision to

423

close their shutters. They estimate there is a twenty per cent probability that the swarm has compromised me too and therefore cannot trust that I am being truthful.

If three or more Minds do not close their shutters, it will lead to catastrophic failure of the Project. I calculate a 42.32 per cent probability for this outcome.

He'd heard enough. *What's the point of entrusting so much to artificial intelligences if they are just as bloody unreasonable as humans?* If he left now the Mind would order the other shutters to be closed. A forty-two per cent chance of disaster was too high. Too terrible to contemplate.

Fuck it. So, this was it, then. He'd have to do it manually.

Hoping that the Mind would understand what he was about to do, Marc Bruckner ran towards the quadrupole casing, searching for the way in. He was shivering uncontrollably now, and his breath came out in great white plumes. There! A gap between two three-metre-high metal towers packed with electronic instruments. He squeezed in between them and there it was. The magnet sat inside its chamber, large enough for a man to fit inside when not operational but it was now under high vacuum.

And the shutter was somewhere inside.

The small porthole in the side wall of the chamber had frosted over, which meant he couldn't see inside.

How much time did he have left? His AR contacts had frozen and were useless now. He knew it couldn't be very long.

Everything was covered in a white frost. At first, he didn't know where to start, but then, as though the gods were finally taking pity on him, he spotted a lever. A good old-fashioned lever. The edge of a metal panel was just visible through the frost beneath it. Using his sleeve to wipe the panel clear, he saw what he was looking for. Bold red letters declared: **SHUTTER MANUAL OVERRIDE**.

Of course, something as important as a beam shutter would always have a mechanical lever for an operator to control during construction and testing. He grabbed hold of the metal bar with both hands. The searing pain of the cold metal scalding his palms and fingers shot up his arms. He tried to pull the lever downwards, but it wouldn't move. He realized that his hands had now frozen to the lever too. He felt himself smile. He wasn't quite sure why but a strange thought ran through his head. *I am one with my experiment. I am now physically part of the Odin Project.* He knew he was becoming weaker – his breathing shallower. Was hypothermia setting in? Probably. He thought of Evie. He could see her. She was admonishing him for taking such a stupid risk. But Evie, and Sarah and Qiang and everyone else he'd ever known, wouldn't be around anyway to know that he'd tried. And with that realization came a renewed sense of urgency.

He leaned his entire weight on the lever and, without warning, it swivelled downwards.

Had he done it? Had he made it in time?

He managed somehow to pull his hands from the lever, ripping away layers of skin but feeling nothing. A voice from somewhere deep in his mind was telling him it wasn't such a great idea to hang around here. But he was feeling so sleepy now. And it didn't seem nearly as cold any more. The Mind – the other one – was saying something too, but he was no longer listening.

His vision was blurring and he tried to rub his eyes with his ruined hands. As his lungs began to freeze, his shallow breath was no longer creating a white fog in front of his face. His mind felt heavy and slow. He tried to recall what he was doing here. Then from deep within his barely conscious self, he remembered. He'd done it. He'd cleared the path to the Earth's core. Come on through, little neutralinos. I've opened the gate for you. The thought gave him the beginnings of a smile on his frozen lips just as he felt a mild tingling sensation followed by a sour taste in his mouth. Then, just as quickly, it was gone.

He had a brief moment of clarity. He *had* made it in time after all. The pulse of dark matter had just passed through Mag-8 and was on its way down to the core, leaving in its wake a burst of high-energy x-rays, and good ol' Marc Bruckner had just received a lethal fifty Sievert dose, equivalent to several thousand CT scans all at once.

His legs gave way beneath him and he slowly folded to the ground. The lyrics of an old song came into his head: *Que será, será*. He began to hum tunelessly.

I'm so sorry, Evie. I love you so much.

And then . . . nothing.

46

EVERYONE WAS RUNNING. AS SOON AS IGNITION HAD taken place, the Mind had raised the temperature inside the Mag-8 and ended the Lockdown. Sarah reached Marc a few paces ahead of Qiang. Maher Haydar, the Mag-8 chief engineer, had been alongside her, going on and on about how Professor Bruckner had saved the world. But Sarah didn't need to be told what had happened. All she knew was that Marc had been inside during Ignition.

She pushed aside two paramedic bots that had arrived at the scene quickest and dropped down beside Marc's prone figure. She lifted his head gently off the ground and cradled it in her lap.

His eyelids slowly opened and he looked up at her. 'Sarah? Sorry, I can't see very well,' he said, his voice a hoarse whisper.

She didn't know what to say and couldn't stop the tears rolling down her cheeks.

'The shutter was closed, Sarah. I had to open it.' His voice was so faint now, she had to bend down to hear him.

427

'I know it was. You did a very brave thing. Very stupid, but brave.' She didn't need to tell him that he'd just received a fatal dose of radiation.

His breathing was shallow now and he was shivering uncontrollably. She looked down at his ravaged hands. The skin hung off them in long red shreds. As she stroked his head, she could feel the cold seeping from him.

'Sarah, have you heard from the other facilities? Did they all work?'

'I guess we'll know soon enough.' She smiled down at him. If any of the eight beams had failed or missed the central collision spot, a seismic wave could come up anywhere on the Earth's surface, but satellites would tell them instantly if it did. Maybe this was the time for loved ones to hold each other tight as they awaited their fate. All she could do now was to sit with Marc and cradle him in her arms, talk to him. Reassure him.

Marc smiled back weakly. 'I expect they'll put up statues of us in years to come. Make sure mine is huge, won't you?'

Sarah laughed shakily through her tears. 'I'm sure it will be. It has to match your ego, after all.'

She felt she should keep talking to him but wasn't sure he was still listening. He seemed to be drifting in and out of consciousness.

Only vaguely aware of the minutes passing by, she tried to care about whether the Project had been successful or not, but found she couldn't. If they'd failed then everything would be over in a few minutes anyway. It was right that she and Marc were together at the end.

It was then that Sarah became aware of a growing and palpable sense of elation and relief around her. People had started clapping and cheering. Dared she hope that the Odin Project had worked? It certainly sounded as if it hadn't failed – not in the way Peter Hogan had planned. She leaned closer to the man she realized she loved. 'Hey, Professor Marc Bruckner. You did it. We did it. I have a feeling it will work, too.'

Marc's eyes fluttered briefly. 'Ah, I hope so . . . Make sure Qiang gets most of the credit . . . He was always the smarter one, you know. And if it doesn't work . . . blame Qiang. It was his stupid idea.' He let out a breath and closed his eyes. His shivering had stopped.

She thought he'd lost consciousness again, but he now whispered so quietly she could barely hear him: 'And Sarah . . . um, thank you. Thank you . . . for making me . . . the man I never . . . I never knew I could be.'

They were his last words.

47

Friday, 22 November – Southsea, England

SARAH'S FEET CRUNCHED ON THE SHINGLE AS SHE walked. The Southsea beach was deserted, which she found surprising considering what a beautiful day it was on the English south coast. There was a chill in the air and she was glad of her thick jacket, but the sun was bright and the sky a clear blue. She looked out to sea; across the Solent, the Isle of Wight seemed a lot closer than usual. Often, she could barely make out its tree-lined hills through the mist and sea fog. Today, its waterfront buildings glittered as their windows reflected the afternoon sun.

The days were getting a little easier now, even though her sense of loss was still so palpable. Wasn't it strange that Marc had now been gone for longer than the length of time she'd loved him when he was alive? She'd wondered whether her feelings for him had been magnified by the extraordinary circumstances in which they'd found themselves – not only because so much responsibility had rested on their shoulders, but because of a sense that they might have so little time together. That last bit at least had been true. She'd wondered too how much what she felt now was guilt – that she and the world had survived thanks to him – or gratitude for his selfless act.

No, this gaping emptiness inside her was real.

But yes, it was getting easier. Now, she did all her crying as she walked along Southsea beach. Marc used to hum one particular tune all the time. It drove her mad: a song by his favourite band, the Killers, called 'Mr Brightside'. So, every day, she walked along the beach, playing 'Mr Brightside' as loudly as she could, over and over again. And the tears would flow freely. Her parents had of course been supportive, but she still preferred to spend most of her time alone, even away from the beach, unable to share in the feelings of hope that so many people desperately clung to.

Two months had passed since Ignition, and the world was getting used to the reality that it still had to deal with the same old problems facing humanity, even if the immediate threat from the Purifiers had now receded. Although there had been plenty of false dawns, with many people claiming they had detected a strengthening in the magnetic field, the official line maintained that these were just isolated remnants that had been there before Ignition. A dying magnetic field wouldn't fail uniformly around the globe – there would be pockets of it that survived for longer.

The fact was, no one had a clue how a planet-sized defibrillator – essentially what the Odin Project had been – might work in reality; how long it would take for the energy from the dark-matter collision to turn the chaotic, turbulent eddies of the molten iron and nickel core into a regular flow that would kick-start and sustain a magnetic field again. But there was undoubtedly a general hope that the darkest days just might be over.

Sarah left the beach and climbed up to the footpath that skirted around the sea-facing battlements of Southsea Castle. The sixteenth-century artillery fort built for Henry VIII offered a stark reminder of permanence and nostalgia. She still recalled long summer days playing here with her brother, racing him to be the first to climb up and sit astride one of its huge, now ornamental, cannons outside the gates.

For a few weeks after Ignition she'd just felt numb. Returning to England, she had tried, mostly successfully, to avoid the media circus. After her testimony in court and her recorded conversation with Hogan had been released, she had insisted on being left alone, hiding away from the spotlight. Many were desperate for her to tell her story, so she felt grateful that there were people around her to shield her from the frenzy.

The hardest thing she'd had to do was travel to New York to meet Evie and Charlotte. At Evie's request, they'd met in Bryant Park. She had wanted to know every detail about what her father had done, and why it had to be him.

It had felt awkward initially with Charlotte being there too and Sarah was grateful to her when she said she would leave them alone for a while. They had sat together on a park bench and talked. After a while, the words dried up, so they sat and held hands in silence.

She'd met up with Qiang on that trip too. He'd been giving evidence to the UN before his return to China. He said he was being hailed as a national hero back home even though there was no indication at all that the Project had succeeded in its mission.

She hadn't heard from Shireen for a few weeks now, but the young woman continued to impress her with her maturity. Despite all the media attention and the lucrative job offers, all the Iranian cyb had wanted to do was to get back home to her parents and to finish her studies.

Now, over the last couple of weeks, the number of reports of a strengthening field had seemed to be growing. Sarah had ignored them all. She could, if she'd wanted, have very easily checked the overall status of the magnetosphere from the hundreds of measurements and simulations being carried out. But that wasn't the way she wanted to do this.

Every day for the past six weeks, come rain or shine, she had come out for her walk along the seafront. And every day she would stop at the same spot, at the base of Southsea Castle below the black and white striped lighthouse, and take out the little compass that had been a gift from her grandfather. He had given it to her when she was eight. They had stood in this very spot, and he'd shown her how its needle always pointed due north, away from the water, past the lighthouse and across the Common, towards the city of Portsmouth.

Today, she stopped as usual and reached into her pocket. She had taken to going through the motions so absent-mindedly these days that the mere act of holding the compass flat on the palm of her hand had in itself become a ritual. She would watch the needle spin around aimlessly for a few seconds and then place it back in her pocket, never truly allowing herself to believe. Today, however, something about the little instrument from a long-forgotten era dragged her gaze back down to it. She twisted and wobbled it between her thumb and forefinger. The needle no longer moved around freely beneath its glass casing. Instead it behaved in a way it hadn't done for a long time. It remained resolutely fixed. But now it pointed across the Solent – not due north as it used to, but due south. The Earth's magnetic field had flipped,

433

and it had recovered sufficient strength to grip and align the tiny magnetic needle.

The Killers played in her ears. Destiny was calling to Mr Brightside to open up his eager eyes.

She felt the familiar warm tears rolling down her cheeks. But this time they weren't just tears of sadness. She looked out to sea, then back at the compass, afraid that, like a holographic projection, it might just fade away.

The needle was holding firm. And it was the most beautiful thing she had ever seen.

Technical Note on Dark Matter

THE CENTRAL PREMISE OF THE ODIN PROJECT RESTS ON the behaviour of dark matter. But how accurate is this scientifically? Well, let me make a couple of things clear. Firstly, dark matter is real. It is what holds galaxies together. In fact, there is five times more dark matter in the universe than normal matter. The problem is that, as of the time of writing in December 2018, we still don't know what dark matter is made of. Whatever its constituent particles are, they are nothing we currently know of. Physicists refer to it as 'non-baryonic matter'. We know dark matter feels the force of gravity but not the electromagnetic force (which is what allows it to pass through normal matter as though it weren't there). The second point is that it is indeed the case that one of the potential candidates for dark matter is called the neutralino, a hypothetical particle predicted by a still speculative theory called Supersymmetry. My concern in using the neutralino in *Sunfall* was that it would either be discovered before the book came out or, even worse, ruled out entirely by some new experimental result; and that another particle would be discovered to be what dark matter is really made of. But, so far, so good. Neutralinos are still in the running.

As for dark-matter beams self-interacting, well that is sort of correct, as far as we currently know. However, I have taken some liberty here in the sense that self-interaction of dark matter is likely to be rather weak, otherwise we would see evidence of it in astronomy. But then if the beams are intense and energetic enough when they collide . . .

The other business of decay of heavy neutralinos into charginos and back again to light neutralinos – all that stuff necessary for the bending magnets to work – is, well, not wrong, just oversimplified. Theoretical physicists around the world are currently working on speculative mathematical models with such technical names as the Minimal Supersymmetric Standard Model with complex parameters (or cMSSM) and the cosmological concordance model, ΛCDM, which is read 'Lambda-CDM', standing for Cold Dark Matter plus the Cosmological constant. Well, you did ask! What's that? You didn't? Oh, OK.

Acknowledgements

WELL, THAT WAS AN ADVENTURE! OVER THE PAST THREE years, whenever I was able to prise open a sufficient block of free time – a day here, a weekend there, evenings and long journeys – I would immerse myself in an exciting world of my own creation. Escaping from my familiar, solid reality of academic teaching and research, broadcasting and, crucially, *non-fiction* writing, I would shut myself away in my study at home in Southsea, shake off the deterministic shackles of having to understand the real world and soar over a universe where I got to play God, proactively deciding for myself where the dice would fall.

Don't get me wrong – imagination and creativity are just as important in my scientific research as they are in storytelling, so it's not as though I had to flick a switch in my brain every time I sat down and teleported myself into this new reality I was building. It's just that, well, I'd not been used to such freedom.

As an academic scientist, I have always been at ease with facts and mathematical truths, with theories and hypotheses that describe some aspect or mechanism in the natural world, tested and checked against empirical data and observation. I am also an *explainer* – what I have understood about the nature and workings of the physical universe, I have endeavoured to transmit and describe as best as I can through my broadcasting work and non-fiction writing over the past twenty years.

So, making stuff up? Really? Was I allowed to do that? Would I be thrown out of the Royal Society of London for besmirching the good names of Newton, Darwin and Faraday? Would my students believe anything I tell them ever again?

Well, to hell with it. I have discovered that writing fiction is just as exhilarating as scientific research. And by freeing myself from the fetters of describing the world 'as it is', I can take the smallest of sideways steps into a world that 'could be'; one, by the way, in which no laws of physics are violated – I could never bring myself to invent bad science – and one that our own world could easily become in the near future. Indeed, *Sunfall* is our world. Of course, I have speculated – here and there I have pushed what we currently know a little beyond the comfort zone of established science – but I reckon I can still look my colleagues in solar physics, particle physics, dark-matter physics, computer science and nanotechnology (it's a long list) directly in the eye. And I am indebted to all those who have reassured me that everything I describe in the book is utterly plausible. I am also grateful to the nearly two hundred remarkable scientists and engineers that I have had the privilege of interviewing over the past seven years on my BBC Radio programme, *The Life Scientific*. These men and women have not made me a polymath – my brain couldn't possibly retain all the information that I have picked up – but they have opened my eyes to the vast range of exciting science across so many different fields being carried out at the moment, and I have tried to include as much of it as I can in this book.

As for my leap into fiction writing itself, with all the aplomb and subtlety of a swimming-pool dive bomb, well, it turns out there's more to the craft than mere story-telling. And so, for all his patient guidance, advice and tutelage, I have to thank, first and foremost, my editor at Transworld, Simon Taylor. When I first started the book, I came clean with Simon that I had never even taken a basic creative-writing course. He reassured me that he was prepared to roll up his sleeves and guide me through-out the process. He has been true to his word. So, thank you, Simon; I am sure that the word count of all your notes and comments that have helped me shape *Sunfall* over many drafts must come close to that of the book itself.

As always, and as I have done repeatedly over the almost two decades we have worked together, I would like to thank my literary agent, Patrick Walsh. As all those many authors under Patrick's wing will attest, he is far more than just an agent. His encouragement, advice, comments, suggestions and amendments to the story meant that I actually had two excellent editors to guide me.

I owe a huge debt of gratitude to both Charlotte Van Wijk and Julie Crisp who went through early drafts of the manuscript so carefully and offered so many brilliant suggestions that have vastly improved and tightened the storyline and plot.

Among friends and colleagues who also read early drafts and offered suggestions and advice, the two that stand out are Richard Millington and Mark Richardson. Thank you both for indulging me, and I hope you enjoy reading the final product. I must also thank my Surrey University col-leagues, Justin Read for his advice on dark matter, and Alan Woodward for his words of wisdom on cybersecurity.

I am indebted to Elizabeth Dobson, a wonderful (and incredibly thorough) copy-editor, for all her corrections and suggestions for tightening up, smoothing over and making the various plotlines consistent. Thank you also to Vivien Thompson at Transworld who looked after the copy-editing and proofreading stages of the book.

I am immensely grateful to, and hopefully forgiven by, the many people I know – friends, colleagues and family members – from whom I have stolen names, identities and personality traits. Particular thanks to my sister, Shireen Al-Khalili (here it really was just your name that I borrowed), to my friend, solar physicist Lucie Green, to my ex-postdoc, particle physicist Qiang Zhao, and of course to CERN director-general, Fabiola Gianotti.

Last but not least, of course, I must thank my wife, Julie, who, as ever, is always there to steady the ship. Her calm, organized mind complements my chaotic, flitting one. Whenever I'm asked how I have managed to fit writing a novel into my schedule, I always say that I have Julie to thank for maintaining order and sanity in my life and for helping me slot the different pieces neatly together. She's always been good at jigsaw puzzles.

ABOUT THE AUTHOR

JIM AL-KHALILI OBE, FRS IS A QUANTUM PHYSICIST, author and broadcaster based at the University of Surrey where he holds a joint chair in physics and the public engagement in science. He has written ten books, translated into over twenty languages. He is a regular presenter of TV science documentaries and also presents the long-running weekly BBC Radio 4 programme, *The Life Scientific*. A recipient of the Royal Society Michael Faraday medal, the Institute of Physics Kelvin Medal and the inaugural Stephen Hawking Medal for Science Communication, he is also the current president of the British Science Association. He was appointed OBE in 2007 for 'services to science' and was elected a fellow of the Royal Society in 2018. *Sunfall* is his first novel. Jim Al-Khalili lives in Hampshire.

To find out more, visit www.jim-al-khalili.com and follow him on Twitter @jimalkhalili

PENGUIN BOOKS

By the same author

Georgia

Charity

Tara

Ellie

Camellia

Rosie

Charlie

Never Look Back

Trust Me

Father Unknown

Till We Meet Again

Remember Me

Secrets

A Lesser Evil

Hope

Faith

Gypsy

Stolen

Belle